BLOOD

✦ OF THE ✦

EAGLE

Cover by Damonza

Maps created by Charles Thompson @whitehawkcreekforge

Internal layout by Jess Chaplin @jesschaplincreative

Printed in Australia

First Printing: September 2022

This edition: December 2024

Paperback ISBN 978-0-6451842-0-4

eBook ISBN 978-0-6451842-3-5

Hardback ISBN 978-0-6451842-8-0

 A catalogue record for this
work is available from the
National Library of Australia

BLOOD
· OF THE ·
EAGLE

· ANTHONY KEARLE ·

An Echo of the Ashes

-

Keeper of the Flame
Blood of the Eagle
Shadow of the Nightingale
Song of the Raven

Dedications

To the Teacher for love and guidance.
To the Carpenter for invaluable wisdom.
To the Brother for friendship and support.
To the Writer for counsel and unwavering loyalty.
To the Soldier for strength and brotherhood.

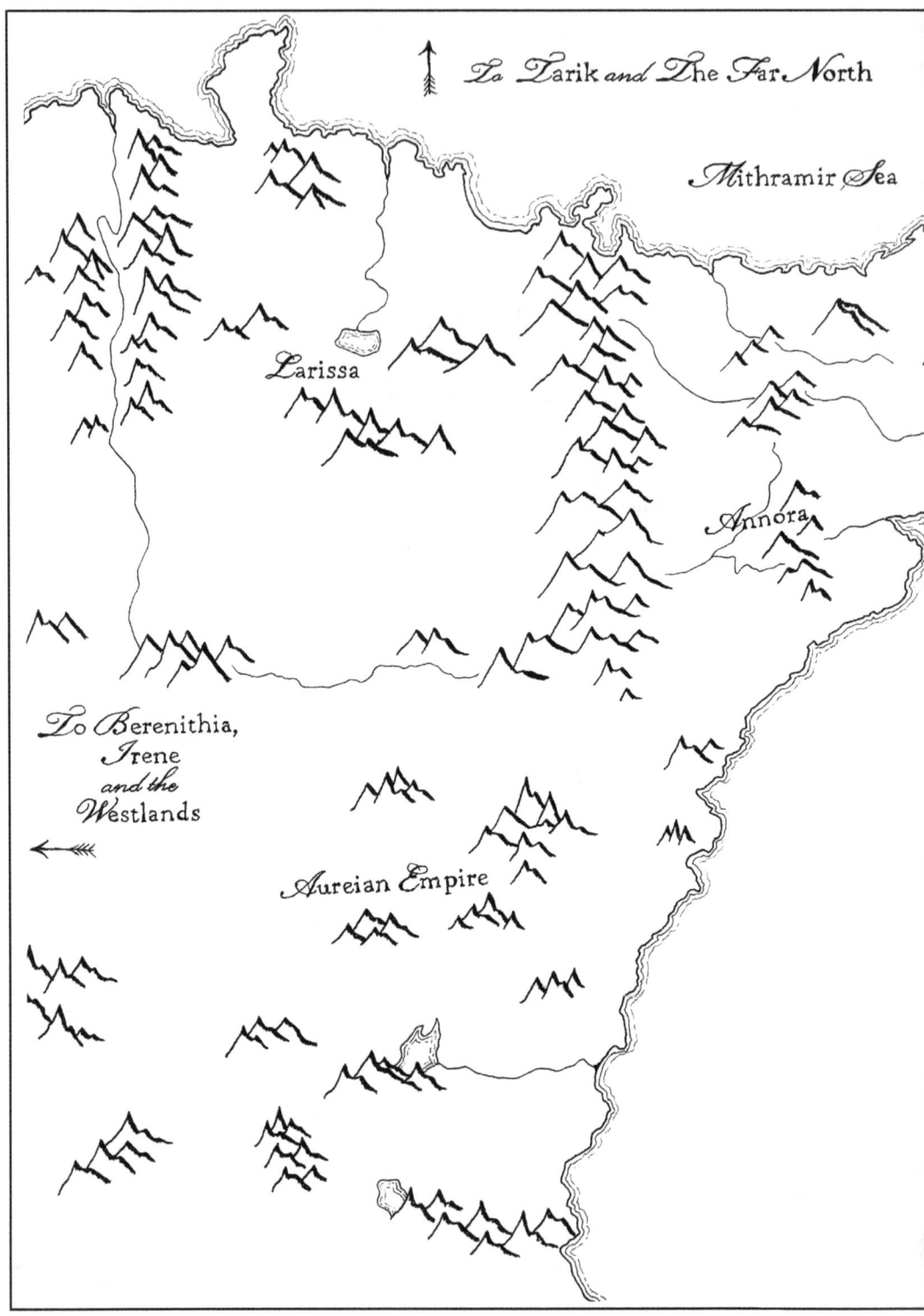

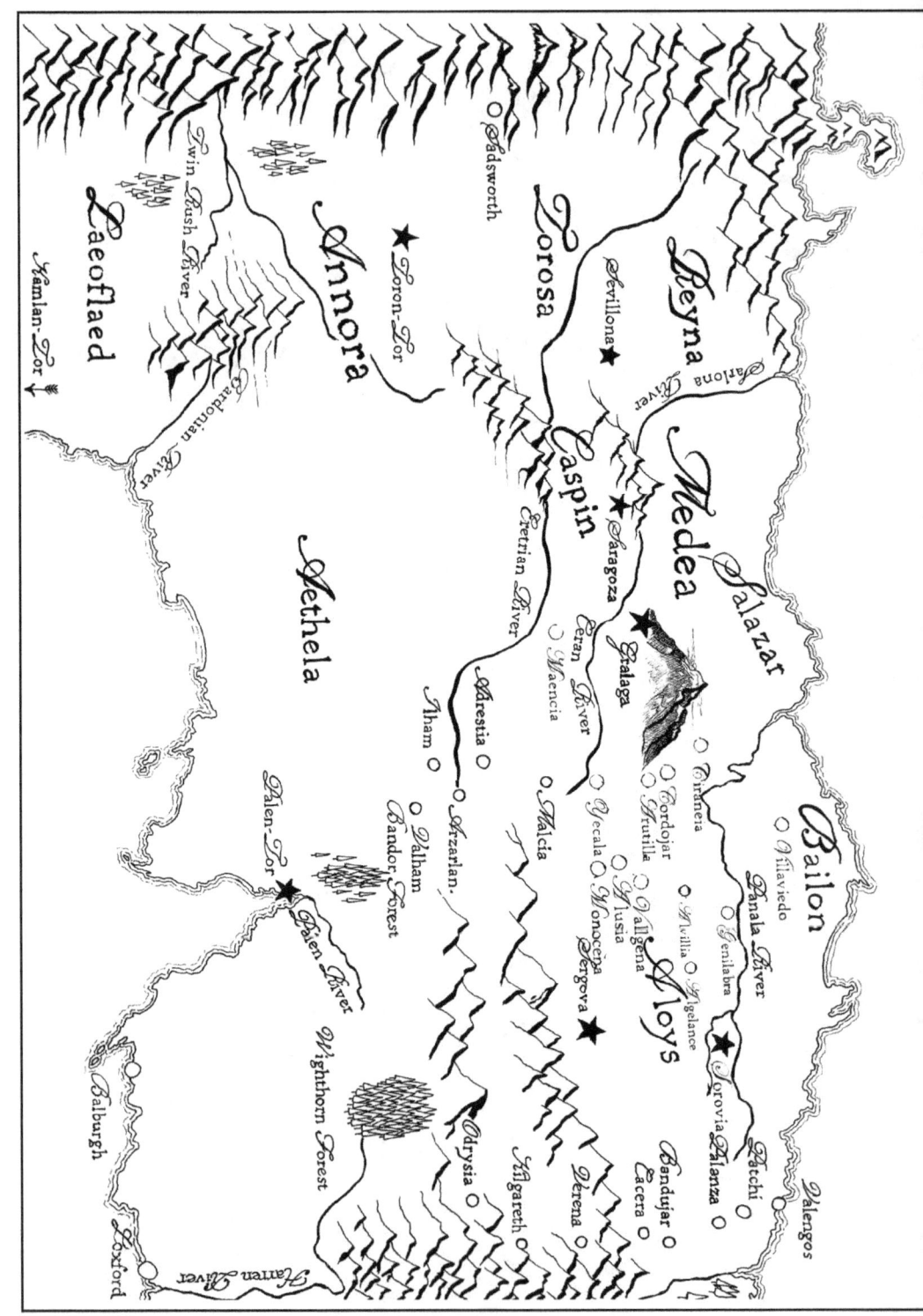

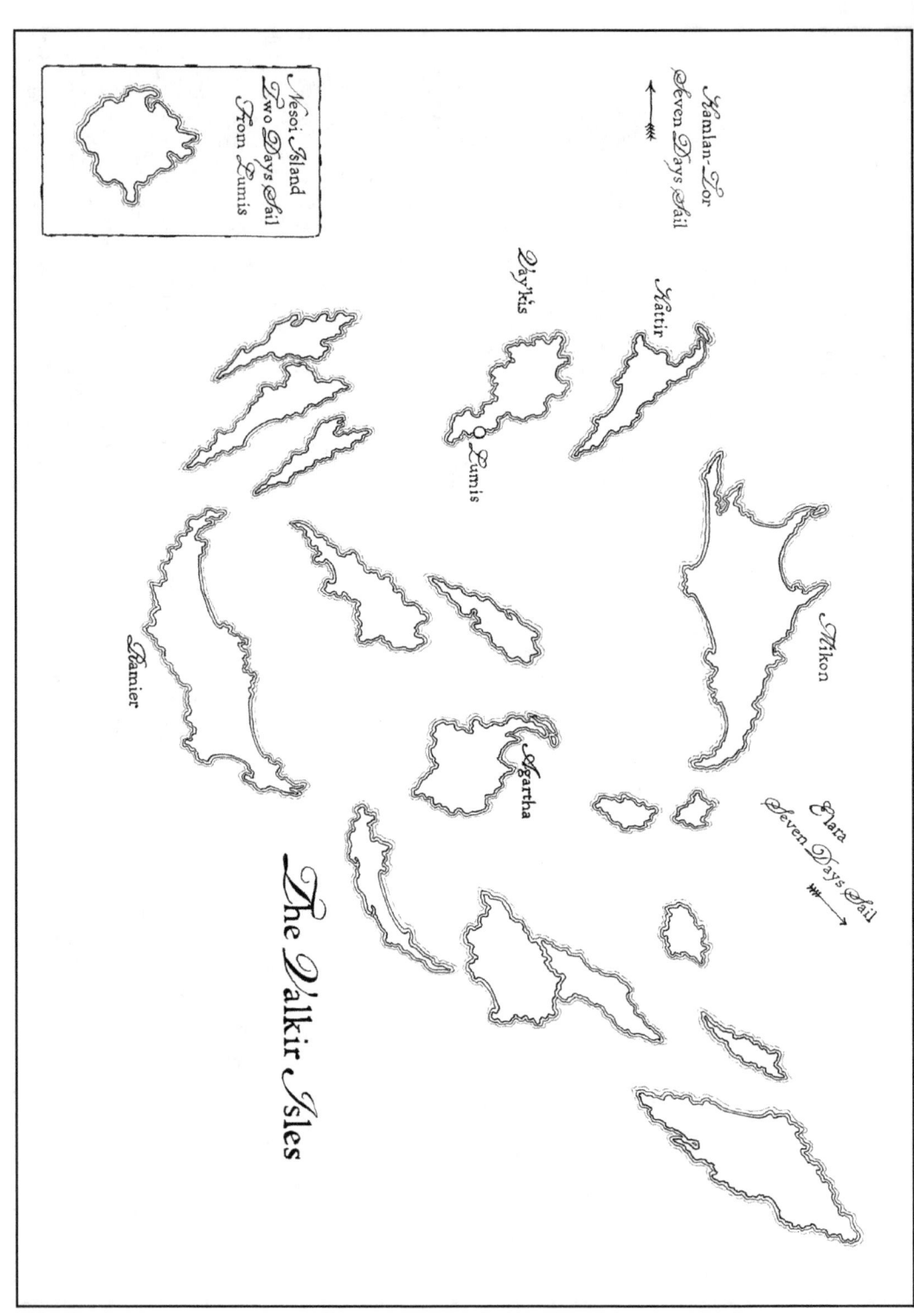

Kamlan-Tor
Seven Days Sail

Daykis

Katir

Lumis

Nesoi Island
Two Days Sail
From Lumis

Ranier

Athon

Agartha

Elara
Seven Days Sail

The Dalkir Isles

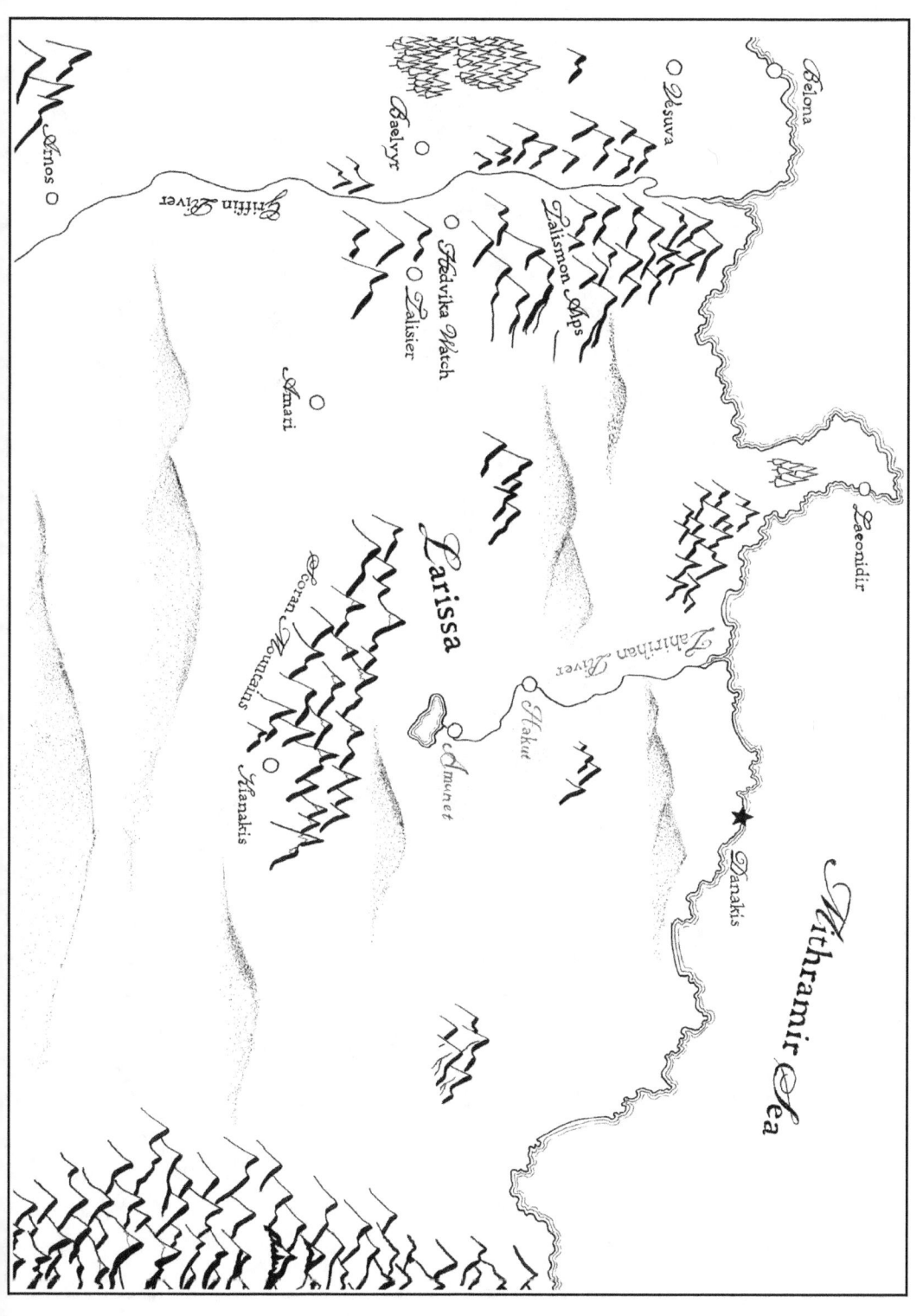

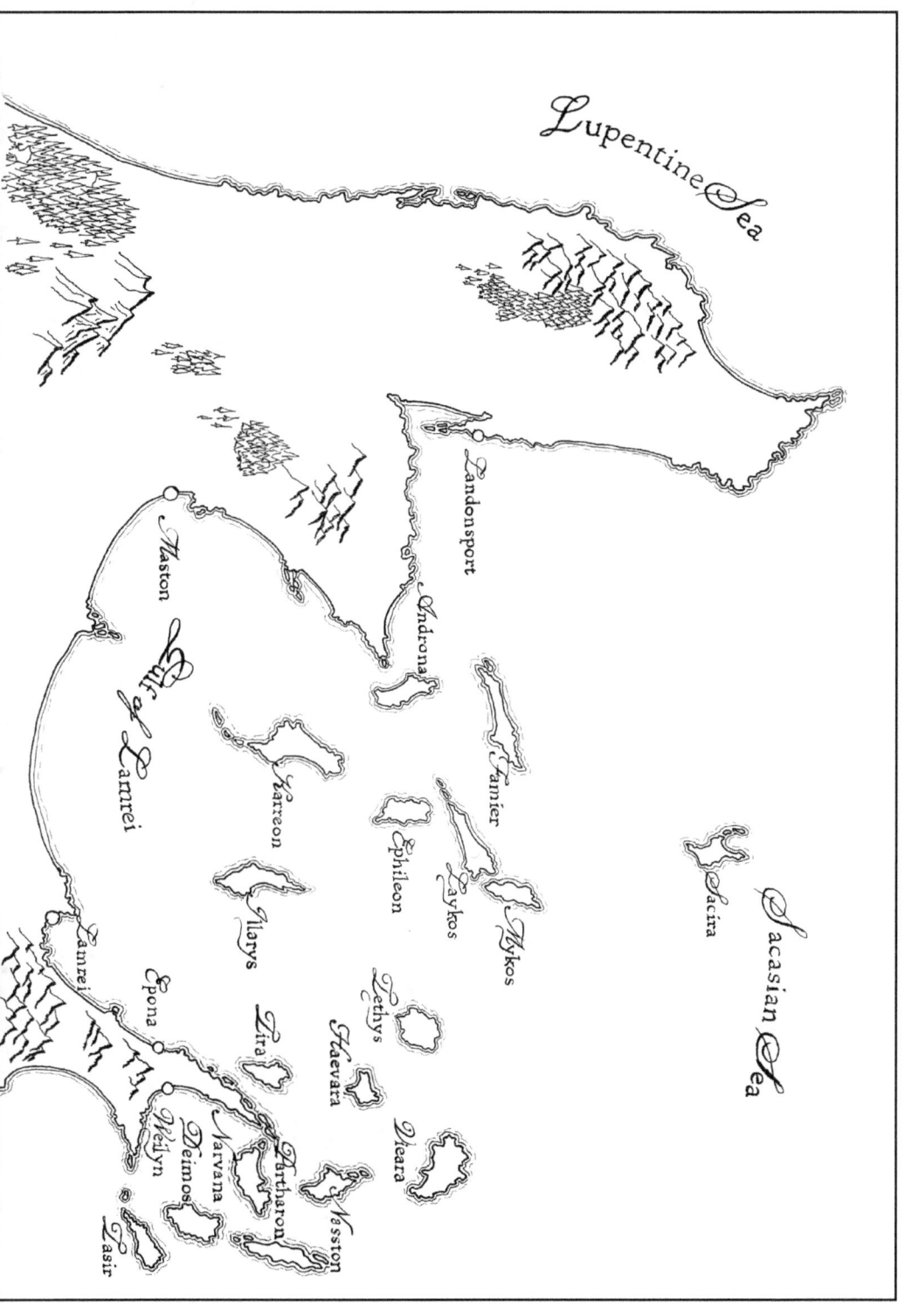

ONE

Holy City of Rovira, The Aureian Empire

The last of the sun's rays seeped into the silent chamber. It wasn't the cold that chilled Bavarian to the bone, nor the wind that howled through the castle's stone corridors. He had grown used to the biting cold of the holy city when the northern winds arrived.

It was the sight of the bedridden man before him that sent an icy freeze clawing through his blood. His commander, the grand master of the southern outpost of the Order of Kil'kara, Evalio Delrovira.

The man who had taught Bavarian the values of being a knight, and the man who had been as a father to him for near three long decades.

He was dying.

The sickness had struck Evalio days ago. It had hit him hard, sapping his strength within hours, and sent the Order into a panic. The grand master had always been strong despite his sixty years. Now he could not stand, and he could barely breathe. It struck like poison yet left no trace. Despite the best efforts of the maija, nothing could be done.

"Bavarian," the old man murmured as his eyes flickered to the warrior he had named his successor. The only one he had not sent from the room. "Come closer."

"Master."

The knight's chainmail armour clinked as he dropped to his knees beside the bed.

"There is something I have not told you, something that you need to know," Evalio told his successor, and his voice was barely more than a whisper. "You have no idea how important this is."

A shiver ran down Bavarian's spine as the man spoke. Whatever it was, Evalio had not wanted the rest of his advisors to know, not even the Circle.

"What is it?"

"The gods came to me last night," he said as his withered hands clutched at his necklace where the symbols of the gods, the sun of Durandail and the crescent moon of Azaria, interlaced. "The bell has been rung."

"What bell, master?" Bavarian stared at the man before him. The man he knew and loved was not one to pose riddles, nor had he lost his wit.

"The bell has been rung," Evalio repeated, and the intensity of his gaze pierced Bavarian's soul. He reached out and wrapped his fingers around his successor's wrist. It was a strong grip. Far stronger than that of a man on his deathbed. "And it has been heard … Shadows are drawing near, and it is nearly time," he continued.

Bavarian met his grand master's gaze; there was no lie in his eyes. Not one shadow of a doubt. Yet he was talking madness.

"I don't understand. Time for what?"

"The gods do not lie," he muttered. "Something is coming, and we need to be ready … You need to be ready. The Order must be strong."

"Who is coming?" Bavarian asked and his voice grew stern. "Answer me."

Evalio let out a deep breath and a shiver ran through his body. "Promise me that you will not let the Order of Kil'kara fall into darkness. Promise me that you will lead in my stead."

Bavarian dipped his head. "I swear it."

Evalio gave a slight nod. "I have left orders. You are to be named Bavarian Delrovira, grand master of the south, protector of this holy city."

"Evalio, I–"

The old man cut him off with a tiny gesture, no more than a slight flick of his hand, the last his failing strength could muster. "You must find it," he said solemnly. "It is the only way. Trust the northerners, Bavarian. The journey will begin where the Sword of the North ends."

Bavarian could only watch as his friend sank back into his bed. He took Evalio's cold hand, but it had already grown limp.

A cold tear slid down Bavarian's cheek as the old man breathed his last and the light in his eyes faded.

The grand master was dead. He joined the gods in the high heavens with his faith placed in one who would have been his son.

Bavarian reached out and closed his mentor's unseeing eyes. "I will not fail you."

The final words of Evalio Delrovira etched themselves in Bavarian's mind like a burning brand.

The journey will begin where the Sword of the North ends. Words that had come with a warning from the gods.

The gods that the Order of Kil'kara served. It would be heeded.

Bavarian would find whatever Evalio had hidden from his brothers. This he swore.

THREE MONTHS LATER

Two thousand miles away, a column of hooves kicked up dust as they thundered beneath the trees.

The final orange rays of the sun descended over the thin dirt road leading to Caelis, painting the forest red. The leader of the small band of riders peered through the unsettling wall of mist that had begun to fall upon them, all but shrouding the surrounding trees from sight. His head was on a constant swivel, his eyes narrow as a hawk's.

There were a dozen horsemen in the party. Each of them was wrapped in thick cloaks over woollen tunics and baggy trousers. The men wore their thick, shaggy hair tied back, some with braids. The few women in the retinue carried themselves with the same pride as the men. All had their hair painted white with grease. It streaked through their dark locks to keep it from their faces. All were armed to the teeth with powerful bows, steel-tipped spears and wicked axes. Malakai, great chief of the Aedei, ran a calloused hand down his dark brown mare's powerful neck as he rode. His equally dark hair blew gently in the chill breeze.

At nearly forty summers, the chief carried himself with the strength and pride of a man in his youth. The large steel longsword at his hip weighed no more than a feather when grasped in his powerful hands. At his side rode his brother, Cyneric, eldest of his two siblings and heir to the tribal lands of the Aedei. Behind the nobles came a detachment of some of the finest killers in their tribe, each and every one of them proven in battle. Each and every one of them watched the tree line for the first sign of trouble.

Though not because the forest that ran for over four hundred miles and was filled with over a dozen tribes was dangerous – far from it. Not for the Salvaari at least.

For the road marked the border of the Aedei lands, running parallel to those of the neighbouring Catuvantuli tribe, one of the most powerful factions in the tribal confederation that made up the Salvaari.

And tribal borders were always treacherous.

As is this mist, thought Malakai bitterly. He couldn't see a thing through the fog aside from the road underfoot and the faint outline of trees to the sides of the path.

They had ridden the better part of a day, from one side of the Aedei lands to the other, aiming to reach the town of Caelis by dusk. Barely two hundred men, women and children called the village home, but its strategic value was great. Running within two miles of the Catuvantuli lands, Caelis acted as an early warning in case the other tribe broke the treaty.

"Less than three miles to ride, brother," the rider beside him muttered in their native language, the tongue of Salvaar.

Malakai nodded and glanced at Cyneric, a reply forming at his lips, and then he heard a rustle from ahead. The faintest of sounds, nothing more than a light footstep, as if something was moving quietly through the forest.

Malakai held up an arm to signal the party to halt.

Malakai's brow furrowed as he peered down the road, his amber eyes attempting to breach the fog.

"Damn the mist," he cursed silently.

"What is it?" his brother whispered, riding to his side.

"I'm not sure. I thought I heard something … there." The sound that hit his ears was soft enough to nearly miss. It was almost like a twig breaking underfoot. He turned back to his men. "Ivar."

One of the riders nudged his horse and slowly made his way to Malakai's side. His silver eyes glinted despite the thickening mist.

"Chief?"

Malakai held up a hand to silence him. He heard the sound again, a faint clinking.

"What do you see?" he said softly as he nodded down the road.

The chief looked at Ivar as he peered down the road with his silver gaze. Malakai had chosen the warrior for more than just his deadly skill with a longbow; he'd chosen him for his eyes. He was moonseer. The Salvaari believed those with the silver gaze were given their gift by the spirits. A gift they called the Sight that allowed them to see near perfectly even on the darkest of nights and through all but the thickest of mists.

"This haze, it grows ever thicker. Even my eyes … Wait." Malakai felt a shiver run down his spine as Ivar spoke. "There is a rider not a hundred paces down the road. I'm sure of it."

The mist seemed to grow thicker and the air colder. Branches creaked overhead as the northern wind whistled through the leaves.

The hair on the back of Malakai's neck stood up as he closed his eyes and took a deep breath. There were two possibilities. One that the rider was Aedei and a friend. The other drove an icy dagger into the old chief's heart.

Malakai wrapped a hand around the hilt of his sword and eased it from its sheath. Behind him steel rang as his people armed themselves.

"On my order, we ride hard for Caelis," he said calmly as he turned to face his warriors. "Do not stop for anything."

Malakai turned back and glanced at his brother for a moment, and their eyes met. Cyneric nodded.

"Now."

Without hesitating, the Aedei urged their horses into a gallop with weapons at the ready.

They had ridden barely fifty paces when Malakai felt his heart skip a beat. He could hear another sound from beyond the trees to his right, even over the sound of his own horse, the thrumming of hooves crashing through the undergrowth. He saw a flash of colour through the mist.

"Ambush!" he bellowed moments before the first arrow hissed out from the tree line.

It caught one of the Aedei in the throat and sent him crashing to the road in a spray of crimson blood.

Bows sang and the trees came alive with a hail of arrows.

Half of Malakai's men were thrown from their horses before they could so much as blink. The steel-tipped shafts drove through muscle and flesh as if it were nothing.

The first of their attackers emerged on horseback through the mists and pelted down the road with a vicious war cry on his lips.

Realisation hit Malakai as he saw the blood-red paint on the rider's face. He was Catuvantuli. A dozen horsemen appeared behind the first. They rode hard towards the trapped Aedei. The treaty had been broken. The Aedei roared their own battle cries and formed a line of steel as they charged beside their leader. They came together in a mighty crash.

Malakai knocked his opponent's axe to the side and swung with his razor-sharp blade. It sliced through bone and marrow. A cascade of hot blood splashed on the chief's face as the Catuvantuli warrior toppled from his mount with a scream.

Without hesitating Malakai kicked his heels in and angled his horse towards another attacker. He ducked under a hastily thrown spear thrust and with a roar lunged forward. His sword pierced the warrior's chest. Malakai twisted his wrist and savagely wrenched his blade free. The red warrior fell. Malakai glanced around as chaos engulfed his people. The churning of the horses' hooves and vicious fighting had turned the earth into a slurry of mud and the blood of friend and foe alike.

He saw Cyneric cut down an attacker with his axe. To his side, Ivar put an arrow through a second man.

Malakai's blood froze as he saw four riders appear out of the mist like demons and angle towards his men. The newcomers were not clothed in pelts.

They were covered in chainmail with helms of steel, longswords and round shields.

Confusion struck the chief. They were Medean knights.

"Behind you!" roared Malakai, but it was too late.

The riders smashed into the side of the Aedei formation and in moments overwhelmed it. Horses and riders alike crashed to the ground as the Aedei fell beneath the blades of the knights. The screams of the dying echoed through the forest as Malakai's people fought for survival.

The chief of the Aedei bellowed and kicked his horse into a charge. He rode back towards the melee even as his people were cut down. Cyneric turned in his saddle as one of the knights crashed into him, his sword coming down hard.

Cyneric blocked the blow and swung back, hitting nothing but the knight's shield. A bow sang from the edge of the tree line and he twisted in his saddle. The arrow drove into his arm and sliced through his skin. Cyneric grunted and nearly lost his grip on his weapon. The knight reacted fast and swung his blade at his wounded foe. Agony ripped through Cyneric as he caught the blow with the haft of his axe. Tears of his blood fell all around Cyneric as his wound screamed. A vicious cry came from the road, and he risked a glance. A Catuvantuli on foot thrust a spear his way. Cyneric's arm burned as he knocked the spear aside. The knight swung his sword again, and Cyneric kicked his horse hard, forcing it to rear. The blade missed by a hair's-breadth as his mount skipped away from the blow.

Malakai appeared at his side and his sword hacked into the spearman's head like a hammer to an anvil. The warrior collapsed as Malakai took hold of his brother's mount's reins and kicked his heels in. He tore them both away from the knight and warriors that were appearing at his side.

Malakai swivelled his head, watching as the Catuvantuli surrounded what was left of his people. The road was blocked. There would be no escape unless they used the forest. Beside him Cyneric ripped the arrow from his arm with a snarl and tossed it to the blood-soaked earth.

The chief felt a cold burning anger rise up in his heart. He was going to die here; he felt it in his bones. Why else would the attackers have chosen to ambush them? He would die, but perhaps his brother might escape.

"Cyneric, get out of here," Malakai growled as he nodded his head towards the trees at his back.

"No, brother."

The chief inwardly cursed. The honourable fool. Malakai pulled his scabbard from his belt and then shoved it and his sword into Cyneric's hands. The blade of a chief.

"Live this life for the both of us," he pleaded. "I cannot follow you."

Cyneric looked to his brother and could see the intensity in his eyes. The meaning behind his brother giving him the sword was paramount. He nodded.

"Tell the tribes what happened here," Malakai said. "Go!"

Then the chief of the Aedei smacked his hand into the flank of Cyneric's mount.

The horse squealed and took off into the trees at a gallop. It crashed through the undergrowth even as a pair of Catuvantuli riders set off in pursuit with howls upon their lips.

Malakai turned back to the battle and took a deep breath as he saw the last of his people cut down by the knights. He tore free an axe from his belt.

Archers were beginning to form up along the road now with their bows coming up towards him.

"Tanris, I come to you," he muttered quietly.

Then he charged, a fearsome battle cry upon his lips.

The arrows took him in the chest before he had ridden five paces. He fell from his horse. His axe slipped from nerveless fingers.

The arrow shafts shattered as he hit the ground hard.

Henghis, chief of the Catuvantuli, rode into the aftermath of the battle. He watched as his men looted the dead. To his side rode a man wrapped in a wolf's skin, a staff clenched in his right hand, while at his back rode a second group of knights. Though many within his tribe had argued against hiring the foreign mercenary knights of Medea, they had proven themselves well in their first engagement. Judging by the dead, Henghis still had close to fifty men in his raiding warband alongside the eight knights. Easily enough for his next move.

"The Medean knights proved themselves," spoke the man at his side.

"As you always said they would," Henghis said with a nod before glancing at his kinsman.

The chief was perhaps the only man who did not fear the mysterious wolfskin-clad Salvaari wanderer who had arrived at his door two months past. Although suspicious at first, he'd grown to trust Kendrick more than many of his own people.

"Though how you knew exactly when and where the Aedei would ride … Your foresight is invaluable, my friend."

A vicious smirk appeared on the wanderer's thin lips. "A druid has his tricks, and I have mine."

The chief chuckled as he swung a leg over his horse's back, dismounted and passed the reins to one of his men. Blood-soaked mud squelched beneath his boots as Henghis walked through the dead. He searched for the face of his rival, the chief of the Aedei.

"Chief Henghis, one of the riders got away."

The chief turned to the voice and saw the captain of his mercenary knights approaching, running a strip of cloth down his blood-stained sword. The knight spoke in the common tongue, for the language of Salvaar was lost to foreigners. While the warriors and leaders of the tribes could speak in both, they reserved the use of the outsiders' language for when dealing with them.

"That is of no consequence," the chief replied in the same tongue.

"Aye," the knight said and sheathed his blade.

"Sir Rowan," called one of the Medean knights rising from a crouch beside a corpse. "Is this him?"

Henghis and Rowan walked through the dead until they reached the body. Henghis took in the aging but strong features of his enemy. The shattered ends of two arrows protruded from his bloody chest.

"Yes," he answered as he looked down at the dead man. "This is Malakai, chief of the Aedei."

"He fought well," said Rowan as he glanced down at the fallen chieftain.

Henghis nodded. Like the knights, the Salvaari respected strength above all else. Despite everything that had led to this moment, a slaughtered village and dozens dead, Henghis respected the very man he resented.

His rival had died a true warrior's death. "What shall we do with the dead?"

Henghis looked at the captain before taking the reins of his steed back.

"Caelis is barely three miles away and we need to take it before nightfall." The chieftain of the Catuvantuli swiftly climbed back up onto his horse. "Leave them to the crows."

"Even the chief?"

Henghis nodded as he glanced at the blood-stained road. "A funeral fit for a king."

TWO

Steel hissed as the blacksmith plunged the red-hot length into a barrel of hot oil. A cloud of vapour ignited and flared cherry red. He didn't flinch as he slowly withdrew the blade from the barrel. He was so used to the steam and heat that he didn't feel the sweat upon his brow.

He ran his expert gaze over the tempered steel blade in his hardened hands. Every inch of the three-foot-long blade was as beautiful as it was deadly.

"Gascon."

The smith glanced over his shoulder as his name was called and with half a smile slid the rod of steel onto clay bricks to cool.

He turned to the man who now approached.

"Ah, Kyler. It is good to see you," Gascon greeted the boy.

At eighteen summers, Kyler Landrey was as strong as an ox. He had needed to be after years of working at the local tavern with his father. Troublesome customers and the like needed to be dealt with, and as his father grew older, the task had fallen to him. Like Gascon, Kyler wore a plain tunic with his sleeves rolled up against the heat of the Adrestian sun. His dark hair was neatly cropped, and his face was clean shaven.

"Is it ready?" Kyler asked the older man, barely able to keep the excitement from his young voice.

Gascon brushed his hands on his heavy work apron.

He chuckled. "Aye, it's ready."

The smith vanished into the back of his forge. The boy glanced around the workshop that had become well known to him in recent days. The rays of the afternoon sun covered the Medean town and filled the smithy with light. He had to return to the tavern within half an hour, but for now he was content to gaze over the rolling hills and green fields of the Adrestian Highlands. The city was close knit, and many of its inhabitants knew the rest by name. Gascon had been a lifelong friend to Kyler's father, Theodore. As such he was as good as an uncle to the boy.

Footsteps.

Kyler turned back to the forge as Gascon appeared again, his hands laden with a sheathed sword.

"Here you are." He passed the weapon to Kyler's eagerly awaiting hands.

How the boy had dreamed of this moment. How he had spent years saving up enough coin to purchase a sword from the renowned blacksmith.

Kyler wrapped his fingers around the soft leather-bound hilt of the sword and, with a flick of his wrists, slid the blade from its sheath. The steel seemed to sing as it left the scabbard. The light of the sun danced upon its length. Kyler twirled the blade in his calloused hand and ran his dark eyes down the steel.

"It is beautiful," he murmured as he marvelled at the smith's handiwork.

Gascon merely nodded, and a slight smile pulled at his lips as the boy praised his work. "Little over three feet long, as you requested. The blade is perfectly balanced and the hilt long enough for both hands. Make no mistake: this is a tool, not a toy."

With a final twirl, Kyler sheathed the blade and pulled a small coin purse from his belt. The final payment that he owed for the sword.

"I cannot thank you enough, Gascon," the boy told the smith as he handed over the pouch. "Father always did say you were the best."

"It was a pleasure," came the reply as the two clasped hands to complete the exchange. "Do pass my regards on to Theodore. I shall be at your tavern when my work here is done."

"I will see you tonight." Kyler grinned back.

With that he began his walk back through the winding streets of the city towards the Sleeping Siren, the inn owned by his family.

Adrestia was a large town nestled tightly in the highlands of Medea. Neither rich nor poor, the town had survived centuries. With long fields rolling over the hills and small forests nearby a large creek that ran alongside the town, Adrestia was a perfect agricultural village, its farmers prospering. The town sat within the borders of the lands of the House of Caspin – one of the five noble families that ruled the land of Medea. The five provinces that made up the nation were led by the wealthy dukes and their families that had ruled for the last century. Each province was deeply embedded with the Twins faith. After its rise in the far south, the religion quickly spread through the Aureian Empire and beyond, until it arrived in the north and seeped into the very fabric of Medea. All who followed the religion were devout believers in the Twin Gods: Durandail, the warrior-god of truth, and Azaria, the goddess of wisdom.

The streets were filled to bursting at this time of the year as hundreds flocked to the city for the Adrestian market. It brought the large town to life and brought travellers from all over Medea to its humble streets. For three days, Adrestia prospered under the wealth of traders, merchants and even the occasional noble. Some of the villagers, like Gascon the smith, the tanners, and butchers, did well. Others, like Theodore and Kyler, prospered because everyone needed a drink and a bed for the night. With the extra travellers, however, it was harder to keep track of thieves and tricksters within the tavern's walls. More fights would have to be broken up and more heads knocked together. Just another day in Adrestia.

The sounds of raucous laughter had faded as the moon reached its peak, leaving the Siren silent, save for the steady roar of the fire. The clientele had left the stench of ale, hot food and sweat throughout the dimly lit tavern. Some had left their dignity. Kyler couldn't help but chuckle at the few unfortunate drunks that lay passed out around the room. There were always a few who drank too hard and paid the price the next morning. Some dice lay scattered on tables abandoned by their owners. Flame-lit candles filled the room, adding a hint of smoke to the aroma. Kyler made his way to the bar. His arms were laden with empty cups and plates. It had been a good night for his family, but then most market days were.

Rain fell outside the walls of the tavern, striking the muddy road and thatched roof of the inn itself.

"A good night," called Theodore heartily from the opposite side of the tavern.

Kyler glanced at one of the unconscious men and then back at his father. His lips barely restrained a grin. "For some."

Theodore finished wiping down a table and joined his son at the bar. He poured a cup of ale and took a long draught. The older man closed his eyes and gave a whistle. "Gods, I needed that."

Kyler snorted in reply. "Careful, old man, you're getting as bad as some of them."

Theodore gave a look of mock indignity and slapped his hand on the boy's shoulder. "Son, when you get to my age, you will discover something."

"And what's that?"

"That there is no smell so fine, nor any taste so sweet as good ale." Theo chuckled and took another swig. "Trust me, Kyler. It helps brace against the cesspit of a day."

"I'll take your word for it, Father," the boy replied sarcastically as his eyes danced with humour.

The door to the tavern shuddered and then was flung open, a pair of dark figures striding into the warmth. Water dripped from their travel-stained cloaks and mud fell from their boots onto the wooden floor. Kyler could see the dull glint of armour beneath their hooded garments, while swords hung from their sides.

Kyler knew they were mercenaries instantly simply from the look of their cloaks. For who else would have ridden so hard that mud now covered their clothing? No doubt their swords would have been freshly cleaned of blood.

Kyler crossed his arms as he watched them curiously. Mercenaries were a common sight in these parts, as every man with wealth in Medea seemed set upon claiming another's land. These ones seemed different. They seemed more dignified despite the mud.

One of the men muttered something to the other before gesturing towards Kyler and his father.

"Father," Kyler murmured. "Mercenaries by the look of them."

The older man looked up, his eyes instantly going to the men walking their way. "Aye," Theo replied, glancing at the approaching men. "We'll know soon enough."

The first of the sellswords glanced around the dimly lit room as he walked. He pushed his large hood back, revealing his weathered face and hawklike eyes. The mercenary looked in his mid-forties or perhaps older. He had long hair hanging loosely down his shoulders and a short beard. The rider's cloak trailed behind his shoulders, revealing a black vest buckled over a shirt of chainmail. He wore a curved sword at his right hip and a dagger at his left.

Strange, thought Kyler. It was rare enough to see a warrior who favoured his left hand, but to see what was clearly a far western-styled sword in Medea, especially carried by a mercenary – that was unheard of. His companion followed suit and pushed his hood back from his face. He ran a hand through his cropped hair as he did. Though near the same height, the second man was broader and looked strong enough to bend steel with his bare hands. His hand never strayed from the hilt of the longsword at his hip.

"Good day," said the man with long hair, the leader, as he nodded to Theo.

The accent was impossible to guess. It was gruff yet it oozed with authority.

"And to yourselves," Theo answered as he ran his eyes over the men before them. "What can I do for you?"

"I have two dozen men taking shelter in the stables out back." The mercenary nodded over his shoulder. "If that is alright with you."

"Of course," Theodore replied. "You are all more than welcome to stay the night, keep out of the blasted rain."

The man gave a slight shake of his head. "That is kind, but I am afraid we cannot. There is a storm coming from the west; however, we must reach the border with haste."

Kyler frowned. Strange. If they did not want to stay at this time of the night, then what did the mercenaries want? Stranger still, the man failed to say which border.

"Can I get you anything?" Theodore asked with a slight furrow in his brow.

"That depends." The mercenary leader stepped in close enough for Kyler to see a series of gold rings running down the length of his left ear. "Travellers come and go, and I'd wager that a man in your position would learn quite a lot. I am willing to pay."

"Information, is it?"

"Tell me," said the gruff voice as a slight smile entertained the man's lips. "What do you know of the wedding?"

Kyler caught his breath, and the room seemed to grow darker. They spoke of the betrothal between crowned Prince Dayne Raynor of Annora and Lady Sofia of House Caspin. The family that ruled over one hundred miles of Medea. With no son of his own, Santiago Caspin, the head of his family, had all but made Prince Dayne the heir to his lands as well as those of the powerful kingdom to the south, Annora. The lands beyond the Eretrian River once stood as three kingdoms led by three kings. That was before the time of Dorian. Once merely the king of Aethela, Dorian Raynor had spent years of his life unifying the lands across from the Eretrian, the lands of Annora. This act had given him wealth and reputation far beyond his closest rivals, and his eldest son, Dayne, would one day inherit the beginnings of an empire. The marriage threatened the very heart of Medea and would cause a shift of power. Caspin would rise far beyond the noble houses of Salazar, Reyna, Bailon and Aloys. It was a dangerous move.

Theodore nodded slowly and gestured towards a table. "Kyler, bring our friends some ale."

"Who would have thought that old Caspin would marry his only daughter to the heir of the Annoran throne?" Theodore said as Kyler brought a jug of ale over and poured it into the cups he had procured. "He must have known what it would do to Medea."

The man with the curved sword shrugged. "He is fifty years old, and his son died a long time ago. The rumours of his ailing health are naught but that. His mind is as sharp as it ever was, and this arrangement may prove the very thing to save his house."

"Certainly has caused a stir among the nobility," muttered the second man before downing a mouthful of drink. "Not seen this much fear since Laeoflaed came under Dorian Raynor's rule and he became king of all Annora."

Kyler joined the men at the table and shared a glance with his father as he sat. He had heard the rumours and whispers. Mumbles among the soldiers and sellswords that often rode through Adrestia.

"There is not much to say," Theodore told them. "Not yet, at least. Santiago held a war council last moon after the betrothal was announced. Word is that he has left orders for his generals to marshal their armies and call in their mercenary companies. Even those from beyond Larissa have been recalled. Though they will not be on their own soil for near a month. Santiago must have a strategy for this game of his."

"Caspin may be playing a game, a dangerous one at that. Yet he is taking no chances," Kyler cut in. He knew something that his father didn't know. Not yet at least. "There was a rider from the north today who–"

"Kyler," snapped his father.

The lead mercenary looked towards the younger man and their eyes met. They seemed like empty vessels gazing hungrily into Kyler's soul.

The man rested his hands on the table as he spoke, his voice a low growl. "No, it's alright. Let the boy speak."

Kyler couldn't help but glance at the hands before him as they caught his eye. Clad in dark fingerless gloves and covered in rings. Some gold, some silver. Some embellished and some plain. Kyler flicked his eyes back up to meet with the man's. The boy had not travelled out of Adrestia often and yet he had seen jewellery from all over. Rings and necklaces that adorned the arms and throats of nobility that traversed tavern and market alike. Many that the mercenary wore were not from Medea, many were not even from nearby nations.

Who are you?

"The man said that Salazar, like the other families, had not taken kindly to the news. That the Salazar army is assembling at Gralaga in a moon's time."

Little before Santiago's mercenary companies from Larissa would arrive. House Salazar was clearly on the warpath.

Theodore snorted. "You mark my words, no good will come from Caspin's greed."

The mercenary smirked darkly and spun a coin in his gloved hand. "Ah yes, all hail our noble lords and their noble games. In this world the dice are loaded. Soldiers fight and die on the battlefield for the greed and ambition of lords. I suppose fighting over a wedding makes little difference to the aristocracy. The poor stay poor and the rich fill their coffers."

That was near treason, Kyler thought as he glanced from one sellsword to the next.

"Best be careful who you say that to," murmured Theo as he leaned across the table. "Even in these parts there are some who would gladly pass those words on to the city watch for chance of a reward."

The man replied dryly, "There is nothing they haven't done to me that they can do again."

That caught Kyler's attention. All mercenaries lived a hard life. Always caught between the space of life and death. Yet something about the sellsword's eyes showed true darkness.

He shot Theo an inquisitive glance. "I didn't catch your name earlier."

"The name's Theodore." Kyler's father nodded to the man. "And yours?"

"They call me Bellec," came the reply. "And this is Galadayne."

"Charmed," the other man added.

Unlike his leader, the second mercenary had shaved the sides of his head, leaving naught but the hair atop his brow and his short beard intact. Swirling dark tattoos adorned the sides of his head.

Kyler barely stopped his sharp intake of breath. The name Bellec sounded part Medean, part something else. Larissan maybe? Kyler wasn't sure. Yet he knew the name and of its reputation, as did his father. Though he could not place the accent or its providence, he knew of its owner's deeds. How he had near singlehandedly won the Reyna Rebellion ten years ago. One of many such battlefields that had given the man power to his reputation.

"Your name precedes you," Theodore told the sellsword. "I've heard the stories."

Bellec let out a growl of a laugh. "They're all true." The mercenary leaned over the table towards Theo and continued in a hushed tone. "Can you wield a sword?"

"Aye." Theo nodded. He had been a part of House Caspin army in his youth and had given near twenty of his years to the duke. "I fought for Santiago for near two decades."

He had also spent the last six summers passing on some of his knowledge to his son. Though, as he often said, Kyler could swing a punch better than he could swing a sword. The boy was forced to agree.

"That is good," Bellec replied his eyes moving to Kyler. "There's a war coming. I can feel it in my bones."

War? Kyler exchanged a glance with his father. Was he serious? None of the five families that ruled Medea had exchanged threats in years. Even with the encroaching wedding, they were at peace. A fragile peace, but peace nonetheless.

Theo leaned across the bench closer to Bellec. "What have you heard?"

"The eastern border is silent. We haven't heard so much as a whisper from the Salvaari tribes for months. No raids. Nothing. Not a hint of the riders though the trees," the mercenary replied sombrely.

"There has to be some kind of explanation behind it," said Kyler. The raids wouldn't just simply stop and especially not with those who had stood as hated rivals for over a century.

Bellec looked back at him. "No doubt. But the forests are quiet, and the ruling families are scared. Duke Aloys sent riders into Salvaar to find out why. None returned. Aloys and Duke Bailon have set aside their past grievances and are watching forest with both eyes while calling in their armies as a precaution. And then." He paused, looking from son to father. "Then we have troubles within our own borders."

Theo nodded. "The wedding."

"Exactly," Bellec continued with a slight chuckle.

"If the encroaching storm does break, if the sky turns red with blood, what will you do?" Theodore asked as he glanced from one mercenary to the other. "Remain and fight?"

"We fight for coin," the second man, Galadayne, said, "yet we are not moths to a flame."

"The future is beholden to the present moment as it is cast," Bellec added as the coin danced across his fingers. "Perhaps we will fight, yet for now at least I have business that must be attended." He turned to his companion. "Ready the men, we have lingered here too long."

"Aye." And with that the second warrior downed the contents of his cup and headed for the door, iron-shod boots ringing on the wooden floor. The mercenary leader flicked his wrist and his coin vanished. He rose to his feet.

"I'll give you some advice. Leave. Leave Adrestia. Leave Medea."

Kyler's blood froze as the man spoke.

"Get out while you can. The nation is about to go up in flames." Bellec tossed a coin pouch onto the table and strode towards the door with his cloak trailing behind him.

Kyler followed him to the entrance and watched as Bellec pulled his hood up and joined his company of mounted men. The mercenary heaved himself into his saddle and gave Kyler a curt nod.

"We ride," was the last thing he said as he kicked in his heels. The horses surged past in a dark wave and thundered down the mud-filled street.

Bellec's last words rang in Kyler's ears. The kingdom is about to go up in flames.

He clasped the double necklace that hung at his throat. The first bearing six beads to show the founding principles of his faith: honour, valour, justice, truth, compassion and allegiance. The second strand bore Azaria's crescent moon joined with Durandail's sun. The symbol of the Twin Gods.

The gods were angry.

Adrestia was about to be caught in the middle of it.

Father and son cleaned the tavern in silence before they made their way home for food and rest.

"So, it's really happening then?" said Maria Landrey as she glanced from Theodore to Kyler.

Kyler looked across the table to his mother as his father replied, "Caspin and his daughter are already well on their way to the Annoran capital as we speak. They crossed the river two days ago. Close to two hundred knights, noblemen and ladies of the court ride with them. Should reach Palen-Tor within a matter of days."

Palen-Tor, the capital city of Annora, was said to be a rare jewel with soaring towers and prospering trade.

"What else have you heard? How are the other houses taking it?"

Theo grimaced. "As well as can be expected … As a threat. Duke Santiago is taking a risk with this new alliance and it's shifting the very foundations of Medea. People are saying that the other families are calling in mercenaries from all corners and gathering their armies. The only thing keeping the peace are the treaties, and we all know how fragile the word of men is."

"Bellec was right," Kyler murmured sombrely. "There is a war coming."

"Yes, I fear so," replied Theo, looking across the table at his son. "Though where it will start, I have no answer. But I do know this … it won't be long now."

"Perhaps we should leave." Maria pursed her lips. "If war does come to Medea, then we will be caught right in the middle of it."

That took Kyler by surprise. "Where would we go?"

"Somewhere … I don't know." His mother shrugged. "I have family in Elara. Maybe they could help us."

"The merchant city," Theo said thoughtfully. "It wouldn't be so hard to set up shop there. I hear they treat skilled craftsmen like kings. Perhaps … perhaps it is time to move on."

Kyler was dumbfounded. He'd never once thought his parents

would simply up and leave their city, even with trouble brewing among the houses. They had lived in Adrestia all their lives, and the thought of them beginning the huge journey to the port city in the southwest was foreign.

"To even get to Elara would take months." The boy spoke up. They would have to make their way to the capital of Annora, Palen-Tor, and from there charter a ship east to the great merchant city itself.

"Think, boy, would you rather get caught up in a war of the scale this threatens to become?" his father said. "Five provinces cutting each other to pieces. Annora will undoubtedly join their new ally and send their soldiers. We have all heard the stories of King Dorian and his eldest son."

Kyler slowly nodded as his father spoke.

Dorian of Annora was a renowned warrior king, while his eldest son, Dayne, was a prodigy.

"To say nothing of the Salvaari. Who knows what is passing beneath those trees right now, right in this moment. If we leave within the month," Theodore continued, his voice containing a hint of sorrow, "we can avoid whatever storm is about to descend upon Medea."

"Well, if that's your decision, then I would like your blessing."

"Our blessing?" inquired Theo looking at his son thoughtfully. "For what?"

Kyler was silent for a moment as his parents watched him. It was time to tell them of a dream he'd had ever since he was a young boy. He took a deep breath.

"I want to help those with nothing, those who can't defend themselves. To serve the gods as best I can." He leaned over the table as passion filled his voice. "I wish to travel to the Citadel in Odrysia and join the ranks of the Order of Kil'kara."

Silence.

His parents looked at him with mouths agape. He'd taken them by surprise. Few joined the fabled Order of Kil'kara, and those that did were devout believers in the Twin Gods. It was a religious order divided into two sects. One devoted to Azaria, known as the maija who studied medicines, languages, histories and philosophy. The other being the dedicated, well trained and highly skilled holy knights who served Durandail. The elite warriors were immersed not only in the art of war, but also baptised in the very heart of their faith. The combination of soldier and priest was a powerful one, as to the knights, martyrdom in battle was one of the most glorious ways to die. They were a force who served the gods with deadly passion and vigour. They fought injustice wherever they saw it.

"The Order of Kil'kara?" Maria was the first to speak. Her voice little more than a whisper. "You wish to join the most sacred order of our faith?"

"Gascon has forged me a blade. I am ready to take my vows and serve as a knight." Kyler nodded and looked from his mother to his father. "If you agree, I will leave for Kilgareth at dawn."

"Gascon made you a sword, eh?"

Kyler saw a flicker of anger flash across his father's eyes as he caught on.

"You were planning on leaving anyway," Theodore continued with a growl. "Without so much as a word."

"Ever since the Order rode through Adrestia when I was a child, I have wanted this," Kyler replied. "I can still see them when I close my eyes. A company of silver-clad knights, mounted on their massive chargers with their cloaks as blue as the clearest sky."

"The knights haven't ridden out in force in near a century, lad. Not since Cardinal Octavan's inquisition and the war," his father told him. "Are you sure you want to do this?"

Kyler felt as if a weight had been lifted from his shoulders. The decision had been made. Nothing would stop him from riding to Odrysia. He had never been so sure about something in his life.

"I do. The Knights of Durandail have always, always defended those in need. I for one do not believe that the Citadel will remain silent if treaties are indeed broken. And I won't simply stand by as our land is ravaged by war. I have to do this."

"Why a knight? Why not the maija?" said Maria. "There is great honour in becoming one of the physicians. Their skill with the healing arts is legendary."

"I know," Kyler replied as he saw the hint of fear in his mother's eyes. "I could save people as a healer, but perhaps I can change things as a knight."

"The gods work in mysterious ways." Theodore ran his aging hand over his amulet. "I fought beside Santiago Caspin and his house for a long time. I bled in the mud for him. I know not how many men I put in the ground for that family. Perhaps countless. But know this: there is little glory in battle. Little glory and for many an early grave."

"I don't seek glory," Kyler said as he leaned across the table. "And nor do those men whose original purpose was nothing more than protecting travellers along the roads. There is more to the world than Adrestia, more than Medea. And besides, you said yourself that the knights haven't left their valley in force for a hundred years."

Maria took her son's hand. "I will ask you one time, please do not do this," she begged. "Stay with us another year. Please."

Kyler could see the pain in his mother's eyes. He paused a moment and his thoughts filled with the possibilities of what his next words would mean for him.

"You know that I cannot spend my life dealing with drunkards. It's not who I am. And besides, who would I be if I stay?"

Kyler's parents exchanged a glance, and he knew instantly what the answer was.

Theo was the first to speak. "Well, if this is your decision, then you have my blessing."

"No, you have our blessing," said Maria as she gazed at her son.

Kyler wrapped a hand around his amulet and felt the excitement flow through his veins. "I swear to you that I will not dishonour you nor the gods."

The dawn sun had barely risen when Kyler buckled on his newly forged sword and said his goodbyes to his father and tearful mother. He mounted his ebony-skinned mare, Asena, and with a last look at his childhood house and family, he rode east. It was two hundred miles to the valley of Odrysia. Kyler sent a quick prayer to Durandail and Azaria that the ride would be safe, that the next time he swung a sword would be within the walls of the Citadel itself.

THREE

The Sacred Grove, Forest of Salvaar

The flames of campfires and torches illuminated the darkness of night and filled the forest with an orange glow. Each tribe had answered the call. The chieftains were gathering, and each brought a small retinue to the depths of the forest of Salvaar. Every tribe warily watched the next with suspicious eyes, for who knew when the old blood feuds would arise again.

All had come. The Coventina from the north, their hair braided and filled with the feathers of birds. The Belcar from the east, civilised and sporting armour over their pelts and furs. The highland tribes and river clans had all come. Even the Sagailean from the deep forest had emerged from seclusion. Something that had not occurred in more than a year.

All of this Cailean saw as he walked through the trees with his hand resting atop the steel head of the axe that hung at his hip. His eyes scanned every last man and shadow, seeing everything about him. The gentle breeze ran through his long, dark hair and beard, its biting chill barely noticeable to one who had lived in the forest for over three decades. His back and arms were powerful, for he had swung his weapon for equal years. His dark eyes shone like those of a wolf.

The undergrowth crunched beneath his heel as he made his way towards his tribe's camp, and more importantly to where his brother, the chief, sat by the fire.

"Cyneric," he called to the other man. "The chiefs are nearly ready, everyone is assembled."

The leader of the Aedei looked up from the stump atop which he sat. "Aye, brother."

Cailean merely nodded and sat opposite his brother. He spared a glance at the eight others with them, warriors to a man. It had been weeks since Cyneric had appeared out of the forest covered in blood and his eyes cold. He had said little, his words replaced with a slow burning anger that had been consumed him since the ambush and the death of his brother, their brother. Less than a day after his return, a scout had arrived. His horse had been near to collapsing from exhaustion. Henghis had led his men on a bloody rampage along the border and had burned Caelis to the ground. Every man and woman had been put to the sword.

Riders had been sent to each tribe and that was why they had come. For all would answer the call to a sacred conclave. A gathering of the chieftains.

Here they would decide upon who stood guilty. Oaths would be sworn and sides chosen, for unprovoked attacks did not go unpunished.

"Every tribe is here," Cailean told his people. "They have all answered the call. Even the druids have come."

Cyneric looked about the fire slowly and his eyes searched the faces of his people. "The first conclave in half a decade. But make no mistake, no matter the outcome, no matter what the tribes decide: we are at war."

"Chief," called one of the warriors his hands holding a large wooden bowl filled with blue woad.

Cyneric took the bowl and glanced at its contents. The Aedei turned to their chief and watched intently as he made his decision. To the Salvaari the blue paint was more than just paint. It meant that they would rather die than fail. It was more than just a declaration of violence or war. It was a pact. A solemn oath to the spirits and to their tribe.

All were silent as the chief dipped his fingers into the blue woad. He closed his eyes and then drew the paint across his face in two strokes. The first from ear to ear and the second from his left temple to his chin. All was quiet save the crackling of the fire as Cyneric passed the woad to his brother. Cailean drew three strokes across the left side of his face and a fourth under his right eye.

One by one, the Aedei warriors covered their faces in the woad and silently swore their oaths to the spirits.

Cailean's eyes blazed as he remembered Malakai whom he loved dearly. Whom he would avenge.

A horn sounded in the distance, and all eyes turned to a small hill barely two hundred paces away. The Scared Grove of Salvaar. The heart of the forest. The birthplace of the spirits.

"It is time," Cailean said.

Cyneric rose to his feet and held out his arm. Cailean took it and the chief pulled him to his feet.

"For Malakai," he said, and his powerful voice emanated around the trees. "For Caelis."

The Aedei followed the path up the side of the hill. Torches burned brightly on either side of the track. Cailean could feel his heart quicken. This Conclave would not just be about a trade dispute or a petty border skirmish. It would be about war. War between well respected rivals that could erupt into something far worse.

But one question had plagued Cailean for days. Why had Henghis attacked? It wasn't in the Catuvantuli chief's nature to strike without reason. Especially since he prided himself on ruling with his head and not with his heart. Henghis did not make rash decisions. For someone who commanded such a following and respect among not just his people but his fellow chieftains, attacking without cause was a bad move to say the least. None of the tribes would stand for it.

The trees started to thin as the Aedei rose higher and higher up the hill. Each step brought them closer to answers and war.

Half a dozen warriors appeared before them with their weapons at their sides and their eyes as silver as moonlight. The guardians of the grove. Only the most steadfast of warriors were chosen for the sacred duty of watching over the grove, and only those with the Sight were admitted into their ranks.

"Cyneric of the Aedei," one of the warriors said. His voice was empty, and it sent a chill over the skin. The warrior stepped forwards and nodded at the chief. "Your weapons."

Cyneric did not hesitate as he unbuckled his sword and handed it over. Violence was forbidden within the grove. The chief nodded to his people, and one by one they handed their weapons to the guards. He said not a word as the warriors stepped back, their arms laden with blades and spears.

"You may pass."

Cailean looked around the hilltop as the Aedei made their way into the grove. He had only been present at a Conclave once before. There was little need for all three of the brothers at such a gathering. In the centre of the grove stood an ancient tree that soared into the sky. Its thick branches were covered in green leaves. A ring of twelve stones ran around its base and each was marked with the runes of the twelve clans. Under the tree there stood a man who was hooded and cloaked. Clasped in his weathered hands was a staff of oak, while his long hair and beard were greying with age. He was the shaman. The only one of his kind. He had no tribe and was answerable to no man save himself. He had a deep connection to the spirits and watched over the gatherings and Conclaves, occasionally providing sage advice.

The grove was tightly packed with warriors from each of the twelve tribes, each differing from the next. The Káli wove bones into their scant clothing, while the Niavenn tribe, closely tied to the Belcar, sported some steel in their attire.

Cailean's eyes wandered as a new delegation arrived. He felt a dull ache in his chest as the Icari made their way through the gathering. Their woven vests and sleeveless tunics were worn only by the highlander mountain tribes. At their head strode a woman. Her flame red, braided hair tied back and her blue eyes fierce. The thick sash that ran from her left shoulder to right hip and bronze torc at her neck symbolised her status as a chief. Etain, chieftain of the Icari, had arrived.

Etain, like the rest of her mountain kin, was a warrior. They had been betrothed two months ago.

She saw Cailean watching and gave him a slight nod. Their gaze spoke volumes as their eyes met. They would talk properly once the Conclave had concluded. He knew how the conversation would end even as he fought to deny it. No doubt Etain knew it too. For among the Salvaari, family came first, and Henghis was Etain's cousin by blood. A tie stronger than any vow they had once sworn.

All the tribes were assembled. Each one was vastly different from the last, save for one thing. Every man and every woman of every tribe wore an arm ring around their wrist. A devout sign of their faith.

The shaman's staff thudded against one of the stones and the clearing grew silent.

"In sight of the spirits, we come here to this sacred grove in Conclave," he began with an ancient voice. "Tonight, we sit in judgement of the tale carried by Cyneric, leader of the Aedei and brother to the slain chief, Malakai."

The look on the faces of those gathered suggested all had heard of the death. Some, Cailean knew, would have mourned it.

All eyes turned to Cyneric as he stepped forwards from the crowd. "Many of you know me. Many of you have fought beside me. What the shaman says is true. My brother is dead. Killed by one who stands among us even as Malakai lies in the cold iron earth."

Another of the chieftains stepped forward. His hair was filled with feathers and his skin was darker like those of his tribe.

"We have all heard rumour that you were attacked within your lands. Is this true?" Dáire of the Coventina asked.

"It is," Cyneric replied. "And tonight, I call for justice against the chieftain of the Catuvantuli, Henghis son of Elidor."

A few gasps came out of the crowd, for none would have expected Henghis to be the culprit.

"What he says is true. The chief of the Aedei fell before my eyes," came a growl as the accused leader stepped forward, his eyes blazing. "I commanded his death myself. And then I led an attack on Caelis and burnt it to the ground."

At Henghis' side walked two men. The first was clad in the robes of a Salvaari wanderer, but the second was not native to their land. Whispers and surprise ran through the crowd as a foreigner stepped into their midst. None had expected to see a Medean knight this far beyond the border. Cailean ran his eyes over Henghis and saw something he had never seen on the man's face before. Anger.

"What cause did you have to break the peace?" called out Etain as she strode into the stone circle. "A peace that has kept civil war at bay for many years?"

"What cause did I have?" Henghis echoed the words before turning his burning gaze towards Cyneric. "My cause was vengeance. You thought your brother was so clever, didn't you, Cyneric? Clever enough to send a warband into my land near a month past to sack one of my villages without warning. It was Malakai who broke the peace, not I."

"That is a lie," Cyneric bellowed above the roar that followed from the crowd. "My brother would never have defiled the treaty he himself forged with your father."

"Yes, that was what I told my people who came to me from the village bringing word of the slaughter. Malakai would not do this,

I told them. Malakai is an honourable man. Or so I thought. That was until I found this." Henghis turned to his wanderer and held out a hand.

The man reached into his cloak and withdrew an arm ring of silver. Henghis took the band and held it up for all to see.

"This is of Aedei make," he said, "and its owner painted in the same blue woad you wear now was found dead at the village he had just laid to waste. He was one of your people. I was well within my right to exact revenge for those slain by your brother's hand."

Etain walked over to her kinsmen and took the band from his out-stretched hand.

"It is true. This is of Aedei craft," she told the chieftains, her voice containing a hint of sorrow.

"Chief Cyneric." The shaman waved a hand to silence the crowd. "What do you have to say in defence of this?"

Cailean watched his brother step forwards and all eyes peered at him closely.

"I know nothing of what you speak. I swear by the spirits," he growled softly. He turned to his brother and gave him a nod. "Cailean?"

The chief's brother shook his head, and his eyes did not leave Cyneric's. The wordless question was as loud as any accusation.

"No," was all he said.

He knew nothing of the attack.

Henghis strode forwards and brought his face to within inches of the Aedei chieftain's.

Fury burned in his gaze as he spoke. "You dare invoke the spirits and lie? An attack was made on my people, on my land. Fifty innocent people lay dead within the Catuvantuli border, the attackers wearing Aedei colours. And yet you claim to be guiltless of the crime?" He gazed around the clearing and his flame-filled eyes flickered from chief to chief. "It is clear that the lordling wanted to prove his iron and blood his sword."

Henghis looked the man opposite up and down before he pulled a small dagger from beneath his cloak.

"In the name of my people. In the name of the Catuvantuli, I declare Raigath on this pretender." He slid the blade of the dagger across the palm of his hand as he spoke the oath.

Henghis tossed the bloody blade into the dirt at his feet and his hate filled eyes bored into Cyneric. He wrapped his blood-covered fingers around his silver arm ring as he spoke. "In the name of the spirits, I will have blood for this."

The tribes grew silent as they watched the altercation. To bring a blade into the grove was a sacred offence, yet to swear Raigath, the most sacred of oaths. A blood oath sworn upon one's arm ring was unbreakable. To break it was to receive a fate worse than death. To break it was to be cursed by the spirits for eternity.

One of the chieftains entered the stone circle with his powerful chest exposed and his hands clenched into fists.

"What have you done?" he snarled as his golden eyes glinted dangerously. "You speak of those who bring dishonour by lying before the spirits, yet you bring a blade into their sacred grove? The very heart of the forest?"

"Peace, Balor of the Sagailean," called out another of the tribal leaders.

The woman stepped forwards as she spoke, and her voice held a dark allure. She wore little more than a small wrap around her breasts that left her stomach bare and a long dress that barely disturbed the ground. A slit in its centre revealed her linen covered legs.

The chief of the Káli looked at the man as if he was her next meal. "He meant no offence."

"You may have forgotten the importance of tradition, Vaylin." Balor spat as he glared at the black-haired woman. "But my people have not."

"Enough!" roared the shaman as he stepped between the two

leaders. "You go too far, Henghis."

"Apologies." The Catuvantuli tapped a fist to his heart, a symbol of his sincerity. "It was not my intention to cause offence."

Cailean held back a snort as the man spoke. Of course, the man meant nothing by it.

"Oh, but it was Henghis of the Catuvantuli," came a new voice, its tone nearly musical.

A man stepped forwards as though he had appeared from nothing. He was clad in gnarled robes, while his head was bald and scarred. His eyes were blacker than the night sky and as piercing as the moon. Silence fell as he walked through the crowd, for all feared the dark power of the druids.

His hands moved as he spoke. "And it is for that same reason that Tanris himself has accepted your oath."

A very real shiver ran down Cailean's spine as the dark spirit was named.

"Why would the Dark One grant such a favour, spirit caller?" asked the shaman.

The druid seemed to sway as he walked into the centre of the gathering.

"This past moon I crossed into the other Plain at the behest of Tanris. I was shown many, many things," he told them.

"What did you see?" asked Vaylin, her dark eyes flashing.

"I saw a wolf rising. I saw a bloodmoon arisen over burning skies. I saw the eagle entangled with a great viper. I saw shadows ripped in two, as if the night itself had been pierced. The spirits whisper that the eyes of Tanris are soon to be revealed, and as day turns night, fire shall follow."

"What meaning did you take from this?" the shaman asked as his eyes bore into those of the druid.

"Events have been put in motion that cannot be undone, wise one." The druid turned around and his eyes flickered from one face to another before they came to a rest on the leader of the

Catuvantuli. "At the next full moon, the Festival of Sylvaine will be upon us. Here we shall gather. But know this: no matter what storm breaks through these forests in days to come, no matter how the crows feast, not one blade is to be drawn at the festival. Or no one will be able to save you."

The Salvaari were quiet as the druid stepped back. All thoughts had turned towards his words. When a druid talked, you ignored him at your peril.

The shaman looked up slowly. "What is it that you want, Henghis, son of Elidor?"

"I merely wish for those responsible for the death of my people to atone for their sins. My tribe will not be humiliated."

"Pah." Cyneric snorted and glared at his rival.

Cailean had seen the look in his eye before. It was a look that said the insult would not go unpunished.

"My people were not responsible for this barbarity, Henghis. You are blind to the truth."

"It is you who is blind. Malakai was a leader, not you. Choose your next words with care."

"My brother may have been trained to lead my people, trained to command. I was trained to fight and kill my enemies. Oh, I have chosen my words very carefully, Henghis," he said, his voice rising as he glared at the Catuvantuli and his men. "If it is war you want, I will bring the rage of the spirits down upon you."

The words echoed through Salvaar as the delegations left the grove. There was no escaping this war and now they all had to choose a side.

Cailean walked through the trees, each step taking him further from the fires of his people. Come dawn they would ride hard for their lands. In less than a week, blades would be drawn and blood would be spilled. The chieftains would be talking now. Some would choose sides and honour past pledges, while others would simply watch as the conflict unfolded.

He should have been at his brother's side, but he needed to do one thing first. A thing that in his eyes went beyond the unfolding war.

To his side branches cracked as another approached.

"Cailean."

He turned to the voice with a thin smile. Her red hair was cast in shadows.

"Etain," he said, feeling the taste of joy as the name rolled across his lips. She crossed the ground to him without a sound. Steel rasped as the chieftain of the Icari drew her dagger and held it to his throat, her face inches from his own.

Pain filled her eyes as she spoke. "Is it true?"

Cailean's breath faltered as he looked into the woman's fiery gaze. "No," he murmured.

"Is it true?" Louder.

"I swear we had nothing to do with the raid."

She could see the truth in his eyes as he spoke. Etain slowly nodded and withdrew her blade while her eyes never left his own. He could see the sadness in them, just as she could see it in his.

She stepped back and slid her knife back into its sheath, "I am sorry."

"I would have done the same."

They stood in silence for a moment before Etain slowly shook her head. "I must go. My people need me. My cousin needs me. I have no choice."

"I understand. Henghis is your blood. A thing that goes well beyond any pledge we once made," Cailean replied.

"Maybe this was always fated so."

The Aedei looked at her and his eyes flashed intensely. "I do not believe that."

"Who can ascertain the will of the spirits?" she said softly as she lightly touched his arm.

Her voice held no sorrow or hint of sadness. Instead, her words were spoken as if no more than fact. As was her way. It would be the only familiarity she showed him now that they were all but enemies. The chieftain stepped back and still her eyes never left him. "Perhaps one day."

"Perhaps one day," Cailean agreed.

It was harder than he had anticipated and he saw a hint of pain flash into her expression too.

Etain held out an arm as she composed herself. "Farewell, Cailean of the Aedei."

"Farewell, Etain of the Icari," he replied, taking the arm.

They stood like that for a moment before Etain let his arm go and dipped her head to turn away.

Cailean realised he may never see her again and his heart began to ache. There was much he wanted to say, but he could not. Not here and not now. Not after what had been said at the Conclave.

Etain started to walk back through the trees. Cailean watched her leave with regret.

"Don't die," she called over her shoulder.

The Aedei's eyes peered into her back as she walked away.

"I will not," Cailean said quietly.

He prayed that he did not meet her on the battlefield.

The moon was at its highest when Cailean arrived back. His brother greeted him, yet there was no question on his lips. Cyneric knew. Many probably did.

"Dáire of the Coventina has vowed his support," Cyneric told him. "As have the Sagailean. No doubt the Belcar and Niavenn will watch from their borders rather than get involved, as is their way."

"As is their way," Cailean agreed.

"As for the others," Cyneric continued after a moment, "all have been swayed by Henghis and his words."

"Those are not good odds."

Cyneric nodded. Even if the Belcar and Niavenn had aided them, they were badly outnumbered. The Sagailean barely had over two thousand spears, while tribes such as the Catuvantuli had near five thousand. At best it would be near five to one against the Aedei alliance.

"No, they are not," the chief muttered before turning his gaze to his brother. "We can bring perhaps six thousand spears to bear over the following days with Balor and his people. The Coventina will arrive in half a moon, but many of their men will be left to watch their own border. With them, we may reach as many as nine thousand."

Cailean glanced at him sombrely. "Not enough."

"The spirits are yet to decide, brother."

"Aye," Cailean replied, deep in thought. "We were outnumbered when the west invaded and still we threw them from our lands."

"Much has changed since then. But perhaps not all." Cyneric clapped a hand on his brother's shoulder. "Clean yourself of woad. I have a task for you."

The sun had barely risen when Cyneric returned to the grove. Watched on by the soulless eyes of the druids, the chief of the Aedei tightened his grip on the axe he bore.

It was a simple tool: a warrior's weapon.

He glanced over his shoulder to take in the faces of each of his own people, the few who had accompanied him to the conclave. They were brave, strong and loyal to a fault. Was he worthy enough to lead them?

Cyneric raised his axe.

He brought it down and the honed steel blade dug deep into the flesh of the Sacred Tree.

There it would remain until the fighting was done. "War,"

Cyneric said quietly as he released his grip.

The Aedei at his back roared filling the grove with a cheer that echoed to the very plains of the spirits.

War was inescapable now.

FOUR

Brilliant rays of the midday sun glimmered along the vast stone walls and soaring towers of Palen-Tor. A gentle breeze lightly caressed the eagle-emblazoned banners of Dorian Raynor, King of all Annora. The city was once merely the capital of the Kingdom of Aethela. It now stood as a beacon to all of Annora. Raynor, formally king of Aethela, had spent decades of his life working to unify the three Annoran kingdoms under his banner. The crown had come at great cost, and yet now it was his warriors that stood in their shining armour along the ramparts of the walls. They gazed out over the green fields and small woodland that surrounded the vast city. Behind them, the city met with a steep cliff and the ocean broke upon rock a hundred feet below. Within the outer wall stood thousands of houses made of stone and wood. They stretched in all directions to fit the growing population of Palen-Tor, over two hundred thousand men, women and children. Beyond the town, a second inner wall surrounded the great castle of Palen-Tor itself, wrapping the keep tightly in a stone embrace.

Thousands of townspeople hurried around the city. They were busy hanging hundreds of red banners bearing the ivory-encircled scarlet eagle of Raynor. Other flags emblazoned with the snake symbol of Caspin flew among them.

King Dorian's outriders had brought word that Duke Santiago

Caspin and the wedding retinue would arrive within the hour, and soon after that, the infamous wedding would take place. The world was shifting underfoot, and in just a few short hours, both the Annoran royal line and House Caspin would be elevated well beyond even their most powerful rivals. A deadly game was about to begin.

Lukas Raynor glanced up into the clear blue sky as he hurried through the streets, his boots thudding on the stone pavement. As the second and youngest of the King Dorian's sons, Lukas had been put in charge of the wedding preparation. For the last month, he had been torn away from his books and his horses in favour of sending invitations, arranging parties and directing hundreds of people.

How he'd hated it.

No expense had been spared on his brother's, the heir's, wedding day. At least, Lukas thought with a smirk, if what he'd heard about Lady Sofia was true, then she was as pious and devout as Prince Dayne was. As it was in Medea, it was in Annora, all worshipped the Twins. Not to mention, the bards sang about the exotic beauty of Duke Caspin's daughter as often as they told the tales of Dayne's near-legendary swordsmanship. They would all know soon enough if what was said about Sofia happened to be true.

At twenty-six summers, Lukas was every bit the soldier that his agile form suggested. As the second son of the renowned warrior king, Lukas had grown up with the sword, though he had always preferred his books and horses to the way of the warrior. His mid-length, light brown hair shone in the sunlight, while his face was clean shaven. His tunic and britches were simple and unembroidered, for like the rest of his family, Lukas saw no need of glamorous attire. The sword at his hip was just as plain except for the golden, eagle-shaped crossguard and pommel. It was a warrior's blade and not a ceremonial toy that so many among the nobility carried. It was a castle-forged, steel longsword, as beautiful as it was deadly. At his throat hung the sun and moon amulet of the Twins.

"Looks like everything is going to plan."

Lukas looked to his side as a deep, heavily accented voice interrupted his thoughts. His lips twitched into a smile. If the man's dark skin, angular features, bright orange headscarf and short, pointed beard didn't give him away, then his clothing would have. Cyan and orange loose robes beneath embellished steel pauldrons and breastplate, while his equally as flamboyant trousers were tucked into high, brown boots. Braided tassels adorned his wide belt, while a wicked khopesh sword hung from his hip. His massive arms were covered in the hard, rippling muscle that only a master of the bow would bear. The man was Sakkar Alsahra, a warrior from the Larissan desert clans to the far west. Two summers past, Lukas had the good fortune of saving his life in a border skirmish, and since that moment, Sakkar had been honour-bound to him until he could repay the debt. Lukas had tried to convince him otherwise, but the pride and stubbornness of the Larissan wouldn't hear of it. In the two years since, the pair had forged a friendship as strong as brothers.

The prince snorted. "You know these weddings, Sakkar my friend. Nothing ever goes to plan."

"Aye," replied the Larissan. "The wine will flow and the streets will fill and even the most honourable will become drunken fools. Myself chief among them."

They both chuckled. Sakkar was always the joker, and he would always say to live everyday as though it was your last. It kept the man in good spirits and gods did the people love him.

"Though perhaps if this Lady Sofia is as beautiful as they claim," Sakkar continued, "your brother at least will be pleased."

"I suppose we will soon find out." Lukas grinned. "At worst they can at least pray together."

"No doubt," came the reply as the pair made their way through the bustling streets filled with men, women and children of all ages hurrying about the city.

Small detachments of the city watch roamed Palen-Tor. Their surcoats sported the red eagle of Annora. Merchants and traders called loudly through the busy streets as they attempted to sell their wares. All things Medean had gained in popularity thanks to the ever-approaching wedding and were flowing through the Annoran capital. Silks, jewels, furs, weapons and even wine from the northern kingdoms sold by the minute. They filled the coffers of all who had thought to set up networks with their counterparts in Medea.

The prince and his companion quickly navigated through the throngs of people and maze of streets until at last they arrived at the outer wall of Palen-Tor. The huge gates of the city were two feet thick and flung wide open, allowing an almost constant stream of travellers to enter the stone walls. Half a dozen heavily armed Annoran soldiers stood at the city's entrance, while an equal number stood atop the gatehouse armed with bows. Many more stood idle along the walls or walked the streets below. Despite not having been at war in near twenty-two years, Palen-Tor was always on high alert. The king wished to set an example for the visiting Medeans. A show of strength. One that was to be expected from the warrior king who had marched straight back from war to take the throne of Laeoflaed from its former monarch.

"Prince Lukas." One of the soldiers walked over to the young prince and his companion.

"Captain," Lukas greeted the man and clasped his outstretched arm. The soldier nodded to Sakkar before gesturing to the stairs that led up onto the walls. "We have just received word that Duke Caspin and his daughter are barely a mile out. Sir Garrik and a dozen knights have been sent out to escort them to the city."

"Good," the prince replied as the three men quickly strode up the stone stairs and onto the wall's walkway.

Lukas leaned out over the wall and scanned the long road that began beneath him and vanished into the horizon. The fertile land surrounding the Annoran capital supported dozens of farms that grew most of the wheat that the capital needed. The Palen River cut through the farmland that surrounded the city, giving life to the farms and supplying the city with a constant source of fresh water, while beyond the river the road vanished into the depths of Bandor forest. From above the wall came a shrill cry as a hawk circled high in the air before gliding down and landing gracefully atop Sakkar's outstretched arm. With a laugh, the Larissan ran a hand over the bird's feathered head as it glanced out across the open fields.

"Aye, Sabra," he said before pointing out across the farmland. "Over there."

The hawk had been with his friend for as long as he could remember and years before that. Sabra served as almost a scout for the Larissan.

Lukas squinted as his eyes followed his companion's gesture. A glimmer of silver signalled a contingent of mounted figures emerging from the forest little over a mile away. After months of talks and negotiations, the wedding between not only Dayne and Sofia, but of two of the most powerful families among the kingdoms, was about to happen. Lukas watched intently as the retinue started to pour out of the forest. The prince was curious about the Medean guests, the only people from their land that he had met being Duke Santiago's many ambassadors and his younger brother Aquale. First came the Annoran knights led by the Palen-Tor master-at-arms, Garrik Skarlit, clad in their shining silver armour and crimson cloaks. Emerald banners of House Caspin flew atop standards carried by chainmail-clad men of Duke Santiago's house guard, wrapped in their equally as green capes. Behind them rode the duke and his bodyguard of elite mercenaries. They were hard men who had been born and raised in the fires of war. Men who would never desert their post. As with the rest of Medea, the Caspin lands were overflowing with soldiers of coin, many of whom stood as knights. Despite working for profit, the Medean sellswords were renowned and highly sought after thanks to their reputation of being loyal to a fault. At their fore was their captain, the grey-haired Lord Garcia Castile. A legendary warrior who had devoted his life to the Caspin linage. First to Duke Alfonso, and then his son and heir, Duke Santiago.

Behind the duke and his guard came brilliant, embossed carriages pulled by fine horses and surrounded by more of the duke's men. Lady Sofia Caspin along with other ladies of court would be travelling within the first carriage. More warriors and knights would be bringing up the rear on the convoy that was already stretching well out of the woodland.

"Well," the prince began as he looked to his companions, "shall we begin?"

Sakkar grinned. "I suppose we must."

"Captain," Lukas said. "Give the order."

"They're here!" bellowed the gate captain as he turned his gaze down into the streets below. "Sound the call."

Lukas glanced around the hall almost uneasily as he waited, as they all waited. The meeting between his family and that of Santiago Caspin had gone smoothly. In some ways, the duke had reminded him of his own father. He was proud and dignified despite his years. Like the rest of his people, the duke's eyes were rich brown with flecks of emerald. He had the look of a man who could easily carve up an opponent with his sword. The rumours about his ailing health had clearly been just that. Sofia, on the other hand, he knew nothing about, save the stories he'd been told. As was the Medean custom, brides covered their faces behind a veil on the day of their wedding and remained silent until the ceremony itself. And as such, neither Lukas nor even her husband to be had seen her face or heard her voice. Though from what he knew of Medeans, Lukas guessed that Lady Sofia would have elegant features, ebony hair that matched her equally as dark eyes and an exotic voice.

He shifted uncomfortably wishing for the thousandth time to remove the silver band that ran through his hair. Lukas had always hated crowns, even when they were no more than a thin band worn for ceremonial occasions.

The young prince gazed around the hall taking in the sea of faces below the dais upon which he stood. Perhaps two hundred people stood within the confines of the ceremonial hall, a mixture of Annorans and Medeans alike. Noblemen, ladies of the court, knights and friends of both nations filled the large crowd. Galan, Lord of Torosa, and Balderik, Lord of Laeoflaed, stood at the forefront of the crowd. An aisle ran down the very centre of the hall surrounded by a guard of honour, made up of the renowned Palen-Tor royal knights in their red colours and those of the Caspin family in their green. The guard stood as silent sentinels.

At the foot of the dais stood the master-at-arms and commander of the guard, Sir Garrik, alongside Sir Tristayn Martyn, general of the Aethelan army. Both were great bears of men who under their armour were covered in hard muscle. Opposite them stood the commander of the House Caspin forces, Rodrigo Santana, clad in his chainmail armour and silver-trimmed, emerald cloak.

Lukas quickly shot the priest a glance and had to stop himself from smirking at the pure white robes that the leaders of the Twins faith sported. He'd always thought they looked ridiculous in their snow-white gowns and heavy golden amulets at their throats. Father Bardhyl had served the Aethelan throne for near forty of his sixty long years, and he had served it well in more than just matters of faith. Lukas saw the man as almost a grandfatherly figure, and despite that he didn't much care for the Twin Gods, Bardhyl had been a patient mentor to the young prince. The altar before the priest was as white as his robes and trimmed in an elegant, golden floral design. In front of which stood Dayne Raynor, heir to the

Annoran throne and soon-to-be heir of the Caspin lands.

Dayne was almost the spitting image of his father in his youth, with a powerful build and cropped brown hair neatly fitting beneath a crown of shining silver. As a child Lukas had always been jealous of his brother's dashing looks, strategic genius and political wit. Not to mention Dayne's renowned swordsmanship. At barely thirty summers, Dayne was rumoured to be an even greater warrior than his father had been, both in battle and in command. No small feat. He was cold, measured and calculated. Dayne was like winter ice while his brother burned as summer fire.

To the heir's left stood Aquale Caspin, Duke Santiago's only surviving brother, clad in his own brilliant ceremonial armour, while to his right stood his father, Dorian Raynor, Lord of Aethela and the first king of Annora. Despite his greying, dark hair, matched with his weathered face, Dorian was as strong as he had been thirty years before when he had earned his title as warrior king.

Lukas barely spared the woman next to his father a sideward glance. Queen Riona Raynor. Twenty years ago, she had been nothing more than the daughter of Torosa's former king – his only child. King Rowland had feared what would happen to her after his death, so he had made an offer to King Dorian that he couldn't refuse. It was an offer that would give the Aethelan lord a chance of realising his dream. If the King of Aethela and Laeoflaed agreed to marry his daughter, Rowland would bequeath to him the lands of Torosa and his crown. Dorian had accepted and now there she stood in her blue dress, bright eyes glimmering in the torchlight and slightly furrowed brow. Lukas' stepmother. How he despised the thought that his mother, his real mother, had been replaced.

"Do you think she's beautiful? Lady Sofia, I mean," came a hushed voice from Lukas' side.

His lips twitched into a smile as he heard his younger sister speak. Lukas shot her a sidelong glance as he grinned. If this had not been a formal occasion, he would have ruffled Kassandra's brunette hair.

The princess at sixteen was just as mischievous as she had been at six. She preferred to spend her time riding her horses and hiding from her mentors rather than embroidering and reading poetry. Despite the difference of age, the pair were closer than anyone, and Lukas loved her to pieces. She had been the only good thing to come out of Dorian's marriage to the princess of Torosa.

The prince leaned down towards his half-sister and he replied, "I hope so, for Dayne's sake."

Kassie smothered a laugh and jabbed an elbow into her older brother's side.

The prince's grin faded as footsteps sounded from outside the hall, and all eyes turned to the open doors. He glanced at Kassandra again as Santiago Caspin strode into the hall. His hand held that of his daughter who was wrapped in a stunning white and gold dress with a veil over her face. The garment was of light cotton and left her arms naked. Half a dozen of Sofia's handmaidens, each as beautiful as the next, walked behind the pair.

The maidens wore no veils and did not hide their elegant faces. Their eyes were dark and their features sharp, but as for the Lady herself? Lukas nearly grinned again. They'd find out soon enough.

"We gather here today to witness the union of Dayne Raynor, crowned prince of Annora, and of the Lady Sofia of House Caspian," Father Bardhyl said, his voice echoing around the hall so that all could hear. "In the sight of Durandail, Father of all Fathers, and the Silver Lady, Azaria, may the heavens bless this union." The priest paused a moment before turning to Sofia. "You may remove your veil."

The room grew silent. All eyes fixed upon the woman standing at the altar as she lifted her hands to the pearly white veil.

Sofia looked to Dayne as she pulled the headdress aside allowing her shining black hair to fall in tresses past her shoulders. The intake of breath that came from the crowd was loud and Lukas couldn't help but stare. The stories about the mysterious foreign beauty were true. Her enchanting eyes were rich brown and circled with long, lustrous lashes. Her slightly coloured skin was perfectly smooth and her lips full.

Aye, thought the prince as he watched as his brother's face lit up. He was captivated by the vision before his eyes. If anything, the stories didn't do the daughter of Santiago Caspin justice. Dayne took Sofia's hands, his eyes glued to her own.

"As your hands are joined, so too are your lives joined," said Father Bardhyl, raising his arms towards the pair.

Then they spoke in harmony. Dayne's strong voice was matched by Sofia's elegant and exotic tones. Even her words were beautiful.

"By the power of the gods brought from the heavens, may you love me. As the sun follows its course, may you follow me. As light to the eye, as joy to the heart, may your presence be with me," they said in union. "I will be the shield at your back and sword at your side and we will remain forevermore as one."

Bardhyl held out his hands towards the couple. A pair of matching wedding bands inlaid with emerald sat within. A wider band with a smaller stone for Dayne, while the more elegant of the two for Sofia.

The prince took the ring for his lady and held her hand softly. As he slid the ring onto her elegant finger, the priest began.

"May Azaria's moon bring you peace and serenity."

Sofia took the second ring and slid it onto Dayne's own finger as Bardhyl continued.

"May Durandail's sun grant you warmth and light" – he took the ringed hands in his own – "and today may the spirit of love find a dwelling place in your hearts."

The priest released their hands as the pair looked back at each other and their eyes met. The cheer as they kissed was deafening, filling not only the hall but the entire palace with sound.

The Prince of Annora and the Lady of Caspin were now one. Dayne Raynor was now heir to his father's throne and the Caspin lands. He was now the most powerful man in the kingdoms north of the empire.

It was a new chapter for Annora.

Laughter filled the throne room as the last of the sun's light slipped behind the horizon. Large tables of the finest oak had been transported into the hall for the feast that followed the ceremony. Musicians played and jesters performed their tricks; no expense had been spared. All of this and more Lukas saw from his vantage point at the side of one of the many food-laden tables. He leaned back to sit half on the table as he watched the nobles mingle.

"This will be you soon enough, little brother."

Lukas barely spared his brother a glance as Dayne joined him. The younger prince snorted. "I'm not so sure."

"Come now." Dayne grinned. "It is no secret that father wishes you to marry the daughter of Torosa's lord."

Lukas held back a sigh. It was true. Two summers past, he had spent the better part of a year with the Torosi to help strengthen their bonds of friendship and bring them further into the fold, for the only man who stood above the high lords of Torosa and Laeoflaed was the lord of Aethela, King Dorian himself.

"Iesha is a fine woman."

"Then why the glum look?"

Lukas merely shrugged. In truth he had little to answer to his brother's question. The Torosi lord's daughter loved to read and ride as much as he and the pair had spent untold hours talking and in the saddle together. Yet still he yearned to be untethered to the role of husband.

"Lukas, we are princes. The burden of choice of who we wed is a thing far removed." Dayne met his brother's eyes. "And besides, you have said yourself how much you admire her and Lord Galan and they you. It could be much worse." The heir sniggered. "Father could have wanted you to marry one of the Hornwood girls."

Lukas couldn't stop the grin from spreading across his lips. "I will drink to that."

The night wore on as the drink flowed.

Not a seat stood empty at the king's own table. At Lukas' side sat his sister Kassandra, while they were joined by the rest of his family and House Caspin. Dorian Raynor, Riona, Santiago Caspin and his brother, Aquale, talked in hushed tones at the head of the table, their meals barely touched. No doubt they talked about important matters of the state and crown, thought Lukas with a smirk. Beside the rulers, the newlyweds smiled and laughed as if they had fallen in love in the space of a few short hours. Apparently his ever-charming brother had finally found his equal. Not only that, but a beautiful one who brought over a hundred miles of land to his name.

Lukas took a swig from his cup and felt the wine warm him.

"Any more of that and you won't be able to walk straight," laughed Kassie from his right shoulder.

The prince wrapped an arm around his sister as he smiled. "I don't think you can talk about drinking too much."

She lightly smacked his chest and looked at him in mock horror. "I'll have you know I'm a princess of Annora. I leave the drinking to soldiers, drunkards and foolish princes."

"A proper princess you are." Lukas snorted. "Those two cups you've had tonight were nothing but water, I am sure."

Kassandra laughed. "That would be about it, yes."

The prince grinned at his sister before finishing the contents of his cup. He turned back to Kassie with a reply hot on his lips when he saw two women approaching the table. Like the rest of their people, they wore dresses of cotton that bared much skin and suited the warmth of the north far more than they did the cold and damp of Annora. He'd seen the ladies at the wedding. They were part of the Medean retinue. They were both beautiful and no doubt had some significance to the Caspin family. The older of the two who led was clearly of noble birth, while the younger who stood about two feet behind must have been a handmaid.

"Ah." Santiago Caspin gave a toothy grin as the pair reached the table.

Clearly, he had arranged this. Whatever this was. The duke nodded to Dorian as all on the royal table looked to the new arrivals.

"May I present Lady Eveline Ayria." He gestured to the first woman. She looked around thirty summers, with gorgeous long black hair and shining hazel eyes. She carried herself with a dignified pride, and even before she spoke, the prince knew Lady Eveline was as noble as her birth.

"My lords," she said with an elegant yet strong voice. Eveline dipped her head as she said the words, her eyes meeting the king's gaze. She smiled with her full lips. "A pleasure."

The king of Annora nodded back as he took the noblewoman's extended hand and planted a gentle kiss upon it. "Charmed."

"Lady Eveline has been advising me of late," continued the Medean duke. "She has a knack for keeping tricky nobles in line. A rare talent, I am sure you will agree."

The king chuckled. "All too rare, I'm afraid."

All eyes went back to Santiago as he continued, "I was hoping that you wouldn't mind if she stayed in Palen-Tor after my departure. A companion to my daughter, if you will, and perhaps she could even put her talents to use."

As his father replied, Lukas turned his gaze to Eveline's handmaiden. She looked around twenty, with elegant features common among the Medean nobility, with a slim but full figure and brown eyes that melted into golden light under the gaze of flame-lit braziers. The prince was captivated. The handmaiden glanced and saw him looking. She returned his gaze with a sly smile.

Lukas returned the smile and turned back to the conversation.

Even so, he couldn't resist a second glance at the woman. Gods, she was beautiful.

"You are most welcome in Palen-Tor, Lady Eveline," his father was saying.

"Our house is yours," Riona added lightly, placing a hand on her husband's arm. "And I for one believe we had best put your skills to use in the next council."

"Thank you, my lady," Eveline replied with a graceful smile.

Santiago waved a hand and nodded to the woman, giving her leave to go.

Lukas watched as she left but his eyes did not leave the mysterious woman at her back.

"That is Isabella," whispered Kassandra, leaning towards his ear.

"Who?" He looked to his sister.

Kassie sighed and shook her head. "Lady Eveline's handmaiden."

Of course, his sister knew. She knew everything to do with noble ladies and their households, servants included.

"I didn't say anything," he replied, despite feeling his lips twitch into a smile as he saw the maid, Isabella, glance back at him with a smirk.

She'd left her mistress and was slowly making her way around the room as if waiting for something, or someone.

"You really are hopeless," snorted the princess as she lightly jabbed her brother with her elbow. "Go on, I won't tell Father."

Lukas chuckled as he rose to his feet and he planted a kiss on Kassie's forehead. "Love you, sister."

"Yes, I know."

Barely an hour later, the prince of Annora was stumbling into his chambers, lips locked with those of Eveline's maid. Their bodies were pressed hard together as the doors shut behind them.

Lukas strode through the white corridors of the castle, buckling his sword belt on with a grin, fond memories of Isabella and their night together fresh on his mind. The prince didn't hear the footsteps from his back until Kassandra was latched to his arm and steering him down a new hallway.

"You look awfully pleased with yourself," she said simply.

"Careful now, you're far too young for these" – he paused a moment – "matters."

"Perhaps I am." Kassie stepped in front of her brother. "But Father is not."

Horror flooded Lukas and he felt an icy chill crawl up his back. He didn't want to think about how bad it would be if his father heard the rumours that his second son enjoyed the company of handmaidens and noblewomen a little too much. As second in line, he was supposed to form alliances through marriage and not bed countless women.

"You wouldn't dare."

"Wouldn't I?" "Kassandra said. Then she laughed. "It's alright, I won't."

Lukas breathed a sigh of relief.

"On one condition."

"Bribery isn't very ladylike." The prince crossed his arms and raised an eyebrow. "Go on, what do you want?"

Kassandra's eyes lit up. "I want you to teach me how to fight."

Lukas looked at her in shock. Women in Annora never picked up a sword. No woman in the entire breadth of the Aureian Empire to the west had ever wielded a blade. The prince had heard stories about vicious shieldmaidens of the Valkir Isles. Never in Annora though. They were god fearing followers of the Twins. Not to mention their father would be in a rage if he learned that Kassandra had even mentioned the idea.

"That is not happening."

The princess snorted. "I had best tell Father why it was that you left the feast early then."

"What if Father found out? You know what he'd do."

"He won't," Kassie replied innocently.

"But what of Father Bardhyl?" The prince shook his head in bewilderment. "The ... the very idea of this is near sacrilege."

Kassandra stepped close to her brother. She wore a sickly-sweet smile on her face. "We both know that you have little regard for the gods, Lukas. As I am sure Isabella is well acquainted with this fact …"

Lukas sighed. It was an impossible situation. To go against his father was to go against the will of the gods. He could hide his indiscretions and show his sister how to use a sword. It was an unusual thing, but he couldn't see the harm in it. Especially if Dorian never found out. Hell, when had he ever said no to his little sister?

"Alright," he said after a moment. "I'll do it."

Kassandra had leapt into his arms before the words had fully left his mouth.

"Thank you, big brother."

"Just don't tell anyone. Not Father, not Dayne, or especially–"

"Mother," the princess chimed in.

Lukas felt his mood darken. He had been but a child when his mother had been killed, yet he still remembered her face. Lukas could not bear to hold Riona, the imposter, as such.

"She is not my mother."

FIVE

Malcia, Duchy of Caspin, Medea

Kyler had ridden for the better part of a week when the rain arrived. It had cascaded down from the sky in a dark wave. The hood pulled up over his ears kept the water at bay. At least temporarily.

Mud squelched below as he kicked Asena into a trot towards the soft glow of fires appearing further down the road. The town of Malcia lay less than a mile away. A small border village that sat at the mouth of the Valley of Odrysia. He smiled; some luck at last.

Nearly all wishing to travel to Odrysia passed through the village. Many travelled there for supplies, but in Kyler's case, he sought a warm bed and shelter from the storm.

The guards at the gate barely acknowledged Kyler's presence as he rode through. There was little reason to fear a single rider. They stood under a small shelter and huddled around a brazier for warmth. A couple played dice atop a table, their eyes hungrily watching the growing pile of coins. Two men walked to the edge of the shelter with their hands resting on the shafts of their spears. After a quick exchange, the older of the two guards gestured to a building further down the street. Its windows were glowing orange from the firelight within. Over the door a sign hung with the image of a bow emblazoned upon it. It indicated the tavern that the locals called The Drunken Huntsman.

Raucous laughter assaulted his ears as he strode into the tavern and the heat of the fireplace drove the cold chill from his bones. The boy pulled his hood back and looked around the room for the first time. Dozens of people sat around tables, some talking in hushed whispers, while others roared with laughter. At least half a dozen were mercenaries armed to the teeth, no doubt spending the little money they earned fighting for one lord or another. The establishment was clearly Medean with the smell of alcohol thick in the air, as well as games of cards, dice and other gambling amusements. His lips twitched into a smile as he made his way over to the counter.

"What can I do for you?" called the innkeeper.

His was voice loud to rise above those of the clientele. "I'm looking for a bed for the night," Kyler told him.

The man ran his eyes over Kyler. "We have a few rooms available. Should do you well enough." He glanced at the boy inquisitively. "Just the one night, you said?"

Kyler nodded. "I'm travelling east."

"Ah, I see," the innkeeper replied knowingly and held out a wrinkled hand. "Five coins for the night."

Kyler looked at him aghast. What? Even rooms in the bigger cities cost half of that. Rooms that were, no doubt, larger.

"That is robbery."

"These are the last rooms this side of the valley." The man snorted as he crossed his arms. He nodded over his shoulder towards the door, and the pelting rain beyond it. He gave Kyler a mirthless smile. "Enjoy the storm. Perhaps you may even avoid the bandits that call the mouth of the valley home."

"Bandits?"

"Aye, bandits." The innkeeper nodded. "Came out of nowhere a month back and began to prey upon travellers and the like wishing to enter the valley."

So the rumours were true. Kyler had heard about a couple of attacks in recent times yet had no proof until now.

"Surely the Order would not let that stand."

The man shrugged. "That is none of my concern. I'm just a simple innkeeper. Now, no coin, no room."

Kyler glared at the man as he turned away. He had little choice.

"Wait," he said, reaching into his pouch and handing over five of the bronze coins.

It was going to be a long night.

"Pleasure doing business with you," replied the innkeeper as he snatched up the coins greedily.

Kyler snorted and gritted his teeth to cut of the sarcastic reply that threatened. He still had to get information from the man.

"One last thing." Kyler leaned on the counter. "Travellers from Odrysia pass through here from time to time."

The man shrugged. "That they do."

"What can you tell me about the Order of Kil'kara? Where would be the place to go if I had a mind to join their ranks?"

Kyler placed the cup on the counter. The innkeeper had clearly been in his position long enough to know the goings on in the only holy city to the east.

The innkeeper ran his eyes over the boy before him with a slight grin. "The memory is a bit foggy, lad." He held out a hand for the second time.

Kyler grimaced. His coin purse was already low.

A weathered hand shot out from behind Kyler and latched around the innkeeper's wrist.

"You'll not get one more coin." An older man, the owner of the hand, stepped beside Kyler with furious eyes. "That is, unless you wish to deal with the very Order that the boy is asking of. Any innkeeping fool who lives this close to the valley could easily give the boy the information he seeks. Perhaps we should seek out another with less of a fondness for coin. That is, if you have further quarrel."

A second man clad in steel chainmail stepped forward. He was wrapped in a dark blue surcoat emblazoned with Durandail's white sun. The warrior's hand dropped to his sword as he glared at the innkeeper. His voice was a growl as he spoke. "I have served the Twin Gods for near to a decade, and among our creed we do not tolerate thieves."

The innkeeper backed away as his hand hastily retreated behind the counter. "I did not–"

"Do not speak," the Knight of Kil'kara snapped.

The older of the two men turned to Kyler. "Right, lad, looks like we will be your companions in this cesspit tonight."

Kyler followed the two men as they made their way back to the far corner of the tavern. It was far enough away that Kyler had barely seen them when he had entered. He definitely hadn't seen the warrior clad in the garb of a Knight of Kil'kara.

The older man's grey-streaked hair suggested that he may have been around sixty. The younger man was perhaps in his mid-thirties. Both men had the darker-toned olive skin of those native to Aureia.

"The name is Gaius Aureilian," said the older man as they sat around the small table. He nodded at his companion, "This is my son, Torin."

The knight glanced at Kyler. "Recently transferred from the garrison in Rovira. Decided to follow the footsteps of my forebears and head north."

"I'm Kyler," the boy replied as he looked from one face to the next. "Kyler Landrey."

"Ah, Medean." Gaius' lips twitched into a warm smile.

Kyler returned the grin. "From Adrestia. Around a week's ride from here."

"And looking to join the Order," said Torin.

"That is my wish," Kyler replied.

"By the sword you carry I take it that you wish to serve as a knight and not as maija," Gaius inquired. It was more a statement than question.

"It is my dream."

"It is a hard road, lad," the knight told him. "Not all who make it to the gates of the garrison get to don the armour. Fewer still succeed the trials and join the brotherhood."

"My father was a soldier, and his father before him. It is in my blood," Kyler said. "And for perhaps the first time in my life, my purpose is clear. Either I will find a way to take up arms for the Order or I will make one."

"Well said." Gaius dipped his head to the boy.

"Aye." Torin grinned. "Though before you arrive at the garrison, you should know of its history. Tell me, what do you know of Duran Cormac?"

Kyler looked at the knight thoughtfully. "He was Medean and lived a century ago. He formed the northern outpost of the Order and took part in the Inquisition. They say he was a soldier of fierce renown."

"He was much more than a simple soldier," Torin replied with a slight chuckle. "He saved Medea from itself and led the war that followed the Inquisition."

"That cannot be true." Kyler snorted in disbelief. "Every Medean knows the story of how it was the five houses who saved the country. Duran rode with them. He did not lead them. If the knights had led the families and toppled the barons of old, we would know."

"History is written by the victors and those who claim the spoils, lad." Gaius crossed his arms and leaned back. "Cormac and the knights' involvement is all but forgotten in part because of the nobility, and in part because he desired no glory."

"Then tell me," the Medean replied curiously, "what really happened?"

"A century ago, Duran claimed the valley of Odrysia at the behest of the cardinal," Torin began, his eyes meeting with Kyler's. "He and his followers built Odrysia and the fortress Kilgareth from nothing with their bare hands. The last and greatest of the Order's four outposts, its very birth being baptised in the fires of war. As you know, Medea had been on the verge of collapse, rocked by bloody war after bloody war, a divided nation filled with warring families, each squabbling with the next for reasons beyond count. A land filled with the dark teachings of the Old Religion that had plagued the nation for a thousand years. Ruled by leaders corrupted by the spirits of the old ways, along with the whispers of tricksters and vagabonds. Men who believed in the mere notion that magic existed and was a force for good. Some said that the barons consorted with demons and other unholy beasts. Cardinal Octavan saw this and demanded the corruption to come to an end. Duran Cormac could not stand idly by as he watched the nation burn under pagan rule. So, he sounded the call, and many answered. The Order of Kil'kara mobilised under his banner and not just from the Rovira. Thousands of knights crossed kingdom and ocean to follow him and fight at his side. He inspired such loyalty that even some of the Medean houses started to flock behind him. None more powerful than the great house of Bailon."

It dawned on Kyler as he listened. Perhaps the families had not thrown out the old ways. They had merely sided with the new and claimed the bounty that followed.

"Over the course of four bloody years, the knights and their allies beyond count gathered their strength. The fighting grew fiercest on the plains of Palanza when the combined armies of Kil'kara, Aureia, Annora and the houses fought the deciding battle."

Kyler knew of Palanza and he knew of the legends it had created. "Estevan Bailon's sacrifice," he murmured.

Torin's lips curled into a thin-lipped smile. "Where the Bear of the North gave his life to ensure victory. Together they drove out the corrupt pagans and the Old Religion, pushing many into Salvaar to the east and cleansing the country. From the ashes of the shattered nation rose the land of Medea, divided into five provinces ruled by the families who had shed blood for the Twins. A land that had thrown off the yoke of feudalism, replacing it with new gods and peace. Peace for perhaps the first time in centuries. It all began when Duran Cormac took up the sword and said, 'Enough'."

"I did not know that the man was so involved." Kyler nodded slowly. "Many of us, all of us, thought that Estevan was the man responsible for liberating Medea."

"He helped, yes. He crumbled the resolve of our enemy in one final attack. Yet in doing so put his son on the throne of his lands. A boy who saw his father as the saviour who deserved all the glory and fame won at Palanza." Gaius simply shrugged. "The knights do not fight for glory and were content for the Medean houses to claim it. Though among the Order, Duran stands a legend."

"As fate would have it, the master of the northern outpost is a direct descendant of Cormac's," added Torin. "Cormac was more than just a soldier. He was a true warrior. A staunch defender of our faith … a man to die for."

Two nights after Malcia, the black sky loomed eerily over Kyler as his eyes snapped open. The trees surrounding creaked as the wind blew through their branches. A snort came from where the horses were tethered. Something had spooked them.

Bandits. It had to be. Many plagued the valley mouth leading to Odrysia, preying on unwary travellers and pilgrims.

Kyler slowly eased his bedroll back with his left hand as he reached for his sword with his right. He glanced across the small clearing and in the soft light of the smouldering campfire he could see Torin resting with his back against a tree, his sword resting on his knees.

He dipped his head slightly. He was awake.

Gaius slowly slid a hand up under the blanket behind his head. He kept his shortsword beneath.

The sound of the crackling fire nearly masked the sound of footsteps scurrying among the trees. Someone was out there.

Kyler locked eyes with the knight as the sound drew nearer. The horses stirred and their hooves pawed at the ground. Whoever walked the woods was close. The footfalls drew closer.

Torin rose to his feet and slid his sword slowly from its sheath. His heater shield leaned against the tree to his side, but it was too late to take it up.

Kyler followed suit and rose to his full height; his blade held in a firm grip. Dark shapes flickered through the blackness. Closer they came.

The three men moved back-to-back with their weapons held at the ready. Waiting.

"Who goes there?" spoke Torin. Loud. Commanding. Without fear.

A chuckle came out of the night as a man stepped forward, the orange glow of the fire shining on his face. His eyes sparkled hungrily, while a scar across his lip matched his menacing voice.

"Look what we have here. A Knight of Kil'kara."

Three more men joined the first, their swords and axes held in their steady hands. Kyler glanced over his shoulder to watch as more bandits appeared from the shadows. He adjusted his grip, loosening his fingers slightly. There would have been at least ten bandits slowly encircling them.

Torin levelled his sword at the leader. "You know what will happen if you take one more step."

The man snorted. "Your faith blinds you."

"Durandail guides my sword. Lust for coin guides yours," the knight replied. "You are beneath me."

"Throw down your blades. Forfeit what you have. Gold, coin, jewels" – a savage grin covered the man's face – "or your lives."

"And if we do that, you would what? Spare us?"

"You have my word."

"Aye," grunted Gaius, "the word of a bandit. The word of a man who steals and kills for no cause save desire. I think I will take my chances with the sword."

The man shot a glance at Kyler. "What about you, boy? If you want to see the sun rise, lay down your sword."

The Medean met his eyes, and the corner of his lips curled. "Come and take it, coward."

"Very well."

The clearing rang with the sound of steel as weapons were drawn. Kyler slowed his breathing just as he had been taught.

Thunder rolled through the earth below.

The sound came from behind. Again and again and again. Fifty paces. Closing.

A whistle came from the shadows. A warning.

The leader of the bandits snarled before barking an order. "Out!"

The sound was close. The thundering of hooves clear. A horn's song grew loud.

The bandits scattered and faded away into the shadows from whence they had come.

The horn sounded again, and the thundering grew deafening. Kyler turned to face the new threat, his sword brought to bear.

"KIL'KARA!" the roar erupted out of the trees.

Out of the woods charged a line of armoured horses. Astride them rode warriors clad from head to toe in armour, their surcoats, cloaks and the plumes of their helms as blue as the ocean.

The Knights of Kil'kara had come.

One of the bandits stood his ground and raised his axe. With a savage cry, the first rider drove his spear forwards with the full force and momentum of the charge behind his arm. The steel tip flashed and drove deep into the raider's chest and sent him crashing onto his back in a crimson spray.

"After them!" bellowed the knight as he tore his spear free.

Eight of the riders surged after the bandits in a blue wave, their eyes glowing with intent. The four remaining knights formed a rough perimeter around the campsite. A fifth man clad in loose cloth rode beside the warrior who now approached. Covered in faded robes, brown gloves and with a satchel slung across his shoulder, the man appeared every inch the scholar he was. He was maija.

The leader of the knights turned his mount towards the three and gave them a quick nod.

"Mount up, I suggest we leave quickly," was all he said. His voice was commanding and left no room for protest.

Without hesitating, Kyler snatched up his bedroll and raced across to Asena. He swung himself into his saddle even as he pulled the reins loose.

A shout went up in the distance followed by the clashing of steel.

"With us," barked the knight, spurring his mount back the way they had come.

Kyler kicked his heels in and then they were thundering through the forest.

The first light of dawn was shining above the horizon when the knights finally called a halt. Kyler ran a hand down his mount's neck before dismounting alongside his comrades. The adrenaline from the night's events had faded and his tiredness threatened him.

He watched as the knights gathered together. Every man was a professional killer. Any doubt of that was crushed by the unrelenting glint of danger in their eyes. Now that the boy could see them clearly, it was clear that the leader of the knights was more than just equal with his brothers. Pauldrons covered his shoulders, and a pair of long, blue feathers stood tall to either side of his crest. A chest-plate of steel embellished with a carved sun covered his body. The knight's blue cloak began with a pure white fur pelt across his shoulders.

"They're getting bolder," muttered one of the warriors.

"Aye." The leader nodded as he turned to face Kyler and his companions. "A year ago, that would never have happened. But this last moon … something has stirred those rats out of hiding and now they plague the land from Malcia to the valley mouth. Though I have never witnessed them this far east before. Little more than three days from Odrysia."

"Things change with time, brother," replied Torin, extending his arm to the knight. "We owe you our lives."

He took it. "It was our duty," he said before removing his crested helm. His dark hair cascaded down to his shoulders as he continued, "I am Matias Valenquez, Knight of the Circle, and warden of the northern garrison."

A warden of Kil'kara, Kyler thought, one of the highest honours granted among the Order. It was barely a step below grand master. From what he knew, the Circle was comprised of half a dozen of the greatest knights and maija in the north, while the warden was tasked with protecting the roads to Odrysia. The knight spared Kyler a glance, and the boy instantly knew him to be Medean, his kinsman.

"My name is Torin Aureilian," the Aureian told the warden. "This is my father, Gaius."

"Aureilian? You were not expected so soon."

"We had no reason to delay." Torin shrugged.

"And there was little trouble along the road," added Gaius, "until that lot last night."

"Then you were fortunate," Matias replied. He turned to Kyler. "And you are?"

They clasped arms. "Kyler Landrey."

"Unless the ears deceive," the knight said, "you'd be from Caspin's province. Adrestian highlands?"

"I called it home, yes," he replied with a grin.

Valenquez clearly had a keenly honed mind, for few could place a name to a province.

"I thought as much."

Kyler looked around at the knights who watched. Their eyes betrayed nothing. Most of the men before Kyler were foreign, he realised. One had the midnight skin of those to the far west, maybe even beyond Berenithia, while another had the brown tones of a Larissan. Any with a sword of steel, fire in their eyes and faith in their heart could face the trials of the Order.

The warden nodded slowly and glanced towards the horizon. "Now, we will escort you safely to Odrysia and the Citadel. It is a three-day journey through the valley, so we ride now. We do not stop until nightfall."

SIX

Lupentine Sea, the Valkir Isles

Small waves rippled through the deep blue waters of the Lupentine Sea, gently caressing the hull of the large twin-masted ship. The Lupentine, which ran through the heart of a series of islands that made up the Valkir Isles, was known not only for its calm waters in summer but its ferocious storms in the depths of winter. Storms that had taken many an unwary captain to his doom.

The waters were painted in a brilliant red hue as the sun started to disappear behind the mountains on one of the nearby isles.

The ship, known as the Wind Rider, glided through the Lupentine as a gentle easterly wind billowed through its sails. The prow of the Wind Rider, carved into the shape of a vicious dragon, glared ferociously towards the horizon.

Lief Farrin, a well-respected jarl of the Valkir, gazed out over the Lupentine. His eyes were fixed upon an island barely half a mile away now.

Home. For the jarl, it was the dozens of acres of farmland that he called his own. Aye, the winters were harsh, and it was near impossible to grow any more than grass, yet the sea of greens, browns and greys that flowed from horizon to horizon was all that he longed for. By day his crew and their families tilled the fields and herded the livestock, while by night they feasted in Lief's longhall, drinking, singing and dancing. A simple life yet a good one.

Despite being nearly fifty summers, Lief stood tall and proud. His eyes were as sharp as any younger man and his mind sharper. The jarl was a powerful man, broad and muscular, much like the rest of his forty-strong crew. His long, black hair was sprinkled with the grey that came with his age. The same grey spread through his long, braided beard. A massive cloak made of a bear's pelt was wrapped around his broad shoulders, while at his side hung a steel-headed axe. His most prized possession was the amulet that dangled by his throat in the shape of a raven's skull with Valkir runes carved into it, a gift from his long-deceased wife.

His lips twitched into a smile. After an entire summer of raiding the mainland, Lief and his warriors were nearly home. Each summer the Valkir would depart their isles and sail to the mainland in search of supplies and plunder to help them survive the harsh winter, some to never return home. They needed to raid, for without the provisions taken from the mainlanders, they wouldn't survive through the winter. It was a harsh truth for any of the Valkir knowing death was around the corner, but they welcomed it.

Gloried in it.

Every single person aboard the Wind Rider was a warrior to the bone, the men and shieldmaidens alike, their bodies forged of lean muscle and weathered by the harsh elements of the Valkir Isles and by the vicious sea. Each wore layered lamellar armour of steel and leather. Some of them integrated mainland chainmail into their gear. All carried a sword, axe or bow. Many sported tattoos that wound around their bodies.

Lief would die for any of them without hesitation.

Once more he leaned out over the railing to watch as they drew nearer and nearer to their destination. The railing creaked as he was joined by another man.

"Nearly home, father," the newcomer announced, glancing at Lief.

The jarl grinned as his accomplice spoke. "Aye, lad, nearly," he replied.

Erik Farrin, only son of Lief Farrin, chucked. "I've almost forgotten what a bed feels like."

Even though he was barely over twenty summers, Erik was just as tall, broad and strong as any of the older and more seasoned warriors. A dark tattoo spiralled down his right arm – a tattoo that few ever possessed. The image of a great snake marked him as bloodsworn, an elite force within the Valkir, a brotherhood of blood that was admired by all and feared by many.

With wild long golden hair, a short beard and piercing blue eyes, he appeared as a ruthless lion.

"A bloodsworn warrior in need of a bed?" came a new voice laced with sarcasm. "Perhaps you should have become a priest."

Lief laughed and turned to face the raven-haired woman who had spoken as she crossed the deck towards them.

"My dear sister, you wound me," replied Erik with a sidelong smile.

The woman grinned and crossed her arms. "We all know you think of but two things, Erik. Drinking and fighting."

"As you only have mind towards your next bed partner."

She snorted and rolled her dark eyes. "Well, what can I say? Only the Sea-Father knows which breath will be our last. Why not take as much joy from this world before we fall from it?"

With a laugh, the jarl clapped a hand over the woman's shoulder.

Astrid shared her father's long, raven-coloured hair, which she tied back behind her shoulders. At twenty-four summers, she was the eldest child of the jarl. As such, Astrid carried herself with the same confidence and pride of a veteran. She had her mother's deep, amber gaze and indomitable willpower. Her eyes were warm and bright as if her intelligence shone through them. Like the rest of the crew, Astrid was covered in lean muscle from years spent at sea. A thin layer of black ochre encircled her eyes, for that was shieldmaiden tradition. She was clad in a simple leather jerkin and wore a knife at her hip instead of a sword or axe, for contrary to her title, Astrid was no warrior. Despite this, she was an invaluable member of Lief's crew. She was able to navigate through the harshest of storms and plan impossible raids. Astrid's wit was as sharp as any sword and twice as deadly.

The squawking of gulls carried across the waves as the Wind Rider sped through the water. Each moment brought her closer to Agartha.

"Astrid, do you see that?" called a grinning Erik. His arm was outstretched as he pointed towards the cliffs of the ever-nearing island.

She gazed intently towards the cliff-face until she saw a tiny speck gliding through the sky towards the ship. "An eagle," she murmured with a grin, even as the bird flew closer. "A good omen."

The crew of the Rider gazed towards the eagle as it soared through the sky towards them. It was almost as if to welcome the seafarers home.

One of the Valkir, a veteran named Torben, pursed his lips and let out three short bird-sounding whistles. Almost instantly the eagle swooped down and glided through the ships rigging and beneath its sails before letting out a beautiful, long cry as it flew overhead.

The crew cheered as the eagle passed over their heads before gliding out over the sea.

Lief laughed as he watched the bird soar away. They were home.

The Wind Rider slid around a bend in the island as the helmsman guided her around the cliffs.

Then Agartha came into view. The large port town sprawled along the coast and up the side of a small mountain where it stopped by the edge of a dense forest.

The brilliant glow of fires began to light up the darkness in Agartha, as the sun had almost completely disappeared behind the horizon. Dozens of houses and long, wooden halls were scattered around the coastal town, while in the bay a small fleet of a dozen ships lay at anchor. Half their number were tied off at the small dock. The animal-shaped prows of the ships glared ferociously towards Agartha as the last of the sun's rays glinted against the polished wood.

From the town came the sound of a horn as they were spotted rounding the headland. A horn blown to welcome those returning back to Agartha.

The ship was filled with cheers and laughter as the horn's notes were carried across the water.

"We're home," roared the jarl, embracing his children with his powerful arms. "We're home."

The Wind Rider eased into port as its sails were furled away by the Valkir in the rigging. A small crowd of their kinsmen had gathered by the pier as the ship had come in and now they stood impatiently waiting to see how the crew had fared on their latest venture. How much plunder had they taken? Which of the warriors had fallen in the chaos of battle?

Lief gathered up his large shield and slung it across his back. Its weight seemed like nothing to the veteran warrior. He took one final look around his ship, his home for the last season, before he strode down the gangplank onto the pier.

He was truly home.

The jarl glanced around, as more warriors joined him, carrying cargo and shields over their shoulders, to see Erik and Astrid at his back.

Lief could see the anxiety in the eyes of the small folk. Not only families of the warriors had come but others with them. Men and women, old and young, nobles and commoners alike.

"So," Lief began, and his eyes darted from one person to the next. His voice suddenly broke into a roar. "Another successful raid!"

The crowd cheered and swarmed the disembarking warriors, eager to celebrate and join in their good fortune. Many of the warriors embraced friends and loved ones even as the questions about the raid began.

Lief couldn't help but grin as he made his way through the sea of smiling faces and received congratulations and claps on the back from his kinsmen.

They had made it again.

The jarl looked back at his weary crew as they mingled with the crowd and took in the look of pure elation on even the most exhausted of faces.

"Jarl Lief," called a man over the cheers of the crowd.

He looked towards the voice as a man of about thirty summers pushed his way through the people surrounding the crew until he stood before the jarl. Sven Joramir was sworn to the earl and leader of Agartha, Magnus. Sven also had the privilege of being his cousin by blood. He was a renowned warrior, but even so, the sight of him left a bad taste in Lief's mouth.

"Sven." The jarl nodded while hiding his distaste.

The sworn warrior peered at Lief's men. "The raid went well then?"

"Aye." Lief gestured to the pier where the first of the chests laden with coin, jewels and gold was being ferried to land. "We have good fortune for our people to share in."

Sven's eyes flashed almost eagerly. "Very good. Earl Magnus will expect his share. I would not keep him waiting."

Lief caught the threat even as it left Sven's mouth. Before he could reply, the warrior was pushing his way back through the crowd.

Scurry back to your lord, Lief thought as anger rose in his chest.

"That man is a snake," Astrid muttered from his side as she glared into the retreating man's back. "He but bares his fangs and everyone falls to command."

Lief nodded his agreement as his eyes followed the road uphill to where he could just make out the top of the earl's great hall. "We had best take the lion's share to the earl before it gets any darker," he said and gave Astrid a sidelong glance.

He turned back to his crew. One last task.

"Erik," he called as he noticed his son talking to a young golden-haired shieldmaiden.

Hélla, her name was. She was one of the warriors from Lief's crew. They had grown close this last voyage. All bonds formed in battle were strong, yet the pair had become almost inseparable of late.

Erik looked up to roll his eyes at his father before muttering something to the woman. She turned scarlet as he made his way towards Lief and his sister.

"Gather ten of the crew and we'll take what is owed up the hill to Earl Magnus," he told his children.

They nodded in reply.

"And then," continued Lief, "then we feast."

Laughter and the sounds of merriment filled the streets of Agartha as the darkness of night descended. The moon's brilliant silver rays glinted on the polished wood of the ships moored in the bay.

Flames crackled from the fire that burned within Jarl Lief's longhall, casting the building in its warm light. The entire crew of the Wind Rider, along with their families, drank and feasted in celebration of their return and the end of the raiding season. Some of the Valkir sat on the long wooden benches, while others gathered in small groups to drink away the night.

The sound of music, barely audible over the celebration, began as one of the warriors started to strum the stings of his lute.

Lief himself sat apart from his comrades, his family. His scâldir.

He felt weary as if his age had finally caught up with him. Perhaps he had just returned from his last raid. Perhaps.

He did not know.

Lief's eyes slowly moved around the room, and he couldn't help but let his lips curl into half a smile. He'd gotten them home alive and well again. He saw Astrid laughing with some of her companions by the fire. She shot him a grin as he looked over. Lief took in every face: men and women he had known for years. Few he had known for over a decade, for with the hard life that every Valkir lived, most barely made it to forty summers.

"Jarl," called a cheery voice.

Lief looked up with a grin as his old friend Torben approached with a cup of ale in each hand. He sat on the bench beside the jarl and held a cup out to his leader.

"The night is too old to not have a drink," he said, his voice booming cheerfully.

At well over six feet tall, Torben stood a giant among the Valkir. Despite being of over forty years, his menacing size was matched by his immense strength. If not for his constant toothy grin and boisterous manner, many may well have been scared of the man. Strong, brave and loyal without fault: he was everything that the Valkir aspired to be. He was the jarl's oldest living friend.

Lief chuckled and took the cup. "Good to see you, Torben."

"Well," the other man replied, "I'd be happy to see anyone who gave me a drink, huh?"

Astrid grinned as she walked through the hall, drink in hand and laughter on her lips.

"I have missed this," chuckled the warrior at her side.

His laugh was as strong as the man himself. Raol Soren stood as a friend, no, a brother, to Astrid. One who had fought countless battles beside her and drank countless drinks with her.

"It's been too long," the shieldmaiden said, shooting her

companion with a sidelong glance.

It had been, for the Valkir months and seasons at sea were necessary for their mere survival. Now each and all longed for the roar of the fire. The taste of ale and the song and dance came with the winds of winter.

"What do you plan to do before the snow melts and we return to the sea?" she asked.

"Drink myself into an early grave." The Valkir's eyes flashed with humour. "No, this winter I have plans."

"Oh?"

He peered through the crowd until his eyes locked with those of a young woman. Astrid recognised her though she was not of the Wind Rider, nor was she trained in the arts of war. Mayrun, her name was, the daughter of a tanner whom Raol had introduced her to last winter. The woman smiled at him with eyes filled with joy. They held each other's gaze.

"She agreed."

"What?" Astrid turned to her friend as she realised what he had just said. "Raol … Congratulations."

"We are to be wed in one moon's time."

"I am happy for you, my friend." She clapped an arm on his back. "We must drink. Celebrate."

Lief wrapped his thick cloak of bearskin around his shoulders as he left the warmth of the hall and strode outside. He'd drunk his fill of ale and needed some air, even though the chill turned his breath into a mist.

He was alone except for the wind.

Then Lief saw the figure, shrouded by shadows, hooded and cloaked.

Curious, the jarl began to make his way over to the figure who stood overlooking the bay.

"Jarl Lief."

It was the sworn sword of Earl Magnus, Sven Joramir. Lief walked over and stood beside the man as he continued, "The earl sent me."

No doubt. "Aye," replied the jarl.

"Congratulations on your latest venture." Sven didn't turn from the bay, but Lief saw his lips twitch into a smirk.

"What do you want, Sven?"

"Magnus sent me to solve his land dispute with you."

Anger sparked in Lief. So, that was it. "The earl knows the land is rightfully mine. And so do you."

"The lord offers to pay two hundred pieces of silver in compensation, but no more."

"Bribery, then?" Lief spat on the ground at his feet. "No … no, this isn't about land. This is about something else."

Still Sven did not look at him.

He knows something. "What is this really about?"

Sven crossed his arms. "I told you. Land. Land that the earl desires."

"No, no, it's not," replied the jarl.

Then it came to him. He'd just returned from another successful raid. That marked over thirty successful raids in as many years, far more than most, and they hadn't just been successful; they had been incredibly prosperous.

"This is about power," Lief growled. "The earl thinks I'm becoming a threat."

Sven shrugged. He didn't even deny it.

"This is just a move by Magnus to depose me of my land and title and you know it."

Sven finally turned to face him. "You ought to be careful who you say that too, jarl. The earl has heard rumours. Whispers about certain things that would cause a shift in power. We have traitors in our midst, Lief." He indicated the hall. "And one name always seems to come before all others. I wonder if you know whom."

The jarl knew it instantly. *It's mine.* "That's a lie," snarled Lief. "I have always served—"

Then the knife plunged into his chest.

Sven had been so fast that he hadn't seen the blow coming.

The jarl's instincts kicked in and he lashed out on impulse. His right fist connected heavily with Sven's face. The warrior grunted and lost his grip on the knife as he stumbled back a step. The blood-soaked dagger sang as it struck the ground.

Lief pushed a hand to his wound watching in horror as blood poured over his fingers in a tide of red. He'd seen enough death to know that his lifeblood was flowing from the wound.

His lips twisted into a soundless snarl as he took a step towards his enemy, propelling himself forwards with nothing but willpower. Then he stumbled and his hands reached out in vain for the railing. He collapsed to his knees; his strength fleeing.

Darkness entered his vision like a black shroud.

The last of Lief's strength failed as he fell into a pool of his own blood.

The last thing he saw was Sven's back retreating into the night as the doors to his hall creaked open.

It had been a long time since Astrid had seen her father in the hall. Too long.

Something is wrong.

The shieldmaiden quickly made her way through the hall clutching the handle of her dagger. Her pace quickened as she felt a sick feeling in her stomach.

She saw her brother standing close to Hélla with a grin on his lips. Astrid made her way over without hesitation.

"Erik, have you seen Father?"

An annoyed look crossed his face as he turned away from the golden-haired shieldmaiden. "No."

Astrid frowned as she made her way back through the hall, and then she saw Torben. If anyone had seen Lief it was him.

The old warrior grinned as she approached.

"Have you seen the jarl?"

"Aye," replied Torben, gesturing towards the large doors of the hall. "Said he needed some air."

Astrid smiled gratefully. "Thank you."

She shook her head to clear it as she strode towards the doors, her pace quickening. Astrid's grip was tight on her dagger, and her knuckles turned white as winter snow. They opened before her as a warrior slowly walked through into the hall. He nearly collided with her and his ashen face spoke volumes.

"Astrid …"

"What is it?" she replied, and she felt her heart falter.

Without waiting for a reply, Astrid shoved the wooden doors open and strode into the cold night air. The first thing she saw was the blood splattered on the ground.

Then she saw her father's body.

"Father!" she screamed as she ran over to his still form and collapsed to her knees. She felt for a pulse. Nothing. "No. No. No …"

"He was gone before I found him," the warrior murmured from behind her. His voice was filled with anguish.

She barely heard the doors being flung open as the crew rushed outside. They must have heard her scream.

Erik dropped to his knees beside her. "Father … No …"

Astrid looked up from her father's body and for the first time noticed the bloody knife lying on the ground. She snatched it up.

"This isn't Father's," was all she said as her voice broke.

Anger rose through Astrid's breast as she looked up from her father's lifeless body. His blood soaked her clothes. Her tear-soaked eyes flashed with pain and rage.

She would find the owner of the knife. Whoever was responsible would die.

SEVEN

City of Palen-Tor, Aethela, Kingdom of Annora

Prince Lukas Raynor of Annora circled his opponent. His boots slid lightly over the stone floor of the castle's cellar. The brilliant orange flames of half a dozen braziers lit the small room.

Armoured in nothing more than his tunic and britches, a hard hit with even a wooden practice sword could leave a mark.

"Keep your sword up," Lukas instructed as he flicked his practice blade into a ready position.

The torchlight glinted off the polished wood.

Opposite him his younger half-sister, Kassandra, similarly garbed, tried to match his steps, her own practice sword held with the kind of awkwardness of a beginner swordsman.

She lunged with a grunt, aiming her sword at Lukas' chest. The prince stepped back, parried the blade with his own, and then the pair exchanged a flurry of strokes. The sound of wood clashing echoed around the small room. The girl swung an overhead blow and her wooden sword whistled through the air. Lukas took the blow on his own and then lightly smacked his weapon into his sister's stomach. The girl sighed as Lukas chuckled and stepped towards her.

"Better," he said.

"Better?" she snapped back in frustration. "We've been at this for days and I still haven't landed a single blow."

Lukas shrugged. "Yes. But at least now you know the correct way to hold a sword. With the handle and not the blade."

A slight grin started to show across her lips, and she punched the prince in the shoulder. "Lukas!"

"Kassandra," he replied sarcastically as he cuffed her on the back of her head lightly and ruffled her brunette hair.

Kassandra shot her older brother with a blazing glare and pushed his hand off her head. "Get off."

The pair broke down, unable to hold back their laughter any longer.

Despite the difference of age, the pair were closer than anything and would do anything for each other, including these secret sword lessons. Something that would send their father into a rage if he ever found out.

Lukas ran a hand through his neatly cropped brunette hair and glanced out the only window in the cellar, a tiny slit in the stone wall. The sun had nearly risen to its peak.

"It's nearly midday," he told Kassandra.

"Ah, yes." She rolled her amber eyes. "Your council meeting."

Lukas sighed. Perhaps something interesting would come up. He doubted it.

Annora had been at peace for near twenty-two years. As such, rarely did anything remotely exciting happen during council.

"But at least I don't have to spend the rest of my day doing embroidery." He held out a hand and motioned to his sister.

She tossed him her sword. "Embroidery and those old crones can be cursed." Kassandra groaned heavily. "But father does insist."

Lukas chuckled. "Aye, you have your old crones, and I have my old men. What a pair we make."

The princess nodded. "We'll continue our lessons tomorrow, won't we?"

"Of course we will, Kassie." He grinned as his sister's eyes lit up excitedly.

She hugged her brother. "Thank you."

Lukas hugged her back tightly with a chuckle.

They ended the embrace, and the prince smirked at his sister. "Now, you had best get back into your dress and to your embroidery before you are missed."

The endless stone hallways of Palen-Tor castle echoed as Prince Lukas strode down them, his real sword now buckled at his hip. It had been days since the Medean contingent had left for their home, eager to return to their palaces and families. With the wedding over, they'd said their farewells and that was that. The ties of a new alliance were stronger than ever.

He made his way through the vast maze of corridors and stairways as unconsciously as someone who had been born and raised in them. He passed guards, knights, servants and nobles, all of whom he knew by name.

The hallways had started to grow cold of late as the warmth of summer seeped away and made way for the bone-chilling cold.

He glanced out the large open windows as he walked and peered up into the hazy sky that had been growing darker by the day.

"Prince Lukas."

He looked down the hallway as Sakkar's deep voice reached his ears.

"Sakkar," Lukas greeted his friend.

He realised instantly that something troubled the Larissan warrior. Sakkar hastened towards him with a frown on his brow.

Strange.

It was unlike the Larissan to appear anything but calm. It didn't matter if he was fighting or if he was simply walking about the castle, he was never rattled. Something had happened.

"What is it?" the prince asked as Sakkar reached him.

"There was a rider. Salvaari by the look of him."

Lukas' eyes widened. Of all the people who could have ridden to Palen-Tor, it was one of the eastern tribesmen? The very same people they had fought a bloody war with for near three years. Not to mention that the Salvaar forests stood near five hundred miles from Palen-Tor.

"Salvaari? Do you know why?" Lukas continued walking, eager now to reach the council. Eager for the first time in years. "The Salvaari homeland is half a month's hard ride from here. Not to mention we were at war barely twenty-three years ago."

"I don't know, Lukas," Sakkar replied.

His use of the prince's first name was uncustomary and would have sent the old nobles into an uproar about class decency, but he was as close as anyone to Lukas. Besides which, the title felt almost uncomfortable to the prince of Annora.

"He's been granted an audience before the council though," continued Sakkar. "Rode all the way to Palen-Tor alone so that he could slip through Medea unnoticed."

An audience with the council? Whatever the reason the Salvaari had ridden to Palen-Tor, it must be bad.

"That is brave." The prince glanced at his friend. The Medeans were not known for their love of Salvaari, to say the least. "The lords of Torosa and Laeoflaed left days ago, and so to my father the decisions shall fall alone. I suppose I should hear what the man has to say."

The council chamber was silent as the grave.

Dorian Raynor, King of Annora, and his wife, Riona, sat on their thrones atop a small dais of perfectly cut stone. At fifty summers, Dorian was as strong and fearless as a man half his age. He carried himself with the same amount of pride as he had when he took the throne of Laeoflaed by force twenty-two years ago. His neatly cropped, greying hair and beard, his penetrating amber eyes and almost common clothing helped to breathe life into the legend of the warrior king. His longsword, the very blade he had used to take

Laeoflaed from its old ruler, was at his left hand leaning against the throne.

As the story went, the last king of Laeoflaed, Balinor Tagenet, had murdered the family of the young Aethelan king. Dorian's family. It had been a power play. Nothing more and nothing less.

After the war with the Salvaari had come to its bloody conclusion, Dorian had become known not only as Aethela's greatest warrior, but Annora's as well. He was beloved by his men and respected by his enemies. Fearing his rival's growing fame, the king of Laeoflaed had arrested Dorian's wife, surviving siblings and his children. With the help of Sir Garrik, the children had escaped. The other members of the Raynor lineage were not so fortunate. Balinor executed them without trial.

Upon Raynor's return from the Salvaari war, he took up arms once again in his grief and marched on Laeoflaed. He struck the king down for his betrayal and claimed the throne. The crowns of both Aethela and Laeoflaed were now upon his brow, and with that, the idea of a single kingdom called Annora had begun.

Ever since that moment, there had been peace.

On either side of the thrones stood the two princes. Lukas stood at his stepmother's left hand with his arms crossed as he looked over the stone room lit only by torches. At Dorian's right hand stood the heir to the Annoran throne, Prince Dayne, his left hand wrapped around the eagle-shaped hilt of his sword, while his amulet was ever present at his throat. At his side stood his new bride, Lady Sofia, who watched the room as curiously as the woman next to her, the mysterious foreign beauty, Lady Eveline Ayria. They may have been members of the council in Santiago Caspin's court, but this was a different beast altogether. This was a council of one of the strongest mainland kingdoms, more powerful than all of the Medean duchies combined.

Throughout the hall stood just over half a dozen noblemen, some in their youth and some well past it. They murmured among themselves. Lukas barely noticed them. Fools, his father often called them. Fools with titles. And after ten years in council, the prince was inclined to agree. Often causing more trouble than good, these men were a necessary evil. Loyal allies who provided tax to the crown and soldiers to its army.

Closer to the throne, two men clad in varying chainmail and plate armour stood at the bottom of the dais: General Tristayn Martyn, and the master-at-arms, Sir Garrik Skarlit. Both had been with the Raynor family for decades and had sided with Dorian in the civil war that had won Lukas' father the throne.

The twelve men and two women made up the council of Annora, and had Lukas' mother still been alive, she would have been with them. Dorian had often said that her mind had helped keep the realm intact and had prevented the civil strife for a decade or more before her untimely death.

Lukas' gaze was drawn to the massive wooden doors of the court as they began to creak open. All eyes went to the entrance of the hall as a pair of Annoran guards heaved the doors open, and a figure strode in. Lukas had never seen one of the Salvaari tribesmen before. He'd only been three when the war had ended. He had, however, been told stories about the fearless warriors of the east who went into battle half-naked, covered in tattoos and war paint. Savages, some called them. Primitive.

His father called them fearless.

As it turned out, he was right, Lukas thought as he took in the man walking towards the throne without sparing the nobles so much as a sidewards glance.

The man had long shaggy black hair that was tied back and painted with white grease. His beard was short and dark. He wore baggy trousers and thick boots with a lining of fur. Leather bracers adorned his forearms, while a golden torc hung at his throat. A sleeveless tunic left his massive biceps bare and revealed his defined muscles covered with swirling black tattoos. A thick woollen cloak pushed behind his shoulders brushed on the stones underfoot, while an arm ring of gold hung around his right wrist. He was a powerful man, one who made even Sir Garrik look small.

Lukas kept his eyes on the man who appeared to be around thirty summers. He watched as the Salvaari walked closer and closer to the throne. The warrior did not take his eyes from the king.

Sir Garrik placed his right hand on the hilt of his sword. "That's close enough."

A warning.

Lukas watched curiously as the Salvaari turned to the master-at-arms and ran his gaze over him. The room grew tense. All eyes were on the silent confrontation. Then the tribesman smirked, unimpressed with the man before him, and glanced up at the king.

"It's a wonder Annora did not fall many years ago with men such as this guarding the throne," he said, and his deep voice was laced with humour.

"Is that why you came, Salvaari? To exchange insults?" Garrik stepped towards the man. "Perhaps a savage such as yourself would care to back your insolence with steel."

The warrior stepped close to the Annoran. Their faces were inches from each other.

"Perhaps."

"Enough," growled Dorian.

His voice echoed around the room as he rose to his feet. Anger flashed across his eyes.

"Apologies, King," replied the Salvaari, shooting Garrik with a grin before turning to the king of Annora.

His eyes flicked up to the red and white tapestry that hung behind the throne. It was emblazoned with the Raynor family crest.

"When last our people met, your banners flew above Aethela alone, yet now the great eagle soars above all Annora."

Dorian glared at him for a moment before replying, "What is it that you want, Salvaari?"

"I am Cailean," he said. "Brother of Cyneric, chief of the Aedei. You fought my father, Raywold, and his warriors at the Argon River twenty-five years ago."

Lukas glanced at his father and watched a brief flicker of emotion cross his eyes.

"Aye, I remember Raywold and the Argon. Your tribe fought well."

Cailean nodded as he replied, "We nearly won the war for our people."

"Nearly."

Lukas' lips curled as the Salvaari chuckled at the king's response. It was clear that the man was without fear and was as proud as anyone Lukas had ever met.

"And then together we stopped the war."

"Indeed."

Lukas had been told the stories about the final days of the war. Stories about how his father, the infamous king of Aethela, had gone against his fellow rulers' wishes. How he had decided not to wipe out every trace of the tribes and had instead met with the Aedei chieftain and sued for peace. The other tribes soon followed the much-respected Raywold, and one by one stopped the fighting. Dorian saved thousands of lives, but in so doing broke the last of his ties to Laeoflaed and its monarch. Some of the Salvaari had even joined with Dorian Raynor to topple Balinor from his throne.

"King, I come on behalf of my brother and my tribe," Cailean said, and his voice was now filled with emotion. "My people are at war."

War?

Dorian gestured for him to continue, "Tell me."

"To tell the full story would take a lifetime, King Dorian." He turned back to face the nobles. "One month past, a detachment of my tribe's leaders was ambushed within our own border by a

Catuvantuli warband and slaughtered where they rode. My brother and chief, Malakai, was slain. An entire village was put to the sword and razed to the ground. Cyneric barely escaped the slaughter that followed." He paused for a moment and his gaze swept around the room. "Cyneric had planned to petition the tribes at the Conclave, a sacred gathering of the tribal leaders. But the man who led the attack on my brothers, the chieftain of the Catuvantuli, Henghis, is well respected among our people. He told the chiefs that we had attacked his people, and he was just retaliating for the offence. By the time the dust settled, most of the tribes had made their intentions clear."

Lukas glanced at the faces of the nobles as the Salvaari paused. They looked thoughtful. Probably more so at the prospect of weakened tribes than ending a civil war.

Cailean shrugged as he continued, "One by one, the tribes took sides. The Icari and the other mountain clans were the first to pledge for Henghis. The Káli were next."

"The Káli?" Dorian cut in as he leant forwards in his throne. "Those poison worshippers?"

Cailean snorted contemptuously. "Remember them, do you?"

"I never forget," the king replied.

"When I left my homeland, only two chiefs had pledged warriors to our cause." Cailean looked directly at the king; hoping he was reaching him. He prayed his words would make a difference. "We are on the verge of a great war among the tribes."

Dorian nodded solemnly. "And you wish for the aid of Annora's armies?"

"He wants us to step into a foreign land and save his savage people," snorted one of the nobles.

Silence filled the room, and all eyes turned to the speaker. Lukas nearly groaned at the owner of the voice: Edmund Hornwood. An aristocrat who had inherited his vast wealth from his deceased father. A man with the world at his fingertips. An incompetent fool both in politics and the arts of negotiation, yet his skill with the blade rivalled the best Annora had to offer.

Rage flashed across Cailean's eyes, and he turned on the noble. "Have you ever been in a war? Have you ever seen rivers run red with the blood of your people?"

"I was in Salvaar," he shot back, and his eyes dared the savage to act.

"Were you now?" The chief's brother seemed amused. "Hiding at the rear, no doubt."

That silenced him. Again, Lukas smiled. He liked the Salvaari.

Cailean turned back to Dorian. "King, my people are prepared to fight and die. I do not ask you to save my people, because we do not need saving." He stepped towards the throne, and his blazing eyes met those of the Annoran king's. "Twenty-three years ago, we ended a war together. Aedei and Annora. Together. What I ask is that you help to end another."

All eyes turned to the king as he crossed his arms, and Lukas could see he was deep in thought.

He wants to help the Aedei, Lukas realised. *But he needs to convince the nobles to send their warriors and knights into a foreign war.*

"I must think," the king said slowly before calling out to his hall guards. "Find this man some food and drink. He's had a long ride."

"Yes, my lord," they replied, walking towards the Salvaari warrior. "Cailean, you'll have your response by dusk. You have my word. The rest of you" – he indicated the council members – "we have work to do."

The Salvaari was led from the hall and only then did the council make their way to a smaller chamber. One for planning war. In its centre stood a large table covered by a map of the mainland and surrounding islands.

"We have two choices. Help the Aedei, or watch them fall," the king's voice rang.

"Let them burn. Why should we care?" muttered Edmund. Some of the nobles murmured their agreement.

"Why?" started Lukas. "Because the Aedei have been allies in the past. Strong allies. Some of them joined us in removing Balinor from power twenty-three years ago. Have you forgotten that?"

"They merely showed us favour for sparing their wretched lives."

"You know nothing of what you speak," Lukas snapped. "If only your skill with a blade was matched by your wisdom in politics. Alas, it is not."

Hornwood's face burned as he glared at his prince. "I was there … my lord. Were you?"

"That is enough!"

All eyes flew to the king as his command shook the chamber.

"These petty grievances end now."

Lukas' flaming gaze burned into Hornwood as he slowly nodded. "If we show them our friendship now, they will return the favour."

Prince Dayne spoke for the first time. "Well said, little brother. There is, of course, military gain by helping this chieftain, Cyneric. Not to mention our old ties with them. You've often said that their skill at arms is great, Father."

Lukas gave his brother a grateful look. *Thank you.*

Dayne continued, "However, I do worry. The fact that they are on the verge of civil war shows how quickly alliances change and shift among the Salvaari tribes. United under one ruler, they could be strong. But they are scattered. Divided. Never in their history have they united behind a single leader with a single purpose. Not to mention they are pagan."

"It is as Prince Dayne says," chorused another of the nobles. "Why should I risk me and mine in the affairs of unwashed barbarians?"

"Who said anything about unwashed barbarians, Lord Molay?" Dayne turned to the man. His voice was as calm and calculating as ever. "I said that they were pagan. Nothing more."

"Surely you jest."

Lukas could see the sparkle in his brother's eyes now.

"Have you studied their art?" Dayne asked.

Everyone was watching the exchange now.

"Forgive me, my prince, but what use would I have for art?"

"Oh, I find that you can learn a great deal about people from their craft. The Salvaari are unmatched when it comes to their wood carvings. It is how they tell their stories, their history and legends. It can be quite beautiful. Do you know what that tells me about their people? No? Well, perhaps one day you shall."

Lukas nearly chuckled as Molay's face reddened and he fell silent. To this day none of them could understand Dayne's study of foreign art. Yet as the older prince always said, if you know a people's art, then you know the people. And if you know the people, then you cannot be defeated by them. Thus far it had worked, and Dayne had not even been close to losing a battle that he had commanded.

"Prince Dayne is right," said Queen Riona, speaking for the first time and breaking the silence. "As much as we may want to help these people, we must also think about this in a diplomatic way. How many borders will we have to cross? How many people will just sit by as a foreign army marches through?"

"Aye, that is true," added Sir Garrik, nodding to the queen of Annora. "The risk is too great. Our army would have to march through Miera, and those men do not trust any outsider. It would be as good as a declaration of war to the horsemen."

"So, we send a rider to King Zoran and ask for military access," Lukas replied with force.

"Perhaps, but that may not be so wise," cut in Lady Eveline.

All eyes went to the woman as she spoke with a captivating voice. "As much as I would wish to help the Aedei tribesmen, it is an impossible reality. The only two passages into the Salvaar forests are through Miera and House Aloys' lands, and as you know, neither would let an army simply march through without repercussions. A message asking to allow access to twenty thousand soldiers would be laughed at. Any army we sent into the Steppe of Miera would be greeted by a line of charging horses on the horizon within a day."

Dorian nodded thoughtfully as the woman spoke.

"Our history with the horsemen will have given King Zoran greater cause not to trust us," he said. "Not to mention their experiences with foreigners for the last few hundred years."

King Dorian turned his gaze to General Tristayn, his most trusted advisor. A man who had served as his right hand during the war with the Salvaari and the following civil war.

"General, what are your thoughts?"

"My king," he said, and his powerful voice reached around the chamber, "the problem is before you."

Tristayn indicated the map before running his finger along its surface as he spoke. "To the south, along the coast of the Lupentine Sea, we get raided constantly by those Valkir devils. Summer has ended, yet they have grown bolder in recent years. They raid and pillage for months without end, stinging and then drifting away into the seas where they cannot be matched or controlled. Not to mention further along the coast past the city-states of Trecento. The Sacasian Sea lies treacherous and the pirates who plague it have remained elusive for near on thirty years. The states, even Elara, despite their efforts are barely able to keep them contained to the south. Word is that even men who hunt the raiders are calling the southern Sacasian a nation of thieves."

"Indeed." One of the Annorans gave a dry chuckle. "The waters are so violated by vermin that many now call the pirates 'Sacasians'. I hear rumour they even have a king of their own now."

"What? A lord of thieves?" Lukas could barely hold in a scoff or the heavily laced sarcasm. It was an absurd notion.

"Even thieves have honour among their own," Dayne replied.

Lukas nearly rolled his eyes. He would not fall for his brother's trap by replying.

"We are not here to discuss the pirates," the king said, his voice loud, commanding. "Proceed, General."

"To the north lays Medea, and while House Caspin will no doubt support us, there is no telling whether the other families will."

All eyes went to Sofia who nodded. "My family would back you, and probably even House Reyna."

"Anejo Reyna was once saved by Annoran steel," Dayne added. "A mercenary's perhaps, yet Annoran nonetheless. If we called, he would march with us in honour of the debt."

"As for the others?" his wife continued. "I am of House Caspin, yet I am now a Raynor. By now they would probably like nothing more than to see my head on a spike. Salazar, Bailon and Aloys will not help us. Not without great cost."

"What of the mercenaries your land is so fond of?" cut in Dorian, crossing his arms as he looked at the Medean women.

Lady Eveline leaned on the table before she spoke. "Medea is a land of mercenaries, it is true. Many of the sellsword armies already work for the houses. Some even have foreign interests as far as Aureia, Larissa and Tarik to the far north. But if you are asking whether they would help our cause … Some would, yes. But it is also likely that many would also side with the other houses. Some might even refuse to fight altogether, rather than get involved in what could quickly become a civil war."

"As is the way with mercenaries," the king replied, and his lip curled upwards. He glanced at Sir Tristayn and gave him a slight nod.

Tristayn looked around the room as he continued, "To the east lies the Steppe of Miera. Even if King Zoran was willing to let a single foreigner into his land, there is no way he would let the entire Annoran army. And then to the west. Larissa and the entire breadth of the ever-expanding Aureian Empire." He glanced up from the map, and his eyes swept from face to face around the table. "Make no mistake, my lords, one day the empire will be at our border, and we need to be ready. We are surrounded on every front by kingdoms and nations that are as good as enemies. What would happen if our army was near a month's hard ride from here and Emperor Darius decides to test his hand? This is a risk that I do not think we should take."

"What do we have to fear from Darius?" Dayne asked. "He is not his great-grandfather, nor is he a fool. The emperor is a good man of our faith, and as such, he is no threat to us. We may well be surrounded, my lords, but from Aureia at least we are safe. However, Lord Tristayn is correct. This is a risk that we should not take."

Lukas nearly swore. Inwardly, he had known it would come to this, and he could only watch in despair as one by one the council voiced their agreement with the general.

He could see the pain on his father's face, how torn he was.

The king knew they were right. No Annoran army could travel through Miera without it being an act of war. Lukas could not sit still while innocents were put to the sword.

"Very well," Dorian said heavily. "The Annoran army will stay in Annora."

Aye, thought Lukas. The army will not go to Salvaar.

EIGHT

Road to Kilgareth, Valley of Odrysia

For the next few mornings, Kyler rose at dawn and was riding within the hour. He was accompanied by Gaius, Torin and the party of knights at his side. Matias told them that the knights were able to keep the bandits in check, barely, with constant sweeping patrols along the valley mouth. Each time, like cockroaches under a rock, they hid and then returned.

The fire that the company sat around burned brightly, filling the darkness with a pleasant glow.

"One last night," Gaius Aureilian mumbled pleasantly, "and then the first decent bed in three moons."

Torin nodded beside him, his mind adrift.

"It will be well deserved, my friend," said Sir Matias pulling his large, crested helmet from his head and sitting down beside the Aureians.

"Hmph," Gaius snorted. "Anything to get out of this blasted heat that you northerners long for."

Kyler chuckled and grinned at the older man. "Did you not serve in the legions for many years?"

"Aye, lad, saw enough of the world to know of such warmth that makes this feel like a frozen desert night. Yet where I come from, the sun warms the skin, it does not burn it."

"I have never seen Aureia, nor journeyed to Rovira," the warden said after a moment.

Torin looked to the veteran. "Rovira is ... well, the beating heart of our faith. It stands a titan among cities, second only to Aureia herself. Imagine great temples white as silver and the banners of our Order flowing high in the morning breeze. By day thousands enter the city walls, while by night ..." The knight felt a smile tug at his lips. "By night there are great celebrations and, though he never partakes, the cardinal will walk among the people."

"The city truly is blessed by the Twins," Gaius agreed as he ran a hand down over his amulet. "One day you must travel south. Though you will have to cross a quarter of the empire to do so. Three moons ride if you take the highroads."

"We are no stranger to the saddle," Matias told him as he nodded to one of his men. "Ask Emir."

There was a dull ring as the knight Matias spoke of ran a whetstone down the length of the blade held within his grasp. Kyler recognised the sound of the name. It was foreign and its origin was thousands of miles to the west. Had he not known the name, then the man's rich ebony skin would have given the westerner away.

"Emir? That's Berenithian, right?"

The knight glanced up as he replied, "Well beyond the mountains of the Irene. Gods only know how many months I spent in the saddle to reach the Order. Even so, I may not have made the journey alive but for this." He tapped the sword with his whetstone.

"I grew up working in my father's tavern barely a week's ride from here," Kyler told them. "He taught me some swordplay, though I am yet untested."

He was no stranger to the sword yet far from skilled. Nor was he a stranger to the saddle, yet after a few days in it, he had begun to feel a dull ache in his lower back.

"Few of us grew up with the sword," Emir replied with little more than a shrug. "Many were farmers, traders, potters, blacksmiths, tavern workers." The knight gestured to the dark-skinned Larissan sitting across from the fire. "Neph over there was a marathon runner."

"A lifetime ago, before the gods saw fit to put me on this path." The man smiled slightly as he glanced into the flame of the fire. "My uncle raised me to run for sport and coin. It was a dangerous game, spending days in the baking sands that were once home."

"Yes, Larissa, little more than a barren desert." One of the knights chuckled sarcastically.

"More sand and dust than you could ever see in one life," Sir Neph agreed with a grin. "Yet above, when the moon arises, a great sea awash with stars."

"You're all a long way from home," Kyler murmured.

"No." Sir Matias spoke up. "This valley ... Odrysia, Kilgareth, that is home."

As the third day dawned, the eight who had seen off the bandits returned after sending some to the afterlife and scattering the others to the wind. Kyler rose and mounted his horse with a new excitement in his gaze. With luck, they would reach the Citadel by nightfall.

"Sir Matias." One of the knights rode up to his leader with his arm extended. "We caught nine. Though where the others vanished ... I do not know. One carried this."

The warden glanced at what the other knight held with curiosity. He took the amulet forged of the purest silver.

"You have done well." Sir Matias gestured to the maija. "Quinn, what do you make of it?"

The scholar nudged his horse and rode over to his comrades. Matias handed him the necklace.

Quinn ran his expert eyes over the jewellery and turned it in his hands before he spoke.

"Triple banded and joined in a way I have not seen before. The engravings in the silver seem to be much akin to those of the Old Religion. Though I cannot say for sure."

"It's not from around here then."

"No, but it is old. Very old," the scholar continued. "It may be nothing. But all the same, Lysandra should see this."

"Then we ride," the warden said, "and when the sun sets, we will have answers."

Kyler watched the countryside as he rode. His eyes raked over the hills of the highlands as they slowly merged into the maze of canyons and mountains that grew the closer they drew to Odrysia. It was a beautiful land that had an almost unearthly feel. The soaring cliffs on either side of the valley appeared as giants to Kyler. It was surrounded by impassable mountains. The small state forged by Duran Cormac was all but impenetrable.

The road leading to the city started to fill with people as he drew closer to Odrysia even as the sun started to lower. Travellers and merchants from all walks of life made their way into the city. Some walked, some rode and some sat within carriages. Many greeted the knights as they rode passed.

They had ridden for the better part of a day when Kyler finally brought Asena to a halt. From atop the hill where they were perched, Kyler gazed ahead to where the road split.

They had arrived.

"Behold," said Matias, "Odrysia, and the great fortress of Kilgareth."

Kyler's eyes followed the left path and washed over the township. He'd heard it was large, but Odrysia was at least a dozen times the size of Adrestia, perhaps more. Its tall walls were manned by the city militia. Magnificent spires soared over the city walls from churches below and the rooftops of tall buildings mingled with the blue banners of the Twin Gods as they soared in the sky.

Beyond Odrysia flowed the Odrysian River. It stretched across the great plain and through the heart of the city in a tide of swirling water before it vanished into the mountains.

He barely noticed the crystal-clear river that flowed nor the massive stone bridge that led across it. From there the road rose and wound up the side of a mountain that was covered in lush trees. Still Kyler did not see, for his eyes were fixed higher. Higher still than where the woodland thinned and vanished. For atop the mountain was a great castle of solid stone. Its sapphire banners were blowing high in the breeze and its spires driving into the sky like lances. Before him stood the great fortress of Kilgareth: a city of faith.

The path rose to meet the huge bronze-clad gates of the fortress, closed and shining in the sunlight. Twin towers stood atop the causeway and merged into the first of the massive stone walls that wrapped the city in a stone embrace. Silver sparkled atop these walls, for the Knights of Kil'kara stood sentinel, watching over the valley beneath. So tall were the walls that he could barely see anything towering above them, save two vast towers and a series of soaring spires.

As beautiful as the great castle was, Kyler couldn't help but feel the cold chill of fear run down his spine. All the stories were true, he realised.

"It's something else, isn't it?"

Kyler glanced to his left where the warden sat atop his steed. He nodded. "That it is."

"Survive what comes next and you may yet call it home."

"Had I not answered the call of the legions in my youth," Gaius spoke up and his lips twisted into a smirk, "I may have had the mind to join myself."

Torin snorted. "And what would my father be without all his stories about foreign lands?"

"Absent an ungrateful son?"

Torin was the first to laugh before the others followed suit. Gaius slapped his son on the back with a grin.

The valley was lit with orange light as the sun started to drift below the mountains behind Kilgareth. Kyler had heard that dusk in the valley was as if a painter had taken a brush to it.

"As the sun sets, the gates of Odrysia seal," Matias said after a moment.

"Aye," Gaius replied.

"May the light of the Twins go with you, Aureian."

"And with you, sir knight," the elder replied as he exchanged a nod with the warden. He turned to the boy at his side. "Kyler."

The Medean took his extended hand. "Gaius."

Finally, the man pulled Torin into an embrace. "Durandail rides with you, my son."

"Farewell, Father."

With that, they continued on their way. Gaius took the left rode to Odrysia. Kyler, Torin and the knights took the right to Kilgareth. Cobblestones crackled under Asena's hooves as Kyler rode towards the gates of the great fortress. They were shut against the encroaching night and locked those within behind an impenetrable wall. Thin wisps of smoke trailed into the sky from torches and braziers that lined the city's immense walls. Kyler's awe hadn't faded in the last mile he had traversed. Each step had brought him closer to his goal.

He had finally made it.

"Here we are, girl," he murmured as he leant down over Asena's neck. His gaze was drawn to the gatehouse as a voice called, "Riders approaching."

Kyler felt a tingle of excitement run down his spine as the call was answered. In just moments, the wide gates of the fortress trembled and began to move as those behind flung them open. Kyler peeked between the opening gates to see buildings of solid stone. Their hue was that of light brown, the same as Kilgareth's walls. Kyler and his companions rode through the opening into a courtyard of stone while the sentries watched them with the same unrelenting gaze of those who rode with the Medean. All were armed in the same fashion with shields slung across their backs and longswords at their sides.

"Sir Matias," called out one of the approaching knights as the party dismounted.

Boots met stone with a dull thud as all turned to the owner of the voice.

"Sir Alarik." The warden gave the man a slight nod. "I need to speak to the grand master."

Kyler looked at the knight who approached with his helmet neatly tucked under one arm. His face was lined and scarred. Shorter in stature than Matias yet with broader shoulders. As far as Kyler could tell, the man was a veteran of many conflicts. His eyes suggested as much. Like Matias, he wore a steel chestplate.

"Follow me," Alarik said with a curt nod and his voice a low growl.

Kyler looked on in amazement as the group made their way through the city. Before him, Matias and Alarik talked in quiet conference as he took in all of his surroundings. The streets were of perfectly laid cobblestone and were filled with bustling crowds. Some were knights clad in silver and blue. Others were maija in their hooded tunics and baggy pants. Yet they were not alone. More than knights lived in the fortress. The crowds were filled with fathers and sons, mothers and daughters, wives and families of the holy warriors and maija. As such, the city was alive.

Each street was filled with houses of wood with tiled rooftops. There were markets and stalls selling food, linen, jewellery and more. Churches of stone with stained glass windows sparkled in the sun's final rays. Kilgareth was more than just a fortress. It was a living, breathing city.

Footfalls. Loud and thudding on the stone corridor. The sound of chainmail and plate rubbing. Even the soft sound of cloaks lightly brushing the ground. Kyler could hear it all as he walked with the knights. Around them a maze of corridors and hallways that led to new rooms throughout the huge palace that was the Citadel of Kilgareth. If the city itself had been impenetrable, then the keep was even more so. With a second, higher layer of walls, a dozen manned guard towers and entire complement of knights on watch at all times, to any invader, breaching the Citadel would be impossible.

Alarik brought the group to a halt outside a pair of large wooden doors guarded by four of his brothers.

He turned to Kyler. "It is not normal for a recruit to speak to the grand master before even the induction ceremony," the knight told him. "But these are dangerous times, and Master Amaris will want to know about the attack. For that reason, and for that reason alone, you are here."

"Understood."

"Sir Matias." Alarik gestured towards the doors, allowing the warden to go first as his rank dictated.

As one, the guards pushed the doors open, and Matias lead them through.

Two men stood before them. One was garbed in the same armour as Valenquez, and the other's chestplate bore more than just Durandail's sun. Carved into the steel was also Azaria's moon. His cloak was trimmed with white, while small etchings ringed his gauntlets. His mid-length beard had a few strands of grey, but his face spoke of a man who dared his enemies to test him. Amaris Delodrysia was a powerful man indeed.

The warden bowed as he spoke. "Grand Master."

Kyler and the other followed Matias' lead and dipped their heads.

"Welcome back, Sir Matias." The voice was powerful. Stronger than any Kyler had heard. "I trust your patrol went well."

"It did, Grand Master. Thank the gods," the warden replied. "Barely a scratch among the men in the last month."

Amaris held out his arm. Matias took it.

"I am glad to hear it, old friend. But what of those raiders? I need them gone, Valenquez."

"That is easier said than done. Each time we chase them away they scurry off into the night like frightened rats and then return in greater numbers."

Amaris slowly turned his back. "We received a rider while you were gone. An emissary from Duke Bailon."

"What did he say?"

"Word is spreading that we cannot defend the valley. The people we were charged to protect. It is hurting our reputation."

"I regret to tell you that those same bandits are now striking within three days of our beloved city."

"What?" Amaris' voice turned cold as he looked back at the warden.

"Three nights ago, we tracked a small force to where they tried to rob and murder travellers on the road." He gestured towards Kyler and Torin. "Among them were our brother from the south, Torin Aureilian, and his companion, Kyler Landrey of Medea."

"Step forward." The grand master nodded to them. "You have my apologies for the rabble that attacked you so near to my hearth."

"None are needed, Master," Torin told him. "Your men saved our lives, and for that we are eternally grateful."

Amaris merely waved an arm. "It is our duty to protect travellers on the road. I will hear no more about it. Tell me about those who sought to harm you."

"They were well organised, not just simple thieves in the night."

"And their numbers?"

"No more than fifteen," Torin replied thoughtfully. "No fewer than ten. If I didn't know better, I would have thought them a scouting party or small warband."

"I thought as much." Amaris turned to Kyler. "What about you, Landrey?"

The Medean looked at the man before him and met his eyes for a moment. "I'm not sure … there was something about their leader."

"Go on, speak freely."

"I have grown up around mercenaries and soldiers my whole life, sir. The man who led the attack reminded me of a mercenary captain. Not one of his men spoke out of turn. They offered to spare us in exchange for anything of value that we carried, as if not outright willing to risk their lives for the sake of a few coins."

"For what use is the coin you earn when you're dead," added Matias. "Simple raiders and thieves. That is what we, what I, once thought."

The grand master crossed his arms. "We know better now, don't we? Each attack is the same. A simple choice. Life in exchange of coin. Or death. These men have a purpose and one that can no longer be tolerated."

"Grand Master." Quinn stepped forwards, holding out the silver ring. "The leader of the bandits held this amulet. I know not where it comes from, nor what the engravings mean."

Amaris studied the jewel for a moment before handing it back. "Take it to your mistress and see what you can uncover. I am certain Lysandra will know what to make of it."

Quinn bowed before he slipped out of the room. His boots did not make a sound on the stone as he left.

"Now," Amaris began, and his voice grew stronger. "We cannot let these attacks go unpunished any longer. It is clear that our patrols are not working, and we cannot afford to let these creatures continue to attack. They strike us from north to south, east to west. This tarnish on our reputation cannot stand." He turned to the man at his side. "Sir Corvo Alaine, Sword of Kil'kara, step forward."

Kyler watched as the huge warrior moved to stand beside Matias. Everything about the man screamed one thing. Fire. Only the greatest warrior in the entire Order was granted the rank of Sword, only a man who lived by the title. As a member of the Circle, he was also a leader of the warriors within Kilgareth.

"Grand Master," Corvo said, dipping his head slightly. Even his voice was as a raging inferno.

"I charge you to bring an end to these attacks. In two days' time, you will take one hundred knights and hunt those who would wish us harm. Do not hesitate and show no mercy. These men seek to harm those who wish to serve the gods in peace. For that you will show them Durandail's wrath."

Kyler could see the spark in Corvo's eyes as he was given his orders. Hunger and longing burned within. He didn't want to fight. He needed to fight.

"By the grace of the gods, it shall be done," the knight said.

"Sir Alarik," Amaris continued, "take the boy to his quarters. The induction ritual will be at dawn tomorrow." He looked meaningfully at the Medean. "So do not be late." The grand master set his gaze upon the Aureian. "Sir Torin, remain here. The Circle are gathering this eve. I would request you tell of our southern brothers and of Rovira. And I believe you bring word from your own grand master."

The older Aureian knight met Kyler's eye and nodded towards the doors. With that, the boy followed the knight from Amaris' hall.

"So, you wish to become one of us?" Sir Alarik growled as he led Kyler back through the city shrouded in the darkness of night.

"Yes," the Medean replied with half a smile. "It has always been my dream."

"Are you familiar with the sword?"

"My father taught me," Kyler told him. "He served in Duke Caspin's army for many years."

"That is good. You will be put to the test soon enough." The older knight chuckled drily.

"A test I plan to overcome. For as long as I can remember, I have always wanted to don the armour of a knight."

The knight snorted. "Aye, have you just? First you will have to pass the initiation and trials. Then and only then will you be granted the chance to say your piece."

"Be that as it may, I will one day call you 'brother'."

"You have heart, boy." Alarik slowly nodded and flicked him a sidelong glance as they came to a stop before a house. "You will sleep here tonight. Dawn tomorrow. I will send a brother for you. Today is your last as a simple Medean. Pass your initiation tomorrow and you shall be welcomed into our Order."

He held out a hand. Kyler took it.

"I will be there."

"Good. Oh, and Kyler? From now you address all knights as 'sir'. Do not forget."

Sound echoed down the staircase as the maija rapped his hand on the oaken door. Here he was at the chambers of the head of his order.

The door creaked open.

"What is it, Quinn?" said the dark-haired woman before him. She wore the robes of a maija, but they were of faded purple and trimmed in blue instead of the brown that the others sported. Her voice was smooth and quiet, and her smile full on her barely lined face.

"Lady Lysandra." Quinn dipped his head. "I wish to seek your counsel on something."

The leader of the maija opened the door and stepped back. "Come in."

Quinn followed her into the office, marvelling at the full bookshelves and tables lined with potions and medicines. He hid his excitement, for few ever got to enter the office of the arc'maija, chief of the maija. "Now," Lysandra said as the door shut. "What did you wish to ask?"

"I just returned from the field with Sir Matias. We foiled an attack on some travellers, and when the dust settled, one of the men found this on one of the raiders."

He procured the amulet from his robes and held it out once more. Lysandra was the wisest within the entire Order of Kil'kara, and if anyone knew what the amulet was, then she did.

Her deep blue eyes flicked over the silver jewel as she turned it in her hands, running her fingers over the etchings.

"This is old," she muttered. "Perhaps even centuries old, judging by the markings."

"But that is impossible," replied Quinn, aghast. There was no way that a necklace such as that could survive so long.

Lysandra met his eyes with her own. "Come now, Quinn, we are scholars, are we not? We seek answers to questions and mysteries such as these. I have seen a lot of strange things in my life, far stranger than an amulet of silver. Let me hold onto it for a while and I will see if I can unshroud this mystery of yours."

"Of course, my lady."

"Oh, and Quinn," Lysandra said. "Thank you for bringing this to me."

"So, Evalio is dead, and his successor sent you to our doors." The statement seemed to echo around the small stone chamber as Amaris spoke. His voice carried a deep sorrow.

"Yes, Grand Master," Torin replied, and his voice was equally mournful. Evalio Delrovira had been beloved by many within the Order and respected by all. "Bavarian leads in his stead."

"He has proven himself many times over," the northern grand

master replied. "No man could ask for a better successor."

"Bavarian was my mentor for many years. It was he who tasked me with riding so far north."

"Then why travel with your father?" Sir Matias spoke up. A good question and Matias knew it. They all knew it.

"Why not simply ride alone or with a company of knights? Surely it would have been swifter."

Torin glanced around the chamber, and his eyes swept from face to face. Trust the northerners, Bavarian had told him in confidence. Trust them with your task.

Yet he could not help a feeling of dread as he looked around the room. The five members who made up the Circle sat around him in wooden chairs. Amaris, Matias Valenquez, Corvo Alaine, Sir Alarik and Lysandra of the maija. Each watched him differently, from curious to expressionless.

Bavarian had put his faith in Torin for a decade. First as a mentor, and then as a brother and a friend. Now he had entrusted him with a task he deemed vital, for, as grand master of the south, Bavarian could not leave Rovira. Now he had to put his faith in Bavarian's words. Trust the northerners.

"My master entrusted me with a message," Torin told them. "One that must not leave this chamber."

Lysandra's brow furrowed. The mind of the arc'maija filled with possibility. "What message is of such importance that only we of the Circle can know of it?"

Torin turned to the lady. "Bavarian believed that until we know more, it is safer that only a few hear it. For who knows what is watching in the dark."

"Then speak," Sir Alarik said with his gruff voice .He gave Torin a slight nod. "You are among friends."

Torin took a deep breath and stilled his thoughts. "Bavarian was with the grand master when he left this world. Said that Evalio told him that we need to be ready, that we need to find it."

Corvo leaned forwards in his chair. "Find it?" he said, and his voice was a low rumble. "What do we need to find?"

"In truth" – Torin shrugged – "we do not know."

Amaris met the knight's eyes. "Then tell us what you do know."

"He said that the journey will begin where the Sword of the North ends."

"What?" Matias was aghast. It made no sense.

To his side, Corvo chuckled. "It's a riddle, brother."

"I think I understand," Lysandra said after a moment as her eyes flashed. "Part of it at least. And I think Bavarian did too. Why else would Torin be here?"

"Aye," the Aureian replied. "Duran Cormac was dubbed the Sword of the South before he travelled to Odrysia all those years ago."

"And from there he became the Sword of the North before donning the mantle of grand master," Amaris finished for him. "I know my great-grandfather's story well ... yet where the Sword of the North ends? It is almost as if Evalio was speaking of Duran's death."

"Perhaps it is meant to be taken as it is?" Lysandra cut back in. "Where the Sword of the North ends ... In my eyes, that can only mean one thing. Where his legend ended. His tomb."

Alarik watched his companions as they spoke. Riddles had never been his calling. Training men to fight was what he was good at.

The grizzled veteran rose to his feet. "Then that is where we begin."

NINE

Isle of Agartha, the Valkir Isles

Lief's hall was as silent as the grave, and the only movement came from the knife that Astrid slowly turned in her hands. The blade that had taken her father's life.

Erik sat across from her, his thoughts lost in the same trance that her own now inhabited. Astrid hadn't slept in the hours following her father's death.

No, he hadn't simply died. He had been murdered.

Her only dreams would have been nightmares. Nightmares about her father. She could still see his lifeless body and feel his blood on her hands. No more would she hear his growl of a chuckle or the glint in his gaze when they were at sea.

Astrid's amber eyes were focused intently on Lief's raven's head amulet. It sat on the table before her as she spun the knife absent-mindedly, her thoughts still on her father. Tears had long since dried on her cheeks. She was too exhausted to cry. Cold anger boiled within her now and it overcame the grief that threatened to pull her apart. No, the time for tears would be when the war was won. When the man who killed her father was dead at her feet.

Astrid remembered when, at the age of six, her father had caught her aboard the Wind Rider in the captain's cabin, running her inquisitive gaze over his collection of maps. She'd always wanted to be a sailor; it was in her blood. After all, there were dozens of shieldmaidens in the Valkir isles, yet so few ever took to the helm or served as navigators. Instead of taking the maps from her or laughing, Lief had simply smiled and given Astrid her first lesson in navigation, the first of hundreds that would take up hours upon hours each day. Any time that Lief could spare, he was guiding her and passing on his experience as a veteran sailor.

Within the next two years, her brother Erik was training at her side. Though he held no interest in maps and books, Lief had instead taught him the sword. A thing that Astrid found utterly dull.

When she was ten, a plague had ravaged Agartha for many months. Dozens had been claimed by the sickness that spread like wildfire through the town. It took both young and old, both strong and weak. Then it claimed her mother's life. Lief had taken her in his big arms as she cried all night, feeling her heart break into millions of pieces. The next day he'd taken Astrid deep into the forests and mountains that ran for miles and miles outside Agartha. They'd gotten lost, and when she was too exhausted for tears, he had told her to lead them home. For a time, the pain of loss was forgotten as she put her mind to the test.

At sixteen, Lief had taken her on her first raid. It was a voyage that lasted nearly four months. Four months of fighting. Four months of blood and sweat.

She had relished it.

Her first time being a proper Valkir raider. Her first time proving her wit in the taking of a walled settlement.

As she sailed the seas, she bonded with her companions. A second family forged and strengthened by blood and tempest. The crew of the Wind Rider became her brothers and sisters.

Her father had been at her side every step of the way, teaching and guiding but never sheltering her from the storm. Until she became the storm.

The memories died in her thoughts as Astrid's finger caught on the leather grip of the knife as she spun it. Strange. The leather used for grips was smooth and never, never loose.

Curiosity got the better of her as she ran her fingers over the leather until her finger caught again. Astrid bit her lip. The leather wasn't attached. She chipped at it with a fingernail for a few moments, and then the tip of the leather came loose.

What's this?

She grabbed the band and started to spin the leather around the hilt, watching as it unravelled. It happened slowly at first before it picked up the pace.

The first thing she saw as the leather wound away was a steel hilt. Astrid's brow furrowed. This was unusual. Valkir used wooden hilts for their blades.

"What is it?" called Erik, noticing his sister pulling apart the leather grip.

She barely heard him, for her attention was fully on what she saw as the last of the leather unwound: a ruby embedded in the steel.

"Come look at this," Astrid said thoughtfully, glancing at her brother. "I think I've found something."

Erik made his way around the table to her with a furrowed brow. "What have you found?"

"Do you know of anyone who inlays their weapons with gemstones?" she replied, holding up the knife by the blade so that her brother could see.

Erik took the weapon, peering at Astrid's discovery. "Certainly not anyone who uses high quality ruby. Or hides it under a leather grip, for that matter." What would be the point of embedding a ruby in a dagger if you didn't show it off?

Astrid nodded. "I think the killer planned that he might lose the knife and wanted to cover his tracks."

Erik handed the knife back before crossing his arms. "So what do we do? We can't tell anyone."

"Aye, we can't let the killer know," Astrid said, an idea springing into her head. "Tomorrow, why don't we pay the blacksmith a visit?"

Erik placed a hand on his sister's shoulder. "Viktor would be hard pressed to forget working with ruby of this quality, not to mention crafting a hilt casing for it."

"That is what I was thinking." Astrid met Erik's eyes with her own. "Once we have the killer's name, we will march into Earl Magnus' hall if we have to and demand justice."

Her brother raised a hand to his bearded chin. "Even with evidence, if the culprit so happens to be one of the earl's friends, then there is no saying whether the trial will be fair."

"Who said anything about a trial?" said Astrid, her lips curling into a smirk. "Once the murderer is uncovered, I'll take the culprit's head myself."

Her mind had been at work. If you gave her a minute, she was good, but if you gave her hours, days, she was great.

Erik shook his head. "If you kill without the consent of the earl, you are signing your own death sentence. No, this has to be done lawfully."

"I know that," Astrid replied. "However, if we challenge the culprit to single combat, the earl cannot do anything. And since false accusation of murder is punishable by death, the only possible outcome is a duel."

Realisation dawned on Erik's face and he grinned. "We will get justice and the earl won't be able to do a thing to stop it."

"And then together we will avenge our father."

Lief's son slowly nodded before turning and heading towards one of the walls. Just like in most halls, the walls were covered with swords, axes and shields – relics from raids and the like. Astrid watched her brother curiously as he reached the wall and took an axe from its clasp.

He walked back and held it out to her. "There is still a murderer walking the streets. Until such a time as he is in chains, you should not go unarmed."

Astrid snorted. "I have my dagger."

"Astrid ..."

"You know I am no warrior, nor do I have skill at arms."

Erik sighed. "You should have trained at my side."

"Then, my brother, I would be no better than middling if even that." Astrid shrugged. "It is better to be no warrior than one of little skill, for the halls of the Sea-Father are filled with their ilk, while those who live either are great warriors or have no knowledge of that craft." Astrid could see the grimace flick across her brother's face, just as it always did when she gave him that speech. She felt a tingle of humour race down her spine. Perhaps he did not understand ... yet to her it made perfect sense. Why fight her enemies and lose when she could simply outsmart them?

"You do not have to be a warrior to bear a blade," he told her after a moment. "Nor do any outside our crew know of your ... disinterest in fighting. At the very least, it would make an attacker think twice before making a move against you."

"Alright ... Since it is law to be unarmed during the procession, I shall wear it after the funeral rites." Astrid shook her head, and for the first time since they returned, felt something of a smile tug at the corners of her lips. She had to admit that he did make sense ... Maybe she could not swing a blade well. At least she would have a length of sharp steel between her and any who would attempt harm. She took the proffered axe.

"Oh, and I believe this is yours." Erik again extended a hand, this time holding the wooden raven's head out to her, their mother's necklace. "You are the oldest, after all."

"I am not the only one of father's children," Astrid replied. "You should have it."

"No. Mother made it." Erik shook his head with half a chuckle. "It belongs to you."

And with that he handed Astrid the amulet and stepped back. He crossed his arms as if to say there would be no argument and Astrid knew none was to be had.

The doors to the hall opened with a wooden creak.

Lief's children glanced up as dawn's first light came through the entrance and Torben strode in, two of the crew at his back.

"It is time," was all he said.

Astrid nodded and shoved the knife into the inside of her boot – one of the few places she knew it would be kept safe. A place where no one could take it but her. With a deep breath, she placed the amulet over her head and let it fall to her throat.

It was time.

Time to send her father to the gods.

The town was quiet. Not even the gulls were squawking overhead. A crowd had gathered in hushed silence as the procession slowly made their way down to the docks. The only sound was that of the aulos pipe. Its sound was both mesmerising and filled with pain. The instrument was played by Nenrir of the Wind Rider, the man who walked before his jarl's coffin. The sorrowful tune carried through the streets and across the bay.

Astrid and Erik walked at the head of the retinue comprised up of the Wind Rider's crew. In the middle half, a dozen of the Valkir carried a lidless coffin that held the jarl's lifeless body. None of those gathered, including those in the procession, were armed. This was a sacred law that all of the Valkir clans shared, for to seek to harm another at a funeral was considered all but barbaric. Murdering someone at a celebration was just as bad, Astrid thought icily. She did not care that if the knife in her boot was found, she'd be headless by nightfall. It would not leave her side until it was buried in the murderer's heart.

Astrid's hand went to the amulet at her throat as she walked. Her fingers brushed over the beautifully carved raven that had been her mother's, then her father's. Now it was hers. Her eyes looked dead ahead towards the approaching docks. They did not once shift to see the crowd that had formed up on either side of the road as almost an honour guard.

Women and children in the crowd threw flowers on the road before the procession and created a path filled with colour. It was a tradition among the Valkir, a way of showing an unspoken grief at the passing of a loved one. A tradition that all could share. Many were grieving the loss of a jarl, a friend and a brother. Some of the Valkir openly wept at the sight of their dead captain.

Lief would be remembered by all, a legend among his people. Now to join the dead.

Astrid looked around as she led the procession to the dock front and noticed for the first time the size of the crowd that had gathered to farewell her father. It was massive; hundreds of men, women and children had gathered to say their goodbyes. Dozens stood in front of one of the long piers, the path that the procession would take, and so that those closest to the jarl could say their farewells in peace. At the fore of the gathering stood Earl Magnus Vedoera and his dozen sworn warriors. Ever present at his side stood Sven Joramir with his arms crossed over his chest.

Astrid felt anger blaze as she saw the earl and his retinue. They almost had no right to be there. The few that her father had spoken ill of were always attached to the arrogant, pigheaded and gold-hungry earl of Agartha.

Long may he reign indeed, Astrid thought angrily.

Earl Magnus' long greying black hair blew in the slight breeze as did his matching beard. Despite his age, the earl was a powerful man. The defined figure under his tunic was testament to that. They said he had once been a great warrior until he followed in his father's footsteps and became lord of Agartha. His eyes were cold and calculating, seeing everyone as an enemy. Aye, he'd killed a lot of warriors in his life. Many were his own people.

With a nod from Erik, the crowd before the docks parted, leaving an open path through to the wooden pier. At the water's edge stood the six grey-clad acolytes of the Sea-Father, priests of Ra'Haven. A long boat was revealed as the Valkir moved aside, the last ship that would carry the jarl. In its centre was a bare table that would hold the coffin, while around it were piles of gifts from those who had known him. Food, beautiful jewellery, carvings, small statues and a variety of weapons covered the polished wooden vessel as it shone in the sunlight. Many had given even more than Astrid had expected.

The sum of the gifts would have been high, as much as even an earl would have received. That would have stung Magnus, Astrid thought, even as she saw a flicker of anger in the earl's eyes. Even in death, Lief was respected more than even he, an earl and lord.

Lief had touched the lives of many. Not just as a jarl and captain, but with his kindness and generosity. Even so he had been murdered with the knife that was hidden in the depths of Astrid's boot. She knew that one of the people present had wielded the blade. It was almost a sixth sense. If the murderer had stayed away from the funeral, it would have drawn attention to their absence. Only an incompetent fool would not have come. The shieldmaiden knew it.

Astrid took a deep breath, quenching all thoughts of revenge, and then with her brother at her side strode out onto the pier.

Everything was silent. The only sound came from the wooden planks creaking underfoot as the party made their way to the small funeral boat. The vessel was tied off at the end of the pier and had room for maybe half a dozen to pay their respects at a time. Flames flickered from torches that adorned each of the wooden posts along the pier, illuminating the walkway with an orange glow. If not for the circumstances, it would have been a beautiful sight.

Astrid turned as the procession reached the end of the walkway. It was time. She nodded to the coffin bearers who clambered down onto the boat without a word and carefully placed their charge on the small table. Lief lay in the coffin dressed in his finest clothes. His axe was held in his hands across his chest. Over his eyes were coins used to pay for safe passage through Ra'Haven, the realm of the Valkir gods. The gifts around him would serve as his wealth after gaining passage.

The coffin bearers uttered a quick prayer as they broke the silence with their chanting voices. After a moment, the six men climbed out of the boat to make room for the children of their jarl and captain. Astrid saw tears in one man's eyes as they strode past. What was normally a sign of weakness among the warriors became a sign of respect to their fallen leader on this day.

She exchanged a look with Erik and then, together with her brother, Astrid made her way down onto the vessel.

"Father," Astrid said quietly as she knelt beside the coffin and glanced at the hay and casks of oil beneath the table.

It was hard to look at her father's body when barely a day past they had shared smiles and laughter. After all of her years seeing her father nearly every day, this would be the final time. The final time until she joined him in death. And when she did, Astrid vowed to bring him tales of glory, tales about how she tore his murderer to pieces.

Erik knelt at her side with his hands clasped in his lap. "Father."

"Soon you will begin your voyage to Ra'Haven to be with the Sea-Father." Astrid felt an icy tear slide down her cheek as she said the words. "I will do all in my power to honour your name and serve your crew. I will not fail you."

"I will fight for you until my last breath," said Erik, his voice filled with emotion. He placed a hand on the edge of the coffin. "We will uphold your legacy."

Astrid felt fire flood her breast and her hands clenched into fists. "You were taken from this world too soon," she said. "But I swear to you that whoever harmed you will die in agony. They will never darken the threshold of the realm of the Sea-Father."

Whoever had killed Lief was as good as dead. Nothing would save the murderer from Astrid's blade.

"The pieces are set, and the hunt has begun, Father," Erik murmured, his eyes ablaze. "It won't be long now until all the players are revealed."

"All I see is the warpath ahead of me." Astrid looked into her brother's eyes. The same fiery expression in her amber gaze was mirrored in his.

"Your killer will be brought to justice."

The funeral boat created ripples in the calm ocean as it was propelled forwards by four men up to their chests in the deep blue water. The streamlined vessel sped forwards as the warriors let go. It cut its way through the bay under a brilliant midday sun.

Astrid and Erik watched from the tip of the pier with the crew of the Wind Rider at their back. This was the last time they would see their father before they themselves gained entrance to Ra'Haven. Tears threatened to pour from Astrid's eyes, but she held them back. Lief had been part of her everyday life for twenty-four summers, and she loved him more than anything. The time for tears was over. Now was the time for revenge. Revenge on all those who had harmed her father.

Astrid turned to Torben who had moved to her side, a bow in his left hand, an arrow in his right. The arrow's tip was covered in a layer of oil-soaked cloth. It was time to send her father to the realm of the Lord of the Sea.

She nodded at the old warrior. The man her father had often called his closest friend. The man who would send him to their god.

Without a word, Torben held the arrow to the last of the pier's torches, setting the tip ablaze. The flames hungrily licked the air. Torben nocked the arrow and drew the string of his bow back. The weapon sang as it sent the arrow on its way, a trail of thin smoke following its flight.

Astrid's gaze never left the boat as the arrow struck. The flames instantly ignited the oil caskets and hay bedding on the vessel. Fire roared as the long boat went up, and the flames wrapped the jarl's body in a brilliant embrace.

She felt Erik slip a hand into hers, his fingers entwining with her own.

As the fire engulfed the boat, the same fire engulfed the shieldmaiden, its burning fury becoming her own.

Now the long game would begin.

TEN

City of Carlian, Steppe of Miera

Carlian, capital of the largest of the northern kingdoms, Miera, was cast in the brilliant silver rays of a full moon. A huge wall of stone wrapped around the city, while within the walls stood hundreds of beautifully carved wooden houses. A great castle stood in the very centre of the city, casting the nearby houses in shadow while its vast stone towers soared into the sky.

The city was seen as impregnable by all. And for over five hundred years, it had been, though not just because of its thick walls. Miera had been invaded countless times throughout the centuries since its founding, with many outsiders seeking to take its vast lands for themselves. The Mierans had fought back bravely, if not stubbornly, each time. Every time, the invaders had been repelled and their conquest had the opposite effect to what they had hoped, for the constant invasions and wars had forged the very people of Miera into warriors. Warriors who learnt to ride by the age of six and fight by ten summers.

Thus gave life to the legend of the infamous Mieran cavalry. For what else but horsemen could traverse the near thousand miles of the vast Steppe of Miera, filled with endless plains and rolling hills? Who else but the Mieran horse lords could ride for days without sleep and still have the strength to fight? It was said that a Mieran rider could hit an egg from near thirty paces with an arrow, and when invaders came, it wasn't the sword that greeted them first. It was the song of a thousand bows followed by the crash of a cavalry charge.

To a man, the Mierans were baptised in blood and battle, warriors to the bone.

Unyielding and uncompromising.

Laughter echoed through the tavern as the moon reached its peak. Although the establishment was small, it was packed to the rafters with its loud clientele, many of whom were drunk beyond measure. The young woman smiled as she downed the last of the contents of her cup. She relished the taste of the hot spirit as it ran down her throat. Proper Mieran alcohol. Not the swill you would find in any of the other kingdoms. She placed the cup on the table before her with a thud, her hand brushing against the sword that leaned against her chair instinctively, though she knew she was among allies. It was a habit that would never change.

Three others sat around the table with the woman. They were all warriors, blooded in battle many times over. They wore swords and warhammers at their hips and were clad in a combination of leather jerkins, gambesons and chainmail armour. The three men were just as any other within the tavern, soldiers between battles.

"Tell me, Kitara." One of the warriors spoke, a thin smile appearing on his lips. "You've been with us a year now and still have not told us where you came from. You rode from Annora, yet you are not Annoran. Why?"

The girl pursed her lips. How she hated questions about her past, even when asked by those who saw her as an equal. Besides which, she could see a dark glint in his eye. "That is none of your concern."

Lucian merely shrugged in reply. "Alright, keep your secrets. But at least explain that."

Kitara held back a snort. It didn't take a mind reader to know what her companion was talking about: the white scar that ran down the left side of her face. It was carved from her temple, across her eye socket and down her cheek. She had been told on more than one occasion that it was the only thing that marred her beauty. She didn't care. It kept people away.

"The scar? I told you," she replied, sarcasm lacing her voice. "I got it in a fight five years ago."

"Yes, but how?"

He was starting to tread on thin ice, and Kitara's expression warned as much. She could tell him that it had come from a man she had called friend, but she did not. Her past was her own; her secrets were her own. Lucian was her ally, yet she could not bring herself to trust him … to trust anyone. Not anymore.

"The day that you beat me in the sparring yard," she told him as her emerald eyes flashed, "will be the day I tell you. And seeing as none of you have given me more than a scratch, I'd imagine I'll get on just fine, Lucian."

"The lass has you there, Luce," added in the oldest of the group, Caidin, with a dry laugh.

"For now," Lucian replied with a snort. "One day I'll get through that strange style of yours and put you on the flat of your back."

Kitara scoffed. "Oh, I doubt that." She took another swig of ale. In all her twenty-three years, Kitara had never been able to relax and let her guard down even a little. Even now, surrounded by the people she'd been with for a year, she couldn't relax.

When the Mierans had first caught her crossing their western border, there had been questions, many questions. Why was a woman of her age riding so hard for the border? Why did she wear a blade at her side? For in their country, women had never taken up the sword and fought beside their menfolk. The questions, however, had ended when the first of them swung a blade her way.

Now the three who sat with her – Lucian, Caidin and Uriah – saw her as something of an ally.

The doors of the tavern boomed open and cold wind from

the street seeped into the large room. Three men strode inside, veterans all, with lined faces and brooding eyes. All three men wore longswords at their sides as was the way with all Mieran warriors.

"Alright, lads," the first man called out, his voice loud and commanding. "Listen up."

His words carried power, and all eyes turned to the man as he spoke. Kitara knew him by face and reputation. Ulric Carac was one of the most feared and ruthless captains Miera had ever known. His men would gladly follow him into the depths of hell if he but asked. A series of gold rings ran down his left ear and his dark eyes spoke of danger, while his lips were curled into a constant smirk.

"We've been sat here for too long," his deep voice growled.

"Two weeks is too long?" called out Lucian.

Carac snorted, and his eyes flicked to the man who spoke. "By the look of you, Lucian, a ride, half rations and a fight might do you some good."

"Yes, captain," Luce replied as the laughs started and his own lips tugged into a grin.

Carac held up a hand and the chuckles died down. "Time to draw lots. Some of us are headed north," the captain told them.

A silence filled the room. They all knew what that meant: the border between Miera and Salvaar known as the Rift. A desolate plain filled with little more than small hills and sparse trees that ran for near on five hundred miles. It was the reason why the northern Mierans were such fierce fighters. They were forced to fend off countless incursions from Salvaar. It meant months of watching the border and months of fighting.

Ulric Carac held up a large bag and pulled its drawstrings open. Within was a collection of stones. The two warriors at his back followed suit, as in hushed silence the warriors within the tavern began to line up before the men.

"Draw white and remain here," Ulric said. "Draw black, as most of you will, and we leave at dawn."

Drawing lots, they called it. Within each bag was a collection of stones, some painted white, the others black. Sometimes used to provide "volunteers" to certain tasks such as building, other times it was used to choose those who would leave and who would stay. All was in the hands of lady luck.

One by one, the Mierans reached into the bags and drew an unseen stone from within. One by one, they glanced at their stones with little more than a small smile or nod. Ride or stay; none cared. Before Kitara, Caidin drew black, and after him, Uriah drew the same. Lucian was next.

"Not you. We'll not leave this to chance," Carac grunted as the man made to reach into the bag. A vicious grin flashed over his lips as he spoke. "You are coming with me."

Some of the Mierans laughed. The talkers were always taken, and Lucian … he was the biggest talker of them all.

"Captain." Lucian nodded, accepting the decision before it was even made.

"Enjoy the north," Kitara said dryly as she moved up to Ulric.

Lucian snorted at that and rejoined his companions as they were given their fates.

Carac met Kitara's gaze as she reached for the bag, and in one swift movement, he lowered it.

"And what do you think you are doing?"

The girl narrowed her eyes and glared up at the veteran as she replied, "Finding my fate."

"Yes." Ulric gave a low chuckle. "Yet you are not one of us, outlander."

"Carac, I have been here for a year."

He shrugged. "Perhaps. Yet until your riding is at least average to us, here you shall remain."

"Do not insult me. The only reason that you do not let me ride is because I am not Mieran."

There was some grumbling around the mess as she spoke, for

it was true. The disdain and distrust that the horsemen held for foreigners was no secret.

"There is nothing wrong with my riding," Kitara seethed.

"Anywhere else, maybe." The growl in his voice was louder now. "Yet this is Miera."

Kitara gave the older man a devilish grin. "Yes, it is. And perhaps until your skill with a sword averages my own, you should not insult me. Even though I am an outlander."

Silence.

All turned towards the confrontation. Carac's expression darkened as he returned her glare. Then he roared with laughter. All of the Mierans did.

"You have some nerve." He chuckled, giving her a hearty slap on the shoulder.

"Do not touch me again." Kitara gave him a sickly sweet smile as she restrained herself from pulling her knife from its sheath.

Despite Carac being a much loved and well-respected leader, Kitara could not remove the feeling of being surrounded by enemies. Had that been anyone else placing a hand on her, then she would have buried her blade in his chest. Carac leaned down and looked her in the eye.

"I know you have courage, Kitara, we all do. Perhaps one day."

She merely snorted at that, and with a spin, she strode back towards her comrades.

"Perhaps one day", he had told her. Kitara had more blood on her hands than many of the Mierans. She had lost more than most would in three lifetimes. Yet still she could not ride with them because she was foreign. Even after living among them for a year. What were another few months trapped in the city? Besides, what could she do about it?

"It's late," spoke Uriah with a grimace. "And we have a long journey ahead of us. One last drink before we ride?"

One by one, the others nodded. The three men would begin a

two-hundred-mile ride at the break of day to reach the northern border that ran along the edge of the neighbouring Salvaari lands.

Lucian called over one of the tavern's serving girls, who swiftly deposited four cups on the table with a smile. She retreated back to the bar in a swirl of skirts for the next order.

Kitara rose to her feet as the three men stood and raised her cup with her companions. The cups clanked as the four smacked them together noisily before downing the ale in a few quick draughts. Kitara placed her empty cup on the table before picking up her sword belt and buckling it around her waist. There were no goodbyes. There was no room for softness in Miera. There was no room for weakness.

Kitara wrinkled her nose as she strode through the city, the smell a mixture of chimney smoke and that of the sweat and alcohol of the many alehouses within Carlian.

Even though she had spent the last year with the Mierans, Kitara was something of an oddment. The sword strapped to her side saw to that, for though most men in Miera carried blades, few women within the mainland ever took up the sword. Those who did were not of Miera. Women who wielded a blade were from the savage north and untamed southern isles. They were thought as little more than uncivilised barbarians by most. Yet, like her, the sword itself was foreign to these lands. Hailing from far to the north, the Tariki called the blade a Dao. Three feet of razor-sharp steel lined the double edged and slightly curved blade. Forged by the northern blacksmiths of Tarik, the blade was lighter than any longsword, yet just as strong. It suited Kitara well. Her lean, muscled body had body had been forged into a weapon as strong as any steel. Kitara stood as an outsider with long flowing hair of golden blonde billowing down her shoulders in a wave, tied back with a simple strip of cloth to keep the shaggy mane from her face and laced with half a dozen thin braids. She sported a black leather brigandine over her white shirt and dark pants. The brigandine appeared as no more than a vest, yet beneath the leather were a series of small steel plates that protected her from shoulder to thigh. It did not slow her down, nor take away from her mobility and the style in which she fought. A brilliant dark green sash was tied around her waist under her wide belt with a long dagger sheathed though it. A simple ring inlaid with a small sapphire hung from her neck yet hidden beneath her shirt. A gift she was told that came from her mother.

Kitara was a survivor. She had been all her life. She cared not for the beauty that many had once remarked upon. Those comments had long since fallen silent thanks to her marking, a white scar that ran down from her left brow, over her eye socket and down her cheek. The steel that had sliced her skin long ago had barely missed her eye. All Kitara cared about was living to see the next dawn.

Her mother died in childbirth twenty-three years before, and she knew nothing of her father, save that he must have abandoned her. She was raised as an orphan among the pirates of the Sacasian Sea to the east for most of her life, until she ended up living in the gutters of Annora. Now she was part of the Mieran warband.

She had been fighting all her life. Born in darkness and raised in shadow. It was the fighters who survived in this world. From the moment she'd been born in what was little more than a rundown shack, Kitara had known she would never get a normal life. Never get a chance to live a life of comfort. Not that she'd ever wanted to.

Even as a child, Kitara had chosen the road upon which she walked.

And nothing since – not the trials, the blood on her hands, nor the things she'd suffered – none of it would make her look back.

Her faith was in herself and herself alone, not in any god or man. As such, there was a dangerous glint in her eye and a self-confidence in her stride.

Kitara's pace quickened as the moon rose higher.

The streets were filled with small groups of people, warriors with swords at their hips and women in their long dresses. Some stood huddled together talking in hushed tones, while others strode the streets in groups.

Carlian was a city that never slept.

Despite being seen by Mierans as one of their own, Kitara knew it was better for her to be inside after dark. She'd been too caught up in the tavern to notice just how high the moon had risen.

Stupid, she cursed herself silently.

When darkness fell, Carlian's many taverns and alehouses, not to mention the streets, were filled with many drunken soldiers – bored, drunken soldiers.

A dangerous combination.

To ease their boredom, the soldiers often fought each other for sport or sought the arms of a willing woman.

Kitara was interested in neither.

What she was interested in, however, was her bed and a night's sleep. She nodded in greeting to a small band of soldiers as they passed her in the street. Likewise, they sported swords, while their clothing was a combination of padded jerkins and chainmail armour.

They replied in kind. One man was more confident than the rest and winked at her as he passed by.

Not far to go, Kitara thought as she turned down another road. She was barely two blocks away from the abode she called home.

Home, as Kitara called it, consisted of four walls, two floors and a roof that she shared with half a dozen Mierans. Warriors: the kind of people she favoured most. One was an older warrior by the name of Zandir. He was a beloved lord and commanded the respect and love of his people. He was one of the first Mierans to throw in with her, along with his family.

Crash.

Kitara whirled around as the door of a tavern across the street was thrown open, its orange light flooding the street. The light was abruptly cut off after a man was thrown through the opening.

He crashed onto the road with a grunt, landing in the mud at her feet, the few passers-by roaring with laughter at the sight.

Kitara gracefully sidestepped the man without a fault in her stride and smirked as a second man in the doorway, the one who did the throwing, rubbed his meaty hands together and walked out onto the street.

This was not an unusual sight.

She couldn't help but chuckle as the fallen soldier heaved himself back up off the ground and stumbled towards the man who did the tossing.

Kitara moved on with a shake of her head. No doubt the man who did the falling would buy the man who did the throwing a drink, and they would happily go on drinking the night away. No doubt.

Kitara's ears pricked at the thudding of footfalls coming from an alley to her right and she whipped around to her side. Her left hand flicked to within reach of her dagger as her instincts kicked in.

Three clearly drunk Mieran warriors boldly strutted around the corner, nearly crashing into Kitara.

"Watch where you're going," she said with a good-humoured smirk as she stepped back and placed her hands on her hips.

She almost sighed as she recognised all three of them. Dastin led the group, while his younger brothers, Radin and Zain, completed the trio.

All three were talented killers. Talented at getting into trouble.

"Apologies, m'lady," the leader of the group began before blinking in his drunken haze as he noticed that she wasn't in a dress. Dastin's eyes flicked to the sword at her side. His lips twitched into a smile. "Kitara."

"Who did you think it was, Dastin?"

Kitara grinned at Dastin's companions, who had clearly had less to drink than their brother.

"A golden-haired beauty," he said.

"Oh," Kitara replied sarcastically. "Am I not?"

Dastin was a well-known womaniser. He was in his early thirties and in his prime. His short beard, long hair, strong figure and emerald green eyes only helped him secure his reputation.

Every woman in all of Carlian's whorehouses knew him.

"I never said that," Dastin replied with a sleazy grin and reached out a hand as if to touch her hair.

What a surprise. Kitara inwardly sighed, and she watched as Dastin's hand came towards her. At the last moment, she caught his wrist with a grip tighter than any vice.

"You're drunk."

She let go of his wrist and shot him a glare of pure fire as the hand dropped back to its owner's side, brushing the pommel of his sword.

Kitara locked eyes with Dastin and slowly wrapped the fingers of her right hand around the hilt of her blade. Her feet slid to shoulder width as her gaze hardened. A warning.

"Come now, brother," one of the other men muttered, placing a hand on Dastin's shoulder. "Leave this rogue to her business."

The Mieran set his jaw as he stared straight into Kitara's cold eyes. Then he nodded and let his hand fall from his sword.

Just like that, it was over.

Kitara folded her arms and rolled her eyes, half a smirk forming on her face. She shook her head as she strode past the trio, her shoulder smacking into Dastin as she passed. She heard him chuckle with his brothers and mumble something under his breath, no doubt something as cocksure as the man himself.

"You should be careful," he called after her. "The streets are dangerous at night."

She didn't even turn back to reply. "Then stay inside where it's safe."

Mierans, Kitara thought bitterly.

Their hatred of foreigners was a thing well known, yet even after a year, she was still treated differently. She was given tempered responses and dark glares.

Yet they had once saved her life.

"I'm back," Kitara called as she pushed the door to her house open. The glow and warmth of the fireplace eased the chill of the outside air.

"It's about bloody time," called a gruff voice from by the fire.

Kitara grinned as she entered the house and shut the door. The house was that of a warrior sired by warriors. A blind man could see it. It was a simple house made for purpose rather than comfort, with little embellishment or luxury. Its only decorations were its fireplace and a display of swords along one of its walls. Each of the blades was different. Each was taken from a different battle or brought from traders and travellers over the last century. There were steel longswords from Annora; shorter, rougher blades from the Valkir raiders; curved scimitars from Larissa; and dozens more. Filling out one of the chairs by the fireplace was an older man in his early fifties. His greying black hair shone in the flame light. Zandir Barangir was a veteran of a hundred battles, and he had the scars to prove it. He was an old warrior who commanded enormous respect, even among the greenest of recruits. It was because of him that Kitara had found a place with the Mierans.

She had been picked up on the Annoran border by a patrol Zandir led. The Mierans had thought it the grandest joke that she, a girl, wore a sword at her hip. They'd nearly laughed her off and sent her back the way she'd come. That was until Zandir convinced his men that perhaps she carried the sword for a reason, and that they ought to see just how well she could handle herself. After putting three of the company's warriors on their backsides, including Zandir's son, Silas, the Mierans decided that perhaps she had some use after all.

"I had some business to take care of," Kitara replied, making her way over to the man.

The old warrior snorted. "Aye, lass, and would that business have been at an alehouse by chance?"

Kitara's lips curled as she unbuckled her sword belt. "I have no idea what you're talking about."

"Right," came the gruff reply.

Most who met Zandir would have mistaken it for annoyance, but Kitara could hear the slight hint of humour in the reply. She'd lived with the old warrior and his family long enough to tell as much. He was perhaps the only Mieran she half trusted. Aye, she had companions in Carlian, but despite that, she couldn't bring herself to trust them fully. She had seen what promises were worth her entire life. She had seen people sell their own families for profit. She bore the scars from what trust really was.

"Any word from Silas?" Kitara asked as she reached the man.

Silas had accepted her as fast as his father and had never tried to interrogate her about her past, a thing she was eternally grateful for. From the moment she'd arrived in Carlian with Zandir and his men, Silas had been the first to silence anyone who made a remark about her rudimentary skill on horseback. He had been the first to teach her how to ride as the Mierans ride. As the stories told, from the moment a Mieran hit the earth, he was a horseman. For the last six months, he'd been stationed along the furthest eastern reaches of Miera.

"Last time he sent word he said he was leaving the eastern border within the week." Zandir glanced up from the fire for the first time and chuckled. "But you know my son. Could be there another two months."

Kitara nodded. Who knew exactly when Silas would at last return.

"Well," she said after a moment. "I'll be off."

Zandir nodded as she started towards the stairs leading to her room on the second floor. He'd be down there a while – he always was.

ELEVEN

City of Palen-Tor, Aethela, Kingdom of Annora

"Do you play games of strategy often?" Dayne asked Prince Lukas as they sat down opposite each other.

Between them sat a small table with the board and pieces of latrunculi set up upon its wooden surface. Each of the princes controlled sixteen small round pieces along with a taller, pointed dux piece. The aim of the game was to capture as many of your opponent's pieces as possible.

"Not so much anymore," Lukas replied as he moved one of his black pieces forward, eyes scanning the board as he made his play.

"Indeed," Prince Dayne said as he moved one of his ivory chips. His eyes never left his brother, not even to glance at the game, for he knew latrunculi well. "The trials of adulthood."

Lukas glanced down at the board as he replied, "I find that you can learn more from books than games."

He pushed another piece forward, and still Dayne's eyes did not leave his brother's face.

"In some matters, perhaps. Yet in the art of war, this is a thing far removed, is it not? For as time goes on, do not the pieces become soldiers, and the boards become battlefields?"

Lukas frowned. "You would liken latrunculi to battle?"

The pieces danced across the board as the two men played their game.

"They are much the same," Prince Dayne replied as he jumped one of his pieces over one belonging to Lukas, capturing it. "Anticipation. The downfall of many men. Most can only plan one step ahead and see only what is before them. Where should one place his archers to take advantage of the terrain? Should the cavalry remain with your army or be sent to harass your enemy?"

There was a dangerous glint in Dayne's eyes as he spoke, yet his face remained devoid of emotion. Lukas' brow furrowed as another of his pieces was lost. He could not understand his brother's moves. Dayne's pieces were moving into the strangest of places without ever getting too close to his own.

"Yet," the older prince continued, "what if there is a second enemy force hidden from sight. Waiting in ambush or looking to flank your position? What if they gain an ally and the odds turn in their favour? One false move could be your undoing."

"Possibilities," Lukas said as he captured one of Dayne's pieces. "A thing well known to me."

"Precisely," the older man told him. "That is all I see. Plan for your opponent's most obvious move yet also for his boldest. Think two steps ahead, five steps ahead … ten. Nudge him move by move until, though he does not see it, you have manoeuvred him to your will, and then …"

There was a slight smirk gracing Dayne's lips now as he spoke. Lukas had finally come across his brother's plan. All the small moves and unusually placed chips had begun to take form on the board before him. One move was all it would take now to beat his brother.

Prince Dayne slowly jumped his last two pieces as he spoke. "The game is over."

Lukas leaned back in his chair and folded his arms. "Ever the schemer," he grumbled.

Prince Dayne met his eyes.

"Now do you see, little brother, why I am hesitant to ride to

Salvaar?"

✦ ✦ ✦

Anger burned in Cailean's chest as he heard the words that poured from the noble and honourable King Dorian Raynor's mouth. He had ridden for over two whole weeks without rest and little food through Medea, whose very people would have almost certainly killed or captured him on sight, just to be turned down by a man he had once called ally. The very man who stood before him in the chamber he had been granted for his stay.

"Near twenty-three years ago, we helped you win your throne," he snarled, unable to hold back his rage as he glared at the king. "We fought and died for you! Does that count for nothing?"

"I am sorry," was all Dorian said.

The Aedei tribesman just looked at him in disbelief. He could tell that the king was sincere, but not even his brother had expected this. He shook his head. The man before him seemed to have become a puppet. Pulled by the strings of his advisors.

"Have you no honour? Among my people there were stories after that war. Stories about the nobility and strength of the Raynor clan. Clearly, they were wrong."

Cailean could see a flicker of annoyance flash in the Annoran king's eyes, and the Salvaari felt a hint of satisfaction. He had hit a nerve.

"Or perhaps that strength died with your family."

"Be silent." Dorian's voice grew loud like a brewing storm on the verge of breaking. "Remember, Cailean, you are but a guest in my house."

The threat was clear. Guest could change into prisoner at but a word from the king. He couldn't push the man any further, but even so, Cailean's hands clenched into fists as he watched Dorian turn his back and stride towards the door.

The power of the Annoran kings had come to an end, Cailean thought with disdain.

First they were plagued by King Balinor. A tyrant who didn't care who got caught in his schemes and a man who saw everyone as a threat. Now they had Dorian. A man who had always done what was good and honourable, until now. Now he turned his back on friends. How long before he started to hunt them down like his former rival?

"Salvaari." King Dorian glanced over his shoulder as he reached the door. "The hospitality of Palen-Tor is yours for as long as you require."

Cailean only watched as the king left his chamber. He would be leaving at first light to ride back from whence he came. He would have to fight an almost unwinnable war at his brother's side. Maybe they could win and maybe they could not. One thing was certain. The Aedei would meet their enemy in battle nonetheless.

Lukas' thoughts were taken by the council meeting as he made his way through the castle. The prince knew in his heart that what had been decided was wrong. He'd never been the smartest of the king's children. He had always preferred riding to Father Bardhyl's many lectures. Hells, the prince had even skipped many, if not most, of his lessons in favour of going on patrol. However, he knew that not aiding those who had once helped you was as good as breaking an alliance. Staying in Annora may well have been the most sensible choice, but it was wrong.

If only more among the council had thought so. That was why he was making his way to the stables. He wanted to talk to the one Annoran in Palen-Tor with any sense. His sister.

Kassandra had received her love of horses, Lukas supposed, from himself. She'd even begun disobeying their father by staying up long after dark just to be around them. The prince smiled as he recalled how their father had flown into a rage when he'd first caught Kassandra grooming one of the horses. It was work for servants, so he'd said, work for servants and younger princes who had helped their sisters escape their tutors and gain access to the stables.

It had been worth it, however, just to see the look of sheer joy upon his little sister's face as she saw the young white mare he had brought for her especially. She'd hardly shut up about her new Ely for near a month. Gods, it had been the same when he'd taught her to ride. Nothing had changed since.

The sun had all but vanished as Lukas strode through the castle's main doors and descended the stone steps into the cobblestone courtyard. Half a dozen braziers filled the square with light, while some sentries stood around them to keep the chill night air at bay.

He passed by a pair of stablehands as he made his way out of the courtyard and into the stables. No doubt they were retiring for the night. Lukas recalled their names were Hugh and Elliot. He gave them a nod in passing and received the customary, "M'lord," in reply.

However, light still flickered in the wooden building. If fire had been left alone around hay and wood, that was dangerous. Lukas smiled. He had clearly been right.

He walked through the stables without a care. The prince had grown accustomed to the smell a long time ago. Horses stood in their stalls and munched away at their food contentedly as they ignored the newcomer. Ahead, Lukas could see one of the stall gates slightly ajar.

He made his way down slowly, and sure enough there was Kassandra Raynor, the chestnut-haired princess of Annora and the groomer of horses.

"I think you may have fed poor Ely one too many apples." He grinned as he leaned over the gate.

Kassie turned at the sound of his voice and shot him a glare. "Poor Ely is in excellent condition, thank you very much," she told him matter-of-factly as she continued to run her brush along her mare's snow-white neck.

Lukas laughed and entered the stall and gave Ely a quick pet on his way in. "Nearly done?"

"Mmmhhhmm," she mumbled without ceasing her work for a moment.

The prince leaned against one of the gate posts. "I'll take you back when you're finished. Don't want Father to have a fit if he caught you out this late alone."

Kassie turned to her brother. She had heard the quietness in his tone. She doubted anyone but her would have noticed. "What is it?" she asked.

"You've no doubt heard about our new guest," he said.

Kassandra nodded.

"Well, it turns out that the tribes are in the middle of a war among their own kind."

"Oh?" the princess replied thoughtfully. "Strange for a Salvaari to travel all this way even for a matter like war."

"Aye … The man, Cailean, is brother to the chief of the Aedei."

Kassie pursed her lips. "And he wants to try and rebuild the old alliance?"

Lukas nodded. He was not surprised that his sixteen-year-old sister had figured it out that quickly. She'd always been smart.

"I had thought that there was only one choice: help these people who once helped us. It would be the honourable thing to do."

"But?"

"But" – he sighed – "the council thinks different. An 'impossible reality', they call it."

Kassandra stopped brushing and turned to look at her brother. Her face was filled with worry. "And what are you going to do about it? You would not have come down here just to pass on what the lords have decided."

Lukas nodded. This was where he made his choice. "These people need our help. And if the old alliances mean nothing to the council, then someone has to do something."

"So what?" The princess crossed her arms. "You're going to ride to Salvaar, aren't you?"

"I … I don't know. To try and cross the Steppe of Miera unnoticed is insanity." Lukas took a deep breath. He knew in his heart that his mind was already made up. "But someone must help these people. And if the council will not, if Father will not … then I will. I have to."

Kassandra placed her brush on the small stool that stood inside the pen and made her way over to Lukas. She reached out and took his hands. "It looks like you have made your decision. But why tell me? You could have just slipped away in the dead of night."

Lukas squeezed her hands. "I know what I must do, it's just that …" He trailed off.

He was afraid. Not of dying or battle. Lukas had been around soldiers his whole life. He had learned how to die a long time ago. He was afraid of what he would be leaving if something did happen to him.

"I understand," Kassie said softly as she rested her head on his chest. "I know you must go. Just promise me that you'll come back safely too."

The prince took a deep breath and kissed his sister's forehead. He leaned down and looked her in the eye. He could see the tears that threatened her ocean-blue gaze. She would not let them fall. Brave girl.

"I promise."

It was late when Lukas arrived back in his chambers, and he still needed to take care of a few things before he left. He had to get himself and the Salvaari out unseen. Kassandra had vowed not to tell a soul about his departure, and no matter what happened, no one could ever know she knew of his plan. He wouldn't have her in trouble over his choice.

The prince looked to the stand upon which his armour and helm were placed. He couldn't take anything with the Annoran eagle upon it, nor anything that would give away that he came from royalty. Besides which, he would be travelling light. Speed would be of the essence, so he wouldn't be taking plate armour. Lukas removed his shirt in favour of a plain, faded-red padded tunic. He pulled on a shirt of chainmail that hung to his elbows and shone in in the fire light. Perfect.

He buckled a black leather vest over his mail as well as bracers of steel and his sword belt. Finally, he shoved his warhammer through his belt. It had a black handle with a head of hardened steel. It was perfect for dealing with those who wore armour. The prince looked little more than a common mercenary in between contracts. Exactly what he had hoped for.

Lukas made his way over to the wooden table by his bed and quickly took out a quill and a sheet of parchment. He paused a moment as he looked for the right words. He would write a letter, a letter to his father the king. A letter about why he would not be seen the next day, or the days that followed. No doubt King Dorian would send riders after him, but they would too late and too slow. By the time anyone could act, he would be twenty miles away or more.

Lukas glanced at the message one last time before pulling on a dark cloak and looking about his chambers for perhaps the final time. For most of his life, Palen-Tor had been his home, and he prayed to the gods that this would not be the last time he walked within its stone walls. He snatched up an unmarked black shield and slung it over his back.

He was so caught up in his thoughts that the prince didn't hear the door open.

"Going somewhere?"

Lukas let out a deep breath as the door shut and he recognised the voice. It belonged to his friend, Sakkar.

"I was planning on heading east," the prince said simply as he turned to face the man.

Sakkar simply nodded. "Dangerous country. Perhaps I would be able to offer some assistance."

It didn't surprise Lukas. Had it been in reverse, with the Larissan riding into war, he would have done the same. Life debt or no life debt, he would have done it.

"I cannot ask you to do this, Sakkar."

"Well then, do not ask," came the reply. "But either way, I am coming with you."

The prince nodded. "You know why I go then?"

"Lukas, I've known you for two years and I have never known you to run from a fight. Besides, you have never excelled at following orders." Sakkar grinned for a moment. "I knew what you would do as soon as you told me about why the Salvaari had ridden so far. You are an honourable man, and the honourable thing to do is to ride to the aid of this chieftain, Cyneric."

The prince looked at his friend. "Even so, you do not need to come. Chances are that we won't even reach Salvaar."

"Perhaps … Perhaps not. You saved my life two years ago, and I will always be indebted to you. Perhaps this is my chance to repay that debt," Sakkar told him. "Now tell me, what can I do?"

The discussion was over. There would be no talking his friend out of this.

"Gather your weapons and then head to the stables. Prepare our horses and that of the Salvaari for the journey through Miera. Enough food and supplies for two weeks hard ride. We will meet you there. There is a hidden passage along the city's northern wall. We'll use that to slip out unnoticed."

"It will be done." The Larissan turned to leave.

"Oh, and Sakkar, be ready to ride. We need to put as many miles between us and Palen-Tor by dawn's first light as possible."

Not to mention, if he was seen, they would have soldiers on their tail.

Lukas was careful as he made his way through the castle's endless maze of corridors. His hands were clutched around Cailean's axe. The prince had made a quick detour to the armoury to collect the weapon. He had easily slipped in and out of the room unnoticed. Had the hallways been full of servants, knights, guards and nobles, passing through unseen would have been impossible. As the moon rose higher, the corridors had emptied of all but a few guards pacing up and down. Lukas had been evading them since he was barely five years old.

The tricks needed to slip past the guards were as simple to figure out as they had always been, but with years of experience up his sleeve, Lukas found it easier than ever. As a prince, he knew which guards patrolled where and when the shifts changed. Lukas smirked. He had only ever used the information to help Kassandra see her beloved horses. He had used his knowledge only once before to leave the castle walls. It had been four years past when his sister had pleaded with him to take her riding. Back then it had been the only way. That is of course, until they were caught.

After a brief scolding from their father, Kassie's teary eyes had convinced the king to allow her to ride with her brother during the day. A thing, he said, that he could not have stopped from happening anyway. Aside from his sister, Lukas had only helped spirit maids and noblewomen alike through the halls and into his chamber.

The stakes had never been as high as they were now. Aye, his father would not have been impressed with his scandal of a son, but to discover one was about to disobey his orders and leave in the dead of night on a quest with little chance of succeeding, Lukas could barely imagine how furious his father would be.

Footsteps sounded from up ahead.

The prince ducked behind a pillar just as a pair of red-clad Annoran guards rounded into the corridor. Lukas held his breath as he heard the guards march closer and closer. They were so close that he could hear their breathing. So close that he could reach out and touch them if he wanted to. Then they were gone.

He waited a moment until the footsteps started to fade before slipping out from behind the pillar and scurrying through the hallway once more. He took care to keep his feet light upon the ground as to make as little sound possible. It was going to be a long night.

"Lukas Raynor, son of the mighty Dorian." Sarcasm laced Cailean's words as he rose to his feet upon the prince's entry to his chamber. "Tell me, what has happened for me to receive such an esteemed guest this night?"

He'd expected the hostility. Especially after the council had given the man false hope and then bitterly crushed it in one fell swoop. The prince crossed the room in a few short strides, until he was standing toe to toe with the Salvaari. He held the man's axe in his hands.

"I stumbled across the armoury on my way here. Thought that you might be interested in joining me on a ride."

"Shall I be receiving a knife at the end of this ride?"

He was suspicious. He had every right to be, Lukas supposed. A guest being taken for a "ride" by a prince late at night was a subtle way of receiving an unseen blade in the dark. It wouldn't have been the first time guests were murdered by their hosts.

"No, you won't be dying today," the prince told him.

"And where exactly would we be riding?"

"I was thinking about travelling through Miera, perhaps even to the great forests of Salvaar."

Realisation dawned on Cailean's face as he took his axe and stared at the prince.

"You would disobey your father, the will of your council?"

"I believe they are wrong." The prince shrugged at the warrior. "Your people helped my father avenge the death of my mother and family many years ago. It's only right that I now help you in return."

"And you'll be coming alone, is that it?"

"No," Lukas told him. "There will be one more."

Cailean looked at the prince sharply. Now he saw the extent of what Lukas was doing. This wasn't just going against his father, the king. It was betrayal, near treason.

"You speak of Miera," Cailean murmured. "I travelled through Medea."

"Miera is faster," Lukas replied, "and the eastern roads make tracking hard."

"This is a dangerous game you are playing."

"We can talk later," Lukas cut him off. They didn't have time for this. Any moment they could be discovered. A servant could enter Lukas' room or someone may stumble into the stable. The possibilities were endless. "We need to leave. Now."

"Aye, lead the way, prince."

The moon was at its highest when the three riders shrouded in the darkness of night slipped though the small stone tunnel that ran under the city's walls. The dark speck of a hawk glided in the sky above them. Lukas spared Palen-Tor a glance as they rode hard to put distance between themselves and the pursuit they knew would come. The home he may never see again. The family. His sister.

He would not stop fighting until he saw them again.

TWELVE

Isle of Agartha, the Valkir Isles

The midday sun was flying high in the sky, sending its brilliant rays down into Agartha, when Astrid and her brother left their hall and walked out into the town. Both wore their axes at their sides as was customary for Valkir warriors, but nothing else. No armour was worn over their tunics, and nor did they wear shields at their backs. To do so would have made their intent obvious, and within moments, they would have been confronted. To wear armour while the intent was not blood was near a sin among the raiders and was considered the mark of a coward.

Astrid had sent a quick prayer to the Sea-Father that no blood would be spilt today, for the next body she wished to see would belong to the one who had murdered her father.

Gulls squawked overhead as the pair made their way through the winding streets of the town. They greeted all those who greeted them so not to arouse suspicion.

They walked along the harbour, and they were swarmed with the smell of salt and freshly caught fish. The dock front was the busiest part of the town. It always had been, from the trade that was conducted each day in the bustling market, overflowing with goods for sale and people to buy them, to the small boats filled with fishermen and their catch. Hundreds of people were packed tightly in the narrow streets leading through, many of which were made out of little more than planks that had been built up from the seabed beneath. Merchants called out to passers-by, hopeful to attract customers and coin. Though none would risk overcharging or else the earl may take their hands. For that was the punishment of thieves among the Valkir and no one, not even the wealthiest of merchants, wanted to attract the ire of a wronged warrior. Let alone the earl.

"Once this is over," said Astrid as they weaved through the throng of people, "we should leave Agartha for a while. Let things settle."

"What did you have in mind?" replied Erik from her side.

Astrid glanced over her shoulder at her brother. "We could run the Annoran coast, maybe even hit Miera." The shieldmaiden shrugged as she spoke. "We could even wait out the storm season on one of the other islands."

"Get away from all this, you mean," replied her brother.

Astrid simply nodded. He knew exactly what she meant. Even when the murderer was dealt with, they would still be facing the pitying looks of others and worse. Among the Valkir, strength had to be proven and earned. It wasn't passed down from father to son, or father to daughter. While the siblings had earned that and more from their comrades aboard the Wind Rider, there were few others who knew as much. Especially in Astrid's case. She was no great warrior. Her brother, on the other hand – well, he was bloodsworn. Some believed that she had survived simply from the skill and strength of her father and brother, as if they were her only claim to honour. Now he was dead, and people would talk. She would be challenged at every turn until she had proven herself. A successful raid without Lief was sure to help in that regard. A thing they all knew.

Astrid looked out to sea as a horn sounded from one of the docked ships. The ship was prepared for its voyage, and now sat idle waiting for its crew.

"Looks like the Harpy is going hunting," Erik said as he

recognised the ship.

"Again? I heard they only docked here two weeks ago."

A second horn answered from the town and moments later a jarl clad in his lamellar armour appeared. An axe was sheathed through his belt beside a longsword while he carried a series of packs over his shoulder with his left hand.

Erik nudged his sister's side as he saw the jarl. "Jorun."

"Aye." Astrid nodded as she spoke.

Had he not been a former member of Jarl Lief's crew five summers past then she would have recognised him for the weapon at his side. Jorun Thorkel, or as he was more commonly known Jorun Bloodaxe, was a powerful man with a near unmatched skill when it came to violence. He was a few summers older than Astrid, and the pair had grown up together on the Wind Rider. That was until he'd been granted the titles of jarl and bloodsworn five years before.

The crowd at the harbour made way as the jarl's men arrived at his back, all armed and armoured, and started on their way to their ship.

Jorun noticed the pair as he led his men through the crowd. He held up a hand, stopping his men as he stopped in his tracks before the siblings.

"Astrid," he said with a nod, and he clasped her arm.

"Jorun."

He repeated the greeting with her brother, and his lips twitched into the ever-present smirk. His crew had returned from their last raid barely two weeks before the Wind Rider had returned. Already they were heading back to sea.

Same old Jorun, she thought.

"We're headed to Nesoi Island," Bloodaxe told them. "Plan to winter there so we can pressure the imperial coast for a few months. You are more than welcome to join us."

So, Jorun and his crew were planning an extended raid along the coast of the Aureian Empire. No doubt there would be a lot of wealth to be had and a lot of danger. Nesoi Island lay but a week away from the Valkir Isles, and another two from the mainland. With a yearlong garrison of warriors, fresh water and dozens of food stores, the Valkir had made the island the staging point of many a raid.

"We may just do that," Astrid replied.

Once her father was avenged.

Erik clapped his friend on the arm. "It has been too long since we last sailed together."

"That it has," Jorun agreed before turning to his men. He nodded to indicate that they were about to leave. "The waters await. Farewell, my friends."

"May the Sea-Father watch over you, scâldir."

The sound of hammer striking steel reached Astrid long before the smell of the forge assaulted her nose. She could feel the heat resonating from the smithy brush against her skin as the siblings made their way towards it. This area of the city was rarely busy as it was located away from the market.

"We're alone," Erik told her, his voice stern. He was ready for whatever was about to happen.

Astrid took a deep breath. If all went well, they would be walking out of the forge shortly with the identity of their father's killer.

She could see Viktor at work in the smithy now. He was wrapped in his leather apron and gloves, and his arms and face covered in a layer of sweat. Despite being over forty summers, the blacksmith was a beast of a man. His arms and chest were huge from a lifetime of swinging his hammer, while his long greying hair was tied back.

Astrid shared a look with her brother that spoke volumes.

The shieldmaiden took a deep breath and turned her steely gaze upon the man barely twenty paces away. Now was the time.

"Viktor," Astrid called out as they approached. Her loud voice rose above the sound of hammer upon steel.

The blacksmith spared the siblings a brief glance, running his eyes over them even as he plunged the blade in his hand back into the fires of his oven. "I was sorry to hear of your father's passing," he told them.

Astrid could hear that he meant it.

Viktor pulled off his gloves and tossed them onto a nearby bench.

"Thank you," Erik said as he glanced around the smithy.

The racks were filled with an assortment of swords and axes, while another bench was covered in lamellar armour of leather and steel. Astrid ran her eyes over the weapon racks, as she walked through the forge. Her gaze was keen upon the handiwork of the steel as she admired it. She pulled one of the swords from its rack and looked at it closely. The fires of the forge danced on the metal and gave it an orange glow. Her father had always said that you could always tell if it was Viktor's work by the quality of the steel. A blind man could see the man's heart and soul had been poured into each of his works, and she knew instantly that the dagger in her boot was crafted by the man before her. For whom else could have created a blade of such quality among the Valkir?

"What can I do for you?" inquired Viktor as he slapped his meaty palms together. He turned towards Astrid as she returned the sword to its place. "Do you have mind to a blade?"

"That we do," Erik said, and he crossed his arms.

"We came to inquire about a knife." Astrid bent and withdrew the knife from the depths of her boot before she approached the blacksmith. She held it out to the man. "This knife."

Viktor took the blade and held it before his eyes. The ruby sparkled in the light of the forge, and its vibrant colours were accentuated by the firelight. The blacksmith ran his hands over the weapon, and he glanced at the siblings. "What of it?"

"It is your work, is it not?" Erik stated, his voice stern.

Viktor nodded. "Indeed it is."

Astrid could see something in his eyes. A flicker of doubt. As if he was afraid. Her hand went to the head of her axe.

"Who did you make it for?"

"I cannot say," he replied. "I've made many daggers in my time."

Erik stepped towards him, and Astrid knew that his expression was that of the quiet before a storm. The warrior's voice was strong but calm. "Cannot say, or will not say?"

"It was a long time ago." Viktor's knuckles were whitening on the knife's grip.

Astrid's grip tightened slightly on her axe. The blacksmith's tongue had slipped. Astrid could tell from the furious look in Erik's eyes that her brother had noticed too.

"A long time ago," Astrid echoed, and her eyes met Viktor, daring him to move. She drew her axe an inch to show that she was serious. A Valkir warrior only drew his blade when its wielder had intent burning within them.

She saw horror fill Viktor's face as he realised his mistake. He saw the shine of steel as Astrid made to take up her weapon and, without hesitation, lunged towards her, the dagger she had handed him now aimed towards her chest.

Astrid moved just as fast and slid backwards. Her weapon was nearly clear of her belt even as the knife neared her heart. Then it stopped only inches from its target. Viktor's expression changed from triumph to surprise as Erik grabbed his wrist with one hand and with the other slammed Viktor's head upon the nearby bench. Erik viciously wrenched Viktor's arm up behind his back. It was over in a heartbeat.

"Drop the knife," snarled Erik, "or I will break your arm."

He complied and released his grip on the blade.

Astrid snatched the dagger from where it fell. She felt a hint of satisfaction as her brother pinned the man to his own workbench. She shoved her axe back into her belt. The man was no longer a threat. In any case, she had the knife once again.

"You tried to stab my sister," Erik growled into his captive's ear.

"I should kill you now."

"No," moaned Viktor from beneath him. "Please."

No Valkir feared death in battle, for in battle you can earn glory. In battle, when you fall, the Sea-Father will take you into Ra'Haven to feast for eternity. If you fell not by the sword, then there would be nothing.

Astrid strode over to the pinned man and held the knife to his neck. The edge of the blade dug into his skin.

"Tell us who, Viktor."

"I can't."

She increased the pressure of the blade. "Who?" she snarled.

He spluttered as he tried to wriggle from the iron-grip that held him. Astrid snorted. Not only was he honourless but he was a coward, as well.

Astrid handed her brother the knife before walking into Viktor's workshop. They needed him to talk. She grabbed one of the swords from its rack and shoved the tip into the burning hot coals of the oven. The shieldmaiden was behind the smith and out of sight. He had no idea what was coming.

"You do not want to cross me, blacksmith," Astrid told him calmly. Her words were controlled but powerful.

He struggled against Erik in an attempt to turn and see her. Erik shoved him back down. Hard.

"What are you doing?" the smith called out. He could hear the oven crackling hungrily.

Astrid ignored his plea as she withdrew the sword from the flames, its tip burning red. She walked over to the man pinned by her brother. The same man who was protecting her father's killer. For that, she had no sympathy. No mercy. Astrid raised the sword and lowered its red-hot edge towards Viktor. He flinched back and cried out as his eyes fell upon it. The blade was only a hair's-breadth away and he could feel the heat of it upon his skin.

"Give. Up. The. Name," Astrid growled forcefully, and her steely eyes did not leave the blacksmith's. She was prepared to hurt him. To give him the pain that she was now in. "You do not want me as an enemy, Viktor."

"No … Please …"

"You don't understand, do you?" the shieldmaiden spat. "Skûra is empty, and all its devils are here. If you do not speak the name, you shall see them." She twitched her arm and the red-hot blade closed in on Viktor's cheek.

"Sven!" he cried out as he strained to get away from the burning sword. "The knife belongs to Sven Joramir."

What?

Astrid exchanged a surprised look with her brother. There was no love lost between them, it was true, but the man was a warrior sworn to Earl Magnus. If he had killed their father, then there was no doubt as to who was pulling his strings.

Astrid flicked the sword away from Viktor. "The earl's cousin?" she replied as her eyes bored into the blacksmith. "You're sure of it?"

"I remember every blade I have ever forged. I would be hard pressed to forget the man who wanted a ruby inlaid into the dagger's hilt."

Erik glanced at his sister. "Earl's cousin or not, it changes nothing. There is only one fate for a murderer."

Astrid nodded as she watched the red glow of the sword slowly fade away. So, Sven Joramir had wielded the knife that had taken her father from her. She could feel a cold anger start to seep through her bones. She knew that the earl would try to cover it up. Even a testimony from Viktor confirming the knife's providence would be waved aside as if little more than a feather in the wind, for Sven could have simply misplaced the blade after all. Besides which, Magnus' ire would be turned upon the blacksmith. A thing that Astrid had considered. It was tempting to leave Viktor's fate in the hands of the gods. However, it would stain her honour if he was drawn into her fight and killed as a result of her actions.

"Let him go," Astrid told her brother, and she tossed the sword onto a nearby bench. "We have all we need."

Erik nodded and he removed the knife from Viktor's neck. The blacksmith let out a deep breath, finally away from the sharp edge of the blade he had forged, a short-lived moment. Erik grabbed his prisoner by the shirt, turned him about and shoved him against the bench. The knife returned to Viktor's throat. He glared into the blacksmith's eyes.

"Keep your life. But if you ever speak of this, I may just remember that you tried to kill my sister. Betray us and you will hear from me again. And I promise you, next time I will not be so forgiving."

"I understand," growled Viktor through gritted teeth. His gaze did not leave the warrior as the knife vanished from his neck.

"Good," Astrid replied as she took the knife from her brother's out-stretched hand. "Then you have nothing to fear."

Sven Joramir on the other hand had much to fear. For Skûra, the tempest-filled underworld, had opened and its devils were taking refuge in Astrid's heart. Nothing and no one would be able to stand in her path to vengeance.

They sent out the call to gather. Astrid glanced around her father's hall and her gaze swept from one face to the next. The entire crew of the Wind Rider stood present. Night had long since fallen and a decision had to be made now that Sven had been named. They knew the stakes. Each of them knew that accusing one of the Earl's own had to be done with the highest caution.

"We need to proceed very carefully," Astrid told them, "and quickly. If word gets out that we mean to challenge Sven, then this could all crumble around us. I won't lie to you, this is dangerous, and if any of you wish to leave, you may do so now without tarnish nor stain upon your honour."

None of the Valkir budged as she spoke. She realised none of them were going to leave, and she felt her heart lift.

Torben crossed his arms as he glanced back at the assembled warriors before turning back to Astrid and her brother. "Looks like none of us are going anywhere," he said simply, and his lips curled. "We're all too stupid to avoid the axeman's block."

Astrid grinned as the older man spoke and gave him a nod in return. Having her father's oldest friend at her side was a blessing. He would never abandon her or Erik.

"Aye, Torben is right at that," spoke another warrior. Raol Soren strode forwards as he spread his arms. "And besides, Lief was family to all of us. He was scâldir. As are you both. We are all with you until the end."

One by one, the Valkir chorused their agreement and soon filled the wooden hall with sound. Astrid felt a weight lift from her shoulders. They were not alone. Erik stepped forwards from Astrid's side and his face was awash with pride.

"Thank you, all of you. Your loyalty does you credit, a balm against the grievous injury inflicted by Sven Joramir."

"What of that toad?" called one of the warriors as he crossed his massive arms over his equally as large chest. "What is to be done?"

Erik turned to his sister. "Astrid?"

The shieldmaiden nodded to her brother and stepped forward. She felt a tingle run down her spine. She wasn't sure if it was excitement or the need for revenge.

"Sven is of the earl's blood, we all know this. He is a great warrior and one of Agartha's finest. Magnus will not let a trial take place. What evidence is there after all? The word of a blacksmith against that of a great warrior. Whatever we say would merely be turned into rumour or hearsay by the earl. On that front there is little we can do, if anything at all." Astrid glanced at Erik and took a deep breath. "What I suggest could easily be turned into treason if we do not succeed. A ploy for Magnus to turn to his advantage. Make no mistake, if we fail, we will all die."

"Treason, is it?" grunted Torben with a half-lipped smirk. "Never much liked the earl anyway."

"That rat can drown for all I care," snorted the shieldmaiden Hélla. The hall was filled with chuckles and guffaws as many voiced their agreement.

Astrid grinned. Only those of the Wind Rider would talk openly among themselves of the resentment they bore their lord. They were all fools. Loyal, honourable fools.

"I suggest that tomorrow at dawn we march to Magnus' hall armed. I suggest that we challenge Sven in front of our lord. And then I suggest we take his head."

The cheer that followed was deafening, and for the first time, Astrid felt hope burn brightly within her heart. They were close now. So close to claiming their revenge.

"It must be me who challenges Sven," Erik leaned down and murmured into her ear.

"I know," Astrid replied, and she turned to face her brother. "I am no great warrior, yet you are bloodsworn."

It was true. With more interest in maps, navigation and the stars than a sword it would be folly to think that she could defeat one of Agartha's finest in single combat. No, she preferred to outthink her enemies and strike where least expected.

"We have only gotten this far because of you," Erik said. "It was all your plan and tomorrow it will bear deadly fruit."

"It may have been my plan," she told him, "yet it shall be your arm tested, not mine."

Her younger brother placed a hand upon her shoulder and pressed his forehead into hers.

"Your will, my strength," Erik replied.

When the sun rose and the truth dawned, it would dawn with fire.

THIRTEEN

City of Carlian, Steppe of Miera

Dawn's first light had barely breached the horizon when Kitara awoke from slumber. She brushed a lock of golden hair away from her face and she rolled out of her bed. Her eyes did not betray any hint of tiredness, for each morning for the last fifteen summers had been the same. She rose before dawn every morning and began her daily routine with the words of her old mentor branded into her mind.

Your skill needs to be as sharp and precise as the finest of blades. For if it is not ... you may as well slit your own throat.

It had taken her near two years to fully adopt this gruelling daily routine, and despite the pain it had caused at first, she was grateful. She would have died a long time ago if not for the constant lectures. She would have been struck down in combat by one of the many who were bigger and stronger than her. The lectures and mentors were from another time and another life.

Kitara felt the chill morning air upon her skin as she rose to her feet. Her shirt and breeches barely kept the cold at bay. She tied her hair back with a band of cloth and took a deep breath. Kitara closed her eyes and felt a steely calmness wash over her body. Everything was blocked out, from the sound of Zandir's snoring emanating from the next room to the light patter of footsteps from early risers on the street below.

The serenity filled her body, relaxed her muscles and slowed her breath.

She stretched to the side and felt the sinews in her back stretch under her skin. They flexed and loosened as she slowly changed position. Her body flowed from one move to the next like water. Each movement called upon different muscles as her body fluidly moved at her command. Her bare feet gently slid across the wooden floor without a sound as she moved in the slow melody of a dancer. Each move found the perfect form of foot, leg and shoulder and stretched out her lean muscles.

One first had to master the body in order to master the sword.

With her routine finished, Kitara pulled on her boots and slipped into her brigandine. Next came her bracers and knife belt before she took up her scabbard and blade. She ran her eyes down the plain scabbard and the empty ring that adorned the Dao's pommel. Some of the Tariki, she had heard, embellished the ring with coloured silk to show their rank and prestige. Yet to one who preferred practicality over looks, such things were far removed. The sword had been with her for near to a decade and was worth more to her than all the gold and silver in Miera.

That had been before Carlian and before Annora. Back when everything had made sense, and she had a place. Before her old life had been sundered by those she had trusted most. The pain it had caused had numbed in the years since and taught her a valuable lesson. Trust no one, for everyone is in this life for themself.

A light breeze brushed against Kitara's cheek and gently wove through her hair as she walked out into the empty street. The sky was still dark with little more than the first hint of an orange glow in the east. The dirt road crunched lightly under the weight of her leather boots.

She rolled her shoulders and felt the familiar and comforting weight of her sheathed sword in her hand. Kitara took a few steps down the dirt road before slowly quickening her pace into a jog.

Buildings flashed by her as she dashed through the winding streets of Carlian. She increased her speed until she was running. Her breath was steady and her footfalls light.

The sword in her grasp she did not notice even as she ran. For in a fight, you had to be ready for anything, and to run without a blade while you trained was stupid. One needed to be comfortable running with the extra weight and awkwardness of a sword. Kitara never missed a beat as she ran and barely noticed the all too familiar streets. After a year of running through them, she could have drawn a map of every inch of the city. The runs gave her time to think and enjoy something that was rare these days. Her own company. The Mierans had never batted an eye from the first time she had taken to the streets. Each soldier had their own rituals, and like the rest of the nation, Carlian was a city of warriors.

Which is why she had remained here among the hardened veterans. If there was an issue, it was resolved by compromise or a brawl. That was where it ended. In Miera, there was no scheming or backstabbing. Everyone knew where they sat with everyone, and no one had to fear a knife in the dark, for which she was very thankful.

Kitara could feel the warm sun rays upon her face now as the sun rose higher in the sky. Soon the streets would be flooded with people.

She rounded a bend and put on a burst of speed. The ground sped underfoot as her stride lengthened.

One, two, three. One, two, three. One, two, three.

Fire filled her veins as she pushed herself into a sprint and felt adrenaline course through her blood. Wind whipped through her hair, creating a trail of gold streaming at her back. It was intoxicating.

She took a breath and slowly lessened her pace to a jog and then to a halt. Her body was warm against the chill air now and a thin layer of sweat covered her pale skin.

The streets of Carlian were filling. The almost mercenary-looking warriors hastened to training halls, stables and the like to begin their daily rituals. Many of the soldiers rode in mounted contingents as the city was home to the horse masters. Women, children and old folk tended various stalls and went about their trade.

Three miles of running and Kitara had reached her destination. Kitara walked towards a large walled courtyard that rose before her. It was one of the many training yards in the city. She enjoyed coming here early even if only to get a little peace before the others arrived in droves. Peace from the endless sarcastic remarks on her foreign style. Remarks that she often smirked at before knocking the seven hells out of the men who made them, much to the enjoyment of those watching. She could understand the amusement of witnessing a girl of middling height putting those far bigger than her on the flat of their back. Her sword moved in ways they did not understand. In the far north they called it tarkaras, the swordsong. A technique created for duels and open combat rather than the tight confines of a full-scale battle. It was refined, graceful and deadly. Kitara had created her own way of fighting with a few backhand tricks she learnt among the Sacasian raiders added to the style. Whatever she had to do to survive.

Kitara walked into the training yard with a bounce in her stride, and her eyes flashed about the enclosure as she belted on her sword. With wooden walls that were lined with racks of wooden staunches and ceremonial blades, for every warrior carried their own steel, and filled with near twenty large sand-filled squares for fighting, the yard was everything that was Mieran.

Kitara ignored the racks lined with the wooden practice swords and walked into the centre of one of the squares. Her boots touched the dry sand with barely a crunch, and everything stilled. Her arm rose as she lightly spun in the square and her fingertips gently brushed the leather hilt of her blade. Her hand wrapped around the handle and in one fluid movement she drew the sword from her side. Kitara twirled the blade in her right hand, and her wrist flexed as it took the familiar weight of the steel with the ease of someone born to the sword. The steel sang as it spun in her hands and sliced through the air as easily as it could slice through flesh. She spun lightly and her boots made no more than the slightest of noises as she moved across the sand. The steel in her hand became an extension of her body. A shift in footwork and flick of the wrists turned a low cut into an upwards slice. Her posture flowed effortlessly from one move to the next. Time stood still as she danced amidst a web of steel.

"I should have known you would be here."

With a final flick of her wrists, Kitara brought her blade to a stop. The sun was rising steadily in the sky, while the yard was filled with the sound of clashing wood, staunch upon staunch, for the other warriors had begun to arrive. Kitara held her final stance for an instant and relished in the perfection of the form before taking a deep breath and lowering her sword. She glanced around the yard as the Mieran's hammered at each other with their practice blades in a very unrefined but deadly manner.

She glanced up as a grin began to form on her lips. She recognised the man. "Silas Barangir." Kitara held her pose for a moment longer before turning to face the young man.

Zandir's son reached her and with a chuckle pulled her into a one-armed embrace. His clothes were rough and travel stained. He would have only just arrived in Carlian and not had the time to change his attire. If he had come straight to find her, then something had happened. Something that did not bode well, judging by the dark expression on his face.

"Care for a ride?"

Together they found their horses and left the confines of Carlian behind. At Kitara's side rode Silas. He was near a head taller, and his powerful body was as broad and strong as the sword at his hip.

His dark hair was mid length, and a pair of gold rings adorned his left ear. The beard at his chin was short like his father's, and his blue eyes had a dangerous glint to them as if fire wanting to be unleashed. He had grown up along the northern border with his family and spent the last half decade fending off Salvaari incursions into Miera. The Rift, as many called the untamed north, bred the fiercest warriors among the horsemen. Born with a sword in hand and fire in their blood, they were battle-hardened by the raids.

She had been tired when they had first met yet had been too stubborn to refuse the Mieran's challenge. Kitara had barely eaten or drank in days and had not slept. He had underestimated her and that had cost him the duel. Had Silas treated her as an equal, then Kitara would probably have been dead.

The wind whipped through Kitara's long hair as they rode and pushed their horses into a gallop. It streamed behind her in a brilliant wave of gold. She held the reins loosely as they thundered across the rolling green plains, and she felt every move her mare made. She had named the mare Lamreil when she fled the Annoran border a year ago. The name reminded her of home. What she had once called home, anyway – the Gulf of Lamrei in the south of the Sacasian Sea.

Lamreil's legs were corded with muscle, and she moved effortlessly as her hooves kissed the ground. They flew through the plain and churned the earth beneath. Silas whistled loudly beside her and gestured towards one of the small hills that had arisen before them. Without a word, the pair angled their horses towards the hill and the mounts never broke their stride.

They rose higher with the sun warm on their backs.

A slight twitch in the reins and the mare slowed to a canter and then a walk as they reached the top of the shallow incline. Kitara ran a hand down Lamreil's powerful neck as she brought the mare to a halt before a small crop of green trees. It was a place that Silas had brought her a few times yet only for things of great importance. He would not have minded another ride after what appeared to be a full night in the saddle. He was Mieran after all.

Kitara swung a leg over Lamreil's flank and slid from her horse's back. Her feet met the hard earth beneath with a light thud. "How was the border?" Kitara asked as she gave Silas a sidelong glance.

"Uneventful for the most part. Spent most of our time keeping an eye on the convoys between Tallis and the Belcar tribe from Salvaar. But then it got quiet. The last convoy we saw was near a month back."

"Strange. Even the Belcar would not be so foolish to end a trade agreement with the Tallisians."

Silas nodded thoughtfully. "And that's not the end of it," he continued. "We got word from the northern garrison that the entire Salvaari border has grown silent."

Kitara stopped in her tracks and turned to her companion. That didn't make sense at all. It was rare to go half a day without seeing tribesmen patrolling the tree line.

"How silent exactly?"

"The final reports of warriors wandering the Rift was near to a month ago. The Tallis traders told us that they had not been met at the border."

The Rift spanned for most of the border between Salvaar and Miera. It was a disputed territory that had led to countless skirmishes over the centuries, an area where the trees melted into the plains and created a near barren land that both sides watched cautiously.

"The Salvaari would not just abandon their border," Kitara replied as they walked. "Nor would they leave the Rift without reason."

Silas nodded. "Your guess would be as good as any. Perhaps they pulled back from the Rift so that they could avoid our northern outposts. Perhaps something happened that they do not want the world to know about. I do not know."

Kitara could hear something different in his voice. A hint of something. He seemed on edge. "What is it, Silas? Why are you back so soon?"

The Mieran stopped in his tracks as he turned to the girl. His brow was furrowed. "Something is coming," he said with an intensity that caught Kitara off guard.

This was not like the Silas she knew.

"The heartbeat of its drums echoes through the earth."

"What are you talking about?" Kitara replied and she felt a chill run down her spine.

"You are not Mieran, so you may not understand, but can you not see? The forges are at work, day and night. The training yards are filled from dawn until dusk. There is a fight brewing. We can all feel it in our blood."

Kitara had noticed something in the air had changed. The Mierans were quieter. They were more reserved as of late, and their eyes were wary. She shook her head in exasperation. He had told her nothing.

"The men are quiet, I have noticed. Almost like they are preparing for something, yet you're speaking in riddles, Silas. What fight?"

The man chuckled without mirth. "I am not certain; none of us are. Yet the feeling is there. A shadow of a doubt. When the Medeans came eight years ago, we felt it, and before them when the Annorans invaded. This time it feels different ... Even the king is unsure."

The king? Now she was curious. This was not the same Silas who had left for the western border.

"Oh, and how do you know what plagues the king's mind?"

"Less than a week ago, Zoran Layin rode into our garrison."

"What?" Kitara looked at him in shock. Even though Zoran rode through his kingdom frequently to meet with his generals and visit his soldiers, this came as a surprise. "I thought ... we all thought he was still in Carlian. Why would the king ride east without so much as a whisper?"

"He had ridden through the night with only a handful of his guard to seek out Azrial Dathmir."

Kitara listened. Her mind was abuzz. From what Silas and his father had told her, Azrial had grown up with Zoran and the two were as brothers. Dathmir had risen to prominence thanks to his skill at command against an attempted Medean incursion eight years before. He had sent the invaders back across the border with their tails between their legs, carrying a warning:

The next time they attacked would be the last.

Now the man served as King Zoran's right hand.

"The next morning, Dathmir brought us news that we were to make haste towards the western border, stopping one day in Carlian for supplies and reinforcement. Seems that Zoran thinks a war is brewing to the west. Wants his greatest commander to keep an eye on Annora and Medea as a precaution."

Kitara let out a breath as she took it all in. With the northern border silent and trade ended between the Belcar and Elara to the east, with rumours coming from the west, King Zoran had right to be nervous. It would not be long before Miera was fully roused, and riders were sent to every corner with eyes on the horizon.

"Why did you come to me first, Silas? Before anyone else?" she asked. "You didn't just come to me to speak of what happened."

"No, I did not." Silas nodded, and his eyes met hers. "You have been in Miera for nearly a year now and you have seen little more than Carlian in all that time. Would you like to travel west?"

Kitara wasn't sure what surprised her more. What Silas had told her or the fact that he was asking if she wanted to ride with the Mierans for the first time. Yet barely days ago, she had been told a firm no by one of the Mieran captains.

"Carac does not think me ready."

Silas shrugged. "I am not Carac."

She could feel the same excitement she had felt when she was fourteen and had first been taken on a voyage across the Sacasian Sea aboard one of the galleons. Once more, she would get the chance to be a part of something. This time she would know to watch her back.

Kitara snorted and gave her companion a grin. "Do you even need to ask?"

Silas extended his hand with a grin. She took it with her own and clasped it firmly.

"We leave at dawn."

FOURTEEN

Isle of Agartha, the Valkir Isles

A cold wind howled through the town of Agartha. It swirled in amongst the wooden walls and thatched rooftops that belonged to the halls of the Valkir. The gentle rays of dawn's first light reflected off the thin layer of pale snow underfoot. It crunched under the heavy footsteps of the small band making their way up the hill towards the earl's great hall. Each of the two dozen Valkir, shieldbrothers and shieldmaidens alike, wore their weapons at their hips. All save their leader bore shields slung over their shoulders.

All of them had the same dark expression. All of them were filled with anger and grief.

The leader of the group, Astrid Farrin, strode towards the great hall with purpose. Her eyes were fixed dead ahead and her left hand rested comfortably on her axe's head. She was about to take a risk. All the warriors of the party knew it. If it went badly, then she could pay with her life. They stood by her anyway. They believed in her.

That wasn't the only reason they stood with her. They wanted blood. To her side was her brother, Erik, his face contorted with rage. No doubt the same expression was mirrored on her own face. As the warriors climbed higher up the hill, a large crowd was beginning to form and grew bigger. Dozens of people began to follow the crew.

Not a single member of the group responded as the crowd began to hurl questions at them.

"What has happened?"

"Where do you march?"

They didn't answer. Not a single word was said. Their business wasn't with the crowd. Their business was with Earl Magnus and that snake Sven Joramir.

Soon they would be through the maze of streets and standing before the earl himself.

Now that Lief had been sent to Ra'Haven, they could have their justice. They could have vengeance.

The great hall of Agartha rose before them as they rounded onto the small street leading up to it. The hall towered above all in the city and was built with large wooden beams of oak. Ferocious gargoyles carved out of the same wood stood guard at the massive doors of the hall. Their crazed expressions seemed to stare into the very hearts of all who approached.

Four warriors stood guard at the entrance to the hall. They were armed to the teeth and bore armour of leather, steel and chain. Huge round shields were strapped to their arms.

Astrid could almost see their eyes widen as the group approached the hall. The guards' hands were within inches of their weapons.

"You there," called one of the warriors loudly as his hand dropped to his sword handle, "what is your business here?"

Astrid ignored the warning, and her own warriors followed suit as they continued their march.

They were within twenty paces of the hall and their stride did not waver. The crowd grew quiet as the band of warriors drew closer to the hall. The only sound was the crunch of their footsteps on the ground.

The guards drew their swords and axes and raised their shields. Astrid almost smirked as she saw a flash of fear cross their eyes.

"Halt," came the call.

Brave man, thought Astrid as she sent a glare his way to show she heard. However, her stride did not falter.

She had – they all had – come too far to simply stop.

"You will obey!" the guard captain shouted as he levelled his sword.

Ten paces now.

Astrid's axe whistled as it cleared her belt. "Move," she said loudly.

The courtyard was filled with the ringing of steel as her companions drew their weapons and slung their shields over their arms.

The guards glanced at each other. They were unsure and afraid.

"Move," Astrid repeated, louder. She glared venomously at the guard as she took a step forwards and raised her axe slightly. She was prepared to fight to gain entry to the earl's hall.

Another step.

"Get out of the way," growled Erik. He strode forwards and shoved his shield into that of one of the guards. The man was pushed back as the shields smashed together. Just like that, it was over. The guards, not willing to die to protect a doorway, stepped aside. A thing that said a thousand words about their love for the earl.

The crew of the Wind Rider looked to Astrid and sheathed their blades. All except for four who stood watch over the earl's men.

Now we begin the game. And if we lose, we die. She glanced at Erik. She knew what she had to do. "For Father."

Then she pushed the massive doors open and strode inside the great hall, her eyes ablaze.

"What is the meaning of this?" bellowed Earl Magnus from his wooden throne atop a small dais as the doors to his hall burst open.

Astrid strode into the centre of the hall, and her eyes locked with the earl. Her eyes continued to stare him down, even as his sworn warriors drew their blades and stepped towards her. Rage and grief flashed across her eyes as she saw Sven Joramir standing beside the earl with his arms crossed over his chest. Astrid tossed the ruby-embossed knife to the floor where it landed with a thud.

"My name is Astrid. Daughter of Jarl Lief Farrin," she shouted so that all could hear the anger and sorrow filling that filled her words. "And in his name, I come for justice and blood!"

Silence filled the hall as Astrid's words echoed through its walls. The earl rose to his feet. His long black hair hung past his powerful shoulders while his hand wrapped around the pommel of the longsword at his waist. Magnus Vedoera, they called him the Wolf of Agartha. His endless plots and schemes, ruthless nature and unrelenting hunger for the hunt had earned him the name. Thus Magnus, the man he was, had taken the wolf as his symbol. It was a symbol that drove fear into the hearts of many through reputation alone.

"So, you think that you have discovered who killed your father," Magnus' powerful voice boomed.

Astrid glared at Sven before turning as she spoke. "No, not killed, lord. My father was murdered."

"Ah, and this blade is supposed to be the weapon responsible," came Magnus' reply as he gestured to the dagger.

Astrid was sure she could see humour in his eyes. *He knows.*

"Aye, lord," called out Erik as he stepped to his sister's side before levelling a finger to the man beside the earl, Sven. "And that is the man who thrust it into his heart."

"In the name of our dead father," added Astrid even as the crowd started to yell, "we demand justice."

The uproar that followed was deafening. They had just accused one of the earl's best and most trusted warriors of murder, a crime punishable by death.

"That is a grave accusation, shieldmaiden," said the earl as the shouts died down. "Do you have any evidence to back up your claim? A witness perhaps?"

He knows we don't, thought Astrid angrily. *None that would be damning, at any rate.*

"No, lord, none save that the blacksmith Viktor forged this knife not two summers past for the man himself."

There was no getting away with it, Astrid thought smugly as she felt the room darken. They were all turning on the earl's cousin.

"I see. Sven Joramir, step forward."

Sven stepped down from the dais. He was barely half a dozen paces from Astrid and Erik.

"Lord."

"How do you answer these allegations?" The warrior crossed his arms.

"I know nothing of the jarl's death."

"That's a lie," roared Erik. "You stabbed him in the heart and left him to die. Have you no honour?"

Shouts came from the crowd now. Some backed the siblings, while others backed Sven.

"Silence!" roared the earl, quieting the shouts. "I will have silence."

The hall grew quiet as all looked to their leader and awaited his judgement.

What would he do?

Astrid knew the answer. The earl was going to find a way to defend his man.

"Murder is a grave crime. One punishable by death. We all know this," began Magnus and his eyes did not move from Astrid. "As is falsely accusing an innocent the same." The earl stepped forwards and gestured towards Astrid and her brother. "However, the accused has said he is innocent of the murder of Jarl Lief Farrin, a man that many of you knew as one of the greatest captains in the history of our people. As neither side has any solid evidence, I must think on this matter."

And there it is, thought Astrid as her eyes blazed. Even a fool knew what would happen next. The earl would think. After he was done thinking, Sven would get away with murder. The murder of her father.

She knew what would come next. Lief had always said that she had the wit, and her brother had the strength. He had said that together they could accomplish wonders that many dreamed of.

"No need to trouble yourself, lord," Erik said as he turned his furious gaze on Sven. "I challenge the murderer to single combat. Warrior against warrior. To the death."

Sven bared his teeth as the crowd roared at the prospect of a fight. He was stronger than most bloodsworn. One of the best fighters in all of the isles. He had nothing to fear even from one who stood as such, for if he won the contest and stood victor, there would be no doubt of his prowess.

"I accept," he bellowed over the voices of the crowd.

He no doubt thought that he could solve two problems at once. If he appeared true in the eyes of the Sea-Father in victory, then he could rid himself of Lief's son in the process.

Astrid felt her lips threaten a smile. Sven was ever the arrogant fool and had taken the bait perfectly.

Magnus slowly walked down the stairs of the dais until he was standing directly in front of Erik and Sven.

"Very well, we shall leave it in the hands of the Sea-Father," he said, and his voice echoed around his great hall. "The victor to be judged true by our god, the fallen to pay for his sins."

Astrid felt adrenaline flood her body as the cheers started. Erik would avenge her father or die in the attempt.

The cries did not end until Erik, Astrid and Torben gathered in a tent to prepare.

"Let me fight as your champion," said Torben as he watched his friend strap on his bracers.

Erik snorted. "Aye, and let everyone think I'm a coward?"

"He is a great warrior. The sole reason he is not bloodsworn is his position in Magnus' hall."

"And like you, my brother stands as a bloodsworn," Astrid said to Torben as she quickly tied her long black hair with a leather cord. "The greater the warrior, the greater the fame. And so, it will be even more glorious when Erik buries his axe in Sven's heart."

"I understand," Torben replied with a nod.

Erik couldn't back down or choose a champion without looking weak and losing the respect of the people, and he knew it. Who would believe Erik's word that Sven was a murderer if he wasn't willing to risk his own life? It was the brand of a coward and a liar.

"Just don't hesitate," Astrid said.

She would never admit it, but she felt fear for her brother. Fear that in a few short moments she could have no family left. She had never been able to say goodbye to her father. She didn't know what she would do if Erik was to fall too.

"I know you're worried." Erik turned to his sister and his eyes glinted with intensity. "But when my day comes, I will not beg for more time nor shall I cry. Until that day, I will fight." The warrior finished tightening his bracer. "I have been killing bigger and stronger warriors all my life. And if there is one inescapable truth, they fall just as hard as anyone else. Sven may have all the advantages you could wish for ... his reach, his strength, and he knows it. But he is arrogant. He will be overconfident because he has every reason to be. An overconfident warrior is a flawed warrior. And flawed warriors can be overcome, no matter the odds."

"One of Father's many lessons," Astrid remembered.

"Yes." Erik looked around his father's hall and took a deep breath.

There was one last thing to be done. Astrid was acting as her brother's second and as such she had come fully kitted out for battle. She was clad in her leather jerkin with her axe buckled at her hip.

"Torben," she said, and she gestured to her second companion.

The big man reached out and handed her a small bowl filled with white ochre. "Jarl."

"I am no jarl," Astrid said as she ran her fingers through the white liquid before smearing it around her eyes, a custom among the Valkir, one that gave them an almost unearthly look.

"Yes, you are," Erik added. "You are the oldest child of Jarl Lief. His title falls to you."

"You are his son," she insisted. "Not me."

"Perhaps." Erik shrugged. "I may have a good sword arm. But you, Astrid, you have a good mind. You have always been brighter than me. Your wit is as sharp as my blade. You'll make a far better leader than I ever could."

That hit her.

They're serious.

"The crew has chosen. They will follow you to whatever end," Torben continued. "And once your plan has put that murderer in an early grave, everyone will know it."

I didn't ask for this, thought Astrid.

"We are with you, no matter what comes next," Erik added. He extended a hand and took the helmet that his sister held towards him.

"Alright. Kill Sven and avenge our father. And then we can talk about the future."

Deafening cheers assaulted Astrid's ears as she left her father's hall and entered the town. A huge crowd had gathered to see the fight between the earl's champion and the jarl's son. No doubt some of them had placed bets on the outcome. The crew of the Wind Rider formed a vanguard around Astrid, Erik and Torben as they made their way towards the town square. Each wore the same calm expression overlaying their emotions of anger and grief. The man who had murdered their beloved leader was about to face justice.

Astrid blocked out the sound of the cheers and kept her steely gaze fixed dead ahead as she walked through the path formed by the crowd. Astrid looked every part the Valkir warrior with white around her eyes, clad in her garb of leather and fur, and an axe at her side. She was ready for blood. Beside her, Erik stood as a demon. He was clad head to toe in his lamellar armour with ochre covering his face that intensified the fire in his burning gaze. Astrid held her brother's broad-bladed axe tightly in her hands.

The cheers grew louder as Erik made his way through the last of the crowd and into the square. It was empty except for the earl, two of his guard and Sven.

It was time.

Astrid clapped her hand on Erik's shoulder. Her brother leaned down to hear her words. "Send him to Skûra," she murmured.

Erik gave her a small nod in reply. He strode into the square, with his sister by his side, to join the earl and Sven. His iron gaze was fixed upon his opponent.

Astrid felt herself glaring at the earl. She bit her tongue and tore her eyes away. For the first time, she looked around at the half a hundred people who had gathered. It was the most that could fit into the courtyard without crowding the fighting square.

Sven grinned mirthlessly as he saw her. He was confident that this would last all of a few moments. Like her brother, the warrior wore plated steel and leather lamellar armour over his chest and bracers strapped to his arms. A helmet covered his head and ochre was painted around his menacing eyes.

Sven's grin widened. The man clearly didn't think that his opponent would be able to land a blow, let alone harm him. Astrid smirked as she saw his lack of humility. It was a mistake that Erik would punish him for. A shield was strapped to his left arm, while he held a vicious axe in his right hand.

One of Magnus' warriors moved to stand in front of Sven while Astrid did the same for her brother.

"People of Agartha," Magnus called out and those who were gathered fell silent. "Erik Farrin, son of Lief Farrin, has challenged Sven Joramir to single combat. The fight is to the death. No mercy is to be shown, no quarter given."

A hush fell over the crowd as the earl stepped out of the square with his two warriors. Erik closed his eyes and took a breath. He slowly placed his helmet over his head. "May the spirits of my ancestors envelop me," Erik murmured.

This was for his father.

Astrid held out her brother's axe. With barely more than a slight nod, he took it and gave it a twirl. The polished steel glinted in the sun as he turned to face Sven. The shieldmaiden stepped back to the edge of the crowd. Her eyes were fixed on the combatants, and her ears blocked all else out.

Sven's grin faded as he faced Erik. His eyes were now cold and watching his opponent's every move. He smacked his axe into his shield.

Thud. Thud. Thud.

"Begin!" roared Magnus.

With a fearsome battle cry, Sven charged at Erik with his axe raised into the air.

The crowd roared as Sven made his move towards Erik. His axe swung into a diagonal slash aimed at Erik's neck. Reacting instinctively, Erik slightly moved his right boot back. He barely disturbed the dirt underfoot and slightly changed the angle of his body even as the blade whistled down. With a flick of his wrist, Erik angled his axe and deflected Sven's weapon to the side. He spun away as Sven launched a new attack.

Erik's shield thudded as his opponent's axe smashed into it with the power of a hammer on an anvil. Erik grunted under the force of the blow before he rammed his shield into Sven's.

Their weapons came together again and again in a flurry of blows. The sound of steel striking steel was barely audible over the roar of the crowd baying for blood.

Erik didn't give the man time to pause before launching himself at him, Erik's axe becoming a blur as it cut through the air. The weapons rang as they collided.

With a roar, Sven struck out and punched the edge of his shield into Erik's exposed stomach. The bloodsworn gasped as he was thrown back. He was barely able to keep his footing on the muddy ground. The steel rim of the shield pushed him back, yet his armour took the brunt of the blow. Erik dodged another shield strike by a hair's-breadth before he hammered the shaft of his axe into Sven's face. The warrior stumbled backwards as his helmet rung out. Blood erupted from Sven's split lips. Erik disengaged and put space between himself and Sven. He growled as he began to circle. His heart pounded. Fire burned through his veins. Sven moved again. His axe sped towards Erik's chest with the momentum of a charging bull. Erik's foot slid back along the ground as his shield came up to punch into the path of the axe. Steel struck wood with a crack. The blow sent Erik back a step. The bloodsworn retaliated but his blade met nothing but Sven's shield.

Erik grimaced as the axe hammered home a second time. His arm burned under the strain, and he could feel his opponent's hot breath upon his face.

A third blow came.

Erik flicked his wrist and deflected the blow with his shield as he whipped around to Sven's side. He lashed out even as Sven sprang into action. Axe sliced through leather and cut into Sven's flesh.

Blood flowed and the warrior snarled.

It was little more than a shallow wound. The armour had saved his life.

Sven's rage-filled eyes turned on the man who had dared to draw his blood. The man who had dared to stand against him.

Erik's breathing was slow. Calm. His fingers flexed on the handle of his weapon. Its leather grip was ever comforting to the warrior.

His shield thudded as Sven rammed his own into it. Hard.

Steel rang as the pair fought for control. No longer was the earl's cousin overconfident. Now he fought with a calculating gaze and deadly intent.

Axe met axe and shield met shield.

Erik swung his shield up as Sven drove his own towards him. Lief's son shifted his footing to brace against the blow.

The shields crashed together. The butt of Sven's axe smashed into the side of Erik's shin.

Erik snarled as his armour caught the weapon. The steel saved his bone, yet the blow buckled his leg.

His foot left the ground as a wave of pain lanced through his shin. Sven charged forwards and threw all of his body behind his shield.

He crashed into Erik.

The bloodsworn felt his knees weaken as the weight forced him down. He was falling.

Erik hit the ground and swung his shield desperately towards the blow he knew was coming. His head rang as Sven's axe smashed home. It drove through his shield and into the side of his helm. For a moment, the world blurred.

The crowd roared as Sven closed in for the kill with a vicious sneer on his lips.

Erik grunted as pain shot through his body. He gritted his teeth. He would not die here. Not when he was this close. Erik bit back the pain and sent his axe towards his opponent's exposed legs. Sven swatted the blow aside with his shield as if it were nothing.

It left him exposed.

Sven's boot cracked into his cheek.

Blood exploded from Erik's lips as the blow rocked him back.

Erik fought to remain conscious as his head rang. Sven stood over him and hovered his axe over Erik's throat. "Now you die," he snarled.

Erik looked up at Sven, and images of his father flashed before his eyes.

This is not how it ends, he thought through gritted teeth.

With a roar, he swung his axe again. Its edge cut towards Sven. The warrior took the blow on his shield with a contemptuous smirk. Sven had not seen the dangerous glint in Erik's gaze. Sven's eyes were blind to his feint.

Erik's shield smashed into Sven's right knee. The steel rim struck with a dull crack.

Sven howled in pain as he staggered backwards. The bone of his knee was shattered. His face contorted in agony as he fought to stay afoot. A lesser man would have been felled by the blow, but Sven was near bloodsworn.

Erik slowly rose to his feet. Blood dripped from his face as he looked at Sven like a wolf eyed its prey. A devil rose from the depths of Skûra to claim its victim. Erik took a step towards Sven. His hand tightened on his axe. His leg burned. He relished it. Turned it into strength. The air sang as Erik's blade leapt towards Sven and smashed into his hastily thrown shield. The blow drove the warrior back. Sven grunted as his full weight fell upon his injured knee.

Erik lashed out again as the fire that burned in his veins gave him strength. Sven's defence splintered as the axe drove his shield to his side. He desperately swung his weapon.

Erik's shield came up as he moved and flowed from one movement to the next effortlessly. His shield thudded under the blow as he countered. His axe splintered Sven's armour and drove deep into the flesh of his shoulder.

Crimson blood flowed as Sven's knee gave way. He crashed to the ground in a ruined pile. A howl tore from his lips. Sven lay face up in the mud. His axe lay just beyond the reach of his outstretched fingers.

The crowd watched in stunned silence as Erik walked over to the fallen warrior. The warrior gazed at him in disbelief, as if unable to comprehend that he had been beaten. Perhaps it had never happened before. Perhaps his reputation was well earned.

Erik kicked Sven's axe aside and tossed his own shield into the mud. He reached behind his back, and his fingers found the hilt of a dagger. Erik slid the knife from his belt. Its inlaid ruby glinted in the sunlight.

Anger and grief filled him as he stood over Sven with his axe at his throat.

He had murdered his father, and now he would avenge him.

Erik dropped into a crouch over Sven. One knee pinning Sven's left arm to the ground while his blood-soaked axe pressed against the other. There would be no escape for him. The bloodsworn glared down at the murderer beneath him. The dagger's cold tip pressed into Sven's neck.

"You will not die by the axe. You do not deserve that honour. You shall not enter Ra'Haven. You shall not walk the golden halls of the Sea-Father." Erik could feel the fury building inside as it sunk its hot claws into him. His knuckles were white from his ever-tightening grip on Sven's knife. "Instead you shall spend all eternity screaming in the pits of Skûra, and all the cursed within shall know: there lies Sven. The fool who thought that murder led to glory."

Horror filled Sven's face as he looked up at Erik and felt the icy fingers of death begin to reach for him. So terrible were Erik's words that all who had gathered looked on in stunned silence, as if the curse had frozen them in place.

Astrid could not help the rush that sped through her veins as Erik spoke. How she had longed for this moment. Her brother raised the knife. His scream was filled with rage and pain as he brought the short blade down.

Astrid's breathing was ragged when she reached Erik's side. Her eyes were fixed on the corpse at his feet. She dropped into a crouch beside her brother, and boots splashed in the pool of bloody mud. The gentle wind that blew through her hair was cool to her cheek.

All eyes were on the siblings.

Astrid pulled the knife free and watched as blood drained from its tip. It dropped onto the earth below. Then she tossed the blade into the dirt beside its owner before she rose to her feet. Anger still clawed at her. It threatened to tear her apart.

He's dead.

It wasn't enough. Astrid spat beside Sven's unmoving body. She almost wished she could kill him for a second time. A tear rolled down her cheek as emotion threatened to overcome her.

Erik rose beside her. His hand was tightly clenched around his axe. His weight shifted away from his wounded leg, yet his face barely held a grimace.

Sven was dead. So was their father.

Sven was like a well-heeled dog. He would only have killed Lief on the word of another.

Astrid wrapped a hand around her brother's wrist. "You did it," was all she said as her brother turned and planted his forehead gently on her own.

"Your will … my strength," he murmured as they were swamped by the crew of the Wind Rider. "The murderer is dead."

She looked past her brother and through the crowd to where the earl was standing. His face was expressionless, but Astrid could see the hidden anger in his eyes. Erik followed her hate filled gaze as Astrid spoke again.

"But who gave the order?"

FIFTEEN

Wighthorn Forest, Aethela, Kingdom of Annora

Prince Lukas set their rapid pace. They had ridden hard for the better part of a night and day and pushed both themselves and their horses to the limit. Had they stopped any sooner they would almost have certainly been caught by any pursuit that Lukas' father had sent. The prince knew that at best the Annoran riders would be little more than half a day behind.

The three had spent the last night and day dodging villages and people. They rode through forests and rivers with no respite. The little food and drink they had consumed had been in the saddle. Small mouthfuls of water from their canteens and morsels of bread and salted meat were all that kept them going.

The sun was starting to set when Lukas brought his horse to a halt. The prince rubbed his mount's brown neck and looked over the terrain before them. The lush, grassy plain melted into an evergreen forest before them. The forest of Wighthorn. His mind conjured a map of Annora and all its territories. The hundred-mile-long forest would be the perfect place to rest for the night. It was filled with dense woods and thick undergrowth; however, travelling through the woods was the fastest way to reach Miera.

"Wighthorn Forest," Lukas said as his companions reached his side. "We can rest here tonight."

"Are you sure that's wise, prince?" spoke Cailean. "Your father's men will not be far behind us."

Lukas grimaced. The Aedei had the annoying habit of using titles.

The prince shook his head as he replied, "They will be stopping for the night soon enough if they haven't already."

"The forest will give us good cover," added Sakkar. "And besides, we may have lost them at the river."

The Salvaari slowly nodded. "Aye, maybe ... we ride at dawn though. And no fires."

They found shelter in the trees and set up a small camp. It was little more than a nook between the trees. The horses were tethered a few paces away, while the companions sat on bedrolls and leaned against the trunks of oak trees.

"This chieftain, Henghis. Tell me about him, your leaders, how has this situation come about," Lukas said as he looked to Cailean from across their makeshift campsite.

Cailean glanced at the prince and then to the Larissan who watched him intently. "What you have to understand is that my people, all the Salvaari, place family and honour before all else. This conflict started because of honour, but rarely do we have a fight on our hands of this scale. As I told your court, the first we knew of was when Henghis of the Catuvantuli led an ambush. He is a man with a fierce loyalty to his tribe and is a well-respected leader among my kind. Somehow, he knew of the exact route that my brother was taking. To this day I do not know how ..." He trailed off for a moment as his eyes flickered skyward. "We turned to the other tribes for justice, but Henghis had planned ahead."

"You said that most fell in line behind the Catuvantuli," Lukas said thoughtfully. "Why?"

"Each had their own reason for joining with Henghis. He is the most admired and beloved leader our people have had in decades. Some will have wished to become allied with him to strengthen themselves and their people. Some will have done it for power, for as one tribe rises, another falls. Some chiefs no doubt will be doing it because of blood feuds their grandfathers swore. Why did they join Henghis, prince? Reasons beyond count. But he killed my brother. In cold blood …" Cailean trailed off and turned to stare at the knife clasped in his hands. "Even now I can feel it. The creature of the deep that leaves a pit in your stomach. Every step we take towards those trees, it stirs evermore."

"So, war is the only way?" asked Sakkar.

"We use the pelts of animals for warmth. We use the white grease to keep our hair from our faces in battle. These things unto themselves are meaningless, no? Do you know why we paint our faces and bodies?" replied the Aedei as he searched his companions' blank expressions. "We call it being marked. It is a pledge, a sacred pact to the spirits and to tribe. It means we would sooner die than fail in disgrace. For us, it means no mercy. There is no turning back. Not from this."

Lukas met the man's eyes and saw nothing but the burning intensity held within them. "No doubt this Henghis feels the same."

Cailean nodded slowly. "My brother tells me the Catuvantuli were marked when they ambushed my people and took Malakai's life. Their faces were painted like blood. You wanted to know about the leaders of the tribes, prince. Many are warriors. Some served as druids before their clans called them. Some inherited their kingdoms; others took them. They say that Vaylin of the Káli won her way to power through guile and a poisoned chalice."

A woman? Lukas had heard a little about the Salvaari, yet his father had failed to mention that any of the chiefs were female. "Women lead your menfolk?"

Cailean's eyes flashed with humour as he replied, "Our women would say that they are the only ones who raise real men."

"My father failed to mention that, as did my tutors."

"Our women hunt, ride and fight beside the men. Any who hold land, be they man or woman, are expected by law to take up arms when the chief sends out the call."

"It does not concern me," Lukas shot back with a snort. "But where I come from, we leave the fighting and leading to men. To do otherwise goes against the gods."

"Not my gods."

Lukas let out a chuckle. "Nor mine. I place no stock in them."

"Is that so?" Cailean grinned as if surprised that one from Annora would not be a firm believer.

The prince shrugged absent-mindedly. "I pray to them as much as the next man to keep the priests happy. Yet I pray in silence. I wear the amulet of the Twins to appease my father. But I do not hold faith in any higher power. Only in men."

The Salvaari couldn't help but stare at the younger man. He was royalty from the west, a prince of the blood no less, and yet was not fully indoctrinated in the beliefs of his own people.

"In Larissa," Sakkar spoke, "Queen Reshada rules alone."

"In Salvaar it does not matter who you are. Be you man or woman, any can fight and die for their people. All deserve the chance to impress the spirits, no? Of the twelve tribes, four are led by women. And the fiercest of them all, her name is Etain."

"You speak as if you admire her."

"She has won more single combats than any chief. Many admire and respect her." Cailean glanced at the Larissan. "She would have joined with my people, save for her blood ties with Henghis. You see, she is his cousin by blood."

"And as such she must follow him into battle, even to death," the prince replied. He finally understood.

"As is our way."

Lukas leaned against the tree and folded his arms. His head was filled with everything he had been told by his father, by his tutors and the old soldiers from the war twenty-five years before.

"My father once told me," he began and his eyes moved towards Cailean, "that your people speak with two languages. That the tongue of Salvaar is not the language of your forefathers."

The older warrior nodded, and his lips twitched into somewhat of a smirk. "Yes, that is so. Once upon a time, my people spoke only the old tongue of your people. Once upon a time, we had little to fear from the outside world. But that changed when the Knights of Kil'kara rode north. I believe your people call it the Inquisition. Its intention to rid Medea of we heathens." There was venom in his voice as he spoke. "When the west triumphed over them, my ancestors fled into Salvaar. And when the fighting finally stopped and the bloodshed ended, those who had been of the north claimed Salvaar as their home. There they learnt the ways of trees and earth and water. There they learnt our tongue. Though now we all speak Salvaari, our warriors and leaders also speak the language of your people."

Lukas snorted as he remembered something he had been told years before, something that he still found utterly absurd. "Those same people who fled to Salvaar believed in fairy tales and superstition did they not? In magic."

Cailean felt a tingle run down his spine. Not quite fear, but something else entirely. "Listen to me, prince, and listen well. If you are to survive the pagan lands, I suggest that you trust in these fairy tales. Or perhaps one day they will be ripping out your heart."

The trees seemed to draw closer as the man spoke, as if his words had awoken something. Lukas could hear the seriousness in his companion's voice as he spoke. Judging by the Salvaari's dark expression, now was not the time to press for answers.

"I know that we cannot change the past, the blood spilt between my kin and yours" – and the prince looked at his companion with a new-found respect – "but if we succeed … if we defeat Henghis, perhaps we can usher in a time of friendship between our people."

Cailean's expression gave away nothing as he watched the younger man thoughtfully. "There are many among my kind, many from every tribe, who hate the west for the crimes committed against us in the last hundred years. You have honour, prince. Maybe you will be able to change how my people view your own."

"There are some who call your kind savages. That you drink the blood of your dead, that you worship battle and relish killing. I see now that that is not the case. You have more honour than they ever will, Salvaari."

Cailean at last slowly dipped his head into a nod. He sheathed his dagger as he took a breath and glanced at the two who had turned from their king to come to the aid of his tribe.

"I do thank you for coming. But two men are unlikely to change the tide."

"Perhaps."

Sakkar felt a drop of blood run down the side of his face as he drew a razor-sharp knife down his scalp. For near fourteen summers, this had been a ritual. He had been shaving his hair ever since he had reached adulthood. Each day as the sun rose, he knelt with the knife in hand and a small bowl of water at his side. Each day he cut the thin growths of hair from his scalp.

"Why do you shave your head?"

The Larissan glanced up from where he knelt to see Cailean watching him curiously. Sakkar ran a cloth over his knife to clean it of his blood.

"To honour a friend no longer of this world."

"Those we love always live on in memory," Cailean said, "and will be seen again when we pass through the Veil."

"It has been many years." The Larissan smiled as he tipped a small bowl of water over his head to wash away the blood. "Yet he awaits my arrival in the Field of Daciana."

"What is this?" the Salvaari asked as his companion rose to his feet.

"The afterlife, friend. The Garden of Amkut, Lord of the Desert."

"Much like the ancestral plain that lies beyond the Veil."

Sakkar merely shrugged as the pair started to walk back towards where they had camped.

"I suppose."

"Tell me of your home."

Sakkar chuckled as he wrapped his headscarf back over his brow. "Far to the west well beyond Torosa is Larissa. Have you ever seen a desert?"

Cailean's blank expression told him all he needed to know. Of course the Salvaari had never seen one.

"Imagine a great sea of sand stretching far beyond the horizon. To the north sits great cities of such wealth and beauty that you could only dream of, while to the south" – the Larissan smiled – "the desert clans roam by day and sing by night. It is here you will find my people, my home. My family."

Cailean came to a halt. The foreigner had kinfolk? "Yet you are in a foreign land without your clan and kin and have been for more than one summer."

"It is ..." – Sakkar paused and met the other man's eyes – "complicated."

"What kind of man abandons his family?" the Salvaari asked incredulously. The very idea bewildered him.

"One with honour," came a voice from further down the stream. Lukas. The prince walked towards them with reins in his hand and horse at his back.

Sakkar nodded. "Honour led me to leave my home and honour led me to stay. Much like you are here in this moment because of your own."

Cailean snorted. "Be that as it may, you know my story. What is yours?"

"Two years ago, I was attached to a trade convoy between my people and the Torosi," the Larissan began, and he crossed his powerful arms. "The first of many, or so we had hoped. We had barely reached the border when we were attacked by the rebels that plague my land. You see, there are those in Larissa who turned from our queen after she made a pact with the empire. They are ignorant, naïve. They rob and steal. They even murder their own people. They decided that us trading with the Torosi was too dangerous to allow. We fought, yet we were outnumbered and outmatched. When the battle seemed dire, and all hope had faded, the Torosi arrived and charged into the ranks of our enemy. And among them rode Prince Lukas."

"My father had sent me to study in the court of Lord Galan," Dorian's son explained when the Salvaari looked to him.

"And in the chaos that followed," Sakkar continued, and his voice was filled with emotion, "he saved my life. From that moment, I have ever been indebted unto him until I can repay this debt. A life for a life. If I return home before the debt is complete, then my honour is forfeit. I would be shunned for bringing dishonour to my clan and I would give up my place in the Field of Daciana. Yet I shall return to Larissa upon a day."

The forest grew quiet as Sakkar spoke his last. Lukas said nothing, for it was not his place to speak. He knew the story and he knew it well. Sakkar was his closest friend aside from his little sister. Lukas trusted him with more than his own life.

"I understand this honour," Cailean said, breaking the silence with his booming voice. "Perhaps you being here is the spirits' will, and perhaps this is your chance to pay your debt and return to your homeland."

"Be it by their will, or the will of my own god," was all the Larissan said.

They rode at dawn. Lukas led the way down hidden goat tracks and narrow paths.

"Are you sure you know where you are leading us, prince?" called out Cailean as his eyes darted from one tree to the next as if expecting danger.

Sakkar grinned from behind the Salvaari warrior as his hand stroked Sabra's soft feathers. "I would not worry, my friend," Sakkar told him. "He has been hunting these woods for near ten summers. He knows them like a sword knows a whetstone."

Lukas ducked under a low-hanging branch and turned in his saddle. "Sakkar has joined me many times. But I am sure that bird of his knows this place better than either of us."

As if on command, Sabra uttered a squawk.

Cailean gave a booming laugh and shook his hairy mane. His eyes were alight with humour. The Larissan had surprised him. Never had he met someone not native to Salvaar who had such a bond with an animal. Many of Cailean's people had a great love for the creatures that called the eastern forest home. It was known that the Sagailean tribe worshipped the Great Wolf, Lycan. It was known that their people hunted with the forest wolves by moonlight.

As the trio rode through the winding corridors of the trees, following a barely visible path, Sakkar raised his arm, and Sabra took flight with a screech. The hawk soared skyward and zipped through the canopy in the treetops and vanished from sight.

"If we stay in the forest and follow the trails for two days, we will come to the river Harren," Lukas told his companions. "From there it is another three to the Mieran border and the plains of Carn-Dair. Five days. And if we bypass the river towns, five days without risk or chance of discovery."

"You speak as if the worst is behind us," Cailean replied, and his tone was suddenly serious. "Yet we are still to reach Miera. Still to navigate the plains and pass through the Rift. I would be a fool to say that anything but good fortune is the sole reason that I did not get caught by Medea when I rode to Palen-Tor. Miera is far more treacherous."

Lukas shrugged and a slight smirk tugged at his lips. "Then perhaps your good fortune will be with us."

"One can only hope."

Sakkar rode up beside Cailean. "I have heard many times that to meet the Mierans on an open battlefield is to beg for death. That many call them the lords of the plain."

"They fight like devils," the Salvaari agreed. "Not once in my life have I heard that the horse masters have been defeated in their own land."

"The reason for that is because they have not been," the prince said as he brushed a small leafy branch to the side with his hand. "At least, as you said, not in their own country. Not in Miera. And not since Zavian took the throne."

Cailean frowned. "Zavian?"

"Zoran may be king, and from what I have heard, a good one at that," Lukas began, "yet Zavian was the first. As the story tells, he was little more than a farmer when the eastern hordes of Idrisir conquered Miera. They went from town to town, burning and killing, and in their wake claimed the lives of Zavian's family. He rebelled and claimed the life of a foreign lord as vengeance. One by one, the Mierans joined him and, like a phoenix from the ashes, cast the Idrisians from their land. Zavian took the firebird as his symbol, and the phoenix banners still fly over Miera to this day."

"How do you know this?" the Salvaari asked after a moment.

"My brother and I were taught history from birth. Every major conflict for the last few hundred years and more. It has all been recorded by scholars and scribes in books and texts," Lukas replied. "The Mierans hate and distrust outsiders like they do because many, many foreign rulers have tried to take their land. In the last half century alone, they have been invaded four times. Outnumbered four times. And victorious four times. Once they were attacked by my father's predecessor, King Aonaran, alongside King Balinor, wanting to test their hand. My father was there. Another time by the City States of Trecento, seeking wealth for their coffers. After that invasion was halted, the Mierans replied in kind and rode deep into the heart of the States. They were only stopped when Elara joined her sister cities and took up arms. Elara's army defeated the horsemen barely a day's ride from their gates. Now the only thing keeping the peace between Miera and Trecento are the Accords."

"Word is that Miera is invaded so because of gold," Sakkar said thoughtfully.

"Miera holds the largest gold deposit this side of the empire," Lukas replied. "Many kings covet the wealth that conquering the plains could bring. Yet to the horsemen, the gold holds no value. They trade amongst themselves and the gold sits under the ground, untapped."

"And the invasions made them strong," Sakkar concluded. "The rumour that one of their soldiers is worth three of any other nation has some truth to it."

The Salvaari snorted. Unlike the others, Cailean viewed such statements as a challenge. "We will see."

Lukas didn't turn around as he replied, his voice wary, "I pray we do not have to."

King Dorian slowly made his way through the palace of Palen-Tor. He had long since sent his guards away. He preferred his own company and longed for what his title granted him so little: peace. He walked out onto a large stone balcony that overlooked the sea. The sun shone down onto the gentle, blue waves as they met the cliffs below. Father Bardhyl had often described this place as serene. After decades of wars and fighting, Dorian had finally grown to know a measure of peace. He liked to come here to contemplate and think. Dorian reached up to take his crown from his head and placed it upon the edge of the wall. He took a breath of air and closed his eyes.

"My lord?"

Dorian bit back a sigh and turned to face the owner of the pleasant voice. He knew the exotic voice even before her face betrayed it. It was that of Lady Eveline. The woman that his daughter-in-law had brought from her homeland as a companion. A woman who, despite her young years, had proven to have the intellect that so few possessed.

"Lady Eveline." The king gave her a smile.

The Medean woman returned it. "Forgive my intrusion."

"No, not at all," he told her as he turned back to gaze out over the ocean below. "Join me, if you wish."

"I find this place strangely peaceful," Lady Eveline said as she joined Dorian on the balcony. "As if it is a dream."

"It is calming, yes," the king replied and for the first time he felt his body relax. "I come here to think … to speak to the gods and relieve my worries."

Eveline glanced at the Annoran lord. "What is it that troubles you, my king?"

He could see a sincere worry in her eyes and not the false sympathy that so many within court were beholden to.

"It is strange," he said after a moment. "I do not know you at all and yet I feel that I can trust you. Why is that?"

"I do not know, lord," she replied. "Perhaps the gods sent me here so that you may unburden your thoughts … or perhaps I have come to steal your crown and pitch it from the balcony."

Dorian met her gaze for a moment and saw the amusement painted across her amber eyes as they sparkled. Her lips twitched, and then they both laughed. It was the first time in days that he felt capable of such an act and, gods, did it feel good.

"The crown is growing heavy," he told her after a moment. "Each day it worsens."

"Tell me," Eveline murmured.

He could see the gulls far below. They were no more than white specks as they soared above the waves.

"There are days where everything is just slipping through my fingers. My errant son is lost to his reckless naïvety. I fear that it will get him killed." He closed his eyes and felt the cool breeze of the wind on his old cheeks. "And then Dayne … You will have heard the rumours about his health."

Eveline nodded sadly. "I've heard."

"Whatever illness he has been cursed with is worsening with each passing year. If nothing can be done …" He trailed off as the dark thoughts took him.

He felt her hand touch his arm and it was as if the darkness fled his body entirely. Dorian gave her a sad smile and glanced at the hand she had placed upon him. She was showing him a compassion that many within his own lands lacked.

"I fear that Annora will crumble and fall back into its old ways. Three kings, three kingdoms. And war. The cycle of blood will begin anew."

"I know in my heart that that will not happen," Eveline said. Her voice was strong, yet it was not loud.

"You are the gods' king, chosen by Durandail and Azaria to save Annora, not let it fall. One by one, you have led the kingdoms into the light, and under your rule, they have flourished. I know this, and more importantly, so do your people. Trust in them … Trust in the gods. They have a reason for allowing all things to happen. We may never understand their wisdom, but we must trust in their will. You will find a way."

Dorian felt hope blossom for the first time since Lukas had slipped away.

"I now understand why Caspin kept you close," he told Eveline with a smile. "It is because you give people hope. I thank you for your counsel, my lady."

SIXTEEN

Fortress of Kilgareth, Valley of Odrysia

The stone stairs rang beneath the iron-shod boots of two knights as they descended deep into the bowels of Kilgareth. Grand Master Amaris took the lead with a torch burning in his hand to light the darkness. With him were Torin and the arc'maija, Lysandra, both holding their own burning brands high.

The lower they got the more the chill of the tunnels seeped through their armour.

"Upon building the fortress" – Lysandra glanced at Torin as she spoke – "Grand Master Cormac ordered the construction of tunnels that run for miles. A network of paths that lead deep into the mountains. Some house the dead, while others lead beyond the valley."

"For evacuation," the Aureian replied.

It made sense. Even the greatest of defences could be toppled.

"Though in near a century, they have not been needed," Amaris added.

"All things change with time," the arc'maija murmured as they reached the bottom of the stairs.

The corridor before them was as dark as a cloudy night and the smell in the air was thick. A series of unlit braziers ran along the walls. Amaris held out his torch and with a whoosh the first brazier roared to life. The corridor slowly came to life as one by one the fires were lit. The orange flames painted the once dark room in rays of light.

For the first time, Torin could see all the runes carved into the stone. *They must be ancient Aureian,* he realised.

Down the corridor there were four large stone blocks, and each was covered by a lid that had been carved into the likeness of a man. Each one was different from the last, but all held steel swords in their stone hands.

"Welcome to the crypt of my forebears," murmured Amaris as his left hand clutched the amulet at his throat. "Where the grand masters of the north come to rest."

Torin followed suit and gently grasped his own necklace. He closed his eyes and dipped his head out of respect. All those who lay here were the embodiment of their faith. Slowly, the three made their way around the tomb until they reached the final coffin.

"Here lays Duran Cormac, Father of the North." Lysandra bowed. "May the Twins always watch over him."

Torin ran his eyes over the stone likeness of the man who had won the north. The man who had become immortalised by the Order of Kil'kara. His face was lined, and his brow furrowed as if deep in thought. The sword atop the coffin was simple steel. It was unembellished save for a small crescent moon and sun drawn on the pommel.

"The journey will begin where the Sword of the North ends," whispered Torin as his eyes searched the lid of the coffin for any kind of clue.

"There has to be some kind of sign," said Amaris as he gazed at the tomb of his great-grandfather. "There has to be."

"The caskets are sealed upon use. So, whatever this mystery is, it must be found here," the arc'maija told them as she ran a hand along the carved stone. "The Sword of the North … This man was the Sword of the North."

"Yet the only thing here is his stone likeness." Amaris glanced at the runes that were carved about the chamber. "Even the runes hold no clue."

"What do they say?"

Torin was curious. Few could speak ancient Aureian now. The Order's grand masters and maija were some of the only who knew the language.

"An old battle prayer in ancient Aureian," Amaris replied. "Areut talc cuun'ect … which, as you are aware, in the common tongue reads, 'Blood or immortality'."

Torin knew those words and he knew them well. No more than a saying uttered before a fight. For those among the order, those serving the Twins, death was a gateway into the realm of the gods and the never-ending life that lay within. The saying was of little use to them now. They had no more to go on than a stone carving and a sword atop it. Torin's eyes widened.

"Wait. We have been looking at this the wrong way."

Lysandra pursed her lips as the two northerners turned to the Aureian. "Explain," she said.

"Perhaps Duran was the Sword of the North. Yet what if the phrase has a double meaning? The journey will begin where the Sword of the North ends."

The woman's eyes lit up like an inferno and swept towards the sheathed steel. "Duran's blade," she breathed.

Without hesitating, Amaris dropped his torch and took hold of the sword held in the hands of his stone ancestor. The grand master gave the blade a firm tug and it slid free. The sound of steel grating on stone echoed through the chamber.

"Where the Sword of the North ends …" he muttered under his breath.

He turned the sword over. One of his gloved hands held the steel blade, and the other held the pommel of its hilt.

"Where the sword ends …" Amaris twisted the pommel.

Torin watched on and his eyes widened in disbelief as the

pommel unscrewed before his eyes. They were never that loose. Never.

With a pop, the circular pommel was pulled off and the edge of a roll of parchment was revealed. It had been hidden within the pommel itself.

Amaris slid the parchment free before he passed the steel pommel to Lysandra. It was small, no longer than a finger, and bound tightly with a small ribbon. Torin took Duran's sword from the grand master as his mind was filled with questions. Whatever it said held great importance to Evalio Delrovira. Amaris unravelled the ribbon and opened the small scroll. His eyes swivelled as he read the words on the page.

"What does it say?" called the arc'maija as she stepped closer to her companion.

Torin felt a cold stab of dread hit his heart as he saw the hopeless look cross the Medean's dark eyes.

"Following the light of the sun, where the young were raised by frail, carved stone draws breath beyond the Maiden's Veil."

The Aureian nearly swore. Another damned riddle.

The chamber was dark and dimly lit. Only a few small braziers gave it light. A banner carrying the sun and crescent moon of the Twin Gods hung before him, white on ocean blue silk.

"Kyler Landrey, son of Medea, are you prepared to pledge your sword, your blood and your life to uphold the principles of our Order?"

Kyler could feel the words Sir Matias spoke reaching into his heart. He could feel a shiver run down his spine as the man's voice echoed around the chamber. Four knights stood watch as Kyler took his vows. To one side stood a pure marble statue of warrior-god Durandail. To the other side stood a similar statue of Azaria.

This is what he had worked towards ever since he had been a boy. Ever since he had seen the silver armour of the Knights of Kil'kara shining in the sun.

"I am," he replied. He had never been so certain.

"Will you stand against all those who seek to bring harm to our faith and all people within it?"

"I will." Kyler turned his eyes to the statues of his gods. "I swear the sacred oath that I shall render unconditional obedience to the gods. I will set aside the deeds of darkness and put on the armour of light. I shall honour the man and honour my faith. I shall give all glory to the gods, and whenever they deem it, as a loyal servant, I will surrender my life for this oath."

"The name Kil'kara comes from the ancient language of Aureia. It means 'I am worthy'. Will you honour the Twins and serve within their holy order?"

"In the name of Durandail, Father of all Fathers, I shall fight to honour his kingdom. In the name of Azaria, Lady of Silver, I shall safeguard all those who seek protection under her moon. And in the name of Twins, I shall serve."

From the shadows behind Matias, a new figure materialised, a woman whom Kyler did not recognise. She was clad in the robes of a maija, yet instead of brown and grey, she wore violet. *She must be the arc'maija*, he realised, the head of her sect. A deep hood covered her face, while in her hands she held a silver cup that was covered in small jewels.

She held out the cup as she spoke, and her words were as sweet as honey.

"Then drink."

Kyler nodded and took the cup from the woman. He felt her warm fingers as their hands brushed lightly. The arc'maija stepped back to Matias' side as Kyler raised the chalice to his lips.

Here goes nothing, he thought as he sent a final prayer to his gods. Kyler tipped the cup back and poured its contents into his mouth.

He bit back a cough as the bitter taste ran down the back of his throat.

"Kneel," commanded Sir Matias as Kyler swallowed the brew.

It was the last thing the boy heard. His knees hit the stone floor, and then it all went dark.

The world turned into shadows mixed with blurs as Kyler opened his eyes. Around him lay the streets and fields of Adrestia. The roads were lined with people as if an important event was about to take place.

What? How had he gotten here?

"Kyler," called out a voice. "Where are you, boy?"

He turned to see his father walking down the road towards him. Something about Theodore seemed different. He carried himself differently. There were no streaks of grey in his hair. He was younger.

Kyler made to speak, but before he could form words, another voice cut in.

"Over here, Father."

Kyler turned towards the voice. Surprise ran through his veins. There in the crowd stood his younger self. He was no more than ten.

What in the name of the gods is going on?

"Ah." Theodore grinned as he made his way through the crowd towards young Kyler. He pushed past people as he walked and closed in on his son. Yet it was clear that Theodore could not see his adult son.

"Father," Kyler began as his father reached him.

His father did not falter and walked right through him. "What?"

As Theodore reached young Kyler, realisation dawned on old Kyler. This was merely an illusion. A phantasm of his mind. His memories.

"What have I told you about running off," Theodore told the boy with a chuckle.

"Sorry, Father."

The thundering hooves reached his ears.

"They're coming," one of the townspeople cried.

I know this, *Kyler remembered. He knew what was going to happen next even as the sound of clinking armour hit him. The crowd cheered. The first rider appeared. He was clad in silver armour and an ocean-blue surcoat. The same blue cloak cascaded down his shoulders and over the back of his pure white stallion. The plume of his helm trailed behind him, and he bore the sun of Durandail emblazoned upon his shield and coat. More riders came into sight. One ... two ... three. Twenty in total. With them rode a pair of maija. Their hoods were pulled up over their ears, making them all but invisible amongst the knights. As Kyler remembered, the company had been sent to sort out a grievance with the headman of Adrestia. Sort it out was exactly what they had done.*

The cheers of the crowd seemed to fade as young Kyler turned to his father, his eyes glowing as he spoke. Five words that he would remember until the end of his days.

"Someday, I'll be a knight."

The scene changed in a wave of shadows, and suddenly Kyler was standing in the Sleeping Siren. The tavern was filled to bursting with patrons, and the roar of laughter slowly faded as Kyler watched the play unfold. He saw his father behind the bar serving drinks, while his now sixteen-year-old self moved around the inn collecting abandoned cups and plates.

"Oi, girl," *a voice called out.*

Kyler turned towards the seated man and saw him gesture to one of the waitresses. The man had a big nose and squinty eyes, while his jowls hung low. The girl made her way over to the man and her lips formed a smile.

Brave girl.

Elena her name was. She was a few years older than Kyler. Her eyes shone and sparkled in the candlelight and her dark hair cascaded down her shoulders. The smile upon her lips was one that brought light even to the darkest of rooms, and yet it was nothing compared to her laugh, a sound that only gave Kyler feelings of pure joy. Gods, she was as beautiful as the day they had met.

"What is it?" she asked pleasantly.

The man grinned at her in the way that half-drunken fools did. "So, you come with the room, I take it."

Both young Kyler and old Kyler watched as Elena snorted in good humour. "I'm afraid not, sir."

She turned to leave, but the man quickly reached out his hand and imprisoned her wrist in a vice-like grip.

"Now, that isn't very nice. My friends and I would like some entertainment, so to speak."

"Please, sir, let me go," she stammered, and her eyes searched around the room for help.

"Oh, I don't think so, poppet." Crack!

Elena's slap caught the big-nosed man across the cheek with a meaty smack.

"Let me go," she growled as she glared fiercely at the man.

The man snarled, and his fingers dug deeper into her wrist. "You are going to pay for that."

A hand appeared on the man's shoulder and clamped down hard. "The lady asked you to let her go," commanded young Kyler.

"And if I don't?"

"Then I am going to have to ask you to leave," Kyler replied.

The man roared with laughter and rose to his feet. He glared down at the boy of sixteen summers like he was nothing.

The room fell quiet.

The man released Elena who backed up behind Kyler, but her eyes never left her attacker.

"Alright." The man grinned, and he glanced back at his companions. "I will teach this boy a lesson first."

Kyler's right fist hammered into the man's face as he turned back. Cartilage smashed and blood wet the air. The man staggered back against the table cradling his broken nose. The blow had been hard, far harder than he had anticipated.

Kyler stepped forward. His left hand drove up into a vicious uppercut. It connected.

It connected hard.

The man was propelled into the air, and he crashed down onto the table. The man lay motionless, and his eyes were still. Unconscious.

"Thank you," murmured Elena gratefully.

Kyler turned to the fallen man's companions. His hands were still curled into fists.

"Does anyone else have a problem?" Silence greeted his ears. "Now, get your friend out of this establishment. And the rest of you" – he turned to the others within the inn – "keep your hands to yourselves."

Again, everything changed and now Kyler was standing in the inn's stables. It might have been half a year after the tavern incident.

"We're leaving," Elena told young Kyler as her eyes threatened tears. "My father ... he fears that Adrestia is no longer safe."

"Where will you go?"

"I do not know, he won't tell me," she replied. "Maybe south."

"Stay, please," young Kyler insisted, and he took her hands with his own.

"Kyler, I can't. My father's leg ... and my mother, she cannot

leave the house. I cannot leave them. Not yet at least. Not until I know they will be safe."

Her father, Kyler remembered, had been crippled when a thief had tried to break into their home. He had been stabbed badly in the leg and it had never fully healed. No one really knew what afflicted Elena's mother. Yet she spent all her days in doors and out of sight.

"I will miss you if you go," was all Kyler said.

"And I will miss you ... trust me," she told him, and her hands squeezed his. "Please don't make this harder than it already is."

The boy nodded. "I understand. You have to go."

"Thank you," she replied. A tear streaked down her cheek as she said the words.

Kyler reached up to run a hand along her cheek. Her skin was cool to his touch, and he brushed her tear away.

Elena felt her lips tremble as she felt his touch.

"I have something for you," Kyler told her as he pulled a pouch from his belt. "Open it."

The girl took the small bag and pried it open. She pulled out a beautiful necklace of silver. A small crystal as white as winter snow sat within a cocoon of knotted silver. The jewel glistened in the light as the sun kissed it.

"You cannot give me this," Elena murmured.

"Here," Kyler said as he took the necklace. He unclasped the silver cord and stood behind her. "With this, I will always be by your side," Kyler told her as he brushed her hair aside. He tied the necklace around her neck and let the crystal fall to her throat.

"We will always be together," Elena said quietly as she turned to face him. She stared at the jewel with sad eyes as she caressed its surface. Elena closed her dark eyes and stood on her toe to kiss him lightly on the lips. He kissed her back. She shivered and then stepped back.

"Goodbye, Kyler."

"Goodbye, Elena," he replied, and he felt the joy of her name on his lips for the last time.

As she turned to leave, the world vanished behind a veil of shadows.

Kyler awoke, and his eyes opened to the dimly lit initiation chamber. He took a deep breath. The memories still filled his mind. He could still hear the words.

Someday, I'll be a knight.

He could still feel his fist connecting with the drunken man's nose, and he could still taste Elena's lips upon his own.

"Through the Chalice of Azaria, the Lady of Wisdom grants us visions of great importance. It reveals truths or principles that guide who were, are and who we shall become. Everything you saw will mean something, whether you know it in this moment or not." Matias' voice once more filled the chamber. "I trust that your truths shall help you succeed in the coming days."

Kyler nodded as his eyes gazed at the cup that sat before his knees on the cold stone floor.

Three truths.

The first memory was why he was here. The second showed that he was a fighter.

As for the third … Kyler wasn't fully sure. He supposed it may have been that he had let the only person he had truly loved go. All so that she could look after her family rather than be with him.

Maybe one day he would understand.

Maybe one day.

"Arise." The arc'maija's voice broke the silence.

Kyler obeyed the woman's command and Matias stepped towards the boy.

"Today, you leave your past life behind. From today, you lay your life in the hands of the Twins," the warden told him.

"I understand," Kyler replied, and he could barely keep the excitement from his voice.

"Then we welcome you into our fold, brother. You are now a novice within the Order of Kil'kara."

The next morning, Kyler was awoken early and directed to an open yard. There were near thirty of them, novices to a man. Each and every one of them was freshly initiated into the Order. Each and all had begun the long journey to knighthood. Kyler glanced around the courtyard as they waited. His eyes flickered from one man to the next. They had come to Kilgareth rich or they had come to it poor. Some were high born and some low born. Some had trained with weapons under their noble masters-at-arms. Others had never held so much as a spear in their lives. All had come seeking something greater than what they were.

The courtyard they stood in was a large training square. Its ground was no more than a layer of soil, and it was ringed by four large stone walls.

Some of the recruits talked in hushed whispers as they waited under the stern gaze of six heavily armed knights. Kyler did not know what they were waiting for. All that had been said was that they were to wait in the training yard until further instruction.

He heard iron-shod boots clanging on stone before he saw the two knights that arrived atop the dais before them. Neither of them wore their helmets, and nor did they carry their huge heater shields. The first of the pair was a grizzled veteran, and his hair had begun to grey at the tips. His eyes were fierce, and his lips curled into a mirthless smirk. He looked at the men before him as though they were beneath him. His hands were wrapped around a gnarled cane.

Sir Alarik, Kyler realised with a slight smile. The same man who had shown Kyler to his quarters. Without his helm on, Kyler could see the pair of intersecting scars that ran across the side of his face.

"FORM UP!" bellowed the grizzled knight. His parade-ground voice was bold and commanding.

Slowly, the recruits started to move into a sort of formation, while their eyes remained glued to the two men to their fore. It was easy enough for some of the novices as they had served in armies or, like Kyler, spent a lot of time around soldiers. For others, it was not so easy.

The knight glared down at the recruits and his eyes blazed. "You call that a formation?" he roared as he rapped his cane sharply on the stone dais. "By the gods, it's a disgrace! If Durandail could see you rabble, he would turn his back in shame."

Kyler nearly winced as one of the men near him mumbled something under his breath.

The fool.

Kyler could have sworn he saw Alarik's ears twitch at the sound. He had to have heard.

"Did I say that you could speak?" the knight bellowed, and he strode down the steps towards the recruit who had spoken.

From the look of his clothes the recruit was of noble birth. The knight stood inches away from the recruit and his breath was hot upon the man's face as he shouted.

"Some of you may have come from privilege and the nobility with servants at your beck and call. But here, you are nothing. Not yet at least. And this" – he swept an arm around, indicating the yard – "this is my arena. Here, my word is law. You speak only when spoken to." Alarik glared from recruit to recruit. "Did you not hear me?"

"Yes, sir!" called the novices.

"You do not move unless I command it."

"Yes, sir!"

The knight strode up and down the line of men, and his eyes swept from one face to the next.

"Break rank or disobey command and you will be punished. Is

that clear?"

"Yes, sir!"

"Good," he growled as he took a step back and glared at the recruits ominously. "My name is Sir Alarik Sindra. I have the pleasure of being battlemaster here in Kilgareth. And do you know what that means? It is my job to whip you lot into shape. To turn a trembling hand into a fist. To turn you into the fiercest warriors the world has ever seen."

He nodded over his shoulder towards his men. They stood side by side, and their eyes gazed intensely ahead. Their armour was shining and their poise proud. They looked deadly.

"There is no barbarian nor pagan who does not live in mortal fear of us. No army that does not tremble before us. I will train you, and by the gods, I will hurt you. But know this … survive and you shall reach knighthood. Survive and you shall earn my respect."

Kyler noticed that Alarik had put more emphasis on gaining his respect, though he did not think it was out of any kind of arrogance.

"Now, I answer only to Grand Master Amaris himself. You answer to me and me alone. Understand?"

"Yes, sir!"

"LOUDER," he bellowed, and he smacked his cane into the palm of his hand.

"YES, SIR!"

Alarik ran his eyes over the men before him.

"Report to Brother Lorencio in the eastern storehouse and gather your equipment. Return here within the hour. After that." He gave a dry chuckle. "After that, you're all mine."

The storehouse smelt musky and only a little light wafted in through the windows. The wooden floor echoed with the thudding of the hard leather boots that Lorencio had issued them. The brown britches that Kyler now wore felt more like a hessian sack than leggings and were equally as itchy. Over that, he pulled a thick, padded, blue gambeson. It was a layered jacket of linen and cloth that could stop all but the sharpest of blades. He buckled on his belt and rolled his shoulders. The unfamiliar weight of the gambeson was lighter than expected.

A rack of sheathed swords ran along one of the walls, while opposite hung dozens of large grey heater shields. It looked as though the shields were the same size as those used by the knights themselves.

The floorboards rang.

All eyes turned as steel hit the ground. A recruit gazed at the sword he had dropped incredulously.

"That," he said with a grimace, "is heavier than any blade I have held before. And what use is a sword without an edge?"

Lorencio approached the novice with a snort. There was a vicious glare upon his face.

"Drop that again and you will be on half rations for a month." He turned so that he was addressing all the recruits, and his voice was gruff. "Now, as this fool has discovered, the blades and shields are weighted to be double that of the real thing. Weighted to make you stronger. The swords are also without edge. Can't have mere recruits flapping around with real weapons absent direction or training. These are sparring swords, and until you prove yourself as worthy of knighthood, these are all you shall wield."

Kyler felt his heart sink as he pulled one of the swords from the rack. He could feel the muscles of his arm strain under the weight of the blade weighted with lead. He sighed. These next few months were going to be hard.

SEVENTEEN

Isle of Agartha, the Valkir Isles

Astrid awoke with a snarl. Her breathing was ragged. Her fingers trembled. The shieldmaiden glanced at her hand and for the first time noticed the dagger she held tightly. Her knuckles were white. A bead of sweat rolled down from her brow.

Everything was quiet.

Astrid shook her head and slid the blade back into its sheath. She sat up and pushed herself up from her bed. The wooden floor was cold on her bare feet, and her warm breath created a wall of mist in the chill air. She pulled on her boots as she sat on the edge her bed and closed her eyes. A shiver ran down her spine and a strange feeling entered her mind. Agartha was never this quiet. Astrid clasped the raven's head at her throat. Something was wrong. She could feel it.

Astrid froze. It was akin to instinct. Her father had told her about it many years ago. How some people were born with a sense that warned of impending danger. Some called it intuition. Her father thought it something else. Something more.

She felt it now. She felt the walls of the hall closing in around her.

Everything was quiet. Not a sound came from the streets. Nothing broke through the veil of night.

A slight clink of metal and the sound of boots squelching mud suddenly cut through the silence. However, no voices accompanied the sounds. Without hesitation, Astrid strode across her room and took up her jerkin. She tightened the straps and belted on the axe Erik had given her.

The squelching of boots continued.

"Warriors," Astrid murmured, and her heart began to race.

A bellow cut through the night. It was a cry that sent a shiver down her spine.

"WAKE!"

The shout came from beyond her doors. The song of clashing weapons erupted as Astrid strode into her hall. She gripped the cold steel of her axe tightly in her hand. The fighting was in the street outside the walls of her home. Flames erupted at the ends of torches and illuminated the hall. Screams filled the air outside as men fell to the clash of steel. Astrid looked around. Most of her crew stood at the ready within the hall with their families. There were many she did not see.

The doors boomed open and Torben staggered in with a grunt. His face was covered in blood and a red gash was visible through his ripped sleeve. Two of the Valkir slammed shut the doors behind the man as he gasped for breath.

"Torben," she called to him. "What in Skûra is going on?"

"They came out of nowhere," he said through gritted teeth. "Bearing the colours of Earl Magnus."

"Only a coward kills his own people," Astrid spat.

She could see the fire in Torben's eyes. It burned in the eyes of all who stood with her. Her breath caught as she looked around. She could not see the face of the one most important to her. Nor could she hear his booming voice.

"Where is my brother?"

"I have not seen him," Torben said after a moment.

"Nor me," added Raol as he sauntered over. "Not since the celebrations last night."

The jarl buried any emotion that she felt, for it would not help them to survive. "He will be fine," she muttered.

The doors to the hall boomed as a heavy weight smashed into them.

"Astrid, we cannot hold them for long. What are your orders?" called out Raol as he drew his sword.

The earl had caught them unawares and unprepared, but they still had a chance.

"Hélla." Astrid gestured to the blonde-haired shieldmaiden.

They were surrounded on all fronts. The jarl knew there was but one way out of this alive, but only if the earl had not discovered it.

"See if the grain store passage is secure," Astrid commanded. "Lead the families to safety. We will buy you as much time as we are able. I pray that they do not discover the tunnels."

"It will be done." Hélla nodded and turned towards the congregation of non-combatants.

Raol glanced at Astrid briefly before he followed Hélla towards the families. He wanted to say goodbye to his betrothed. It may be the last time he did.

The warrior reached Mayrun and planted a kiss upon her lips. He leant down and met her eyes.

"No matter what happens, I will find you," he told her.

"Everyone with me," Hélla called out behind Astrid, and she gestured towards the back of the hall. "We make for the grain store. There is a way out."

There was fear in their eyes as they moved away from the crew. Many of them would never have wielded a blade in their lives. Some had known many summers, while others had not yet reached adulthood. Some may die, but Astrid would give her own life to make certain that many would go on to see the next dawn.

Astrid gathered up a shield and then turned to the rest of the crew as they assembled before her. Their faces were lit with anger. Torben and Raol stood at her side. They were ready for whatever came through those doors.

"We hold this hall," she growled, "no matter the cost. They bring fire and death to our home and for that we will show no mercy." Astrid raised her axe above her head. "No mercy."

A great roar filled the hall as the chant was taken up by all.

"No mercy."

Weapons met shields in a thunderous crash.

"No mercy."

The floor shuddered under heavy boots.

"No mercy."

The doors shook as a hand-held ram smashed into them and sent a cascade of dust through the room.

"FORM!" bellowed Astrid.

The Valkir hastily moved to the entrance and stood side by side, three ranks deep. Fifteen-strong held their shields at the ready and prepared to form an impenetrable wall. Behind them stood more of the crew waiting to fill gaps. At the rear, the brothers Laerke and Nenrir stood atop a table with their powerful bows aimed at the door.

Astrid stood a few ranks from the front and her eyes gazed at the great doors of her father's hall. Her hall.

Crash.

The doors shook, and the bracing plank splintered. One more thrust and the earl's men would be upon them.

"SHIELDS!"

The Valkir roared and locked their massive round shields together. Their swords and axes rested atop the steel rims.

"Paint the hall with their blood!" growled Torben from the first rank.

With a crash, the doors caved in from the weight of the ram behind it. The attackers cheered and the screech of a horn filled the night.

"And send them to the afterlife!" Torben's lips twisted into a vicious snarl.

The earl's men charged.

Shields came together with a crash as the two sides met. Torben's body moved unconsciously as a warrior swung a sword his way. His shield took the blow and sent it to the side. His axe flashed and struck the attacker across the chest. Blood sprayed and the warrior fell. He was dead before he hit the ground.

From behind, Astrid watched as the battle for the door unfolded. The initial rush of attackers had been finished off as quickly as they arrived. They had sprinted to the fight without formation.

Fools.

Now they came locked in a shield wall. A bow from one of her men thrummed and an attacker crashed to the ground. The bladed tip of an arrow had ripped through his throat. The two walls of steel-rimmed wood came together in a great crash. Both sides heaved against the other. Astrid could see the savage gleam in their attackers' eyes and feel their breath on her face as they pushed. The shieldmaiden's arm was firmly planted in the back of the warrior before her. She could feel the tide turning as her boots started to slide on the wooden floor, and inch by inch, they were pushed back. One of her men cried out as a sword drove into his chest. He sank to the ground, and his weapon fell from his nerveless fingers.

Raol roared and lashed out. His own blade darted over the shoulder of the man in front and sliced into the neck of his friend's killer. He wrenched his sword free as another of the earl's men took the place of the dead man at Raol's feet.

Astrid was barely twelve feet from the fore of the fight. She could feel sweat, the iron taste of blood and the hot breath of friend and foe upon her face. Her muscles tensed as she pressed hard with her arm as she gripped the worn leather of her axe's hilt tight in her hand.

A warrior fell. And another.

Shields splintered as the battle raged, yet still they held the earl and his men at bay. The hall was slick with the blood of the dead and dying. A man screamed as Torben cut him down. A second of the earl's men sensed an opening and charged at the old warrior.

There was no such thing as an opening against a bloodsworn. Torben blocked the axe with his own and slammed the edge of his shield into the man's stomach. The warrior staggered back. Torben's axe smashed the man's shield to the side, and then with a flick of the wrist, he sent the steel head into his opponent's chest.

A vicious cry went up and Astrid felt her sweat chill. Her breath created a mist in the cold air as shiver ran down her spine.

A warrior pushed his way through the earl's men as they chanted. He clutched a sword in one hand and an axe in the other. He wore a roughly hewn leather and steel lamellar chest plate. The tattoos that spiralled down his arms spoke volumes. It was a tattoo much like that etched upon Torben's flesh. He was bloodsworn.

Sindric Einar. Another of Magnus' dogs.

The first of Astrid's warriors snarled and lashed out. His sword flashed towards the newcomer.

It was over in a heartbeat. Sindric's weapons moved as a blur. A flurry of strikes carved through his opponent's defence and sent him to the ground in a crimson tide.

Sindric pointed his sword at Torben. His eyes were murderous. There was no greater glory than defeating a famed warrior.

"Don't do it," Astrid muttered to herself. She prayed. She knew of Sindric's reputation. They all did. "Don't do it …"

Time slowed as Torben stepped towards the warrior with his shield and axe held at the ready. No one spoke and a circle was formed in silence. Enemy stood beside enemy, their fight forgotten, for two great warriors, two bloodsworn, were about to test their strength.

Astrid pushed her way to the edge of the circle as the pair locked eyes and began to move. Their boots gently brushed the wooden floor. Sindric moved and Torben replied. Steel met steel in a crash.

It was the only sound. Everything stood still. Torben's shield thudded as axe met wood. He struck out, and his own weapon cut through the cool air where it met Sindric's sword. Torben's eyes never wavered from his opponent's, for eyes could show an attack coming before it was made. His breathing was slow and measured. He moved, and his axe sliced towards Sindric's exposed leg. Sindric anticipated the blow and caught it with his sword as he stepped back. Torben lunged forwards and punched the edge of his shield towards the man. Sindric hastily caught the attack with his weapon, but the shield smashed through and slammed into his chest. Sindric stepped back with the blow. He barely seemed to be rocked by it. He acted as the flurry of blows rained down, and his weapons moved with lightning speed. His sword slipped through Torben's defence and drew a line of blood across his cheek. Another blow chipped Torben's armour and then he was on the back foot.

Astrid gritted her teeth as her friend gave ground inch by inch and blow after blow.

Sindric lunged, his sword hungry for the blood of his enemy. Torben moved as Sindric's blow slipped through his defence and under his shield. Then Torben slammed his shield into his own side and pinned the sword as he spun back. He wrenched on the blade as his momentum carried him away. Sindric's face contorted in surprise as his blade was torn from his grasp. Sindric started to move. Too late. Torben's spin drove momentum into his shield as it smashed into his opponent's head with a dull crack.

Sindric stumbled as he blocked Torben's axe in a daze. Without pause, the old warrior drove the shaft of his weapon into Sindric's face. The blow rocked. Sindric fought for consciousness as another strike tore the weapon from his hand. Blood entered Sindric's vision and his feet gave way. His knees met the wooden floor with a crack. Torben raised his blade. His opponent looked up into his eyes. He was fearless to the last. Bloodsworn to the last. With a savage cry, Torben buried steel in his enemy.

Cheers filled the hall and broke the silence as the defeated warrior toppled over. He hit the floor as a pool of blood washed across the floorboards.

Astrid let out breath she didn't know she had been holding.

"Jarl," a voice muttered to her side.

Astrid didn't so much as turn. The voice belonged to Hélla. The shieldmaiden slowly made her way to the jarl. Her expression betrayed nothing. The two sides eyed each other, and hands went to weapons. Hélla leaned in, and her lips nearly brushed Astrid's ear as she spoke.

"The way is open."

Astrid slowly started to back away from the enemy, and her axe slowly rose. Hélla slipped into the same stance as the rest of the crew hastily formed a shield wall. Their feet slid back across the floorboards as one.

"Back," she ordered as she watched the earl's men starting to move. "BACK!"

Astrid stood over a hole in the floor of the grain store. An unlit tunnel beneath led to within fifty feet of the harbour. Hélla dropped down into the darkness. Torben shot Astrid a glance. "You next," he said.

The jarl shook her head. "I am going back for them."

She turned to leave but the old warrior planted a hand on her shoulder.

"No. I will get them. You must lead our people to safety."

"I cannot."

"You are our leader, our jarl."

"Torben, we do not have time for this!" Astrid cried as she shoved her friend's hand aside.

She met his eyes, and her glare was fierce as she began to draw her axe.

He returned the glare. "Lead us out of here. Go!"

Astrid moved to step around Torben. He stepped in front of her and gave a slight shake of his head. "Go!" he shouted.

The jarl snarled and jammed her axe back into her belt. Rage flashed across her eyes and without word she turned and dropped into the hole.

Blade splintered shield as Raol led the Wind Rider's rearguard. Four others stood at his side. They were a wall of steel, leather and hard muscle. Behind them stood an open doorway and a small corridor that led to the grain store.

The earl's men surged forwards and drove the defenders back towards the doors. One of Raol's companions fell to a sword that drove under his shield and between his ribs. Four became three. Raol bellowed and heaved against his shield. He pushed the man before him back a pace and lashed out at the one who had killed his comrade. Sword bit into flesh and the warrior vanished under the feet of those behind him. They were but two paces from the doors now and closing, step by step. He could feel the weariness entering his muscles. Each move became harder than the last.

"RAOL!" Torben yelled from behind as he ran towards the fight. "Fall back!"

The warrior brought another of Magnus' men down. Two more filled the fallen man's place.

Raol flicked his gaze to his companions and then back to the horde before him. Reality hit him. If one of them fell, it was over. If one of them left the shield wall, it was over. They would die. Their crew, their brothers, their sisters and their families would all perish. Mayrun.

"We cannot!" he shouted over his shoulder, and he slammed his shield forward.

Torben felt a chill run down his spine as he watched the fight. Raol was right. The earl's warriors were locked together with the defenders. Their faces were inches apart as they pushed against each other with their shields. If even one of the rearguard retreated, the attackers would overwhelm their defences in moments. Astrid and the crew would be found easily.

"We will not abandon you, scâldir," growled one of Raol's men through bared teeth.

"Leave us!" roared Raol as he dug his feet in and heaved. "Do not let this be for nothing!"

The warrior grunted and gritted his teeth as he pushed. He could feel his boots sliding back another step.

"Torben, shut the doors. NOW!"

The old warrior let out a deep breath. He would give his life for Raol's without hesitation, but now the choice had been removed from his hands.

All he could do was obey his friend's final command.

"Mayrun," Raol murmured, his voice little more than a whisper. "Goodbye, my love."

The doors closed at his back.

The tunnel was dark. Any lights would give away their presence. It was narrow and barely wide enough for the twenty survivors to move in single file. The earth beneath them was damp, and each step threatened to topple them. All were on full alert. Their weapons were ready for any sign of a flickering torch or the echo of footsteps.

Astrid walked at the rear of the column, and she constantly turned to check for followers. Moments before, she had heard the sound of the wooden entrance being pulled closed. Torben and the others would be close behind. A flash of light came from ahead as she rounded a bend and saw one of her crew hoisted up through the exit and into the storehouse above.

Astrid waited as the man before her was pulled up, and then she raised her right arm through the hole. Someone on the other side gripped her wrist and pulled. They lifted her from the darkness. She nodded her thanks to the man. Who knew what lay outside the storehouse doors? She made her way through her crew towards their exit where Hélla stood. Hélla peered through a small gap in the wooden beams and into the darkness beyond. She raised a finger to her lips as the jarl approached and Astrid stopped.

The crunch of footsteps came from outside the walls.

Two men. Astrid let out her breath. A patrol. Nothing more. They waited and the footfalls faded into nothing.

A dull thud from behind.

All whipped around with their weapons brought to bear. Astrid's axe was half drawn when she saw the hand on the lip of the hole. With a grunt, Torben pulled himself out of the blackness. Hs face was ashen.

"Seal the tunnel," was all he said.

Astrid's heart skipped a beat. She looked over at Mayrun as Torben spoke. Her blood chilled as Mayrun's face turned to the coldest shade of ice.

A tear streaked down her cheek, and her voice shook. "Where is Raol?"

Everything blurred together as Torben led the way to the harbour. They jogged through winding streets and passed the empty market. The air was cold and still. Astrid could barely think as they moved. They followed the old warrior blindly as they ran. Her only concern was the dark-haired woman at her side. Tears ran freely down Mayrun's icy cheeks, yet she would not give in to grief. Raol had been her world, yet she held back her emotion as much as she could. To fall apart now would lead to their destruction.

Astrid felt the loss keenly, for the warrior had been as a brother. She sent a vow to the Sea-Father that she would watch over Mayrun until the day she died.

Wood creaked under their boots as they reached the dock. The Wind Rider came into sight. The sea churned beneath the thin walkways. It crashed into shore and broke across beams of solid oak. Four warriors stood before the ship. They watched with horror as the crew materialised before them. They closed the distance.

"ESCAPE!" shouted one of the guards.

The nerves in his voice betrayed his fear. With their cover now lost, the crew roared as they surged towards the four guards. The planks beneath them thundered under their heavy boots.

Three of the four guards fell quickly as Laerke led the charge. He swatted one to the side as if he were no more than a fly. Two crashed underfoot as the crew fell upon them in a tide of steel. Torben engaged the last. His rage gave strength to his blows. The bloodsworn slammed his axe into the warrior's shield before looping it around and slicing it into the guard's legs. He fell with a shout, and Torben finished him with a quick blow to the neck.

Without stopping, the crew started to pile onto their ship. The families went first as the warriors formed together to protect against any attack. They needed to get under way, or they would die here.

Astrid glanced around the bay. They were alone. Yet she felt cornered. Even if they were upon the waves in minutes, the earl would pursue. Then an idea hit her.

The ships.

"Torben, get the Wind Rider ready," she commanded as her eyes locked on the earl's vessels. "And get the families aboard first."

"Yes, jarl."

"What of the ships?" Laerke called, and he gestured to the vessels that lay moored all around. "Some will catch us, and we will have to fight."

"Many have just returned from the summer raids." Astrid looked to the warrior. "They will be full of food, supplies, weapons ... oil." She could feel the sparkle in her eyes as she spoke. "Laerke,

Fargrim, Hélla." Astrid gestured to them. "Bring casks from the hold. Nenrir ... prepare a torch. We are going to set the ships ablaze."

Astrid jogged down the pier with her axe hanging at her side. The oil, which the Valkir harvested from flaxseed, was used to help waterproof tents in the depths of winter. It helped keep the rain at bay, but by the gods, it burned fast and hot.

The shieldmaiden and her companions spread along the docks, and their eyes watched the streets. A warning cry would be heard half a mile away and there was no doubt they would have company soon enough.

Astrid clambered up the side of a ship and made her way down to the hold. Crates of salted beef, tents and large barrels of flaxseed oil lay before her. Astrid dropped into a crouch before one of the smaller barrels. She drew her knife and with a grunt shoved it into the small barrel of oil. The steel smashed through wood and created an opening. Astrid pulled her blade free, and a small burst of black oil covered her hands.

She quickly splashed the liquid over everything she could see. The grain, linen and the oil barrels were all covered in a dark tide. Astrid made her way back up into the open and poured a line of oil from the hold to the deck. One spark and it would all be over. She tossed the empty barrel to the side and dropped back down onto the pier. One by one, the others joined her and leapt down onto the walkway.

A crash came from the city and a rush of footsteps followed. A pair of warriors appeared from the darkness. They had emerged from the city like wraiths in the night. A howl came from the streets as they were seen. Astrid saw the torchlight first and then the shadows of the horde behind.

"Run!" Astrid shouted.

The pier shuddered as they sprinted towards the safety of the Wind Rider. The shudder turned into a thunder as the pursuers reached the planks and surged after them. Astrid glanced over her shoulder to see the snarling faces of the warriors behind them. They were no more than thirty paces away and closing. Moonlight glinted on steel as Astrid took up her axe.

"Form!" Torben's voice boomed across the pier.

Two of the crew leapt down from the Wind Rider and brought their weapons to bear as their companions powered towards them.

Fargrim and Hélla reached them first. They ran through the gap in their shields as an arrow was launched down from the deck. It buzzed over Astrid's head and caught the first pursuer in the chest and tossed him down into the sea in a spray of blood. Another arrow followed. It drove into the shield of the next man. Laerke raced by the shield wall. Astrid risked another glance over her shoulder. The first man was less than fifteen paces from her. It was not him she was looking for. Her eyes met the first oil-soaked ship.

"Nenrir!" she bellowed towards her ship. "Now!"

The hiss of a torch catching alight met her ears, and it was quickly followed by the orange glow of flames. The archer slid an arrow into the torch, and the oil-soaked rags around its tip flared to life. His powerful muscles took the weight of his bow with ease as he drew the arrow back. The owl feathers of the bow's fletching brushed his cheek lightly.

His fingers slid from the bowstring.

Everything slowed as the flaming bolt sliced through the night. The arrow vanished over the railings of the vessel. There was a whoosh, and then night became day.

The sound of a wall of fire engulfing the ship was deafening. Its wave of heat caught Astrid off guard. She stumbled. Astrid cried out as the inferno singed her cheek and nearly sent her to the ground. She ran past the rearguard as Nenrir sent another arrow on its way. Astrid turned as she caught her breath and watched the arrow's flight. Behind them, some of the earl's men had been sent reeling from the blast and were staggering to their feet. They were still determined not to let their prey escape. Another ship vanished with a roar as the flames washed across its deck and painted the sky with fire.

Fargrim heaved himself up onto the Wind Rider and reached down for Hélla.

Astrid reached Laerke's side. Her heart raced.

Perhaps they would escape. Perhaps.

"Torben, get out of here," she bellowed as she raised her axe.

A crash came from behind and her heart sank. The pursuit collided into her rearguard with the force of an enraged bull. Her warriors snarled and fought back. They were all willing to sacrifice their lives so that their comrades could live. A warrior fell as an axe caught his neck. He screamed and then the waves enveloped him. Another of the earl's men was driven back as an arrow punched into his shoulder. The pressure was too much. One of Astrid's men stumbled under the onslaught and lost his footing on the wet planks. The tide surged forwards. It was a wall of steel, shield and muscle. It was over in a heartbeat as the defenders were overwhelmed. Their bodies hit the wooden pier and then vanished over the side and into the dark waters beneath.

Astrid turned to face the assault. She took up the shield of a dead man at her feet. Laerke stood at her side. He blocked the way to the ship as the rest of the crew boarded. The first warrior arrived and barrelled forward. Astrid locked her shield with her comrade as the man smashed into them. His momentum forced them back. Astrid lashed out with her axe. It was an awkward strike, and the man blocked it with ease. The earl's man's attention was taken away from Laerke. Astrid's companion drove his blade between the warrior's ribs. He wrenched his blade free as the man crashed onto the planks. The next warrior arrived, and his armour was covered in blood. He had an axe gripped tight in his right hand, while his shield bore the wolf symbol of Earl Magnus. A helm covered his head and shrouded his face.

Laerke acted first and drove his blade towards the attacker. The warrior saw it coming. He moved like a blur and trapped the blade to his side with his shield. The warrior hammered the haft of his axe into Laerke's exposed face. Laerke fell back. His feet slid on the wet planks. He cried out and then toppled from the pier. There was a splash. Then there was nothing save for the ripples in the water.

Astrid was alone as she backed away. The man before her mirrored her moves. He attacked. His axe sliced through the air with a whistle. Splinters flew as it bit into Astrid's shield. She retaliated with a blow of her own, but he easily swatted it aside. She could see the mark of the bloodsworn on his arm. A flurry of strikes came down and forced her back. They smashed her shield and buckled her knees. His axe slipped through her weakening defence. It sliced through leather and then blood flowed. The steel bit into the flesh of her arm. Astrid cried out as a wave of agony surged through her muscle and threatened to overcome her. She screamed, and the axe ripped away in a haze of blood. Her left arm burned. There was nothing she could do. He was too fast. He was too strong. The man rushed forward. He raised his shield and prepared to use it like a ram. She raised her own. She was barely able to keep it up with her near nerveless fingers. He slammed into her hard. Astrid's feet left the pier and then she was flying. Her axe and shield fell from her grasp. Steel rang as her blade hit the planks, and then she crashed down. Her vision wavered as her head met wood and agony lanced through her body. She buried the pain with a grimace as it threatened to overwhelm her. Astrid reached out, and her fingers brushed the hilt of her axe.

A bow sang.

An arrow drove towards the warrior.

The steel tip easily cut through the wood of his shield.

Nenrir.

Relief cascaded over her even though she knew she was not yet safe.

Astrid's arm burned with pain and her arm ran red with blood. She groaned as she rose to her feet. She took up her axe. The man stepped towards her. A smirk played on his lips as the Wind Rider began to move.

She had to leave.

Astrid turned and pushed herself into a sprint, her axe held tightly in her hand. An arrow sped over her shoulder and thudded into the bloodsworn's shield. Astrid panted as she pushed herself faster. Planks creaked underfoot as she reached the end of the pier. Without a second thought, she propelled herself forwards and leapt towards the vessel as it edged away from the dock. Her body smashed into the side of the ship and then she was falling. Her fingers reached for something. Anything.

They found purchase on the ship's stern.

Her wounded arm screamed as it took her weight. Hot blood ran down her arm as her arm began to shake, and her grip loosened.

Footsteps.

She turned her head and saw the warrior approaching. There was a gasp from above followed by the snap of a bowstring.

The bloodsworn caught the arrow on his shield and swatted it from the air. Astrid felt her fingers slip. The pain from her wound was too much. Suddenly she was falling, and the water called her to its depths. A hand latched around Astrid's wrist, and she was jerked to a halt. She cried out through bared teeth as white-hot pain seared through her arm. A grunt came from above and then she was pulled over the railing and onto the deck of the Wind Rider. Astrid gasped as she fell onto the planks below. Her bloody axe fell from her hand as she struggled to control the agony spreading from her wound. Astrid caught her breath and rose unsteadily to her feet. She turned back to look at Agartha. The fingers of her right hand were wrapped tight around her wound. The city shone in the light of a dozen burning ships. There would be no pursuit. Not for a while at least.

Her eyes met the man on the pier. He dropped his axe and then did the strangest thing.

He removed his helmet and a wave of golden hair cascaded to his shoulders. The bloodsworn who bore the mark of the wolf upon his shield stood at the end of the pier and gazed out towards the Wind Rider as it sailed away.

"TRAITOR!" Torben bellowed towards the harbour.

His words were filled with venom and rose louder than the waves down upon the harbour.

"No …" breathed Hélla, as her dark eyes stared at the bloodsworn on the pier.

Her voice was filled with anger and sorrow, for she had grown close to the warrior. Astrid slowly dipped her head. She had grown up with the armour and the man within. He had fought beside them for years, and now against them.

It was Erik.

An arm shot down from above. It wrapped around Laerke's wrist and heaved him up from beneath the waves. The sound hit him first, and it drove away numbness in his body. The roar of burning ships, the shouting of warriors and the crash of boots upon the pier filled his ears. He gasped for breath as he was heaved up onto the planks. He coughed up what felt like an ocean of water. At last, he flicked his eyes open and looked up at his saviour.

"Still in the realm of the living, my friend."

His eyes locked on the face as a cold shiver ran down his spine. "You …"

Erik stood above him with a dark look in his eyes. Magnus stood beside the bloodsworn with a sword clasped in his hands.

"Kill him," the earl said after a moment.

Laerke chuckled. At last, he would enter Ra'Haven and feast in the hall of the Sea-Father. At last, he would be given what all Valkir wished for, but few ever received: a glorious death.

"No, lord." Erik glanced up at the earl and raised a hand. "He could still be of use to us."

"So be it," Magnus' cold voice replied. He gave a slight nod to the bloodsworn.

Erik's fist came down, and then Laerke saw naught but darkness.

EIGHTEEN

Ruins of Israfil, Steppe of Miera

The Mieran warband, led by Azrial Dathmir, rode at nearly a thousand strong. They rode with purpose, and that purpose was clear: to send back any who trespassed upon their soil. It had been a four-day ride from Carlian, and many had been in the saddle since the eastern border, which was over nine hundred miles away. Those who had travelled that far were more restless than tired. The Mieran warband was used to spending weeks, if not months, in the saddle.

A vast line of horses and steel-tipped spears galloped beneath the red phoenix banners of Miera. It was a great sight to behold for those lucky enough to bear witness to it.

They had arrived at the fortress of Cardna in the dead of night and spent the dark hours within its stone walls. The stables and barracks had been filled to bursting, and many of the warriors took refuge in the houses of the townspeople. Mierans always welcomed the riders as if they were family and fed and sheltered them accordingly. From there, Dathmir had ordered the companies to divide. He had sent the riders to outposts and border towns to keep a weather eye on the horizon. Kitara and her band had been sent north to watch over the plains of Carn-Dair. It was a fifty mile stretch of open land filled with little more than a few hills, small towns and ruins.

The apple crunched as Kitara bit into it and sent juice flowing down her chin. The sun was hot upon her face as she sat atop the ruins of a stone wall with one leg dangling off its edge. She stretched as she leaned back and rested her back on the higher wall behind. It was the ruins of a small outpost that had fallen in the Annoran war. Israfil, it had been called. Now only ghosts inhabited its broken walls.

Ghosts and a small grove of apple trees. Beneath her, in the overgrown courtyard, the twenty horses of the band were tied, and they happily munched on the lush green grass of the orchard. Some of the warriors leaned on trees as they caught up on some much-needed respite. Others tended to their horses, while some patrolled the ruins. Silas had sent a man up into one of the few standing watchtowers to keep an eye on the plains. His position as commander of the men had been well earned in the north fighting against the Salvaari screamers. She could hear Silas talking as he gestured at his map of Miera and ran a finger along Carn-Dair. Two others were with him. Both were veterans who had seen much fighting in their time. They both had joined the company in Cardna, and as such they knew the terrain.

They may have thought Silas was a bit green, yet after growing up in the Rift, they knew he was capable. They listened as he spoke and occasionally offered advice to one who had rarely been this far west. Kitara closed her eyes and blocked it all out. She wanted to enjoy the little downtime she had. The light northerly breeze tickled her cheeks as she took another bite from the apple. Her left hand rested gently on her sword belt where it lay across her thighs.

The camaraderie of the Mierans on the ride had surprised her, for though she knew them to be a close-knit people, there seemed to be no boundaries between the riders. They shared food and drink, among other things, yet subjected each other to mockery when the occasion arose. Kitara had decided that they were a real brotherhood in arms. A brotherhood that, just like in Carlian, did not extend to her.

A whistle came from beneath and she glanced down to see Silas rolling the map up.

He shot her a quick look as he called out, "Gather around."

Kitara sighed as she swung her legs over the edge of the wall and dropped to the ground beneath. She held her scabbard in one hand and clasped the apple safely in the other.

All the Mierans, bar the man in the tower, made their way into the courtyard to their captain. Some of them rested their hands on their swords, axes and warhammers, although it was not out of anger or wariness. It was little more than a habit that had been instilled in them. "Alright, lads, Dathmir sent us north to watch over the plains of Carn-Dair. Not to rest," Silas told them with a grin.

Kitara's lips twitched into a smile and some of the men sniggered.

Silas grew instantly serious as his gaze swept over his men. "The ruins provide good watch of the surrounds, and they provide cover," he said. "Yet the well has fallen into disrepair."

"We will need to fix it yet. Until we do, we are low on water," added one of the men.

"Exactly." Silas nodded. "Now, we can all go a few days without it … We all have."

Many of the men mumbled their agreement as their leader spoke. Kitara remained silent. She had been without water for days in the past. She knew of cracked lips and a parched throat all too well.

"But that does not mean that we should," Silas continued. "Imalric is a few hours ride north."

One of the veterans from Cardna stepped up to Silas' side.

"For those of you not of the west, Imalric is a small town built around the end of the Rinar River as it flows down from the mountains to the plains," the veteran told them. "It has prospered in recent years, as the Valley of Odrysia shields them to the northern border, while to the west the Annorans have been quiet for years."

"As we all now know, that time may be at an end," Silas finished for the man. "So, we cross the plains, ride to Imalric and rest there for the night. Tomorrow, we shall return here with supplies that we need and repair the well. The ruins are simply too good a position to abandon. Now, mount up. I for one would rather travel by light of the sun."

A simple plan, thought Kitara, as the men voiced their agreement.

She started to make her way back to Lamreil. Her boots lightly brushed the stones and grass beneath as she walked. She had been forced to learn to ride well in her retreat from Annora the year before. There had been a company of soldiers hot on her tail when she fled. Men like that did not take kindly to a thief, and it would not have mattered to them that she had robbed to survive the gutters. She merely supposed she had robbed the wrong noble, one who wanted his revenge for the large purse of coin he had carried. Kitara had deprived him of it. She wished she could have seen his face turn a deep shade of crimson when he had discovered that his gold had vanished. She had lost any feeling of being saddle-sore after she had spent a year with the Mierans. The joy of the thundering speed and the wind on her face was all she felt.

Kitara took a last bite of her apple and tossed it to the side. She swung up onto Lamreil's saddle, and with a piercing whistle from Silas, the Mierans galloped away from the ruins and onto the plains of Carn-Dair.

The sun was high in the sky when the horsemen finally rode into Imalric. Kitara felt her lips twitch into a smile as she looked down at the village. It was like nothing she had seen before. Though the houses were of the traditional Mieran style – wooden walls with thatched rooftops – the town was built in a semi-circle around what appeared to be a small lake. It was the end of the Rinar River. To the north lay the soaring peaks of the Valley of Odrysia. They drove up into the sky and vanished beyond the clouds.

The soft earth beneath thudded gently under the weight of hooves as they rode. Smoke wafted from chimneys pleasantly, and the townspeople stopped to wave at the company as they made their way towards the heart of the village. Farmers worked the fields, and the sound of a blacksmith's hammer reached Kitara's ears. The village seemed almost peaceful.

A large structure rose before them and dwarfed the houses around it. A party of heavily armed soldiers stood at its doors. No doubt this was the headman's lodging.

The lodge stood in front of the town square, which was empty save for a large stone pillar covered in old carvings. It was a gathering point. Every Mieran village had one.

The guards turned to face them as the riders approached. They started across the square towards them without hesitation. Kitara could see six warriors, hands all clasping sword hilts, yet she knew there would be more out of sight. There always were.

"Welcome to Imalric," called one of the warriors as his dark eyes swept from rider to rider warily.

Silas nodded in reply. "Azrial Dathmir sent us to patrol the west lands. We come seeking resupply." He gave the man a smile as he ran a hand down his mount's neck. "It has been a long ride."

The guard snorted at that, and his eyes shone with humour. He knew of the long journeys and sleepless nights in the saddle. All Mieran soldiers did.

"Our village is yours, brother," he told Silas.

"Thank you." Silas slipped from his saddle, and his boots crunched on the road.

With the exchange over, the rest of the company dismounted. They were eager to explore the unusual village and stretch out the stiffness gained from days in the saddle.

The lead guard made his way over to Silas as he tied the reins of his horse to a nearby fence.

"You're from the north," the warrior said.

It was more a statement than question. He must have picked up on the slight ruggedness in the captain's accent, a ruggedness found only among the northerners.

"Aye, I grew up there," Silas replied, and he nodded over his shoulder towards his men. "Most are from the east, though we come from all corners." He extended a hand. "Silas Barangir."

The man clasped it with a slight smile. "Illiran. I can imagine that you will want to speak to the headman."

"I bring word from the king," Silas said seriously. "Tidings that your leader must hear."

"Very well."

Silas turned back to his company, and his voice boomed loudly as he spoke. "Restock and resupply. Camp by the river. We leave at dawn."

Kitara walked through Imalric. For the first time in nearly a week, she was alone. She felt as if a weight had been lifted from her shoulders. She always relished time alone after spending years fending for herself.

The locals paid her no mind other than to throw her the occasional curious look. To see someone dressed with a sword at their side was no strange thing, yet on a girl was unheard of.

Who were they to judge?

It did not matter so much among the Mierans. She rode with a company of their riders, and to the townspeople that was good enough. It was why she had stayed in the kingdom. It was the time she had lived somewhere that she was not outcast by those whom she lived with.

After filling her waterskins from one of Imalric's wells, and watering Lamreil at a nearby trough, Kitara had decided to see what the peaceful town had to offer. The warm rays of the sun lit the village from the lake to the plains and covered it in golden light. The pastures and farms that surrounded the town were lush and green, while the roads were little more than earthen trails. It was a simple place, yet unlike any she had seen before. The lake shone light blue as the sun's rays danced across its rippling surface.

Kitara ran a hand through the reed grass that lined the sides of the streets, and she smiled as its tips tickled her palm. It was a beautiful village, quiet and almost serene. Even the air she breathed was clear.

So, this was what the small towns of Miera were like, she marvelled.

Before Imalric, Kitara had only ever seen the capital and the fortress of Cardna. She had never seen the places that were built for anyone other than warriors.

As she walked along the edge of the lake, her eyes sparkled like the water itself. A ring of buildings circled the lake. Some of the buildings were houses, while Kitara could tell that others were traders and merchants from the signs hanging from their thatched roofs. Kitara didn't have to read the first sign to know that it belonged to a bakehouse. The sweet scent of baking bread that filled her nose as she walked past said as much. Next to the bakehouse stood a store marked by a hanging barrel that had the word merchant inscribed upon it. She started towards the store. Curiosity had gotten the better of her. Silas had given them an hour, and very little of that time had passed. Most of the men were no doubt having a drink at the tavern. Kitara could see lights flickering through the merchant's doorway, and with a shrug she walked inside.

The room was lit by candles and the flicker of light that crept through the windows. The store was filled with dozens, if not hundreds, of items. Strange orbs, staffs, jewels, rugs, clothes and more filled the tightly packed and dustless shelves. Kitara's nose twitched as she caught the smell of incense burning. It was mingled with the feint aroma of things that were far older than she was. It was almost musty.

Behind the counter sat a man fiddling with something beyond her view. It looked as though he were cleaning with an old rag. He barely gave her more than a glance as she entered the store. He was far too occupied with the thing in his hands.

Her boots thudded gently on the wooden floorboards as she strode through the store. Her gaze swept over old carvings and shining gems. A banner covered in the likeness of a burning phoenix hung atop one of the walls. The banner of the first king of Miera. Beneath the flag sat a counter with racks of necklaces and bracelets, but those were not what caught Kitara's eye. Beside them, almost hidden by a pile of scrolls, sat a simple knife sheathed in a small leather scabbard. It was plain, featuring no embellishment, while the wooden hilt was notched with over a dozen small lines. She shifted the scrolls to the side and picked up the small blade. It was no larger than two of her fists. She drew the knife and flipped it. Its balance was near perfect, and the blade was very well made.

"Pretty lass like you deserves something better than that dusty old thing," a hearty voice boomed as the man behind the counter hurried towards her.

Kitara held back a chuckle as the man approached, and she turned to face him. "Is that so?" Kitara replied.

She saw the flicker of shock run across his eyes as he noticed the white scar that ran down her face. It was the same expression that everyone bore when they saw it for the first time. Pity.

"Apologies."

Kitara's lips curled. "Not what you were expecting?"

"No," the merchant agreed with a shrug before his lips broke into a toothy grin. "Yet we all have scars some place, eh?"

Kitara returned the smile and handed over the knife. "The markings on the hilt. What do they mean?"

The man examined the knife for an instant before speaking. "Ah, now, this is a blade from the far west. Well beyond the mountains and Larissa. Dangerous folk they are. Each notch in the hilt is carved for each kill. For every life taken."

It was well made, and from what the merchant said, she doubted it had fault. Perhaps in Annora it would have cost five or six pieces of silver, but Mierans did not put any stock in coin. She reached into her pocket and pulled out a small white orb.

"Will this do?" she asked. "It's a pearl from the south of the Sacasian Sea."

"The Gulf of Lamrei?" the man murmured.

He reached for the pearl and his eyes sparkled. Kitara nodded and closed her fist to stop the merchant's greedy hand.

"Do we have a deal?" she muttered.

To her, the pearl held little value. She had a handful of the things tucked safely away in her pouches. It was little more than the shadow of a memory from a lifetime ago.

"Perhaps the knife is far too simple for you, no?" The trader grinned sweetly.

Kitara nearly rolled her eyes as he spoke. He had seen one pearl and no doubt thought she had more that he could get his greedy little hands on.

"I have jewel-encrusted blades from Medea, ivory-handled daggers from Aureia–"

"This will do." Kitara interrupted the merchant with a wave of her hand. "Let the fine ladies play with their jewels. I have no use for them."

The merchant took the pearl and the deal was made.

Kitara sheathed her new blade and made for the camp of her companions. It was not long before the moon rose and she found sleep. A chill night breeze blew gently through the Mieran encampment along the banks of the Rinar River. Instead of taking up lodging with their kin in the village, they lay beneath the starry night. They rested upon simple rugs, and they were ready to mount up and ride within moments if the need arose.

The gentle snores of the warriors carried across the waters of the

Rinar as they rested. Kitara's body tensed in her sleep. Her muscles contorted. Darkness clouded her dreams and seeped into every corner of her mind. She grimaced in pain. With a gasp she awoke, and her hand instinctively went for her sword that lay at her side.

Agony.

It ripped through her skull like a wave and seared from the back of her eyes to her temple.

Kitara gritted her teeth and closed her eyes. She clutched at her head as the pain grew blinding.

She prayed to the gods that she did not believe in.

Please not again ... Please.

Horror rolled through her mind as suddenly she could feel everything. From the Mierans sleeping all around her to the trees and waters of the river. From the birds flying through the trees fifty yards away to the very earth itself. It was as if they shared the same mind. The same awareness.

It burned though her.

Kitara staggered to her feet. She had to get away before the Mierans saw what she knew to be true. She had only felt this pain once before and it did not come alone. She fought back the strangled gasps and cries of agony that threatened as she left the campsite. Sweat ran freely down her face.

One of her trembling hands held her head, while the other was wrapped into a tight fist.

She reached the river. Each step she took was as hard as the last. She could still feel it all. Still see it all. Her eyes screamed in pain, and she dropped to her knees upon the riverbank.

Then it faded. Her thoughts became her own, and the awareness seeped back into her own body and mind. She could feel a dull ache around her temples, an ache that made her feel something that she had not felt in years. Fear. Kitara opened her eyes and gazed into the moonlit waters of the river.

No ...

She could see her reflection. She could see that where they had once been emerald her eyes now blazed purple. As the pain faded so did the colour. Her natural green began to return.

Kitara called it the change. The violet shade that had awoken her from her slumber many years before had returned. The last time it had happened she hadn't understood what was happening. She had felt everything back then just as she had this night. The ocean as it rippled against the ship. The beating hearts of the fifty pirates slumbering around her.

Perhaps it had been more than just some kind of vision or hallucination. Perhaps it had been some kind of warning. For soon after it had happened the first time, she had been betrayed by all those she had called friend. Most of her dreams were plagued by nightmares, but this had only happened to her twice. She had told no one of what had happened on the pirate ship. Who could she have told anyway?

The Mierans would simply laugh and call her mad, for a person's eyes did not change colour, and there was certainly no way to see and feel everything that transpired around you.

Kitara rubbed her brow as the ache begin to dull. She watched the last of the violet in her eyes fade away in her reflection.

She slowly made her way back to the encampment. She gathered up her sword belt and buckled it to her waist. Kitara spared a glance at her companions as they slept. Without a backwards glance, she left the Mierans behind. Her boots barely made a sound on the grass beneath as she retreated.

Kitara had been searching for answers ever since the first incident. Books held none and nor did any scholar she had met.

She followed the river as she walked, absent-minded and lost in thought.

"What is it?"

She whirled around as her hand reached for her dagger. The blade was half drawn when she saw Silas glancing at her with a look of bemusement.

"Just a dream," she told him, and she slid the blade away as her companion made his way over. "It was nothing."

Kitara looked her companion in the eye and could see that he was struggling to hide some amusement. The Mierans, ever practical people, could never understand.

Kitara sighed and crossed her arms as she turned her gaze to the river. The waters were clear, and they reflected the silver moon that flew above them in the night sky. The waves caressed the banks of the Rinar and gentle whispers of the wind. It reminded her of home. It reminded her of Lamrei, of ships upon the ocean and banners flying high in the breeze.

It was almost calming.

She turned and gazed out over the river. Her eyes flickered down towards Imalric. The faint light of candles burned brightly through open windows as the village slumbered.

"It is peaceful here," Kitara said quietly. More so than any place she had seen before.

Silas nodded slowly. "If only all places were so."

The woman gave her companion a slight smile. It was a smile tinged with sadness.

"If only."

The sun rose all too soon and the Mierans rose with it. There were no goodbyes between the riders and the people of Imalric. The plains of Carn-Dair flashed beneath as the Mierans raced across the open terrain. The wind whipped through Kitara's hair and lashed her face. It was a feeling she had grown to love. The thundering speed of the gallop comforted her. Yet right now her thoughts were taken by the visions that still plagued her thoughts.

What did it mean?

The earth churned beneath the hooves of twenty horses as they sped across the plains and over the rolling hills.

Kitara's ears prickled as something reached them over the sound of the horses. It almost sounded like a cry, but Kitara could not place the sound.

Silas held up a hand and let loose three sharp whistles to call the party to halt. He had heard it too.

With a slight flick of her wrist and a gentle pull of the reins, Lamreil began to slow to a walk. None of the Mierans spoke as the horses came to a halt. They were now all on full alert. Kitara's eyes scanned the plains. Nothing.

Then she saw it. A dark speck in the sky to the west. Little more than a dot against the sun as it dipped below the horizon. Kitara pulled her spyglass from her belt and extended it. She flicked it towards where she had seen the speck. Her gaze locked on a bird that hovered in the sky to the west. The sound of its screech came to her ears again. It was followed by silence. It mirrored the sound that she had heard moments before.

Kitara lowered her spyglass and breathed a sigh of relief. It was just a hawk.

NINETEEN

Fortress of Kilgareth, Valley of Odrysia

The training yard echoed with the thudding of sword upon post as the recruits swung their weapons. Sir Alarik and his instructors watched with keen eyes as Kyler and the men trained. The instructors never failed to give advice to the willing or to punish the unwilling with their gnarled canes. Each day had brought on new torment. They were forced to run and march in their full kit while they spent long days learning the horse, lance, sword and shield. The most fearsome weapon that the knights had at their disposal, the crossbow, was able to carve a hole through chainmail as easily as a knife carved a cake. When the sun finally set, the recruits took it in turns to stand watch atop the fortress walls.

Now they stood in the yard, shoulder to shoulder, with their fellow initiates, their weapons held at the ready. Kyler's arms ached under the weight of the sword and shield that he held. His muscles were nearly failing after weeks of this torture. The unfamiliar weight of the armour and the heavy weapons sapped their strength within moments. The boy's breath was ragged as the sun started to lower in the sky. Warm sweat ran down his chin, soaking into the padded tunic beneath.

"FORM ONE!" roared Sir Alarik, and his voice boomed around the yard.

The recruits swung their blades at the posts lined up before them.

One. Two. Three.

"SHIELDS!"

Kyler's shield came around. He was ready to block an invisible blow.

"FORM THREE!"

With a grunt, he propelled himself forwards and slammed his shield into the wooden post. Kyler moved instinctively to the next move. He raised his shield and lunged forwards with his sword.

One. Two.

Kyler stepped back, and his sword returned to rest upon the lip of his shield.

"Landrey."

The Medean lowered his guard and turned to face Sir Alarik as the knight approached.

"Sir?"

"You crossed your feet as you stepped back into position, a weakness that an opponent could exploit." The battlemaster gestured at Kyler's feet with his cane. "Raise your shield and ready yourself. Your sword." He held out a hand.

Kyler obeyed. He handed over his blade before he raised his shield and slid his foot back. A strong stance.

Alarik drove forwards and slammed his shoulder into Kyler's shield. The boy hardly budged.

"Good," the knight said. "Now the same yet cross your feet."

Once more Kyler fell to command, yet already he could see what the veteran was getting at. His footwork already felt awkward. He raised his shield.

The battlemaster charged again, and his armoured shoulder crashed into the shield with the strength of a bear behind it.

Kyler's feet locked as he slipped back, and he was sent crashing to the ground. Alarik's cane lowered over his neck. If it were a real sword, in a real fight, Kyler would be dead. The knight held his form for a moment to let it sink in.

"I understand," Kyler told him as Alarik clasped both his weapons with a single hand.

The battlemaster reached down with his other. Kyler took his hand and was pulled to his feet.

"Set your foundation strong" – Alarik returned Kyler's sword – "and the gods themselves could not move you."

The day wore on as the initiates were drilled. Their weapons became heavier than the largest of boulders to the weary recruits. Alarik and the other tutors stalked the line as they gave out sage advice to those they were training.

Thud! Thud! Thud!

"What in the hells are you doing?" Kyler heard Sir Alarik scream from further down the line. "You drop your shield and swing a flurry of blows at that little wooden man absent command?"

The Medean turned to see the knight stride towards a hapless recruit standing over his shield. Kyler winced. The recruit had dropped his shield, and whether by exhaustion or choice, it was not acceptable.

Alarik's grip tightened on his cane as he stepped to within an inch of the man.

"Pick it up."

"No," the initiate mumbled, as he rolled his shoulders back.

"I GAVE YOU AN ORDER!" bellowed the battlemaster.

He was preparing to strike. In his weariness, the recruit had forgotten one very important thing: always refer to rank by their title. The cane slammed into his stomach with a meaty smack. The recruit doubled over in pain and gasped for air.

"I do not need to hide behind a shield, sir," came the garbled reply.

"You think shields are cowardly, eh?" muttered Alarik in disbelief. He sneered at the recruit. "Then perhaps you would like to just train with the sword. Forget the shield weighing you down."

"It is how I was taught in Annora."

The battlemaster snorted and swept his gaze around the square. "Initiates, attend your eyes." He paused a moment as all thirty men and the four instructors turned his way. "The lands from which you come matter not. What you were taught matters not. Hugh Karter here was raised in the Annoran aristocracy and trained by them to wield a sword. He wishes to fight without a shield to slow him down. It is true, there will always be a time when you neither have shield, nor armour, nor ally. A time when you are not prepared for a fight. A time when the only thing between you and death is the blade you carry. It is this very reason that we have devoted much of our training to the sword and the sword alone." His smirk said it all, and the instructors chuckled drily. "I served in the Aureian legions for near to fifteen years. I fought in battlefields beyond count, killed more than I can remember. Seen friends die, struck down by savages who took the heads of those slain by their hand. I have seen a lot of things in my time, more than any of you will ever witness. Yet let me give you one piece of advice." He held out his cane and gestured to a nearby recruit's shield. "That is not just your life. It is the life of your brother who stands beside you. For we fight in a shield wall, a thing that can allow no weakness. One broken link and the wall will fail. I could teach you the sword, teach you to fight unencumbered by thirty inches of hard wood and steel. Yet what would happen when you're slogging your way through a battlefield, the ground a slurry of mud, blood and the bodies of friend and foe alike? What would happen if you have no shield? What would happen when one who has never held a pike in his life points a crossbow at you? What would save you then? The sword? I do not think so."

The silence that followed was deafening. Sir Alarik started to walk through the ranks of initiates.

"The weighted shield may be heavy, and you may curse it now. Yet when the real thing weighs as a feather, when it saves your life … you will praise the gods for it. Then you will understand."

Many of the initiates slowly nodded as their mentor spoke. The grizzled veteran had spent fifteen years in the legions. Fifteen years of endless fighting and bloodshed. Even most seasoned fighters would be green compared to Alarik.

The battlemaster pointed his cane to the fallen shield, a new glint in his dark eyes.

"Now pick it up. Learn the shield or lose your life. The choice is yours alone."

The recruit gritted his teeth and obliged. His arm screamed against the weight of the shield. He was in agony. They all were.

"Now you will train. You will bleed. You will strengthen yourself, and you will remember this day as the last that you so much as think about dropping it again," Alarik told the recruit with a slight nod. The Aureian swept his eyes over the initiates before continuing. "Work the posts until sundown. Then you can rest."

"Yes, sir!" cried the initiates.

They all turned back to their posts with a newfound strength.

"BEGIN!" roared one of the instructors, and his voice echoed throughout the arena.

Kyler raised his shield with his aching arm, yet he would never drop it. With a snarl he lashed out. His sword struck the wooden practice post with a crack.

The mess hall was filled with the smell of cooked food and warm ale as the recruits sank exhaustedly into their seats around the small round tables. A smoky tang came from the crackling fire that burnt towards the back of the hall.

Kyler had exchanged his chainmail and steel armour, along with his sweat-soaked padded tunic, for a clean shirt and britches. They had all learnt within a day that not to do so would be far worse than pulling off the heavy gear after the day's training. It had become a ritual to the trainee warriors.

Two other men sat with the Medean. The first was a boy, no

older than Kyler, who hailed from Torosa. Haylan his name was.

The other man, Evander, had the rougher accent and olive skin of one from Elara, which was to the east.

"I heard Sir Alarik talking to one of his men," muttered the Torosi with a slight grimace. "Tomorrow we are to fight each other."

Evander winced. "I have never swung a blow in anger, let alone at something that swings back."

"Nor me," added Haylan as he stared absent-mindedly at the cup in his hands. "How about you, Kyler?"

"On more than one occasion." The Medean's lips twitched into a cocky grin. "Growing up in a tavern was ... interesting." He shrugged, and humour danced across his face. "Had to deal with many drunkards lacking manners. Though all those brawls were decided by the fist and not steel."

Evander chuckled and glanced at the Torosi. "You see, Haylan, my friend. Medea truly is a brutish land."

Kyler grinned. "Trust me, you haven't seen anything from this brutish Medean yet."

Evander snorted and took a gulp from his half-empty cup. "I'm trembling."

The trio laughed at that. It had not taken long for Kyler to form a bond of friendship with his companions. Haylan's mind was as sharp as any that the Medean had seen before, and Evander's dry humour made the long days pass even more quickly.

"Forget what I have been taught, he says," a voice groaned behind them. "As if Alarik thinks that I am a stranger to the art of the sword."

Kyler didn't have to turn to recognise the voice. A slight smirk crossed his lips as the voice continued.

"I'm better than any of them ... Hells, I could probably show the warrior himself something about footwork."

Kyler grimaced and glanced over his shoulder to where the man sat among a ring of other recruits. Hugh Karter, the son of a wealthy Annoran noble, was as arrogant as they came. Yet the noble had proven himself deadly with the sword from the beginning. Hugh had all but shunned the idea of using a shield, even after Alarik had spoken to him about the need to bear one.

"You think that you could teach a knight now?" Kyler rolled his dark eyes and chuckled dryly.

Karter shot the Medean with a withering sneer. "Something to add, Landrey?"

"Just that the man training us has swung a sword for longer than many of us have been alive," Kyler shrugged. "You would do well to follow his example. We all would."

Hugh's booming laugh filled the mess hall. It was a laugh that was taken up by his companions who were all of noble stock.

"Follow the old man? I have been trained to fight since birth under the best swordsmen and masters-at-arms that coin could buy."

Kyler felt his lips twitch into a grin. He could no longer help himself. "Then it is a shame, Kartie, that not one of them taught you how to hold a shield."

Silence.

All thirty of the recruits watched on. All thirty of them knew how good Hugh was with a blade. Some of them visibly winced at Kyler's bold words. He was lowborn and not only had he insulted one of noble birth, but he had also branded him with a shortened name.

Evander reached across the table and clapped a hand on his friend's shoulder. "Kyler …"

"What was that?" Hugh growled as he rose to his feet.

The Medean finished the contents of his cup in a single gulp before he turned to face the Annoran. "You say that you were taught by the best."

"I have trained to kill for years," scoffed the man. "What were you doing? Serving drinks."

Karter's companions laughed and sneers covered their pompous faces.

"Oh." Kyler let out a loud sigh. "Now it all makes sense. Instead of learning a decent manner, you were taught what few men have and so few crave."

"And what's that?"

"The arrogance that only one of noble birth may possess," Kyler told him.

The Medean knew he was pushing the Annoran too far, but he needed to be taught a valuable lesson.

"You believe yourself better than all of us, Hugh." He gestured around the room. "And you even believe yourself a match for one of the most respected and formidable knights of this Order. Of this, we all know you are mistaken."

"Be careful," Hugh snarled, and his hands balled into fists. "I could take you apart with one blow."

Kyler's grin widened. "I don't think so."

Karter's fist drove towards Kyler's face. The Medean's feet slid backwards as his reflexes kicked in. He blocked Karter's blow with his arm before he retaliated. Kyler's left hook slammed into Hugh's stomach and rocked him back.

The silence broke and the hall was filled with cheers. Some voices backed Kyler, while the others backed Hugh.

The Medean followed up with another strike. He hoped to catch his opponent off guard. Karter ducked under the strike and barrelled into his foe. His arms wrapped around Kyler's waist as he dove forward. They both crashed to the ground in a pile of flailing limbs. The Annoran landed on top and drove down with a fist. Kyler knocked the blow to the side before hammering an elbow into the man's chin. Blood erupted from Hugh's lips as the blow struck, and it struck hard. He snarled and rolled away from Kyler. Karter leapt to his feet. The Medean followed suit and pushed himself up. He was too slow.

Hugh's boot connected heavily with his stomach. Kyler gasped as air fled his lungs. He threw up an arm as another kick came down. Kyler's wrist screamed as the kick smashed into his hastily thrown defence.

Suddenly, he was back on his feet.

His left arm caught the first punch with a thud. The second slipped through and struck his face. The blow rocked Kyler back as blood began to pour from his aching nose. Red tears streamed down his chin and dripped down onto the wooden floor beneath. He couldn't tell if it was broken.

Kyler's instincts took over as Hugh moved to end the fight.

Karter's blow flew through the air fast, yet Kyler was faster still. He blocked the punch and launched his own at the same time. It caught Hugh on the chin with a meaty smack. The Annoran stumbled as a second blow crashed into his ribs. Kyler blocked out all sound as he sauntered towards his enemy. Fury was etched into his gaze. He felt a slow-burning anger well up inside his chest. He glared at Hugh and raised his fist.

Crack!

Kyler doubled over as the cane struck him hard in the side.

He gasped as he struggled to take in the precious air. It was at this moment that he realised the hall had fallen silent.

"What in Durandail's name do you think you are doing?" The bellow filled the room.

The boy looked towards Hugh and then flicked his gaze towards the voice. Horror sent a numbing shiver down his spine. It belonged to the battlemaster himself.

"A misunderstanding, Sir Alarik," muttered Hugh, as he sent a small nod to Kyler. "Nothing more."

The knight turned his fury-filled gaze down to the other recruit. "That true?"

"Yes, sir," Kyler told him, and he winced as he rose to his feet.

"Nothing more."

"As you say, Pisspot," Alarik snorted.

There was no doubt that he could see right through the lie.

"You are both on half rations for three days. See that it does not happen again." He swept his eyes across the mess hall. "What are you waiting for? An order? Back to your chambers now!"

Kyler shot his friends a quick glance as they made to leave. His red lips curled. He ran a hand across his chin to wipe some of the blood away. It had felt good to bring Karter down a step or two despite everything that had followed.

"You two," the battlemaster growled as he turned his furious gaze back to the pair. "See yourselves to the maija and get yourselves cleaned up before I have you thrown from the Order. And make no mistake, if you test my patience again … you will be."

"Sir," they chorused before doing as Alarik commanded.

Night came and went. Dawn's first light crept over the mountains and lit the training yard. The dull ache in Kyler's face had all but faded thanks to the skill of the maija. Some of the bruising still remained. Hugh Karter stood further down the line. His face was equally as dark from the punishment Kyler had inflicted.

"The sword is the weapon that forged our order," Sir Alarik told the recruits as they gathered around their mentors. "Yet for all its strengths, it has one weakness. The inability to cut through armour. And so how do you defeat an armoured foe?"

He switched his grip on the sword so that one hand clasped the hilt, while the other wrapped around the steel edge halfway down its length.

"There is a very simple answer. Half-swording. Now, you could take up arms like this and try to drive the tip of your sword through the chinks in another man's armour. It is difficult, chinks are small and, more likely than not, your opponent will be moving."

Once more he adjusted his grip and twirled the sword now so

that both hands were firmly latched around the blade. Now he held the weapon in reverse, with its hilt and crossguard in the air.

"With this grip you will not kill a man in plate, but you can hurt him just as if you were holding a hammer. Knock him to the ground ..." – Sir Alarik freed his right hand and snatched out his dagger – "and go for the throat."

Kyler ran his fingers along the steel crossguard of his training sword. It was sturdy and strong. As lethal as Alarik had told the recruits. The battlemaster sheathed steel and took his cane back from one of the other instructors. They trained for the better part of the day in the reverse grip Alarik had shown. They learnt to take their opponents from their feet and deliver a final blow with a knife. A few hours before sundown, Alarik ordered them into formation once again.

"To be a Knight of Kil'kara means to be more than the sword you carry and the skill you bear it," Sir Alarik called as he strode before the recruits with his fist clenched tightly around his cane.

Kyler held back a wince. He could still feel the lash of the wood upon his body.

"We are more than just warriors serving the will of our father, Durandail. Many a time we are called upon by village elders, counts, dukes, even simple farmers. All of them seeking our judgement and counsel. We have the right and privilege to act as the voice of Azaria herself. For as her instruments, we adjudicate and judge the innocent from the guilty. We advise those who seek our counsel, and we can act as priests if required. To join the ranks of our great Order, you must learn more than the sword and shield." The knight stopped before Kyler and ran his angry, dark gaze over the Medean. "You must learn to judge without emotion. You must show compassion to even those many deem unworthy. You must show wisdom befitting your rank, and for this, each and every one of you will be presented with a task. Some of you may question this, yet I tell you ... the Order that separates its scholars from its warriors will have its thinking done by cowards and its fighting done by fools."

There was some mumbling among the recruits. Kyler shared a glance with Evander who stood at his left shoulder. The Elaran merely shrugged at Kyler's inquisitive expression.

How could any of them have known about this?

Sir Alarik extended his cane and gestured towards his instructors. A familiar face stood among them with a scroll clasped in his hand.

"Brother Lorencio has brought with him a list. Each of you have been allocated a task," the battlemaster said.

The smirk on the maija's face told the recruits that he was looking forward to this.

"Starting tomorrow," Alarik continued, "you will be taught the sword from dawn until your end of day meal. From there you will work on whatever task that the maija have seen fit to grant you. Understood?"

"Yes, sir!"

"Good." He turned to the scholar and gave him a curt nod.

Lorencio's lips slipped into a slight grin as he took a step forwards and extended the scroll.

"Alright lads, form up. Let's get this done in an orderly fashion."

On command, the recruits moved into a single line. They moved with the swiftness of men who had been drilled constantly. They were men who had felt the smack of cane upon their flesh whenever they had taken a misstep or broken formation.

"Once you have been given your orders, stand to the side," Lorencio commanded as his eyes peered at the Torosi initiate before him. "Haylan Lindell …"

One by one, the recruits were given their tasks. Many of them shook their heads in a mixture of dismay and disbelief as they moved away from the maija quartermaster.

What could be that bad? Kyler could only watch as his new brothers' expressions fell.

"Kyler Landrey." The older man raised an eyebrow as the Medean stepped forward. "Have you been fighting?"

"Fighting is my job," he replied.

"Quite the tongue you have, eh, Landrey?" Lorencio snorted and glanced down at his parchment.

His eyes lit up for a moment, and Kyler's heart sunk.

"Ironic," the maija said with a chuckle. "You are to translate the works of the renowned philosopher Herodys of Delios."

Kyler stared at the man for a second. Had he heard the correctly? Herodys had lived and died more than a century ago.

"Translate?"

"Did I forget to mention that the philosopher wrote in Delion? The language of his kin."

"That tongue has been all but extinct for over a century." Kyler was incredulous, and his face paled in shock. "I cannot speak it, let alone read it."

"Well then," Lorencio told him, "I suggest that you visit the maija's library this evening. There are many books on the subject within. Perhaps you will learn more than just the language, eh?"

The Medean suppressed a groan as he moved to join his companions for the day's training.

All he had to do was translate an all but extinct language into the common tongue. To do so he had to first learn the ancient language itself. It was a test he had to pass or he would never become a knight of the Order. It was going to be a long night. The first of many.

TWENTY

"I regret to inform your majesty that we lost the trail at the river Harren," said one of the scouts as the pair knelt before their king.

The voice was little more than a murmur as it left the soldier's lips. He was quiet from the first word and trailed off as his face paled. He could not so much as look up to meet King Dorian's thunderous gaze, for he felt such shame. He and his accomplice had lost the trail of Prince Lukas.

Fury leapt through Dorian Raynor's eyes as he descended from his dais. "You lost my son?"

"My lord, we do not know that region. Tracking them through Wighthorn was hard enough–"

"Quiet!" roared the king.

His anger was directed more towards himself than at the two men at his feet.

Had Lukas not been vocal about helping the Salvaari? Had he not always gone against the wishes of his king? His father?

Perhaps Dorian should have just killed the Aedei, Cailean, and spared them all much grief.

The king gave a small gesture, little more than the shake of a finger, and the two scouts rose to their feet. The king glared around the hall. Plan after plan had already begun to fill his mind. He needed to act. He needed to decide upon his next move.

"Sir Garrik, General Tristayn, and you, my son" – he nodded to Dayne – "remain. The rest of you, out." The king continued as he turned his gaze to his councillors, "All of you. Out."

Within moments, the room that had been filled with nobles and soldiers was empty, for none would disobey the great Dorian Raynor. Aside for the three men, only Riona remained. Dorian, despite his reputation as a warlord, would never send his queen from his side. The doors boomed shut and then they were alone.

"We need to act," the king said as his most trusted advisors gathered before him, "and we need to act quickly if we wish to save my errant son."

"By now he will have crossed the border and be riding through the Steppe of Miera," said Prince Dayne.

"We must send riders at once." Tristayn spoke up. "Perhaps–"

"Riders?" cut in the master-at-arms and captain of the royal guard, Sir Garrik. "We sent twenty men after them with less than a night's lead and they still lost our prince. Now they are near to a week ahead of us."

"I do not believe that the general was going to suggest sending riders after Lukas, my lord," Queen Riona said as she crossed her arms thoughtfully.

"Aye, my queen," Tristayn replied. "That was not my intent."

"You wish to ride to Carlian and beg an audience with Zoran of Miera."

The Annoran general held back a chuckle. The queen had read his mind.

"It could be our only chance if we wish to avoid war," Tristayn continued.

"Avoid war?" The king spoke, and he crossed his arms. "Because of Prince Lukas' actions, we are unmistakably, if not undeniably, at war. Perhaps not with Miera, but almost certainly with this tribal leader, Henghis. For there is no possible way for us to stop my son from reaching Salvaar."

"And even when our riders cross the border, even if they herald miracle and the Mierans do not engage, King Zoran Layin would rather die than help any bearing the title of Annoran," added Dayne as his brow furrowed. "Though perhaps we should send riders north."

"Medea?" Garrik glanced at his lord. "We stand shoulder to shoulder with Caspin, and as Lady Sofia mentioned, Reyna may yet offer support. However, Bailon and Aloys lands border with the tribes and they are not our allies. It is folly to believe that they will be more inclined to help than the men of Miera."

"I believe it is so that we can manoeuvre the eastern Medeans to a more favourable outcome. I can foresee only one possible path that will lead to getting my brother back," the Prince Dayne replied, and his eyes began to shine as his mind went to work. The mind that had studied the works of countless philosophers and read the journals of the great Vesperan, the general who had forged the empire at the tip of his sword.

"Father, give me leave to ride to House Aloys with a company of mounted knights. Allow me to speak to Duke Alejandro and I swear to you that I will return with my brother."

"Need I remind you that Duke Alejandro Aloys wants your wife and her family dead, my son?"

"So we offer him something that all the houses crave yet only one thus far possesses. A thing that will turn foe to fiercest ally."

"What do you suggest we offer?" Sir Garrik asked.

Dayne merely shrugged and held up his left hand to show his wedding band.

"Marriage. The duke's son, Emilian Aloys, passed his nineteenth summer last season. As of now, he stands unmarried."

"You want to offer the hand of my daughter, your sister, to that of a man who would call you enemy?" Riona's face paled. "Is that wise?"

"Aloys would not dare harm her," Dayne replied. "He knows

what would happen if he did." The prince turned to Dorian and hope etched onto his face. "Father, please, this may be the only way to save Lukas."

The king's lips twitched into a slight smile. It was heartening to see just how much Dayne cared for his brother.

"It is a thing known, is it not, that there is nothing greater than the bond between brothers?" He placed a hand upon the shoulder of his eldest child. "I am inclined to agree with your proposal, my son. However, it shall not be you who rides to Aloys with this offer."

"Father, I–"

"No." Dorian held up a hand to cut off his son.

"If I leave now, I can easily reach Sergova in–"

Dorian's eyes turned cold and his posture stiffened. "I do not speak to you as your father. I speak to you as your king!"

Dayne returned the cold look. He understood his father, yet he had to fight to keep the sliver of annoyance slip into his tone. Control at all times, that was Dayne's code. "Then what does the king decide?"

"Sir Garrik" – the king turned to the knight – "gather a company of three hundred of the guard. Ride to Sergova and make the deal. Tell Alejandro that in two summers, when Princess Kassandra comes of age, she shall wed his son and heir, Emilian. Do whatever it takes to turn them to ally … You must not fail."

"I will not let you down, sire," the master-at-arms' voice boomed.

Dorian dipped his head. "You never have, old friend. Once the deal has been made, remain in Sergova."

"Remain?" the master-at-arms looked incredulous. "Forgive me, my king, but I do not think that the duke would allow a force of three hundred professional soldiers to stay within his walls absent of reason."

"Father, let me go in his stead," Dayne said as he stepped forward, and his eyes locked with the king's.

"No, I need you here."

"My king …"

"For who else will raise my army?"

No one spoke. The king had just undeniably declared war.

"Prince Lukas has flouted the law, flouted the authority of the king and in so doing forced us upon the warpath. That cannot, that will not, be tolerated. In time, he will be dealt with, but now," King Dorian continued as he strode back up his dais and sat back in his throne, "I can hear the beat of war drums. Sir Garrik, you must leave at dawn tomorrow. Tell Duke Alejandro that you remain in his city under my instruction. There you will await reinforcement. Tristayn, send word to Lord Galan of Torosa and Lord Balderik of Laeoflaed. Their king requires them to call their men to arms."

"It will be done, my lord," the general told him.

"And you, my son." The king turned his stern gaze towards Dayne. "You must assemble two thousand of our mounted warriors and follow by week's end. You will ride to the border between the lands of Caspin and Aloys. There you shall wait for word that our proposal has been accepted. Then you ride for Salvaar, and war."

"And what of you?" Dayne said after a moment. "What will you do?"

"The general and I shall remain in Palen-Tor and gather the full might of Aethela. We will join with Laeoflaed and Torosa, and together the men of Annora shall become as one. We will not abandon my son to the east, nor shall we forsake our land or our friends. By the gods, I swear it."

"Why the change of heart, Father?"

"Many years ago, the idea of Annora being united under one banner would have been met with mockery and scorn. When the council of Aethela appointed me as their king, I could see this dream as clear as I see you now. When I was your age, I took Laeoflaed from Balinor." He took his wife's hand. "Torosa joined by choice. I did not inherit this Kingdom of Annora; I won it.

Never in the history of our people has a king successfully passed his kingdom from father to son. I plan to be the first. Not just with the crown of Aethela, but that of Annora."

✦ ✦ ✦

"Miera."

Lukas glanced to his companions as they gazed across the barren plain before them. It was filled with little more than a few shrubs, hills and a crag of gullies.

"And the plains of Carn-Dair. Be on your guard, for there will always be riders watching the horizon."

Cailean nodded and gestured across the plain. "We should head for those crags and use the gullies to shield us."

Thundering hooves churned the sea of earth as the three horses galloped across the open plain. Their manes whipped back in the breeze. Lukas' heart raced as he rode, for they had left the safety of Annora behind and had crossed into Miera. His eyes warily searched the rugged land. Every shadow could hide danger, and every hill could conceal riders that lay in wait to spring their traps. Yet as far as Lukas could see, they were alone. Even still, he was unable to shake the sense of impending doom. With every inch they rode further into Miera, his muscles grew ever tighter. With every hill or gully they passed, a cold shiver ran down his back, colder still than the chill air that lashed Lukas' face.

Sakkar had called Sabra down as to not attract attention from far away threats. Now the hawk circled in the sky just above their heads. They had crossed the border hours before and had seen no sign of pursuit. Lukas began to feel a small ember of hope bloom in his chest. Perhaps they would pass through the realm of the horsemen unnoticed.

At his side, the Larissan rode tall, with one hand wrapped loosely around his reins. Skill in the saddle was taught to the people of the southern desert clans in Larissa from childhood.

To his fore rode the Salvaari. Long, shaggy hair cascaded behind his head as the wind whipped though his dark locks. His eyes were as cold as the expression upon his face, and his hand lingered by the axe at his side.

Now that they were in Miera, the companions had decided to ride until nightfall. They would rest for a few hours, and then set off again with the moon to guide their way. The less time that they spent in this foreign untamed land, the better.

Sabra's shrill cry reached Sakkar's ears. He flicked his eyes towards the hawk even as she soared higher into the sky. His hand grew tight around his bow.

"Lukas!" he bellowed.

The prince turned to his friend and dropped his hand to his hammer. He could hear nothing. He could see nothing save for the small hills and gullies that surrounded them.

Then he heard it.

It started as little more than a whisper kissing his ears. It was little more than a gentle thrumming that echoed through the earth. The sound grew louder and Cailean glanced back at his companions. He could hear it too.

It came from the left. Then the sound grew on their right as well. With each heartbeat, it drew closer. The unmistakable sound of racing hooves.

A piercing whistle and then a flash of white as the first horse galloped into sight. Lukas' heart fell as the icy embrace of fear sank its claws in. He swung his shield from his back and snatched out his warhammer. More riders materialised from the hills. They came from both sides. They poured from the gullies like ants.

Miera had come.

Another whistle cut through the sound of thundering hooves. Lukas glanced to his right as a rider angled towards him in an effort to push him closer to Sakkar.

"YAH!" Lukas bellowed, and he kicked his heels in.

His mount accelerated and, with a sharp tug of the reins, barrelled in front of the rider. Yet the rider was Mieran. A lord of the horse. He swung to the left and with a cry cut between Lukas and Sakkar. The Annoran prince spun in his saddle and swung his warhammer. The air sang as the steel tip angled down and smashed into the Mieran's shield. Steel rang to his side as another rider engaged Sakkar. They closed the distance and drew Sakkar into combat before he could put his bow to use. Now the Larissan moved, and his wicked khopesh flashed. The Mieran at his side snarled. He was close enough for Lukas to see the darkness in his eyes, the hatred that was held within. Lukas acted, and his hammer struck out in one fluid movement. His opponent skilfully countered and deflected the prince's weapon to the side. Lukas swung his shield around and caught the counter. The Mieran feinted and then attacked again. He slid inside Lukas' defence and the edge of his blade sliced the prince's exposed cheek. Only a well-timed duck had saved the Lukas' life. With a flick of his wrist, the Mieran angled his faster mount in front of the prince's. A calculated move.

No ...

Lukas felt sheer horror as his horse panicked and veered to the right and drove him away from his allies. More riders closed in. Most of them headed for Cailean and Sakkar. Two shot after Lukas.

His horse was laden down with saddlebags and the Mierans gained ground rapidly on horse and rider. Lukas shot a glance over his shoulder. A plan had begun to take shape. He had one chance.

It was a foolhardy idea.

The first rider was no more than ten paces away. It was the black-haired man who had so artfully separated him from his companions. The other, no more than five horse lengths behind the first rider, rode a white-skinned mount and had a trail of golden hair streaming behind them. The prince eased back on the reins, and his horse began to slow ever so slightly. Lukas took a deep breath. This might be the death of him, yet he had to try. He risked another look behind. The first rider was now five paces and closing.

Three … Two …

Lukas cried out and wrenched back on his reins. He drove the full force of his weight into the stirrups. His horse bellowed and obeyed. The horse pulled up dead in its tracks. Lukas swung his hammer to the side. Steel struck steel, and then the Mieran flew past with a scream. Lukas flicked his wrist to turn his horse.

There was a crash and then the world blurred. Lukas flew through the air as his mount crashed to the ground with a shrill scream. Instead of stopping or angling away as expected, the blonde-haired rider had rammed his horse.

A wave of pain hit Lukas as he hit the hard earth and rolled to the side. He barely avoided his falling mount. His head boomed as his ears were assaulted by the sound of ringing. Lukas struggled to his feet. He coughed as he spat dirt from his mouth. His horse rose and staggered to the side.

He'd been lucky. If the stallion had landed on top of him, then he would be dead. Adrenaline filled his veins, and he snarled. He forced the pain that sought to cripple him. His arm burned. Lukas glanced about. His hammer lay to the side as did his shield. He drew out his sword without a second thought. The familiar weight of steel comforted him.

The first rider was cantering back now. Blood ran through his clenched fist as he clutched at his side.

"He's mine," the other Mieran spoke up.

Lukas nearly gasped as he turned to the second rider who dismounted barely twenty feet away.

The other rider was a girl.

Kitara's boots met the earth with a light thud.

She had almost been caught by surprise when the rider had abruptly pulled up. Almost. Her companion, Darian, had been too close to react in time, but she had not. Now the man had managed to rise to his feet, and he stood facing her. He clutched at his sword with his mouth agape.

It was the same way that they all looked at her.

She glared at the man as she stalked towards him, and her lips curled into a sneer.

Kitara stopped barely fifteen paces from him and slowly raised her sword into a ready position. Take them alive had been Silas' order. He needed to know why these men had crossed into Carn-Dair.

Ten paces.

She highly intended on sparing the man, yet it would be on her own terms.

"Lower your sword," she commanded.

His vicious glare met with hers. His ocean-blue gaze locked with her emerald stare.

"No." His voice oozed with authority.

Despite the mud on his clothes and despite his bloody and bruised face, he carried himself with noble purpose.

Her heart barely seemed to beat as the man's blade rose. Everything was calm and her breathing slowed.

He moved. His blade darted towards her neck. He meant to meet her style with strength. It was the downfall of all who had never properly witnessed tarkaras. It was natural for her to shift her position. Her posture turned as the blow came, and her foot slid back as she angled her blade. She effortlessly deflected the warrior's stroke. Kitara flicked her wrists as her movement flowed. Her sword intercepted the incoming strike. It was a heavy blow, but her sword was her arm, and she could not drop her arm. Perhaps she could have ended the fight there, yet her purpose was not to kill.

Kitara danced backwards as the third move came. His blade sliced towards her stomach as she moved. It missed by a hair's-breadth. Her footing did not miss a step and her form was perfect. Her feet moved again. She glided atop the ground as she countered with her sword. The man hastily retreated a step and caught the first of her strikes with his own blade. As steel struck steel, Kitara stepped off her line and slid around his blade, around his strength. Kitara used his power to spin her blade as she released the hilt with her left hand. In a swift movement, she used it to push the warrior's arms down. Her sword was through his defence and slicing towards his throat. With a slight change of angle, the hilt of her blade crunched into his jaw. Blood exploded from the man's lips as he staggered back a step. The grunt of pain turned into a snarl as he wildly swung his sword to create distance. His eyes grew wild with surprise at the underhand move. She gave him no time to think, no time to breathe before she drove forward.

Fire danced in Kitara's gaze as she attacked. Her sword was no more than a blur. The warrior intercepted the blade with his own. Kitara moved into a second stroke. She pushed him off balance as he attempted to knock her blow aside with a hastily thrown parry. Steel collided twice more as her opponent fought for advantage. His sword sliced through the air. Kitara met his blade with her own before she flowed into a third move. Her wrists turned as she danced forwards. She sent his weapon to the side as she kicked his feet out from under him.

He crashed to the ground, and his sword flew from his grasp.

The man groaned as he turned to face her. He bared his teeth. His expression was a mix of pain and humiliation. Kitara held her form for a moment as she relished the move that had sent the man to his knees.

She shifted, and her emerald gaze watched curiously as he reached for his sword.

He wasn't giving up.

Lukas felt the rough leather of his sword's hilt rub against his fingers. Then it was gone. The sword was snatched from his grasp by the warrior, the girl, who had beaten him. He pushed himself to his knees with a groan. His battered face was coated in mud and a thin trail of blood from where the first rider had hit him. His body ached in a thousand places. Each move he made brought on new agony. He turned his glare up at the golden-haired woman and squared his shoulders. He was a prince of Annora, and he would die as one. In her right hand she held her sword at his throat, while her left was clasped about the eagle-hilted sword. A man appeared beside the woman. Blood ran from a wound across his side.

Lukas sneered through red lips. At least he had bloodied one of them.

His ears pricked at the sound of hooves thudding. A contingent of Mierans appeared from the way he had ridden. All of them were mounted, and all had weapons clasped tightly in their eager hands. At their fore rode a man who appeared little more than Lukas' own age. His pale eyes glinted dangerously and were as cold as a winter's night. His hair was dark, and a line of golden rings adorned his ear. Lukas knew him to be the leader.

His eyes flickered shut. They had failed.

Sakkar and Cailean walked beside the Mieran. Their hands were bound to the lead rider's saddle by a pair of long ropes, and they had been deprived of their weapons.

The Mierans wanted them alive.

The golden-haired girl didn't take her gaze from Lukas as she spoke. "Silas."

He looked down at the prince thoughtfully. "Bind him."

TWENTY-ONE

Isle of Agartha, the Valkir Isles

Erik barely grimaced as the ink-tipped steel needle was hammered into the exposed flesh of his back. The artisan who stood behind him, Rusikora Bannik, worked his hammer and needle with the steady hands of one who had used them for near three decades. The craftsman was renowned throughout the Isles for his legendary skill. There were few who could afford the privilege of his work.

Again and again the razor-sharp point bit in to his skin. Each strike drew ever closer to Erik's right shoulder, ever closer to the dark, swirling patchwork of tattoos that rolled down his shoulder to the back of his hand. A great serpent wrapped around his upper arm.

The tattoos were a tradition among the Valkir, yet only the bloodsworn bore the mark of the snake. From there the tradition was added to with each successful raid.

The tattoo grew larger for each kill. As did its bearer's fame.

The warrior sat on a small wooden stool. He was clad in his pants and hard leather boots. He leaned atop the bench and rested his tunic and axe well within arm's reach. It was habit. One could never be too careful. Especially after what had taken place in the small hours.

It had been a long night and the stench of burnt ships still filled the city like a dark cloud. Some of the vessels had been completely destroyed. Some were barely afloat. Even those barely touched by the flames would not be seaworthy for at least a couple of days. Erik couldn't help but let his eyes drift to his weapon. Its blade was freshly cleaned of blood.

The blood of Astrid. The blood of his sister. Many had fallen that night.

Erik gazed out across the bay. Bannik preferred the gentle ocean breeze upon his face as he worked to the thick air of a craftsman's lodge. The Wind Rider had sailed east from the bay and headed towards the heart of the Isles. It was out of Magnus' reach.

The thudding of iron-shod boots made Erik's ears twitch. He glanced towards the sound as three men strode onto the walkway atop which the artist worked.

"Earl." The bloodsworn dipped his head slowly as Magnus and his pair of guards made their way towards him.

"Earl," echoed the artist.

"Rusikora Bannik." Magnus nodded to the man out of respect for his craft. "If you would give us a moment."

"Of course," replied the older man, and he gently dabbed a clean cloth on Erik's back to remove any excess ink that had not set into flesh.

Erik turned around to watch as Bannik sauntered off into the market with a merry whistle on his lips.

"Many of my men wish to see your head parted from your shoulders," Magnus told him.

The earl's eyes bore into the man before him. His weathered hand dropped to the sword at his hip as he looked down at Erik.

"Perhaps I should grant their request and end your life here in this very moment," he continued.

"Perhaps you should," Erik said simply as he glanced up at the two men at Magnus' back.

Both bore the serpent of the bloodsworn. The earl was taking no chances. Both men stood with hands wrapped about their weapons. Erik knew them both by name. Yet was it possible that either of them wished him dead? It was not unlikely. He was of the Farrin line, and they were sworn to the earl.

"These last few days have cost me a great deal. That little trick of your sister's. Five of my ships lie at the bottom of the bay, and the rest are in need of repair. Two dozen of my warriors have been sent to the halls of the Sea-Father." He met Erik's eyes as he spoke, but his own betrayed nothing. "Among them, the bloodsworn, Sindric Einar, and my cousin, Sven. Two of my finest swords. Dead."

Erik had heard of Einar's death during the attack. He had been told it was a great contest between Einar's youth and Torben's experience. The old man had sent the rage-fuelled warrior to the afterlife.

"How many?" Magnus inquired, and he ran his cold eyes across the patchwork of tattoos that covered the bloodsworn's back and arm.

Erik merely shrugged. "I lost count after sixty."

"Sixty lives taken, sixty marks upon flesh." The earl looked across the bay "Tell me, what am I to do with you?"

"Earl?"

"You slaughtered my cousin, my own blood."

"He killed my father."

"And you wanted revenge, as any son would." Magnus did not turn his gaze from the horizon as he spoke.

His voice was calm and measured. His body was relaxed yet wary. He was a wolf stalking his prey. His face betrayed nothing as he spoke.

"Sven was a fool. My cousin, alas, but a fool. Family is a strange thing, is it not? You fight and bicker amongst each other … sometimes even to blood. Yet there is an almost unconditional devotion to your kin." He paused a moment and spared Erik a glance. "Therein lies my problem. You see, you pose something of a riddle, Erik Farrin, and though I greatly admire your skills as a warrior, I cannot help but question your purpose here."

"My lord." Erik met the man's steely gaze. "What question do you seek answered?"

"You were known as a loyal man. That much is obvious. Yet you knowingly turned on your sister and your crew. Why? By what means would you willingly give up your place in Ra'Haven by betraying your oath to your kin?"

Erik slowly nodded. It was a fair question.

"All my life, I have been living in the shadows of others. First my father, whose accomplishments will be sung about as long as men have tongues to sing. And then" – he snorted – "then my sister cast her own. I am bloodsworn." Erik tapped the serpent tattoo twice. "Yet my deeds went unnoticed. Shrouded by those of my 'betters'. I wished to leave the darkness and see the sun hot upon my face. In time, everything falls and fades, yet legacy lives on. Now, perhaps, I can forge my own path."

"How can I trust a man loyal only to himself?"

Erik was silent for a moment. Perhaps there was a way to prove himself in the earl's eyes. He reached out a hand and drew his knife from his belt. Steel rasped as Magnus' guards drew their weapons and stepped towards Lief's son. Erik flipped the dagger and caught it by the blade. Its hilt was extended towards the earl.

"If you wish it, take my life. Get it over with. Yet, if the Sea-Father wills it, perhaps I can earn your confidence."

Magnus took the knife, and a cold fire emerged in his eyes. "Tell me and tell me true. Must I fear your sister's blade?"

"In truth" – Erik shook his head – "she is no great warrior. I could finish her within three moves."

"What of the man who killed Sindric? That bloodsworn, Torben?"

"You would do well to respect him," Erik replied. "He may be old, yet he is one of the finest warriors that Agartha has ever seen. Though among that crew only he bears the mark of the serpent."

He could see Magnus' mind at work as he listened. That is what had won Magnus his throne.

"You were there when they escaped aboard the Wind Rider. How many follow Astrid? How many warriors?"

Erik thought back to the night and remembered the sight of those he had once knew scuttling aboard the ship.

"No more than thirty warriors remain, my lord. Though all are blooded in battle and the recent raid has made them sharp. Perhaps equal the number of women, children and old folk."

Magnus turned back to the waters of the Lupentine.

"I have near a thousand seasoned men at my command," he said. "In a matter of days, the first ships will be seaworthy enough to again sail the isles and pursue that band of traitors. They cannot run forever."

With that, the earl turned his back and made to leave. He had what he came for. Another great warrior added to his ranks, and knowledge of the crew that he faced.

"Lord?" Magnus looked over his shoulder in reply as Erik spoke. "That man you captured, has he spoken yet?"

He meant Laerke. The man whom Erik had known for years. The one he had pulled from the waters during the night.

"He will."

The crew were near silent as the Wind Rider surged through the Lupentine. All canvas was dropped, and the ship sped forwards under the full strength of the winds.

Astrid stood beside Fargrim as he helmed the ship. Her hands were tight on the railing beside the massive wheel used to steer the Wind Rider. Her gaze barely shifted from the horizon ahead. She did not turn as they sailed by the islands and sandbanks that made up the Valkir Isles.

By now they had put the better part of a night and a day between them and any pursuit. Astrid doubted there would be any attempt to follow them for two days at least. Like the rest of her crew, her clothes and face were covered in dried blood. Her wounded arm had started to colour during the night as purple bruises started to arise in her skin. Astrid had merely ripped a length of cloth from her shirt and tightly bound her arm. Astrid could still taste the ash from the great blaze she had started, ash that still painted her face black. The thought of burning ships did little to ease her mind or grant even a whiff of satisfaction. Many had been lost during the night. Many she had known since she was but a young girl. Raol had been as a second brother to her.

"Jarl." Torben's booming voice cut through her thoughts.

Astrid inwardly cursed. She was so caught up in her mind that she had not even heard the man approach.

"What is it?" she replied.

His face was just as covered in ash as hers. "We have little food and water in the hold," he said.

"I know … God, we should have sailed as soon as Sven fell," Astrid cursed. "I should have foreseen this. I knew there would be repercussions, just not so soon."

"No one could have seen this coming," Torben told her with a shrug. "The earl moved fast to reassert his control. But worrying about the past does not help the present, nor does it keep us alive." He gazed out across the waves. "Nowhere is safe now. It will only be a matter of time before we are pursued by one who knows where we would seek sanctuary."

Astrid shot a dark glance at her companion. "We do not speak of Erik," she growled. "He made his choice, and we shall deal with him when the time is right. Until then, we do not so much as speak his name."

"Alright." The old warrior nodded slowly. He was silent for a moment before, "How is your arm?"

"I will live, I promise you," she replied.

In truth it hurt, and it hurt badly. The axe blade had cut her flesh and muscle almost to the bone. She would seal the wound with fire when she got the chance. Until then, she would weather such blows as she always did.

"Where do we sail?"

Astrid's lips twitched slightly. "Two hundred years ago, the shieldmaiden Freydis Bluksvier sailed out from these Isles with Iren Brightblade. The very first to ever achieve such a feat and reach the mainland."

"Everyone knows the tale of the Queen of the Shield."

"Yes." She nodded. "When the crew was set upon by a company of mainlanders and Iren fell to their blades … she took up his sword. Outnumbered and surrounded, she led a desperate charge towards her enemies." Astrid's eyes glowed, for Freydis was something of a hero to her. "They say she fought as if all the demons in Skûra guided her hand," she continued. "They say that when she led her warriors into combat, the Sea-Father wept for the souls of those slain by her hand. She left these isles no more than a warrior and returned a queen upon a throne of blood. As the years went by, her fame grew ever greater. Tales of her exploits travelled far."

Torben snorted. "Each more outlandish than the last. They say she slew a great serpent."

"And after all we have seen and heard, you don't believe these stories?" Astrid countered. "Though among the tales and sagas of the queen there is but one story that repeats itself in my mind. One that, if I am right, may just be our saviour."

"What can a two-hundred-year-old legend have to offer us?"

"Before her death, Freydis spent years travelling across the Lupentine, exploring every crack and crevice within the Isles," Astrid told him. "There is a river that runs through the Isle of Vay'kis. It meets the sea like a gentle kiss and travels far inland. The queen ordered her crew to sail into the river. The crew said the hull was too deep. The ship was sure to get beached. Yet still she persisted, and at last the crew agreed. With the wind behind them, they sailed into the river's maw. For miles and miles, they travelled, each more miraculous than the last. For the riverbed was deep. Soaring mountains rose and fell to each side. Great canyons nearly blocked out the sun. As the tides turned and the ocean receded, the mouth of the river became impassable to all who wished to travel its currents. It was left hidden to the outside world. That's when they found it: a lake large enough to keep a ship afloat sat at the river's end. Around it was a deep forest filled with plentiful game and shelter from the wind and rain. The great queen wept at the sight, for such beauty was unparalleled. They had found a haven safe from the outside world. The lake became known as the Tears of Freydis."

"That story is naught but the shadow of a legend." Torben chuckled. "Many have tried to sail that river and have floundered on its bed. Our kinsmen who settled the coast found the mountains an impassable labyrinth, and the river currents too strong for simple boats."

"I believe it exists," Astrid said, barely hearing her companion speak. "In the tale, Freydis made the crossing at midday and all those seeking to discover her tears in the years since attempted the same. Yet the tides grow with the moon and fail at dawn's first light."

Astrid met Torben's gaze once more, and at last he understood. Perhaps the path would be open when the tides rose.

"We can reach the river mouth in a few hours when night falls, and so it shall be our heading." Astrid continued on with no more than a sidewards glance to the helm. "Fargrim, take us north-west. We sail to Vay'kis."

Night had fallen when the first sign they were drawing near came. A voice shouted from the lookout atop the crow's-nest. Soon after, the soaring mountains of Vay'kis came into sight. They were little more than darkened peaks revealed by the dim light of the moon.

"Keep us below the horizon until we reach the shore. From there, we hug the coast and sail west until we reach the river," Astrid said to Fargrim. "Let us pray our presence goes unnoticed."

The helmsman nodded and adjusted course. She sent the Wind Rider tracking north-east away from the thin trails of smoke that had appeared to the west.

"Is it wise not sailing into the harbour? You have heard the stories about Earl Arndyr."

Astrid glanced at her companion. "I know that he and his crew served Darius of Aureia for many years in the emperor's private guard, the Arkin Garter. For that feat alone, I know that he is a man of honour. Before we meet with the man, I would like to establish a camp and deliver my people into some kind of safety."

The nearest settlement that Astrid knew of was the trading city of Lumis. It was a successful town that had grown much in stature soon after the infamous Earl Arndyr Scaeva rose to power four summers before. He had fought alongside Magnus of Agartha many times, yet his skill as a warrior and reckless nature had seen him travel to the heart of the Aureian Empire. There, he and his crew won great renown, and for near ten years they served in the highest office a warrior could dream of. The Arkin Garter. An elite company of Valkir chosen to protect the emperor himself. Many Valkir despised the idea of the Arkin Garter. The idea of serving a man not of their kin was not welcomed by everyone. Many Valkir even led raids into the empire. Though there were those who emperor Darius traded with, and those he hired as paid killers. Some were even paid to prevent raids and stop those who would do the empire harm. It worked for Darius, and his father before him, though it often caused issues among the Valkir clans. Issues that often escalated to the point of bloodshed.

Hours passed as the Wind Rider drifted through the currents

under Fargrim's steady hand. Astrid almost allowed a sigh of relief when the ship rounded a split of land and came to a head with the mouth of the river.

There it was. It was barely four ship lengths way. All else was forgotten. Her weariness from the last two days vanished. The ache in her arm was forgotten as a newfound excitement gripped her.

"Sea-Father, please let me be right ... The passage is only open when the moon reaches its peak," Astrid murmured as her eyes darted up into the night sky. "When the tides return and join the river. By day, the passage is blocked by the low tide."

Torben merely grunted. He was sceptical, and that was the very thing that had kept him alive all these years.

"Keep us steady," the jarl said as she glanced at Fargrim, who replied with a nod. "Two notches to port."

The helmsman turned the wheel slightly and the ship eased to the left. They drifted away from the coast and the large rocks that Astrid had noticed spearing out of the water. Her dark eyes lingered on the rippling waters as she searched for rocks, reefs and other dangers that could hole or scuttle the Wind Rider.

Two ship lengths.

"Five notches starboard."

The ship began to turn.

One ship length.

"Hard to starboard!" Astrid called, and her voice filled with intensity.

This was it. Fargrim pulled hard at the wheel. The turn had to be perfect or they would smash against the land.

Astrid's heart raced. Fear gripped her.

The Wind Rider eased into the river.

TWENTY-TWO

Kilgareth, Valley of Odrysia

"Your return is sooner than expected, brother," Sir Matias said with a smile as he extended his arm to Sir Corvo Alaine, the Sword of Kil'kara.

Corvo took Matias' arm and gripped it tight.

"The Twins saw fit to guide my hand and speed my return," he said. "Much has happened since you rode out," Matias replied as he gestured to the seats. "Come, Amaris shall explain."

One by one, the leaders of the Order assembled and made their way to their seats.

"Members of the Circle," Grand Master Amaris began, and he reached up to clasp his amulet as he gazed around the room. "Today we give thanks to Durandail, Father of all Fathers, and Azaria, the Silver Lady, for the safe return of Sir Corvo and that of our brothers who rode with him." He bowed his head and closed his dark eyes as he continued, "By the grace of the gods."

"By the grace of the gods," the council echoed.

"Be seated," the grand master said.

Amaris turned to the Sword of Kil'kara as they all took their chairs. "Sir Corvo, if you would give your report," Amaris said.

All eyes turned to the warrior as he began his tale.

"Two days after setting out from these walls, we received a blessing for the heavens and were fortunate enough to capture an outrider. He was sent by the bandits to scout the highroad. It was not long before he talked and led us right into the very jaws of the beast. We rode in hard and caught the vagabonds off guard. We charged among them like a wolf among sheep. Most fell to our blades while those few who lived scattered like frightened rabbits. We burnt the bodies and destroyed their camp. The rogues are gone," Corvo said, and his powerful voice was triumphant. "No longer shall they plague our land."

"That is glorious news, brother." Sir Alarik spoke up. The old warrior leaned forwards in his seat. "Though tell me, what of the survivors?"

The Sword shrugged. "Sir Neph and twenty of our finest pursue them as we speak. It is over."

"Then the gods truly were with you." Lysandra smiled.

Corvo inclined his head to the arc'maija.

"For many months we have endured their raids and were never able to find their camp let alone drive them from our lands," Alarik stated. "Yet they are gone in only a matter of days? I cannot believe it."

"And yet it is so," Lysandra replied. "Perhaps their leader was slain by Sir Matias and his men when Sir Torin arrived and without him they fractured. We do not know. All we know is that they are gone."

"You have done well, my friend," Amaris told Corvo.

It had taken far too long, but finally the raiders and bandits had been dealt a mortal blow.

"Now we must look to this message from Rovira. Lady Lysandra, if you will," the grand master said, as he gestured to the lady.

"Of course," the woman replied. "In the crypt of the grand masters, we uncovered the first clue sent to us by Evalio Delrovira. Within the sword of Duran Cormac, we found this."

She reached into her wide sleeve and withdrew the small piece of parchment.

"It reads: following the light of the sun, where the young were raised by frail, carved stone draws breath beneath the Maiden's Veil."

The room seemed to inwardly sigh as she spoke.

"Thus, the riddle continues," mumbled Sir Alarik with a grimace.

"And so, it does," agreed Sir Corvo. "Though its meaning begins to take form. For does the sun not rise in the east and set in the west? Following its light can mean only one thing. We must follow its path across the sky. We must travel west."

"I agree," Matias added. "Though where the young are raised by frail … of that I have no clue."

"I sense a story unfolding through the tale," Lysandra muttered, and she bit her lip as her mind went to work.

This puzzle had been on her mind for days.

"The first clue spoke of Duran, of his journey north to this very city," Lysandra continued. "May not the second also speak of the man himself? For was he not born and raised in Medea to the west?"

Amaris slowly nodded as he replied, "That he was … In fact, my ancestor spent his childhood little over a week's ride from this very fortress. Though the town was little more than a small village in his time, it still bears the name Adrestia. When his parents fell to pagan ideals and the Old Religion, it was his grandparents who took him in, before they too suffered the same fate."

"And so, the first verse reveals itself," Alarik said as his hand clamped down tight on the arm of his seat. "We must ride to Adrestia and find the end of this tale."

Lysandra glanced at the battlemaster. "Patience, brother. None of us here is from those highlands, and would it not be unwise to charge head on into territory that we do not know, absent an idea what we are searching for? I do not know of this Maiden's Veil."

"What do you suggest?"

"There is one within my sect who hails from that region. A

young woman who came to us years ago seeking sanctuary and is now one of the most skilled maija I have had the privilege to train."

"A maija … and a warrior." Alarik rubbed his chin thoughtfully. "Another lad, a recruit freshly initiated into our Order, comes from the same."

"I met the boy," Sir Matias said. "He shows potential."

"Yet lacks discipline," the battlemaster offered.

"Very well then." The grand master nodded as his eyes flicked to Lysandra. "My lady, do you trust this woman?"

"With my life."

"Then speak with her … yet reveal nothing of our plans."

"It will be done."

After a moment, Sir Corvo broke the silence. "Grand Master, if I may?"

Amaris waved a hand. "What is it?"

"This riddle which we pursue must be of great importance for it to be so well hidden. Indeed, even Evalio and his forebears believed it unnecessary for nigh on a century," the Sword said. "It comes to me that we may be on the hunt for something of great value. Perhaps it could be–"

"Another artefact," Lysandra breathed, and her eyes widened. "We have not heard more than a rumour of one the gods' devices in years."

"And that in turn raises another question," Sir Matias added.

A chill seemed to enter the chamber. They all hid their expressions well. The betrayal had been keenly felt, especially by Corvo, for they had been betrayed by one who was beloved by all in the chamber, and so they had been forced to send him to the gods.

"What if Wa'rith resurfaces? In the last eight years, this so-called shadow has followed every rumour of an artefact and taken the lives of every knight sent to trace them," Matias continued.

"That is why I shall follow this trail west," snarled Sir Corvo.

"That murderer shall not take the life of another knight while I still breathe. The shadow shall fall to my blade."

Amaris gazed around the room. Each person present was family to him. Each of them had been by his side for years, yet only now would he speak his mind.

"We speak of many possibilities, my friends. Perhaps Wa'rith will strike once more. Perhaps we do seek an artefact of the gods'. Yet what of this? If it is one of those mighty instruments ... would not the cardinal demand a crusade against the pagans? Perhaps an attempt to finish what was started by Duran."

"You mean invade Salvaar?" Lysandra looked to him sharply.

Amaris nodded. "With such power at our command and the blessing of the cardinal, the armies of our faith would once again assemble."

"Good," Sir Alarik growled, and his eyes blazed like wildfire. "We should strike those beasts from this land. They do naught but pillage and burn in the name of their dark spirits."

"I concur," Matias agreed. "Each year they cross the border into Medea and kill good people, godly people."

"If the cardinal commands my sword, I shall give it gladly," Sir Corvo added. "For are those people not the enemy of our gods? Would they not, if they had the chance, do the very same to us?"

Amaris sighed as his companions spoke. Somehow, he had known they would answer as such.

"What if there was another way to live with them? Perhaps even peace upon a day."

"Peace?" Alarik was incredulous. "Peace with those pagans is a fantasy. To think any different–"

"To think any different is what? Sacrilege?" Amaris interrupted.

He met the steely eyes of his friend with his own. Sir Alarik was his oldest living friend and his brother in all things, yet, gods, could he be stubborn.

"The Salvaari raid along the Medean frontier because the

Medeans do the same. Things can change," Amaris finished.

"Do you forget what those people nearly did to this land? What your ancestor prevented? First it was those savages, the ruskalan who sunk their claws into Medea. Those pointy-eared brigands had more in common with snakes than man. Poisonous words and mouths filled with fangs. When Duran Cormac purged them into extinction alongside the elves, it was their human allies who tried to intervene. Allies who would become Salvaari. Salvaari who burnt Medean towns and villages to the ground. Have you forgotten?"

"Unfortunately, Sir Alarik, I never forget."

Amaris closed his eyes for a moment. He would win his friend around one day, but at least for now he had spoken.

"We can speak of this later, yet for now we all have work to do."

The grand master rose to his feet. His hand was itching to swing his sword and relive him of tension. Perhaps he would spar with Corvo later.

"We shall gather again in three days' time. By then, Lady Lysandra will have gathered the information that we seek. Light of the gods be with us all."

All who were gathered could see the darkening look on the grand master's face. It would take a fool to speak up now and challenge him. The council was indeed over.

Kyler was at a loss as he gazed at the massive library. His mouth had nearly dropped open in shock when he had entered. Thousands of volumes adorned the shelves of dozens of bookcases that were spread around the huge room. The initiate let out a sigh as he began to stride through the maze of knowledge.

Gods, did it never end?

Dozens, if not hundreds, of maija flitted about through the aisles with books and scrolls clutched tightly in their hands. Kyler was surprised to see that there were more than a few knights within the walls of the library. The sight of heavily armoured warriors sifting through shelves of books amused him. He could see little reason that soldiers should need to know how to read. Then again, his own father, a lowly tavern keeper, had been a learned man. He had seen fit to give Kyler something of an education.

"May I be of some assistance?"

The boy turned to see a wizened old maija standing behind him. The wrinkles that adorned his face complemented the large, greying, black beard and mane-like hair. His kind eyes seemed to show a deep intelligence.

Kyler smiled. He could barely keep the sigh of relief inside. He would have been wandering the maze of bookshelves for days, and probably still would not have found what he was looking for.

"I would be most grateful," he told the maija with a slight nod. "I don't suppose that you could direct me to the works of Herodys of Delios?"

"But of course." The man chuckled. "Follow me if you will."

With that, he turned and started to walk through the maze with Kyler hot on his heels.

"My name is Rene Aristo," the maija explained as they walked. "I help oversee things here in the library. And let me guess ... Two decades old, Medean heritage and the garb of an initiate ... You must be Kyler Landrey."

Disbelief hit Kyler for a moment. He had not set so much as a foot towards the quarters of the maija. Yet this man, Rene, had guessed who he was.

Wait ...

It hit him like a hammer and his lips curled as he replied sarcastically, "Did the bruise give it away?"

The blow struck by Hugh was yet to fully fade.

Rene grunted, "Sir Alarik did mention that you had a sharp tongue."

There was no malice in his words that Kyler could make out. It was merely an observation.

"I won't deny it."

They rounded a corner, and Rene came to a halt in an aisle of shelves covered in books and tomes small and large.

"Here we are," the old man said. He slowly ran a finger along the spines of the books and squinted closely at the titles. Some of the words were in the common tongue, yet many were little more than alien runes and symbols to Kyler's eye. They were clearly Delion. Rene's hand came to a rest against a book that sported no common words. The maija pulled it from the shelf. His fingers clutched at the brown, leather book and gazed over its gold leaf writing.

"An Odyssey of Delios," Rene read aloud. "Written by Herodys centuries ago. Though this is no more than a humble copy." He held out the massive book to Kyler.

"You speak the language?" the Medean asked.

"Only a few words," Aristo told him with a sparkle in his eye.

The boy took it and flicked the cover open. He slowly turned the pages, and each and every one made his heart sink further.

How was he supposed to learn an entire new language? It could take months if not an entire year …

"I did not know there were so many words in any language." Kyler grimaced.

"Then this particular text may be of help with your endeavour." Rene grinned and held out yet another book.

The Medean took it and breathed a sigh of relief. This one was titled in the common tongue.

"*A Study of Delion* by Arc'maija Khemar Osborn," Kyler murmured.

Rene Aristo nodded. "Khemar was one of the finest scholars that our Order has ever seen, one with an affinity for languages. In it you will find every known word and phrase in Delion and its translation into the common tongue."

"Thank you," Kyler told the man sincerely.

The librarian smiled. "Though I may offer you some advice." He placed a hand on the boy's shoulder and met his eyes. "A blind man could see that you have pride, lad. It is good to have pride, yet do not forget that it is pride that turns angels into devils."

Before the boy could reply, Aristo turned his back and vanished into the maze of bookshelves.

Angels into devils?

Kyler knew his meaning, but even so, if the maija wanted to quote arrogance, he should speak to Hugh Karter. The thought made Kyler smile as he tucked the second book under his arm and made his way from the aisle. He crashed straight into the path of a dark-haired woman and nearly knocked her into one of the nearby shelves. He had been so lost in thought he had not bothered to see if anyone was walking down the path.

"Watch where you're going," came the woman's annoyed yelp as she turned to him.

"Sorry ..."

His eyes widened and he froze. The same expression was mirrored on her face. A face that he knew well. Despite the fact he had not seen her in years, he could remember every small detail, from the freckles that lined her cheeks to the dimples the sat beneath them.

"Kyler," she breathed, and her hazel eyes showed nothing but disbelief.

"Elena ... What are you doing here?" Kyler stammered. "You're maija?"

"That I am." Elena nodded, and her lips broke into a smile.

"It has been two years ... two years since you left Adrestia," the boy managed.

Two long years. He had missed her greatly for much of that time. That was until he had turned those memories from his mind. Yet now here she was.

"Aye, here I am," she replied, and she indicated down the aisle for Kyler to walk with her.

Elena gave him a sidewards glance as they walked. "Much has changed since our days in the tavern," she said.

"Not all is different," Kyler told her. "Yet in some ways everything is."

"Trust me, I understand that better than you know."

She turned to face him as they strode into a more open space filled with half a dozen tables. Maija sat at some of the tables with their eyes glued to various scrolls and texts.

"Now, tell me," Elena continued, and her brow furrowed slightly as she eyed the books in Kyler's hands. "What brings you to the library?"

Kyler placed the books on an unoccupied table with a grunt. "Sir Alarik has given us all tasks to complete if we wish to be sworn into the Order as knights. Mine is to–"

"Translate the works of Herodys," Elena finished as she picked up the book and flicked through its pages with shining eyes.

She had always loved learning new things and uncovering the knowledge of others. Her amber gaze scanned the pages as if she was reading the foreign language.

"Though why is beyond me," Kyler added with a snort.

"I am sure you will understand when the time is right," the maija told him with a grin. "I have not known the man to be wrong."

"Well, whatever the cause, I must learn a near extinct tongue," Kyler replied with a shrug.

"Perhaps I can help with that," she told him, and she looked up from the book for the first time. "In my time in the Citadel, I have learnt four languages, and as it happens, all maija are learned in Delion."

For the first time, Kyler's heart soared. Perhaps this trial would not be so bad after all. If all maija learnt the tongue, then that meant that the old man, Rene Aristo, knew more than a few words.

Of course he did.

"I don't suppose that you would be able to help?"

"With your endeavour? Of course," Elena said. "Though I shall not complete it for you. For finding knowledge is its own reward, don't you think?"

"I suppose ..." he said as he looked at her gratefully. "Thank you."

Elena's lips twitched skyward as humour danced across her eyes. "Well, you never were much good at study," she told him.

Kyler chortled and made to reply.

"Elena," a voice called from behind.

The pair turned to see Lady Lysandra making her way towards them. Her voice was as elegant as the woman it belonged to.

"Arc'maija." Elena dipped her head to the leader of her sect.

Kyler followed suit and bowed in the presence of rank as he had been taught by Sir Alarik.

"And who is this?" the lead maija said sweetly as she gestured to Kyler.

"Kyler Landrey, my lady," the boy told her.

He knew that, just like Rene Aristo, Lysandra was most likely aware of his name thanks to his run in with Karter. Yet she asked his name out of courtesy anyway.

"We grew up together," Elena explained to her mentor. "Though until today we had not seen each other in years."

"And now you are reunited. The gods must have fated it to be so." Lysandra smiled. "In that case, I am most sorry, but I require a word with Elena."

"Of course," the younger woman replied before turning to Kyler. "Meet me at the western tower tonight. I have so much to tell you."

"I will be there," he replied sincerely.

Elena followed her mentor with a backward glance.

Kyler could barely stop the grin from lighting up his face as he turned back to his books. His hand went instinctively to the pendant at his throat. Lysandra was right. The gods had fated their paths to cross again.

✦ ✦ ✦

"You grew up in Adrestia, did you not?" Lysandra asked as the pair of women walked down an empty corridor.

"Some of my childhood was spent there," Elena told her mentor. "Yet I only called it home for five years."

"And before that was Saragoza." The older woman nodded. "I remember."

Elena turned to her companion. "My lady, what is this about?"

Lysandra paused a moment before sighing and walking over to one of the massive windows that overlooked Kilgareth and the valley beyond.

"I am told that there is a place not far from Adrestia, a place sacred to the gods, and a place of great importance both to myself and to the Order."

Elena frowned. For the first time in the years they had known one another, this was the only time that the arc'maija had not been forthcoming.

"Then tell me, how can I help?"

"They call it the Maiden's Veil."

"The Maiden's Veil?" Elena bit her lip and cast her mind back to her years in the town. She had been a little under thirteen when her family had moved from the Caspin capital of Saragoza into the smaller country town. She had been eighteen when they had moved on, and by the gods' will they had ended up at Odrysia. Yet she had never heard of the Maiden's Veil.

"I cannot remember such a place."

Lysandra's eyes flicked shut and she let out a deep breath. "That is most unfortunate," she said, and she almost sounded sad.

Elena stood with her in silence as they both stared out across the valley.

"My lady … I may have only called Adrestia home for a few years, yet Kyler was born and raised there."

Lysandra pursed her lips, and she was suddenly deep in thought. "Perhaps I shall speak to him when the time is right."

Elena glanced at the older woman. Curious. What could be so important about the Maiden's Veil that her mentor was unwilling to speak to Kyler?

"How goes your study?" Lysandra said after a moment. "If I recall correctly, you were last looking into the Bludvier plant."

"Aye, the leaf has remarkable healing properties," Elena said, and she returned the smile the arc'maija offered her. "Yet the flower is far more deadly than even nightshade … it can cause painless and rapid death. And it leaves no trace."

"Nasty little thing, eh?" The arc'maija chuckled. "It holds the power of life and death yet bears no consequences."

Steel-shod boots rang in the corridor and the women turned to see a knight making his way towards them.

"Lady Lysandra," the warrior called.

"Ah, Sir Mortimier, what can I do for you?"

"The grand master has requested your presence."

"Very well," she said, and she glanced back at Elena. "If you think of anything at all, come to me at once."

"I shall," the girl told her.

TWENTY-THREE

Ruins of Israfil, Steppe of Miera

Pain.

It was all Lukas felt as he trudged across the plains. Yet it wasn't his bloodied and mud-covered face that made him grimace, nor was it his bruised body that brought on new torment with each step. It wasn't even that his hands were bound tight by a rope attached to the saddle of the Mieran leader. For all that was physical pain. Pain that he hid behind a stoic face. He had failed the crossing of the Steppe.

Hells, they had barely been on the plains for an hour before the riders had come.

Ahead, the leader, the one they called Silas, and four other Mierans served as a vanguard of sorts. Lukas could only see their backs and the rear of their mounts.

Sakkar and Cailean trudged along beside him. They were both similarly bound. Both covered in the same mud kicked up by Mieran horses. The Larissan marched in silence, and his eyes scanned the skies for any sign of Sabra. Cailean walked with anger driving each step. His eyes blazed with fire, and he stood tall and proud in defiance of their captors. His venomous gaze rarely strayed from the blonde-haired girl who rode side by side with her leader. Cailean had something on his mind that vexed him. It was something to do with the woman who fought unlike anyone he had seen before.

The prisoners were encircled by the rest of the riders. Their wary gazes flicked between the horizon and the men they had bound. Lukas shot a quick glance over his shoulder to where one of the horsemen led his mount and the mounts of his companions.

Lukas' mind went again to the woman. She was a mystery that he could not solve.

She did not dress like the Mierans, and nor did he feel the same hate in her eyes that came from the men. Never in his life had he read that the Mierans let their women fight. She merely regarded him with a smirk when she met his eyes.

A whistle came from Silas' lips. As a boy, he had been told of how the riders to the east communicated on the ride with whistles. The stories in this case had been true.

Lukas kept his gaze straight ahead as he nudged Sakkar. "We're moving south," he murmured.

The Larissan dipped his head a fraction and kept his voice low. "Half a day's walk. Maybe a few hours ride."

"Nightfall is nearly upon us," the prince whispered. "We may only have one chance."

"Quiet!" growled one of the Mierans as he rode up beside the prisoners.

The horseman glared down at Lukas with one hand lightly on the reins of his mount. He had not heard the exchange. The prince allowed himself a moment of satisfaction. The man who spoke was the man he had bloodied. Lukas glanced up at him without reply.

"You fight in the saddle with more skill than most of your kinfolk," the Mieran said, and his lips curled into a sneer. "Though you ride as a child."

Lukas snorted.

Let the man gloat, he would not waste his words.

Instead, his eyes were drawn to the structure that rose before them. A cobblestone road overgrown with grass and weeds led into the crumbling walls of what had once been a small town or outpost. The Mierans had brought them to a collection of ruins.

They were led through the crumbling outpost. The earth beneath them turned into a road of cobblestone. Lukas glanced around. A portcullis of sturdy steel and oak stood within the gatehouse. It was tethered by a great wheel to keep it raised. In some places the stone walls were so crumbled that a man could climb them without a ladder or climbing spikes, although only one could breach the walls at a time. Perhaps this was why the Mierans had left them in a state of disrepair.

The Mierans dismounted and led their prisoners on foot into the bowels of the former outpost. It was clear that their captors considered it safe even though the walls and floor had fallen long ago. A fire was started in what appeared to be the remnants of a hall. Half the roof above had been destroyed, allowing the light of the rising moon to spill into the sanctum.

"Sit," the Mieran leader called to his captives, and he gestured to a crumbled pillar that lay along the stone floor.

His hand never strayed from his sword, and nor did his wary eyes ever leave the three men.

Lukas and his companions sat. It was the first time they had been able to do so since they had been taken hostage. The prince gazed around the room. He was searching for some kind of weakness. All he found were the cold glares of the Mierans who watched them with hatred spewing from their eyes. The rider that Lukas had dealt a blow to was binding his wound with a long rag.

"My name is Silas Barangir," the Mieran leader said after a moment. "My purpose is to watch the western border. Who are you?"

None of them spoke.

Cailean glared menacingly at Silas but betrayed not a single word.

"I see," Silas said. "Now, that offers some difficulty. An Annoran, a westerner and a warrior of Salvaar ride into our land from the west. An unlikely grouping. One that poses many questions." He turned his gaze to Lukas.

The prince felt his heart drop. If he said nothing now, then the Mieran's may come close to guessing the truth.

"We are mercenaries seeking work," Lukas said.

"Is that so?" Silas smirked. "Beneath the mud I can see that you wear mail that could only have been forged by castle smiths. So, you are either of noble birth or a knight. Yet you do not bear the mark of Malius O'Lacey and thus would not be in his sellsword company of nobles."

The Mieran flicked his eyes to Cailean and nodded towards the man.

"I was born in the north and grew up fighting his people in the Rift. The torc that you wear at your neck tells me that you have relation to a Salvaari chief."

"Pity that my people didn't kill you when we had the chance," Cailean growled venomously.

"Oh, they tried," Silas countered before turning to Sakkar. "I have never had the pleasure of meeting a Larissan before. Though from what I have been told, your people rarely travel east. This is where the riddle begins. For what business would an Annoran noble, a Salvaari with chief's blood and a Larissan warrior have in Miera? The Rift has been quiet for many a week and all of our outriders have been met with arrows upon attempting a crossing." He returned his gaze to Cailean and met his eyes. "Yet here you are. From there my questions only multiply," Silas continued. "A state in which you do not want to keep me in."

Lukas made to speak. He meant to give a false name in the hopes of giving them a little more time.

"My name is—"

"Save whatever lies you are about to speak," Silas cut him off, and his voice grew loud. "I have been doing this a long time, and in that time I learnt to tell when a man is being dishonest." The

Mieran raised an arm and gestured around the crumbling hall. "Do you know where we are, Annoran?"

"No."

A few of the Mierans chuckled. A few of them sneered.

"This was once the outpost of Israfil," Silas said.

Lukas let out a breath and his eyes shut. Every Annoran knew this tale. Silas glanced around the hall as he spoke. "Many years ago, Balinor, King of Laeoflaed, along with King Aonaran of Aethela led an army into our land without warning. They killed all in their path until he reached these very walls and rained down fire upon them. It took three days for us to muster our forces, three days for the Annoran kings and their army to destroy this place and kill every man, woman and child within."

"Balinor was a bloodthirsty tyrant who got the end he deserved," Lukas spat, and he was barely able to keep venom from slipping into his voice. Of all the cretins in the world … he hated the former king the most.

"A sword in the chest from his very own kinsman, Dorian Raynor," Silas replied. "A man who rebelled against his own people and usurped Balinor's throne."

"And a king who saw fit to murder the family of his most loyal ally because of a rumour based on a lie," Lukas snarled. The prince felt a tingle of anger spark and fought the urge to scream. He had been barely a child when all of his family, save his father and Dayne, had been killed by the order of that monster.

Silas grunted, "Let us not forget that it was Dorian who led the attack upon land at Balinor's request and sacked Israfil."

"We did not come here to fight nor dredge up the past," Lukas told him.

"No?" Another of the Mierans smiled mirthlessly. "I was fifteen when my country called me to fight against Annora, here at Israfil and then on the plains of Carn-Dair. I was there when we pushed your kin out of our land with great cost to my own people. Many were lost on those fields, yet to me and all of Miera, Carn-Dair is the place of heroes. We sent your king and all his men back across the border with the promise of great reparation if they ever returned. Perhaps today is that day."

Lukas met his steely gaze as he replied, "I swear to you we come in peace. We are no more than travellers passing through."

"Aye, travellers passing through," snarled one of the older Mierans as he strode forwards with eyes that blazed with fury. "On a pilgrimage? Doing your gods' bidding? It matters not. I have heard every reason there is. We all have. Three of you today, five tomorrow. Within a month … thousands. We have all seen it before." His knuckles turned white as he clutched the pommel of his blade. He turned his head and pointed to his ear. It bore five rings. "The first ring I received when I took my first life. I was thirteen. The second I gained in combat when a warband of Salvaari crossed the Rift little over a year later." He glanced at Cailean darkly for a moment before he continued, "From there, each link gained is for each war. I have fought in three. Annora. The League of Trecento. Even those cursed Idrisians. Some of the invaders wanted land. Others sought wealth. Some wanted to serve their gods. Others to conquer the pagan lands of Miera." He snorted. "All failed. Each time it began with travellers passing through."

Silence filled the hall as the warrior spoke no more.

"Maybe now you understand the gravity of what you have done," Silas told Lukas sternly. He glanced over his shoulder towards the golden-haired woman. "Kitara, take them to the dungeons."

Kitara and another of the Mierans led their captives through the small maze of tunnels under Israfil until they reached the old dungeons. It was one of the few parts of the ruins untouched by the conflict from years before. The hallway and room connected to the dungeon were lit by half a dozen torches. The solitary cell had a small crevice for a window that allowed a small strip of moonlight to slip inside. The steel gate squealed as it was shut behind the three men.

It was strange, Kitara thought as she locked the door by key, to see the most unlikely of groups.

It had been decades since the last son of Larissa had travelled this fast east. Yet today history repeated itself.

"This place bears the stench of a sewer," the Annoran mumbled as he sat down against one of the walls.

Kitara rolled her eyes as she spoke. "Your naïvety shall be your undoing. Think what you will, yet this place smells far grander than any sewer."

"You speak as if you are familiar with them." The Larissan looked at her curiously. There was no poison in his eyes, nor malice in his voice.

Kitara snorted in reply. For three years she had called them home. She pulled her small leather ale flask from her belt and took a long gulp before tossing it onto the nearby table.

It may burn her throat, but damn did it feel good.

Kitara drew her sword and sat down on a nearby stool. She ran her expert gaze over the steel. Kitara grimaced as she spotted the smallest of imperfections in the blade. That would have to go. She rummaged around in her pouches for a moment before withdrawing a whetstone. Kitara drew it slowly down the length of her sword over and over again. She worked out any tiny dents and sharpened the blade to perfection.

"You fight well," the Annoran said as he turned his gaze to her. "Though had you not unhorsed me as you did, it would not have mattered."

"You show great humility," Kitara replied sarcastically as she worked. "Truly, you must be of noble birth. You may have been hurt, yet I was not trying to kill you. Had I been so inclined, had you not been injured, it would not have mattered, for even your gods could not have saved you."

"Hubris" – Sakkar snorted – "often boasted by fools who perish from it."

"Tell that to your man there," the girl replied and gave him a devilish grin.

"The way you fight is … strange," Lukas told her. "Almost elegant in a way. That is, of course, until you kicked in a swordfight."

"That's just it, isn't it?" the woman said, and her grin widened. "There is no such thing as sword fighting. There is only fighting with a sword."

"There was no honour in it," Lukas snapped.

Kitara looked over at the Annoran, running her green eyes over him briefly. Despite everything, he still held an air of arrogance. He was not yet beaten. He had to be some kind of noble.

"And now you wish to understand it in the hope of gaining advantage if we have future contest?"

"You mistake me," came the grunted reply.

"I do not think so."

"In the court of Queen Reshada, there is a man who fights like a dancer," the Larissan said. "Like water, he moves and flows, never once being touched by sword or spear. And just like water, he crashes upon his enemies with the fury of the sea."

Kitara tensed slightly as he spoke. She had no doubt that he knew exactly how she fought.

"That man hails from Tarik," Sakkar said as he gestured towards the steel in her hands. "By the look of it, so does your blade."

Oh, he was good. He was very good.

Few on the mainland had ever seen a Tariki blade. Fewer still knew of the vast qualities of the northern steel, steel that created lighter and thinner blades that were just as strong. Kitara knew of the warrior the man spoke of. There were few among the Tariki who had not heard of the swordsman.

Kitara sighed. "I have heard mention of Palagius Altmira, and I know that some call him the Stormslayer. You are near to the mark, Larissan. I do fight similarly to the men of Tarik."

"Tarkaras."

"Yes," Kitara said, and she allowed a brief smile. "In our tongue, it is known as swordsong. Do you know why?"

"Tell me."

"When you fight with someone well versed in tarkaras, you enter a dance that can only be ended by the tip of a blade. Their blade. It is like swatting at the very air you breathe. You can try and try again, yet every attempt to land a blow will fail," she said, and her smile turned vicious as she eyed the prisoners. "Until at last the melody ends with the single swing of a sword." She ran the whetstone down her blade one final time. "They say that just as tarkaras is the soul of Tarik, a Tariki sword is the soul of its bearer."

"If this is so," the Salvaari growled softly, "why do not the Tariki rule us all?"

There was scepticism in his voice. He was clearly a man who needed to see a thing to believe it.

"They have no armies nor want for war," Kitara said, and she shook her golden mane.

"Or perhaps they are too cowardly to try us," the tribesman chuckled.

"You would underestimate foreigners merely because you do not understand them?"

"No, yet to hear you of all people speak of foreigners," the Salvaari said and spared her a glance. He grinned at her inquisitive look.

"Perhaps while you explain yourself, you may be so inclined as to tell me why exactly you have been watching me ever since we took you captive," Kitara replied with a sneer.

What did the man have to say that he had kept quiet about up until now? Why had his eyes never left her?

"Do not think that I have not noticed," Kitara said.

"I have been trying to decide where you fit into this," the Salvaari said. "You do not wear the garb of a Mieran, nor do you ride like one. You do not fight as Mieran or bear their weapons, for no woman in this land has ever wielded a blade. Your voice is not from here ... Indeed, I cannot place it. And your name is clearly not Mieran. So, I will ask you, why do you fight beside these people who are not your own?"

"I have no people," Kitara snapped and turned a malicious glare towards the cell.

The man had struck a nerve, yet anger was a part of who she was. Her hand tightened on the hilt of her sword.

"They never told you? Those men of northern Miera?" the Salvaari asked, and his dark expression turned into curiosity. "Yet by your face, I can tell that you have the blood of my kin running through your veins."

"You lie."

The words came out as a growl, and Kitara slid her sword back into its sheath. Her father was a man she had never met. He was probably dead in a ditch. Her mother had died in childbirth. She had grown up two thousand miles from Miera. Even further from Salvaar. No Salvaari had ever stepped foot on anything larger than a fishing boat, and none had ever reached the Gulf of Lamrei. It was impossible for her to be the blood of a Salvaari. She glared at the Salvaari, and her blood boiled.

"What would I have to gain?" he asked.

"I do not know your mind," Kitara fired back. "If I had your blood, I would know."

Despite this, she could not understand the truth hidden in the warrior's eyes. He had nothing to gain whatsoever, and yet Silas and the other men of the north would have told her if she were Salvaari.

"No," the Salvaari told her, and he met her fiery gaze. "Now you only lie to yourself."

With a snarl, Kitara turned and snatched up her wine flask.

How dare he attempt to dig up her past.

She strode away with anger burning through her body.

Prince Dayne of Annora gazed at the pearl-white marble statue before him. It was the sculpture of a warrior clad in traditional Aureian armour. It had the added flair that only the Trecento colonies possessed.

Sir Garrik and the royal guard had left mere hours before. That left the older prince to ponder his next move. For now, he stood in a room that he used to store hundreds of pieces of art from each of the mainland kingdoms. The tables and shelves were covered in paintings, illuminations, busts, carvings and sculptures.

The prince's attention was glued to the statue though. His gaze was drawn to the complexity that the artist had put into the cloak that the statue bore. The sculptor had managed to make the marble look like real fabric.

The door to the room opened behind him, but the prince barely reacted to it. His attention remained on the statue.

"My prince," called a man as his footsteps drew nearer. "The king has requested your presen–"

"Ah," Dayne muttered, and he held up a hand to silence the general.

After a moment, the prince glanced over his shoulder at the older man. He indicated to the statue.

"I had this shipped in from Elara … See the detail of the eyes and the cloak. Already I begin to see how those of Trecento think," Dayne said as he turned to face Sir Tristayn. "Pray tell, what do you think of them?"

"The city-states?" The knight shrugged. "Little more than

Aureian colonies with a penchant for trade, my lord."

"Indeed," Dayne replied as he suppressed a chuckle. "My father has never agreed with my use of spies, yet today they have proven their worth," he said as he took up an open letter from a table beside the statue. "The League of Trecento has at last mustered its fleet and has sent it deep into the Sacasian to reclaim what is rightfully theirs. To reclaim the Gulf of Lamrei from those devils that plague it. I am told that no fewer than two of the pirate strongholds have been put to the sword and razed to the ground, while Landonsport has turned upon those retches and has banded with the League," he said, and he folded his arms. "It will only be a matter of time before the region is once more civilised."

"Very good, my lord," was all the general said.

The prince had noticed his face was pale and ridden with something else. Anguish perhaps? Dayne could see it clearly. Something had happened.

"Tell me now, what is it that grieves you? What word do you bring from my father?"

"It is the princess."

"What of her?" Dayne asked and he felt a flush of worry. "What has happened to my sister?"

"She's gone."

The slight furrowing of his brow was all the heir gave away. He would not show weakness. He would only show control. Without a word, he followed the general from the room.

"What has happened?" Dayne said calmly as he entered his father's chambers. "Where is Kassandra?"

The few present turned to him with startled expressions. Some were angry, others sad. Dayne kept his emotions well under control. They would only stop him from doing what needed to be done. His father, the king, stood in conference with Queen Riona and the lieutenant of the royal guard. He was the highest-ranking officer from the guard still within Palen-Tor. Sir Garrik had taken all but two hundred of their finest. Elion Montbard was his name, and he had been as a second brother to Dayne for many years.

With them stood a girl about Kassie's age. She was no more than fifteen or sixteen. Marian Martyn. She was the princess' handmaiden and niece to Sir Tristayn.

"Peace, my son," the king said as his son and the general strode into the room.

Tristayn closed the door behind them. They were cut off from the outside world.

"No man outside these chambers knows what has transpired," the king said.

"The castle is crawling with hundreds of people," Dayne replied incredulously. "How can she have simply vanished?"

Riona gestured to the girl as she spoke. "My daughter's handmaiden, Marian, found her chambers empty."

The queen gave the girl a smile despite the tears that threatened in her eyes. She loved her daughter more than anything in the world.

"Go on, tell the prince what you told me," Riona murmured.

Marian took a deep breath as all eyes turned to her. The poor girl looked as if she were about to burst into tears.

"My prince, two hours after the sun's first light, I wake the princess from her sleep," the girl began, and she bit down on her lip nervously. "I rose this morning to find her gone. Her bed had been slept in, but she was not there … I found a note bound and sealed by her ring."

"A note?" Dayne said softly.

The girl had done naught but her duty and harsh words would only make matters worse.

"What did you do next?"

"I thought it was best to remain a secret. So, I went to find my uncle."

Despite the worry he felt for his half-sister, Dayne could not help but smile as the ever-stoic general placed a protective hand on Marian's shoulder and gave her a gentle squeeze.

"Smart girl," the prince told her.

"Yes." Dorian nodded, and he held up a sheaf of parchment. "After reading this, I called for Lieutenant Elion and sent Sir Tristayn to find you. The note is in Kassandra's hand and as Marian said ... her unbroken seal."

"What does it say?" the prince asked.

He crossed his arms as a sickening feeling started to enter his chest. King Dorian held up the note and read aloud, "I am a princess of Annora, not a pawn to be bargained away. I shall return upon the day that the High Mass begins and then we will discuss my future. I am beholden to no man whom I do not I choose. Kassandra." Silence filled the chamber as the king spoke his last.

"How did she come to find out about Aloys?" Dayne said after a moment.

If this was true, then this whole thing was his fault. If she planned to return only at the High Mass, then they wouldn't see her for over a month.

"I know not," Dorian replied. "And yet it is so. At this very moment, Sir Garrik and the royal guard ride for Sergova. The message has been sent. There is no recalling it."

"This is the kind of recklessness that I expect from Lukas ... but not her. Not my sister."

The king nodded sombrely and clutched at his amulet. "Only the gods know where she ran to," Dorian muttered.

"And I for one will not rest until she is found," Dayne said. He stroked his chin. His mind was filled to the brim with ideas that had been circulating ever since he had been called to his father's chambers. "We must proceed as planned," Dayne continued.

"And lie to House Aloys?" the general asked as he turned to Dayne. "Is that wise?"

"We can deal with the duke later. While I pray for the best outcome, we must prepare for the worst. And if it comes to it, one duchy cannot contend with us," the prince replied.

Riona flicked her gaze from Dayne to the lieutenant. "Sir Elion, you lead what remains of the royal guard."

"I do, my queen," the knight said.

"Please inform them that Princess Kassandra is bedridden with a fever," Riona told him. "Have her chambers guarded at all times. No one is allowed in without the authority of myself or the king," the queen said and then she turned her amber gaze to her companions. "This is what we must tell the people until such a time as my daughter returns to us."

"I agree," King Dorian said, before he raised his powerful voice. "Not a word of what we have discussed can leave this chamber. For if it does, you will need to worry about more than just spending the night in a cell."

TWENTY-FOUR

Tears of Freydis, Isle of Vay'kis

The hull of the Wind Rider kissed the water of the river gently. It parted the current and slipped through the cool surface. Astrid stood by the helm with her hands clamped down on the vessel's railing. The corner of her lips began to curl.

Only a fool would have dreamed this fantasy into reality.

By now the ship should have squandered on the riverbank. Yet despite all odds, and despite the fear that had set in when the ship had scraped along the riverbed, the panic had all been over in moments. Twelve agonising feet of sand and mud later, and the Rider pulled free of its hungry embrace.

A silence had come to those aboard the ship as they sailed deep into the beating heart of Vay'kis. They had done the impossible. They had accomplished a feat that none had so much as come close to in hundreds of years. The further they sailed, the quieter it got. Peaks started to soar into the sky on either side and created a barrier that was impassable on foot. The river turned into a canyon, and only the howling northern wind that whistled through the earthen corridor kept them from coming to a halt.

They sailed for another mile until at last the canyon walls left the churning waters of the river and melted into a valley.

A hand clapped down on Astrid's shoulder as she stared out across the open space, a newfound hope burning to life in her heart.

"You've done it," Torben whispered.

Groves of trees littered the valley and encircled the great lake that lay before them. It was not the lake that captivated Astrid. Nor was it the serenity that the valley wore like a cloak. A waterfall cascaded from the mountains and drove deep into the lake. It gave life to the river beyond.

"The Tears of Freydis," Astrid breathed.

The crew moored the Wind Rider in the lake and then used smaller long boats to make their way ashore. Fires crackled to life along the sandy beach and illuminated the valley for the first time. Tomorrow they could venture out and explore the valley, but tonight Astrid had much to consider.

She needed to think about her next move, and how Magnus might counter it.

Plans within plans.

She could not defeat her enemies by the sword, but she would be damned if she could not defeat them with her wit. She stared at the fire burning before her. Astrid rolled her shoulders and rose to her feet.

"Crew of the Wind Rider," she said as she took up her axe and ran her keen gaze down its length. "We have a choice to make."

The fire snarled as Astrid slid the axe's head into it and engulfed half the blade in its burning maw.

"Magnus' treachery has cost us dearly," she said as she clasped at the medallion at her throat. "Fathers and mothers, brothers and sisters ..." Astrid glanced at Mayrun as she spoke and felt the woman's sorrow as fiercely as she felt her own. "Husbands and wives. Family. We now stand upon the edge of a knife. If we stray even a little ... it is over. We will have been for nothing. Not even a page in a history book," she said as she raised an arm and gestured down the river. "We could sail away, leave the isles, leave the Lupentine. For if we stay ... we will have nothing. And I for one would rather die."

"What other choice do we have?" called one of the Valkir. Despair clutched his voice. His lined face spoke of an elder whom age had finally caught up with.

"Do you want to go home?" Astrid asked.

"Aye."

The low mumbling reached her ears as many spoke.

"Then we have to start fighting back," Astrid shouted.

"But they have an army," another of the warriors said.

"And the bloodsworn," chorused another.

Astrid pointed to Torben. "Not all of them."

The old bloodsworn glared at the man who had spoken.

"We are not Magnus' lackeys, falling to command at but a word from that worm's tongue," Torben snapped. "Few will follow him."

"There are few warriors among us," said the first man. "What would you have the rest of us do? Fight with rocks in our bare hands?"

Astrid could see the anguish written in his face, yet there was fierce, unbridled anger. It was in all their faces. It just needed to be directed.

"I will make you no promises, save one," she snarled, and her voice rose as a strength flooded her veins. "This is not over. Not while I still breathe. Until we give up, we have not lost. Agartha is my home. I can't walk away from that. Can you?"

Astrid tore off the blood-soaked bandage wrapped around her arm and took up her axe. The flames of the fire hungrily clawed at her as she raised the red-hot steel.

"For by the Sea-Father, I intend to strike back," she growled venomously.

Astrid pressed the blade of the axe against her wound. She gritted her teeth as it melted her flesh and sealed the bloody gash. Astrid barely made a sound as the pain hit her like a wave. She turned her agony into strength. She lowered the axe, and its steel still glowed red from the heat.

"What say you?" Astrid shouted.

Hélla drew her blade and rose to her feet. "I am with you, now and always!"

"Now and always!" boomed Torben as he moved to stand by Hélla with his axe in hand.

One by one, the crew rose. Nenrir, and then Fargrim, until all of them were standing.

"We have all suffered under the hand of Magnus," Astrid called. "No longer."

The cheer that followed was deafening.

Astrid strode through the small encampment that her people had put together. They had pitched a few small tents and hangings, and they had started a few fires. Some of her people had already drifted off into slumber. They rested for the first time since the attack. Others sat around the fires in silence or quietly talked to their companions.

The Wind Rider was anchored in the lake and Astrid had posted half a dozen warriors aboard the vessel as a precaution. She doubted that they would be found here, yet she was not willing to risk all their lives on the chance she was wrong. Perhaps the earl of Vay'kis had discovered a hidden path or trail leading to the Tears of Freydis. Astrid had sent a party of her warriors out to scout the area. She wanted to know if there was a hidden path that led into the mountains. The Story of Freydis spoke of no such tales, yet she would rather be cautious than dead. While the rest of her crew slept under the silver light of the moon, she had a task that had to be done. She reached the man sitting alone by one of the fires. Beside him sat a shield with a great serpent emblazoned upon it. Unlike Astrid, the dark-haired man wore a suit of lamellar armour.

"Torben," the jarl murmured as she reached the fire.

The bloodsworn warrior glanced up from the flames. "Astrid?"

Astrid simply gestured down the shoreline without any

explanation. "Follow me."

They walked in silence for a time. It was a companionable silence that only came with a lifelong friendship.

"I keep thinking to myself," Astrid said as she gazed out over the water, "what would have happened if we had simply stayed in Agartha and not challenged the earl?"

"I think you know that he would have come for us either way," Torben replied. "Had we not stood against Magnus and Sven … perhaps we would be swinging over the harbour at this very moment."

"In my heart I know that to be true," Astrid told him. "The course we have followed was the only choice. Yet now we find ourselves in unknown waters surrounded by wolves. We need allies."

Torben nodded. "More than that, we need warriors. Real warriors," Torben replied. "Among us we have children, old folk, craftsmen and those who never took to raiding. Men and women who have never so much as swung an axe. And yet what time do we have to train them? It takes years to learn to wield a blade."

"Time we do not have," Astrid agreed. "And for that I see but one possibility."

"What is that?"

"We may not have many warriors, yet look at what we do have."

Her words were filled with the same intensity that had driven her to speak with such fervour to the crew mere hours before.

"Among the carpenters, butchers and boat builders, we have blacksmiths, fletchers and Hvitsred the bowyer. Tell me, Torben, why do we not attack Annoran towns that are aware of our presence?"

"Because of Dorian Raynor," the older man said, and he finally understood.

"Indeed." The jarl smirked. "When he took the throne and made it law that every man in his kingdom had to learn the bow … well, everything changed. No longer were we able to sail straight into the ports and harbours of the Annoran coast with impunity."

"And this valley" – Torben gestured about the cove – "has many trees."

"Exactly," Astrid said at last. "Tomorrow we will get to work. Any spare sword or blade is to be melted down to forge arrowheads. We have wood for weapons, craftsmen to make them and people to use them."

"Many among us hunt in the mountains of home," Torben added. "Even those untrained for battle will have some knowledge of the bow."

"Yes, that will save us some time." Astrid turned back to face the camp. "Nenrir can train all those able, and in a matter of days, we could have near to forty archers. Each ready to follow our warriors into battle."

"It may not be enough to defeat Magnus, yet it is a good start."

"It will take time and no small amount of luck, yet I believe we can win," Astrid said as she met the warrior's gaze. She could see the same hope reflected in those dark eyes that burned ever so brightly in her own. "I have sent Hélla to scout the cove. I have this feeling that our presence has not gone unnoticed. Perhaps there is a track … a hidden goat path that leads here."

"I have heard of no such trail," the man replied. "However, this place does not exist … and the men of Vay'kis play their cards close."

It was true. Those of this isle rarely said more than was needed. Especially to outsiders. The discipline instilled by their earls for generations had left their clan shrouded in mystery.

"I cannot do this alone," Astrid said after a moment.

"Jarl?" the bloodsworn asked as he looked at her curiously.

"Do you know what it means to be a leader?" Astrid asked as she once more gazed out over the ever-moving waters of the lake. "It means making the decisions that no one else will. It means doing what you believe to be right, no matter the consequences. Plan for every outcome, anticipate your opponent and surprise him. I want you to be my second. If I fall in battle … you will lead these people."

"Astrid, I am no leader," Torben told her sternly. He was taken aback by the notion of becoming jarl. He could not assume any kind of command over the crew. He was just a warrior. He was no more or less than any of them. "I am a warrior. I am not like you."

"No, you are not," Astrid replied. "I could navigate us from one side of the Lupentine to the other with my eyes closed. I could hunt someone for days across the entire breadth of the sea, and they would not know of my presence. If you give me a town, I can give you a ruin. The gods gave me wisdom. They gave me this gift, and I will do all in my power to use it. Yet I can only wage wars of the mind. I am no fighter of legend. Nor can I lead warriors into battle as Freydis once did," the jarl continued without hesitation. "But you, Torben, you are a great warrior held in high esteem by friend and foe alike. You have the respect and loyalty of the crew. More than that, you lead from the front. I have seen it. We all have. This is a thing that I could never do. I ask you this now … Are you with me?"

Torben was silent even after his friend and leader trailed off. Astrid was like a daughter to him, and he would die for her without hesitation. Yet in this matter, they were not of the same mind. He had never thought to be more than a soldier.

Aye, bloodsworn maybe, yet no more than that.

Everything he had done on the battlefields from Torosa to Miera had been naught but instinct.

"I will follow you to whatever end," Torben said. "I will be your second. Though I pray to never assume the mantle of jarl."

"You are a loyal friend," Astrid told him. "You always have been."

Wood echoed underfoot as Erik walked through the earl's hall. The bloodsworn had decided it was time to visit his old friend, his former brother-in-arms, Laerke Redleaf, who now rotted in the dungeons of Earl Magnus.

A pair of guards stood sentinel before the locked and bolted door of the jail. The warriors watched him warily as he approached. Their hands did not leave the hilts of their blades.

"I am here to see the prisoner," Erik told them.

The warriors were the private guard of Magnus himself, and they could not even be cowed by the bloodsworn.

One of the guards held out a hand. "Weapons."

Erik returned the hard stare that came his way. Without dropping his gaze, he unbuckled his sword belt and handed it over. With that, the second guard unlocked the heavy oaken door with a key and heaved it open. Erik strode through and into the dark room. It was lit by nothing more than a thin stream of moonlight that came through a small, barred window. One of the guards entered with him and the door closed at their backs. Steel clinked as the bolt was pushed home. Erik's gaze was now drawn to the shadow of a man sitting against the far wall.

"Laerke."

"Come to gloat?" he asked with a growl. "Traitor."

"Are they feeding you?"

It was a simple enough question, spoken ever softly.

"Well enough," came the reply.

There was a rustle of chains as Laerke rose to his feet and finally revealed himself to Erik as the light of the moon lit his face. Erik held back a wince as he saw the bloodied and bruised flesh that covered Laerke's face. So, he had been tortured by Magnus. Though far more than even Erik had anticipated.

Laerke saw his face change and chuckled again. "Surprise you, does it?"

"I shall speak to the earl," Erik told him sincerely.

"To what purpose?"

"You will not be harmed, not by his hand or any other."

"I have known you a long time, Erik." Laerke snorted contemptuously as he stared at the bloodsworn. "Do not play games with me."

"This is no game, I can assure you of that."

"What would it matter? Torture or not, even if I did know where Astrid sails … I would not utter so much as a whisper of it. I will not betray my brothers. So let Magnus and his dogs have their fun," Redleaf growled as he glared deep into Erik's eyes. "Nothing would give me more joy than watching that snake writher and squirm without an answer."

"Laerke, let me help you," Erik said after a moment. Despite everything, he did not wish to see his old friend harmed.

"What? Like you helped Astrid? I think not," the warrior snarled, and he took a step towards his rival. The chains tightened and brought Laerke to a halt even as his glare darkened. "What did it cost to forsake your honour? Coin? Position? Want of power?"

"You would never understand." Erik crossed his powerful arms. "None of you would."

"Pah!" Redleaf spat. "You turned on us, Erik. Your crew. People you have known all your life. Your brothers and sisters. Your family. Astrid, Erik, your own blood!" Laerke strained against the chains as he yelled, and his hands clawed towards the bloodsworn. "You betrayed your oath. You betrayed us. There is no going back from that."

"Everything I have done, everything I will do, is for my people," Erik shot back, and his eyes never left Laerke's hate-filled gaze.

"Is that what you tell yourself at night?" Redleaf muttered. "It's all for my people?"

Erik hid his growing anger behind a blank mask. Blood raced through his veins as he felt a very familiar feeling threaten to overcome him. The fight. He longed for his blood to run hot, and his heart to race. It was what he lived for. It was what fuelled him. He slowly closed his eyes and suppressed the rising need for violence.

"That is none of your concern," was all Erik said.

Laerke never once lowered his eyes. He did not let Erik look away from the ever-growing inferno that burned within.

"Skûra welcomes traitors like you."

"Then I will go there proud," Erik snarled before he turned on his heel to stride towards the door. He thumped a fist on the wood. The bolt squealed, and the door was pulled open. The bloodsworn turned back to Laerke.

"You will not be touched again."

With that, he marched out of the cell and snatched his weapons back from the guard. Erik's knuckles whitened as his fingers wrapped around his weapons belt. With that, he started towards the sparring yard. He needed to clear his head.

TWENTY-FIVE

Kilgareth, Valley of Odrysia

The last of the sun's orange rays had slipped behind the horizon when Kyler at last made it to the western tower. Watch duty had made him familiar with every section of the great fortress' vast stone walls. The tower was one of many that stood astride the inner wall of Kilgareth. Not only did it give a view of Odrysia and the valley but also the small town within the outer wall as well.

"You made it." Elena grinned as she saw Kyler emerge from the stairwell.

"Of course," he said, and he returned the smile as he made his way towards her.

It was all he could say before she pulled him into a tight embrace. Kyler felt a tingle of joy run through his body as he hugged her tightly.

Gods, it had been so long.

After a moment, Elena pulled away and moved to stand by the edge of the wall.

"A beautiful thing," she mused softly. "A city at night."

Kyler made his way to her side and leaned out over one of the merlons. The lights of torches and braziers lit up the township. It mingled with the first silver rays of the moon in a tumescent glow. She was right. It was beautiful.

"Despite everything, it reminds me of home."

"Do you remember when we used to watch the sunsets in

Adrestia?"

Kyler chuckled. "On top of the headman's lodge."

"Old Ignacio wasn't very impressed." There was a faintly amused sound in her voice now.

"Yes, well, perhaps he should have built taller walls," Kyler said.

Elena laughed as she stared out across the city. Kyler could remember the first time the pair had snuck out. It had been a warm spring night three years ago. He had been fifteen summers. He may have convinced her to sneak out in the wee hours of night, yet she had persuaded him to follow her to the very top of the headman's lodge. They had climbed its walls and watched from the roof as the sun dipped beyond the horizon. Kyler would be a fool to not admit that it had been that night when he had fallen for her.

"What happened, Elena?" Kyler asked after a moment. "How did you get here?"

Elena turned and met his dark eyes with her own. The light of the torches along the wall seemed to make her eyes sparkle as she pursed her lips.

"My father wished to give us a new life." Elena sighed. "Kyler, Adrestia was not safe for us. My mother's sickness was growing worse by the day, and my father could hardly walk after the attack."

"And so, Odrysia." Kyler nodded.

"Odrysia," Elena agreed. "Where better than the holy city to seek sanctuary? Father told no one until after we had left in the hopes of leaving misfortune behind."

"And did it?"

"For a time," she told him, and she flicked a stray strand of hair behind an ear. "The maija came to see my father. They made a brace for his leg ... He was able to work again. And then a year later, he passed away."

"I'm so sorry," Kyler said, and he reached out to lightly touch her arm.

Her father had been a good man. Kind and considerate of all.

"I'm not," Elena said, and she gave him a slight smile. "He went in his sleep having known peace for the first time in many years. What more could anyone ask for?"

"He will always be remembered … The kindness he showed me," Kyler said.

"Well, he did like you." Elena smiled at the thought. "As for my mother, Lysandra herself visits her every week. It is because of her kindness that I decided to commit to the maija trials and don the robes. Lysandra took me under her wing … gave me a new life, a new family. And now …"

"Now you are maija," Kyler finished for her.

"And what of you?" Elena reached out and gently turned his chin. "Been here for a short time and already you seemed to have caused quite the commotion." There was a faint glint of humour in her eyes as she ran her fingers over the bruising.

Kyler nudged her hand away with a devilish grin. "You were always a bad influence." Kyler smirked.

"No." Elena snorted in indignation. "You were a worse one."

The Medean boy laughed as a feeling of contentment wrapped around him like a cocoon. Perhaps things between them had changed since the day she had left, yet at least now he had a friend whom he could hold to heart.

"Tell me," Elena said after a moment, and she gestured once more to the bruising.

"It is nothing," Kyler mumbled, and waved a hand innocently.

The woman chuckled. "Yes, well, I did hear something of a brawl occurring in the mess hall a few nights ago. I take it that you have no knowledge of that?"

"None whatsoever," grunted Kyler. "Though Karter is something of a ponce."

"Perhaps he is, perhaps he is not. Yet if the last two years have taught me anything, it is that everyone is fighting their own battle. From what I hear, Karter is in this castle for decisions not of his own making. And be he fool, naïve or ill-mannered … he is still your brother. For did he not take the same oath?"

"He is a noble." Kyler sighed.

"And yet no different from you or I," Elena said. "Do not be so quick to judge. A man may possess some noble character yet."

Kyler nodded, and he let the conversation drift into a companionable silence as they both gazed out across the city. Elena had changed a little in the years since their parting, and yet she seemed almost wiser for it. It was true. She had always been smarter than him. She was less prone to anger, but now she was more focused than ever. Perhaps it was in the maija training she had received. Perhaps it was not. Then he noticed the necklace. A simple chain with a snow-white pearl wrapped in silver attached.

"You kept the necklace?" Kyler murmured.

Elena reached up and lightly touched the jewel. "Always. It was a gift from you," she told him with a smile. "Come with me. I have something to show you."

Kyler followed Elena through the winding roads and passages that ran through the castle. They passed under arches and down narrow corridors. They continued past the maijas' library until at last the girl brought them to a halt.

"The Garden of Azaria," Elena told him.

Before Kyler was a part of Kilgareth that he had never seen before: a small garden filled with small stone pathways that wound amongst small shrubs. It was simple and overgrowing with green, yet Kyler's eye was drawn to the statue that stood in the very centre of the yard. It was a stone likeness of the goddess Azaria. She stood atop a small stone pedestal and clasped an open book in her hands.

"It's peaceful," Kyler said as he looked over the garden.

He felt at ease here. It was quieter away from all the bustling that was the fortress. The small, secluded grove seemed to drive some of the weariness from his bones.

"I come here to think," Elena told him seriously. "Meet me here tomorrow evening and bring your books. It is time you learnt Delion history."

The moon rose and fell all too swiftly. Night turned to day. The baking Medean sun glared down into the training yard. It roasted the very skin of those who toiled beneath its vicious gaze.

Kyler felt a trickle of sweat run down his chin as he watched the confrontation that was about to unfold. Ever since the midday sun had risen, they had been fighting each other under the stoic gaze of their instructors.

Gods, he was tired.

The moon had been high in the sky when he had parted with Elena, and after that he had found it an impossible task to sleep. His mind was haunted with memories of his life in Adrestia.

The boy squinted and wiped the drop of sweat away. Alarik stepped back from the two men standing within the ring of initiates. Evander stood opposite Hugh Karter as they awaited their mentor's command. Kyler had noticed something about Alarik was different. The battlemaster wore only his blue and silver tunic in place of his usual armour.

Kyler's eyes went to the initiates standing inside the ring with their mentor. The pair were clad in their padded jerkins and chain armour, yet they carried naught but their heavy training swords.

They were weapons of the sturdiest wood and filled with weighted lead. The swords were perfect for combat training as they were almost non-lethal, but they did leave marks.

By the gods, did they pack a punch.

Evander adjusted his grip on his blade and set himself into his fighting crouch.

Hugh Karter stood opposite him, and his expression was filled with confidence as he twirled his sword expertly. The Annoran locked eyes with his opponent and shut out the crowd of recruits that encircled them.

Everything was still.

"Begin!" roared Sir Alarik as he stepped out of the circle.

Evander attacked first. He powered forwards and lunged towards his foe. Karter stepped back and deflected Evander's strike with a flick of his wrists. Now Karter moved. He sent two lightning blows towards Evander. Evander blocked once, and then again. He moved to block a third as Hugh lashed out. He realised Karter's feint too late.

Karter twirled and changed his angle. The feint opened Evander up to a devastating blow on his side.

Evander gasped as the sword landed hard. It tore the air from his lungs. He staggered back but never dropped his guard. Karter danced towards him, and Evander was barely able to stop his onslaught. Staunch struck staunch three times as the Annoran sliced through his defence. Strength sped through Karter's arm as he struck Evander's blade with the full weight of his body. The Elaran's sword flew from his fingers. Hugh's weapon whirled through the air and sliced towards Evander's throat. Evander did not have time to blink before the wooden edge of the staunch was pressed tight against his neck.

The initiates erupted in applause as the fight came to a close. It had ended before it had even begun.

Kyler could not help but join the clapping despite his dislike for Karter. It had been a masterful display from Hugh Karter's part. The noble had beaten his friend with ease. There was a barely a drop of sweat on his brow. The fight had seemingly been won without effort.

Kyler watched the man intently as he clasped Evander's proffered hand and then swaggered back to his companions to celebrate his swift victory.

The ponce.

"You hesitated," Sir Alarik said as he made his way back into the circle. The battlemaster gestured towards Karter. "There were at least two points in which you could have ended the fight sooner, had you wished it."

The noble shrugged. "Aye, I could have, sir. My first opening was two strikes in."

"And yet you did not take it."

Kyler nearly winced as Hugh met Alarik's dark stare rather than keeping his eyes fixed over his superior's shoulder.

"Why risk sending a brother to the maija for the sake of a duel, sir? Was I wrong to do so?"

The battlemaster nodded slowly.

"A difficult question, Karter. You showed mercy to a fellow warrior. A commendable act. And yet foolish, nonetheless," the old knight said as he swept his gaze around the ring of recruits. "You may think our ways here are harsh. The lash of the cane. The iron fist used to turn you into warriors. We do this much like the Aureian legions of the south. Because each hurt is a lesson. We do this because beyond these walls and mountains … the world is unforgiving. It is for that reason that here we demand discipline. You may ask why I say that it is foolish to spare your fellow man injury, yet out there" – and Sir Alarik gestured out past the walls with his cane – "none will spare you. My time in the legions taught me that. Twelve years ago, we were sent to the west, deep into the mountains of Irene. Aureia had been invaded, you see, and that cannot be tolerated. So, Emperor Darius charged us with bringing those tribes to their knees."

Alarik's eyes gazed into the distance as he walked as if the recruits around him were forgotten. His voice was filled with something new. It almost sounded like sorrow.

"A week into the campaign, we were set upon by the natives. They attacked in the night without warning, when we were absent armour. It would be the last time we made that mistake. And not just one tribe … They had all come. Thousands of them. Teeth filed into fangs, bodies covered in scars and screaming for blood. They threw themselves at us like madmen. Their teeth were as much a weapon as their spears. They came at us … again, and again, and again. Without mercy. Without respite. Each time we were fewer. Each time we came closer to defeat. We were surrounded and cut off from reinforcement. We stood back to back, side by side. The only thing keeping us from being overwhelmed was the shield wall." The battlemaster trailed off and offered his cane to a fellow knight. "Attend your eyes."

With that, Sir Alarik untied his bracers and tossed them into the ground at his feet. His tunic followed.

Kyler gasped. They all did.

Over the muscle that covered the man's body lay a patchwork of scars. Some were thick and knotted, while others thin and pale.

"I received this," he said, and he ran a hand down the mark that stretched from his left shoulder to his stomach, "when the man before me fell and three of those savages attempted to overwhelm our position." And he turned as he talked to show a pair of scars running down the length of his back. "These came when they forced us back. The sheer weight of their numbers turned the earth beneath them into a river of mud. For every man they took, we killed a dozen more. They tried to make us give in to our fear. They fought like monsters from the depths of hell and screamed like demons as they came at us. Every officer they captured was executed before our very eyes. Cut to pieces on altars of stone." Alarik snorted, and the memory of those three nights was as fresh as it was the day it happened. "We were outnumbered, outmatched and surrounded. And yet we triumphed. I tell you now, so that you will understand why we are as we are," he said.

Alarik nodded to his fellow knights. He let his words sink in before he gestured to Karter.

"Mercy is an honourable trait, and we should all follow it. Yet do not let it be the death of you. Landrey, what is the founding principle of which our Order is built upon?"

Kyler looked to the knight as his name was called. The Order of

Kil'kara had many tenants, and yet one was above all. The one for which Durandail stood.

"Justice, Sir Alarik."

"Precisely." The veteran nodded. "Durandail commands it. Too much mercy leads to crimes going unpunished. Too much mercy and the innocent suffer. Innocents who would not have been victims had justice been given. Show mercy to those who are deserving of it. Not to monsters. Not to men who come at you swinging a blade. Upon a day, there will always be a choice where you must decide whether to lower sword and show mercy or to not. Whatever the outcome, do not let that moment be your last. Do not let it lead to the suffering of others."

Sir Garrik Skarlit made his way through the makeshift encampment under the watchful gaze of the moon. The scale armour he wore had once been heavy and unforgiving, but now it felt light as a feather. Its weight comforted him. It had been many years since he had first donned the scale armour and cloak of the Laeoflaeden and then Annoran royal guard. Many years and countless battlefields.

He unbuckled his helm and tucked it under his arm. Once more he wished that he had brought Elion along with the three hundred.

No, he silently cursed himself.

Someone was needed to command Palen-Tor's defences and watch over the royal family. Who better than his lieutenant? After all, oaths had to be fulfilled, or the gods would not smile kindly upon them. Garrik could only pray that Azaria and Durandail judged him kindly for the only oath he had ever broken. It had been over two decades since that day and yet he remembered it all. The clear blue sky and the peaceful corridors within Kamlan-Tor. It had been just as a normal day. That was until the army of Dorian Raynor had descended upon the city to lay claim to the throne and avenge the unjust murder of Elodie Raynor and the rest of that line.

King Balinor had commanded him to fight Dorian and to kill him. He had refused and instead Garrik opened the gates for his friend. The oath he had sworn to protect his king was for naught. It was a vow he would not break again. No harm would come to Dorian or his family.

He was halfway through the long line of knights curled up on their bedrolls when the first sound of alarm came. The guards erupted to their feet, and swords leapt into their hands as a trio of horses galloped into the encampment.

Why had the sentries not stopped the rider?

Garrik fumed as he stalked though the ring of warriors that had begun to surround the horsemen.

"What the hell is going on?" he thundered as he pushed his way through the throng. "Why was the alarm not sounded?"

Suddenly, he saw why. Two of the riders were his own men, clad in their armour and blood-red cloaks. The third was hidden between them.

"Forgive us, Sir Garrik," called one of the knights as he dismounted. "There was no threat, and we did not want to cause her further distress."

"Further bloody distress?" the master-at-arms snapped.

Then his eyes flew to the young rider. The blood drained from his face, and a sickening feeling entered his stomach as he recognised the girl before him.

"Your Highness."

Kassandra, Princess of Annora, sat atop a white steed. "Sir Garrik," she said as she smiled back to the knight.

Skarlit stared at her in shock for a moment as he took in her windswept hair and the garments of a servant.

"What are you all waiting for?" he said after a moment. "Give her some room."

How in Azaria's name was Kassandra here?

Garrik approached her horse and extended a hand towards her. "Princess, let me help you."

"No need." She chortled, and she swung herself out of the saddle with the grace of one who had been born to the horse.

The knight could see a slight shiver run through the girl's body as she turned to face him.

Damn Annoran weather, he inwardly cursed. Cold through every bloody season.

He unclasped his cloak and handed it to the princess. "For the cold, my lady."

"Thank you," Kassandra said gratefully as she took it and wrapped it about her slender frame. "I need to speak to you," she told him with authority. "Alone."

"If I may, my lady," Garrik said once they were out of hearing, "what are you doing here? The wild is no place for a princess."

"My own land is not safe for me?" Kassandra snorted.

The master-at-arms stopped in his tracks and looked at her seriously. "My lady—"

"I know it is not safe, alone at least," she cut him off. "Which is why I borrowed this from the servant's quarters."

Smart girl.

Garrik almost smiled at that. It was better to look as a peasant than royalty when she was alone in the wilderness.

"You should not be here," he told her.

"No ... yet here I am," Kassandra said, and she looked him in the eye. "You are aware, of course, that my father and brother wish to marry me off to Duke Aloys' son. That is why you ride north, is it not? To secure this alliance between our two peoples."

"It is." The older man nodded.

"I do not wish to be sold as livestock."

Skarlit bit his lip. Neither of them had any say in the matter. "Then what do you want?"

"What any sister would want," Kassandra said. She turned to face the camp and watched as the royal guard slept around their fires. "To find my brother."

"My lady, you must return to Palen-Tor. I will have two of my men escort you back tomorrow."

"No, you will not," she replied forcefully. "For if you do, I shall tell Father that it was you who took me from the castle. That it was you who planned to hold me hostage. Now tell me, Sir Garrik, do you believe that my father would turn aside the pleas of his tearful daughter? Do you think that he would take your word over that of mine, especially after what happened with Balinor? It is a long ride back to Palen-Tor, and I am certain that whoever you chose to escort me would prefer life over the gallows."

Garrik's jaw dropped. He had seen a lot during his lifetime, yet now a sixteen-year-old girl had gotten the better of him. He saw no way past it. He could send her back to Palen-Tor, yet he knew Dorian. The king had been changed ever since the brutal murders of his first wife and family. He was colder and less forgiving when it came to family. He was a lion protecting his cubs. No matter what Garrik said, Dorian would surely take his daughter's side of the argument. Within days, Garrik would be swinging over the town square.

"What did you have in mind?" he said at last.

Kassandra smiled. She knew that she had won.

"We ride to Sergova as planned, and you bargain with Aloys exactly as my father wishes. You will proceed as planned and deal with the Medeans to allow Dayne and his men passage through Aloys' lands. We shall join them and ride to Salvaar. Then, Sir Garrik, we shall end this war and return home with Lukas. I will not marry Emilian Aloys."

"You want me to lie to Alejandro Aloys?" Garrik replied incredulously.

"We can deal with them later," she said with a nod. "Lukas comes first."

The master-at-arms sighed, and his shoulders slumped. "What choice do I have?"

"None."

"The ride will not be easy. We travel over fifty miles per day and only stop to water the horses and sleep."

"Do not take me for one of those noblewomen who would break after riding half a mile." Kassandra grinned. "I did not expect this to be easy."

Garrik suppressed a laugh as she spoke.

Brave girl. Naïve maybe, yet brave nonetheless.

"We cannot travel with you looking like that. This needs to be held as a secret until such a time as we return to Annora. Do you understand, my lady?"

"Then you had best stop calling me my lady," the princess said.

"Some of the lads may have spare equipment that we can tailor for you," Skarlit told her thoughtfully. "People would notice if a company of royal guards travelled with one not bearing their colours. And you must not talk to anyone who is not one of us."

"This may help with the illusion," Kassandra said.

She bent down and reached into a boot and pulled out a long knife. The jewelled sheath was beautiful, yet the blade was of the finest quality. It was steel from Tarik. Garrik had no time to act. Kassandra quickly took hold of her tied back hair and sliced the blade where the tie met her brown locks. Moonlight glinted on steel, and her shaggy hair fell to the sides of her face. She tossed the sheared clump to the ground. Kassandra ran a hand through her locks and shook her head to flick her hair back into its natural position. It was now shorter than even shoulder length.

"Oh, and Sir Garrik … to save issue, if the time arises when we are with Aloys or anyone else and you need to speak to me … call me Kassian. For why come so far only to let my name give us away?"

TWENTY-SIX

Ruins of Israfil, Kingdom of Miera

Steel sliced through the air as Kitara spun. Her feet glided atop the ruined cobblestone courtyard as if it was smoother than glass. Years aboard ships had taught her a balance that would not fail under the wrath of the most severe of storms. In comparison, a few broken rocks were no trouble. She could feel everything. The light breeze on her cheek. The gentle rays of the dawn sun warming her skin. The rough leather of the sword's hilt was more comforting to her than the finest of silks.

The sword glinted in the sunlight as she moved. A flick of the wrists turned a downwards cut into a sidewards slash. Kitara spun inside the move and lunged. She could feel the muscles of her leg, back and arm stretch with the movement. She angled her body as she twirled back. She arced her sword over her head with a single hand. Her feet slid across the ground as she caught the blade with two hands and turned a spin into a cut. Her hair whipped through the air as Kitara turned her sword skyward. She drove the razor-sharp steel edge towards the heavens. Once more she turned, and her blade carved a path through the air as she threw a high kick. The momentum of the move spun Kitara around. Her boot touched down as she pivoted, and her blade sliced through the air. There the movement ended. Her form was ever graceful.

Kitara held her pose. It was perfect – from the strength of her muscle to the reach of her arm. She still thought her technique could use work. Her old mentor had taught her that tarkaras had many flaws. Foremost among them was that it was an honourable way to fight. Graceful. So, Kitara had taken what she had learnt from the gutters, what she had seen among the pirates of the Sacasian and combined them to create her own way of fighting. Kicks to stagger opponents and break joints. Punches and knee and elbow strikes could be devastating when used at the right time. For if there was one thing she had learnt, it was that she would lose if she tried to fight bigger and stronger opponents in their own way. Had she tried to learn the mainland way of fighting, she would have died a long time ago. Instead, she had found her own way. In her experience, precision beat power and timing beat speed. One perfect blow is all it took to end a fight. Add in a few nasty tricks and she could take most opponents by surprise.

Kitara took a deep breath as she lowered her sword. For the first time she noticed the thin layer of sweat that covered her body. She had been going through her motions since before the sun rose in an attempt to clear her mind. Now she might have time to think about what the Salvaari had said.

Was it really possible that she was one of those people? The very same people that the Mierans called savages?

The man they had captured seemed anything but savage. He was a little rough around the edges. He didn't appear to be savage though. Kitara snatched up her belt from a nearby post. She sheathed her sword and swiftly buckled it to her waist. She took a long draught from her wineskin. She was glad to have purchased more during their trip to Imalric. A fiery warmth seeped through her body as she drank and sent a slight shiver down her back.

A piecing whistle cut through the silence. It was followed by an arrow that arced down from the battlements and drove into a patch of earth.

The lookout.

Kitara sprinted towards the stairs that led up the wall. She took them three at a time. Her hand dropped to her sword as she reached the walkway. Her emerald gaze swept over the countryside. She had been the first to the wall, but within moments the battlements were crawling with Mierans armed to the teeth.

Her eyes flicked to a growing speck coming towards them with haste. She didn't need her spyglass to tell that it was a rider.

A single rider from the south.

That could mean only one thing. He came from Cardna. Azrial Dathmir had sent word.

Iron-shod horseshoes rang on stone as the rider galloped into Israfil and dismounted in a single move.

"I come from Cardna," the rider gasped to his brethren as they assembled around him.

He looked exhausted. He must have ridden faster and harder than the wind to reach them in this state.

"You bring word from Dathmir?" Silas asked of him.

The rider nodded. "And from the king …"

The Mierans exchanged looks. They all knew that this meant.

"Something has changed?" Silas asked as he met the man's eyes.

"Salvaar is at war."

There was a sharp intake of breath as he spoke. His very words chilled the air around them.

"With whom?" Darian asked.

The rider turned to the other Mieran, and his voice was little more than a whisper. "With themselves."

Lukas growled as he and his companions were hoisted to their feet by a group of Mierans and led out of the cell. Their hands were bound by rope under the stern gaze of their captors.

"Darian, was it?" the prince snapped when he recognised the

warrior whom he had injured. "How is the wound?"

"You speak when spoken to," Darian snarled as he gave Lukas a rough shove and forced him into the hall.

Lukas glanced around the room and was met with the grim faces of the Mierans, though now a curiosity had joined the anger that burned in their eyes. The girl, Kitara, leaned against a wall and eyed them for a moment before she turned to Silas.

The Mieran leader rose to his feet, knife in hand, as he saw the three men enter the room. Silas swiftly and gracefully flipped the knife, caught it by its blade and then hurled it towards the ground. His eyes never left Cailean. The blade thudded as it bit into a small clump of earth.

"You," was all he said, and he pointed towards the Salvaari. "I know who you are."

Cailean merely snorted.

Lukas crossed his arms. "And who might that be?"

"Do you take me for a fool?" Silas asked as he strode towards Cailean. He stopped inches away from that of the Salvaari. "Did you think that we would not discover the answer as to why you are here?"

"The only fools here bear the title of Mieran," Cailean growled, and his eyes threw daggers at the man before him.

Silas chortled before gesturing to one of his kin. A man whom Lukas had not seen before. A man who had not been a part of the company that had captured them. He appeared to be little under forty summers and wore the same cold expression as the rest of his kin.

"This is Caradoc," Silas called. "He rides from the north."

The man walked to Silas' side, and his eyes never left Cailean. "Days gone we captured one of your kin in the Rift. We know what is transpiring beneath those trees. We know," the newcomer said.

Lukas felt his shoulders slump, and his eyes flicked shut. So the secrecy had been in vain after all.

"And in so doing," Silas added as he nodded towards the prince, "we know why you are here. The alliance between Annora and Salvaar was once strong, was it not? So, who are you? Some kind of ambassador? No … You ride too well for that. A noble perhaps."

"I am just a warrior," Lukas snapped. "A warrior who believes in honour."

"Honour? What do you know about honour?" Silas let out a mirthless chuckle. "You, who has never faced true fear. Learn what honour is before pretending you are a warrior."

"Let us go," Sakkar growled. "Or let the blood of thousands be on your conscience."

"What care have I for Salvaar?" The Mieran turned to face him, and he indicated Cailean. "His people have slaughtered mine without regard or mercy for generations. Each year new raiding parties cross the Rift, slaughtering and killing at will. And yet you would have me let you go so that you could what? Save them? Those trees can burn for all I care."

"You speak as if one tribe represents all of my people. The men who raid you, the Catuvantuli, are a bloodthirsty people," Cailean snarled. "Yet the other clans live in peace."

"Clearly they do not," cut in Caradoc.

"Aye, maybe we do fight and bicker amongst ourselves." The Salvaari glared. "Yet do not believe yourself innocent. For it was not the Catuvantuli who first crossed the Rift. Nor was it them who took first blood. And the Catuvantuli … they always remember."

"Enough of this," Silas snapped. "Soon we will ride for Cardna. Dathmir shall decide your fate."

"Shall he indeed?" Sakkar asked, and he gave the man a savage grin. Too late did they see the rope that bound his hands was gone. The Larissan drove his fist into the face of the nearest Mieran as the shouts began. He leapt forwards as blood exploded from his captor's lips and sent them both crashing to the ground in a pile of limbs. He hit the man, once, twice.

The swords of the Mierans were drawn and soon blades pressed to the throats of Lukas and Cailean. Finally, Sakkar was pulled from his foe. Two men held the Larissan tightly and pinned his arms up behind his back. The man whom he had attacked rose to his feet and wiped the blood from his face. He spat to the side and then struck Sakkar hard in the stomach. Lukas nearly winced as his friend doubled over with a grunt. The heavy blow nearly drove him to his knees.

"I thought you were fighters." The Larissan managed a chuckle as he rose back to his full height with a sneer. "Yet you have such soft hands."

Silas knelt over the rope that had once bound the westerner's hands tightly. He picked it up and turned his dark gaze upon the man.

"Where did you learn that?"

"That trick?" Sakkar grinned once more and nodded skywards. "The creator came down from the heavens and taught me himself."

Silas snorted as he glared towards the man.

"You should learn to watch your tongue," he growled. "Or someday someone will cut it out."

The prisoners had been returned to their cell for a long time when curiosity finally got the better of Kitara. The Salvaari had appeared to be telling the truth about her heritage, but she couldn't wrap her head around the idea. The idea of a Salvaari crossing the seas was unthinkable.

She breathed a sigh of relief as she reached the ruined hall. It only had one sole occupant. Silas.

Half of the company had ridden out to scout Carn-Dair, while others would be keeping watch atop the walls or training in the courtyard. Not their leader though. Much had been on Silas Barangir's mind ever since Caradoc had arrived. Now he sat by the fire and stared into its burning flames, as his mind danced around the choices he had yet to make.

"Silas."

His gaze did not shift from the fire. "Hmmm?"

Kitara sat down on one of the small benches opposite Silas. "I need to ask you something," she said.

Silas' eyes finally flicked up from the flames and he looked towards her.

"What is it?"

Kitara took a deep breath. She was suddenly nervous about what she was had to do. A cold tingle ran through her veins, and she shivered despite the warmth of the flames on her skin.

"Your people still do not trust me," Kitara stated.

"Kitara." Silas sighed, and looked her in the eye. "Not this again."

"It can wait no longer," her voice growled as she fought back the irritation the clawed at her. "I have been in Miera for over a year. Do not think me stupid. I have trained and ridden beside your kin since the day I arrived, yet still they look at me as I am the enemy."

"Don't be absurd." Silas snorted.

"Let me finish," Kitara snapped back. She glared at her friend and a new darkness entered her gaze. A darkness that had been a part of her life since the day she was born. "I have met people, foreigners, who travel these lands. Men granted the favour and seal of King Zoran himself. Men free to travel Miera without fear of death. Men that your people greet as a brother. I spoke to one such man months ago in Carlian, and at the time I thought nothing of it. He had earned the trust of Miera by fighting as a mercenary against Annora all those years ago. He said that your people welcomed him with open arms within weeks of him first stepping foot on this soil. I did not see it then, but now I do. It is not because I am foreign that I am distrusted, is it?"

Silas let out a breath, and his eyes never left hers. Not for a second did they waver.

"Where does this come from?" he asked. "You who speaks of distrust yet does not trust anyone."

"It comes from the dark looks and harsh words. It comes from the intolerable hatred in the eyes of even those I would call friend. I have done nothing to warrant such suspicion."

"You have been speaking to the prisoners, haven't you?" Silas said after a moment.

There was no doubt he could see it in her eyes.

Kitara dipped her head slowly. "It is no secret that most of the northerners despise me, and now perhaps I know the answer to that."

"What answer would that be?"

"The men of the Rift have always viewed me with the utmost suspicion, a suspicion that has bled into the rest of Miera." Kitara set her jaw. "I want you to tell me the truth. When you look at my face, when you look into my eyes … what do you see?"

"You know what I see," Silas muttered.

"I want to hear you say it," Kitara shot back. "You owe me that much."

The Mieran was silent for a moment.

"Alright," he said at last, and his voice turned hard. "I see the fire of burning villages. I hear the screams of my people as woads stream across the Rift. I feel fear … fear as the night beckons and we are cut down by an unseen enemy. You want to know what I see? I see Salvaar. You want to know why we distrust you? Ask yourself this: Would you be so willing to accept one who unmistakably looks like your enemy? An enemy who has killed a number beyond reckoning. Thousands of your people. An enemy that you have been at war with for generations. It is the pain my kin feel every day when they see your face."

"Why did you not tell me?" Kitara's voice was soft.

She felt as if a knife had been slipped between her ribs. They had lied to her. All of them. Zandir, Darian, Lucian, Uriah and Caidin. Even Silas.

"We believed that—"

"I had a right to know," she snarled.

She could taste the poison in her words as she spoke them. She relished in the anger that burned to the surface. Kitara leapt to her feet, and her hands balled into fists.

"I had a right to know!"

She could feel moisture well in her eyes as she turned and strode away from Silas. Kitara took a breath and composed herself. She had not cried in many years. She would not start today. No man was worth her tears.

Cries flooded the Aedei encampment as a company of riders cantered through the rows of blue-painted warriors. Those atop steeds wore little in the way of clothing yet sported war paint black as the night sky. The Káli had come.

Vaylin, Chief of the Káli, rode at their fore. Her eyes never strayed to the baying crowd on either side. Nor did they move when those of the Sagailean tribe, long time enemy of the Káli, snarled and cursed at her. For she was proud. Each of her warriors held aloft an olive branch. None of them looked down. To do so would be to show weakness, and the Káli were not weak.

A great tent arose before the warriors. The humble dwelling was made of wood and animal skins. The antlers of a massive stag were fixed above its entrance. Three men stood before the tent. One wore the white paint of the Coventina, another the thin black and red stripes of the Sagailean, while the third merely wore blue. He was Aedei. Dáire, Balor and Cyneric were the three leaders of their alliance. Each man was vastly different, yet each was powerful beyond all measure.

"Why do we play host to these people?" grunted Balor.

His hand itched to take up the sword at his side and run his mortal enemy through. Yet to do so would be to go break a sacred truce between the tribes. To do so would incur the wrath of the spirits.

"Peace, Balor," Cyneric told his fellow chief. "The Káli must have cause to bring the olive branch and come to us with their hands extended."

Vaylin brought her ebony mount to a halt and tossed her olive branch before her.

"I seek an audience with Cyneric of the Aedei," she roared, and her fiery eyes never left those of the Aedei chief.

At a word from Cyneric, the black-painted chief was led from her horse to him.

"You being here does come as a surprise," Cyneric of the Aedei said, and he glanced back at Vaylin as she followed him into his tent.

"And yet, here I am," the Káli chief replied proudly.

They were alone. Her business was not for Dáire or Balor. At least, not yet. Cyneric led his alliance, and so it would be with Cyneric she would speak. Vaylin pulled her wineskin from her belt and held it out for Cyneric. The Aedei extended a hand and then, with something of a smirk, withdrew it.

"I mean no disrespect, yet you understand, of course," Cyneric told her.

"Had I wished you dead, I would not have come here, Chief Cyneric." Vaylin suppressed a chuckle as she spoke. "Say what you will about my people, but we honour the spirits ... We honour guest rights. To poison a man beneath his own roof is tasteless, don't you think?"

"Indeed," came the reply.

It was hard to put the rumours of Vaylin from his mind. There were tales that she had poisoned her own chief in the safety of his own hall.

"Why have you come?" Cyneric asked. "You must know that many beneath my command would happily take your life."

"Balor first among them," Vaylin replied. "I know. Yet my trust has been wavered."

"What has Henghis done to make you reconsider your position?"

"Henghis? Nothing," the Káli woman told him. "It is his pet wanderer that I have no faith in. Nor his Medeans."

She said Medean as if it were a curse. It was true. The deep forest clans had no love of outsiders. Even those bearing the name Salvaari. Yet her simmering hatred seemed to go beyond that.

Cyneric folded his arms. "Tell me."

"This wanderer … this Kendrick … has blinded Henghis to his cruelty," she spat. Even the mention of the man's name left a bad taste in her mouth. "By day he plays the part of stoic advisor, yet by night he turns monster," she continued. "People who sought his counsel were vanishing, and yet I had no proof. He is cunning … manipulating those about him with a forked tongue. I fear that magic is involved, Cyneric, dark magic."

"And you believe that this is the reason why the wanderer has a hold over Henghis?" The Aedei stroked his beard.

It was possible that some kind of sorcery was involved. Ever since the days of the Inquisition, the purge, magic in many of its forms had vanished. Yet there were always traces that lingered. Especially in the deep forest.

Vaylin slowly nodded. She was Káli. Her blood flowed with the beating heart of the deep forest in which she was born. A lot of strange things happened beneath those trees, and the idea of dark magic did little to faze her.

"And then last moon … I confronted the man. I told him that I saw through his act, that Henghis would not take kindly to the disappearance of his own kin ..." She trailed off and leant heavily on the bench that separated the two chiefs.

Vaylin bared her teeth and gazed at Cyneric with her dark eyes.

"I made to warn Henghis when the knights attacked. My cousins were slain at their hand, my brother taken. Whether he is dead ... I do not know."

"I share your grief," Cyneric told her sincerely.

He could still see his brother facing off against the knights as he had been forced to flee. One day he would avenge Malakai's death. He pushed those thoughts from his mind. He needed to think clearly and without emotion if he were to lead.

"Yet why come to me?"

Vaylin moved around the table and stepped by Cyneric. Her long hair gently brushed his arm as she walked past. Cyneric suppressed a shiver and resisted the fire that burned through his veins after so brief a touch. Malakai had often told him about Vaylin. That she used her captivating eyes and mysterious beauty to ensnare any she chose. Seduction was as much a weapon to her as the poisons that she mixed.

"I believe that our ends coincide," she said. "I believe that Kendrick has played us all for fools and that there may be some truth in the idea that Malakai did not start this war."

"And now you wish to ally yourself to me."

"Exactly."

Her dark green eyes bore into Cyneric. There was a spark within them. They almost looked hungry. Cyneric couldn't say what for though. Yet if what she said was true, then she was offering him five thousand warriors. The men sorely needed aid that could light the first fires of hope. So far there had been little more than minor skirmishes and conflicts between the scouts. Yet a fight was brewing to the east. A compromise would have to be made before he could add the Káli to his ranks.

"Very well," Cyneric told the chief of the Káli.

The corners of her lips twitched, and she stepped towards him. She was no more than half a foot away. He could feel her breath tickle his chin even as the smell of wild berries reached his nose.

"Kendrick has wronged us both and I would have his head upon a day. However, if we are to complete this alliance, then I have a condition of my own."

"Yes?"

"Make your peace with Balor. End this dispute between Káli and Sagailean, and we shall have our peace."

Vaylin pursed her lips and Cyneric knew he had caught her off guard. As much as it pained her, she would have no choice but to accept his terms.

She dipped her head as she whispered in reply, "Give me your knife."

The assembled warriors snapped their eyes towards the command tent as the two chieftains emerged from the darkness. Aedei, Coventina, Sagailean and Káli all watched intently as the lady of the deep forest spoke.

"Brothers and sisters of Salvaar, for too long have we fought amongst ourselves. A great change is upon the horizon. I can see it. And we to must change with it," Vaylin said as she turned to face Balor. "No more shall I be beholden to feuds so old that no one alive knows of their providence. Balor of the Sagailean, for too long have our people killed each other in the name of our ancestors. Names long forgotten. For too long has the forest been divided."

She held aloft the blade that Cyneric had offered her. She drew it across the palm of her hand in a single swift moment. She did not so much as wince as the blood spread across her hand. She held the blade out towards Balor.

"I offer peace."

All eyes went to Balor as he fought with the decision. Many of his own family had perished in the fight against the Káli. Now Vaylin, a woman he distrusted, offered to end the bloodshed.

He closed his eyes. Then he took the knife.

Silence overcame the warriors as the chief looked to Vaylin. He slid the blade across his own hand. He extended his open palm towards the Káli chief.

"In the name of the spirits, let us be as one."

Vaylin took his bloody hand in a firm grip with her own. A new pact with the spirits had been made. It was an alliance sealed in blood. The roar that filled the forest was deafening.

TWENTY-SEVEN

Tears of Freydis, Isle of Vay'kis

The burning sun was greeted by the hammering of axes and grating of chisels as Hvitsred and the other craftsmen went to work. The few hunters of the party had risen before dawn to stalk the forest. Thus far, game had been plentiful and the feathers of owls, pheasants and other birds were being used for fletching. A pile of arrows that had been crafted by women and old folk steadily began to grow under the gaze of Hvitsred's son. Hélla and her party of warriors were yet to return, though it gave Astrid no concern. The shieldmaiden was fearless in battle and had a keen mind for strategy. They would return soon enough.

"Astrid."

Astrid turned as Nenrir approached, and a grin spread across his face. Another of the Valkir stood at his back. They both clasped a selection of bows within their grasp.

"We found these in the hold," the archer explained, and answered Astrid's unspoken question.

"Add them to those Hvitsred has made," Astrid told him as her lips twitched upwards. "Then get to work. I want all who are beyond fourteen summers to be ready by the next moon."

That gave them little over a week, and yet none save the hunters and craftsmen had tasks to complete. Time enough for her people to learn the bow. Astrid had seen the power of the weapon in

Annora.

Her fear had been held at bay by only a single steely nerve as arrows fell all about them and splintered shield and flesh alike.

"Jarl." Nenrir nodded.

Within moments, he was handing out bows to the first volunteers. Six bows from the hold, plus the three that the bowyer had crafted. With Nenrir and the half dozen hunters as well, they were starting to look more and more deadly.

A few of the women who were skilled in the crafting of fabrics had taken up spare canvas and filled them with the long grass. They attached them to some crudely lashed together branches to create some basic targets. The crew placed them at the edge of the forest. They were about sixty feet from where Nenrir was now lining up the first of the chosen recruits. Some of them seemed confident, while others seemed less so.

Astrid slowly made her way through the campsite until she stood alone. She sought comfort in her own company. She was alone save for the gentle breeze on her cheek and the silent company of the Sea-Father. She watched on, half in eagerness and half in uncertainty, as the archers began to line up.

"This should be good," Torben said with a grin as he walked to his jarl's side.

The flicker of irritation that arose within her quickly receded as the silence was broken. There would be time to be alone in the days to come. Astrid grunted, and she barely looked at the older man.

"Many of them have used a bow to some degree over the years, whether they be the older folk who learnt on the raiding path or those who merely hunted in the mountains of home. A head start … Yet some …" Astrid trailed off.

"Some will have never so much as skinned a rabbit let alone wielded such a weapon," Torben finished.

She didn't reply. Instead, her amber eyes stayed locked upon the men and women as they began to draw their bows. Astrid could only watch as Nenrir gave the signal and arrows began to fly. Their bladed tips sliced through the air towards their targets. Some arrows found their mark with a dull crack. Some speared into their target, while others bounced off or missed by a yard. Astrid closed her eyes and let out the breath that she had been holding. Only two of the arrows had met their mark. Only two would have counted in a fight.

Torben placed a weathered hand on her shoulder. "There is still time," he said.

"I pray that you are right."

"I would not have thought of this," he replied.

He gestured around the cove with a long branch he held in his hand. She had not noticed the branch. She silently cursed.

Yes, she had not slept last night and very little the night before … yet she needed her mind to be sharp. It was often the smallest things that got people killed. She met Torben's eyes as he continued.

"You got us to safety. The archers were a stroke of brilliance that no one else would have so much as dreamed of. No doubt you are working on our next move … and more than that." He gripped her shoulder tightly, and his eyes glowed like fire.

It was as if he could see the thin strand of light she was clinging to. That last ounce of hope that was nearly lost. He had known her for many years, and if anyone knew her thoughts, it was Torben. Astrid knew he could see that pain that she hid so well. The loss of her mother still weighed deeply. Her father's murder. Many of her scâldir were gone. Laerke. Raol. Erik. On top of that, she had to lead these people who were on the verge of defeat and find a way to bring them victory. She had to find a way to give them their lives back. They all looked to her to lead them, and by the gods, she would do it.

"You gave them hope when there was none," Torben said. "You gave them hope."

Astrid felt her heart soar as he said those words. The man was a mentor to her. He was the uncle she never had. She clasped his arm.

"Just as you now give me."

That was as sentimental as she was going to get. No more words needed to be spoken, nor emotions made bare. She was a jarl of the Valkir, and she would show no weakness.

"Now tell me," she said as she nodded towards the stick that the warrior held. "What use do you have for that? Are you so old that you can no longer trust your own two legs?"

Torben roared with laughter as Astrid's lips curled.

"I may be old, but I could still teach you a thing or two."

"Of that I have no doubt," she replied. "Now tell me before you grow soft."

"I am not soft," the warrior growled, and he planted the end of his branch in the earth. "None of us are soft, and the raids have made our skills as sharp as any blade. Yet rather than grow fat and lazy, should we not keep ourselves keen to the ways of battle? We have no practice blades here, so sticks and branches will do."

"I agree," Astrid told him.

He was a veteran of many battles. He was a man who had fought for well over thirty summers. A man with the skill to be welcomed into the ranks of the bloodsworn. If anyone knew how to prepare them for the coming storm, it was him.

"Keep them sharp, for our warriors must be as a wall."

"They will be," Torben vowed.

With that, he headed into the campsite where many of the warriors had gathered to watch Nenrir's recruits. Astrid swept her gaze around the camp towards the river that ran down from the mountains. Further up the ridge stood a figure that stared almost blankly towards the horizon.

Mayrun.

She had not spoken a word since receiving news of her betrothed's death. Maybe now she would be willing to speak. Astrid had to try.

The jarl took a deep breath as her mind searched for words that might help Mayrun. She started to climb as she heard Torben's parade ground voice booming.

"Alright, lads, get off your arses. There is work to be done."

The clash of wood began as Astrid reached the top of the hill.

"You should not wander alone," Astrid said as she approached Mayrun. She was a woman who, thanks to Raol, was as good as a sister to her. "There may yet be danger here," Astrid continued.

Mayrun did not even turn to look towards the jarl as she spoke. Her voice no more than the faintest of whispers when she spoke. "There stands no such place that is safe … Not anymore."

Astrid walked to stand beside her. Mayrun simply gazed down past the camp and lake towards the river mouth. There was a ring clasped tightly in her hands. Raol's last gift to her. The jarl felt a pang of worry in her breast.

"You have not spoken since Agartha … You have not eaten," Astrid said softly.

She held out a small loaf of bread that she had taken from the camp. The Rider had only recently returned from raiding season and had almost been emptied. Almost. Lief had instilled in Astrid to always be prepared. So, the Rider had provisioned with some food and water. This was some of the last of the bread they had, but that did not bother the jarl.

"Take this," Astrid said.

Finally, Mayrun glanced at Astrid and the proffered loaf. Her eyes were raw, and her cheeks were covered in tears.

"Would it make any difference? I am but a shadow … one that haunts a world without meaning."

Astrid lowered her extended hand. She tried to catch Mayrun's eyes, yet the girl would not shift her gaze from the cove.

"You live."

"Hardly," she said, and a fresh tear slid down her cheek. "Astrid … He is dead. Raol is dead."

"I know," Astrid murmured, and she lightly touched Mayrun's arm. "He is in the golden halls now, feasting and drinking with the Sea-Father."

"Would that I could turn back time and exchange my life for his."

The jarl took her hand and clasped it gently. "I wish that I could have done the same. That I could have fallen and spared you this grief," Astrid told her. "Raol … he gave his life so that we may live."

A fresh wave of tears threatened Mayrun. "I loved him," she murmured.

Astrid pulled the girl into an embrace. She barely noticed the girl's wet cheek against her own, and nor did she feel the tears that ran from Mayrun's eyes and onto her neck.

"He loved you … more than anything."

Astrid felt the girl's arms wrap around her back as she returned the hug.

"He would not want you to weep for days long past," the jarl told her. "Nor shed tear over what could have been. Embrace the present and live each day as it comes … I swear to you that the man responsible for his death will die for his betrayal."

"Astrid!" Hélla yelled as she sprinted into the camp with a band of warriors at her back. "ASTRID!"

The shieldmaiden's legs had begun to burn a mile back, but she needed to find her jarl. Hélla was used to travelling great distances over land, yet she had just run over seven miles laden with heavy armour and a shield. Hot sweat ran down her face as her aching lungs made her breath ragged. She came to a halt and all eyes turned to her party. She could almost feel the shock that they felt. Hélla unbuckled her helm and pulled it from her head.

The shieldmaiden tossed it to the ground and doubled over as she gasped. Hélla attempted to suck in as much air as she could take. One by one, the crew of the Wind Rider began to assemble around the exhausted warriors. Hélla took a long breath and rose back to full height. She was composing herself even as she saw the jarl push through the crowd towards her.

"Hélla?" Astrid called, and her eyes flashed with worry. "What is it? What have you found?"

The warrior's hand dropped to her sword as she replied. Hélla shouted loud enough for all to hear.

"There is a small path … some kind of goat trail that leads into the mountains little over a mile from where we stand." Hélla panted as she stepped closer to Astrid. "We followed it for some time … no more than seven miles. It leads towards Lumis, Astrid. It leads towards the city."

Astrid's heart began to pound. It was the only sound she could hear over the silence that now emanated from the crew.

"What are you saying?"

"I am saying that this place is not safe. I am saying that Earl Arndyr and his people know of what Freydis discovered all those years ago … There are warriors heading for us as we speak."

Astrid crossed her arms as a feeling ran down her back. Not fear or doubt. It was anticipation.

"How many?" she asked.

"Forty strong, at least."

"So, they must have seen us enter the river after all."

Hélla nodded. "I left Fargrim and Osval to watch them. They will be here before nightfall," she told Astrid.

Astrid glanced towards the horizon. The sun was starting to draw close to the mountains. "Whether they mean us harm or not, one thing is clear: we do not have much time. Hélla, take your men. Eat, drink, rest. Prepare yourselves," the jarl said as she swept her gaze around the assembled crew. "Nenrir, call the hunters in.

We will need every man and woman ready. We make for the goat path. In friendship or battle … we meet them head on."

✦ ✦ ✦

The sky had turned into a vibrant orange as the sun began to dip behind the mountains. Astrid had climbed up atop a small ridge that overlooked the mouth of the goat path. A small canyon that ran deep into the mountains lay below. Fargrim stood beyond her, his piercing gaze not leaving the path. They could see roughly fifty paces into the gorge before it rounded the bend and vanished from sight.

"Osval is but a little way up the track," Fargrim told her as she reached his side.

In his hands the warrior clutched a bow. An arrow already sat nocked atop it.

Astrid nodded. "Good."

Osval was taking a very real risk, but this was the last vantage point they could get without taking a step into the path before them. It would do them well to have eyes further within. The jarl spared a glance to the mouth of the track where it opened up into the cove. Torben, Hélla and the other warriors had formed into an arc shape two dozen paces from the goat path. It would give the newcomers space to properly form up. However, it would mean that the crew could surround them on three sides. Not to mention that, if it came to it, the archers under Nenrir who stood behind the warriors could unleash Skûra upon them. Even the greenest of recruits couldn't fail to hit a target at this range. They're opponents would soon be pincushions. All they had to do was wait.

Once more Astrid went over the carefully laid plan that she had constructed. Her crew had followed her command to the letter and stood ready. It had not taken long to absolve her people of the idea of blocking off the goat path. The trail was narrow, and at best only two warriors could fight another two. It would take far too much time to accomplish anything. It would negate any advantage that her archers could give her, even if there were only a dozen thus far. Arndyr's men would assume that an attack was imminent if the very mouth of the path was blocked.

"It's quiet," Astrid murmured, and she fingered the head of her axe. It still felt alien at her side.

"Aye," Fargrim muttered. "We're in the eye of the storm now."

Astrid made to reply when she saw a flicker of movement from the goat trail. A man clad in the armour of a Valkir warrior rounded the bend at a sprint. It was Osval.

"THEY'RE HERE!" he roared.

"MAKE READY!" Astrid bellowed towards the crew as she pushed herself into a run and dashed down from the ridge.

The warriors hustled into position as Astrid made her way to the front beside Torben and Hélla. She was their leader. She was their jarl. It would be her who first issued challenge to Arndyr's men. Her fist tightened on the head of her axe. She was ready to draw it at a moment's notice. All around her the crew took up their weapons. Their shields were slung onto their arms while swords, axes and steel-tipped spears were at the ready.

Astrid took a deep breath.

The first of Arndyr's warriors rounded the bend and came into sight.

Arrows were nocked as more and more warriors streamed out of the goat path. Yet, as Astrid commanded, her troops did not react. Their shields were not hefted and locked together into an unbreakable wall. Nor were their bows or blades raised in defiance. Instead, they stood still. Their eyes were cold as ice as they watched the new arrivals form up opposite them. One of the men of Vay'kis stepped forwards and removed his helmet. It was made of beautifully crafted steel and unlike anything that could be found in the Valkir Isles. A wave of dark hair fell down his shoulders and blended into his long, dark beard. He wore an oval shield on his back and bore a blade at his hip. A steel cuirass was sculpted over his chest. It matched his helm and was embellished with the image of a griffin. The symbol of the Aureian Empire. Around his right arm he wore a band of violet. It was the sacred band. The mark of the Arkin Garter. Astrid knew that he was not Arndyr himself. Yet at least fifty of his people had served in the emperor's elite guard. The man who now glared towards them with hawk-like eyes was not to be trifled with. He was, above all else, a warrior. A man who could easily gain entry into the ranks of the bloodsworn if he wished.

"Who are you that would step foot on our land?" he called out.

He was now no more than fifteen paces away. His men approached and came to a halt at his back.

Astrid stepped forwards to meet him. "My name is Astrid Farrin of Agartha, Jarl of the Wind Rider."

"Ah, the daughter of Lief," the man said, and he slowly nodded. "Word reached us days past that he was killed by one of his own people."

"He was, and the shadow of his murderer now stalks Skûra."

Astrid looked deeply into his eyes. She was searching for any hint of false sympathy. Her father had always told her to beware of snakes in the grass.

"And now you stand as jarl."

His gaze gave nothing away. He betrayed nothing. There was no emotion in those cold, blue eyes.

"That you found this place is a thing unheard of … yet what is this? Some kind of invasion?" he asked.

"We did not come here looking for a fight," Astrid said as she shook her head. "We only seek sanctuary for a few days."

"Yet you did not come directly to Lumis. Nor did you seek audience with the earl of this isle," the man replied. "Why?"

"My reasons are my own."

The warrior snorted. "Then what is to stop me ordering my men to attack? What is to stop me from killing you all here and now?"

"Nothing."

Astrid hardened her gaze until she was all but glaring at the man. She stood tall and proud. Without fear. Without compromise. She spread her arms and stepped towards him.

"Strike me down if you wish. I do not fear death."

The man returned her stare, and they locked eyes for a moment. It was as if he could look within her. It was as if those eyes that had seen so much of the world could look into her very soul. Something new seemed to flash within his eyes as he watched her.

"You have honour," he told her. "A rare thing in these times."

"Rarer still to meet my equal," Astrid pressed. "Allow me to speak to Earl Arndyr. Perhaps we can come to some sort of understanding."

Time seemed to slow as the warrior made up his mind, but at last he extended an arm.

"I am Jormund Scaeva, formally of the Arkin Garter and brother to the earl."

Astrid clasped the man's proffered arm.

Brother to Arndyr? It was no wonder that the man carried himself with such pride and strength if he was once part of Darius' elite guard. "Run to Lumis, tell my brother that he will have company," Jormund said as he gestured to one of his men.

"Lord," the warrior said, and he turned and jogged back down the trail.

"We leave now." Scaeva turned back to Astrid. "You may bring two companions, and if you wish it, you may carry a blade. Things are done differently in Vay'kis, and you have earned that honour."

TWENTY-EIGHT

Ruins of Israfil, Steppe of Miera

A thin sliver of golden sunlight slipped through the small, barred window of the prison cell. It mingled with the orange light of the torches just beyond its steel door.

Sakkar danced a coin across his fingers, and the moon's rays kissed it. The Larissan flicked his wrist and rolled the coin over the palm of his hand before sending it back along his fingers. Again and again, he rolled it. It had not been hard to smuggle the coin past the Mierans.

"We need to get out of here," Lukas said from where he stood looking out the window. "And it has to be tonight."

"How do you propose we do that?" Cailean asked as he glanced up at the prince. "We are locked in this cell with naught but a single coin."

"So what? You heard the Mieran … Tomorrow we ride for Cardna," Lukas grunted and turned to his companions. "I have heard of Azrial Dathmir. He is a man who is not afraid of bloodshed. We'll be gutted and hung to dry within days."

"Perhaps I have a solution." Sakkar spoke up. "Though its risk is great."

Cailean growled, "If we do nothing then we're already dead."

"What is it?" Lukas dropped into a crouch as he looked to his friend. "You have a way out?"

Sakkar shrugged and reached into the folds of his robes.

"I may not be able to spirit us from this cell. Not without my tools ... yet some tricks require no physical means."

"Ever fond of riddles." The prince gave an exasperated sigh.

The Salvaari stared at Sakkar. "What do you mean, tricks?" Cailean asked.

"Some men grow to work steel, others to till the fields or train horses ... I dabbled in being a performer of sorts," Sakkar said as the coin danced faster across the top of his hand. "Maybe I need tools to free us from this cell and spirit us from iron bonds, yet perhaps now I have them."

He withdrew his free hand and opened it. A key glimmered in the palm of his hand.

"That's why you struck the Mieran," Lukas stated incredulously.

The prince's eyes glowed. His friend had often entertained the people of Annora with his parlour tricks. He had even showed them in the court of Palen-Tor upon occasion.

"These people may be great warriors, yet a child could tie a knot better." Sakkar chuckled, and he slid the key under his bracer. "I easily slipped my bonds ... and in turn the Mierans supplied me with a way out of this cage. They plan to take us south tomorrow to meet whatever fate they have in store. We have to move tonight."

Lukas nodded. "Numbers count for nothing in these corridors," he said. "If we can get to the hall ... if we can capture their leader. We can do this."

"Precisely," the Larissan agreed. "We get Silas. We get the horses and then I suggest we get the hell out of here."

"A bold strategy ... The kind that I favour most, Larissan," Cailean told Sakkar. "Though answer me this: The bond with your bird, and these tricks of yours ... where did you learn them?"

A smile came across Sakkar's lips. The coin rolled faster.

"Many years ago, a man came through my village. It was said that he could escape chains with naught but his own hands. That he could vanish in a puff of smoke. His name was Caheira. So skilled was he that his talents were sought after by even the most noble of the aristocracy. So naturally, I asked him to teach me ... And after days of begging, he finally agreed." Sakkar chuckled as he spun his tale. "Many things I learnt from Caheira ... That is, of course, until he attempted his greatest trick of all."

"What was it?" Cailean asked.

"To slow his heartbeat down until it stopped," Sakkar said, and his grin widened. "Though in truth he only did manage to pull it off once."

Cailean blinked in shock and then roared with laughter. He slapped the Larissan on the shoulder as he fought to compose himself.

"You nearly had me."

"Nearly?" a new voice came from outside the cell. "Sounds to me like the man had you right where he wanted you."

Three sets of eyes flicked towards the barred door. It was the golden-haired girl. Kitara.

"What do you want?" the Annoran snapped, and all traces of humour left his face.

Kitara rolled her eyes and turned to face the Larissan. "Not bad." She nodded to him. "The coin."

He smirked and with a flick of his wrist the coin vanished as if it had never been there.

"Illusion opens many pathways."

"Do you not have other travellers to capture?" the Salvaari said. The malice in his eyes from days before had all but gone. Now it was replaced with what seemed like pity. "Kitara, that is your name, yes?"

"Indeed." She shrugged. There was no need for secrets. Not

anymore. "Though now you have me at a disadvantage. You know my name, yet I do not know yours. You who may be my kin," Kitara said.

"Do you mock me?" He snorted. "But days ago, you spit in my face and called me liar. And yet now you come here seeking what?"

"I believe that there might have been some truth to your words," Kitara growled and then she turned her back. "Perhaps I was wrong."

She started to walk away. Anger had begun to stir within her.

"Wait," the man called out, and Kitara came to a halt as he spoke. "Wait. My name is Cailean, son of Raywold."

"Where are you from?" she said, and she glanced back at the man.

"Does it matter?" the Annoran cut in.

"Please," she said as desperation edged its way into her voice. Kitara walked over to the cell door and placed her hands upon the cold steel of the bars. "I need answers," Kitara whispered urgently. "Please."

"Alright," Cailean said after a moment, and he looked up at her. "I was born in Noyon, a small village in the heart of my tribe's lands."

"Your tribe?"

"Yes." His lips twitched fondly. "The Aedei."

Kitara leaned on the door. "The Mierans speak only of the savages that inhabit the forests to the north. They say that your people care for nothing but blood."

"And do you make a habit of judging an entire people based on the stories told by those who hate and distrust them?"

"No." Kitara shrugged. "Yet the Mierans took me in. Gave me a home. Until you, I had never so much as met one of your kind."

"What of your family?" Cailean asked as curiosity got the better of him. "No Salvaari would ever abandon their child."

"They are both dead, for all I know," Kitara muttered, and

bitterness crept into her voice.

"What do you mean?"

"That is none of your concern," she warned. A vicious look flashed across her eyes. It was only there for the briefest of moments, but it held true meaning. "I shall tell you once and once only. Do not speak of my past," Kitara said.

"Apologies." Cailean tapped a hand to his heart. "I did not mean to offend."

"I do not want your pity," Kitara grunted.

It was still there. It crawled under her skin. The anger. The hatred. The feeling that she had been abandoned. It made her blood boil. Yet she had adjusted to it a long time ago. She had learned to live just fine without a family. She had learned to trust no one save herself.

"Tell me about your home," Kitara said.

"Home," Cailean whispered, and he closed his eyes and leaned back against the stone wall of the cell. "Where the birds sing and the trees are evergreen. To the west there lies a small river for the children to play in." He grinned as he spoke. "You can see wild horses gallop through the forest beneath the open sky ... In any village, the people will welcome you with open arms and call you brother. And then" – Cailean opened his eyes at last and looked to Kitara – "and then we have the Festival of Sylvaine."

"Sylvaine?"

Kitara could not help the corners of her lips from twitching into something of a smile. If what the Aedei said was true, then Miera was wrong. Maybe they had let decades of distrust and hatred seep into their idea of the northerners.

"Every five years, the tribes come together in celebration. A celebration of the spirit mother ... of life itself," Cailean told her. "On the first night of this sacred festival, the Great Queen, Sylvaine, paints the sky with violet. The shaman speaks, and then it begins. An entire moon of feasting and drinking. We dance and sing around the fires and the druids tell their great stories. We give offerings to the spirits and then the forest truly, truly comes alive. Everyone is happy."

"That doesn't sound so bad," Kitara said, and she finally allowed the smile. She could almost picture it clearly. Everything from the song of the birds to the warmth of the fires.

"No, no it doesn't," Cailean replied. "The solstice that marks the beginning of the festival will be upon us soon."

"The autumn solstice?" Kitara asked, and she bit her lip. "That is barely a few weeks away."

Cailean nodded. "The fighting will stop for the festival," he said, "and by sacred law, it cannot resume until the festival is complete."

"Perhaps this will give us a chance to end the conflict," the Annoran added.

Kitara's gaze swung to him, and her eyes widened even as his face paled. The fool had given them away.

"Tomorrow we are bound for Cardna," Kitara told him. "It is a two-day ride south and Dathmir is not known for mercy. You plan to escape."

Cailean turned on Lukas. "What have you done?" he snarled at his companion.

"She will not betray us," Lukas said as he met Kitara's eyes. "Is that not so?"

Kitara crossed her arms and returned his stare. She could tell Silas now and the prisoners would be watched with utmost care. They would be separated and maybe even killed in the cell this very night.

"I should. By all reason, I should," Kitara growled. "If you lived to see dawn, then Azrial Dathmir would seal your fate. And yet if I were in your position, would I not be planning my own way out? For surely a chance at freedom is better than the certainty of death. Will I tell this tale to the Mierans? No."

She could remember a time when she too had needed to escape

from the confines of a ship's brig. A time when death was on the horizon. Yet she had not given into despair. Just like these three would not.

"What is this? Some kind of victor's remorse?" the Larissan said as he rose to his feet.

Kitara merely shrugged. "Aye, something like that."

"Then you are one in ten thousand," Cailean told her. "Most would not be so kind."

"I am not most people. Though I should warn you, whatever this plan of yours is … do not go through with it."

"Oh, and why is that?" the Larissan asked as he stepped towards the cell door.

Kitara watched him carefully. Her fingers were barely inches from the hilt of her sword.

"Because these men are Mierans. Do you not think that people have tried to escape from them before? They will watch you eagerly, hoping that you try something rash. The moment that they so much as suspect something foul, they will leave you with more than just a bruise. Try to escape and they will kill you before you make it ten feet."

"Well." The Annoran rose beside his friend. "You said it yourself: if we get to Cardna, we're probably dead already."

"You don't get it, do you?" Kitara snarled as she glared at the two men. "Maybe I won't tell the Mierans, yet if you try to escape … if you so much as raise a blade, I will kill you."

"I don't believe you," the Annoran said softly. His voice was little more than a whisper.

"Believe what you wish," she snapped.

Her golden hair lashed the air as she turned her back. Kitara snatched up her wineskin and strode away. Her mood darkened once more.

The warmth of the fire seeped into her bones as Kitara took a draught from her wineskin. What Silas had said was true. What this man, this Cailean, said was true. Salvaari blood ran through her veins. Whether it came from her mother or father, Kitara did not know. One had died giving birth to her and she had no clue about the other. Kitara ran her thumb over the sapphire ring pulled from beneath her shirt. She had been told it was her mother's ring. She had been no more than twelve summers when the women who had raised her had given her the sapphire-inlaid band. They had said she was finally old enough. Kitara pulled the cord from her neck and rolled the ring over in her hand. The light of the fire cast its light on the blue gemstone. It seemed to blaze with life.

Who did it belong to? Who was her mother?

It was a question that had often plagued her. All she knew had come from the women who took her in. They said that her mother was not from the Sacasian. That she had arrived mere weeks before giving birth. No man had been with her. Her mother could have been anyone. She could have been low-born or high-born. Noble or peasant. The widowed wife of a soldier or a courtesan.

In all her life, Kitara had never been any closer to finding her family. That is until the three companions had ridden into sight. From their first meeting, she knew that the Annoran was both reckless and of noble birth. She could barely make anything of the Larissan save for the loyalty he showed to his friends. As for the Salvaari, Cailean, he was the only one who had given her a name. If nothing else, Kitara knew that he was an honest man. A man who only cared for the simple things and damned those who tried to take them from him. He had answered her questions without complaint and had earned her respect.

The people will welcome you with open arms and call you brother.

There had been no lie in his eyes. She knew in her heart that Silas and his people were wrong about those they called barbarians. Kitara would not follow anyone blindly, for that could get you killed. Yet if what Cailean said was true, then Salvaar was a place that longed for peace. Maybe they even deserved it. Yet if the Mierans held or killed him and his companions, then perhaps the war would never end.

Thousands would die.

Kitara took another swig of alcohol. She relished the taste as it burned down her throat. It had been a year since the Mierans had taken her in, the first time in many summers that she had known a kind of safety. Yet it would not last. Already the dark looks were beginning to turn into words. Even those she called ally were starting to let the feeling that she was the enemy affect them. It might not be long before the dark looks turned into action.

And yet what if they did not? What if it was just her distrust that was pushing them away?

She had a choice. She could stay with the Mierans and hope that nothing changed. Perhaps they would eventually accept her. Or she could leave. Perhaps one day the Mierans would come for her with their blades in hand.

Kitara was a survivor. She always had been. It was written in her blood. Leaving Miera would be a survivor's move.

Where would she go though? Annora? She was wanted there for crimes against the crown.

The Gulf of Lamrei? She would be captured or killed on sight.

Medea? The Medeans might see her as the enemy for her Salvaari blood. They would be less forgiving. To them the forest-dwelling pagans were a blight on the world. The Salvaari were considered no more than heathens and barbarians.

She could travel east and make for the lands of the League of Trecento. Elara perhaps? Yet the League was plagued by the same evil as the western nations: the religion of the Twins. She would be forced to put down her sword and wear a dress.

Kitara raised her flask again to take a sip. She stopped with its lip just shy of her mouth. Kitara took a breath and calmed her nerves before she lowered it. She could already feel the warm tingle flooding her body from the alcohol. Kitara knew that she drank too much, yet it helped her to forget what had happened in the Sacasian all those years ago.

Who was she?

She had spent over two decades looking over her shoulder. Lamrei and the Sacasian had only been the beginning. The horrors she had witnessed. The scars she had been given. She could still remember being curled up in the brig. Covered in blood from the wound to her face. The wound had healed into the scar, but the memory of that night still haunted her. It was the first time she had been betrayed, yet it had not been the last. She needed to find her people. Her real people.

Kitara swept her emerald eyes around the hall. A few of the Mierans sat around the hall talking in hushed groups. Most of them would be outside either with their horses or riding the plains. It finally hit her now. They would never trust her. Never see her as more than a stray dog. Never treat her with more than a kind of mild neglect. She turned her gaze to another of the small fires that filled the ruin. Above it hung a pot. Inside a soup was boiling for the Mierans to eat at sundown. Kitara put the necklace back on and let the ring fall to her chest. She knew what she had to do.

TWENTY-NINE

Prince Dayne Raynor glanced across the huge map of the mainland that sat atop the circular table in the war room. It covered the edges of the Aureian Empire through to Miera and some of Salvaar. The map extended further south to include the Lupentine and the Valkir Isles.

"How goes the assembly?" Dayne said as he glanced up at his accomplice.

General Tristayn looked to his prince with the same almost eager expression that had covered his face when he had ridden to war twenty-five years before. Fighting and battle were all he had ever known. There were no politics or backstabbing on the battlefield.

"At the last count … over four thousand have arrived. Most of the knights are here as well," Tristayn replied.

"Good," Dayne said as he leaned on the table and gazed towards Salvaar. "All this waiting … I should just take what cavalry we have and ride at first light."

If he rode with nearly two thousand knights and nobles, a force comprised of nothing but heavy cavalry, perhaps they could deal with this pagan civil war and get his brother back. Two decades ago, a force of knights had more than evened the playing field against the heathens. It was said that the Annoran-heavy cavalry could rival even the Mierans in mounted combat. If Dayne left now with what men had arrived, perhaps they could swing the odds in favour of Lukas.

"Sir Garrik knows what he is doing."

"I know." Dayne nodded as he clutched his sun and moon medallion. "Yet with only three hundred of the guard, only the gods know if it will be enough."

"Durandail and Azaria ride with him," the general told him, and his voice was full of conviction. "They will protect him and your brother."

"All glory to them," Dayne said quietly.

To him the gods came first, and he would give everything to honour them. Being the crowned prince of the realm came second to those who ruled in the high heavens. He bit his lip.

"You rode to Salvaar by my father's side … by King Balinor's side."

"We all did," the general replied almost bitterly as he heard the old king's name. "For the first time in our history, a united army of Aethela, Laeoflaed and Torosa marched together."

"I have heard tales of what happened," Dayne said, and his lips curled. "Some seem too fantastical to be true."

Tristayn tightly gripped the edge of the table as he remembered. "When we first left Annora, near to twenty-six summers ago, we left with a purpose: to end the conflict that was spilling into Medea. We had no reason to fear those trees nor what lay within them. We had never been so wrong. It took barely three days for us to realise that it was more than just another war … it was a fucking nightmare. By day we saw not even a shadow, while by night … the forest was filled with the screams of the dead and dying. It wasn't until the men threatened mutiny that the king of Laeoflaed gave in to your father's demands to build marching forts."

"Much like the Aureians," Dayne said thoughtfully.

It was a thing he had learned during his time in the court of Emperor Darius. At the end of each day, they would construct a small fort comprised of wood and earth to protect them from any outside threat. The following morning the army would raze the fort to ashes and resume the march. It reduced the distance that they travelled yet gave them a means to defend themselves from raids. It was ingenuity such as this that had seen Dorian send his heir to the imperial palace as a boy to learn from those who had conquered much of the known world and had defeated the Delion Empire.

The general nodded as he spoke. "They worked and, with your father commanding the heavy cavalry, helped turned the tide."

"This could prove vital knowledge in the days to come," Dayne told him.

A feeling of sadness crawled into his heart. Lukas had been too young to remember, yet Dayne could remember his uncle who had died in that war. He was a man who, like his brother Dorian, had been betrayed.

"A pity that it did not save my uncle," Dayne said.

"Few things can save a man from those closest to him. Always remember that," Tristayn replied.

He could still remember the day he had been forced to bring word to Dorian of his brother's death. The day that had changed everything.

"Just know that the man who led Eldred into that ambush was hunted down like a dog. He died a long time ago," Tristayn snarled.

"Words of comfort," the prince said. "But, alas, that is in the past. Now we have other problems to solve. Namely in Medea."

"Pay them no mind, my prince," Tristayn told him. "If the duke rejects our terms and will not let us pass peacefully, then we could take his city with an army of cooks."

Dayne's lips curved upwards as he met his friend's eyes. Pain hit Dayne as suddenly as a spring storm. It seared through his gut like a hot iron. Shivers hit his body and blood drained from his face.

"My prince!" Tristayn dashed around the table to his prince's aid.

Dayne winced, and he suppressed a grunt as he doubled over. He gripped the edge of the table tightly to stop himself from falling to the ground.

"No," he barked at the general. He fought back the pain and clutched at his gut in an attempt to stop the agony that racked him. "It will pass," Dayne growled.

His knuckles began to turn white as his grip on the table tightened. He could feel the fire burning within. It scorched his innards and threatened to burst them.

"Dayne!"

The prince heard Sofia rush into the room. She reached his side even as the pain began to fade. Sofia reached out a gentle hand and placed it over his own.

"It's alright," Dayne said, and he straightened his back as his body shook no more.

Dayne released the table and clasped his hands together. It was gone. All that remained was a dull ache in his gut.

"Shall I fetch the physician?" the general asked as he ran his worried eyes over his prince.

"No," Dayne replied. "Tell him if you must. I will see him later." He could see the shock in his friend's eyes.

"I … Of course, my lord," Tristayn said after a moment.

The prince of Annora could see the worry etched in his face clear as day. He prayed that Tristayn and Sofia could not see the pain in his own face.

"Thank you, Tristayn. You may leave us."

The general glanced from Dayne to Sofia. He was still unable to remove the worry from his heart. The prince was the future of his country.

"Prince Dayne. My lady," Tristayn said as he bowed and made his way from the chambers.

Sofia waited until the wooden door had boomed shut before

turning to her husband. "Are you alright?"

"I am fine," he told her as he took a deep breath.

Her eyes never left his as she took his hand. She moved with the pride of one born and raised to be nothing short of a queen despite the fact she was a duke's daughter. There was a softness in her eyes and a calmness in her touch that comforted Dayne.

"What is it?" she asked softly.

"In truth I am not sure," he replied. "The royal physician and Father Bardhyl have no answers."

"I had heard the rumours ... Does anyone know?"

Dayne shook his head. "Few enough. To this day only they, my family, and Tristayn knew of this ... affliction. Soon I fear the whole nation will know the truth."

Sofia ran a thumb over his hand. "Is it bad?"

"It comes and goes as the seasons pass." The prince shrugged. "And yet it is of little importance. There is much to be done, and this sickness, whatever it may be, will not stand in my way."

He turned back to the table and ran his keen gaze over the maps that lay strewn across it. He seemed unable to tear his gaze from the map, nor remove his hands from the table's edge. Sofia reached out and gently pulled his hand away from the desk.

"I have seen that expression before," she murmured.

"These days have been trying," he told Sofia as their fingers entwined.

He ran a thumb across the smooth skin of her hand. She extended her free hand and stroked his chin softly.

"You worry too much."

Dayne met her beautiful, deep brown eyes.

"There is much at stake. My sister is missing. If I fail in my task, my brother will die. If I fail, we could have war on three fronts. I try to do what is right. I try to do what will save lives. What the gods will. Yet here" – he ran his hand across the map – "my father's life work. A single kingdom called Annora. United under one faith. Under one king. A nation born of great tragedy. No matter what I feel, no matter what I believe, I am heir to Annora. And that is all that is important."

"Believe me, I understand," Sofia said quietly. "When the plague confined my father to his bed and took my brother ... the safety of my people fell to me. I was seventeen. All of them were scared and afraid. I used to walk the streets to show that I was not afraid. And yet I was terrified. Each day brought new horrors. They all looked to me to make things right. To take away their pain and wash away their fears. Yet it grew and grew, and I thought that the burden would crush me. I prayed to find a way through. A way to stop the nightmare that had ravaged my city. The choices we had to make ... who would live and who would die ... and then the plague ended."

There was no trace of pain on her face as she spoke, no trace of the unending sorrow that she had felt during those dark days. The screams of the mother watching her child die before her eyes had stopped haunting Sofia's dreams. She remembered it all, but she had decided years ago to not let it control her. The horrors had ended. She smiled up at her husband.

"I know that I do not have your experience, nor have I led soldiers into battle as you have. Yet I know that you will not fail. You will face whatever evil comes your way, and you will defeat it. Not because you are the son of Dorian Raynor, but because you are Dayne of Annora."

Dayne listened as she spoke. He was not one to show emotion nor even feel much of anything. It was a thing well known that arranged marriages were rarely happy affairs. Sofia was more than just the beautiful daughter of a Medean duke though. She was wise beyond her young years and burned as brightly as the sun. Dayne placed a hand on her smooth cheek.

"Soon things will be as they should be," he told her. "I will make it so."

Sofia took his hand and stepped closer. "Trust in the gods and they will guide you. They always have."

Dayne pulled her close and kissed her soft lips. He relished the taste as she returned it.

The prince had always given everything he had to earn renown as both a swordsman and leader, yet to him the gods always came first. They gave him everything. Every skill he possessed.

In their infinite wisdom, the gods had guided Sofia to his arms. An act for which he would be forever grateful.

"Malakĕn andros a'læn diora … makĕr ni a'læn … mala dresta," Kyler stumbled across the sentence as he read.

He was already exhausted from the day's training, though he would never admit it. Despite the fact that he had been sitting on a bench in the Garden of Azaria for the last few hours, he did not feel at all rested. It was not the intense training that left him wanting. It was the study that came after. He had never taken to any sort of academic art. So far as he knew, the only Delions who still spoke the tongue were those descended from the old bloodlines. The nation of Delios itself was gone. Reshada, Queen of Larissa, was called the last Delion. Though her father was of Larissa, her mother's blood could be traced back to the great conqueror, Nykalous Gaedhela. He was the man who had forged the once great Delion Empire with his sword. Though it had fallen to ruin upon his death, remnants and relics of the empire still remained. Now Kyler was forced to learn their tongue. By day he trained and by night he read. His only comfort was Elena and the ever so fleeting moments that they spent in each other's company.

"Dræsta," Elena corrected from beside him. "Makĕr ni a'læn mala dræsta."

Kyler sighed as he saw the slight twitch in his friend's lips. "You're enjoying this," he said.

"I haven't the faintest idea of what you are suggesting." Elena grinned before gesturing to *An Odyssey of Delios*. "Try again."

Kyler bit his lip as his tired eyes looked over the sentence once more.

"Malakĕn andros a'læn diora, makër ni a'læn mala dræsta … Stand up for what you trust, even when alone."

It made no sense. It sounded like a riddle within a riddle.

"No, not quite," Elena told him. "When separate 'mala' reads as 'stand'. While 'dior' on the other hand is often used as a combination of trust or believe. Add the 'a' and you get …"

"You get 'in'," Kyler muttered as realisation dawned. He ran his finger along the writing again as he read, "Stand up for what you believe in, even if you stand alone."

Elena nodded slowly. "It was Herodys' belief that every man or woman had the right, the responsibility, to discuss their beliefs. To never back down from what you hold to heart. No matter who stands against you … be they serf or king. It was this very belief that led to the end of slavery in Delios. Many may stand against you, yet you must never betray yourself. For if you do, they win."

"Was not Herodys executed for his teachings … his beliefs?"

Elena glanced at him. "Should he have backed down to Aureia when they came, this so-called law of the land? The man who burned Herodys' library and threatened to arrest him for 'treason'. No … Herodys was brave. He lived and died for what he believed in. I can think of nothing more worthy of my respect."

They continued for a few hours before at last Kyler found his way to his bed. The sun rose all too soon.

"To win any battle you must fight as if you are already dead!" Sir Alarik's voice echoed across the training ground as he roared. "For the gods will welcome you when your time comes!"

Kyler Landrey flicked his wrists as his longsword sliced through the air. His muscles strained under the weight of the heavy training blade. The sword rang as his opponent's blade slammed into his defence. Kyler was strong and his technique was good. Constant weeks of drilling from sunup until sundown, under the keen gaze of Alarik and the other instructors, had begun to turn him into a weapon.

Kyler's arms barely trembled as they took the weight of the blow. He reacted instantly and stepped inside the strike. He drove the edge of his blade towards Haylan's chest. Haylan hastily retreated and barely blocked Kyler's attack. Kyler advanced as he struck again. Haylan met staunch with staunch.

Once. Twice. Three times.

Kyler watched his opponent carefully as he moved. He left himself open when he attacked. If Kyler played it risky, perhaps he could end the fight far sooner than anticipated. After all, Haylan had taken quickly to the sword.

Haylan lunged. Kyler danced to the side and lashed out. The tip of the Haylan's sword clipped the side of Kyler's padded gambeson. The edge of Kyler's blade drove into Haylan's hip. Haylan winced and stepped back as he tried to create distance. The blow that hit Kyler would barely leave a bruise, for his sidestep had carried him out of harm's way. Kyler could see the grimace as it covered Haylan's face. The weighted sword had hit hard. Haylan had shifted his weight from his lead foot to switch his stance away from his injured hip. His centre was weak. Kyler charged. He was determined not to let Haylan back into the fight. He deflected a hastily thrown cut and slipped inside Haylan's guard. Kyler slammed into him with his shoulder. Haylan crashed to the ground in a spray of sand. Kyler leapt forwards to press his advantage. Still Haylan grasped his sword. He refused to let it fly from his fingers. Just days past, Alarik had drilled into them the need to never be disarmed in a fight.

Lose your sword in a fight and you are dead, he had told them.

Kyler levelled his blade and watched as Haylan pushed himself up onto one arm and met Kyler's eyes. Haylan pulled a leg up and prepared to push himself to his feet at a moment's notice. Kyler's staunch pressed into his chest. It was over.

"I nearly had you," Haylan muttered as he slapped the blade away.

"Nearly." Kyler extended a hand to his fallen friend.

Haylan took it and pulled himself to his feet. With their fight done, Kyler finally became aware of the ringing of staunches from other recruits. They had been at it all day. Each and every initiate aimed to defeat their opponents. Kyler wiped a bead of sweat from his brow. He had grown used to this feeling in recent days, just as much as he had to the sticky and sweat-laden tunic that he wore beneath his gambeson. On hot days like this, the garment stank.

"Pisspot."

Kyler glanced towards Sir Alarik's beckoning form. The battlemaster stood away from the other recruits. He was alone save for the man at his side. A man whom Kyler recognised instantly. It was Hugh Karter.

What did he want now?

Since their arrival, Hugh had become something of a hero to many of the new recruits. The posh fool was favoured by the recruits for his considerable charm and sword skills.

"You charged at your opponent like a wild animal," Alarik told Kyler. "All aggression and no thought of defence had it failed. A weakness that could be exploited."

Kyler saw the brief flicker of humour cross Karter's face as the battlemaster spoke.

"It is hard to exploit weakness from the flat of your back," Kyler replied, unable to fully keep a hint of bitterness from his voice.

"Your tongue is as reckless as the way you fight." The battlemaster glared at Kyler. "Another thing that you would do well to contain."

"Sir." Kyler gave a simple nod.

He knew that what the knight said was true, and his tongue had gotten him into trouble countless times. Yet it was a part of who he was.

Alarik flicked his gaze from Kyler back to Hugh. "I have a task for you," the battlemaster said.

"A task?" Hugh inquired, and he crossed his arms.

"Indeed," came the reply. "Tomorrow one of the maija is travelling to Odrysia to gather supplies. She will require an escort, and as such, the pair of you shall go with her. Think of it as a test."

"When do we leave?" Kyler asked, and excitement edged its way into his voice.

His first test. There had to be a reason that Alarik had chosen both he and Karter. It was true that Hugh was the best of the initiates when it came to the sword. He was a prodigy. Yet if Alarik had chosen Kyler, then he must think him not far behind.

"You will meet her at the gates an hour after dawn," the battlemaster told them. "Expect to be back no later than midday. Though I feel that I should warn you: the recent bandit attacks have made the people on edge. So be on your guard."

"Yes, sir," Hugh said. "Though if I may ask, who is the maija that we will be travelling with?"

Alarik gave Kyler a knowing look. "Her name is Elena."

THIRTY

Ruins of Israfil, Steppe of Miera

Kitara's boots echoed on the stone as she walked up the stairs of
the watchtower with a bowl of soup clutched in her hand. The rest
of the Mierans were eating their fill as the girl entered the lookout.
A small brazier cast light across the stone walls of the small room.
Thin rays of moonlight slipped through the windows and open
doors that led out onto the wall. Kitara made her way out onto the
parapet. Her stomach was filled with a mixture of confidence and
nerves. There was a slight chill running through her veins. It was
almost a sickening feeling of dread, yet she was committed to her
decision. She pushed the emotions that she felt to the side. She had
not eaten a morsel in many hours, but she barely felt her hunger.
She had gone days without food or water in the past, and if need
be, she would do it again.

"Beric," Kitara called as she made her way towards the man
standing on the parapet.

A powerful war bow was held in his clasp. It was a weapon that
he had mastered long ago.

The warrior glanced at her. "Ah, Kitara."

"It has been a long day," Kitara told him, and she held out the
bowl. Beric nodded his thanks and took it from her. He leant his
bow against the wall of the lookout. The Mieran gulped down a
mouthful of the broth. He savoured its taste as it filled him with

warmth, and then he tensed.

Kitara watched as Beric's smile faded and he tried to speak. No words could spill forth from his tightening throat. The bowl fell from Beric's shaking fingers. It hit the ground. Soup spilled across the floor. Beric reached for his blade. Kitara's hand dropped to her sword as he took a step towards her.

Then Beric's eyes rolled back into his head and he fell. His unmoving body thudded down next to the ruined bowl. Kitara watched his still form for a moment. He was only unconscious, but his head would hurt like hell when he finally awoke.

Now she had to move, and she had to move quickly.

"Are you ready?" Lukas whispered as he sat down beside Sakkar. "What tomorrow brings, we do not know."

"It is in the hands of Amkut now," the Larissan replied. "Taking Silas as a hostage is our only path."

The prince chuckled drily. "Sakkar, my friend, if we make it out of here in one piece, then your debt is paid. You can go home."

Sakkar smirked. "If we make it out of there, you can build a statue in my honour."

Laughter came from outside the cell as two of the Mierans swaggered into the prison. Each of them held a bowl in their hands, and the contents of which dribbled down their chins. Mierans cared not for appearance.

Sakkar sauntered over to the cell door with a dangerous glint in his eye. "And what have simple travellers such as ourselves done to warrant such esteemed company?"

"Of all the years I have been riding the Steppe, there is a thing that has become abundantly clear." One of the Mierans snorted.

"And what is that?" Sakkar replied sarcastically.

The warrior chuckled. "There is always one … the one who

always talks. Perhaps one day we shall see if you could ever add weight to your words with a blade."

"You had best pray that day never comes."

The Mieran who spoke stepped towards the cell. "I..." he started.

Then he coughed, and his eyes widened. He turned to his companion who had doubled over clutching at his stomach.

Lukas rose slowly to his feet. His mouth dropped open as the Mierans fell and thudded to the ground in a tangle of limbs.

Footfalls echoed as Kitara ran down the stairs and sprinted across the courtyard. Her hand never strayed from her sheathed blade. She crossed into the keep and barely spared a glance at the sight that greeted her. The Mierans were strewn around the hall. Some had barely moved from where they sat. Others had tried to reach the doors perhaps to sound an alarm. Yet now they all lay still, as if life itself had fled from their bodies.

Yet they still breathed.

In one of Kitara's pouches, she stored three small vials. Each one was filled with a different kind of brew, the first of which now stood empty, its contents having been poured into the broth while no one was watching. Physicians and apothecaries alike knew it by its proper name, erims'mir, though to many it was called the Black Dream. It was brewed using the seeds of the erims leaf plant, and it created a powerful drug that sent its victims into a groggy sleep. It affected people differently. Some would sleep for hours, while others would sleep for mere moments. Yet all would awake with a pounding head and sluggish movement. Erims'mir was hard to create, and its cost demanded great expense, but to those who acquired it, it proved invaluable. Just as it had many times for Kitara.

Silas had nearly made it to the doors before the drug got the better of him, and now he lay against the wall as if he had merely dozed off in an armchair. Kitara ran past his prone form. He would never forgive her for this. None of them would. She gave no backwards glance.

There was no turning back now.

"What is going on?" called Cailean as he saw Kitara running towards them.

The three prisoners looked from her to the Mierans.

"Did you do this?" Cailean asked.

"No time to explain," she snapped back as she crouched over one of the fallen warriors.

Her eyes ran over the warrior's belt.

"Looking for this?" the Larissan asked as he removed the key from his bracer.

He reached through the cell bars and slid the key into the lock. With a click, the cell door opened. Kitara raised her eyebrows at the man.

How had he got that?

Kitara decided it did not matter, for every moment they delayed brought closer their doom. She gestured towards the corridor.

"Why are you helping us?" Cailean asked with a furrowed brow.

Kitara met his eyes. "I do not believe that your people are monsters under the bed, nor the nightmares that the Mierans fear."

The Salvaari nodded and strode from the cell.

"You killed them?" the Annoran asked as he followed his companion.

"They aren't dead," Kitara told him. "The horses are ready, and your weapons are with them. We leave now."

It was all she said before she turned on her heel and pushed herself into a run. A sadness filled her as she glanced at the two Mierans lying across the stone floor. The last year she had spent would now count for nothing. She was forced to ask herself if it ever actually meant anything.

Kitara led them through the ruins and out into the courtyard where their horses were saddled and ready to ride. She pulled herself up onto Lamreil's back and ran a hand along the mare's powerful neck. Once more they would be riding for their lives. She did not want to think of what would happen if the Mierans caught them.

Kitara looked towards the doors of the ruins. Each sound they made threatened discovery.

"Hurry." She couldn't help the panic from edging itself into her voice.

The three men buckled on their weapons and heaved themselves up onto their mounts. Kitara clicked her tongue and Lamreil started to move. She glanced over her shoulder as the companions, her companions, followed. Kitara's eyes flicked to the doors. Erims'mir was strong, but the Mierans were hardy. Perhaps some of them had received a lesser dose than others. What if they had already awoken and were at this moment moving to stop the escape?

A cry went up from inside the building. The alarm.

Kitara kicked her heels in as they raced through the courtyard. She risked a glance up at the watchtowers. She prayed, though she had no god, that Beric and the other archers were still dreaming.

"What of the pursuit?" shouted the Larissan from behind.

If they rode away without first hindering the Mierans, then the horses of the Steppe would catch them by dawn. Kitara flicked a foot over Lamreil's back.

"I'll deal with it. GO!"

Kitara dropped down onto the stones as the three riders raced by and thundered through the gates with Lamreil.

Kitara's sword rang as it cleared its sheath. Its blade glinted in the light of the braziers.

"There!" Silas shouted, and one of his men ran from the hall.

They looked almost drunk. The erims'mir had done its work. She ran for the gatehouse and pushed herself faster with every stride.

Kitara could hear the thudding of boots as her pursuers closed in. She did not look back. She did not glance over her shoulder, for that would slow her down.

The huge wheel that operated the portcullis jutted out from the bottom of the gatehouse. It took two men to raise it. So if she simply dropped the heavy steel gate, it would do nothing to stop a pursuit.

Kitara aimed for the stairs that led up the wall and into the gatehouse. Her feet barely made a sound as she moved.

She took the steps three at a time and finally spared a glance at the men hot on her heels. They had run after Kitara instead of going for the escaped prisoners. She was their biggest threat right now. They were halfway to the gatehouse, and their weapons clutched firmly in their hands. The man who ran beside Silas was Caradoc. He was the messenger from the north.

Kitara cleared the ramparts and sprinted into the gatehouse as the Mierans reached the bottom step. Around her stood racks. In days gone they would have been filled with bows, blades and spears. Now they were only adorned with the remnants of a few broken halberds. A doorway stood at each end of the house and led onto the walls of Israfil. A series of arrow slits overlooked the plains and gate from above, while the portcullis mechanism stood in the very centre of the room. It was a great wheel that held the steel gate up with ropes that were attached to heavy weights. The defenders of Israfil could raise and lower the gate from this room. However, in here the cables and ropes were exposed. The ropes were thick and strong. They would take more than a single cut to sever.

Kitara flicked her eyes over the mechanism and followed the ropes from the wheel to the floor. If even one broke, then the portcullis would crash down without a chance of being raised again. With the right materials, it would take days to fix. Materials that the Mierans serving under Silas did not have. There was still a week before the changing of the guard, so that would give them time.

Kitara ran a hand over the rope. The weights of the portcullis had it pulled tight.

She raised her blade and with a snarl lashed out. Her two-handed grip sent the sword through the air. It landed heavily on the rope. Some tendrils ripped apart with a snap. She swung her sword again and hit the tightly pulled rope in the same place.

Again.

The rope jerked and the steel portcullis beneath groaned. It was close now. Kitara raised her blade.

"Stop!"

Silas and Caradoc ran into the gatehouse. Kitara froze as she was about to make the final swing. They could all see the last tendrils that held the rope together.

"There is still time to make this right," Silas called. "Stop this madness."

"I can't stay here," she told him.

The man stepped towards her.

"Stay back," she warned, and she flicked her sword up.

"You will not be punished for this," he replied, and he stopped in his tracks. "You have to trust me."

Kitara felt her heart seize as she fought back any emotion. Still, her anger surfaced.

"Trust you? Silas, I can't trust you. I can't trust anyone. The last person I trusted … the last person I called friend gave me this." Kitara gestured to the scar on her face. "I have been sold, I have been beaten and I have been betrayed by all whom I have ever trusted."

"Kitara, I …"

"You do not understand," Kitara snarled. "I have no one. And now you wish me to turn down the only chance I have ever had at finding where I came from. At finding my people. Silas, you know what will happen if I stay. Though I never asked for his help, how long before your father can no longer keep the northerners at bay? How long before your kin turn on me? Days? Weeks? To them I will always be Salvaari. Nothing more."

Silas stepped towards her. "I can protect you."

"I do not want or need your protection," Kitara snapped.

She would let no one treat her as a weak child. It was insulting that he had implied that she needed someone to protect her.

"If you do this," Silas said, and his voice was cold now, "then there is no coming back from it. And I swear you will hear from me again."

Kitara flexed her fingers over the hilt of her blade. "So be it."

She brought her sword down.

The rope snapped.

"Go!"

The words still echoed in Lukas' head as they cleared the gates. He did not know Kitara as anything more than a name to a face. Yet he found himself bringing his mount to a halt barely fifty feet from the gates of Israfil.

"Why do we stop?" roared Cailean, as he pulled up on his reins and turned his horse.

"We can't leave her," Lukas yelled back.

"We have to," the Aedei snarled. "The Mierans …"

"She saved our lives," cut in Sakkar.

The Larissan drew his curved blade and nudged his mount back towards Israfil.

"Her fate will be the same as ours," Lukas said, and steel glinted as the prince snatched up his warhammer.

Cailean cursed and spat into the mud.

"You westerners," he snapped as he pulled free his own weapon and rode to Lukas' side. "Determined to die."

"We hold the line."

The prince spared his companions a glance. Both were more experienced than he in the arts of battle. In this moment, there was no one else he would rather fight beside. He tightened a hand on his reins.

A snap came from the gatehouse above. Steel screamed.

And the portcullis thundered down before them.

Caradoc came at her first. His eyes were filled with bloody intent. He was a northerner, one of the best warriors in all of Miera, yet the erims'mir slowed him. When she had fought the Annoran, she had needed to capture him alive. With Caradoc, she was under no such obligation. The gatehouse was narrow, and the mechanism was large. Only one could attack. His first strike was rushed. He clearly hoped to end the fight with a single blow. His stance was weak as he half staggered towards her. Her boots slid back across the stone floor as she parried his first two strikes. Kitara slipped inside his third attack, sidestepping around the blow so that she could catch it near her crossguard. His sword met hers as the edge of her blade ripped into his hip. Blood erupted from the wound.

Caradoc screamed in pain and staggered back. Kitara's follow-through knocked the Mieran's sword to the side. She could have killed him then. She could have sliced her sword down across his neck and sent him from this world. Yet despite everything, Kitara did not want to take his life. The Mierans had taken her in. That meant something to her. With his sword out of the way, Kitara used her forward momentum and cracked the steel pommel of her sword into the side of his head. He fell back as the blow dazed him, and he lashed out wildly to keep her at bay. Kitara deflected the strike and countered. She slammed the crossguard of her sword into his face. Blood erupted from his shattered nose as he was sent crashing into a weapons rack. Spears and halberds fell to the ground with Caradoc's body.

The pile of steel and flesh separated Silas from Kitara and prevented him from charging towards her. Behind Kitara a second door opened onto the ruined wall. She locked eyes with Silas. Rage and anguish burned bright in his gaze. Then she ran through the door. Kitara sheathed her blade as she sprinted along the wall. She charged towards the hole caused by the siege many years ago. A gap jutted deep into the ruins. It was near six feet deep, while a further drop led to the ground beneath. Kitara neared the hole. Her golden hair whipped in the breeze as she leapt and propelled herself into the air.

She fell and the wind rushed all about her.

Her boots hit the ruined wall hard. Stones crumbled underfoot. Kitara slipped and slammed her shoulder into the side of the hole. She hit it with force. Her hand came up to stop the fall. Her palm smacked into the sharp stones and stopped her from falling from the edge. Pain seared down her arm like a furnace. Her hand felt sticky. Kitara did not have to look at it to see the blood. She had been taught to rise above pain and agony, and with a growl, she pushed it down. The next drop was smaller than the first. Just.

Kitara swept her eyes towards the road before Israfil. The three travellers were waiting with their weapons in hand. They had not left. They had not abandoned her. Kitara jumped from the hole. This time she fell onto grass, and this time the ground was more forgiving. Instead of sharp, broken stones, her feet met soft earth. She hit the ground with a roll. Kitara broke into a run and accelerated towards the three riders. Kitara reached them, and with a grunt, she swung herself into the saddle of her horse.

"With me," was all she said as she kicked her heels in and galloped down the road away from Israfil.

They rode for hours until at last Kitara allowed them to stop. There was no pursuit. Dawn's first light had crept up on them and now covered the plains with its light.

She had not said a word when they had stopped. Instead, she had made for the river that lay before them. Kitara felt a dull ache in her shoulder. It was not broken nor dislocated, for she knew what those felt like. Instead, it would be covered in nasty bruising. Her left hand was covered in drying blood. The wound was nothing to Kitara. She had seen her own blood a thousand times before.

Kitara crouched beside the river and let the waters wash over her wound. She bit her lip as she scrubbed it clean of blood and stone. Finally, she tied a strip of cloth around it to keep it clean and help with the healing.

Footsteps.

She turned to see the men walking towards her. There was an itch in the back of her mind. An itch that told her to draw a blade. She did not know these people nor trust them in the slightest.

"What you did back there ..." the Annoran said as he approached, "thank you."

"No need." She grunted and crossed her arms.

"No need?" Cailean told her. "You freed us against the wishes of your people. You turned on them."

Kitara snorted. "They are not my people. They never were. As you said, I am Salvaari and in time they would have turned on me for it. They were already starting to."

The Larissan pursed his lips. "So what now? What will you do?"

"I cannot remain in Miera, not now, that much is clear. Not after I poisoned them ... not after I drugged them. They are probably all awake by now, trapped within the ruins until the next changing of the guard. After that ... I will ride with you to Salvaar ... to meet my real people," she replied. "With me perhaps you will make it out of Miera alive."

"You draw your blade on us, throw us in a cell and now you want to pose as friend?" the Larissan replied incredulously.

"Friend?" Kitara glared at him. "I offer you no friendship."

"Your actions speak otherwise."

"That could change," she said.

Silence. Kitara watched them carefully as she awaited a response. Would they welcome her, or would they reach for their blades?

"Alright," the Larissan said after a moment, "but if I get even the slightest hint of betrayal ... I will not hesitate to cut your throat."

"Betray you? I am an outlaw in Miera now. Once word spreads of Israfil, they will not hesitate to kill me ..." Kitara told them. "I do not even know your names."

"We have reasons for holding our tongues that have to do with more than pride," the Annoran said.

He stepped towards her. Kitara flexed her hand, ready to snatch out her sword.

"However, if you are to be with us, then you should at least know who we are. You've met Cailean." The Annoran nodded to the Salvaari before gesturing to the Larissan. "Sakkar of Larissa." He extended his hand. "And I am Lukas Raynor, son of Dorian and prince of Annora."

THIRTY-ONE

City of Odrysia, Valley of Odrysia

The road to Odrysia was filled to bursting with travellers and pilgrims. Some wished to make the great city home, while others came in search of coin. It mattered not, for each and every one of them was merely wishing to make their way in the world.

The three riders had left Kilgareth at first light and before long were riding through the gates of Odrysia. Elena rode at the fore with her maija robes flapping in the breeze. She wore a satchel over one shoulder, while a long, slender knife adorned the back of her belt. Behind came Kyler and Hugh Karter in their blue gambesons. They sported steel gorgets, pauldrons and bracers. Durandail's white sun adorned their armoured jackets. After a month of training with double-weighted weapons, the longswords they wore at their hips felt like nothing. The sapphire cloaks at their backs fluttered in the breeze.

The bright colours of a dozen nations bloomed all around them, while loud voices of traders assaulted their ears. The guards at the gate waved them through without a second glance. Aside from the wave, the trio were mostly ignored, for those among the Order were often seen to frequent the city. Elena led Kyler and Hugh a short way down the main road to one of the city's many stables.

"We'll leave the horses here and continue on foot," Elena said as she dismounted. "No reason to attract any more attention."

"I imagine it's for the best," Kyler said as he swung his leg over his saddle and dropped to the ground.

Hugh followed and glanced down the street. His gaze seemed to be drawn to something.

"Karter?" Kyler asked.

"I thought I saw something." The other initiate shook his head. "It's nothing."

He looked serious. He had looked that way ever since they had met in the courtyard at first light. It was strange behaviour from one usually so ready to talk. Kyler could see nothing down the street that warranted concern. He turned back to see Elena smiling at a young stablehand as he spoke to her. He looked no more than twelve or thirteen summers and had a mischievous glint in his dark eyes.

"Thank you, Luca," Elena said as she grinned and flicked him a coin.

With that, the lad pocketed the coin and led the horses inside the stable.

"Sweet boy," Kyler said as Elena made her way to the initiates.

"Looks after the yard with his father. They have always been good to us," she told him. "Marius is expecting us."

"After you," Kyler said and gestured to the road.

"Old Marius lives only a short way from here," Elena told them as she led the way down the thronging streets of Odrysia. "He runs a trade network that stretches all the way from the very heart of the empire. It brings us supplies that would be impossible to find this far north."

She glanced at them as she slid gracefully through the crowd. Elena had lived in Kilgareth for two summers and had ventured into Odrysia countless times. The thick crowds that had once proved near impossible to navigate had become no more difficult to conquer than an empty corridor.

Kyler rested his hand tightly upon the hilt of his sword and kept his head at a constant swivel so that he could always keep Elena within his sights. Every member of the crowd that slightly brushed her made him tense. Every sharp move from a stranger gave him a cold shiver. Though Odrysia was known as a peaceful city, Sir Alarik had warned them to be on their guard; the city had changed in recent months. The bandit raids had made the people scared, and those who were ruled by fear could turn hostile in the slightest of moments.

He looked to Hugh and could see naught but the slight smile that he always wore. He was confident, though his hand never strayed from his weapon.

Elena led them into a wealthier district of the town where the houses all soared into the sky. The crowds were thinner here, and many of the residents had hired guards to watch the doors of their homes and villas.

"Here we are," Elena said as she gestured towards one of the buildings.

The house before them stood three floors high and was made from white and black timber. It had a jettied frame and rich ebony tiles covered its slanted roof. A pair of armed guards also stood outside its doors. Kyler could see a dark wariness in the guards' eyes as the trio approached. It was as if they suspected everyone of foul play. The wariness did not leave the guards' eyes even though the three of them wore the colours of Kil'kara.

"We're here to see Marius," Elena told them.

The guards led them through the tall house, up the stairs and into Marius' study. The trader neatly laid out an assortment of goods upon a large wooden table.

"It's all here," Elena said with a brief glance at Kyler.

The table before them was covered in strange veils, elixirs, stones and colourful plants. No doubt they were all important in some regard to the Order, yet to Kyler they were no more than a pile of oddments. He tossed the coin purse to the man who sat at the other side of the table.

Marius looked as Aureian as his name suggested. His skin was olive like the rest of his kinsfolk, while his thinning grey hair was cropped. There was a glimmer in Marius' eyes that seemed to speak volumes. Perhaps he used to be a soldier. Perhaps he had served in the legions during his youth.

"I remember a time when the maija did not need protection when they walked within these walls," the trader said as he watched Elena start to fill her satchel with the goods.

"Times have changed." She shrugged.

"And not for the better," Marius said as he rose to his feet. "Ever since those vagabonds started to hit the roads this last moon, the city has gone to hell."

"What do you mean?" Hugh asked.

"What I mean is that the many rats of this world have grown in daring thanks to those bandits. The streets are not as safe as they once were, could you not tell?"

"The people are quiet, as if suspicious," Elena explained as she finished her task. "Even of us."

"Why would they doubt the Order?" Kyler asked.

"Why would they not?" Marius gave a dry chuckle. "The bandits only began their attacks because of you. They robbed and murdered for a month because of your complacency. Many people lost their livelihoods and more thanks to the inaction of your Order."

"Now wait just a minute," Kyler growled and stepped towards the man. Perhaps he did supply them with goods, yet he was openly showing disrespect.

Elena gently laid a hand on his arm and said, "He means no disrespect."

Marius nodded. "I just want you to understand. The people are scared."

"Then one day soon, things will be as they should be," Kyler promised.

If the people were living in fear, then someone had to do something. When they returned to Kilgareth he would inform the Circle.

"I will hold you to that," Marius replied. "Now, if you will forgive me, I have work to do."

They were quiet as they left Marius' house, for what he had said still plagued their minds. The Order had tried to destroy the bandits from the very first attack. Matias had ridden with his men, yet like cockroaches in the night, the bandits had vanished. For months there had been a deadly game of cat and mouse, yet the raiders had always been one step ahead. That was until one of their number had been captured. It still puzzled many within the Order that simple thieves and criminals had managed to keep away from the knights for so long. A great stroke of luck many called it.

"Help!"

The tiny scream snapped Kyler's thoughts back to the present. A young girl pushed through the crowd and ran up to them. Her breath was ragged as she gasped for air. Her cloak was covered in mud and filth, and she clearly stood no older than twelve or thirteen years.

"They have my sister," she cried desperately as tears streaked down her face.

Elena dropped to a knee before the child. "Who has her?"

"I … I don't know … They came from nowhere … My brother, he tried to stop them." A sob wracked her small frame. "But he's …"

Dead.

Kyler felt a sickening feeling enter his stomach. He glanced at Karter and could see that his smile had vanished. It had been replaced by a cold mask.

"Hush now," Elena told the girl. "We will find your sister. Can you show us?"

The child bit her lip and seemed to fight to compose herself. She gave the faintest of nods and took the maija's outstretched hand.

They followed the girl as she led them through the winding streets. Down alleys and backstreets they went, past a labyrinth of walls and houses so tall that they blocked out the sun. Kyler's hand never left his sword as they jogged through the roads. Cobblestone turned into mud beneath their feet as they were led further away from the streets. They could neither see nor hear the crowds anymore. The alleys grew darker, and the stench grew ever more potent with every step. Yet it was quiet. The only sounds were those of their hurried footsteps and breathing.

"Stop."

It was Hugh.

His eyes were locked on something behind them. Kyler followed his gaze as a pair of men materialised from the shadows. He shivered as adrenaline flooded his blood. A slight breeze tickled his cheek as he started towards the two men.

Were they the ones who had killed the girl's brother and taken her sister?

They approached, and even in the dull light Kyler could see the glint of steel in their hands. Not knives. Swords, axes and clubs.

Scurrying footsteps.

Kyler turned to see the young girl dash further down the alley. Three more men appeared before her. The Medean felt a sliver of fear in his pounding heart as he saw the weapon that one of the men carried. A crossbow.

They were surrounded.

Without a word, one of the newcomers tossed the girl a coin as she ran by.

Kyler closed his eyes. It was a trap. They were surrounded in a narrow alley by five armed men.

"Back to back," Hugh muttered. "Elena, stay between us."

Kyler moved without hesitation. He slid around to face the original threat, while Karter looked to the three men.

The two initiates drew their longswords in unison. Elena took up her dagger.

"In the name of the Order of Kil'kara," Hugh called out, "be on your way or there will be violence."

The five men drew closer. They were now no more than ten strides away on either side. They wore little more than rags and cloaks.

One of the men before Kyler sniggered. His face was still shrouded in the gloom.

"Looks like we had best get out of here, lads," the man said.

The others chuckled.

Kyler levelled his sword towards the man who spoke. "Turn back now."

"Oh, you don't want to do that boy," he said as he flicked his wrist and absent-mindedly twirled his blade.

The voice was familiar as it reached Kyler's ears. He had heard it before, but he couldn't quite place it.

"Show yourself," the Medean called. "Or are you too cowardly to reveal your face?"

The man stepped into the light, and Kyler could not stop surprise from edging into his voice.

"You!"

The shadows fell from the man's face revealing those hungry eyes and the pale scar that ran across his lips. It was the leader of the bandits who had attacked he, Torin and Gaius on the road.

"You know this man?" Hugh asked, and he did not let his gaze slip from the three men at his fore.

"We have met before," Kyler replied.

The man sneered. "And how things have changed. Now you are what? A baby knight?"

"You would brand me as such," Kyler shot back. "You who grows in stature as he grows in numbers?"

The five rogues closed in. The only thing holding them back was a word from their leader.

Scar Lip pointed his sword towards the boy as he spoke. "Might I have the pleasure of your name before I run you through?"

"Kyler Landrey of Adrestia."

"Well, well. Landrey, welcome to Odrysia," he said, and he nodded towards the three as he barked his orders. "Kill them."

The man with the crossbow raised his weapon.

Hugh's arm shot forward, and a knife flew from his fingers. The bowman jerked as the dagger struck his weapon. He had already pulled the trigger, and the motion sent the bolt flying over Kyler's shoulder. Hugh turned back and then the first clash of steel came as he was engaged by their attackers. The man who stood with Scar Lip charged. His boots splashed in the mud as he raised his blade. Kyler stepped towards him as the blow came down. He blocked it overhead and deflected the sword to the side. Kyler lunged. The man countered.

Steel met steel. A scream came from behind followed by the thud of a body as it hit the filth underfoot. Kyler ignored the cry, and instead he swung his blade as the sound distracted his opponent. The man made to block it. Three underhand strikes drew his opponent's focus. Steel rang as sword struck sword. His hard training had paid off. Kyler effortlessly flowed from one stroke to the next. Kyler changed stance and led with an overhand strike. The man barely caught the blow with his blade. Kyler followed through and lunged forwards as the man's blade slid down the length of his own. It met his crossguard as he drove forwards with all his strength. He sent the point of his sword into the throat of his attacker. The man's weapon fell from his fingers as he gasped. There was an explosion of blood as Kyler kicked the corpse to the ground.

"BEHIND!"

Kyler spun back as Hugh screamed the warning. One of the other men had lunged past Hugh as a second hand engaged the Annoran.

Kyler reacted on instinct. He flicked his sword up and deflected the club as it came his way. Elena lashed out with her dagger. Steel sliced the man's shoulder open as Kyler shoved him down the alley.

The Medean glanced back. The man facing Karter was good. Very good. If he hadn't been, he would have died as quickly as the first bandit. Elena met Kyler's eyes briefly and she tipped her head slightly. She was alright. He turned around as the man with the cut arm grunted and composed himself. Three bandits remained.

With a roar, Karter engaged his opponent. Kyler raised his sword and stepped towards the man who now stood between him and Scar Lip. Without warning, the man charged. Time seemed to slow as Kyler blocked two blows with the edge of his sword. Then he saw it. The man had overextended, and his feet were about to cross. He knocked the man's club aside and rushed forward. Steel met wood again as the man tried to retreat. The bandit's feet crossed. Kyler lunged. He deflected the strike aimed at his side and slammed his shoulder into his opponent's chest. The man's feet locked, and he fell. The club flew from his fingers as he crashed into the mud. The air was driven from the bandit's lungs, and then Kyler's blade plunged down. It slid through his ribs and drove deep into his heart. Kyler took a breath and ripped his sword free.

"Look out!" Hugh shouted.

Something heavy crashed into Kyler and shoved him to the side.

Kyler's back hit the side of the alley. His gambeson took most of the impact. Air fled his lungs. Steel rang as a sword fell to the ground. There was a gasp, and then Hugh toppled over. A bolt was embedded in his side. Scar Lip cast his dead companion's crossbow to the ground.

"NO!" Landrey shouted.

Kyler pushed himself off the wall to engage the last attacker, but he was gone. Scar Lip had vanished like footprints in sand. The darkness had shrouded him in its arms.

Hugh growled and tried to push himself to his feet. He barely got to his knees. Kyler looked at him in shock. Hugh had taken the bolt in his stead.

"Put him on a table," Elena cried as they carried Hugh into the first inn they had found.

He was barely conscious. The only thing keeping him up was Kyler and Elena holding his arms. Hugh's blood covered them both, but they had still left the bolt inside him. There was no way of telling how much damage it had done, and there could be a mortal risk if they had removed it in the alley. Kyler swung an arm across the top of the nearest table, sending plates and cups to the ground.

"Out, all of you," the innkeeper shouted to his patrons as Kyler and Elena placed their companion on the table. "By the gods, give them room! OUT!"

The tavern emptied in moments. The clientele gave them shocked looks as they fled the room.

"Bring wine and hot water," Elena called to the innkeeper. "Kyler, help me."

Together they removed Hugh's cloak, gorget and sword belt. Within moments, the innkeeper was back. He deposited a bowl of hot water on the table alongside a wine flask. Kyler took up the flask and held it towards Hugh's lips.

"You will need this," he said.

The initiate grunted and opened his mouth. Hugh gulped down three mouthfuls before Kyler took the flask away and turned back to Elena. The maija sifted through her satchel. Her calmness soothed Kyler. She was experienced and had done this kind of thing many times before.

She withdrew a needle, thread and strips of cloth from her bag. She dipped the cloth in the hot water, and after rinsing it, she handed it to Kyler.

"I am going to pull the bolt out now. Press down there hard," she said as she indicated the wound.

Kyler nodded. He could feel his heart racing. He had seen the wounded and dead many times, yet this was different. Now he was trying to save a man's life. Kyler got his hand ready. Elena gripped the bolt and with a firm tug slid it from Hugh's side. The initiate snarled as the wave of pain hit him. Kyler pressed down as soon as the arrow left the wound. Blood covered his hand within moments.

"I need to see the wound," Elena told him. "When I say, remove your hands." She took up the bowl. "Now!"

Kyler lifted his hands as the maija tipped the bowl to pour some of its contents over Hugh's gut. She cleaned the wound with another soaked cloth. The blood flow was already starting to slow.

Kyler hoped that was a good sign. He prayed.

"Press down again."

He did as instructed, and he watched as Elena readied her needle and thread. They worked for a long time to stop the bleeding and repair the wound. Hugh had been lucky. Had the bolt stuck a few inches higher and had there not been a maija present, he would have almost certainly died.

Kyler looked at his blood-covered hands for a moment before he lowered them into a bucket of water and scrubbed them clean with a cloth. Kyler splashed his face and rubbed off the last traces of blood. He leaned on the bench for a moment and stared into the water. Hugh had saved his life. A man who hated him had almost sacrificed himself for Kyler. The door creaked open.

"How is he?" Kyler asked as Elena walked into the room.

The innkeeper had given them a pair of rooms for the night for a small handful of coin. One for Hugh while he recovered and one for the pair of them. It was all he had spare.

"I have dressed his wound and given him some valerian to help him rest," Elena told him as she made her way over to the bench where he stood. "He will make a full recovery."

"Good," Kyler whispered as Elena washed and scrubbed her own hands.

Their skin was clean, but blood still covered their garments.

"I know that look," the maija and she nudged his arm as she smiled. "What is it?"

"He saved my life," Kyler said. "Karter almost died to spare me such a fate."

Elena leaned on the bench. "Ah, and you believed that he hated you."

He nodded. "Perhaps I was wrong about him."

"Well, when he wakes up, you can ask." Humour danced across her eyes as she spoke. Despite the mud and filth that covered her robes she looked, to him, as she always had. Beautiful.

"Thank you," Kyler told her.

He reached out and touched her hand gently, feeling the softness of her skin under his fingers. Kyler's heart raced as she intertwined her fingers with his own.

"For what?" She met his eyes and leaned towards him.

"Proving me wrong," he said softly.

Then he kissed her.

Kyler could taste nothing but the sweetness of her lips as she returned the kiss. He closed his eyes as she leaned into it, yet he could still see her face clear as daylight. He stroked her cheek gently as Elena pulled him further into the kiss. He felt her smile beneath his lips. Then she pulled away. His eyes slowly opened, and he could see his own grin mirrored upon her face.

By the gods, he had missed her.

The years they had spent apart had been agony for him, and yet here they were as if nothing had ever changed.

"I have been waiting two years for that," Elena told him, and she reached out and ran a finger over his chin.

"As have I."

Once more he leaned towards her. He was stopped by her finger against his lips.

"Wait." She smiled. "There is something I need to ask you."

"What is it?" Kyler asked with a frown.

Elena paused for a moment, as if trying to choose her words. "During your time in Adrestia, did you ever hear of a place called the Maiden's Veil? It could be anything. I don't know."

"The Maiden's Veil?" Kyler pursed his lips as he thought. After Elena had left, he had spent a lot of his time exploring the highlands around the village. A maiden's veil was a ceremonial veil used by Medean brides during their wedding. It was a white lace headdress that covered their faces. It hit him.

"I think I know what it is you seek."

THIRTY-TWO

The goat track ran for miles on end. It rose through soaring peaks and carved a path through the thick vegetation of the forests of Vay'kis. At times the group were forced to travel in single file, for the cliffs were steep and the trees large. The track, Jormund explained, had been discovered a few generations ago and was one of the best kept secrets in the whole of the Valkir Isles. The people of Vay'kis had left it untouched, so that in the event of an invasion, they could have a safe haven.

The column of warriors talked in hushed whispers as they walked. It was as if it was some kind of unwritten law while on the path to the Tears. Astrid barely said a word to her two chosen companions, for she was taking in every detail. It might all be of great importance come dawn.

The two she had chosen, Torben and Hélla, talked among themselves quietly, their eyes constantly flicking to Scaeva and his men. The pair had been close for as long as Hélla had been alive, for her father had been a shieldbrother to Torben. For over ten summers, she had been the bloodsworn's apprentice. His teaching was vastly apparent in her skill with the blade.

Finally, the trees began to thin, and Jormund Scaeva led them out of the forest and into the open. The full moon shone overhead and sent its silver rays down onto the city that lay before them. The port was large, perhaps even larger than Agartha's. The thatched houses that began by the port slowly wound their way up the hill to where they met with the biggest hall that Astrid had ever seen. It loomed over the city. It was so mighty that it made Earl Magnus' hall look like a common hovel.

It looked much like a Valkir court, and yet nothing was the same. Huge pillars of granite ran around the palace, and its roof was tiled. A huge flight of stairs ran from its doors down into the town. A large wall encompassed the palace. Fires burned brightly along the walls and in the watchtowers. Astrid could make out the tiny figures of soldiers patrolling them. She shared a glance with Torben. The movement did not go unnoticed by Scaeva.

"Behold Lumis and the great hall of Auraeva," Jormund's voice boomed. "As you can see, Emperor Darius sent some of his finest craftsmen to help with its construction. A show of gratitude for years of service in his guard."

"The stories I have heard do not do it justice," Astrid told him as she gazed at the magnificent palace in wonder.

"The poets could sing of its glory for ages to come, and those words would slip from even the tightest of tongues," the warrior said proudly. "Now, this way."

The stone underfoot echoed as Jormund led them deep into the massive hall. Roaring fires lit the palace from end to end and filled it with warmth and light. Huge banners adorned the walls, yet none were grander than the pair that flew high above the earl's throne. One pictured the great dragon sigil of Vay'kis, a blazing red wrym over a field of the darkest black. The other banner held the snarling griffin of Aureia, a great silver beast atop a violet backing. Together they showed the brotherhood that bound the people of Vay'kis to those who called the empire home.

All traces of raucous laughter and merriment fled the room as Jormund led Astrid and her companions inside. Wary eyes turned towards them as the hush swept through the room. No horns had been sounded down by the docks, so their arrival came as almost a shock to some within.

Astrid did not shift her gaze from over Jormund's shoulder as they strode towards the head of the hall, and yet she saw everything. The people looked not unlike those of the other Isles. They carried themselves more upright and with more pride perhaps. Their clothes were a little more embellished and Aureian, yet they were not as different as the stories would have her believe. The warriors, however, were a completely different animal from those of the bloodsworn. Few among the hall were dressed for raids and battle. Those that were wore shirts of mail over their broad frames, while steel bracers and greaves of the highest quality wrapped around their arms and legs. None among the Valkir could afford such armour. Astrid knew it; they all did. She supposed that for the warriors of Vay'kis, standing side by side with the empire had its benefits.

Four guards stood by the throne. They were dressed alike to Jormund Scaeva, and each had fought in the Arkin Garter. Vicious blades hung from their sides, while shields were slung across their backs. They wore the same griffin-marked armour as Jormund, yet atop their heads were their helms. They covered all but the lower face and eyes of the warrior in an unbreakable steel mask. Their gazes gave away nothing and sent out the cold chill of the darkest winter. Yet their coldness was nothing compared to the flaming eyes of the man atop the throne, Arndyr Scaeva, the Earl of Vay'kis and former commander of the Arkin Garter. He did not wear his armour yet looked every part a warrior as the men by his chair. He wore a thick tunic over his large frame and a pair of rings adorned his right hand. His long, brown hair was pulled back into a single braid that fell behind his neck. His short beard was closely trimmed in the Aureian fashion. His face was rugged, for it had seen much despite his years. He was perhaps a year or so older than his brother. He could be no older than mid-thirties.

"My men tell me that you are spies or the precursor to invasion," Arndyr's strong voice growled as he looked down at the companions.

Jormund held up a hand to halt Astrid and the men at his back. The jarl snorted and pushed past. Her shoulder knocked his arm to the side. One of the guards reached for his blade. It was the only sound as curiosity turned into shock and anger.

"Forgive me, earl," she told him. "We travel alone and mean no disrespect."

"Disrespect?" Arndyr asked as he rose to his feet to reveal a broad frame. He was at least the same height as Torben, and he towered over them from atop the dais. "You arrive unannounced and uninvited and attempt to slip through our defences unnoticed. Should this not cause concern?"

"I understand how this may seem," Astrid replied, "yet we had nowhere else."

"And you did not merely stumble across the Tears of Freydis, did you?"

The jarl shrugged. "I have been a sailor all my life, Earl Arndyr. It seemed only natural to try the crossing when the tides were at their peak."

She could see a slight smirk tug at Arndyr's lips as he replied, "A thing untested by outsiders in the centuries since her death, and a place that I should like to remain secret."

"And so, will you kill us then? Still our tongues forever?"

Arndyr looked deeply into her eyes as if searching for something. "I am … undecided," he told her without shifting his gaze. "You have me at a disadvantage."

"I am Astrid Farrin, Jarl of the Wind Rider," she said before nodding to her companions. "This is the shieldmaiden Hélla and Torben of the bloodsworn."

Arndyr made his way down the three steps of the dais, and his eyes swung to Torben. He came to a halt before the warrior.

"It has been many years since any man of this isle has borne the mark of the serpent. Not since the time of my grandfather."

Torben eyed the earl as he spoke. "And now you ask why?"

Arndyr Scaeva snorted. "Few of our kin venture this far west in the Isles, and fewer still ever lay eyes upon our hearths and home. They find our relations with the empire … distasteful."

"Indeed," Torben told him bitterly, "and despite their lord or earl, the bloodsworn fight for their own. They do not bloody their blades for the wishes of foreign rulers."

"The Arkin Garter is the sword that defends the empire," Arndyr shot back.

"Under the order of a bloodthirsty conqueror."

"Under the order of a good man," the earl told him. "I would not expect you to understand. You who has never seen the world beyond raids. For now, you are my guest, yet do not expect to insult Emperor Darius and go unpunished."

Torben made to reply, but Astrid smacked her hand upon his chest and glared at him. She could see his quick temper building like a stoked fire. The bloodsworn could not understand the mind of a man who had spent so long fighting for a nation that was not his own.

"Do not say another word," Astrid commanded, and she could see the earl smile as he turned back to face her. "We did not come here to insult you, Earl Arndyr. We came to ask for your help."

"My brother's man said as much," the earl replied. "I am told that you have taken up arms against Earl Magnus."

"He is earl only in title," Astrid growled. "Not manner."

"And yet he is your rightful leader," the earl said.

She glared back. "He is."

"Some may see this as rebellion."

"Oh, it is," Astrid snarled.

It was the first time she had spoken it. Spoken the words that gave legitimacy to her undertaking. Magnus was their rightful earl both in name and title. He had inherited the title of earl from his father. It was his blood right. That made her a rebel, an outlaw.

"I have fought by Magnus' side in years long gone," Arndyr said after a moment.

This was it. This was the leap that she had been forced to take. She had to turn a former ally of Earl Magnus against him. It had been not long after his return from Aureia, Astrid recalled, that Arndyr had fought together with Magnus. Odair, an earl of one of the other isles, had started pressing a claim that would make him king of all the Valkir. The earls had laughed at his request, and words had turned to blood when Odair attacked without mercy. Over the course of four months, Arndyr and Magnus joined their fleets and toppled this would-be king from his throne. That had been two years ago.

"Tell me," Arndyr continued. "Why should I support your cause? Why risk my people in a fight not of our making?"

"Because he has less honour than the lowest of beasts. He steals from those who cannot fight back and murders in cold blood." Astrid paused as she looked to the earl, and her eyes ignited like fire. "He killed my father for our land, and when we resisted this injustice, he sent men to slaughter us in our sleep. I have lost my father, my brother, my friends and my home to a monster. Now I am here. I have thirty men to take on an army."

There was silence as she finished. Arndyr shared a look with his brother before he replied. The earl motioned to Torben.

"The bloodsworn has already spoken as to why helping you would be of great difficulty and could come at a great cost to us. Most of the Isles see us as foreigners thanks to our ties to Darius and the emperors of old. I could call my men to arms and together we could bring Magnus to heel. Yet how would that look to the rest of our people? We would be seen as conquerors and invaders. A song would be sung and then ships would be at my door. I cannot help you."

Astrid felt her blood freeze as the words reached her ears. The worst part was that she understood.

"You gutless coward," Hélla snarled from her side.

"Hélla, no!" Astrid snapped before she turned her cold eyes upon Arndyr. "Despite his bleak outlook on the empire, my father often spoke of the honour among the Arkin Garter. I can see now that he was wrong."

Anger flared to life in Arndyr's eyes. "Honour, is it? Do not think that I have not heard of the daughter of Jarl Lief. Do not think that I have not heard tell of your promiscuity."

Astrid met his glare with her own. It seemed that at last her habits had finally caught up with her. She cared not what others thought, for it was her life.

"Speak plainly, earl," she growled. "You call me a whore. No, I do not sell myself. I lie with those whom I choose … Though you of all people speak of whores, Earl Arndyr? You who spent nigh on ten years bending over for a foreign ruler?"

There was a sharp intake of breath as she spoke.

"You have nerve," he told her, and he stepped in close.

Astrid could feel his hot breath on her face, yet her gaze never wavered.

"So I am told," she said.

"Nerve that it will take to defeat your enemy. Answer me this: If Magnus falls … what then? Will you take his crown?"

"I do not aspire to be earl," Astrid told him. "I do not long for that power. I just want to find some measure of peace."

It was true. Being jarl was power enough for her. Sailing and farming was all that she cared about. It was all she needed.

"When Odair tried to claim the Isles and become king two years ago, it was Magnus who stood at my side against the would-be conqueror. He was my shieldbrother … and yet I fear in the years since, I have made a grave error in trusting him," Earl Arndyr said.

Astrid's watched him closely. She could see his mind at work. Arndyr looked around the hall and locked gaze with his brother.

"There was darkness in him then, and we, the earls, all turned a blind eye. The towns he took suffered under his hand. We should have stepped in after he sacked Ramier. Yet he had guarded himself well. His plans entangled all like a spider entangles its victims. The Wolf of Agartha he is called, yet his words bear the poison of a snake."

The air seemed to grow still at the mention of Ramier. It was once a prospering trading outpost under the rule of Odair. Now it stood as no more than ash. Its people had been slaughtered down to the last child. The bloodlust had taken Magnus that day.

Arndyr slowly nodded before sweeping his gaze over the crowd.

"Perhaps we have remained apart from our people for too long. I cannot invade Agartha for you, but I can help."

Shock made its way down Astrid's spine. Arndyr had been testing her. He wanted to make the right choice for his people.

The earl made his way back up the dais and turned to face his kin. "We are Valkir, we are warriors. For generations we have hidden ourselves away from our brothers. That ends today. I, Arndyr Scaeva, Earl of Vay'kis and former commander of the Arkin Garter, pledge my support to Jarl Astrid. Tonight, we celebrate our newfound alliance. Tomorrow, we plan our war."

"It is nearly time." Earl Magnus' words echoed through his longhall.

Erik Farrin spared the small crowd a glance as they ate up their lord's words. To a man, they were jarls, advisors or great warriors. To the earl's side stood a younger man, yet one with great reputation. Jarl Sigfried Dagma. His long, black hair was shaggy and loose, while his beard was darker still. He could hunt anything over any terrain. He was a man known for his wit and his lack of compassion. If anyone could catch Astrid, it was him.

"Friends," Magnus continued, "jarls, warriors. The time has

come for us to hunt down the Wind Rider and the traitors aboard her. Come dawn tomorrow, Jarl Sigfried shall take six ships and pursue them to the very doors of Skûra itself!"

Cheers erupted though the hall. Sigfried merely tipped his head, and his black eyes were devoid of emotion. He said little and showed less. Sigfried was a man that you did not cross.

"I know that there are some within Agartha," Magnus told them, "perhaps even some of you, that disagree with what has transpired in days past. Speak now, if you wish, and fear no repercussion."

One of the older men stepped forward. His hair was as grey as dull iron.

"Jarl Ulfric." The earl gestured to the man. "What is it that ails you?"

There was not a man in Agartha who did not recognise the jarl, for he had once stood as their greatest captain. Erik's father had often said that if you had Ulfric, then you had Agartha.

"Lord Earl," Ulfric began, "there are whispers that your attack upon Astrid was not legitimate. Indeed, it appears that her actions were well within the law."

Magnus allowed a smile.

"You do well to speak up. My grievance began many years ago. As many of you are aware, the land held by the Farrin clan belongs to me by right. It is good land, farming land, entrusted to me by my cousin, Sverri, upon his deathbed. The last person that my cousin spoke to before his passing was his close friend and shieldbrother, Lief Farrin. Without witnesses or evidence, Lief claimed that Sverri had changed his mind and granted him the land. The jarl took my land without a word. I pressed my claim … offered him silver, yet still he refused to hear me," Magnus said as he swept his gaze around the room. "His daughter, Astrid, was soon to follow in his footsteps. She falsely accused my cousin of murder and forced him into a battle that he could not win. She even threatened torture upon my dear friend, Viktor."

The blacksmith, ever close to the earl and a trusted friend to him, now spoke up. "It's true. She held a burning blade to my face."

There were gasps throughout the hall at that. Erik folded his arms over his chest. No doubt the smith had sought out the earl as soon as the Wind Rider had sailed away. Many of the jarls would already have been bought by Magnus' coin.

"Not to mention the ships she sent to the bottom during her departure," growled one of the other captains. "Our ships."

Anger rolled through the hall at the mention of the fire. While only a few of the ships had been destroyed, many had been damaged. More than just those of the earl. A ship was more than just a vessel to the Valkir. It was the heart and soul of their culture. It was their soul. It was freedom.

Erik could see the sparkle in Magnus' eyes as he spoke again. "And so you see, Astrid believes herself above the law, and as such she must be considered an outlaw to be hunted down and shown the error of her ways. One among her crew, that she holds most dear, has already abandoned her for going against our laws and the Sea-Father," the earl said, and he finally turned his gaze to Erik. "Her own brother."

Erik felt his stomach turn as they all looked to him. His reasoning was his own, yet now this was Magnus' game, and he had to make the right move.

"Astrid turned her back on this place long ago," Erik said. "She cares for nothing save herself and her own desires, and the crew are too blind to see it. Earl Magnus has opened my eyes."

The lord smiled, for if Astrid's own brother was by his side, then that would be enough to persuade most of the jarls.

"Forgive me, Jarl Ulfric, for not speaking up days past. I feared that if I had sent word before taking action, then the traitors would have slipped away in the darkness to avoid their fates," Magnus said.

Ulfric nodded thoughtfully. "And where, may I ask, shall the search begin?"

"West," Sigfried said with his low voice. "To the north lies Annora, which holds no sanctuary. The southern waters beyond the empire only grant one thing. Death. The Elarans hold the passage into the Sacasian to the east. Perhaps they will sail for Nesoi Island to meet with Jarl Jorun. Either way, it is to the west that we must turn."

He was right, and Erik knew it. There was no man in Agartha who stood Sigfried's equal when it came to matters such as these.

"Then let it be done," Ulfric said almost hesitantly. "Leave no stone unturned."

The delegation broke apart. Jarls and their warriors returned to their homes, while Sigfried began his preparations.

"Earl, I beg a moment," Erik called out as he followed Magnus and his retinue through the street.

The earl turned and nodded to grant his approval. His guards let Erik through to their lord's side.

"I wish to speak to Laerke once more."

Magnus' brow furrowed. "Why?"

"Sigfried leaves tomorrow. Would not a proper course be preferred to sailing for days, if not weeks, searching for a sign?"

The earl snorted. "The warrior did not seem ... cooperative the last time you spoke. I have half a mind to slit his throat and be done with it."

"Allow me to speak to him one last time. Without guards at the door," Erik insisted. "Let him see me as a friend, and I know he will speak. Let me help bring the outlaws to justice."

The bloodsworn could see his companion thinking as he waited for a response. The earl had every faith in Sigfried to bring the Wind Rider in, but why wait? Without a word, Magnus took a hold of his dagger. Steel rasped as he drew the blade, and his cold eyes bore into Erik. Erik did not shift his gaze. He did not show weakness.

"Until dawn," Magnus told him, and he handed his blade to Erik. There was meaning behind the gift.

Erik clasped the handle of the blade, yet the earl did not let him take it.

"By whatever means necessary," the earl said firmly, as he held Erik's gaze.

He meant for Erik to use the blade on Laerke.

"Yes, Earl Magnus."

THIRTY-THREE

Plains of Carn-Dair, Steppe of Miera

They rode hard and left Israfil far behind them as they travelled north-west. The golden-haired woman led them at a mile-eating gallop and barely said a word. Her gaze never left the horizon. Lukas rode with a grimace, and his left hand barely gripped the reins. His wrist still ached even though it had been days since he had been knocked from his horse. It was not broken, he knew that much, so the prince pushed it from his mind and rode without complaint. The sun was close to setting when Kitara brought them to a halt. Her eyes were glued to the columns of smoke billowing from the settlement a mile away.

"Chausac," Kitara told the three men with a brief nod towards the town. "It's a supply and waypoint garrison for the northern and eastern borders. We'll find what we need there."

Lukas gave her a wary glance. "And what is it we need exactly?" he asked.

A sneer appeared on Kitara's lips as if it was some kind of joke. "Miera has been roused and we must cross the most heavily guarded border in the entire kingdom. Should we not discover which paths are less watched?"

Cailean shook his mane of shaggy hair as he spoke. "No. It is too much of a risk. We are barely three days from Salvaar and have already made it this far without handing ourselves to the Mierans."

Kitara snorted and rolled her green eyes. "You were captured during the crossing from Annora. Without me—"

"We would have found another way," Sakkar cut in, and he gestured towards the town. "Lukas, this just gives her a chance to hand us in. She knows who we are now. At but a word from her lips, we could be in chains once more. What do you think King Zoran would do to you?"

"Hand you in?" Kitara said incredulously. "I saved your lives. The Rift is impassable once Miera is called to arms. I am not just talking about a few riders. I mean thousands. If you wish to travel north without knowledge" – she shook her head – "good luck without a guide."

Lukas looked from his friends to Kitara and back. The decision was up to him. Whatever course they chartered began with his word.

Perhaps they could slip through Miera unnoticed. Perhaps they could make it to Salvaar unaided. Yet the girl's words held meaning.

"We have trusted her this far," the prince said. "I do not believe she will lead us astray."

Sakkar growled, "Be it on your head."

Lukas glared at the Larissan warrior before turning his gaze to the woman. "What is your plan?" Lukas asked.

Kitara bit her lip. "It can only be you and me," she told the Annoran.

"Out of the question," snapped Sakkar. He looked to Lukas, searching for any kind of denial, and yet he knew the look in his friend's eyes. "Lukas, you cannot be considering this," Sakkar murmured.

"She is right," Lukas told him, and his voice was as serious as his expression. "You would give us away, and as for Cailean … one look at him and they would clap us in chains or worse."

The Larissan gave no argument and nor did Cailean, for they both knew he was right.

"Wait in the woods," Kitara told them, and she nodded towards the grove of trees that stood to the north. "We will meet you there tonight."

With that, she flicked her reins and started towards Chausac. Sakkar looked at Lukas and the prince made to follow.

"I do not like this … following her," Sakkar said.

Lukas shrugged. "We need her."

Together the prince and the outcast made their way towards the town.

Lukas kept the hood of his cloak pulled up to cover his face and hide his ears, for any Mieran his age would have at least one ring adorning his lobe. The prince felt his nerves rise as they rode towards the open gates of Chausac. This could be where it all ended.

What if one of the soldiers questioned them? What if they pulled his hood down?

Then an even darker thought came to him.

What if Kitara did betray him?

The girl at his side had him at her mercy. The unease grew as they entered through the gates. Riders came towards them and Lukas tensed. He was half tempted to reach for his sword. One of the Mierans chuckled at something his companion said as Kitara and Lukas rode by. Unease grew into surprise as he looked down the street and at last understood. Soldiers walked in every direction with swords, axes and spears well within their reach. Some walked in groups, while others walked alone. Some talked in hush whispers, and some laughed merrily with their friends and companions. The only glances they received were reserved for Kitara. In Miera, women rode often, yet never did they wear blades at their sides, and never did they fight. Chausac was just like any garrisoned fortress or outpost in Annora.

"Hold there," a gruff voice called.

Lukas turned to the voice and saw a dark-bearded warrior walking towards them with three other soldiers in tow. He could not help but notice that their hands rested atop their swords. Kitara dismounted and turned to face the newcomers.

"Welcoming party," Kitara told him as he followed suit and slipped from his saddle.

They looked anything but welcoming. They were in the wolves' den now, and this, whatever it was, would be their first test. The lead soldier ran his eyes over Kitara from head to toe before glancing at Lukas with a smirk.

"You let your woman carry a blade?"

The woman glared back at the Mieran as she replied, "He does not let me do anything. I do what I choose."

"That how you got the scar?" he replied with a chuckle.

"Something like that," she said tersely.

Suddenly he squinted as he looked at her face. "You look like you have northern blood," he said.

He meant Salvaar. They both knew it. Kitara rolled her eyes and shook her blonde hair.

"Zandir Barangir is my guardian," she said.

Lukas nearly laughed as the man's face paled in shock and his mouth gaped open.

"Then that means you are ..." the soldier trailed off.

Kitara nodded.

"Welcome to Chausac," the soldier said hastily.

"Your guardian?" Lukas asked as they led their horses through the town.

Had Kitara not told them that she had no family?

"As good as," she replied without so much as a sidewards glance. "It was he who took me in when I arrived in Miera a year back. Zandir has great reputation among his people, and so when he took in a gutter rat with nothing to her name save the sword at her side and a scar across her face, well they said not a word."

Lukas' eyes widened. "Then Silas..." he murmured.

Kitara gave a slow nod as she led him off the street and into an inn's stable. If what she said was true, then not only had she turned on her people, but her adoptive family as well.

"Why?" Lukas could not help but ask, as he tied his reins off on a nearby post.

Kitara met his eyes, and her own grew serious.

"That is of no consequence. You do not know the first thing about my life, and that is how it shall remain. All you need know is that I am here with you now. You may have a use for me," she told the prince as her gaze narrowed, "but I have one for you."

Lukas returned the glare. She would have a use for him? Who did she think he was? "Is that so?" the prince asked icily.

Kitara's lips curled. "If you have argument, it can wait until we are rid of this place," she said.

The tavern known as the Northerngate Inn was anything but delightful, Kitara thought as they entered through its oaken door. It stank of ale and sweat, and Kitara couldn't be sure, but she thought there was a faint odour of blood in the air. Unlike the inns and taverns in Carlian, the Northerngate only serviced the rough soldiers of Miera. It did not play host to wives, sisters, daughters or the scant nobility that Miera had to offer.

Kitara scanned the room as she led Lukas towards the bar. It was better for them to move than stand at the door and attract attention. They needed to act like they had been there before. She ran her gaze over faces and more importantly the rings. For the men of northern Miera would have more rings and scars than the rest of their kinfolk combined. That was the price of living along the Rift. As she scanned the room, she only gave one table a second glance. Four men sat around it, although they were clearly not Mieran. Mercenaries by the look of them, for the man she took to be their leader wore an abundance of rings along his fingers. They were too extravagant for any Mieran, even a noble. She could see the sheath of a curved blade at his right hip. The Mierans thought her own blade was exotic, yet this was something different entirely. King Zoran must be getting desperate. She turned the mercenaries from her thoughts as they reached the bar.

"Two ales," Kitara told the innkeeper.

They took a spare table in the corner of the inn, and away from any prying eyes. It was a place where they could talk. They couldn't talk freely, but they could talk. Kitara took a sip from her cup and closed her eyes. It was not just the taste of the alcohol that she enjoyed. It was also the feeling that came with it. It helped her to forget. It helped her to push back the reawakened memories such as the scar that crossed her face. She would never know how the blade had missed her eye. The luck had undoubtedly saved her life that night. She took another gulp.

"What are we looking for?" Lukas asked from over his ale.

"Four or more rings." Kitara shrugged. "Scars ... I will know when I see them." Kitara took a deep breath and fingered her necklace as it slipped from her shirt.

"Where did you get that?" Lukas inquired.

"Hmm?"

"The ring," he said as he gestured to the jewel in her hand.

"It is just a trinket," Kitara told him with a shrug.

"Hardly," came the reply. "I may have little interest in such things, but it is clear to me that sapphire of that quality would demand great expense."

Kitara tensed. She had been careless. "What is it to you?" she said suspiciously, and she covered the ring with her fist.

"Nothing," Lukas said as he shook his head. "What need have I of jewels? I only ask because I would like to know who is riding at my side."

Kitara watched him carefully. She was looking for the lie. She almost hoped there would be one. Yet she saw nothing in his eyes but sincerity. A thing hard to find in one of royal birth. However, she had been wrong before, and it had cost her. She met the prince's eyes. One hint of truth would not harm her cause, and there was a growing chance that they could both be dead come the new moon.

"It belonged to my mother. I am told that it was her wedding ring."

It was the only thing Kitara had to link her to her people. The only thing that tied her to her parents, whoever they were. To her the necklace was worth more than the world, and she would die to defend it. She pitied anyone who tried to take it.

"And she left it for you?"

Kitara gave him half a smile. "Something like that."

It was then that she noticed eyes upon her. A pair of dark brown orbs that belonged to the long-haired mercenary. The one with the curved sword. Kitara leaned back in her chair and crossed her arms as she met his gaze. He reminded her of a wolf. Her lips twitched into a sneer. His eyes were piercing and held a menacing edge. She held his gaze as she glared back. Her eyes scanned the rings that adorned his fingers and the necklaces at his throat. It was clear that he was some kind of wanderer or traveller.

Thud.

Both Kitara's eyes and the mercenary's gaze flew to the doors as they flung open. A small band of warriors strode into the warmth. They were tall, proud men, yet they were also rough and talked with growl-like voices. Their hair was shoulder length and shaggily cut, while their hands never strayed far from their blades.

Kitara nodded her head slowly to Lukas as she spoke. "Northerners."

The companions watched as the men of the Rift filtered into the room. Some of them moved to tables, while others made their way to the bar. A veteran with dark, greying hair stood with a companion by one of the walls. They talked in whispers and seemed not to care about the rest of the inn's occupants. His nose was slightly crooked, as though it had been broken. A single scar ran down the side of his head from top to bottom, yet it was his ear that took Kitara's attention. Seven rings adorned it. That was more than most living Mierans. Rings that could only have been earned riding the Rift.

"Find what you were looking for?" Lukas asked before taking a swig from his drink.

She glanced over her shoulder at the prince. "Let me do the talking," she said.

With that, Kitara pushed herself from her seat and led Lukas through the maze of tables towards the northerners. The broken-nosed man ceased his conversation as he saw the pair heading his way. His companion turned to follow his gaze. He was slightly younger than Broken Nose, yet still wore six rings. If there had been any doubt that these men were not from the north, it was gone now.

"Yes?" Broken Nose asked and gave them a stern look. He was very forthright, very Mieran.

"You from the north?" Kitara asked.

The man nodded and with half a sneer replied, "And you carry a sword."

It was a barbed comment. Kitara had received them from the very moment she had taken up a blade. Do not let it anger you, her mentor had once told her, for if it comes to it, your sword can speak for you.

"Silas Barangir sent us from Israfil," Kitara told him.

She gave away nothing. There was not a single hint that she was lying. For years she had needed to lie to survive, and now it came as second nature to her.

"We are travelling to Roricsford," Kitara continued.

"And you have never seen the Rift?" Broken Nose asked.

"No," Kitara admitted.

It was true. Though she had studied countless maps of Miera

and its towns, until recently she had never travelled further from Carlian than the fields and hills that surrounded the city.

"Then you will want to take the eastern road past Barona," the man said. "It's quicker ... safer and more heavily watched." Broken Nose snorted at her inquisitive expression. "The heathen often cross the Rift and raid those lands. So now with a larger garrison in those parts, they would be lucky to reach the border."

"What of travelling north and then east?" Lukas asked.

The man shrugged as he spoke. "Slower ... unpredictable. It is rough country, and the crossing is made hard."

Kitara cast her mind back to the maps. She recalled the large body of water that completed the river flowing from Salvaar and into the Rift. The lake had made the northern crossing near impenetrable.

"Lake Thirlryda," Kitara said.

"Precisely." The warrior nodded. "So, there are fewer raids. As such it is a passage less watched. If I were you, I would take the eastern road. It is better suited to someone such as yourself."

Anger flared in her veins. "Because I am a woman?" Kitara seethed. She watched as his lips curled.

"And an outlander," Broken Nose sneered.

What was it that an old friend had said to her? Never let an insult go without reply.

"Better an outlander than a weakling such as you," Kitara snapped back.

"You would find more strength in a cripple," Lukas added as the man's face contorted with anger.

Hands went to swords. This was Miera and no one, no one, questioned another soldier's manhood. Men had been killed for less. The northern leader nodded over Lukas' shoulder, and suddenly the prince's hood was ripped off. Kitara twirled to face the third man who had crept up behind them, but it was too late. Lukas' hair fell from his hood and his face was exposed. His ears were exposed.

"I thought I smelt an Annoran rat," the northern leader snarled, and his fingers twitched on the hilt of his longsword.

Kitara winced as she looked back at Broken Nose. There was only one way this ended now.

Blood.

Instead of reaching for her sword, she slowly wrapped the fingers of her left hand around the pommel of the knife at her back. Swords were a bad option at this range. Her knife would be sliding across the throat of Broken Nose long before his sword was drawn. Broken Nose began to make his move. A hand clamped down over his wrist before he could draw his sword.

"Hold!" the growl commanded.

Kitara glanced towards the voice. It was the mercenary leader. The one who had been staring at her. At his back stood half a dozen of his own men.

"These runts with you, Bellec?" snapped Broken Nose.

Slowly Bellec released the man's arm. "That they are," the man named Bellec said.

"Said they were with Barangir," the northerner stated.

"He sent us."

The Mieran glanced from Lukas and Kitara to the mercenaries who watched them with savage looks. It was clear that he did not believe them, but he had only three men against many. He took a breath and lowered his hand.

"Tell your woman to hold her tongue," he told Bellec. "Else what's left of her pretty face will be marred."

It was the last he said before the northerners turned and made their way from the tavern. His words hit Kitara like a hammer. She could still feel the sharp blade of the knife slicing through her face like it was carving a cake. She could still feel her own blood as it dripped from her wound. She could still feel it as her eye was nearly blinded.

"Whoever you are, I suggest you leave quickly," Bellec muttered, interrupting her thoughts. "Miera is no place for outsiders."

Without a word, Kitara nodded her gratitude to the mercenary and then led the prince back to their horses.

"So, what next?" Lukas asked as they left the tavern.

"Next?" Kitara asked. She did not even look at him as she replied, "We travel north."

The prince gave her a sidelong glance. "You want to make the crossing near Thirlryda?" he asked.

Kitara's eyes flashed open, and she stared at Lukas. Her eyes blazed with anger. He had spoken far too loud for her liking. They were all but alone in the street, but that didn't mean that no one was listening.

"Keep your voice down," she hissed as she grabbed his arm and pushed him into the tavern wall. "Or you will see us undone."

"Apologies," Lukas said as his face paled.

Kitara realised he was not used to these kinds of things as she glared at him. Her face was barely an inch from his own. Lying. Deception. These things did not come naturally to him. She had once been like that, but that had been a lifetime ago.

She released him and crossed her arms as they headed down the muddy road once more.

"You will need to do better than that in the days to come."

Lukas nodded slowly. "I will."

THIRTY-FOUR

The Great Northern Road, Aethela, Kingdom of Annora

They had ridden far since Kassandra had joined them near Palen-Tor. Over one hundred and fifty miles. Now they moved down the Great Northern Road towards the crossing at Ilham. It was the closest border town along the Eretrian River. Ilham was garrisoned heavily and guarded the major crossing between Aethela and Medea.

As night threatened, the Annorans slowed their mounts and made their way to the cover of a nearby grove. Kassie winced as she swung a leg over Ely's back and dropped to the ground. She was accustomed to riding back home, but she had never travelled this far on horseback. Her body ached from the journey, but she would not offer complaint or ask for help. She would not even accept it when one of the men offered to help her to and from her saddle. The fires were soon lit, and the meals were cooking over them.

During the days, Kassandra rode up and down the column of knights. She talked to them and offered words here and there. She did the same when they made camp at the end of the day. Kassandra had always walked the streets of Palen-Tor when she lived there. It was important that she got to know her people. She saw it as no different here among the soldiers. These were men whom Lukas and Dayne had often praised. So now she sat atop a tree stump in place of chairs.

"Twenty-eight years," one of the guardsmen was saying, "twenty-eight long years since I took the red."

"You served my father before the unification then?" Kassie asked as she took a sip from her water flask.

The royal guardsmen wore red, but the colour had once belonged only to the Aethelan guard.

"And King Aonaran before him." The knight nodded.

Kassie knew only three years of the knight's service could have been under her father's predecessor. King Aonaran had fallen just after his forty-fifth summer to some kind of infection.

"Tell her about that night in Balburgh, Edward," another of the knights called out cheerily.

Edward looked aghast. "I'm not sure that it would be suitable in present–"

"Did my brother ever tell you about the time that we put horse shit under Master Aelfred's bed?" Kassandra cut across the knight.

Silence.

Kassandra could actually hear jaws dropping as she spoke. Princesses never spoke of such things and never, never used such language.

"Yes," she continued with a grin. "He spent all night searching for the cause of the smell ... and attended court the next morning reeking of it. The looks he was given as he walked into the hall ..."

Kassie couldn't hold back her giggles any longer.

The silence lasted a moment, and then the men roared with laughter.

"I have never seen Father so furious," Kassandra said as she wiped away a tear.

She remembered it as if it were yesterday. It had been three summers before, and until this day only she and Lukas knew what had really transpired. The pair had thought up their revenge after Aelfred, their writing and history mentor, had forced Kassie to listen to another one of his tirades. This particular one had been all about how a princess of the blood must know her history, dating back to when the very first explorers had founded Aureia. He had berated her and told her she would never achieve anything if she did not memorise the last two thousand years of history. Lukas had offered a solution after Kassandra had been locked away for a whole week to study.

"We were at Balburgh when your father was still an Aethelan lord," Edward said after he had composed himself.

Kassie leaned forwards on her stump. A grin was plastered upon her lips.

"Dorian got himself into an argument with the town drunkard and decided he could best him in a drinking contest."

Edward was struggling to hold the chuckles at bay, as were a number of the older guardsmen.

"He made it through eighteen when he … he started dancing naked on the beach before running into the waters. He thought that there was an island of beautiful women waiting for him on the other side of …" He burst into a fit of laughter before he could finish.

Kassie's grin widened. "The Lupentine," she breathed before the laughter took over.

Armour clinked and footsteps thudded as two men made their way towards the group.

"I trust you aren't filling the princess' ears with your usual swill, Edward," snorted Garrik as he arrived.

"Nothing of the sort, sir," the knight shot back.

"Good. Highness, this is Landon Montbard." The master-at-arms nodded to his companion. "He has some skill with metal and cloth."

Kassandra glanced at the knight and recognised him immediately. He was cousin to Elion Montbard, lieutenant to Sir Garrik. He was one of the stoic, quiet types who followed his orders to the letter. The perfect soldier, Dayne had once said.

"My lady." The knight gave her a small bow before holding up a blood-red, padded gambeson. "It was not easy without all my tools, but I have managed this. Some of the lads bring spare gear on the march just in case."

Kassandra rose to her feet and took the gambeson from the warrior. "Thank you, Sir Landon."

It was heavy and strong. The layers of linen and wool helped to slow blades. The weight of the padded shirt alone was enough that even Kassandra could tell its worth.

"It's beautiful," she murmured.

Landon gave her a small smile. "I have managed to adjust a set of bracers and cloak to your size. However, I do not think that we could find a helmet to fit your head."

"And it is for that very reason," Garrik cut in, "that it may be best if you are seen as my squire."

"That is of no consequence," the princess said, and she waved a hand absent-mindedly.

It mattered not. Arriving in Sergova without arousing suspicion came before everything else. She turned her gaze back to Landon and then swept it around the encampment.

"And from now on I would like you, all of you, to stop with the 'my lady' nonsense. Kassandra will do fine. That is an order."

Garrik raised an eyebrow as he looked to his princess. He saw a leader in her. A true leader who would have the love of her people upon a day.

"As you wish," he told her, "Kassandra."

Lukas found himself unable to sleep the night after they left Chausac. Sakkar stood on watch fifty feet away. His eyes were on the horizon as Sabra soared far in the sky above. They had found a small clearing in an even smaller wood to spend the night. Now they had all the information they needed, and Kitara was leading them down the road to Thirlryda. They made sure to keep off the path, for there was no telling who would be riding it. Cailean slept like a rock as he always did. Spending a night beneath the trees in Salvaar was little different to sleeping beneath this grove of oaks. Kitara on the other hand was twitching in her sleep as she did each night. She was restless and whatever it was that plagued her dreams must have been dark. The prince's thoughts were of home. Of his sister. No doubt she would be hating life in Palen-Tor without him and would be making life hell for her teachers. His father and brother would no doubt have sent men after them. Lukas had even spotted them in Wighthorn forest. After that, the group had backtracked and traversed the river for a mile or two. Their pursuers had eventually been lost. Even if the men Lukas' father had sent managed to find the trail, they would have had to stop at the border.

"No!"

The scream cut through the clearing and shattered Lukas' thoughts. His hand went for his sword, and then he realised that the shout had come from Kitara's lips. The woman sat bolt upright. Her fingers were digging into the ground beneath her. Sweat covered her face and her breathing was ragged.

Lukas watched as she swiftly composed herself. She closed her eyes and took a deep breath. She glanced around the camp briefly with those green eyes of hers before she gathered up her sword and walked away. Whatever she had dreamed of had shaken her.

The prince looked across the clearing towards Cailean who crossed his arms and gave Lukas a knowing look. With a sigh, Lukas took up his own blade and followed Kitara. He found her by the edge of the grove. She looked out from the trees and gazed over the rolling hills and plains of Miera. Her sword was slipped back into her belt, while in her hands she clasped her wineskin.

"What do you want?" was all she said without bothering to look at him.

"You alright?" he asked.

Kitara shrugged and took a gulp from her wineskin. Still, she did not look at him. He could clearly see the sweat on her skin and her tight fists. The moonlight illuminated her scar and there was a small trace of moisture in her eyes.

"You drink too much," Lukas said and gestured towards the wineskin.

"And you were clearly not taught manners," she replied sharply. "Did you not learn from your mother?"

Lukas crossed his arms and turned his own eyes to the plains. "My mother was killed many years ago."

Finally, Kitara spared him a glance, and for the first time, Lukas caught an emotion other than cockiness or anger. It was sorrow. She held out her wineskin.

"Killed?"

Lukas took it and drank a long draught. "By Balinor, the tyrant king," he growled. "And replaced by Lady Riona of Torosa."

"How old were you?"

Lukas sighed for he could not even remember Elodie's face. "Two summers," he told her. "Now she is dead. Balinor is dead. His supporters are dead. And my father sits atop a throne stronger than any before. Yet it is built upon blood. The only good thing to come of his godsforsaken union to Torosa is my sister."

"I didn't know," Kitara said quietly as she took back the proffered wineskin.

The prince shrugged. "So you see, we are more alike than you supposed."

Kitara snorted as her brow twitched into a frown. "We are nothing alike, rich boy. You were given the world, your every desire met. You know nothing even of your own people. Nothing of how the poor starve while you sit in banquet."

Lukas nearly shook his head. Her stubbornness made even that of the fool, Edmund Hornwood, look very much reasonable. A screech came from above, and it was followed by the snapping of branches underfoot. The pair whirled around to see Sakkar running words them. He raised an arm, and Sabra soared down from above and landed upon it.

"What is it?" Lukas called to his startled friend. "What do you see?"

"Riders," Sakkar shouted. "Sabra spotted them two miles out."

Kitara stepped towards the man. "And?"

"They strayed from the road and are on our trail."

Lukas cursed. They had done everything they could to remain hidden and yet they had been found.

"Get the horses. We leave now," Lukas said.

Hooves thundered beneath them as the four riders sped across the plain. The sun had begun to rise in the east, and it illuminated the path ahead as they rode north. They had been riding for less than two hours when Kitara risked a glance over her shoulder. Their pursuers were barely two hundred paces away. They were gaining fast. All that Kitara could see were the dark smudges of their silhouette and the occasional glimmer of silver as the sun struck their armour. They rode in tight formation that suggested what could only be Mieran training.

"They're closing!" Kitara shouted to her companions. Damn Mieran horses. "We have to get to higher ground!" Kitara called out.

She pressed harder with her heels and Lamreil shot to the lead. Her mane streamed in the wind as she accelerated. With a flick of her wrists, Kitara began to lead them northwest towards a crop of mountains. The mountains were small, no larger than tall hills, and yet if they got there, perhaps they had a chance. By the time they reached the hills and began to climb, their pursuers had eaten up the distance between them. They were no more than one hundred paces behind.

Kitara felt Lamreil slow as she led them into the mountains. They rode through chasms before Kitara led them out and onto the mountain side. They raced up, and their horses panted as they were pushed to their limits. The ground began to even out. The companions picked up speed as the Mierans closed the gap further. The ground grew flat as they reached the mountain's peak.

"No!" Kitara roared as she pulled hard on her reins and yanked Lamreil to a halt.

The mountain path had suddenly given way to a sheer drop. It was not a mountain. It was a cliff and below lay razor-sharp rocks. To fall would mean certain death. Kitara drew her sword as her companions formed up. She flicked her gaze over the terrain. The ground was too steep and uneven to move well on horseback. It did not matter how good they were at fighting while mounted, for the Mierans were better.

"Dismount," she snapped, and she slid from her saddle. "Quickly. We can't beat them on horseback, and they will not be able to ride well on this ground."

Kitara watched as the Mierans came to a halt. She kept her expression devoid of emotion as her fingers twitched on the hilt of her sword. Cailean and Lukas stood at her side, weapons in their hands, while Sakkar slid his small shield onto his arm and nocked an arrow in his powerful bow. Kitara ran her gaze over the lead rider as he pulled his horse up. She recognised the rings gracing his ear, as she recognised the man who bore them. It was the broken-nosed northerner from Chausac. The man that they had insulted.

"What is it you want?" she called to him.

"I was taught to never trust the word of a mercenary," the Mieran replied darkly. "Turns out I was right not to do so."

His hand adjusted its grip on the spear it grasped as his men formed up around him. The pursuers encircled the companions.

"I followed you from Chausac, and when two tracks became four … Well, you understand, of course." Broken Nose sneered down at them.

Sakkar flexed his fingers on his bowstring. "If you wish to lead your men to their deaths, then this will be the day that you do it," Sakkar snarled.

"Words can be forgotten as the wind blows. However, King Zoran has offered reward for every foreigner captured in Miera without his mark. You are not with Bellec, that much is clear. And once you are food for the crows, then that treacherous dog too shall fall. Throw down your arms."

Kitara never let her gaze shift from the man as she spoke. "We will not be prisoners."

The northern leader leered viciously and hefted his spear. Earth sprayed forth as he kicked his mount into a gallop. His lips drew back into a soundless snarl.

Kitara's thrown knife embedded itself in his ribs. He crashed to the ground. His weapon flew from his fingers as he landed at Kitara's feet. The Mieran started to rise, and the woman's sword rose to meet him, carving a bloody path through his throat. He toppled to the ground as the Mierans surged forward. Sakkar's bow sounded, and another rider crashed from his horse with a shout. Kitara felt her heartbeat slow as the first rider neared. She felt the steely calm engulf her as she slipped to the side and slid under the thrusted blade of the Mieran. Like water, her movements flowed. Her arms rose as her wrists straightened. She sent the razor-sharp edge of her blade across his stomach. Blood spilled and the man roared. He fell beneath her sword.

To her side Cailean struck out, slicing his axe towards the exposed belly of a rider's horse. The horse reared with a screech. Lukas lunged forwards as the Mieran fought for control of his mount. Lukas grabbed the man's arm and pulled him from the screaming horse. He hit the ground with a sickening thud before the heavy spike of Lukas' hammer found his heart.

Kitara slid back as a sword missed her face by a hair's-breadth. It was impulse that kept her alive as the next rider directed his blade at her head. She sliced his leg with her second dagger and deflected a third blow with her sword. One of the horses smashed into her. Air fled her lungs as she was hurled to the ground. She rolled to the side without thinking as a pair of hooves slammed into the ground where her head had been moments before. Earth filled her mouth. She rolled back, barely evading the horse a second time.

She looked up at the sneering face of a Mieran. He kicked his heels in, and the horse reared. Kitara held her blade up as a desperate defence, a last sign of defiance. Then the horse screamed and crashed to the ground as a spear drove into its side. Roars filled her ears and hooves shook the ground. She saw riders surge forwards from behind the Mierans.

Instinct kicked in and she rolled to her feet. She snatched up her fallen dagger and turned towards the new arrivals. She was in combat, fighting beside those whom she did not trust. Everyone was an enemy. Men clad in rough cloaks and the assortment of armour belonging to mercenaries rode into the heart of the fight. Bows, spears and swords were turned upon the Mieran riders. Their steel turned the tide. Kitara watched as the mercenaries carved a red path through the Mierans. The clash of spear and sword filled the cliff. Two of the northerners had dismounted and were charging at Sakkar who stood alone at the cliff's edge. He tossed his bow aside and drew his wicked khopesh blade. The first man reached him and the Larissan lashed out. Their blades came together in a ring of steel. Sakkar desperately fended off an attack from the second man with his shield. Kitara charged the Larissan's foes from behind. Her sword sliced through the back of a Mieran's legs. The man screamed and dropped to his knees. Sakkar knocked his opponent's blade to the side, and with a single swing of his sword, he severed head from shoulders. Kitara looked at the man she had sliced and watched as he fell to the ground in agony. He rolled over to face her. Calmly, and without emotion, she drove her blade between his ribs and into his heart.

Then it was over. Stray horses roamed the hilltop that had become a slurry of mud and churned earth. Kitara turned to face the newcomers, the mercenaries, her eyes wary. She held her blood-covered blades in hand and kept her guard up. Lukas and Cailean were alive. Covered in dirt and bloodied, yet alive.

Kitara watched as one of the mercenaries mumbled something to one of his men and dismounted. He crouched beside the body of the broken-nosed northerner. The mercenary cleaned his sword on the dead man's cloak and sheathed it over his right hip before he pulled Kitara's knife from the Mieran's chest. She knew him. The man was Bellec.

THIRTY-FIVE

Kilgareth, Valley of Odrysia

It was two days after the attack in Odrysia, and still the maija would not allow access to Hugh Karter. Kyler had fully committed himself to his training in the days since. Each blow he struck was dedicated to the knowledge that if he had been better, perhaps Hugh would not have been so wounded.

Kyler remained in the yard after the sun had slipped beyond the horizon and Sir Alarik had dismissed the initiates. His arms and hands ached from the day's training, yet still he forced his tired body to move as he sent blow after blow at the training post. His feet moved atop the sand beneath him. Sweat ran from his brow, hindering his vision.

One. Two.

The post thudded under the weight of his two-handed grip.

"Pisspot!"

Landrey, panting, lowered his sword after a moment and turned to the voice. He took a breath and noticed for the first time that his hands were shaking.

"Sir Alarik," Kyler greeted the battlemaster.

The use of the name bestowed upon him by Sir Alarik still annoyed him, yet what could he do?

"What is it?" Kyler asked.

Alarik snorted at the boy's irritated tone. "Hugh Karter."

"What of him?"

He stepped towards the knight and tried to find a clue in the man's face. Alarik gave away nothing.

"Bad news, I'm afraid."

Kyler felt his face pale. Hugh had saved his life. "Is he …?"

The knight's lips twitched. "Ugly? I'll say. He has woken up."

Kyler couldn't help the grin from crossing his lips, nor the chuckle that came from within them.

"Thank the gods," Kyler murmured.

"You can see him if you wish," Alarik added. "He is strong but needs rest."

Kyler let out a sigh of relief. "Of course."

"And before I forget. Well done in Odrysia, Pisspot. I hear you fought bravely."

"Thank you, sir."

Kyler felt his smile fade. The conversation forced memories of that day in Odrysia into his mind. He had killed people. He had sent men from this world for the first time. His hands, face and body had been covered in the blood of his enemies as well as the blood of Hugh. Yet he hadn't felt a thing in the heat of battle.

"Sir, those men in Odrysia. I know it is Durandail's will to punish criminals … I have never killed before."

The battlemaster looked at him thoughtfully. "What did you feel?"

"That is just it, sir, I felt nothing," Kyler admitted.

"And you want to know if what you did was right," Alarik suggested. "Lad, what you did saved lives. Not just yours, but those of Hugh and Elena. This may have been the first time you shed blood, yet it will not be the last. It gets easier in time, though the feeling never really fades. It is a question as old as the gods themselves. If someone is trying to kill you, should you not take up arms and kill him first?" the knight asked as he reached out and placed a hand on the recruit's shoulder. "If I may offer some advice?"

Kyler nodded for the man to continue. The man had been through more than most men alive. He had seen more. He had done more. His wisdom was as invaluable as his sword arm.

"The harder you work, the harder it is to surrender, Pisspot." Alarik met his eyes meaningfully as he spoke. "Never forget that."

Kilgareth's hospital was mostly empty. There was barely half a dozen injured and sick. Those who were there were watched over by a couple of maija who flitted through the stone rooms. The large room was grey, but it was anything but dreary. The windows were flung wide open to allow light and clean air in, while candles burned brightly on the tables.

Karter lay alone in of the snow-white beds. He sat propped up by his pillows as he gazed aimlessly into the pale blue sky. His chest was bare save for the bandages that wrapped his torso. His amulet hung from his neck.

"Still alive then?" Kyler asked as he made his way over to his fallen comrade.

Karter glanced at his fellow initiate and gave him a small nod. He clutched his necklace as he spoke. "I would go to the gods without any regret, brother, and I would go gladly. Yet there is much to be done, and I do not plan on seeing them just yet."

"The way you fought ..." Kyler told him. "Durandail must have some purpose for you."

Hugh shrugged. "And yet I would not be here but for you."

"But for Elena," Landrey corrected.

For had it not been her who had cleaned and sewed his wound? Had it not been her knowledge and calmness that had kept him in this world?

"You both had your parts to play."

"There is one thing that I do not understand," Kyler confessed as he looked at his bedridden companion. "That arrow was meant for me, and had you not acted, I would be dead. There is no question about that."

"And?"

"You risked your life to save a man that you hate," the Medean stated.

It was true. The pair had butted heads ever since their arrival in Kilgareth.

"No," Hugh told him as he grimaced against the pain of his wound. "I did not save a man I despised. I risked my life to save a brother. Yes, it is true that your desire to be right always is maddening. As is your need to make situations worse."

"As is your arrogance." Kyler raised an eyebrow.

"And now perhaps we can find some common ground," Hugh said with a sigh. "I was born into one of the most noble families in Laeoflaed, a hair's-breadth away from its lordship. From that day, I have never had a say in my destiny. They taught me to master the sword and lance so that I may one day have the means to lead more than just my house. My father had great ambitions, and I was his puppet in all things. I would fight for him, lead his men into battle, marry whom he willed. What I wanted was of no consequence to the lord."

"Then why are you here?" Kyler asked. Everything he thought that he knew about Karter was wrong.

"I fell in love." Karter closed his eyes for a moment. "When my father found out, he told me to spurn her and marry the daughter of Balderik, Lord of Laeoflaed. I refused … and so he had my woman killed."

Kyler could see the pain in his face as he spoke. It was an anguish that threatened darkness. An anguish that would send most men close to the edge.

"After that I left," Karter continued. "Had I a choice growing up, I would have ridden to Kilgareth in my sixteenth year, and so here I stand. I lost my childhood and my future to my father's cruelty. The one thing he cannot take is my faith, for I know this is the gods' will. And now they have set me upon the proper path."

Kyler let out a breath, for now he understood. It had not been arrogance driving Karter's actions. It had been the pain of those ever-present memories. The loss of a woman whom he had given his heart to and then had been cruelly taken from his arms.

"The Fiodine tells us," Kyler murmured, "that nothing of significance comes without sacrifice. Your faith, and your heart, will always be measured by the size of your sacrifice."

Hugh gave his companion a small smile. "Azaria's words."

Kyler nodded. It was a line from the sacred text of their religion, the Fiodine. In ancient Aureian the word meant 'rebirth'. The Twins had taken the ashes of the old world and forged it anew.

"I am sorry for your loss, brother," Kyler said.

Karter extended a hand. "Thank you, brother," he said.

Kyler took the proffered hand.

Kilgareth was lit with silver moonlight when Kyler at last began to make his way back to his chambers. It was quiet. Peaceful. The silence was interrupted by the thud of iron-shod boots upon stone. A single knight stood before Kyler in the corridor. The knight's arms were crossed as if he were waiting for something, or someone. Kyler recognised the armour before the light revealed the knight's face. It belonged to Matias Valenquez, Warden of Kil'kara.

"Landrey."

"Sir Matias," Kyler greeted the knight.

It was only then that Kyler noticed the older man's frown and serious expression.

"You need to come with me now," was all Valenquez said. It was an order that prompted no explanation. "The Circle is waiting."

Matias led him through the winding corridors of stone and deep into the heart of Kilgareth. There a door led into a small round chamber. Kyler held a sickening feeling at bay as the Circle members gazed towards him. The greatest warriors, teachers, mentors and scholars in the world all looked to him as if he held some kind of knowledge that they desired.

"Initiate Landrey." Grand Master Amaris spoke up and broke the silence. "No doubt you are wondering why we have called upon you at this hour."

"Whatever the reason, master, I will do whatever I can to help," Kyler replied.

Amaris leaned forwards in his chair, as if his eyes were peering into the boy's very soul. "Tell me now and tell me true, do you know of the Maiden's Veil?"

So that was it. The very question that Elena had asked him barely days ago. Now he had been brought before the Circle to answer the same thing.

"Yes, master," Landrey told him. "I have been there many times. The Veil is—"

"No." Corvo's voice was as sharp as his sword as he cut the boy off. "Do not speak of it. Not here. We do not know who else may be listening."

"There have been incidents in the past," Lysandra said, and she gave Kyler a sad smile.

Landrey had spoken to the arc'maija only a handful of times, and yet she had always been kind and compassionate. He knew that she cared for Elena a great deal, and that was all he needed to know.

"But what matters is that you are here now," Lysandra finished.

"And it would be best not to speak until we are on the trail," Sir Matias added as his gaze swept to his fellow masters. "For if this place is real and you know of its whereabouts, then we must be ready to ride out at dawn."

"Then it is settled." Amaris nodded. "Landrey, you will meet Brother Lorencio in the armoury and tell him to prepare you for the road. Be ready to ride come break of day. And do not speak of this to anyone. You are dismissed."

✦ ✦ ✦

The doors closed behind the initiate.

"Do you trust him?" the grand master asked as he looked to Sir Alarik.

"Only time will tell," the battlemaster replied, and he ran a hand over his chin.

Amaris turned his thoughtful gaze to the lady of the maija. "Lysandra?"

"Elena trusts him, and that is enough for me," she replied.

If her apprentice, the woman she was grooming for command, trusted and loved someone, then Lysandra was of the same mind.

"Give a man a little time and he may prove his worth," Lysandra continued.

"Very well," Amaris agreed. "Now we must decide, for this quest may change everything. Wa'rith's blade may be hungrily awaiting our arrival, and so we must be prepared for it."

"I shall go," Corvo said.

"And I," added Matias. "For if this phantasm is indeed on the road ahead, then we shall give him the full might of Kil'kara."

"I will go as well," Alarik called. "I have not left these damned walls in years."

Lysandra looked to the warden, Matias.

"Since he has served you for many years, Quinn shall travel with you," Lysandra said.

"We should take your apprentice as well." The Sword spoke up. "For she grew up in Adrestia, and as you say, knowledge is the most powerful tool of all."

Lysandra felt a sudden chill of fear run down her spine. She loved Elena like she was her own. If this quest did indeed happen to be one the artefacts, then Lysandra would be sending the girl into the lion's den. It was a grave risk, even with three of the most accomplished warriors this side of Aureia. It was a risk that she did not want to take.

"Alright," Lysandra agreed.

"Very well." Amaris rose from his chair. "Corvo, Matias and Alarik, you shall lead twenty of our brothers on this quest of my great-grandfather's. And by the grace of the gods, we shall triumph."

Lorencio was the only one present in the armoury when Kyler arrived in the hours before dawn. The quartermaster had been roused by another of the maija at the behest of the grand master.

It was a thing near unheard of for an initiate to be upon the road with knights, and yet it was so. Lorencio had gathered the armour without questions, and now stood in silence as Kyler pulled a shirt of mail over his gambeson. Next came the blue surcoat emblazoned with the white sun of Durandail. A set of steel braces and greaves joined the suit, as did a gorget. The helmet he was given did not bear the crest of a knight, nor was Kyler afforded their steel pauldrons or one of their cloaks. Kyler buckled his sword to his waist and took the shield that Lorencio had found for him. A large heater shield covered in a field of blue with Durandail's sun upon it. Kyler slung it across his shoulder, shoved his dagger through the back of his belt and gathered up his helm. With a nod to the maija, Kyler made his way to the stables.

Sir Matias sat atop his stallion before the gates of Kilgareth as the company assembled before him. His crested helm rested on his saddle, while the white fur atop his cloak warmed his neck. The sapphire cape fluttered in the morning breeze as the first rays of the dawn sun glinted upon his steel breastplate. He was ready to ride. Ready to fight.

Kyler held his helmet under his arm as he nudged his horse

forwards to join the ever-growing company of Durandail's soldiers. Each and every soldier represented the pinnacle of what a warrior could become. Relentless days of hard training had forged them all into ferocious weapons ready to serve the justice of the Twins.

Kyler smiled as he saw a familiar face in the crowd and made his way over to join her.

"You ride with us?" he asked Elena as he reached out and ran his fingers down her mount's strong neck.

"I do. Someone has to keep you out of trouble."

Landrey looked around as the last of the knights assembled. He saw Alarik and Corvo ride to join Matias. Their breastplates were as strong and fine, mirroring that of Sir Matias. In the crowd he could see the maija, Quinn, alongside the knights, Emir and Neph, who had escorted him to Kilgareth. A pair of small boxes adorned Quinn's saddle, and through the small square holes Kyler could see the feathers of pigeons, the message carriers of the Order.

"Have you ever ridden with the knights?" Kyler asked.

Elena shook her head. "Not like this. Something has changed," she said, and nodded towards the three masters who sat before them. "I can see it in their eyes."

They seemed to be ill of ease, as they had been when Kyler had met with them during the night. It was as if something plagued their minds.

"Still breathing then?" came the accented voice of an Aureian.

Kyler grinned as he turned to face the knight who had ridden up beside him.

"Good to see you, Torin," Kyler said.

Torin clapped his friend on the shoulder. "Who'd have thought, the two of us back on the road," the knight said before he glanced at Elena. "And who is this?"

"This is Elena," Kyler introduced her.

"Good to see someone is keeping an eye on him," the Aureian said, and he gave Elena a smile.

Elena shrugged and replied with sarcasm lacing her voice, "Two eyes."

"Knights, brothers-in-arms!" Sir Alarik bellowed, silencing the murmurs coming from the company. He waited a moment as the last of them died off, before gesturing to Corvo Alaine.

The Sword of Kil'kara closed his eyes as he began to speak. "And Durandail spoke … when it rains it pours. When the tides turn and the heathen is at your door, know that I stand with you. When you do battle in my name, I shall be your mighty instrument. Put your faith in me. Follow that path I have set where no misstep is allowed. A path where glory is the colour of blood. Do this and I shall stand by your side. For on the precipice of slaughter is the Lord."

He trailed off as he finished the line from the Fiodine, and silence swept the courtyard.

"By the gods' grace!" Sir Matias bellowed as he drew his sword and drove it into the sky.

Steel sang as the knights followed suit and swung their blades up.

"By the gods' grace!" they roared.

Matias took up his helm and placed it over his head, and with a kick of his heels made his way through the open gates. Kyler took a deep breath. He could feel his heart pound as the knights began to trail after their leader. He met Elena's eyes before flicking his reins and setting forth. Over a month of hard training each day had prepared him. Now he would find out if he was ready.

THIRTY-SIX

The Road to Thirlryda, Steppe of Miera

Kitara kept her sword and dagger at the ready as Bellec approached. His hands clutched her blood-stained knife. The mercenary and his men had just saved their lives. One question remained. Why? Why had Bellec ridden to their aid? He had risked his life for them, and not for the first time. He had risked his entire future in the Steppe when he had interceded in Chausac.

Her gaze scanned the ridge as she took it all in. Lukas and Cailean were slowly making their way over. They stayed close together. Their eyes were constantly swivelling, and their hands were clutching their weapons close. All around the cliff top milled the riderless horses of the fallen Mierans. The mercenaries talked in huddles. Some of them remained atop their horses and some were now on foot. Kitara counted a score of them. Two dozen hardened men whose sole purpose was blood for coin. Kitara exchanged a glance with Sakkar. She could see it in his eyes. He was wary. They both were. Her fingers twitched on the hilt of her sword. She barely noticed its weight as she prepared herself for what could quickly become another fight. The air was still. Sabra soared through the clouds somewhere above them.

"That is far enough," Kitara called out to the mercenary as he drew near.

She did not trust him or his kind. Men whose loyalty could be bought were not men you should turn your back to.

"A warm welcome." Bellec shrugged as his eyes betrayed a hint of amusement. "Time once was that when a man saved your life you thanked him."

"You have our gratitude," Kitara told him as she watched his every move with suspicion.

She had seen it before. It was all too often that one claiming innocence could attack without provocation. A wolf in sheep's clothing.

"Why are you here?" she asked.

Bellec looked over his shoulder and pointed Kitara's dagger at the Mieran leader's corpse.

"That man, Azian. One of my men overheard him on his way from the tavern. Ruthless bastard planned to follow you after that business in Chausac. Said that he smelt a liar, and that he would have you skinned and gutted by daybreak."

"That does not answer the question," Sakkar told him. "Why help those to whom you hold no allegiance?"

Kitara snorted. "It's obvious," she said. "The Mieran said it himself. For stepping between us in Chausac, he would have lost King Zoran's mark, and his life would have been forfeit."

Bellec raised his eyebrows and flipped Kitara's dagger so that he now grasped the blade. He flicked his eyes over the notched hilt and held it out to the woman. "I believe this belongs to you."

She sheathed her dagger without taking her eyes from the mercenary. With her eyes still on Bellec, she reached out for the proffered weapon.

As she grasped its hilt Bellec spoke up once more. "Pray that you never meet its makers."

She took the knife. What had the trader in Imalric told her? The folk from that far west were dangerous. Kitara could see something glimmer in the depths of Bellec's eyes.

"You've been there?" Kitara asked.

He nodded and made to speak.

"Do I know you, sellsword?" Cailean's rough voice boomed.

Kitara glanced to the side as the Salvaari and Lukas reached them.

The question that had come from the Aedei seemed innocent. How could it be possible for one from beneath those trees to have met a mercenary?

Bellec looked up at the bigger man wrapped in his huge bearskin cloak.

"Not unless you make habit of crossing the Rift, for I do not."

"Then I am mistaken," Cailean said with a shrug.

Kitara had only known him for a couple of days, and yet the Salvaari did not seem the kind to make such a remark unless he was certain. Though perhaps she was wrong. He would have seen many such men when Annora had crossed the border years before.

"What is it you seek? Do not think that I do not know your name, Bellec. I know of the regard with which the Medeans hold you in," Lukas told the mercenary. "You risked your life and those of your men to help us. Yet I have never known a sellsword to do anything without promise of coin."

So, the prince knew of the mercenary, Kitara realised. Perhaps the name was spoken of by the nobility in hushed whispers of awe and fear as so many sellswords had been before. She knew not. The corridors to power were closed to an orphaned girl from a faraway place.

"Unless my eyes are cheated, you come from wealth," Bellec said as he gave Lukas a cold stare. "What is your name, boy?"

"Lukas Torren," the prince replied. "I am a knight in Dorian's court."

It was important he give the man a false name. He kept his first name, however, for the greatest lies always had a hint of truth.

"Keep your money," Bellec said with raised eyebrows. He looked over his shoulder and whistled. As if on some invisible rope, the sellsword leader's horse cantered over. The mercenary took a hold of the reins. "We have lingered here too long. By your tracks you travel north. We shall accompany you," Bellec said.

"Now wait just a minute." The prince looked incredulous. "We are grateful for what you have done, truly. Yet this is where we part ways."

"Then what are you going to do, boy?" Bellec growled angrily. "What happens if you are caught again and lack Zoran's mark? Perhaps you will make the border uncontested. Perhaps you won't."

"And you think we will talk?" Lukas challenged. The prince ran a hand over the hilt of his sheathed sword. He took a step towards Bellec and met the mercenary's gaze with a withering glare. "I am no traitor," Lukas swore.

"You I do not trust," Bellec met his stare. "I will not have you risk the lives of me and mine if the Mierans catch your scent."

"Is that so?" the prince snapped. His hand balled into a fist around his sword. His lips curled into a sneer. Kitara let out a deep breath. It was his passion that had caused him to leave Palen-Tor against his father's wishes, yet this was foolishness.

"Do not test me," Bellec warned.

Sakkar stepped up beside his friend. "What do you propose?" the Larissan asked Bellec and gave Lukas a sidelong glance as if to warn him.

"We will help you to the border. Though why you wish to cross the Rift ... I know what is transpiring beneath those trees," the sellsword told the Larissan. "Once you are free of Miera, we can part ways."

Bellec swung himself up into his saddle with the ease of a veteran. He had first ridden out into battle when he had come of age. Now, nearly thirty years later, the fires in his blood had begun to die.

He had travelled far and seen more than most men alive, yet his journey was not yet done. He had wealth and reputation in Medea and Miera alike, yet neither was a shield. His second in command, Galadayne of Aethela, mounted beside him. Bellec could not take his eyes off the Annoran who sat atop his horse twenty feet away. He knew that face. He knew that blood. And it made his anger rise.

"Keep your eyes on that one," he muttered to Galadayne with a nod to the Annoran. "His blood is tainted."

When night fell, they made camp barely two days ride from Lake Thirlryda. Each mile they closed in on the border made Kitara's heartbeat faster.

Were the Salvaari her people?

The thought seemed to stick in her chest. She never once looked back the way they had come. Not towards Israfil and Silas, who would have sent a runner to Imalric by now. Nor did she look to Carlian, a place that had served as a home of sorts. There was no point in looking back, for she was not going that way. Now that Bellec was with them, a man bearing the mark of Zoran, they could light fires and be safe. For if any Mieran dared challenge them, the sellsword had to but show the mark and they would be left in peace. The sound of a lute echoed through the trees as one of the mercenaries began to play.

"Kompton," called Bellec, halting the tune with a shake of his head. "I would not draw the Mierans down upon us, not while we have guests."

"Aye." The Annoran slowly nodded before he placed his instrument down.

"What do you know of him?" Kitara asked Lukas who sat beside her. She meant Bellec, who now sat across the camp from them talking in hushed tones to one of his men, Galadayne. The man stood shorter than his leader, yet he had broader shoulders. The dark tattoos that covered the sides of his head appeared Valkir to her. She watched Bellec through the flames of the fire as they burned bright.

"He has Annoran blood, that much is clear. His man, Galadayne, as well," Kitara said, and she let her gaze sweep over the rest of Bellec's men. "But of the others, some Medean, some Annoran."

She trailed off and spared Lukas a glance. His eyes seemed drawn to the flames and his brow was furrowed slightly. It looked as though he knew something. Something that disturbed him.

"I was just a boy when word began to go around about a mercenary riding the Medean roads. A skilled warrior they said, a man who could both fight and command," Lukas told her. "To begin with, they were just rumours that seemed to have little truth behind them. That was until Santos Reyna rebelled against his brother and rightful heir to the Reyna lands. Santos, despite being the younger brother, was a feared swordsman who fought like he led: without mercy. Slowly, he sacked the nation, taking one castle at a time until he arrived at his brother's door. He laid siege and all hope was lost. And then mere days before he was about to take his brother's throne ... Bellec arrived. With no more than fifty men, the mercenary cut a path through Santos' guard in the dead of night. He burnt the rebels' catapults and towers to ash and then descended upon Santos himself. It is said that Bellec cut through Reyna's bodyguards with a single swing of his sword and then took the rebel leader's head before delivering it to his brother as a souvenir." The prince paused and glanced at Kitara. "And that was just the beginning. Father often said that whoever owned Bellec's sword was assured victory ... At least so was his belief."

Kitara flicked a lock of golden hair over her ear as she replied with sarcasm, "So he is a mercenary more gifted than most?"

"Duke Caspin once told me that Bellec would only sell his

sword to those he deemed worthy." Lukas shrugged. "Not to those with the fullest purse."

That was strange. She had never known any kind of cutthroat, mercenary or pirate who would not trade his honour for coin. Then again, who knew what this Bellec thought worthy.

"And now it would appear that we are stuck with him," Cailean added, pulling his warm cloak over his shoulders. "I for one do not trust a man who sells his loyalty."

"Come now." Sakkar gave the Aedei warrior a grin. "We are only two days from the border. And unlike you, big man, the mercenary does not smell of goat."

Kitara could not help the beginnings of a smile cross her lips as the Salvaari boomed with laughter. Cailean slapped a meaty hand on his friend's shoulder.

"Pah, you speak of piss, Larissan." Cailean laughed.

Footsteps.

They looked up as Bellec approached. Kitara saw Galadayne call to three other men, and they swiftly mounted and rode off into the darkness. Kitara felt her heart freeze.

Why had riders been sent off in the dead of night?

They were in the heart of Miera. They were surrounded by those who would happily send them from this world. She snatched up her scabbard from where it lay as the companions scrambled to their feet. Kitara took a hold of the sword's hilt. The feeling of its worn leather comforted her.

"Bellec, what is this?" Lukas snarled.

"You send riders in the middle of the night absent word?" Cailean asked as he glared towards the warrior. "Do you call for Miera?"

Bellec raised his hands. "Fuck the gods, no," he told them. "I sent Galadayne to scout the road north. I like to know what is ahead before riding into it. Would you not rather pass this way without dealing with the stubbornness of the Mierans?"

Kitara slowly let her fingers ease away from her sword. The mercenary had a point. She had to admit as much.

"He is right," she told her companions after a moment, but her eyes never left Bellec. "With or without Zoran's brand, they would make the passage harder than it needs be."

The tension that had filled the clearing evaporated as suddenly as it came. Anger and suspicion left eyes and hands fell from steel.

"I could not help but notice that the path you have chartered has started to track west," Sakkar said, and he crossed his arms as he frowned at Bellec. "Why?"

"I have ridden the Steppe for many years," the mercenary leader told them. "It is true, the best crossing is near to Lake Thirlryda. Upon its east bank sits Vadon, a town which has become an outpost in recent years. That means soldiers."

Kitara rolled her eyes. She had studied the maps. She had partaken in conversation with countless Mierans in her time in Carlian.

"But unless I am mistaken, the river to its west is impassable," Kitara retorted.

"Perhaps to some." Bellec's lips curled.

It was all he said before he turned and strode back towards his own. The companions exchanged looks. There must be some kind of ford in the river that had gone unnoticed.

"Mercenaries," Cailean cursed in distaste as he glared into the man's retreating back.

"A necessity," Lukas grumbled. "No more than that."

Kitara rose before the first rays of the morning sun had crossed the horizon. A few of the mercenaries were awake. Bellec was among them. She ignored their prying eyes as she rolled her shoulders back, took up her blade and made her way into the small amount of unused ground that the clearing had to offer. She closed her eyes and pushed everything from mind. The sellswords that slept all around her, snoring gently, and her own companions. She took three slow breaths before she gently slid her sword from its sheath. Maybe they were surrounded on all fronts by hungry Mieran blades, yet still she had to centre herself and still her mind. After days in the saddle, it became even more important to complete her morning routine. She started slowly. She flexed her wrists and shoulders as she turned the steel in her hands. Kitara weaved her sword through the air. Carving it. Slicing it. Her feet began to move as she slid atop the dirt below.

A sidewards cut became a diagonal slice with but a slight flick of her wrists. She may have been young compared to most, yet with the sword she was a veteran. Kitara was one with the steel blade that she wielded. She cut through the air with deadly precision. Kitara moved unconsciously. She created new patterns as she slid through the motions. Each movement was as perfect and graceful as the last. Each movement just as deadly. She felt a flicker of light on her face as the first rays of the dawn sun crept through the trees. It was time. Her breathing was steady, and slowly she lowered her blade. Her body had relaxed as the warmth of her dance seeped into her bones. Yet she felt eyes upon her. She knew the gaze long before she turned to face it. It was the same gaze that she had felt in Chausac. It was Bellec. Kitara gathered up her sheath and slid steel back within.

"Yes?" She raised her eyebrows at Bellec as she buckled on her belt.

"I have not seen tarkaras in many years," he told her with half a smile.

"You know it?" Kitara asked.

"I do."

He rose from the stump atop which he sat. That was a surprise. Few among the mainland had ever witnessed it. She doubted whether the wealthiest lords and dukes had even heard of the foreign art. Kitara had thought Bellec a traveller from the moment she had first laid eyes upon him.

Yet had he been to Tarik? Hell, even if he had been to Queen Reshada's court in Larissa, that would mean he was of some importance.

The man looked no more than his mid-forties. He was little over twenty summers beyond her own age.

He met her emerald eyes as he continued, "You interest me."

Kitara examined his face. There was no malice nor lack of mirth. "Oh?"

"You have spent time in the Steppe, the way you ride tells me as much," he said simply. "Yet I have never known any Mieran to allow a woman to wield a blade."

The golden-haired woman snorted. "They are a superstitious lot. Some cultures believe it brings bad luck to have a woman on board a ship. The Mierans, like most other civilised nations, believe that it is a bad omen for a woman to carry a sword. Though as I am sure you have noticed, I am not Mieran."

A woman who fought and rode as the men did. It was for that very reason that she had been forced to live with mockery and scorn since the day she had crossed into the Steppe.

"Then I applaud you." Bellec smirked. "For surviving for so long. Lady Fortune must indeed be smiling upon you."

If only he knew, Kitara thought darkly as she began to make her way back to camp.

"I make my own fortune."

THIRTY-SEVEN

City of Lumis, Isle of Vay'kis, the Valkir Isles

The great hall was filled with life as Scaeva and his people gathered around huge tables to feast and drink the night away. Astrid ate sparingly and drank only water. Despite Arndyr's words of friendship, she knew it was better to have a clear mind if conflict threatened. A few seats to her left sat the earl, while to her right was Torben. The old man downed the contents of his mug in one long draught. Nothing ever bothered the veteran warrior, not even the fact that they were now in the wolves' den. In fact, he seemed to relish it. Hélla sat to his side and seemed only too happy to follow suit. She was as good as a daughter to him and had adopted more than just his love it seemed. The people of Lumis had long since given up any pretence of suspicion and were now roaring with laughter. Their faces were covered in smiles. Despite what many thought, the earls of Vay'kis had made this city a place of joy.

"Quite the change of heart." Torben's voice cut through Astrid's thoughts.

The jarl glanced at her friend as he nodded towards Arndyr.

"No. I think he judged us the moment we walked into his hall," Astrid said.

"Why do you say that?" the old warrior asked. "His words–"

"Were chosen with care," Astrid told him. "I believe Earl Arndyr is far wiser than he lets on. He was testing me. He wanted to know if our motives were just before he made a decision that could cause his world, and that of his people, to sunder."

Torben merely shrugged in reply. "If you say so."

Once more Astrid let her eyes flick to where the earl sat. A grin adorned his lips as he laughed with his brother. There was light in his sapphire eyes as he spoke. Those eyes had seen so much in so few years, and they fascinated her. Arndyr was a handsome man, but it was his intelligence that interested her most of all. He must have felt her gaze, for he locked eyes with her. The earl smiled and dipped his head. Then he rose to his feet and gestured to her.

"Jarl Astrid, I have something to show you," the earl said.

He led her through the corridors of his palace until, with a grin, Arndyr heaved open a large wooden door and slipped inside. Astrid followed. The room was lit by torches and the sight took her breath away. Tables filled the chamber. Each one was covered with artefacts from the empire and beyond. There were scrolls, books, weapons and jewels. Grandest of all was the great tapestry that adorned one of the walls.

"This map charters from the heart of the empire to the lands of the far north. From Tarik to the Sacasian and far beyond," Arndyr said as he gave her a small smile. "It is the known world."

The tables and artefacts were all but forgotten as Astrid made her way through the room. Her hungry eyes devoured every inch of the great work.

"It's beautiful," she breathed.

"I heard you were something of a traveller," Arndyr told her as he moved to her side.

Astrid nodded as she felt pure joy flood her veins. "I cannot deny that my heart longs for it. There are many joys in this life, yet sailing and navigation, that is what I truly love."

"There is nothing akin to discovering new places and meeting new people," the earl agreed.

Astrid tore her gaze from the map and made her way over to

one of the tables. A scroll lay unbound atop it and she ran a finger down its length ever so slowly.

"Then in that regard we are kindred spirits. One day I should like to read these," Astrid said.

"Then you are learned?" Arndyr chuckled as if the thought amused him. "I thought as much."

Astrid shrugged. "It is a rare beauty ... being able to read. A thing that so few of our people can or wish to do. However, I have sailed the breadth of the Lupentine ... from the coasts of the empire to the shores of Miera, and in that time, I have learnt that no weapon can match a sharpened mind," Astrid said.

The earl placed a weathered hand on top of a small pile of books. "Then once this is over, you must return here," the earl told her.

"I may just do that."

They exchanged a grin.

"Though there are many secrets to this world not beholden to the written word," Arndyr added.

"A thing well known to me," Astrid said as she glanced at a brown, leather-bound book.

Curiosity got the better of her and she flicked open the first page. It bore the image of a half-moon and blazing sun. It was a symbol that she knew all too well.

"Is this ...?"

"The Fiodine." The earl nodded. "Aye, the sacred text of those who follow the Twin Gods."

It was the religion that had founded Aureia centuries ago. If the earl had a copy, then maybe he also followed the Twin Gods.

"But you're not?" Astrid asked.

Arndyr snorted as if it were a grand joke. "No. Despite how hard Darius' priests tried, I kept to the faith of my forefathers."

"That is good," Astrid told him.

The religion of Aureia, and other nations like Annora and the League, lacked much of the joy that the Sea-Father brought. It was a cold faith. It felt like ice to her while her own religion burned like the brightest fire.

"There is one thing that puzzles me," Astrid said.

"Oh?"

"Your map, grand as it is, stands incomplete," Astrid said, and she gestured towards the bottom of the tapestry where the ink faded not far from the southern Aureian coast.

Arndyr nodded. "The south is yet undiscovered and thus untamed."

"No one has been there?"

The thought interested her. An empire known for its discoveries, as much as its conquests, had not ventured far from its own shores.

"Many years ago, there was one who travelled south. Cillian Teague. He returned to the empire as a madman. After him, none have made it more than a few days from the coast," Arndyr told her. "They say that to sail its waters is to invite death on board."

He looked anything but scared at the thought … In fact, his eyes burned with some kind of excitement.

"Intriguing." Astrid turned her hungry gaze to the tapestry. "I should like to go there."

He met her gaze as his reply slipped from his lips. "Then once more, we are of like mind."

Astrid knew he was flirting, and yet she could not help herself. It was in her nature. She stepped closer to the man.

"Tell me, earl, what is one secret that you have discovered during your travels? A thing that you have told no one."

Arndyr met her shining gaze, and Astrid knew that he too saw her intent.

"You would not believe it," the earl said.

"Is that so?"

"Alright," came the reply.

Astrid could just make out the hint of wonder in his voice as the man spoke. In that instant she knew his next words to be true.

"Within the court of Emperor Darius is one thought to be extinct. It was not until I saw it with my own eyes that I believed it possible. Yet there it was. An elf."

Astrid could not stop a dry chuckle from leaving her lips. "Really?"

Those creatures were little more than phantasms of the mind. The mad thought them extinct, while the sane thought them naught but fairy tales.

"It is not a pleasant story," he whispered as they drew closer. Astrid gave him a flirtatious smile and slightly dipped her head, beckoning for him to continue. "I know not how long it has been with his family, perhaps since the time of his great-grandfather. The elf has served as a kind of neglected pet."

"And this elf, what does it look like?"

Astrid could feel his breath on her cheeks now as he spoke.

"It is a woman with hair the colour of fresh snow. Her ears sharpen into the narrowest of points. And her eyes, bluer than any sapphire."

"And as beautiful?" she asked.

"I have seen their match but once," Arndyr murmured, their lips nearly touching. "Though they are of the deepest amber, smouldering like the embers of a flame in a desert night."

Astrid felt a warm shiver run up her spine as her blood ran hot. She had barely noticed that their fingers had begun to come together. She could feel the slight prickles of his beard upon her chin. The light blue of his eyes that would not leave her own.

Astrid gently pressed her hands into his chest and pushed him back half a step. His back met a table and then she kissed him hard on the lips. She pressed her body into his, even as he wrapped his arms around her.

They never returned to the celebration that night.

Astrid's unbound hair blew gently in the morning breeze as she crossed the courtyard. She relished the warmth of the sun as it kissed her cheeks. Hélla stood across the yard with Torben. They were alone and obviously awaiting her arrival.

"You're late," Torben growled as she reached them.

Perhaps she had been slightly late, yet Astrid did not care. Not in this instance.

"Then we had best leave. Fargrim—"

"Can wait," Torben snapped, and he gestured towards one of the storerooms. "Hélla, apologies," he told the shieldmaiden. "I need a word with our jarl."

Astrid pulled a strip of cloth from her belt and pushed her dark locks from her face. She used the strip to tie her hair back and began towards the storeroom.

"What is it?" Astrid asked after the pair hustled into the empty room.

"You know." The older warrior glared at her.

Astrid raised her eyebrows.

Torben rolled his eyes. "You think I do not know what you did last night?"

She could see anger in his eyes. Real anger. Though she could not see where it came from. "What is your point?"

"By the Sea-Father, Astrid, is this a game to you?" he snarled. "We are here trying to win allies so that we can reclaim our home. And yet here you are, sating your appetites."

Rage flashed across the jarl's eyes, and she made to push past her friend. "I will not hear this."

"Yes, you will!" he bellowed and wrapped a hand around her wrist.

Astrid was pulled to a stop by Torben's grip. He met her eyes and lowered his voice.

"In Agartha, your intimacies caused no alarm. Raised eyebrows perhaps yet carried no danger. Yet here, now, we are fighting for our lives. And you think that we have time to what? Bed someone else? A man whom we do not know. Worse. A man who once had ties to Magnus. Did Lief teach you nothing?"

"Be careful," Astrid warned as anger rushed through her veins. She turned to face Torben. She flexed her fingers to stop them from balling into fists.

What was it to him what she chose to do with her own body?

There were many wondrous experiences that this world, this life, had to offer. The pleasures of the flesh had always appealed to her.

"Astrid," the bloodsworn murmured, "I love you like you are my own daughter. Yet this amusement is not like other amusements you have sought to enjoy. Arndyr is dangerous. We do not know him. We do not what he is capable of."

She could see the worry in his eyes. It almost looked as though he were in pain. Just like that, her anger mellowed. It faded as swiftly as snow under the sun's gaze.

"I know you mean well," she said quietly and placed a hand on his arm. "Yet do not treat me as a child. I am aware that we know little of the man, though I do think that I understand him. I don't trust him. I don't trust anyone not of the Wind Rider. I trust you. Please, Torben. Know that I am doing what is best for our people."

Erik held the blood-covered blade out to Earl Magnus. He had left the crimson upon the steel as a sign to the ruler of Agartha. A sign that he was truly at his side. At first, Redleaf had refused to speak when Erik had visited the man last night. That was when Erik had used the knife. That was when Redleaf had spoken.

"It is done," Erik told the earl. Erik wiped the blade across the hem of his cloak to clear the blood. "He breathes," Erik continued, "but I left Redleaf a cloak to cover the mess."

Magnus took the blade from the bloodsworn warrior's proffered hand. "And?" Magnus asked.

"Vay'kis," Erik said. "That is where they were headed."

"Strange," the earl replied thoughtfully. "I know Arndyr. He was my shieldbrother once."

The bloodsworn nodded. He knew as much. "Perhaps Scaeva is harbouring them. Perhaps he has killed them. Yet there is a thing that will not still in my mind."

"What is it?" Magnus asked, fingering the knife in his hands. "You know Astrid better than any man."

Erik felt something of a smile flicker across his lips. He knew exactly where his sister was hidden.

"There is an old wives' tale, no more than a legend. Yet my sister took great stock in these myths. There is always a hint of truth, she used to tell me," he said as he ran a hand through his short beard. "The Tears of Freydis."

A horn blew in the distance, sounding the call to the town square.

"Then that is where we begin," Magnus told him as he beckoned towards the doors of his hall.

Jarl Sigfried was making his last preparations down by the dock and would be leaving as soon as Magnus gave him his blessing. An offering was made to the Sea-Father to bring Sigfried good fortune in the days to come. Then, and only then, would he sail.

"Come, it is time," Magnus said.

The town square was overflowing with warriors when Erik arrived. All were armed to the teeth with sword, spear and axe. All were clad in their armour with shields slung over their backs and helms clasped under their burly arms. Three hundred warriors in all. Six ships to carry them. Sigfried to lead them. The crowd formed a ring around the centre of the square. It was left bare for the purpose of the sacrifice.

Magnus led Erik and a contingent of his household guard through the throng towards the centre of the square. With them the jarls serving under Sigfried stood with their leader. Jarl Sigfried was clad in dark pelts and leather. The sword at his side was vicious and Sigfried's eyes appeared almost empty. He was a hunter. A tracker. A warrior. And a ruthless cutthroat.

A roar went through the crowd and then there was silence. Drums began to beat, and the tune of the aulos flute sounded. It was soft at first, but it rose steadily. Erik closed his eyes as the music hit him. It reached within him as if it was driving into his very soul. The crowd began to part, allowing a column to form that led directly to the heart of the square. There they walked. Grey robes brushed the dirt underfoot as they made their way down the opened maw. They were the six acolytes of the Sea-Father. The crowd was lost to them as they walked. The eyes of the six never left the path before them. They murmured under their breath as they walked. Their lips moved as if to the beat of the drums. The leader of the priests carried a wicked knife in his hands. Its handle was bone, while its blade stood as no more than rough iron. The acolyte at his side led a ram. Its horns were painted the purest gold. It was the offering. A beast for the slaughter. The melody rose as the contingent reached the square.

"Sea-Father," the high priest called to the heavens, "we offer you this sacrifice in the hopes that in your infinite wisdom you will show mercy to your servants who stand about to embark across the waters."

The ram was brought before the high priest.

"May you see that those whom you grant fortune are but your instruments upon this world. May those whom you deem worthy feast at your side, while those desolate souls who profane your will fall to the coldest pits of Skûra. From this day until our last, we serve. Know this, Storm Lord, and let your will be done."

Iron shone in dawn's light as the blade was held aloft. The music stopped. The knife came down. It slid across the ram's throat. The beast bleated, and its lifeblood flowed. A great tide of crimson poured forth. Red tears fell into the depths of the bowl held beneath. Robes rustled along the stones beneath as the acolytes made their way towards Magnus and his six jarls. They were all strong men who would sail under Sigfried's command. Erik stood with them, watching. Waiting. He was one of them. The high priest held the blood-filled bowl towards Magnus. The earl met the man's empty gaze and took it. Magnus closed his eyes and mumbled a prayer as he slid his fingers into the crimson. He stirred the blood slowly and then withdrew his hand. Blood dripped as he raised his red hand and ran it down over his face. The bowl came to Erik next. Like Magnus, he dipped his fingers into the oozing ram's blood. He felt the warmth under his touch as he closed his eyes. The liquid moved upon his command as he stirred it once before lifting his hand free. In the eyes of the Sea-Father, Erik had chosen. Blood met skin as he ran it down his face. He tasted iron as it met his lips and covered his beard. It was done. Soon three hundred men would sail. Yet here he would remain at his earl's side. He was now, and forevermore, a warrior in Magnus' household guard.

THIRTY-EIGHT

Lake Thirlryda, the Rift, Steppe of Miera

The great Lake Thirlryda filled Kitara's vision. A sea of blue that in the summer would have been basking in the golden rays of the sun. Now it stood covered by clouds. Its majesty forgotten. It ran for miles, cutting from north to south, and east to west. At a glance, Kitara knew that it would take a day's ride to fully circumnavigate its shores. They had steered far clear of the road and strayed miles from the towns and villages along the journey north. Far to the east, thin trails of smoke arose into the air from the Mieran outpost.

"There lies Vadon," Bellec told them as he brought the group to a halt.

Kitara felt her gaze shift from the town and flick across the waters. Perhaps a mile from its bank she could make out the distinct outline of trees. It stretched from horizon to horizon.

"Salvaar," Cailean murmured. "Home."

To him it was.

Yet what would those woods be to her in the coming days?

The chill air met Kitara's skin. It had grown cold as they had ridden further north. She suppressed a shiver and pulled her rough cloak more tightly around her. Kitara could smell the distinct hint of moisture in the air. The clouds had turned grey, and the rains were nearly upon them.

"The skies grow dark," Galadayne muttered at his leader's side and spared a glance at Kitara and her companions. "There is a storm coming."

"The closest cover is the forest," Lukas said with a nod across the lake. "We should not stay here long."

Bellec raised an arm and gestured to the west. "We follow the lake's shore and river for a few miles. Then and only then can we make the crossing."

Bellec kicked his heels in and led the party, galloping along the lake's bank. Kitara had pulled her deep hood up against the rain an hour before they reached the crossing, yet now it served little purpose. The heavens had opened, and she had long since been drenched. The ice-cold downpour froze her to the bone. The earth beneath Lamreil's hooves was soft, and with each stride the mounted party churned it into mud. None of them looked back. Even with the rain pouring down around them and deafening their ears, even with the icy cold wind lashing at their cheeks, they did not look back.

At last, Bellec flicked his wrists, and turned his horse to the north. They moved confidently into the surging waters. He said not a word, for none could be heard. The river stood near seventy paces from bank to bank.

It looked impassable.

Kitara was convinced that to attempt crossing was to invite death. Yet Bellec charged into it without hesitation. He had been here before. The lack of expression on his men's faces suggested many of them had as well. Kitara suppressed a shiver as the biting rain bit into her shoulders and face. The clothing she wore had long since stopped being a blessing. She adjusted her reins and followed Bellec into the river.

Slowly, the waters grew deeper. The river lapped at her boots, and then it rose hungrily to cover her knees. Higher and higher it grew until little more than Lamreil's head and neck stood outside its lips. Panic began to set in. An icy dagger far more deadly than the storm. The current was growing stronger. It threatened to pull them to their doom. One false step, one slip in the mud below, and it was all over.

Then the waters began to recede. Step by step, they shrunk back. Kitara let out a sigh of relief when at last they clambered up the opposite bank and onto steady ground. The ford had been hidden well. The chances were that only those blessed with a stroke of good fortune would ever come across it.

One by one, the party of warriors formed up. Their wary eyes darted to the forest that stood before them. Hands strayed to weapons and silent prayers were made. Kitara couldn't help but let her hand rise to her mother's ring. She closed her eyes as she gripped the pure sapphire. Its smooth edges calmed her.

Had the woman who had passed in childbirth called this place home?

"Take cover in the trees until the storm ends," Bellec roared. His voice barely carried over the lashing wind and heavy rains.

"Be on your guard," Cailean shouted above the storm. "These lands belong to Henghis."

Thunder snarled and lightning flashed to life as they rode under the soaring trees. Kitara felt a sickening feeling as she pulled her hood back and brushed stray locks of waterlogged hair from her face. Her blonde hair had turned dark under the storm's wrath. Yet it was not the cold nor the echoing thunder that chilled her blood. It was something else. She dropped a hand to the hilt of her blade. The leather stopped the trembles in her fingers. Cailean had drifted not far from the group. His hand rested atop his mount's strong neck and his eyes gazed deep into the forest.

Kitara clicked her tongue and nudged Lamreil with her knees. "What is it?" she asked as she reached the older warrior's side.

"I am not sure," he told her, eyes never leaving the trees. "Something is wrong."

Kitara nodded. "I can feel it," she murmured.

"The lifeblood of the forest flows through your veins," Cailean said. "As it flows through my own. It grows cold ... A warning."

She glanced around. She was taking in everything. She could almost feel it all. The earth and bushes under hoof and the rough bark of the huge trees that soared all around. The icy drip of rain upon her cheek. The lash of the wind and the silence. In that moment, she knew it to be true. In her heart, she knew that she was Salvaari. She met Cailean's eyes and saw that he could sense it all.

"Eyes watch us," he said. "We are not alone."

A scream erupted over the roar of the storm. It screeched through the air and crashed against their ears. It came from the east. The mercenaries turned their wide eyes towards the noise. Their horses grew skittish. They pawed at the ground as they flared their nostrils. Lamreil snorted and kicked at the earth with wild eyes. Kitara placed a comforting hand on her powerful neck.

"Easy girl," she whispered.

Another screech echoed in reply. This one from the west. Heads whipped towards it. Branches broke, and then a rider appeared. He materialised from the darkness. His chest was stripped bare, while his face and body were covered in red war paint. His hair was slicked back with grease. His beard grew wild, while the spear in his hand ended in a wicked point. The man snarled, baring his teeth, before kicking his heels into his horse's flank and charging across the uneven ground towards them. Sakkar's bow sang, and the warrior fell. An arrow sprouted from his heart and sent him crashing to the ground. The air grew still.

"A scout," Cailean whispered as he stared at the body.

It had been a warning. Nothing more than that. They were outsiders and the alarm had been sounded as the scream had died on the Catuvantuli's lips. Horns blared from all around. Bellec drew his sword. His eyes whipped from left to right. Galadayne and the others followed suit. Steel rang and arrows were nocked.

"We cannot fight here," Cailean shouted to Bellec. "Nor can we retreat. Follow me to the river!"

Kitara's blade leapt into her hand as she kicked her heels in and charged after the Aedei. Lamreil's legs accelerated as her hooves bit into the ground. Mud sprayed behind her as she sped through the woods. They took no road, for none existed. Instead, they relied upon their wit and instinct alone to keep them alive as trees flashed towards them. All around her, the riders galloped after the Aedei chieftain's brother. Perhaps if they could put a river to their back, they could face the enemy with some kind of advantage. Thunder clapped and the wind grew ever wilder. It lashed through the branches and stung Kitara's face. Despite the cold, her blood flowed hot and filled her with fire. Screams came from every direction. They joined the deafening roar of the sky as it unleashed its fury. Shadows flickered through the trees. Riders charged forth and surged towards the galloping column. The Catuvantuli all bore weapons. All bore the red paint.

The first Salvaari to fall did not make a sound as one of Bellec's men turned in his saddle and launched his spear with deadly precision. It caught the man in the ribs and tossed him from his saddle as if he weighed no more than a feather. The Catuvantuli rider hit the ground hard and spun, his bones shattering as the shaft of the spear snapped against the earth. Ahead, Cailean ducked under a low branch and lashed out with his axe to deflect a blow aimed at his neck. He replied in kind and struck the warrior across his throat. The man fell and blood cascaded through the air, drenching the victor in a crimson wave. The first sellsword slipped from his saddle as a pair of arrows sped from the darkness and drove deep into his chest. More Catuvantuli erupted from the undergrowth. Four men became ten within a heartbeat. Ten became a dozen. The red warriors angled into the column. Their weapons drove towards the foreigners.

Kitara glanced to her side as one of the red-painted warriors came at her. His mouth curled back into a wordless snarl as he thrust his spear towards her face. Kitara twisted, angling herself out of harm's way, before lunging and sliding her blade into his stomach. She twisted her arm and carved her sword through his vitals. Blood washed over her skin. Kitara pulled her sword free as the man cried out and then vanished into the undergrowth. Another of Bellec's men fell under the blow of an axe. Screams of the fighters and the cries of the fallen joined the thunder of hooves and the roar of the skies. Kitara could not hear. Could not think. A rider crashed into Lamreil's left flank and forced Kitara to the right. Another rider joined the first and cut a hole through the column. Trees flashed towards them. Kitara pulled hard on her reins and charged to the east. A branch slashed her cheek, and red tears ran from the stinging wound. The trees grew close as Lamreil increased her pace. Catuvantuli appeared from the west and cut her away from her companions. No longer could she see the flicker of shadows that belonged to Lukas or Sakkar. The Catuvantuli closed on her.

"With me!" A shout came from her side.

It was one of Bellec's men. In his hand was a sword covered in blood. She recognised him as Vasquez, one of the Medeans. He too had been separated by the Salvaari. Without hesitation, she lashed her reins and hurtled after the sellsword. Each stride took them further east and away from the Catuvantuli who pursued them. Away from Lukas and Sakkar. Away from Cailean, their guide. Away from Bellec's men.

Their pursuers closed fast. They had ridden through the forest their whole lives. Their horses did not fear the trees that flashed to either side. One of them charged at Vasquez. The fight was fast and bloody. The Medean's riposte and counter stroke carved through his opponent's defence and spilled his guts across the forest floor. Kitara slew the other and then they were alone. Silence fell. Only the cold whispering of the wind and rain greeted them. Shadows still flickered in the distance and the crack of hooves was nearby. Soon enough the Catuvantuli would be upon them once more.

They rode hard. They did not care for the branches that clawed their hair and sliced at their skin. Kitara barely felt the rain even as it clattered all around. Screams came from the forest. A rider flashed towards them and angled his horse to run parallel. He raised his arm and roared. A spear left his hand as he launched it through the air. Kitara had no time to react as it caught Lamreil in the chest. The mare bellowed as Kitara yanked on the reins and fought for control. Lamreil fell. Blood flowed. She hit the ground in a spray of hooves, dead before the earth around her had settled. Kitara came down hard. She barely managed to protect her head as she was driven into the mud. It filled her mouth, her eyes, her hair. Her sword flew through the air and vanished with a splash. Air fled her lungs as she fought to breathe. Then the pain hit her like an avalanche. She cried out in agony as it rolled through her body. Her ribs burned and her arms ached. Her head rang as she tried to rise. Kitara couldn't see her submerged hands. Coldness rocked her body. Boots splashed into the stream in which she had landed. A stream. Little more than mud and a few drops of water. Its stench filled her nostrils as she fought for breath. Kitara felt her throat cry out and with a cough she spewed out the slime and filth that had filled it upon her fall. Cold steel met her cheek and for the first time she glanced at the owner of the boots.

A Salvaari stood above her. His lips twitched into a sneer as he raised his spear. Her sword had gone. It lay somewhere in the mud-filled stream. With a grunt, she went for a knife. The spear came down. The Catuvantuli screamed as a sword ripped through his back. Blood sprayed from his chest and splashed hot on Kitara's face. She tasted iron, and then he fell. The Salvaari splashed into the filth beside her. Vasquez stood in his place. Kitara barely managed a nod as the warrior reached down and helped pull her to her feet. Where his horse was Kitara did not know. Yet now they stood back to back covered in mud and slime. Waiting. Her sword was gone. She splashed through the mud searching for anything. All she found was muck. Not the comforting leather handle nor the length of Tariki-forged steel.

Branches snapped and her skin crawled. Three red-painted warriors emerged from the woods before them. Their hands were clutched at their weapons as they glared towards their enemy with hate-filled eyes. Her waterlogged and mud-stained cloak dragged at her as she walked through the sludge. It slowed her down. With an annoyed scowl, she cast it to the side. Kitara wrapped a hand around the knife at her back. A spear-wielding warrior whipped his arm back. He was too close to miss. His arm came forward. Kitara flicked her wrist. Her dagger drove blade first into the palm of the Catuvantuli's throwing hand. The blow sent his spear splashing harmlessly into the stream. He bellowed and ripped the knife free as he turned his dark gaze towards her. Without blinking, Kitara reached down to her boot and withdrew her second blade. She had two knives left. No sword. No tarkaras. Only instinct.

The red warriors charged. Vasquez engaged the first with his sword as they charged. The second man tossed Kitara's bloody knife to the side and reached for his own blade. The third ran at Kitara with an axe in hand and a snarl upon his lips. The Medean mercenary and his foe were forgotten as the Catuvantuli neared her. She slowed her breathing and dropped into her fighting stance. The mud on her boots was heavy, yet her footfalls were light. She slid back across the ground as the man roared and lashed out with his axe. Kitara danced back. Once, twice. The blade of steel missed her by a finger. Fire flooded her veins as Kitara waited. A third stroke came and barely missed as she leaned back. Kitara launched herself forwards as the axe swung past. She grabbed the Catuvantuli's arm with her left hand to slow his back swing and then she thrust her dagger home.

Blood spilled as steel bit into the warrior's thigh.

He bellowed and sprayed his hot breath over Kitara's face. The man reacted fast by slamming his left fist into the girl's cheek. Kitara grunted as pain exploded down the side of her head. She felt the Catuvantuli tense as she fell back from the blow. She knew what was coming. Fast as lightning, his axe sliced through the air. The punch had slowed Kitara as she stepped back. The blow landed. His close-angled shot carved a path through the leather of her brigandine before it slammed into the plates beneath. Air was driven from her lungs, and she screamed as agony ripped through her ribs. She fell to a knee as the axe slid from her armour and continued its deadly path. Kitara moved. She leapt forwards and jammed her knife into his chest. She forced the blade forwards until only the hilt protruded. Blood flowed and the man roared. He collapsed into the mud in a spray of filth.

Kitara staggered back and clutched at her ribs. Her jaw ached from his punch. It had once more awakened the agony that coursed through her body. Mud, sweat and blood covered her face and clothes. It was all she could feel. It was all she could taste. The Catuvantuli's blow had split her lip. She glanced up to see Vasquez turn to face her. His enemy was covered in gore and dead at his feet. Kitara felt blood enter her mouth. She spat it into the ground as she panted for breath. A splash came from behind and she whirled around. Too late did she see the injured man come at her. Too late did she see his blade angling towards her neck.

Crash.

Kitara was bowled over as a heavy weight smashed into her side. She was flung into the mud. A scream rang through the trees as Vasquez took the blade in her stead. Its steel tip drove deep into his vitals. Vasquez lashed out as he dropped to his knees. His sword carved a hole into the injured man's neck. The red-painted man fell. Then Vasquez toppled into the stream.

"No!" Kitara shouted as her ally crashed down.

He was all she had now. Her only ally. A strangled breath came from his lips. She took his hand and saw nothing but the pain etched upon his face. Kitara could hear branches snapping and the braying of a horse. More red-painted Salvaari drew near. She met Vasquez's eyes as he spoke.

His voice was no more than a faint whisper. "You have to live ..."

He breathed his last and slipped from the world of men even as his hand slipped from her own.

You have to live, he had said.

Kitara pushed it from her mind as she heard a rush from behind. Mud squelched as a warrior barrelled towards her. The steel blade of his spear drove towards her face. She slid to the side, lunged inside his strength. Her free hand angled his weapon away. Kitara thrust her knife forwards, but the man narrowly dodged it. He moved aside as the blade flicked towards him. Without hesitation, he brought the shaft of his spear up and smashed it into Kitara's stomach. Kitara cried out and then she slipped. The mud beneath her pulled her down. The wooden shaft smacked into her head and sent her sprawling. All she could hear, all she could feel, was the ringing in her ears and the splitting pain that thundered through her temples. Kitara coughed as she fought to stay conscious. Her empty hands clutched at the mud, for she had lost her dagger on the way down. A boot thudded into her side and flipped her onto her back even as her ribs screamed in protest. Blood ran from her nose as she managed to roll away from the spearhead that drove into the earth beside her head. The stream rippled as five more Catuvantuli joined their kinsman. Kitara ran her hands through the mud. Hoping. Praying. The man drew near. Her fingers found leather. The warrior tossed his spear aside and drew his own long knife. Kitara pushed herself onto one knee. Her hands remained submerged in the filth as her enemy neared her back. He raised his blade. Kitara spun around extending her arms as she lunged towards the warrior. Surprise contorted on his face as her steel sword ripped through his chest and punched out his back. With a snarl, she wrenched it to the side. The knife that had once been in his hand vanished into the stream with a splash. Kitara watched the light leave his eyes as she savagely pulled her sword free. He dropped to his knees before his last breath had left his mouth and then he toppled over. Kitara took a breath, and everything seemed to slow.

They gazed at her in surprise. The Catuvantuli had thought her as good as dead. Confusion turned to anger. Tarkaras took over as the first painted man charged. Kitara slid to the side, deflected his blade and then opened him from stomach to shoulder. Blood cascaded into the water as the second man attacked. She blocked two strikes as she stepped back to avoid his strength. Kitara deftly slipped around his blade and used her sword to angle his into the mud. Her first cut opened his thigh and her next took his life. Her ribs screamed. The three remaining warriors surrounded her. Now they would not underestimate her. Now they saw her as a threat.

Kitara took a breath and prepared herself. She felt the cool air upon her cheek and the droplets of rain as they washed through her hair. The roar of thunder as it crackled overhead followed by the flash of lightning. She was prepared. Kitara swivelled. She turned from one man to the next. Watching them. Daring them. She held her sword at the ready. At least one would fall with her. She had no regrets bar one. She had never known a place to call home.

The first warrior moved and sent his sword towards her face. Kitara blocked the stroke and danced to the side. Her arms came up for the blow the second man had thrown. It never landed. Instead, he crashed to the ground, gurgling blood as the bladed tip of an arrow ripped through his throat. All eyes swept to the forest and searched for the hidden archer. Nothing greeted them save the chill breath of the wind. Kitara buried her surprise as the Catuvantuli roared and attacked once more. She blocked. Once. Twice. She slid back through the stream. The second man fell as an arrow found his heart. Kitara's blade cut a jagged line of crimson across the last red man's chest. He fell to his knees and her sword took his head. Then it was over.

Kitara found herself panting as she gazed into the forest. She did not drop her guard. The arrows had come from the north. That much was clear. She turned her mud-coated and blood-stained face towards those trees. Her eyes searched for something. Anything.

A shadow emerged from the undergrowth. The archer's face was covered in blue woad. An arrow was nocked in a powerful bow. Kitara took in the face. The blue of the war paint. The silver eyes that seemed to shine. The face of one about her own age. The face of a woman. A woman as wild and untamed as any she had seen before. The archer tilted her head slightly and ran her moonlight gaze over Kitara. Her eyes sparkled in curiosity as she spoke. The first Salvaari voice that Kitara had heard other than that of Cailean.

"Who are you?" the woman asked.

Bellec snarled as he drove his sword down. He forced steel deep into the warrior who lay at his feet. Just like that, it was over. The Salvaari, Cailean, had led his men to a shallow river so that they could put their backs to a wall and face their enemy head-on. A wall of water had stopped the Catuvantuli from surrounding them. It had worked, and now the waters ran red. He looked around taking in every face as Galadayne approached.

"We lost three," his lieutenant told him. "Though where Vasquez is, I do not know."

Bellec nodded as he swept his gaze around. Cailean stood with his Larissan and Annoran companions. Yet something was wrong, and it drove a blade deep inside the sellswords chest. "Where is the girl?"

"Who?" Galadayne sheathed his freshly cleaned blade.

"Kitara ... she's gone."

THIRTY-NINE

Road to Adrestia, Valley of Odrysia

They rode in tight formation. Steel armour glistened in the sun's golden rays, while blue cloaks trailed behind like ocean waves. A magnificent sight to behold for any travellers or passers-by on the road to Odrysia. For when the Knights of Kil'kara journeyed forth, they rode in full glory. The party had barely stopped for respite since the morning they had left their mountain fortress. They had broken formation for only a few moments at midday and then again for sleep come nightfall. They had made camp on the first night with little more than thin sheets between them and the hard earth. A slow-burning campfire was lit to cook their food and keep them warm. Some of the warriors sharpened their blades, while others oiled their crossbows. They were preparing themselves for whatever mission they had been sent upon. Thus far they had been kept in the dark by their leaders.

"Pisspot!" Sir Alarik called out.

Kyler glanced at his mentor as the man tossed him a wooden staunch. The Medean felt his heart sink as he caught the practice sword. He ached from riding all day in full armour, yet now it appeared that his day had barely begun.

"We train; it does not stop," Alarik told him as he tossed his sword belt to the side.

All movement ceased in the camp as eager eyes turned amused

eyes to the confrontation. Kyler rolled his eyes and followed suit. He unbuckled his belt and rid himself of the cumbersome weight of his sheathed blade. The battlemaster spared him a nod.

"Suffer now and live the rest of your life as you wish it. Now, defend yourself," Sir Alarik said.

Kyler raised his staunch as Alarik came at him. The light of the fire danced across his armour.

They had trained for an hour when at last the old warrior tossed his staunch and caught it by the blade. The practice was over. Kyler barely noticed his ragged breath and he lowered his guard. A new series of aches joined his saddle-soreness. The blows from the weighted staunch left him sore despite his armour. Sir Alarik clapped him on the arm before offering one last piece of sage advice.

"Your body can stand almost anything, Pisspot. It is your mind that you must convince."

Kyler wiped beads of sweat from his brow with the back of his hand as he sat against the rough trunk of a tree. No doubt his tunic and gambeson would be soaked. A new series of bruises would appear come morning. Though he would only see those come his return to Kilgareth. The knights rode, ate and slept in their armour while on the march.

Hope for the best, yet prepare for the worst, Sir Matias had explained to him.

They had to be ready to fight at a moment's notice, and besides, they did not want to waste valuable time each day dressing and undressing their kit.

Kyler pulled off his rough leather gloves and rested his exhausted head back upon the rough bark. Though it was tiring, there was no place he would rather be than here. This is what he had dreamed of ever since he was a boy.

"Here," Elena said as she sat beside him and handed over a thin piece of salted pork.

Kyler took it gratefully. He was all too eager to bite into the meat. After a day in the saddle, it tasted better than anything he had ever eaten. He smiled as he felt the softness of Elena's skin as her fingers interlocked with his own.

"I'm glad you're here," he said, quietly giving her hand a squeeze.

The maija smiled and closed her eyes. She rested her head back against the tree trunk. It was not much, yet even her presence comforted the boy and took much of the sting from his aches.

"Alright lads." Corvo's voice broke the silence.

Kyler flicked his gaze to the great warrior as he made his way to the centre of the encampment. Matias and Sir Alarik were at his side.

"It is time you learnt why exactly we are here," Corvo said.

Everything stopped as he spoke. Whetstones left swords and conversations were halted.

"Last moon, Torin Aureilian" – Corvo nodded to the Aureian – "brought us tidings from the south. A message left by Evalio Delrovira himself."

Torin shared a glance with the Sword of Kil'kara before he spoke. "Upon his deathbed, Evalio gave a mission to my friend and brother, Bavarian." Torin said. "Some kind of riddle that he intended to be solved. It led us to the grave of Duran Cormac."

"And from there we found yet another riddle. This one speaking of Adrestia. The place of Duran's birth," Sir Matias added. "It reads: following the light of the sun, where the young were raised by frail, carved stone draws breath beyond the Maiden's Veil."

Kyler felt his face pale. He glanced at Elena who gave him almost a sad smile.

"Some of you may be wondering why an initiate rides with us, and it is for this reason. Like Cormac, Kyler was born and raised in Adrestia. He knows this region and he knows it well. He is the only one that can uncover this next clue," the warden said. "And thus, it is of vital importance that no harm befalls him."

"Harm? What harm?" Sir Neph asked.

"Do you expect an attack, Sir Matias?" Torin asked the warden.

Sir Matias stood proudly, and his voice was as strong as ever. Shadows lingered beyond his gaze. "Ten years ago, we first heard rumour of a divine artefact, the fabled Staff of Azaria," the warden said.

Kyler's eyes widened. That could not be true. He lived and breathed for the gods, yet the mere notion that they left behind such artefacts was impossible.

"It was no more than the breath of a myth, yet we were sent to investigate," Corvo said, and a sad note entered the knight's voice. "And I tell you now that I did not believe it true. That was until I laid eyes upon the staff myself. A miracle granted by Azaria herself. It shone white as silver and filled the soul with joy. What happened in that cave … was my greatest failure." He trailed off and let silence reign as he took a long breath. His gaze was distant as if he were reliving the memory. "The staff was lost, along with my brother," Corvo finished.

"In the years since," Sir Alarik continued as he clapped a comforting hand on Corvo's shoulder, "we have heard tell of other such artefacts. Each time, knights were sent forth to do the Twins bidding. Each time, none returned. We searched for them for months. And all that we found were their bodies left to rot in the sun."

"Wa'rith," Matias whispered.

The air seemed to grow chill as he spoke, as if the wind itself feared that name.

"The Shadow," Matias continued. "That is what we call him. This phantasm who has caused us so much pain … so much grief."

"That is why I am here," Sir Corvo said, and his hand wrapped around the hilt of his massive blade. "To do my Lord Durandail's bidding. The Fiodine tells us to show no mercy to non-believers. I am here for Wa'rith's head."

"And you believe that this path upon which we now find ourselves will lead to another such artefact?" the maija Quinn asked.

"Perhaps, perhaps not," Alarik replied. "Regardless, my heart tells me that we are not the only ones following this riddle."

They left at dawn and rode in silence. Much now plagued their minds. The further they got from Odrysia and Kilgareth, the more Sir Corvo Alaine seemed to be drawn back to his past. Whatever had happened ten years ago had changed the man in ways that none save Matias and Alarik would ever understand. Some of them believed that they were hunting another one of these divine artefacts. Others believed they were looking for some kind of tool or scroll that could prove vital in the days to come.

Yet Kyler could not stop his mind from wandering to Wa'rith. This shadow that could even now be hunting them. If what Matias, Alarik and Corvo said was true, then this ghost, whoever he was, was more than just a threat. He was a nightmare made of flesh. The thought terrified Kyler. If the mention of his name was enough to send a shiver down the spine of those in the Circle, then what could he do to the rest of them?

Over the course of the next few days, they ate in the saddle and made camp only when the sun had all but vanished beyond the horizon. Sir Alarik would train with Kyler for an hour or more. The young Medean would then collapse in an exhausted pile of limbs and sweat where he could finally sleep. They followed the road for days. They travelled by Malcia and the inn of the Drunken Huntsman. No doubt that if he saw Kyler in his full armour, the innkeeper would not dare to try and rob him again. Then at last they reached the Adrestian Highlands, the rolling hills that Kyler had called home for so many years. Sir Matias brought the column to a halt as they looked down towards the town that lay no more than a hundred paces to the west. Where the young were raised by frail. Where Duran Cormac had been raised by his grandfather.

Kyler felt his heart yearn as he gazed at Adrestia. He saw Gascon's forge. It glowed orange and spewed steam and smoke into the sky. It was the place wherein the sword that sat at his hip had been forged. He recognised each house. He knew each street and each face, even from a distance. Then he saw the Sleeping Siren. His father's pride and joy.

Who ran the establishment now that Theodore and Maria had left for Elara? Would it still be as welcoming?

"It feels as if a lifetime ago," Elena said quietly.

Kyler nodded. It had been little more than a month ago that he had left those streets, and yet everything had changed. His family no longer lived in that town, and he now rode with a company of the most renowned knights in history.

"Perhaps one day we could return." He gave Elena a smile.

"I would like that very much," she told him, and her own lips twitched up.

"Do you remember when we broke into Murilo's orchard?" Kyler's eyes sparkled as he spoke.

Joy filled him as he remembered when the pair had ran laughing through those trees. Apple juice had streamed down their lips as old Murilo had given chase. That had been three summers ago when life had been simpler. That was when it had been the two of them against the world.

Elena sniggered. "I swear he would have killed you."

"Most likely." Kyler laughed as he recalled the look on the man's face.

"Landrey," Sir Matias called from the head of the column of silver and blue.

Kyler's grin faded as he was brought back to the present by the warden who beckoned to him. Kyler kicked his heels into his horse's flank and cantered to the veteran's side. It was only then that it hit him. He had been nothing but the muscle in a tavern, and now he sat ahorse and surrounded by three members of the Circle itself.

"Sir." Kyler nodded to the knight who had summoned him.

"Sir Alarik has spoken highly of you," Matias told him.

At his side, the battlemaster offered nothing more than a slight dip of his head.

"Now is your chance to show us that you are worthy of such. Do you remember how to find this Veil?" Matias asked.

Kyler cast his memory back to when he had first discovered this place. He had used much of his spare time to explore the highlands. The plains, rivers, lakes and hills were well known to him. He could remember all of it.

"I would know blindfolded," Kyler told the knights. "It lies less than two miles north."

Sir Alarik gestured to the road, and said, "Lead on, Pisspot."

Kyler led them at a mile-eating gallop. He was all too aware that the eyes of the Circle were upon him. Over the hill and through forest they rode until they at last reached the banks of a small stream. For a mile they followed its clear waters until at last it began to broaden into a lake. The sun shone its brilliant rays upon the calm blueness of the water.

"This place looks untouched by the hands of men," Sir Matias said as he turned his inquisitive gaze to Kyler.

The boy shrugged. "It is a place that few Adrestians ever travel, for there are closer sources of water and forests where game was plentiful. Why travel for that which they already have?"

The knight nodded as he swept his eyes over the water. A thin waterfall fell from the cliff that faced them. It splashed down into the lake and forced the current down the stream.

"How is this a Veil?" Corvo muttered as he gazed at the lake.

"It lies there, sir," Kyler replied as he slowly raised a hand towards the waterfall.

It took a moment, and then the knight at last saw it. The stream of white water, clear as glass, that flowed down from the cliff like a wall. His eyes widened.

"A maiden's veil is white, like a waterfall," Corvo exclaimed.

"I'll be damned." Sir Alarik grinned and slapped a meaty hand on Kyler's back. "He's done it."

"And now," the boy said, "we must go beyond. Follow me."

They followed Kyler as he rode around the riverbank. They stopped only to dismount, for the path grew too treacherous for a horse's hooves. The boy led the way with Alarik, Matias, Corvo and the two maija, Quinn and Elena, at his back. There was no visible path, for none existed. Indeed, it had been only by the will of the Twins that Kyler had found this place to begin with.

The earth of the bank turned into rock as they made their way along the edge of the cliff face. It grew slippery underfoot, and they were forced to hold onto the steep wall of the cliff for balance. Droplets of water struck their armour and clothes as they ducked beyond the Veil. Breaths were caught in throats as they saw it. It was the entrance to a cave. Light flickered across the rock faces of the cave walls as it fought its way past the cascading waterfall. It was small, no more than ten paces deep, yet here it was. A hidden cave.

"I found this place last summer," Kyler told the knights as he led them, open-mouthed, into the tunnel.

Exploring Adrestia had been the only thing to keep him occupied once Elena had left.

"I had thought it undiscovered, that is until I saw this," Kyler said as he gestured towards one of the rugged stone walls.

"Carved stone draws breath," Elena whispered as she followed Kyler's gaze.

Carved into the walls of the cave was a language that few knew and fewer still ever spoke. A language kept alive solely thanks to the Order of Kil'kara and old religious sects.

"Ancient Aureian," Matias breathed, and he reached out as if to touch the text. He stopped his hungry hand mere inches from the stone as he mouthed the words that it read.

"What does it say?" Kyler asked glancing at Elena.

He knew little of the language save a few mumbled prayers and sayings. They all grew silent as the maija spoke. Her awe-filled voice filled the cavern.

"In the Bear's jaws where fabled glory began, a nation would arise where the accursed were doomed to lie."

It stood as another riddle.

"I think that we can all agree now," Corvo said as his eyes swept to the faces of his companions, "that whatever Cormac hid nigh on a century ago is more than just any old artefact or a page of lost wisdom."

Quinn nodded as he looked to the poem. "That path has led from Rovira to Kilgareth and now Duran's birthplace. This riddle, as it is, can only be following his life. I am sure of it," Quinn said.

"But this new verse ... I can make no sense of it," the Sword of Kil'kara cursed. "A nation would arise where the accursed were doomed to lie. What lie, I wonder."

Quinn pursed his lips. "As it is written, lie stands as death or die, it does not speak of falsehoods."

"And the accursed?"

Elena ran her hand over the text. "The accursed were doomed to lie. They knew they were going to fall. But the bear ..." Elena trailed off.

"I think maybe it suggests a title, or name, rather than the beast," Quinn told her. "In the Bear's jaws ... There is only one family I know that holds that symbol."

"House Bailon of Medea." Sir Alarik clapped his hands together as at last he understood. "And who was Duran Cormac's greatest ally and friend? A man he wrote highly of?"

"Estevan Bailon," Matias finished for him. "The Bear of the North."

Quinn nodded. "It was only his sacrifice in Palanza that won the war. Only when he led his cavalry in a desperate attack that saved Cormac. He and all his men died that day, and they knew that they would. The price of freedom," Quinn said.

Bailon had been a martyr in the war, and it had worked. One by one, the houses rallied and drove the pagans and heathens, the devil worshippers, out. The monsters who had been hell bent on driving the land to ruin. There had been stories that had come from that war. Stories that more than just man had walked those hills and plains. Tales of warlocks and elves, wraiths and, most feared of all, the ruskalan. Creatures who been spewed forth from the doors of hell and nearly driven the land to ruin. Had those beasts and nightmarish creatures ever been real, then they were now extinct.

"And then his son took all the glory that rightfully belonged to Duran and Estevan for himself. A great fable, as it would seem," the warden said. "And yet, it was to be that from the grave of his father sprung the unification of Medea. No more was the north just a collection of warring fiefdoms."

"And it began that day in Palanza," Sir Corvo added.

It was as Kyler knew it. He had only come to know of Cormac's involvement last moon, but he had always known of Bailon and the fields of Palanza. Estevan was a hero to his people for what he had done. As such, a great monument had been created in memory to the man and his brave warriors. Medea had arisen from the smoke and chaos of the Inquisition and the war that followed. That day in Palanza the five great families had forged their nation.

Quinn turned back to face the knights and excitement made his eyes shine.

"Then that is where we ride," Quinn said.

FORTY

Catuvantuli lands, Forest of Salvaar

"Who are you?" the woman asked again as she tilted her head ever so slightly.

Kitara ran her gaze over the archer. She was Aedei, that much was clear. The blue woad that she wore in a cross shape over her right eye said as much. White grease was streaked through her raven-black hair to help push it from her eyes. Those dark locks were loosely tied back and hung in curling drapes down her back. A single thin braid fell down her shoulder. She wore a fur across her shoulders to keep the chill at bay. The long-sleeved tunic and trousers that she bore were just as plain and rugged as Cailean's. The fur-trimmed quiver at her back complemented the powerful weapon in her grasp. To wield such a bow the muscles of her back and arms would have been strong enough to match it. Though it was not the bow in her hand nor the bladed arrow atop it that cut short Kitara's breath. It was the woman's eyes. As silver as the moon.

"My name is Kitara," she said as she finally lowered her sword.

The Aedei nodded as if satisfied and unnocked her arrow. She flicked it around so that she held it with her bow hand.

"Aeryn," the archer said.

Kitara returned the nod and finally dropped her guard. She let out a deep breath and pushed back the pain that rolled through her ribs.

Kitara glanced around the churned mud. The horses belonging to the Catuvantuli had long since fled and left their fallen riders in the filth. Nine red-painted warriors lay in and around the stream, each as bereft of life as the others. Vasquez lay with them. His sword rested beside his cold body. Then there was Lamreil. Her ever-constant companion. The once proud horse lay on her side, the huge shaft of a spear still embedded in her chest. The sight chilled Kitara to the bone. She splashed her way through the slurry of blood, water and churned earth until she dropped to her knees at her faithful mare's side. To Kitara she had been more than just another horse. She had been as a friend. She did not hear Aeryn walk to her side, for emotion churned within.

"It is never an easy thing," the Aedei said sadly, "to see one so loved no longer of this world."

Kitara ran a hand down Lamreil's flank until it reached the wooden shaft of the spear. She took hold of the wood. Her knuckles whitened as she gripped the weapon. She yanked it free and cast it away.

"She once saved my life," Kitara told the Aedei woman. "Carried me over two hundred miles to safety, and a thousand more since."

Aeryn mumbled something. It could have been a prayer in her own tongue. Kitara did not know.

"She is at peace now," Aeryn told her. "One with the spirits."

Kitara rose to her feet and looked to the silver-eyed woman. "Why did you save me?"

The Aedei shrugged. "I am a tracker ... a scout. I have been following those Catuvantuli for two days. I caught your scent before they did; however, they were closer. I was too late to help all of you. And for that I am sorry. Though I may ask the same question of you. What are you doing beneath these trees?"

Kitara made her way over to one of the fallen Catuvantuli and used his cloak to clean the blood from her blade. She sheathed it before turning back to Aeryn.

"I ride with Cailean, brother to Cyneric," she told the other scout.

Kitara felt a wave of panic crawl through her body. What had happened to the Aedei warrior? What had happened to Lukas and Sakkar? The mercenaries?

"You ride with Cailean?" Aeryn's mouth dropped wide open. "Then he has returned to us at last."

"We got separated thanks to the Catuvantuli," Kitara explained. "We have to find them … Cailean mentioned a river."

"A river?" Aeryn asked and she gestured to the trees with her bow. "Then they will be miles from here by now."

Kitara shrugged as her boots squelched through the mud. She found her daggers lying in the stream and took them up. "Then we had better start moving."

"We cannot." Aeryn shook her head at Kitara's frown. "Listen to me, Kitara. We are in Henghis' lands now. The path west that your friends took will be swarming with Catuvantuli warriors. To go after your friends is to court death. We would never catch them."

Kitara swore and slapped her hand angrily into her thigh. She knew that Aeryn was right. Whatever fate Cailean and the others had found, they were well and truly alone.

"Then what do we do?"

Aeryn looked to the north. Her silver eyes shone, for she was deep in thought.

"Cyneric has set up camp to the northeast. It is a place that Cailean knows well and would expect his brother to be. So, we go to Cyneric, and if the spirits will it, your friends will be there already."

It was a plan that made sense. Kitara was forced to agree. "Alright."

The fires that ran through her blood had begun to fade and finally Kitara felt the biting cold of the wind. She shivered inside her waterlogged clothes. She snatched up a waterskin from one of the dead Catuvantuli and used its contents to wash her face clean of earth and blood. Her cuts stung and her temple throbbed, yet she gave no complaint.

"Take this," Aeryn said.

Kitara turned to see Aeryn holding out a thick woollen cloak. A light layer of mud clung to its hem. It had been used. It had belonged to one of the dead men.

"It will help with the cold," Aeryn said.

Kitara took the cloak and pulled it over her icy shoulders. The Aedei woman gave a single piercing whistle and a horse answered. It cantered out from the woodland. Kitara watched curiously as the girl touched her forehead to that of the chestnut-coated horse before she pulled herself up onto its back. She did so with grace. It was almost done in Mieran-like fashion. She was a born rider. Kitara took a breath before she gathered up the reins of Vasquez's mount. It was the only horse that had not fled. She gave a final look over the battlefield before she knelt at her fallen companion's side. She slowly reached out a hand and closed Vasquez's unseeing eyes.

"Rest easy now, brother. Drift deeper and deeper. The sirens are calling your name." It was an old saying that she brought with her from the Sacasian. One which still held great meaning to her. "It feels wrong to leave them unburied," Kitara said quietly.

"In war one does what one must," Aeryn replied.

Kitara caught the hint of sadness in her voice. Perhaps there was more to the Aedei scout than she let on.

"I shall offer them a prayer tonight," the woman added. "If you wish?"

Kitara gave a slow nod. Then they made their way into the forest.

Lukas spared Sakkar a glance as they made their way down the riverbank towards Bellec. The pair remained quiet as they felt the same guilt. The woman who had saved their lives was gone. She had been taken like a leaf in the wind.

"We should have stayed with her," the prince cursed.

Sakkar placed a hand on his friend's arm. "Whatever fate has befallen Kitara is of her own making. She chose to ride with us just as she chose to turn from the Mierans. Whether she is alive or dead, Kitara made a choice."

"I know that," Lukas replied, for in his heart he did truly understand. "Yet I ... I failed her."

The Larissan shook his head. "We all did."

They reached Bellec as he gazed to the east. What he was looking for, Lukas did not know. Yet there was a genuine pain in his eyes. Galadayne stood at his side, as did a number of the other sellswords. They stood in silence, for at their feet they had laid the body of one of their men. The man who had so bravely given his life for a cause not of his making. Another two had fallen in the forest, while a fourth, Vasquez, had vanished into thin air. That made four. One of the mercenaries crouched over the bodies of his companions and murmured a prayer. He swept his dark gaze to the forest that surrounded them.

"These trees remain as cursed as they were twen—" He cut off as he saw Sakkar and Lukas approaching.

Yet Lukas had heard his words. The prince ran his eyes over the man who had spoken. His voice, like his face, was clearly that of an Annoran. Once more, the words of Cailean rang in his ears.

"Do I know you, sellsword?" the Aedei warrior had once asked.

The man who had spoken, the one they called Jaimye, certainly looked old enough to have fought in these forests twenty-five years before. Though he would have been a young man then. In fact, Lukas realised, many of the Annorans among the mercenaries could have been a part of that same army. Galadayne, and even

Bellec himself, could have fought with Lukas' father.

If it were true, then what were these men doing here? Why were they not in Annora with the rest of their kin?

"This day carries a heavy toll," Bellec muttered as he glanced at Lukas and Sakkar.

There was something near hatred in his eyes, and Lukas felt his skin crawl. Thank the Twins that he had not revealed his ancestry to the man.

"We must find Cyneric," Cailean said as he made his way over to the forming group. "Every moment we delay brings us closer to death."

"You know how to find him?" Lukas raised his eyebrows. Cyneric would not be at his capital, that town that they called Noyon, of that Lukas was certain.

Cailean nodded and took a deep breath of air. The air of his homeland. "I have walked these trees for decades, my friend. There is a place not two days ride from here that my brother favours in times of war. But before we leave, there is one thing I need to know," he said as he turned to face Bellec.

Cailean's voice filled with power as he spoke. The power of a commander, the power of a great chief's brother and sole heir.

"Are you with me?"

All eyes went to the sellsword leader who gazed so distantly into the forest. He said nothing and gave no sign that he had even heard.

"What now, boss?" one of his men asked. "Do we turn back?"

"Turn back?" Bellec growled. "I will give you five reasons that we cannot. Ander" – he gestured to the body of his dead friend – "Maceo, Raylor and Vasquez."

Bellec flicked his eyes to Lukas and Sakkar. In them Lukas could see a glimpse of raw emotion. Anger, bitterness and, hidden beneath, sorrow. Bellec gave them a small nod.

"Kitara. Do you want to run from those who have already taken so much? Turn from those who killed our brothers? No … I will not let their deaths go unpunished nor let their passing be in vain. The men who took them from us will watch from the trees, laughing, if we turn tail and flee like cowards. I would not have it so. I will do great violence upon those men."

The eyes of the mercenaries began to fill with fire as their leader spoke. Heads began to nod, and voices spoke in agreement. Bellec turned his gaze to Cailean. The man who would help to guide them and kill their enemies.

"You wanted an answer, and I freely give it. We are with you. To the death."

Cailean extended his powerful wrist and clasped Bellec's own. They locked eyes and an unspoken agreement was forged.

The storm had long since stopped, yet the smell of moisture in the air was still strong. Kitara followed Aeryn as they rode through the woods in silence. The sun had finally set, and night cloaked the forest in a shroud of darkness. Every crack of a branch underfoot or the screech of a bird far off made Kitara's heart flutter. This place was strange to her and held an almost eerie pull. Despite the darkness that had enveloped them, Aeryn did not make a sound. Her head remained on a swivel, and her eyes seemed to stare through the trees themselves. Kitara felt her shoulders tremble. Although she wore a thick Salvaari cloak, her clothes beneath were still soaked through. She took a breath and rubbed her hands together to force back the cold. The Aedei scout led them at a brisk pace, her bow in hand and her eyes ever watchful. She occasionally turned those silver eyes of hers to Kitara as if to make sure she was still there.

A bird call rang through the trees. It seemed far away, yet this time Aeryn stopped in her tracks. It seemed as if nothing to Kitara, but Aeryn clearly felt differently.

"Catuvantuli," she murmured, and she shared a look with Kitara. Perhaps it was how Henghis' men communicated through the trees.

Perhaps right now they were stalking the pair. Waiting and watching. Without a word, Aeryn slid from her saddle. Kitara watched on in curiosity as the woman placed her ear to the earth and closed her eyes.

"What is it?" Kitara asked as she glanced towards the Aedei scout.

"They communicate as birds … An ambush," came the quiet reply. Aeryn opened her gaze but let her ear rest open the ground. "A few miles west from here," she continued.

Aeryn rose to her knees and faced her companion.

"How do you know?" Kitara asked. "The call sounded close."

"Sound carries in the woods at night." The Aedei's lips curled upward as if she were amused. "I have known the woodsman's craft since I was a child. I can hear things in the earth … feel them. If you look close enough, the truth will reveal itself to you. The Catuvantuli were mounted, that much is clear. The path west is being watched."

"What does that mean for us?" Kitara had to ask, for perhaps these warriors could force them to take a different road.

Aeryn shrugged and rose to her feet. "Very little. I do not think that they will cross our path."

"I hope you're right."

"Do not worry." A grin danced across the scout's lips as she pulled herself back up onto her horse. "I will be."

Kitara snorted and her eyes flashed with humour. For a fleeting moment, she felt as if some kind of weight had been lifted from her shoulders. They were surrounded in enemy territory. Her clothes were soaked through and covered in filth and blood. Her face hurt and her ribs ached, yet as small as it was, Aeryn had made something of a joke despite their bleak situation.

"A week ago, I was told that I have Salvaari blood," Kitara said as she glanced up into the tree canopy.

It was dark, yet somehow seemed comforting. Aeryn watched her in silence as she spoke.

"I'll be damned if I said that I believed it," Kitara continued. "Yet I have not been here a day and somehow I know it to be true."

"I could see that you were one of us from the moment I saw you," Aeryn said and looked at her thoughtfully. "You never truly know where you come from until you have been there. It is the call of the forest that you feel in your blood, and now as the spirits have willed it, here you stand. Whether you have a thimbleful of Salvaari blood or more ... we are your people."

There was only kindness in her eyes as she spoke. No judgement nor hidden motive. There was an old saying that Kitara had heard once about those who wore their heart on their sleeve. Aeryn reminded her of that. For the first time in as many years that she could remember, Kitara smiled. Truly smiled. A light gust of wind rolled through the air and with a shiver Kitara pulled her thick cloak tight around her. Aeryn reached out and took one of her hands. She bit her lip.

"Your hands are cold as winter ice."

Kitara nodded. She could barely feel the warmth of the Aedei's hand through her numb fingers.

"I need dry clothes," she said as a wave of pain rolled through her body. She winced as she fought it back and clutched at her ribs where the Catuvantuli axe had driven into her armour.

"You're hurt?"

"Nothing I can't handle," Kitara replied as a slight growl entered her voice.

Aeryn gave her a concerned look before glancing through the trees. "There is a cave not far from here. We can take shelter there."

The rains had begun anew as the Aedei scout led them through the forest and up the side of a mountain to a cave. Its entrance was little more than a crack in the earth, yet it opened into something far larger. They were forced to dismount, yet the crack was wide enough to allow the horses into its safe confine.

"I found this place a few days ago," Aeryn told her as she led the way through the darkness. "I cannot be sure; however, I do not believe it to have been used in many years."

"Let us hope it remains so," Kitara whispered.

No light seeped in through the mouth of the cave and she could barely see her arms let alone the ground underfoot. Aeryn seemed to have no trouble navigating through the dark. She heard the Aedei rummaging around through her pouches.

"What are you doing?" Kitara hissed when she heard flint stones cracking together.

"The cave will hide the flames from prying eyes while the rains and wind will cover the scent of smoke," Aeryn explained as the first of the flames caught. "It is a risk, yet we cannot reach Cyneric if you cannot move from the cold."

The moonseer worked patiently and skilfully. The fire grew by the moment.

"Let me see," the Aedei said and gestured to Kitara's ribs as the orange glow lit up the cavern.

"I'm fine," Kitara replied from where she sat as she warmed her hands over the fire.

She pushed back her cloak and unbuckled her sword belt. Her boiled leather brigandine followed, and she looked across at Aeryn with a half scowl. She wore nothing more than her white shirt, travel-stained trousers and muddy boots. The dark-haired Aedei girl made her way around the fire and knelt beside the other woman. Kitara met her eyes and then with a grimace pulled the hem of her shirt up. She held it just under her breast as Aeryn ran her gaze over the wound. The hard muscles of her stomach glinted in the firelight, and then she saw the look in Aeryn's eyes. She looked down at her ribs and saw the bruising that engulfed her. It washed over her skin in a wave of pink, purple and dark grey. Aeryn extended a hand and looked to Kitara for permission. The golden-haired woman nodded. Slowly, with the gentleness of a newborn, Aeryn placed her thumb over the bruising. Kitara winced at her touch.

"That hurt?" Aeryn glanced up at her.

"Yes."

The Aedei pursed her lips. "You have no trouble breathing. Your ribs are not broken."

Kitara let out a sigh of relief and leaned back against the wall of the cave. The brigandine had saved her bones from cracking under the Catuvantuli warrior's axe. She lowered the hem of her shirt and Aeryn sat beside her with a thin smile playing on her lips. What amused her, Kitara did not know. Kitara took up the leather brigandine and rested it upon her knees. Next, she took out her waterskin and a strip of cloth. Kitara ran her expert gaze over the armour. She took in every spot of mud and drop of blood. She pursed her lips and then tipped some water upon her cloth strip. *Take care of your armour and it will take care of you.* It was an instruction that had long since been drilled into her. With that, she began to scrub, taking care to remove every last ounce of filth. The Catuvantuli's axe had carved a line through the leather and revealed a slight line of silver steel beneath.

"In the forest it is hard to see at night," Kitara began as a thought came to her. "Yet in here, before the fire it was all but impossible, and yet you did not so much as trip or lose your footing."

"I am moonseer," came the reply.

Kitara shook her head. "What is that?" she asked.

"Can't you tell?" Aeryn grinned. Her silver eyes locked with Kitara's green gaze for a moment, and at last she understood.

"You can see in darkness."

It made little sense, and yet she knew it to be true. No one, man, woman or child, outside of Salvaar had even known that kind of power.

"Through mists and on moonless nights," Aeryn told her with a shrug.

There was so much that would be made possible by that gift.

"Outside of this place it does not exist nor does anyone know its name," Kitara stated.

"No, it does not," the Aedei said knowingly, "for it is a gift granted by the spirits. And unless times have changed the people outside these trees, then they shall never know of it."

Kitara looked to her. There was so much that the gift could make possible. You could run through the meadows and feel the breeze upon your cheek in darkness without fear of falling. Without fear of judgements. How the pirates of Lamrei would have worshipped one with that skill, for hunting and sailing alike would have been made easier tenfold. No wonder the Aedei had chosen Aeryn as a scout.

"It sounds … interesting."

"Despite the fact that you had not heard of this, you do not seem surprised," Aeryn stated, tilting her head.

"I have seen a lot of strange things," Kitara told her.

"This world has many wonders, no? Yet even here, this gift – few of us are ever born with it. One in many hundreds even. As such, it is our sacred duty to the spirits to put all thought of another life aside and instead learn woodcraft. Hunting, tracking, the bow … becoming unseen. All of this we learn."

Kitara turned her gaze to the fire and felt a pang of pity towards the other woman. In some ways she reminded her of herself.

"It seems part blessing, part curse," Kitara said.

"Being moonseer is not a choice, it is a calling," Aeryn replied quietly.

Kitara could understand the pain. She was with her kinfolk yet forced to take a path not of her own choosing.

The Aedei glanced at her. "Tomorrow we will leave before

sunrise. With a little luck, we can make good time and reach the camp in a few days. Cyneric and your friends await," she said and then frowned as she saw Kitara's furrowed brow. "Though perhaps they do not stand as such."

"Perhaps," Kitara muttered. She glanced at Aeryn and for some inexplicable reason found herself talking. "It is no secret that I do not hold them to heart. For how could I? To them I was just a means to an end ... to help them cross Miera in safety. I am nothing to them, so why should they be to me?"

"So, you do not trust them?"

Kitara rolled her shoulders back and bit back a retort as it formed in her lips. It would do her no good here, and somehow the other woman's presence was almost soothing.

"Trust is weakness."

"That must be lonely," Aeryn murmured.

Kitara did not reply as she gazed into the fire. For in her heart, she knew those words to be true.

FORTY-ONE

Sergova, Duchy of Aloys, Medea

The road north had been long yet the journey easy enough. No dangers had come snapping at the heels of Sir Garrik and his contingent of royal guard. For that he thanked the Twins. Though they had travelled countless miles in the week since they had ridden out from Palen-Tor, passed many towns and villages and traversed the crossing at Ilham, none had even guessed that a girl rode with them. The disguise had worked, and Garrik had to admit the princess was a thinker. Not once did she speak when they were not alone, and not once did she reveal her face. If a girl was spotted with so many knights, then questions would be asked. Sir Garrik did not like questions. The guard had grown fond of Dorian and Riona's daughter over the course of the ride. She had been popular back home, yet this was different. She shared in their hardships and wasn't afraid to help when it was needed. She even went out of the way to make herself useful. By day she rode up and down the column and talked with the knights. She asked about their own families, and by night they ate, sang and laughed around the fires. One day the girl would make a fine leader.

She damn well already was one.

They had been riding for eight days, from the safe walls of Palen-Tor to the allied lands of Caspin, and then onto those beholden to the Duchy of Aloys. At last, the soaring towers and grey stone walls of Sergova came into sight. The knights held the scarlet banners of Annora aloft as they rode forth. The wary eyes of the Annoran knights watched the gates of the city in case of deception. The capital of Aloys' lands was nearly as large as Palen-Tor itself, yet it lacked much of the Annoran grace. Medea was a land of sellswords and mercenaries. The fortifications of the great castle towered well over the height of the outer city walls. A great shadow was cast to the west by the sheer magnitude of city. Silver glints of armour shone in the sun and sparkled upon the city and castle walls. Like his rivals, Duke Alejandro Aloys was a cautious man. Some called him "a soldier's soldier". Garrik had met the man once many years ago. Aloys had given the army of the Annoran kingdoms safe passage into Salvaar and even pledged warriors to the cause. But that was another time. They had been young men then. Like all things, people changed with time.

The gates of Sergova boomed open and four mounted knights rode from the city. Each and every one of them was clad in steel armour. Their faded yellow cloaks flew behind them. One of their number carried an equally as bright banner with a great silver lion emblazoned upon it. The symbol of Aloys. Garrik glanced back at Kassandra, and she pulled her hood up with a nod.

"The duke's guard," muttered the master-at-arms as the riders neared.

"An honour," chirped Sir Edward with a snide grin.

Garrik gave the man a glare that would have frozen the sea. "An honour that you would shut your mouth," Garrik commanded.

"Sir," the knight replied.

Garrik turned back to sit still in his saddle as the men approached. He had ridden this same path twenty-six years ago on the ride to Salvaar. Now, as then, he felt the same restlessness. The worst action was inaction, and now he had to beg his way through Aloys' court to achieve his goal. Not to mention it would be selling the Princess of Annora to a foreign, arrogant piece of work. The thought made him sour.

The Medeans reached them, and their eyes measured up the Annorans from beneath their helmets. The man who stood as the leader rode half a foot in front of his companions. He wore a steel breastplate over his chainmail and yellow gambeson. His hands were clad in thick leather gloves studded with steel pieces, while a helm and coif sat atop his head. A bristling, brown beard hung from his jaw. Dark eyes peered towards Garrik, and they never left the face of his equal.

"I am Sir Berwin Isandro," the lead knight called, his proud voice as loud as any, "captain of Duke Aloys' private guard. What business do you have this far north?"

Garrik could not help but notice that the warrior's hand strayed not far from his sword. This place had almost gone to hell since the wedding of Dayne and Sofia Caspin. Everyone was wary of what could happen in the days to come. The soldiers, it appeared, were all but unwelcome.

"Light of the Twins be with you, captain," Garrik told him with a nod in greeting. "Sir Garrik Skarlit, master-at-arms of Palen-Tor and commander of the king's royal guard. I come on behalf of Dorian and beg an audience with your duke."

The Medeans stirred uneasily at his words. Berwin seemed to bite his lip as he tossed up the decision that lay before him. He nodded slowly.

"This way then," the knight said before he turned his horse and started back towards the city.

The Annoran guard were given quarters in the city barracks upon arrival, though they were kept under the stern gaze of Aloys' men. It seemed as if the whole city had been put on high alert. The people of Sergova, much like the rest of Medea, all had the same sharp features matched by dark hair and eyes. Skin tanned by the burning northern sun was revealed by loose, flowing garments that left little to the imagination. Garrik did not trust these Medeans as far as he could throw them, just as he did not trust the mercenaries that walked the streets. How a nation could be built upon the backs of such people, the old knight did not know. He shuddered to think what would happen if they ever discovered the identity of the girl who rode with him. He kept his eyes tightly on Kassandra until Sir Berwin returned from meeting with the duke. He had left orders that the guard was not to drink anything but water until they left this city. Nor were they to partake in any such games that the locals tried to force upon them. Instead, he had assigned four of the finest swordsmen in the guard to Kassandra's side. They were never to leave her alone or give her so much as a moment's peace. The rest of the men had made an unsaid agreement to watch over her like a lion watches over its cub. She was as safe as she would ever be in this city of vipers.

"The duke will see you now," Sir Berwin Isandro told Garrik, and with that, the master-at-arms joined his escort of Medean knights.

The castle corridors were warm and filled with light of both the sun and torches. The city may have been that of a mercantile culture, yet the castle itself was grand. It was awash with the bright colours of tapestries and banners, while servants and nobles were clad in equally as bright clothing. The benefits were indeed reaped when one sent his soldiers to fight in the wars of other men. Lives for coin. It was an ugly trade, though one that the people seemed most intent on continuing. Shedding blood demanded great expense after all. Garrik's hand longed to reach for the comforting hilt of his sword, and yet it only found the empty air at his side. He had been deprived of his blade upon passing through the castle gates. The duke's guard did not say a word as they wound their way through the passages of the fortress. Garrik knew that their minds would be preoccupied with other thoughts.

Why had King Dorian sent his best warrior as an ambassador?

Was something more at work than a simple visit to their capital?

The Medean captain came to a halt before two large doors of the finest oak. The doors were guarded by a pair of his own men.

He shot Garrik with a knowing glance before he pushed the doors open and led the way into the room. The great hall of Sergova.

"My Lord Alejandro," Berwin said as he bowed to his duke, "may I present Sir Garrik of King Dorian's guard."

The Annoran followed suit and bowed before the duke of House Aloys. "Lord."

"Welcome to Sergova," Alejandro Aloys replied with a smooth tongue.

His voice was as poetic as any Medean. Garrik ran his eyes over the man as he rose. It was the same man he had once known many years before. Unlike many of the other dukes, Aloys had kept himself in form. There was not an ounce of fat upon the man. His dark eyes looked as fierce as that of a hawk, while his nose was beak-like. A broad-bladed rapier with a curling steel hand-guard sat at his hip. It was the traditional weapon of the Medean nobility. A one-handed blade near to the length of a longsword and made from Medean steel. It was light but strong and relied upon its wielder's speed rather than brute strength. The duke's clothes were almost robe-like in appearance, while a thin band of silver ran across his brow. Aloys' hair was streaked with the grey that came with his age, while his short beard stood equally as coloured. Like so many of his people, the duke had grown a long moustache, although it took nothing away from his soldier's frame.

A younger man, no more than eighteen summers, stood at his side. His face was clean shaven, though his attire matched that of Alejandro.

"It has been many years, Sir Garrik," the Medean lord said with something of a smile. "Twenty-three, by my count."

"Since Salvaar," the master-at-arms told him.

"Then you will not have met my son" – Alejandro indicated the young man at his side – "Emilian."

"Well met, lord." The knight dipped his head.

"And you, sir." The boy returned the nod as he ran his eyes over the veteran.

Perhaps the lad had heard stories, and perhaps he wanted to see if they were true. Aloys clasped his hands behind his back as his brow curled into a frown.

"And now I hear that your king has allied himself with my enemy," the duke said.

"Santiago Caspin is not your enemy, lord," Garrik replied as he took a step towards the duke.

One of the guards gave Garrik a warning glance. The guard was daring him to take another step.

"And nor is my king." Garrik continued.

Aloys snorted. "We all know how men change. When I first met Dorian, he was but King of Aethela. Now he rules Torosa and Laeoflaed – indeed, all of Annora. And now it would seem that when Santiago Caspin falls, his lands will become but another piece of Annora. Dorian's lands shall extend beyond the river that for so long has served as a border between our two nations."

"Then let me assure you that you and your people are safe from even the mere idea of an attack," the knight told him. "King Dorian would never–"

"Greed corrupts all men," Aloys interrupted and held up a hand to silence the master-at-arms. "As does power. We in Medea know that best of all."

Garrik ground his teeth. Alejandro remained as stubborn as he had once been, if not more so.

"My lord, I do not claim to know Dorian's mind, yet I know his heart. And it is for that very reason that I am here," Garrik said.

Emilian Aloys rubbed his chin thoughtfully before he spoke. "You say that your king means my people no ill will, yet he has already laid claim to Caspin's lands and now has sent three hundred armed knights deep into our territory without first sending word. Tell me, Sir Garrik, why would my people not have good reason to be nervous?"

Garrik raised his eyebrows. Like his father, Emilian was no fool, for the same question had long since plagued his own mind.

"My lords, there was no time to send a rider before us," he said.

Alejandro pursed his thin lips and motioned for the man to continue. "Why?"

"You will by now of course have an understanding of what is going on beneath the trees in Salvaar," Garrik said.

"Once more those barbarian heathens spill their own blood," Alejandro replied. "What does that mean to me?"

"Near to a month ago, one of the pagans rode into our court," the Annoran told the duke. "He begged my king to send aid, to help his people end this war. Dorian refused and no warriors were sent. He would not risk his men in a war not of his own making."

"And?" Emilian asked and gestured for the knight to continue.

"And Prince Lukas disagreed. He rode from Palen-Tor when night fell. He took the west road towards Miera in the company of another warrior and the Salvaari himself."

"Brave of him … yet foolish," Alejandro replied. "He rides to the aid of godless pagans while attempting to cross the Steppe of Miera. A land filled with nothing but bloodthirsty savages."

Ah, the Dukes of Medea, Garrik thought. Zealous in their following of the Twins and slow to forget. For it had been their own lands that had nearly been destroyed a century ago by these people.

"What of this proposal?" Emilian inquired. "What does King Dorian request of us?"

"An alliance, lord," Garrik replied, "and safe passage for his army."

Silence filled the hall. Requesting military access to another man's nation for his entire army was a thing not lightly spoken of.

"If he wants to send an army to Salvaar ... to reclaim his son, through my lands, then the price will be high," Alejandro said seriously. "For no man, no man, will merely allow so many swords to pass by so close to his hearth."

Garrik nodded, for he could only agree. It was a risk. "And for that he offers the grandest prize of all. He offers the hand of his daughter, Kassandra. He offers a union that will last, a union of Annora and Aloys."

Duke Aloys let out a breath. "A bride for my son. That is indeed a high price. He offers me much more than a daughter. It comes with great wealth and a claim to his throne."

It had been a desperate move on Dorian's behalf. For the king was growing older by the day, while his eldest son lacked an heir and was of ill health. Then there was Lukas who could be dead in a ditch by now. If the king fell and Dayne's sickness took him without first siring a son then Emilian Aloys, a Medean, could inherit the Annoran throne. The thought made Garrik's skin crawl. Alejandro gestured towards the knight.

"When would this match take place?" he asked.

"Prince Dayne awaits my word at the border. If you accept the offer, he shall discuss terms of the betrothal upon his arrival. Though as for a wedding, the princess comes of age in two summers time. Only then would the union be complete."

Alejandro turned to Emilian. His only child and heir. "What do you say? This decision falls to you alone."

"I will do whatever I am required for my people, Father," the young man replied. "Just as I always have. Sir Garrik, you may send word to your prince that I accept these terms. In return, you shall have your access to our lands. Though I fear it would be remiss not to say ... your king does this all for his blood. He sends his only daughter away from her home in an attempt to save his son, when he is probably dead already."

Garrik left the duke and his son with a bow. He passed on word of the deal to Edward and Montbard, who in turn had dispatched a rider to the southern border. Then he had come here. To one of the temples in Aloys' castle. He knelt before the likeness of Durandail and Azaria carved into pillars of stone. He clutched at his amulet as he spoke. Desperation edged into his voice.

"Oh, merciful lords, I am in such need of your wisdom now," Garrik said quietly. "Help me now and I shall repay this kindness tenfold. Do not let this sacrifice be for nothing. Do not let my prince fall at the hands of the pagans. Guide me, Lady Azaria. Show me the light; show me the way. Do I do as I am bid and await reinforcement? For each day that we delay brings Lukas closer to death. Or do I ride absent command and attempt to save him myself? And in so doing risk the lives of my own men. Please, lady … do not abandon me in this time of need. Do not abandon my prince. Help me now and I shall forever be your servant in all things."

The knight finally looked up and glanced into the eyes of his gods.

A tear slid from Azaria's stone gaze. In that moment, he knew what he must do.

Garrik returned to a room filled with drinking and laughter. His men filled the tables and chairs. Some were playing games of dice, while others wrestled. A few had found the company of willing women who were now perched atop their laps. Voices were raised in song. They were happy. Content. As soldiers, even those of the royal guard, such moments like these were hard to come by. Garrik could not do it. He turned to leave.

"Garrik!" roared one of the knights as he caught sight of their leader.

Cups were raised and the men cheered.

The old knight sighed, and his shoulders slumped under the weight of what he was about to do.

"Men, brothers-in-arms," Sir Garrik called as he gazed around the barracks at his friends. "You will have heard by now that Aloys has accepted this proposal, and that even as we speak, a messenger is riding to the border and to Prince Dayne. In four days, they could be with us, and then in another two, we could be at Salvaar. That is time that I do not believe that we have. Prince Lukas is by now more than likely in those trees." His voice grew quiet, for he was plagued by memories two decades old. "Many of you will remember the horrors that we saw when we rode to war many years ago ... Lukas does not have six days, not when he is alone." The old knight took a deep breath as he remembered a vow he once made. "I made a promise to my king that I would let no harm befall his family ... and so I ride for Salvaar without delay."

"Then you do not ride alone, sir," called out one of the knights.

"No," Garrik told him. "Do not be so quick to answer. This is not an order. You may freely stay here without stain upon your honour. Only those who choose to come shall be at my side. It is likely that I ride to my death, and I would not have you join me absent thought. You all have things to live for ... families, children ..."

"Aye, sir," Edward said, "and I would live to return to them upon a day. Every man here would follow you to the realm of the Pale Horseman. To whatever end. Lukas is our prince, and I will not – I cannot – abandon him nor forsake the vows we all swore. Until my last breath, I will serve the Raynor line and ride under the eagle."

"Under the eagle," called out one of the knights.

"Under the eagle," cried another.

The words were echoed as the guard spoke as one, and their voices filled the hall in union. Landon Montbard rose to his feet and swept his gaze around the barracks.

"It would appear, sir, that we have already made up our minds," he said. "When you ride, it will not be alone ... It will be with three hundred swords at your back."

All laughter and cheer had left the room. The knights put down their drink and returned to their beds in silence. Few would find rest this night.

They rose come morning and prepared. Garrik ran a gloved hand down his horse's flank. How far they had travelled together in the years since they had come together. This could well be for the last time.

"Sir Garrik." Kassandra's voice came from behind. He turned to see the girl leading Ely by the reins.

"What are you doing?" he growled. "You are to ride to Prince Dayne at the border along with four of my men."

Kassandra rolled her eyes. "When will you learn, Sir Garrik? I made my choice a long time ago. Either I ride with you to Salvaar or I will find my own way there."

The knight bared his teeth in anger. "Gods, it was hard enough to protect you here, let alone when Salvaari screamers are changing at us."

"I have made my decision," she replied.

Kassandra spoke not as a girl or a princess, but as a queen. She pulled herself up onto Ely's back.

"Now make yours," she finished.

FORTY-TWO

Catuvantuli lands, Forest of Salvaar

Kitara's eyes snapped open as she burst awake. The cries of her nightmares died in her throat. Her breathing was laboured. Sweat dripped from her brow. Each night it was the same. The terrors that haunted her dreams grew worse every day. Her face had not been the only thing scarred on that ship. Kitara snatched up her wineskin as she slowed her breath and fought back the rush that roared through her veins. She took a draught and welcomed the burning sensation that the strong Mieran alcohol produced. It was the only thing that helped. Across the remains of the fire, Aeryn watched her with those silver eyes. She said nothing, yet her gaze was edged with a worried look. The Aedei woman held a small bowl in her hands along with a small stone that had a blue paint-like substance upon its end. Beside her sat a small piece of bark covered in black.

"What is that?" Kitara asked, nodding towards what lay in her companion's grasp.

"You are Salvaari," Aeryn replied with a shrug. "Though you are unfamiliar with our ways, you should wear this as protection," she said as she tipped the bowl forwards slightly, revealing the blue war paint that lay within. "This woad is sacred to our people … With it, the spirits will protect you."

Kitara snorted. "I could have used that a long time ago."

"But they have already blessed you," Aeryn told her with shining eyes.

"How?" Kitara raised an eyebrow.

The Aedei tilted her head. "Your hair, golden like the stars. A thing rarely seen among our people, and a great gift granted by the spirits. It shows that they favour you."

Kitara couldn't help the smirk that played across her lips.

Blessed? Her life had been anything but.

The Aedei clearly believed her words fervently, but to Kitara it signalled only naivety.

"Is that so?" Kitara replied.

Aeryn leaned towards her and her lips twitched into a playful smile. "Well, they guided me here to you, and that has to count for something."

"Then if the spirits are real, and if they favour me," Kitara returned mischievously, "then why the woad?"

"To show faith," Aeryn told her simply.

She rose to her feet with one hand clutching the bowl, and the other the small piece of bark covered in ebony paint. Aeryn crouched in front of Kitara and dipped the fingers of her right hand into the dark charcoal paint. Kitara's eyes flashed in warning as the other woman extended her hand. Then the fires left her gaze. They vanished as if they were never there. For some reason, her reflex to go for a blade at the mere thought of touch had not arisen for the Aedei woman.

"Black around the eyes," Aeryn whispered as she lightly touched the paint to Kitara's skin, "to ward off the dark ones."

Kitara closed her eyes as slowly Aeryn drew a small black circle around each one in turn. Her touch was gentle as she worked. Aeryn placed the bark to the side and took up her bowl of woad. Kitara opened her eyes and locked them with the Aedei's pleasant gaze of moonlight.

"Blue," Aeryn murmured as she dipped her fingers into the

woad, "to show that the will of the spirits is that of your own."

Slowly, she drew three lines down the right side of Kitara's face. They ran diagonally from the centre of her forehead, across her brow, over her eye and down to the bottom of her cheek. She drew a fourth line under Kitara's left eye. It nearly touched the bottom of her scar. The war paint that she now bore was a tradition. It was a sacred rite of which only those of Salvaar were welcome. If there had been any doubts about her ancestry remaining, then they were dashed. Kitara and Aeryn locked eyes for a moment longer before Aeryn drew back and cleaned her hands with the contents of her waterskin. A slight orange glow began to seep into the cave.

"The sun rises," Kitara said as she rose to her feet and buckled her brigandine back on. Next came her scabbard and knife belt. Finally, she flicked a stray strand of golden hair over her ear so that it sat with the rest of her tied-back locks.

Blessed, Aeryn had said.

Kitara smiled at the thought. Her hair had turned near brown from the mud that still ran through its strands, but the thought gave Kitara some comfort.

"Cyneric awaits." The Aedei woman gestured to the cave entrance as she slung her quiver over her shoulder and took up her bow.

With that, they walked their horses into the light.

"Here."

Lukas glanced up from his mount as Bellec tossed him a strip of blue cloth. The mercenary threw another to Sakkar who stood at the prince's side. Lukas gave the man an inquisitive look. Bellec tapped the bicep of his left arm where he had tied his own strip of cloth.

"Protection," he explained. "The Aedei wear blue ... Would be a shame to have made it so far only to be killed by our own ally."

Lukas nodded his thanks and said, "Cailean believes that we can make his brother's camp by midday tomorrow."

Bellec gazed out into the forest. "Good," the mercenary replied.

Lukas exchanged a glance with Sakkar as the sellsword left without another word.

"There is something unusual about that man," the Larissan muttered. "I can't quite place my finger upon it."

"About them all," Lukas said as he swept his gaze around the camp where the other mercenaries were readying their horses. The prince wrapped the band of blue cloth around his arm. He tied it tight so that it would not fall. "Even this reminds me of the Arkin Garter in Aureia. There the emperor's guard do the same yet with bands of purple," Lukas muttered.

Sakkar pursed his lips. "These men have been to many places, that much is obvious. Though their number is Annoran and Medean alone, many have Valkir tattoos or carry foreign weapons. Bellec himself carries a Larissan blade," Sakkar said.

Lukas had wondered about the sword that the mercenary leader carried. It was as wide as his own blade yet curved. The steel widened as it neared its tip. Those to the east called their curved swords scimitars.

"I had thought as much," he said.

A horse snorted, and with the light jingle of reins, Cailean emerged from the forest. He led his mount over to the companions. His eyes were ringed in a thin layer of black paint, while his face was covered in blue woad markings. There was a lightness to the man that they had not seen until they had reached the forest. He seemed more alive. Even without the woad and white grease in his hair, it was obvious that he was Salvaari to the bone.

"A sight to terrify children, big man." Sakkar grinned as the Salvaari approached.

Cailean clapped the Larissan on his shoulder and laughed. "Like your bald head, eh?"

"That is why I cover it." The westerner snorted and gestured towards his bright headscarf.

"Well then perhaps you should have chosen something a little less flamboyant," Lukas added.

How seamlessly Cailean had fit into their camaraderie in days past. The three of them had formed a bond, and not just because of what they had been through together since leaving Palen-Tor.

"Lukas," Cailean said quietly after a moment.

The prince glanced at the Salvaari as he nodded slightly towards Bellec.

"I swear I know that man. Each day his face plays on my mind, as if a memory," Cailean continued.

Lukas pursed his lips as he replied, "Yesterday, his man, Jaimye, mentioned that they had been here before, over two decades ago. I am no mind reader, yet most of these men are Annoran. And were my people not beneath these trees twenty-six years ago?"

"And stayed for another two summers, I remember," Cailean added. "I was a boy, yet I remember well."

Lukas frowned as he thought. Each new idea added to the mystery that shrouded the mercenary company.

"If it is true and they fought in Salvaar, then they would have been young men at the time," Lukas whispered.

"That begs the question," Sakkar muttered as he ran a hand down his mount's powerful neck, "why are they not back in Annora? Why did they not return home?"

"Wait until tonight," Lukas said at last, and he turned his eyes to those of his friends, "and then we unshroud this mystery."

The moon shone overhead and glistened above their small encampment when Lukas made his move. They had ridden for the better part of a day and forged their own path through the trees. As day turned to night, they had barely seen a sign of the natives. They were out there though. Watching and waiting, Lukas was sure of it.

The mercenaries were on guard and paid no heed to the prince as he slowly crept up to their horses. It was Bellec's dark-skinned stallion that Lukas made for. Lukas glanced around as he quietly trod over the wet grass. His eyes were peeled for the first hint of discovery. Sneaking around the castle had been something that he had excelled at. It was how he had managed to see so many of the women that had given him the pleasure of their company. Yet it was his other moonlighting pastime that would aid him so fully tonight. Even before Kassie had been born, Lukas had spent many a night in the stables or going for rides in the darkness. His skill with horses went further than just riding them. He was good with them. They barely made a sound as he quietly slipped between them. He took care that each step made as little sound as possible. He bent his knees and slightly crouched as he navigated between the horses. How the mercenaries would react if they caught him snooping through their saddlebags, he did not know. Yet it was a necessary risk to discover who they truly were. Over two decades ago, these hard men had ridden these paths. That much was certain. In the years since, they had travelled across sea and land.

Yet what had made them leave Annora and take up with an ideal that so few of their people agreed with?

Lukas finally reached Bellec's horse and tentatively ran a hand down its side as he slowly moved towards his goal. Glistening hide and powerful muscle turned to brown leather as his hand rolled from skin to saddle. He reached out with his fingers and unclasped the buckle of one of the saddle bags. Lukas lifted the leather flap and then reached inside. The rough cladding of a bound book was the first thing that the prince found. The wooden box that housed a whetstone came next, along with a large pouch of coins. Nothing of importance. Lukas tightly buckled the saddlebag closed before moving onto the second one. A series of maps. Each of them was tightly bound in oilskin to protect them from the elements. With them were a few letters. No doubt they were promise of payment for the cost of his sword. Then his fingers brushed something small.

The roughness of leather covered something metallic. He could feel the hard metal winding beneath the fabric. It felt as though it were some kind of pattern. Lukas knew the symbol it bore by its touch. He grasped the object and pulled it from the bag. It was no bigger than the width of his closed fist, but it was heavy. Heavier than it should have been. Lukas took a deep breath, and then pulled the object from its leather wrappings. There it was. The thing which he had known by touch. A disc of steel with the image of an eagle forged upon it. His father's symbol. The eagle of Aethela. It was a sigil that only one body of men carried with them. The royal guard.

Lukas cast his mind back. There was only one man of the guard who had fled and was believed to be dead. Cold steel was placed upon his shoulder from behind.

"Find what you are looking for, boy?"

Slowly, Lukas turned and met the dark eyes of Galadayne. Yet another name that was burned into his mind.

"I know your name," Lukas said.

The sellsword pressed the blade into Lukas' neck. "Is that so?"

The prince glanced from the sword to the man who bore it.

"You were once of the royal guard same as your master. You bore the eagle banner same as him. You were a wolf who many believed dead. You are Galadayne Eralys," Lukas said, and he gestured towards the camp, "and the Annorans among you your men."

He was the man whom Dorian had sent to kill the traitor who had betrayed and murdered his brother, Lukas' uncle.

"What a clever bastard you are." The mercenary sneered savagely. "Come with me."

Lukas was deprived of his weapons as he was marched across the camp to Bellec. He stood, talking in confidence with two of his men, Jaimye and another of the sellswords. The three men turned as they heard the sound of boots upon grass. Bellec frowned.

"He knows," Galadayne explained as he pressed his sword into Lukas' back.

"Does he now?" Bellec growled as he glared at the prince.

Lukas tossed the eagle symbol into the ground at the mercenary's feet.

"Oh yes," he snarled as he felt his rage stir. "There is only one man I know who turned tail and fled the guard after murdering his own prince."

"Is that what they taught you?" Bellec said dangerously as his hand dropped to his sword. "That I killed Lord Eldred?"

"Many know it to be true," Lukas shot back at the man who had killed his own flesh and blood. "Just as many believed you long to your deserved grave, Theron Malley."

The mercenary bit his lip as anger filled his face. He did not raise his voice, yet Lukas could hear the rage seething into it.

"Raynor," he said coldly.

Lukas felt his heart stop. The man had guessed his name after all.

"Yes, I know your name too. I could tell of your wretched blood from the moment I laid eyes upon you, boy."

Bellec glanced up as Sakkar and Cailean charged towards the assembling band of mercenaries who held their friend.

"Stay away from him!" shouted Sakkar as he drew his blade.

"Hold," Bellec barked the command.

As one, the mercenaries drew their own weapons and formed a wall between the two sides. Bellec turned his hate-filled gaze back to Lukas.

"Now, the only reason you still breathe is because I am curious to know why a Raynor rode out of Palen-Tor alone and into a war not of his making."

"Honour," Lukas seethed, "a thing that you would know little about. My father–"

"HUNTED ME LIKE AN ANIMAL!" Bellec roared as he

pressed the edge of his dagger to the prince's neck.

Lukas barely felt the cold steel, for fire ran through his blood.

"YOU KILLED MY UNCLE! Led him into an ambush!"

"That is a lie," the mercenary snapped as he pressed his face close to Lukas'. Bellec kept the knife hard against his captive's throat as he slowly moved behind the boy. "A lie that took everything from me," Bellec snarled.

"You are nothing but a traitor."

The mercenary wrapped a powerful arm around Lukas' neck. His grip was tight and nearly cut off Lukas' breath. The prince grabbed at the arm, and Bellec's boot smashed into the back of his knee. Lukas crashed to the ground in a pile of flailing limbs. He tasted earth and mud. His head rang. Lukas rolled onto his back and made to push himself to his feet. The icy tip of the mercenary's newly drawn sword met his chest and stopped him in his tracks. There it waited for its master's command to slice into flesh and drain life from body.

"I should kill you now!" Bellec shouted. "Avenge myself upon your father for all these years of torment. His sins are your own."

"Then take my life and be done with it." Lukas glared up at his attacker. "Kill another Raynor. Show your true colours and kill an unarmed man."

The air grew still as Bellec dropped into a crouch over the boy's prone from. Both his hands wrapped tightly around the hilt of his blade. He drove a knee into Lukas' stomach and pinned him to the ground. One thrust and it would be over. The son of his enemy was at his mercy. Bellec tensed his arms. All it would take was one move. Dorian had destroyed his life, and perhaps in a small way, this could ease his pain.

"Prove my father right." Lukas bared his teeth. "DO IT!"

The mercenary bellowed and brought his blade down. It drove into the ground beside the prince's head.

"I am not a murderer, boy. I did not kill your uncle, and I will not kill you this day."

Lukas' eyes never left the sellsword as the scimitar was pulled from the earth. Bellec slowly rose to his full height and lifted his weight from the boy. He twirled his sword and pulled Lukas to his feet.

"It is time you learnt your history."

The prince did not lower his gaze. "I have heard the story a thousand times. How a Salvaari woman turned you against your own people."

"And where did you hear that exactly?" Bellec replied. "From your father's lips, I am sure. Yet it was Balinor who told him of Eldred's death. Those are his words, boy. Tell me, do you trust the word of that man?"

"No," Lukas growled as he fought the emotion that tore his heart. "Yet he had no cause to lie."

"No cause?" Bellec sheathed his sword and turned with a grunt. "To divide a rival king from a captain of his guard mere months before moving against that same king?"

"This cannot be true," the prince cried incredulously.

It made sense, yet what his father had told him could not be false. It simply could not be. They all knew the story of Eldred's death.

"If it was true, then why did you not return? Why did you not tell your story to my father?"

The mercenary rolled his shoulders back.

"King Dorian does as King Dorian pleases. He had already made his mind up. A hint of truth is all it took to turn him. I was his ambassador, and when he learned that I held a Salvaari woman as wife … Balinor was well able to take advantage of that. He hired sellswords to kill us," Bellec said, and he nodded to Galadayne. "Sent his own guard to finish the job. But unfortunately, some men know more about honour and loyalty than he ever will. For ten years, he pursued me until finally he believed me dead. I took this name to survive."

Lukas took a breath. His mind was reeling from the mercenary's words. It could not be true, and yet much of it was fitting together like a puzzle.

"Tell me this, Theron—"

Bellec turned fast as lightning and pointed a finger towards Lukas. "Theron died over twenty years ago. All that stands before you is the shadow of a man once of Annora. However, I will say this" – and his eyes flashed darkly once more – "the blood of the eagle runs through your veins, just as it runs through your father's. The same weakness. I believe that like him, you have the mind of a traitor. If I ever have reason to doubt your intentions, I will not hesitate to kill you in payment for his treachery. An eye for an eye."

Lukas slowly nodded. He was wholly and completely at Bellec's mercy now. Three men could not fight two dozen. Not even if the Twins stood with them.

"Then the woman—"

Bellec shook his head and cut Lukas off. "We are done here."

It was the only answer he needed to give. Lukas could see the pain written in his eyes. The woman, whoever she had been, was long dead. Lukas made to leave, yet he could not quiet his mind or tongue. "You came back here, even after such pain … without qualms nor explanation. You decided to help us, despite knowing who I am."

The sellsword leader sheathed his dagger and after a moment tossed something to Lukas. "This will explain," was all he said.

The prince instinctively caught the item with his closed fist. He opened his hand. Lukas eyes went to Bellec's back as the man walked away. In his palm was a ring. It was plain except for one thing. A sapphire.

FORTY-THREE

The Tears of Freydis, Isle of Vay'kis, the Valkir Isles

"LOOSE!" Nenrir bellowed as he thrust his arm towards the line of targets.

The bowmen reacted upon command of the archer who trained them. Bows sang as the Valkir released their grip and sent steel-tipped arrows towards their targets. They landed with a crack. All reached their marks and drove into the near-human-shaped targets of hessian, wood and straw. The first row of archers stepped back two steps to reload while a second line slid through their ranks and raised their weapons. As one, they drew their already nocked arrows. Feathers touched cheek and then, without command, they released. Once more, the bladed shafts punched deep into the targets. Each one hit home with enough force to bring even the strongest soldier to his knees. The first row of warriors came forwards again, raised their bows and ...

"HOLD!" Astrid called as she raised an arm.

Her crew lowered their weapons and watched as she walked before them.

An unlikely assortment, she thought with half a smile.

Youngsters of fifteen summers, women and old folk all comprised the ranks. Men who had sought out a craft rather than raid. All had raised a hand when called upon and shown a willing heart. They had become quite deadly guided by Nenrir's seasoned hand though as yet were untested.

"You have made great progress in the week since we have arrived here in this sanctuary. Know that I am proud to call you my scâldir from this day until my last," Astrid said as she swept her gaze over her people.

Their greenness would be hardened by the raiders among them. They made their way over to where she spoke. Torben had put them through their paces each and every day since their arrival. He was keeping them ready for battle at a moment's notice. They were sharp both in mind and body.

"Come midday, Earl Arndyr will meet with us to discuss our final preparations, but make no mistake … we leave tonight," Astrid said, and she met their eyes.

She looked from one man to the next. Hélla, Fargrim, Mayrun, Torben, Nenrir, Hvitsred. She knew all of them by name. Now they stood captivated by her words. She had never been a warrior. She was never more than a sailor and strategist, yet now the role of leader had been thrust upon her. She would be damned if she would fail.

"Today, my friends, we sail to Agartha. Today we sail home. By nightfall tomorrow we shall be upon those shores, and by the Sea-Father, we shall bring the wrath of Skûra down upon Magnus and his dogs!"

Torben thrust his mighty axe into the sky and let loose a vicious battle cry. The roar was taken up by all and soon the Tears of Freydis rang with it. Astrid felt her heart race. She took a breath and stilled it. She wrapped her hand around the head of the axe she wore at her hip. That weapon was almost alien to her. She had never once drawn blood with it or used it in anger.

Would Agartha be its first test? Astrid held up a hand to still the cries. "I urge you this day … lay down your weapons and hold your loved ones close, for who knows what fate awaits us on those faraway shores. Quiet your nerves and laugh hearty … for in life we regain our homes, yet in death we reach for the halls of the Sea-Father!"

Her words echoed through the valley and across the lake. They rose through the trees and into the sky above. Perhaps even to the steps of Ra'Haven.

The sand crunched pleasantly underfoot as Astrid walked down the length of the beach, her mind lost in thought. Much had changed in the week since they had landed here. Arndyr had thrown his support her way, while the families of her crew had become archers. Now they were poised to return home.

"Lief would be proud of you," Torben said from her side.

Astrid glanced at her mentor and gave him a quiet smile. His words meant the world to her. How she missed her father. How she longed to be in his arms once more.

"Some days I hardly recognise myself," she murmured.

"That is because you are changing," Torben said with a shrug.

"For better or worse?" Astrid asked.

The old warrior gave the low growl of a chuckle he always did when amused. "You have lost more than any man here in recent days. Yet you led us to safety, found a strong ally, kept us together and" – he gestured back to the camp – "you made them strong, gave them hope. All without complaint or thought for yourself. You have always had wit. A great deal more than most. Yet this, words cannot describe what you have done. And you have not so much as shed a tear of grief."

Astrid met his eyes. Torben knew how she would be feeling inside better than anyone. Rage, pain and sorrow warred within. Yet she would not let it out. Not yet.

"Father once told me that there is a time to grieve when the battle is won. To give in to sorrow and fear while lives hang in the balance is the mark of one unfit to lead. For in that moment, all those lives become forfeit. I bear this pain so that they do not have to."

"And that," Torben told her, "is why the crew follow you, why they love you."

Astrid gave him a smile. He was the one who had always been there since the time she was but a girl.

"You are both my greatest friend and stand as a second father to me. I shall always hold you as such."

Arndyr Scaeva arrived when the sun reached its peak. He rode into the camp atop a white mare. He had put aside his tunic and bore armour in its place, the same cuirass as his brother who rode at his back. It was steel and engraved with a pair of griffins. His bracers and greaves were embossed with the same swirling imagery, while a violet cape fell from his shoulders. A steel, oval-shaped shield trimmed in wood was slung over his back. A snarling dragon curled upon the shield's surface wrapped around the heavy steel boss in its centre. Arndyr's hand rested on the sword at his hip. It was a magnificent sight, made more so by the crested helm that sat atop his head. The sunlight glinted on its surface and shone brilliantly down upon the dragon-shaped crest. Astrid knew that the leader of the Arkin Garter wore such a helm, yet it carried the image of a griffin. Arndyr had clearly changed the design upon his return to the throne. Jormund Scaeva rode at his back along with a dozen other warriors. They were all former members of the Garter. They looked indestructible. Arndyr gave her a nod before he swung a leg over his horse and dismounted on the sands. The rest of his retinue followed suit, and the earl passed his reins to Jormund.

"Jarl Astrid," Arndyr greeted her as he made his way over.

"Earl," Astrid replied as she extended her arm.

Arndyr took it and then the pair pulled each other into an embrace. They all cheered, both the warriors at Astrid's back and the men of Vay'kis. Earl Arndyr unbuckled his helmet and removed it. "Let us begin," he said.

The leaders of Vay'kis and the crew of the Wind Rider gathered.

"My men cannot directly attack Agartha nor can we land on those beaches," Arndyr said as he glanced around those assembled.

Astrid, Torben, Fargrim, Nenrir, Hélla and Jormund. They were the captains of this raid.

"To do so would be an act of war, a thing of which I would rather avoid," Arndyr said.

"You cannot be serious," growled Torben. "We are already at war."

"No, he is right," Astrid said and shook her head. "I have thought of this in great detail of late. If he attacks, then all of Agartha will rise. Even those who have not fully backed Magnus. So far, the earl will have maybe four hundred men who are loyal to the bone, while the other jarls and leaders may not be so easily swayed. You know how the people look upon Magnus better than anyone, my friend. A direct assault with Earl Arndyr is not possible."

Hélla looked at Astrid questioningly. "Then what do you propose?" Hélla asked. "We cannot fully attack, and yet we cannot stay here either. Not to mention you said that we would sail today."

Arndyr nodded to Astrid. "We believe that there is another option that we may choose," Arndyr said. "Another path that we may take."

"Then enlighten us," Torben bid him.

Astrid shot him a glare. The old warrior had set himself against Arndyr ever since the night in Lumis, despite the fact that the earl had an army and had taken their side. Torben had not cared about the others with whom Astrid had shared a bed, yet to him this was different.

"Torben," she said warningly, "this will work."

"Without an attack there can be no victory." The old warrior scoffed. "If that coward will not send his men—"

"Coward?" Arndyr glared towards the other man. "You ought to be careful, for may I remind you that my warriors and my ships are mine to command."

"Enough," snapped Astrid. "Both of you. Now listen, this is what we are going to do …"

Erik Farrin's gaze was drawn to the harbour down below. The bloodsworn warrior had climbed up one of the mountains that surrounded Agartha as the sun had risen. It was his home, his life. A thing that he would bleed for and, if the Sea-Father willed it, die for. He had grown up with great warriors sired by great warriors. Men who, in time, had become heroes of their people. Men who, in time, he had surpassed in skill and deed, and now it was his tales spoken of in hushed rooms. Yet those of his sister were whispered in awe. He remembered a raid a few summers past. It had been his fourth, and Astrid's sixth, time making the crossing. To begin with, the crew had settled for plundering small towns along the coast. Each one gave much risk and little reward. It was then that Astrid had conjured up a plan to raid Loxford. It was a large town encircled by an even larger stone wall. It was a place that had never fallen to the Valkir raiders and with good reason. It was impenetrable to those without siege weapons. Not to mention it had a garrison of nearly two hundred well-trained and professional soldiers. Many had called Astrid mad. Even her own scâldir had thought so, and yet she had dreamed up the impossible. As fate had it, two days after they had landed, the Annorans had celebrated one of their saints. The Annorans had gathered in one of their sacred churches to give thanks and praise. As the morning sun crept over the horizon, the townspeople had all hurried into their holy buildings for this sacred day. It had left few men atop Loxford's walls. Nenrir and the other archers among the crew dealt with the few defenders while the main body of the crew climbed a section of poorly fortified wall. The wall had seemed strong to the untrained eye, yet Astrid had been watching the town day and night. She had found weaknesses. Like wraiths, they snuck over the walls, blockaded the temples and sacked the city. They had returned to Agartha as heroes, and their coffers had burst with newfound wealth. It was all on Astrid's shoulders.

Now here he stood. He watched as Jarl Sigfried and his ships sailed from the harbour and began their journey out into open sea. Six ships and three hundred men made for Vay'kis. It was a magnificent sight to behold. Each vessel was triple-masted in the Valkir way. Their sails unfurled and were pulled tight by the wind that whistled against the white canvas. In little over a day, Jarl Sigfried and his warriors would land, and then the full fury of Skûra would be unleashed upon those accursed souls. Erik would remain here by Magnus' side. He was now the first bloodsworn in Magnus' guard. A great honour.

The ships had sailed beyond Erik's thought when he at last returned to his hall. His eyes flicked to the small wooden likeness of the Sea-Father that sat atop a shrine. It was simply crafted in the Valkir way, but it always filled him with fire. He made his way over to it and knelt before the shrine. He rested his hands on one knee as he bowed his head low.

"Sea-Father. Give me the strength to stand against my enemies. Grant me the knowledge to overcome them, and the courage to achieve victory. For I know that a thousand swords can only damage a wall in which a single idea can destroy."

Erik kissed his fingers and brushed them against the wooden carving. His faith was as strong as that of any of his people. It gave him strength in the darkest of times and helped quiet his nerves.

By God, he would need it in the days to come.

He took a deep breath and rose to his feet. His eyes swept to his armour atop a rack. Erik reached out and touched the leather and steel with his weathered hands. It had been with him for many years and countless battlefields. It had never once failed him. He took it up and buckled it over his powerful frame with the ease of a veteran. Next, he braided his long hair back in the Valkir way. He strapped his sword and axe to his belt. The blades were both freshly sharpened into fine edges. Both were hungry for blood. Erik slung his viper-emblazoned shield across his back before he gathered up his helmet and made his way to his lord.

"Jarl Sigfried has sailed," Erik told Magnus when he at last stood before the man. "It will not be long now."

"Good," the earl said with a nod. Magnus moved to stand beside his newly sworn warrior. The earl was silent for a moment as they gazed out over the city. His city. "My bones ache," Magnus said.

Erik glanced at his leader with concern. "Earl?"

Magnus let out a breath and ran a hand over the pommel of his sword in almost a soothing way.

"I am old, Erik. Too old for this. Fifty summers I have walked this realm and now I find that my time grows short."

The bloodsworn turned his eyes back to the harbour. Magnus had been a part of Agartha for as long as he could remember. For many years, the city had prospered under his rule, even if some believed it cruel.

"When at last your time comes, lord, the Sea-Father will welcome you," Erik told him. "You will feast and drink with him in his golden hall, and he will bask in the tales of glory that you bring with you."

"Those glories are from a lifetime ago, my friend," Magnus said. His face and voice betrayed no emotion. He had seen too much, done too much. He turned his eyes to the younger man who stood at his side. "One last battle, I suppose. One last chance to add to my legacy and bring an old man a final taste of glory."

Night had fallen, the tides had returned and the moon shone ever bright when at last the Wind Rider eased out of the river. Slowly, it began to cut through the waves of the ocean. Astrid stood at the helm by Fargrim's side as he sent the vessel carving a path through the waters. He chartered a passage to the south-east. A passage towards Agartha and home. She had made her peace with her god before setting sail under the gaze of the midday sun. She had said goodbye to Earl Arndyr and his brother in her last moments on Vay'kis. They knew the plan, and now it was up to their honour to uphold it. In her heart, and with every fibre of her being, she knew that those men would stand true to their word. For with Arndyr at least she had a common understanding.

She felt her old excitement return as at last they were once more upon the ocean. She could feel the sea breeze upon her cheeks and whip through her hair. It made her blood race. The sea was her first and only love. Wild and untameable. Harsh and gentle. Pure. The sea was everything. It made her feel at peace. Yet Astrid's mind was bursting with thoughts and ideas. Her mind would not be silenced until this was all over. She would have no rest until the war was won. She turned to Fargrim.

"Turn the ship around. Take us north."

"North?" he asked incredulously. "But Agartha—"

"Lies to the south-east, I know," Astrid replied. "However, we cannot sail directly into the beast's jaws. Take us north-east and follow the coast of Kattir. From there we sail onto Mikon. We will slip around the Isle and then descend upon Agartha from the north."

Fargrim frowned.

"But that will slow us down by half a day or more."

"It will," Astrid agreed. "And yet it must be so. Turn us around, and we shall see this to its end."

The helmsman pulled down hard upon the wheel, and slowly the Wind Rider changed its course.

FORTY-FOUR

Catuvantuli lands, Forest of Salvaar

Kitara awoke with a cry. The remnants of her nightmare nearly sent her reeling. Sweat covered her skin and her muscles were tight. Her right hand ached and with a glance she could see why. The knuckles of her hand were pure white, while the handle of the dagger beneath her fingers dug into her skin. Kitara took a breath and closed her eyes. She slowly eased the tension from her hand and released the drawn blade. It fell to the ground at her side with a dull thud. Her hands trembled as the fear of her dreams coursed through her icy blood. Those images and memories that flashed through her mind were as fresh as they were years ago. She could still feel the pain. She could still feel the terror. Kitara took another breath. She willed herself to relax.

"You have nightmares." Aeryn's voice broke the silence.

Kitara's green eyes flickered open, though they did not so much as turn to the other woman. She withheld a curse. Aeryn had seen her weakness. It was a thing that consumed her each day more than the last. It stopped her from ever knowing peace and forced her to wake trembling with each dawn.

"Everyone has nightmares," Kitara snapped back.

There was a kind of sadness in Aeryn's silver gaze as the woman replied, "Not every night … Not like that."

"What business is it of yours?" Kitara said at last, and her voice went quiet as it began to break.

"None," Aeryn told her. The moonseer did not lower her eyes from Kitara. When she spoke her voice was gentle, calming even. "Yet no one should bear that kind of pain alone ... that kind of burden."

Kitara tipped her head back and closed her lashes. She felt the first hint of a tear slide down her cheek. This fear that she felt was destroying her day by day, and yet she had never spoken of it. Not once had she told a soul of it. Not her former companions in the Annoran slums, not Zandir Barangir or Silas. Yet somehow, she felt herself beginning to open up to the Aedei woman. Perhaps it was Aeryn's kindness, or perhaps it was Kitara's lack of judgement. Kitara did not know.

"I have never told anyone," she whispered, and she shivered as she sucked in a gulp of air. "But somehow, though I do not know why, it is different with you."

Aeryn watched her with those soft, grey eyes and said not a word. Instead, she slowly dipped her head and gave a small smile. Kitara's last wall broke.

"I was born many miles from here in the Gulf of Lamrei. A small settlement deep in the Sacasian Sea ... a place built by outcasts. Thieves, pirates, cut-throats, escaped slaves. All called it home. A place of freedom, far from the reaches of dukes and kings," Kitara began, and she crossed her arms as the memories rolled through her mind. "The six captains who had struck their bonds with the empire to create such a place set themselves up as lords of the sea. Yet they watched over their colonies like they were their children. Yet in a paradise without law, one must watch your back. My mother died giving birth to me. She had arrived in Lamrei mere days before that. This is all I have to remember her by," Kitara murmured as she pulled her ring out from her shirt.

The blue sapphire glinted in the moon's light.

"As for my father ... he abandoned us to the world of men far before that. I was raised by whores and thieves, and then, then I met her. Luana Marquez. I was ten summers. She twice that. Luana, along with another, Calvillo of Tarik, took me under her wing. They taught me to fight. Taught me to better myself. Luana was as good as an older sister, a mother even. She was captain to one of the finest crews in the Sacasian and a demon in battle. In my eighteenth year, she got sick, and I was forced to take to the sea with another captain. Barboza, they called him. He was one of the six. One of the old guard. A man as great as any legend," Kitara said as she fought to stop a tear from spilling down her cheek. "Four days on the sea was all it took for us to take our prize. A treasure galleon bound for Elara. I have never seen so much gold. In the celebration that followed, Barboza got drunk. Very drunk. He came for me that night."

Kitara closed her eyes. She could still feel his hot breath on her face. She could still remember his words in her ear. Beautiful, he had called her. He had not been the first to do so, but he was the last.

"When I refused his advances, he got angry. He lashed out. I went for my sword but, but he was too close. He threw me down and beat me. This man I had trusted. This man, who Luana ... who they all held to heart."

She could remember the blood pouring from her lips and nose. The pain in her head where it had struck the deck.

"He tried to force himself upon me, yet I fought. I got back to my feet and then he went for steel ... Gave me this."

Kitara slowly ran her fingers down the scar that marred her face. It was a thing that had caused her so much pain. A thing that had received her nothing but scorn. She could still feel the hot blood on her face even now. Blood which had covered her eyes and filled her mouth. She had been drowning in it.

"I fell and he came with me. He was stronger and his fists like hammers. He hit me. Again, and again, and again. I managed to take his knife. And I drove it through his heart." Her words were bitter and filled with anger as she spoke.

That night had taught her what fear truly was. To have someone far stronger than her pin her down and smother her in her own blood.

"As drunk as they were, the pirates would not forgive me for killing one of their own. For killing one of the six. Liar they called me when I tried to speak. They caged me, treated me as a beast. Those who I held as friends struck me. Those who I held dear spat on me. Murderer they called me. Whore. I was judged upon my return and all of them, even those that I loved, even Luana, turned their backs. I was sold as a slave."

Kitara near spat that last word. She had been nothing but a caged animal to those people. Covered in bruises, piss and her own blood. She had even appeared as such.

"To a pleasure house in Annora. I escaped and lived on the gutter for the next four years. That was before Miera. Before here." Kitara took a deep breath and sucked in the sobs that threatened. "It is a thing hard learned, yet a thing shown to me time and time again in those years. That everyone is in this life for themselves. Friendship, love even, is just an illusion to hide dark intent. Nothing more."

Kitara sighed as she finished her tale. She felt exhausted. The thought of even standing was too much.

"You yet live," Aeryn murmured.

Kitara took a sip from her wineskin and looked away. "What if I am just broken?"

The Aedei woman leaned towards her. Her silver eyes searched for Kitara's. "Then we will find a way to make you believe in the promise of better days" Aeryn replied.

"Do you really believe that to be possible?" Kitara asked as she glanced back at Aeryn. "To unburden myself of the past and cast out these horrors?"

"I know it to be true." Aeryn nodded slowly. "The past is never as we would have it, while the future is yet to be known. Embrace the day. Live life with every breath. And remove all else from concern."

Kitara fingered the ring at her throat. "I do not believe it possible," Kitara breathed.

"Do not doubt yourself," Aeryn told her. "You are strong. You know who you are. To know clear purpose of who you are and what must be done, that is a thing that calls to me."

Aeryn bit her lip for a moment before she extended her right arm and pulled the silver arm ring from her wrist.

"Do you know what this is?" the Aedei woman asked.

Kitara eyed the band and shook her head.

"It is a sacred arm ring," Aeryn said. "Any vow made upon these rings must be kept, else you forfeit your place the next life."

Aeryn wrapped her fingers around the band and met Kitara's gaze. There was something fierce in Aeryn's eyes. Kitara could see it. Something wild like fire.

"I swear to you," the Aedei began, "that I will stand by your side for a day, a month, however long it takes to slay these demons that haunt you."

Kitara dipped her head. She was lost for words. Aeryn's soothing voice was comforting, yet her words more so. She had learnt how to spot lies and she had learnt well. There was no deception in the Aedei's voice nor within her eyes.

Though Kitara could not stop the fear in her heart.

What if it all happened again?

They had been met three miles from the camp by Aedei outriders. Eight men in all. They were all armed to the teeth and their faces awash with blue woad. Cailean rode with a pair of the newcomers. They were talking animatedly in their own tongue at the head of the column. It was no surprise that he was glad to be back with his people and no doubt had much to catch up on. The winds were always changing beneath these trees, and Cailean had been gone for over a moon.

Galadayne and Bellec rode behind them. Two men whom Lukas could not take his eyes from. He could not believe that the stories he had been told were false. One had to be a lie, but both sides believed their stories so fully. One would bend under the weight of truth.

Had Bellec killed Eldred Raynor, or had he tried to save him?

"Lukas," Sakkar muttered from his side, nodding down the column.

The prince followed his friend's gaze, and his heart soared. The makings of tents could be seen through the trees. Blue-painted warriors began to appear in droves as they rode closer. Their eyes were wary at first but quickly turned to joy as they saw Cailean at the head of a mounted column of warriors. Perhaps they had some luck at last, despite there being little over twenty warriors at Cailean's back.

The cheers began as the riders entered the encampment. There were few cheers at first, yet they grew with each passing moment. It was the people themselves that took Lukas' gaze from Bellec's back. To a man, they were soldiers, for this was no mere camp. It was a warband. They were clad in little more than ragged tunics, trousers and fur cloaks. The Aedei wore no more armour than some steel chainmail beneath thick pelts and furs. Simple jewels adorned their ears, while all bore arm rings on their wrists. Their hair was shaggy and long, often tied back in braids. All wore the same white grease as Cailean, while their faces, a sea of blue markings, were each different from the last. They all carried weapons. Some held longbows and spears, while others gripped savage axes and heavy oval shields. They stood proud as they formed a column leading to their chief's tent. They were strong and had more discipline than most gave them credit for.

Then Lukas saw them. There they stood, as proud and fierce as the men. The ones often beholden to rumour and myth. The female warriors of Salvaar. They were armed as heavily as any other warrior with bows and spears. Axes and daggers adorned their belts, while their eyes were like fire. Lukas couldn't help the smile that flickered across his lips. They were a long way from Annora. A long way from the palace at Palen-Tor. A long way from the rules that held him captive to tradition and the responsibility of rank. Here he felt free.

He turned his gaze to the tent flaps of the chief's great tent as they were pulled open. Three men walked through the opening and into the light.

The first man was as large as an ox. His bare arms and chest were covered in layers of hard muscle. His long hair was tied back, while some beads adorned his dark beard. A helm sat atop his brow, while a torc was at his throat. A gold-handled sword hung from his hip, and a cloak hung from his powerful shoulders. Blue woad covered his arms, chest and face. He was too young to be Cyneric. He looked around his mid-thirties. He was closer to Cailean's own age. A commander perhaps.

The next man was smaller, younger still, and wore dark skins. A dagger and small axe adorned his belt, while a quiver of arrows and a bow were slung over his shoulder. His eyes shone silver, and his short beard was cropped. His long hair was dark, while the paint on his face was darker still. It was black. Cailean had taught Lukas the tribal colours. Black was Káli, yet the last Lukas had heard, the Káli were sworn enemy to the Aedei.

Then the third man stepped forward, and Lukas knew him to be Cyneric. His very being seemed to ooze authority. The chief wore armour unlike the rest of his people. Not steel, yet a leather brigandine of brown. It was matched by bracers and greaves. A huge bearskin cloak fell from his shoulders. His long dark hair was streaked with grey, yet it took nothing away from his powerful frame. A sword hung from his hip, while a massive golden torc sat at his throat. His face was fierce and covered in blue. He looked like a true warrior.

Cailean dismounted and motioned for his companions to follow suit. Lukas' boots met the hard earth, and he felt a sense of relief. They had arrived. For now, at least, they were safe among allies and friends. The prince watched as Cailean marched up to the three men. Cyneric pulled his younger brother into a massive hug with a grin.

"Welcome home, brother," the chief said in the tongue of Salvaar as he slapped Cailean's back and turned to his people. Cyneric's voice was as a roar. "THE SPIRITS ARE WITH US!"

The cheers grew deafening.

"It is good to be back, brother," Cailean replied in the same tongue.

The Aedei who stood with Cyneric clasped arms with Cailean and pulled him into a one-armed embrace.

"You return at a good time, my friend."

"Well met, Bleddyn," Cailean told him as they ended the embrace. "I came here looking for a fight."

"Then you will get one," the warrior replied.

Cailean turned his gaze to the man who wore black paint. "The Káli stand with us now?" Cailean asked.

Cyneric nodded.

"Many things have changed in your absence. We stand shoulder to shoulder with Vaylin and her kin. Now tell me, who rides with you? Unless I am mistaken, they do not bear the colours of Annora."

"Dorian has forsaken us," Cailean replied. "And yet we are not alone in our fight."

Cailean glanced over his shoulder and gestured to Lukas. The prince walked over to the chief as his companion spoke, this time in the common tongue.

"This is Lukas Raynor, son to Dorian and Prince of Annora."

"Chief Cyneric." Lukas nodded and extended his arm.

The Aedei lord hesitated before he took Lukas' arm in his powerful grip. "Tell me, prince, why do you ride to our aid absent your father? Against his wishes?" Cyneric asked.

"I am not my father," Lukas told him bitterly. He had his own mind and his own thoughts. Too long he had been constricted to what Palen-Tor deemed right. "Nor am I his faithful hound. Some forget what your people did for us, yet I do not," Lukas said. "Your cause is just, and so I am here."

Cyneric released the younger man's arm. The Salvaari lord seemed satisfied with the response. "Then you are most welcome," Cyneric said. "You and your companions."

"You have my thanks," Lukas said before he gestured to his allies in turn. "This is Sakkar of Larissa, a great warrior and my closest friend."

The desert clansman gave a theatrical bow as was common among his people.

"And that is Bellec, a mercenary beholden to no lord or master."

Bellec handed his reins to Galadayne, locked eyes with Cyneric, and made his way over.

"I know you." Cyneric frowned.

"Aye." The mercenary nodded. "We have met before, many years ago. I was Dorian's ambassador."

"I remember you well." The chief slowly nodded. "You left in a great hurry, and now you are returned to us. Tell me, what happened to the Aedei woman who rode with you? The one you held as wife?"

Lukas' jaw nearly dropped from his chin. Cailean had barely remembered Bellec, yet he had been a child. Cyneric, no more than five summers older, remembered him clearly. Not to mention that the woman, who Bellec had supposedly betrayed the three kingdoms of Annora for, was of Aedei blood.

"With the spirits," Bellec replied, and his voice betrayed no emotion.

"Then we share in your sorrow," Cyneric said sadly, as if somehow the woman had meant a great deal to him. "We welcome you back into our fold, brother."

The two men embraced.

"Now come." The Aedei chief gestured back to his tent. "We have much to discuss."

FORTY-FIVE

City of Palanza, Duchy of Bailon, Kingdom of Medea

Even at the pace that Sir Matias set, it had taken a week to reach Palanza. The great city came into sight. It emerged atop the plains once belonging to the final battle of the great war. Palanza lay to the very north of Bailon's lands and was well within sight of the Mithramir Sea. Many thousands had fallen in the final confrontation between the two sides where the armies of faith had stood fast against a horde of beyond reckoning. A force of heathens and pagans. This place, Palanza, was the birthplace of heroes.

"Behold ... Palanza," Sir Matias called out as he brought the column to a halt.

His voice was filled with awe. The same kind that gripped Kyler. The boy uttered a prayer as he gazed down over the field. The great plain stretched for miles. To the north lay the sea, while a little over a day to the east was the border with Salvaar. To the eyes, the great tracts of land were plain and held no meaning, yet to those of the Twins faith, Palanza was the most sacred of places. The holiest site north of Rovira itself. The warden glanced at the man who rode at his side. Matias gave him a nod.

"Quinn," Matias said.

"In the beating heart of Palanza," the maija began, "sits a monument dedicated to the sacrifice of all whom perished upon these fields. It was built atop the very place that Estevan fell in battle, giving his life for Medea. It is there that I believe we will find answers long forgotten."

It was from that very place that Duran Cormac had spoken the words to usher in a century of peace. Kyler shared a glance with Torin, the man who had begun this quest many miles and countless days from where they now stood.

"If only Bavarian could bear witness to this journey," the Aureian said.

"Aye, you'll have a tale or two to tell when you return to Rovira," Kyler told him.

Torin met his friend's eyes. "You should come with me," he said.

"Perhaps one day," the Medean replied.

Everything he had heard of the great city to the south was glorious, and yet he had not passed his tests. Nor did he wear the garb of a knight.

"But first, there are things here that I must finish. Trials in which I must succeed, and then I will have a future here," Kyler said.

He could not help his gaze shift to Elena who rode beside her fellow maija.

"Well, until then." Torin's lips curled. "We share a drink upon our return."

Kyler returned the smile. One day he would ride south. That he vowed.

"And so, Cormac rode to the head of his great army and looked to the gods' kingdom," Corvo Alaine intoned, his gaze washing over the plains before them. "Hear my prayer, he said. Let the wrath of the heavens fall upon these heathens who desecrate our lands. The Twins answered, and the Pale Horseman rode, and the fields ran awash with the blood of the non-believers."

The company rode through the open maw of the Palanza's gates, and instantly their ears were hit with the sound of a bustling city. It was the chorus of voices and buzz of the marketplace as traders sold their wares. The clinking of armour reached their ears too as mercenaries walked the streets. Atop the walls, men stood clad in their maroon garb, shields and standards emblazoned with the snarling bear of House Bailon. Many stopped and stared as the fabled Knights of Kil'kara rode through their midst. Their reputation was as fierce and proud as the warriors themselves.

Sir Corvo and Sir Matias led the column. Their eyes ever watchful. Both were Medean and both had ridden these streets before. Then came the rest of the knights riding three abreast. The sun glimmered brilliantly upon their armour. The maija, Quinn and Elena, rode in the centre of the formation. Cries came from ahead. Angry shouts followed by the unmistakeable sound of a fist striking flesh.

"Find the clue," Sir Alarik called to Matias and Corvo. "I will handle this."

The Sword of Kil'kara glanced at the older battlemaster and spared him a nod.

Alarik turned back and swept his gaze over the column of warriors. "Neph, Emir, Landrey," Alarik called, "with me."

With a flick of his reins the battlemaster turned his horse towards the cries of anguish. Kyler looked to Elena as the formation divided. She met his eyes and that was enough as she vanished down the street in the wake of Matias and Corvo. Kyler dropped his hand to his sword and kicked his heels in as he followed the veteran towards the noise. Whatever the cause was, the commotion was growing. They rode towards a jeering crowd as it formed up in the streets. The horde was hurling obscenities to whatever and whomever lay in its midst. They did not notice the knights until Alarik's horse was almost upon them.

"Make way!" the battlemaster roared.

The people scattered with terrified expressions and opened a path through the crowd. The five heavily armed and armoured knights rode through with expressions devoid of emotion.

At last Kyler could see what lay before them. Two burly men had pinned a third to the ground. They had stretched his arm out over a wooden block. An older Medean stood before them with a small hand-axe in his grasp. A blind man could see what they intended. All eyes turned to Alarik as he dismounted before the scene and stepped towards the four men. His eyes were fiery as he spoke and his voice powerful.

"What do you think you are doing?"

It was a simple question, but it came from a knight whose hand rested calmly atop his sword. Kyler and his companions followed their leader to the ground as the older man, the one who held the axe, replied.

"He is a criminal, sir," the man told him as he gestured to the one who struggled desperately. "A thief. Two times over."

"And they?" Alarik nodded towards a tear-stricken woman and a young boy who watched on.

They looked as desperate as the thief, and their thin frames suggested they were just as hungry.

"My family," the captive cried out.

"Indeed," Sir Alarik said thoughtfully. "He is a thief twice over, and so you take his hand and make his family bear witness."

"It is the law," the axe-bearing man told him after a moment. He gestured towards the criminal. "You are a Knight of Kil'kara and as such have the power to judge the guilty. What say you?"

"I serve the Twins, wherever and however they choose," Alarik replied without taking his eyes from the man. "Landrey."

Kyler hid his surprise and made his way to the knight's side. "Sir?"

"How would you judge this man?" the battlemaster asked as he gestured to the thief.

The older man made to speak, but the knight silenced him with a raised hand. The crowd grew quiet under Alarik's words, for when a Knight of Kil'kara spoke, all listened. Slowly, feeling the weight of the crowd's eyes upon him, Kyler made his way over to the thief. He shot a dark look at the two men who pinned him, and as if on some unspoken command, they stepped back. Kyler crouched beside the thief.

"Is it true? Did you steal from these men?"

"Yes, sir," he spluttered, his face downcast.

"Twice over?"

"Yes."

"What did you steal?"

The man turned his desperate gaze to the initiate. "Bread ..."

"Is that all?" Kyler frowned.

In his heart, Kyler knew the man's reply even before it was spoken.

The thief nodded.

"We were robbed on the road ... had all our coin taken from us. We were starving. We needed food or we won't survive the winter."

"So, you turned to thievery yourself?" Kyler asked.

A tear ran down the man's cheek. "I am not proud of it ... but my son."

Kyler glanced at the boy who stood huddled in his mother's arms. "By law these men have the right to take your hand," Kyler said.

"I will not be able to work to feed my family," the man pleaded. "Please, sir. I do not care for myself, only my family. They have every right to follow the law, as I would in their place. Take the hand."

"Yet still you stole, knowing the risk?"

Kyler glanced back at the man whose only reply was to hang his head. The initiate rose to his feet. The man was guilty of his crimes and had freely admitted as much. Yet Kyler made his way over to the thief's wife and child. The lad was no older than twelve summers.

"What is your name, boy?"

"Leon, sir," the child replied.

Kyler ran his eyes over the boy. He was thin, almost frail from hunger.

"Have you eaten, Leon?"

The thief's son shook his head sadly. Kyler bit his lip. The law was the law, and yet he could not help but feel sympathetic for the thief's cause. Almost. Kyler placed a comforting hand on Leon's shoulder before he walked back to Sir Alarik.

"The boy is half starved," he murmured to his mentor.

Alarik's stern gaze met with his. "This decision, and its consequences, rest on your shoulders," Alarik told him simply.

Kyler took a breath as he glanced from the thief's family to the accusers to the man himself. The man had to be punished. That much was certain.

"This man is a thief. He has admitted as much," Kyler told the crowd loud enough that all could hear. "And as such must be punished accordingly for his crime. However, if he loses his hand, then he and his family will die come winter. Are three deaths truly just punishment for thievery? The lives of two innocent from such crimes? Should we not give them some godly charity and set them upon the proper path? I suggest that we show mercy in that regard, and let the man keep his hand."

"You would let him go free?" the man with the axe exclaimed angrily. "Where is the justice in that?"

"You misunderstand me, friend," Kyler told him. "I said that he will not lose a hand for his transgressions. I did not say that he would escape punishment for them. For if we begin to pardon thieves, then what is to stop one man's crimes from becoming that of hundred's?"

"Then what do you suggest?" The old man frowned.

"I suggest trial by fire," Kyler told him, "and if he fails, he loses the hand."

At Alarik's command the gathering made for the nearest blacksmith.

A length of steel was thrust deep into the heart of a blazing furnace and there they waited.

"You do not have to do this yourself," Sir Alarik told him as Kyler reached out with a set of tongs.

"No. I passed the sentence," Kyler replied as he withdrew steel from the flames. "I should see this done."

Together they walked out into the street to where the thief stood. The crowd formed up in the street. A narrow passage was created between the lines of men and women. An empty passage, a void. The thief spared a glance at his family before he held out a hand. Kyler gave him a nod and opened the tongs. Steel hissed as it dropped into the thief's waiting hands. The man cried out as flesh began to melt. He started to walk down the street. The steel burned hot and sweat streamed down the thief's face. He gasped as the pain threatened to make him lose his grip, yet if he did, he would lose the hand. Step after step he walked as the crowd watched on. They jeered at him, daring him to drop the hot steel. Then he reached the end. The thief doubled over. He dropped the iron and fell to his knees with a cry. His hands were charred, his flesh melted. The old man from whom he had stolen walked over to his side and dropped a bucket of water at his feet. Without hesitation, the thief thrust his hand deep into the water. He screamed. The crowd cheered. Kyler closed his eyes. It was over. He made his way to the thief and placed a hand on his shoulder.

"You have passed your test this time, but do not steal again. Your life will be forfeit if you do."

"Gods bless you, sir," the man replied.

With that, the knights mounted their powerful steeds and set off after their companions. Kyler glanced back at the crowd towards the thief's son and wife who even now cuddled with the man. Kyler bit his lip and reached into his pouch before he tossed a single golden coin to Leon. He clicked his tongue and rode off. The family could eat a whole winter on that.

The great statue at the heart of Palanza arose before them. It was the only thing that adorned the town square. It stood on a small stone dais ringed with carved stairs. A great stallion reared. Its mane as its tail seemed to fly in the wind. Upon its back was a stone warrior with his sword thrust high into the sky. Upon his shield was the sigil of his house. A snarling bear. There he was. The greatest hero that Medea had ever known. The very embodiment of their faith.

"Estevan Bailon," Elena breathed as she saw the great sight. "The Bear of the North, I wonder, what secrets do you hide?"

They dismounted and made their way over to the legendary figure. Sir Corvo tapped a fist to his heart and dipped his head to the man as a sign of respect.

"Here lies Estevan, son of Rodrigas, saviour of the north and father of Medea," he read as he ran his eyes over the carved words that lay at the top of the dais before the statue. "Tell me the riddle again."

"In the Bear's jaws where fabled glory began, a nation would arise where the accursed were doomed to lie," Quinn told him.

The party circled the stone. Their eyes flicked across over every last inch, hunting, searching. Elena looked up at Estevan's stone face. A sadness gripped her. It was a sadness that only those of Medea would know.

"He gave his life for his people, for us even. He fell here, in this very place, so that Medea might be born."

"And therein lies our clue," Quinn said. "The rhyme does not speak of any falsehood. It speaks of where Bailon and his men fell, where they now lie."

Elena looked to her fellow maija as it hit her. "In the very ground beneath this stone," she murmured.

They all looked to her as she made her way to the dais and crouched before the carved epitaph. It was written on a single square stone, yet something about its edges drew her gaze. Had she not been looking for it she would have missed it entirely. It did not seem as attached as the other stones on the dais. Elena drew her knife, and then cracked its pommel down upon the edge of the epitaph stone. It moved. She did it again, this time on the other side of the stone. It shifted again. The knights circled around her. They watched closely as she slid the tip of her blade through the mortar and pushed. It drove under the stone with ease.

"It wasn't properly sealed," she told her companions.

Elena pushed down on her knife and forced the stone up. Then she saw it.

Beneath the epitaph sat a carved wooden box. The figures of Durandail and Azaria were carved upon its lid. Elena sheathed her blade and pulled the box free. She lifted its lid. There they were.

A small piece of parchment alongside a strange wooden object. It was like six separate squares of wood pressed together.

"I have seen these before," Quinn said as he picked up the object. He examined it closely and turned it over in his hands as he spoke. "It is some kind of cryptex. They hail from Tarik … it is a puzzle."

"And this," Elena said with pursed lips as she held up the parchment, "bears both the seal of our order and that of Bailon."

Sir Matias took the paper from her proffered hand. He eyed the crescent moon and sun alongside the bear of Bailon.

"It is true," Matias said.

The knight pulled the ribbon that bound it undone and unravelled the message. The sound of hooves greeted their ears as Sir Alarik and his men arrived. Boots thudded on the paved stones as they dismounted and hurriedly made their way over to the new discovery.

"What is it?" Sir Corvo asked. "What does it read?"

"Upon the crossroads of faith did this path begin, forged alone in hands of Delios' kin. There in the shadows it lies still; what was lost shall be found by Durandail's will."

They drifted into a silence as the knight spoke his last. By the message's words, this may well be the final path.

"It would appear that this is the last clue," Sir Alarik said.

"So, it would seem," Quinn replied with a furrowed brow. "Each of the other rhymes have been used as a play on words. This one will be no different."

"A crowd begins to gather. Too many eyes," Matias muttered as dozens of townspeople had begun to form a circle around them.

They looked on in a kind of awe at the knights who stood around the statue of their hero. Their eyes grew suspicious as they huddled around the epitaph.

"We should leave," Matias told the company.

Elena placed the stone tile down and then those of the order mounted up. They rode two miles south from Palanza and set up camp as the sun began to set. Here, alone in the clearing of a small wood, they would rest. First, they needed to solve this rhyme.

"Crossroads," Elena murmured.

She glanced up at Quinn. Her eyes sparkling. She had an idea. "Do you remember the stories of Stefanos?" Elena asked.

"The maija who rode at Duran Cormac's side. They say he had Delion blood. I remember." Quinn's face lit up. "Do you think …"

Elena nodded and drew her knife once again.

"What are you thinking?" Sir Matias asked.

Elena leaned forwards and marked four places on the ground with her blade.

"A century ago," the maija began, "Stefanos was tasked with hiding many religious relics, things that, if needed, could be easily found by the Order, yet hidden completely from our enemies. So, he devised a kind of code. Four places are named in some kind of writing, while the object itself lies directly between them. These places could be countless miles away, yet if in line, the items could always be found. The Cross of Stefanos they called it. This journey began in Rovira to the south, and thus far, the most northerly point has been Palanza," she said as she slid her knife through the dirt to create a line between two of the markings. "To the east and west lie Kilgareth and Adrestia."

Once more she joined the markings. Before her, carved into the soil, lay a cross shape.

"And if this is right," Quinn said, nodding at her work, "then our journey ends where the cross meets."

Elena stabbed her blade into the very centre of the cross. "Precisely," Elena told them.

She reached into the folds of her satchel. From it she pulled out a map. She ran her eyes over the map. She was looking from Rovira to Palanza, Kilgareth to Adrestia. Elena put her finger upon its surface over one of the mountains that arose at the entrance to the valley of Odrysia. It was barely a few miles east from Malcia.

"Unless I am mistaken, that would be here," said Elena.

"The gates to the valley. This path takes us to North Sword's Peak," Alarik stated.

The mountains that led into the Valley of Odrysia were named after the northern wars. North Sword's Peak after Duran Cormac. While to its south, Octavan's Crest was named for the cardinal of old. The very man who had ordered the assault upon Medea a century before. They drifted into silence. All their thoughts were on the same thing. The end of the line.

"Good," Sir Matias said after a moment, and his voice was filled with purpose. "This journey, and whatever lies at its end, is but the will of the Twins. It is fated. We ride come break of day."

Elena turned her gaze to Quinn. "We should send word to Kilgareth," she told him.

The other maija nodded his agreement.

As the moon grew ever higher, one of the pigeons began its flight back to the beginning. Back to Kilgareth.

FORTY-SIX

Catuvantuli lands, Forest of Salvaar

Kitara had long since lost track of the miles that they had travelled. All she knew was that slowly, one step at a time, they were closing in on Cyneric's camp. What they would find there, she did not know.

Would her companions have arrived safely? Were they yet alive?

It did not matter so much to her, for these people, the Salvaari, could well be her salvation. In Aeryn at least she had discovered a kind of peace that she had all but forgotten. Kitara let her gaze travel up Aeryn's back as she led the way through the trees. The woman with the dark hair, silver eyes and silent footfalls had begun to intrigue her. Despite the wolf-like instincts that the woman bore and the blood on her hands, Aeryn had kept her compassion. She was her own person. One whom Kitara knew would not change her steadfast convictions.

"Leave the horses here," Aeryn said as she glanced back at Kitara. "The forest is thick, and there is a stream up ahead. We can fill our waterskins and be on our way without fear of leaving hoof prints in the bank."

Kitara followed her companion over a large fallen tree. All her years aboard the slippery decks of ships had given her balance. She dropped to the ground behind the girl and took a breath.

"This place is peaceful," Kitara murmured as they walked. The embrace of the forest felt comforting.

"It is home." Aeryn gave her a smile. "The trees are old and filled with thought and memory ... It is wild, no?"

The blonde-haired girl chuckled. "Yes, it is."

The Aedei glanced up into the canopy. "Wild, untamed ... beautiful."

"Just like the sea," Kitara agreed.

Few things would ever be as perfect as being aboard a ship as it flew over the waves and sailed from coast to coast.

Aeryn's silver eyes sparkled as she looked to her companion. "Then you understand?" the Aedei asked.

Kitara met her stare. "Yes. I think I do."

They reached the small river within moments. Large rocks cut into the waters from the shore, while much of the grass-ridden bank overhung the river itself. Kitara pursed her lips and ran a hand through her hair. She could feel the remnants of the filth still coating her locks. She had not had the time nor chance to clean it in the days since the fight in that muddy stream. Besides which, her water canteen was close to running dry.

The pair made their way down the bank and dropped onto the rocks below. Kitara pulled the stopper from her canteen as she crouched by the stream before she dipped the container beneath the clear waters. Aeryn knelt by her side and dipped a cupped hand into the river. She brought it to her lips and savoured the taste for a moment. Kitara tied her canteen back to her belt before at last she reached up and unbound her hair. It fell to the sides of her face in a dirty blonde wave. Its formerly golden colour was all but lost to the dirt that stained it. Kitara leaned forwards and slowly began to wash the cool waters through her locks. She barely heard Aeryn rise and turn her wary eyes to the trees. Kitara looked into the river as she worked. She stared almost absent-mindedly into the waters. She could see her reflection clearly. The newly added blue woad across her face and black paint around her green eyes. A dull ache began to edge its way into her head. She closed her eyes and rubbed her temples. Her gaze flickered and then her emerald eyes turned to violet. Pain drove its blade into her head. Kitara gasped as she fought back against the agony that sent her to her knees. She bit down hard, grimacing as she struggled. Her heart pounded faster. Then she felt it. From the waters before her to the trees all around. Animals in the undergrowth. It was as if she was them.

"Kitara!"

She barely heard Aeryn drop to her side and place a hand upon her shoulder.

"I can feel … everything." Kitara gasped.

She forced her blazing purple eyes to the other woman. Kitara could feel her too. She could almost see herself through the eyes of the Aedei. She clawed at the rock beneath as the pain burned through her mind.

"Look at me," Aeryn murmured.

The Aedei reached out a hand and touched Kitara's cheek. Kitara didn't hear speak.

"Look at me!" Aeryn said louder and turned the other girl's head to face her.

Aeryn met her eyes as she spoke in a language foreign to Kitara's ears.

"Remember the sea. Remember her voice. Feel her anger as she rises around you, lashing as she reaches towards you, threatening a storm."

Aeryn did not drop her gaze as she stared deep into Kitara's eyes. One hand cupped Kitara's cheek. The other was placed comfortingly on her shoulder.

"Feel the tides rise. Feel them begin to slip away, taking the pain with them. Remember the sea's voice as the anger fades, replaced with the calmness of the quietest of nights. Remember how it flows through you, feel her strength, remember it."

Kitara did not notice how her breathing had slowed nor that

the tension had faded from her body. What had begun as fire had all but gone. It had been replaced with no more than a dull ache around her eyes. For a fleeting moment, she could still see everything.

A red-painted face.

Aeryn felt her relax, yet a tremble ran through Kitara's body.

"I'm here," the Aedei murmured as she spoke once more in the common tongue. "I'm with you."

Kitara took in a deep breath as her gaze faded back to green and the awareness vanished from her mind. It was over. She could not help but look for some kind of fear in Aeryn's eyes. She must see some kind of monster. Some kind of freak.

"What do you see when you look at me?" Kitara asked.

"I just see you," Aeryn told her.

Kitara rested her forehead gently on her companion's. Then she remembered. The red-painted warrior from her visions. He was heading their way.

Aeryn frowned and snatched up her bow before Kitara could speak. Without a word, she grabbed Kitara and tackled her. They fell beneath the overgrown bank. They did not make a sound. Kitara felt nothing but the weight of Aeryn's body, her steady heartbeat and her quiet breaths upon her cheek. Aeryn's scent reached her nose. Dark hair tickled her cheek. Wildflowers. That was what she smelt of. Kitara saw the moonseer slowly reach for the hand-axe that hung from her belt. Footsteps. They came from nowhere and barely made a sound. Yet all the same, there they were. Kitara dared not move as they drew closer. She held her breath. It could only be the red-painted warrior, and who knew if he was alone.

The footfalls reached the bank above where they lay hidden. He must have heard her cries. If he dropped down onto the rocks, then they would be seen. They would have to fight. Kitara felt her heart race as she waited. The only things she could see were the earth of the under-bank and Aeryn's face. They waited. Then the footsteps began once more as its owner walked way. Still, they waited.

Aeryn released her grip on her axe and glanced down at Kitara. "We're alone," Aeryn whispered.

With that, she rolled off her companion and slowly rose into a crouch. She gazed up over the bank as she nocked an arrow. Kitara joined her. She wrapped her hand around the hilt of her sword as she looked into the woods.

"Strange," Aeryn muttered.

"Hmmm?" Kitara looked to her.

The moonseer pursed her lips. "Catuvantuli never travel this far north. It's too exposed," Aeryn muttered.

"Why don't we find out where he came from," Kitara suggested.

They followed the Catuvantuli warrior on foot for little under half a mile to the east. Kitara never caught sight of the man. However, Aeryn always seemed to know which way to go. Whether it was by scent or by tracks so faint that Kitara could not see them, she did not know. The Aedei's training as moonseer had given her the skill required to hunt anyone over any terrain. It was almost unnatural. She was part sense, part instinct. Kitara never let her hand fall from her sword as they made their way through the forest.

Slowly, the trees began to thin, and then they ended completely. Kitara caught a glimpse of the man they were tracking. He was no more than fifty yards away. There, across open ground, was a wall. Aeryn dropped into a crouch. She peered through the undergrowth as he greeted another warrior at the edge of what appeared to be some kind of camp. Small palisade walls sprung up in intervals blocking whatever lay beyond. Where there were no walls stood near impassable barriers of sharpened staves. Aeryn led the way through the trees, which despite thinning slightly never turned into a clearing. The moonseer made not a sound as she crept through the woods, while Kitara made little more than that. Closer and closer they neared those small walls. They kept beyond sight of the warrior who stood at the opening. Another two men watched over the spiked fence. Their hands clasped spears close while they gazed out from their base.

"Wait here," Aeryn said quietly.

She spared Kitara a sidewards glance before she pulled herself up into a large tree. Within moments, she was high up in its branches overlooking the camp. The camp was small, no more than eighty paces from end to end. No fires nor torches or braziers could be seen. The smoke from such things would have attracted their enemy long ago. A yard filled with horses tethered to a long wooden fence stood to one side. Warriors patrolled the base. Each one bore the red markings of the Catuvantuli. All except one. He was covered in chainmail, with a steel longsword at his hip and a heater shield slung across his back. He could only have been one of those mercenary Medean knights that Henghis' wanderer, Kendrick, had hired. Yet Aeryn only spared him a quick glance, for her eyes were drawn to a sight that made her blood chill. Steel cages. Some atop wagons and some merely tied to the ground. Each of them was filled with people. Men, women and children. Some bore war paint, but most did not.

Aeryn's face paled as she watched a pair of armed Catuvantuli parade an unarmed man covered in black war paint towards a solitary post. He was Káli. The markings said as much. The man said something to one of the Catuvantuli. The Catuvantuli shoved him to his knees in reply and slammed a fist into the side of his head. The Káli fell. Moments later he was chained to the post by his captors. It was the last thing Aeryn saw before she clambered back down to the ground.

"They have them," she told Kitara, unable to keep anger from her voice.

"Who?"

"My people," Aeryn growled. "Locked in cages. There are iron wagons and one of those western knights leads them."

Kitara felt a very real shudder run down her spine. "I have seen this before," she said. "This is a slave camp. From here, they will take their prisoners in those wagons and sell them to the highest bidder."

Aeryn ground her teeth. "This is not right."

"No, it is not," Kitara agreed.

Once upon a time, Kitara had nearly found herself in one of those caged wagons.

"Yet it is so ..." Kitara muttered.

"You do not understand," the moonseer murmured sadly. "My people have never dealt in slavery."

"Everyone has a price," Kitara told her.

"Not Salvaari," Aeryn replied. "We cannot do nothing."

Kitara looked towards the camp. She eyed the palisade walls. "How many are they?" Kitara asked.

"Fifty spears, perhaps more."

The golden-haired woman gave her a bewildered look. "I cannot take on fifty warriors. Can you?"

Aeryn closed her eyes. "No ..."

Kitara placed a hand on her companion's wrist and turned the moonseer to face her. "You saved my life, and I will follow you no matter what course you charter. But what would you have me do? We cannot take on that many, not without help. We would be slaughtered."

The moonseer met her eyes. "There is one that we might save. We wait until night, then we go in."

They slowly crept towards the spiked fence as the moon rose and darkness fell across the forest like a blanket. Aeryn would deal with the two who guarded that entrance. At thirty paces, the moonseer pulled two arrows from her quiver and held them with her bow hand. Kitara frowned as she watched her companion curiously. She had never seen this before. Aeryn kept her silver eyes upon her targets as she drew her first shaft back. It all happened in a blur.

She did not seem to aim at all, for as soon as the feathers touched her cheek, she loosened her first arrow. It had barely left the bowstring when a second followed in its wake. It was done in little over two heartbeats. The arrows sliced through flesh. Razor-sharp steel tips carved paths through throat and heart. The Catuvantuli fell without a sound.

Aeryn led the way as they scurried through the undergrowth. They reached the sharpened staves and slipped through the opening. There they crouched, watching and waiting. Most of the Catuvantuli stood by the wagons and cages. That was near forty yards from the lone Káli. A maze of tents stood between them. Even so, Kitara could only make out dark smudges.

Who knew how many there were?

Kitara counted three guards surrounding the Káli. They seemed at ease, as if nothing could touch them. So far, they had not noticed that their companions had vanished at the entrance. The tents and camp equipment obstructed their view.

Aeryn nodded towards the Káli and gestured for Kitara to move. The other woman obliged. Her hand went to the knife at the back of her belt as she ran across the open ground towards the first tent. Kitara had to trust her companion, for the moonseer could see perfectly. Perhaps the Catuvantuli had looked away. Kitara could only guess. She glanced back, and Aeryn had vanished. She prayed that whatever Aeryn was doing would work. Kitara took care to gently ease the blade from its sheath. She did not make a sound as she slid through the tents. Closer and closer she scurried until she could hear their voices clearly. She was no more than ten paces away now. Kitara edged her way around the last tent. She kept her back to the wall of dried pelts. Kitara glanced around the corner. Eight men, just as before. Around five steps separated each man. Too many for her to take alone.

Suddenly, a shout rose through the night, followed by the roar of flames as fire engulfed something in the north of the camp.

Kitara nearly grinned. Aeryn. Warriors were belched from tents as they ran towards the fire that threatened to consume them. They charged to the water troughs with buckets in the hopes of saving the camp. Five of the men guarding the Káli prisoner followed their kin. That left three. Those were odds that anyone trained in tarkaras would find easy. Kitara clamped her hand on the handle of her sword as she stepped out from behind cover. Surprise was all the first two men could manage. Her thrown knife buried itself in the chest of the furthest soldier. It slid between ribs and drove into his heart. The second warrior, the closest one, had barely reached for his axe when Kitara's newly drawn sword glinted in the moonlight and sliced him from neck to hip. She continued the move, dancing forwards across the ground as a spray of blood wet the air. She lunged and drove her blade home deep into his vitals. Kitara slammed her shoulder into the warrior as she pulled her blade free. The warrior crashed to the ground. Life had left his eyes long before he hit the earth.

Kitara spun to face the last warrior as he cried out a warning. The tip of his spear angled towards her throat, but she was ready. Kitara slid to the side even as she deflected the shaft. She countered the blow and darted forwards before the Catuvantuli could bring his spear back. Steel met flesh with a sickening thud and blood sprayed from his lips as Kitara's sword drove into his throat. The spear fell from his fingers as life left his eyes. Kitara flicked her blade as her enemy collapsed into the dirt. She spared a look towards the maze of tents. She saw nothing. Heard nothing.

Satisfied, Kitara snatched up her bloody dagger and turned back to the Káli prisoner. He watched her with curious eyes. She raised a finger from the hilt of her red-stained dagger and held it to her lips to silence him. The Káli man nodded. Kitara swiftly wiped her knife free of blood on her own sleeve. There was no time to clean it with the dead's clothing. She sheathed it and crouched before the black-painted warrior. His wrists were bound tight by chain above his head. She ran her gaze up over the steel until they reached a small lock.

"The Medean has the key," the Káli hissed quietly.

Kitara bit her lip and glanced back towards the tents. It would not be long before someone found them, and she could not fight them all. To try and get the key now would be suicide.

"I have seen these locks before in Annora," Kitara told him quietly as she ran her hands over it.

They were strong locks, but they had one weakness.

Thank the gods for her time on the streets ...

She reached into one of her pouches and pulled from it a pair of thin steel lengths. They were pointed at the end and not much bigger than nails. Kitara shoved them into the lock and began to work. Light footfalls came from behind. Kitara glanced over her shoulder as a shout went up. Fifty paces away, one of the Catuvantuli was pointing towards them.

"Hurry," the prisoner whispered.

Moments stretched. It seemed like an eternity. Every sound made Kitara jump. The shout grew as a dozen armed warriors thundered towards them. Twenty paces. Then the lock gave a tiny click and fell from the chain. Kitara snatched up her sword and turned. There was no time.

Suddenly, the scream of a horse assaulted her ears, and a cry of alarm went up. Dozens of horses poured through the camp in a wave. They surged forwards towards her. They drove between Kitara and the Catuvantuli like a knife. Aeryn led the way atop the back of a stallion. Without hesitation, Kitara snatched up the reins of the nearest horse and pulled herself onto its back. The Káli followed suit, and then they were off. They hurtled into the night surrounded by a wall of horses. She spared a glance back as they fled the camp. The Medean knight roared after them. His words were lost in the wind, but his voice lashed her ears.

They returned to the river, to Aeryn's horse.

"I learnt this long ago," Kitara told them as the chains that bound the Káli's hands fell from his wrists. "During my time in Annora."

Kitara exchanged a knowing look with Aeryn. For only she knew of those years and how they had changed her.

The Káli rubbed his wrists as they were finally freed. He ran his hands over the rawness that the chains had forced upon his flesh. "Thank the spirits you found me. I am Kiernan."

Kitara dipped her head towards him. "Why did they separate you from the others?"

"Turns out those bastards don't like it when you give them compliments." The Káli gave a savage grin.

"Forgive me," Aeryn said with a half a frown, "but you are Káli. Why are you this far east?"

"It was not of my choice," Kiernan replied. A low growl entered his voice as he spoke. "Yet Henghis' wanderer is a snake. My kin were riding to meet with Henghis when we were attacked by these men who appeared his own yet serve Kendrick. That was the first we knew that the alliance between Káli and Catuvantuli had broken. A dozen of us were captured, my lord among them."

"Your lord?" Kitara glanced at him. "I thought that the Káli served Vaylin."

"And we would all die for our chief, yes," Kiernan said, fingering his arm ring. "Yet I ride with her brother, Morlag."

"Does he live?" Aeryn asked.

"He does," the Káli told them with a small nod. "Locked in one of those very cages."

"Then we have to tell Cyneric," the moonseer said. "This goes against everything our people stand for. It goes against the spirits."

"Then take me to him."

✦ ✦ ✦

FORTY-SEVEN

Isle of Agartha, the Valkir Isles

The moon shone silver and cast its tumescent rays over the Isle of Agartha. A deep mist hung thick over the waters of the Lupentine and crept up the shores into the mountains themselves. The Wind Rider was hidden from sight in the darkness and fog half a mile off the coast. It took the four small boats that the Rider carried to get the crew onto the beach. There they emerged from the mists as Skûra's demons. They trudged silently through the sand and into the mountains. They were quiet, for no words needed to be said. The only sound came from their heavy boots and thick armour. Thirty hardened warriors carried sword, axe and spear alongside equal their number wielding bows and the occasional hand-axe or knife. All bore white ochre upon their faces. They were ready to die for their cause. Astrid loved these people and would give her life for each of them. Some of them would die this night. That much she knew. It was inevitable.

The truth was that to be a leader on a raid, one must be willing to look into the eyes of their warriors and, if the Sea-Father willed it, send them to their deaths.

Astrid did not so much as spare Torben a glance as they began their ascent into the forest-covered mountains that lay between them and their city. The plan had been laid, and now was the time for action.

They had walked for miles when at last the port town came into sight. Far below the mountains upon which they travelled, burning torches and braziers brought the silent city to life. Thatched houses merged into shadows under the fiery gaze of the lights, while black silhouettes of the patrolling watchmen and guards broke the stillness.

There it was. The thing that drew Astrid's eyes like a moth to a flame. The hall of Earl Magnus Vedoera. The Wolf of Agartha. The prize.

"Agartha lies ready to welcome us," Torben murmured from her side.

Her gaze remained upon that hall. The place where it would all end. "Then we should not disappoint them." Astrid fingered the head of the axe hanging at her belt.

To this day, she had not fought in battle nor drawn blood from even her most hated of foes. She could not help but wonder whether that would change this night. She uttered a quick prayer to the Sea-Father before she turned to face her crew. These people had followed her from the day that her father had been struck down. They had done it without complaint or hesitation.

"May the spirits of my ancestors envelop me," Astrid murmured in prayer. "Let it begin."

The column of warriors divided beneath the trees.

Erik stood at the doors of the earl's great hall. He watched over the bay with his keen eyes. His hand had not left the axe at his belt since the morn that Sigfried had sailed. All pretence of peace had faded, and now he stood guard. He was covered head to toe in his armour. His sword and axe hung over his left hip. Erik held his helm under his right arm. He was ready.

"They are here."

Erik turned to see Magnus emerge from his hall. Like him, the older man was ready for battle. A sword was buckled at his side atop his fine armour.

"They were seen in the mountains. It will not be long now," Magnus said.

Erik nodded. "They must have slipped past Sigfried to the north."

"It is of no consequence," Magnus told him. "We are prepared, and the men ready."

The son of Jarl Lief allowed his lips to curl. "Then we should greet our guests."

"We will await them here." The earl clapped a hand on the bloodsworn's shoulder. "Bring Redleaf. Astrid will fall knowing that one held above all others betrayed her."

They moved silently through the outskirts of Agartha. They passed house and hall as they kept to the shadows. Twenty of her shield warriors, including Torben and Hélla, stood with her. They made up the main body of Astrid's small force. Elsewhere in Agartha, Nenrir led another group, while Fargrim led the final. She could only pray that they found success.

Astrid felt her heart race as they came into sight of the first of men of the watch. Two warriors stood by a fire with their hands resting lightly over their blades. The first man turned her way. His ears had pricked at the sound of trudging boots on the earth. He made to shout. Torben's thrown axe buried itself in his throat, cutting off the cry in an eruption of blood. As he fell, the other warrior went for his own blade. Too late. A bow sang and an arrow sent the second guard to the afterlife. They kept moving and stopped only to recover Torben's axe and pull the bodies from the light. If they were discovered in Agartha too soon it could all be undone.

Hélla and another of the crew took the lead as the raiders wound through the maze of streets. Each step brought them closer to Magnus. They had reached the corner of a hall when Hélla held up a hand. The crew stopped in their tracks. Astrid planted her back firmly against the wooden wall. She stilled her breath as they waited for Hélla's command. Astrid could see Hélla tighten her hand on the hilt of her sword. Footsteps. Three of Magnus' warriors walked into sight. Eyes widened as they saw the group arrayed before them. It was the last thing they saw. Hélla swung her blade. It sliced across the first man's neck. She pivoted and plunged steel deep into the chest of the second. Another of Astrid's band did not hesitate as the shieldmaiden led the way. He leapt on top of the final warrior and drove him to the ground. He clamped a hand down tightly on the soldier's lips. The watchman's muffled cries were his last words. The raider plunged his long knife deep into his vitals again and again until life left the man's eyes.

They were the last of Magnus' hounds that Astrid would see before they finally came into sight of the earl's long hall. There it was. Sitting barely thirty paces away across the courtyard of stone.

Astrid made her way to the head of the column. She did not dare to leave the cover of the house to her side and the shadows it provided. Four of Magnus' sworn warriors guarded his doors, yet they had not seen Astrid yet. Slowly, almost tentatively, she leaned forwards. She turned her gaze from the hall and peered down the streets that led into the courtyard. Nothing. The streets stood empty. Only four men stood between them and a vengeance that had begun to consume her. Astrid glanced back at Torben and the two exchanged a look. Their eyes met, and the meaning was clear. It was time. Astrid rolled her shoulders back. She felt fire surge through her blood. She adjusted the grip on her shield. Then she walked into the courtyard.

The first cry of alarm went up as the crew began to form into a shield wall. The yard looked empty. Yet only a fool would charge into an open space without so much as raising a shield. They locked steel-trimmed wood together in an unbreakable wall. Torben took the lead and allowed Astrid to slide back into the second rank of warriors. When it came to plots and schemes, she had no equal, yet this was the old warrior's calling.

"I have come for Magnus, and Magnus alone," Astrid called out to the guards. "Let us pass and you will not be harmed. I swear it."

The four men did not budge. They planted their feet and readied their blades. Then she felt it. The itch that tickled at her spine and the icy feeling that ran down her neck. She could hear nothing, yet there was something in the air that she could feel.

"Form a circle," Astrid roared as the thudding footsteps began to ring through the darkness.

As one, the crew of the Wind Rider formed up and created an unbroken circle of shields two men deep. Astrid raised her own shield as they huddled closer together. She slid into the second row. Her eyes flicked over Torben's shoulder as they all dropped into a fighting crouch. Roars filled the night, and then warriors surged from the streets and hall.

"We hold the line!" Torben bellowed above the din as he planted his axe atop the steel rim of his shield. His voice grew louder. "We are a wall!"

Fifty warriors encircled them, weapons brought to bear. Lips curled back into snarls. Shields were locked together as they jeered.

"KILL THEM ALL!" one of Magnus' men roared as he struck his axe into his shield.

Everything grew still. Then they charged towards Astrid and her small crew.

Astrid drove her shield into Torben's back as the wave of steel and flesh crashed into them. She braced the warrior as they were all driven back. Boots slid atop stone. Screams filled her ears. The sound of steel striking steel was the only sound to break through the roar. This was the closest Astrid had come to an actual battle.

Hot, stinking breath filled her senses and sweat ran down her brow. She saw a warrior fall under Torben's axe. Blood cascaded into the air as the man crashed to the ground only to have his place filled by another. Astrid heaved with her shield. If Torben lost his footing and fell, then he was dead.

Magnus' men began to chant. Their voices filled the sky with words that she could barely make out. She strained and pushed as warriors fell all around her. The first of her crew was taken by a sword that slipped over his shield. Another fell as an axe ripped into his neck. The circle began to grow smaller as men fell and the pressure on the shields grew. Astrid keenly felt each soul lost. She had led them to this. They had to hold.

A great cry went up and one of their foes punched his arm into the air. His hand was wrapped around the hair of a severed head. Astrid felt her face pale. It was Hvitsred. Blood fell from his neck and the cheer grew. A shieldmaiden leapt forwards in anger and drove her sword into the warrior's heart. She slid her blade into her foe up to its hilt.

"HÉLLA!" Torben shouted as she broke the shield wall.

Everything grew still, and suddenly the jeers and shouts of the horde seemed to fade in Astrid's ears. All she could hear was Hélla's war cry as she pulled her axe forth. She fought like a demon. Her eyes filled with fire as her axe hacked into flesh. She killed two men within seconds and raised her shield to block the sword of a third. The shieldmaiden felled him with a single swing of her axe and drove him to his knees. His chest ripped open and spilt his life blood onto the stones beneath. Hélla twirled and made to step back into the shield wall. A spear ripped through the back of her thigh. Its tip carved through her leg and drove her to the ground. She cried out as the spear was ripped from her wound and took her ability to rise with it. Hélla met Torben's eyes for but a moment as she bared her teeth and tightened her grip on the shaft of her axe. Steel sliced through the air as she lashed out. A rough hand caught the axe, and a blade sliced her arm. Her weapon was freed from her grasp. Then the spear drove down once more. It tore into the flesh of her neck. Astrid felt her heart stop. Blood ran from her friend's mouth as she fell to her knees. Shield fell from nerveless fingers. The spear was pulled free, and then Hélla fell. Her lifeless body crashed down onto the stones.

"HOLD!" The roar filled the courtyard.

As one, Magnus' warriors stepped back. Their shields were still locked and ready. Their eyes were hungry as they watched on like jackals. Bloodied and broken bodies filled the yard. Many had fallen, yet Astrid only had eyes for Hélla. She could hear Torben panting before her and knew that his blood-covered face would be filled with fury. The woman he had trained, the one whom he held as daughter, was dead.

"Astrid Farrin," Magnus called down from the entrance to his hall as he spread his arms. "Welcome home."

Magnus felt a fierce joy run through his heart as he gazed down towards his enemy. Erik stood at his side with his sword pressed tightly to the throat of Laerke Redleaf. The captive wore Erik's thick cloak around his frame to hide the mess that the bloodsworn warrior had inflicted. Before the day was done, Magnus would show Astrid what had become of her friend. Magnus watched as the dark-haired woman turned her gaze from the body of one of her dead friends and looked towards the hall. There were only fifteen of her warriors left alive after the slaughter, and that could change at but a single command from the earl.

"Step aside," Magnus heard her mutter as she tossed down her axe and glared defiantly up at the earl.

"Astrid," growled Torben and his face filled with fury and pain.

"That is an order," she barked.

Torben snarled and then allowed her to pass beyond his shield and protection.

"And so, it ends without a single swing of your axe," Magnus called down to her with a mirthless smile. "You who clung to the title of shieldmaiden yet has never partaken in battle nor knows what it is to take a life." He nodded to Erik. "Yes, your brother told me all about you."

Astrid glanced at Erik, and Magnus fancied he could see agony in her face. The earl clamped his hand tightly on the pommel of his sword.

"Before you die, know that your friend, Redleaf, was all too happy to give away your plans for Vay'kis. By now, Earl Arndyr will be dead. I am afraid it is over."

Magnus started his descent from the hall. He took the steps slowly.

What was it that Erik had once said? He could have killed his sister in three moves, for she was no warrior. He would like to test that.

Suddenly, Magnus frowned. Three moves.

Had not Erik engaged Astrid during her flight from the city?

He turned and glanced back towards the bloodsworn who stood with his sword to Laerke's throat. The cloak around Redleaf blew gently in the cool breeze and slipped back from his chest. It had been days since anyone except for Erik had seen the captive. Magnus' blood froze. There was no wound.

Laerke sneered.

"NOW!" Astrid roared.

Erik's sword sliced through Redleaf's rope bindings as he tossed the man his axe.

"FOR THE JARL!" the bloodsworn bellowed.

Surprise lit up the faces of Magnus' guards as Erik struck out with steel.

Astrid saw fear slip across Magnus' face as Erik made his move. Warriors fell beneath Erik's blade. He was an artist who painted with blood. Disarray and panic swept Magnus' ranks. They did not see the streets behind them fill with warriors led by Fargrim and Nenrir. They did not see the archers that led the newcomers. The first they knew of the attack was the song of the bows. Arrows rained down on their backs, while the streets were blocked by the few shield warriors that stood with them. Spears were thrown and they ripped into flesh and muscle. Everything seemed to grow still as Torben and the other encircled warriors charged into their foes.

Astrid felt the cool wind on her cheek as she began to walk towards the steps of the hall. She felt not the heat of battle nor heard the sounds of steel upon steel. Warriors began to fall in droves as the crew attacked from all sides. Torben rushed before her, two men at his back, and carved a path to the earl. Astrid's hand went to the back of her belt where her hand brushed the hilt of Sven's knife. The blade that had begun this war. Her eyes never wavered from Magnus as the last of his guards fell to Erik, Laerke, Torben and his men. Yet still men fought around the yard.

"I HAVE ONLY COME FOR MAGNUS!" Astrid shouted, her voice fierce. "Lay down your arms and return to your homes."

The fighting paused. Weapons were cast down. No one moved or made to leave. All eyes turned to Astrid as she walked towards Magnus. Redleaf took the earl's sword. Erik slowly walked down the stairs and made his way over to Astrid.

"Brother," she said quietly as she held out an arm.

He took it and then the two touched their foreheads together. She did not care for the blood that covered his face and ran through his hair. This moment was theirs, and theirs alone.

"Your will, my strength," he breathed.

Astrid fought back the emotion that threatened. He had risked more than his life by going along with her plan. Yet here they stood. Covered in blood and surrounded by the bodies of friend and foe alike. With Magnus at their feet.

"Erik," the earl muttered as he glared at Astrid. "Did he always stand with you?"

The jarl dipped her head and tapped her wounded arm. "Even when he gave me this."

"And the blood on the blade that you showed me?" Magnus turned his weary gaze to Erik.

"Every beast carries blood," the bloodsworn told him. "From the birds in the sky to the sheep in the fields."

Astrid glanced over her shoulder as more warriors began to filter into the courtyard. Men who were untouched by the fighting and with not a trace of blood among them.

"Explain yourself," called out one of the warriors. His face was drawn into a frown beneath his helmet, and yet Astrid recognised the man.

"Jarl Ulfric," she greeted the man. "My father often spoke highly of you. I am pleased that you did not join Magnus."

"You should not be here," the old jarl growled. He said nothing more, yet he seemed at war with himself. Did he go for his sword and lead his men against Astrid? Or did he do nothing?

"My place is here," Astrid told him. "This is my home. Magnus ordered the death of my father and came for us without warning. Many have died … I am here to collect payment for this blood debt. It is our law, is it not?"

Ulfric ground his teeth and gave her a nod. "So be it."

Astrid turned back to Magnus and toyed with the knife in her hand. "No one will mourn your passing," she said. "Nor will the Sea-Father welcome you into his halls."

"Tell me." Magnus met her eyes. He showed no trace of fear. "Was this all conjured in your mind?"

Again, Astrid nodded. "I knew you would attack us not long

after Sven's death. Erik and Laerke remained in Agartha to lure you into my trap."

"Many of your people died," he told her. "For no cause but your schemes."

Astrid snorted. "This was war, Magnus. People were going to die. At the end of the day, all of the pieces go into the same box. It is only how we live that makes a difference. You started this, not I. I knew that Erik could win your trust. However, I also knew that you could have placed a spy in my crew or even had eyes in Vay'kis. Which is why for a long time only my brother and Laerke knew of this plan. The only thing that was uncertain to me was whether Earl Arndyr would support my claim to your life. He was once your shieldbrother ... however, my father told me about his honour. I may have been uncertain, yet I believed that he would trust me. And as it would happen, he did."

"Arndyr or no, it does not matter. Take my life if you wish it, for soon enough Jarl Sigfried will return with three hundred swords at his back, and he will take your head."

For the first time, Astrid allowed a smirk to play across her lips as she twirled Sven's knife. "Sigfried won't be returning," she said.

Earl Arndyr and his ships had sat dormant for the better part of a day. There they waited, hidden in a cove not far from Vay'kis. Night had fallen when at last Sigfried arrived. He was not expecting to be attacked this far offshore. Astrid had been right about the path that Sigfried would take, and now he understood why she had sailed northeast and taken the long way. Sigfried's ships had sailed right by Arndyr's fleet in the darkness. Only then had the jarl of Vay'kis made his move.

Warriors roared as they charged across the gangplanks. Shields locked together as they ran in a double column. Blood covered the deck of Sigfried's ship in a dark wave as the men of Lumis slaughtered their foes. The warriors of Arndyr's guard, each and every one of the Arkin Garter, fought with the skill of the bloodsworn. They gave no quarter or held any thought of mercy. None could stand before them and live.

Arndyr Scaeva cut down a warrior and viciously caved his skull in with his steel-trimmed shield. He turned his hungry eyes to the jarl of Magnus' fleet and tossed his shield to the side. With a roar, he engaged Jarl Sigfried. Earl Arndyr's sword was as fast as it always had been as he attacked with the full fury of one born for battle. Sigfried blocked once and barely survived the follow-through. Arndyr's blade slid across his thigh. The earl cut through his opponent's fragile defence with his third strike and drove sword into flesh. Steel ripped into Sigfried's stomach and carved a path through his vitals. Arndyr gave his blade a savage wrench and spilled blood and guts across the deck.

"A game well played, Astrid," Magnus murmured as at last he understood. "A game well played."

The jarl of the Wind Rider glared at the man before her as she spoke. "And that is why you lost. This was never a game to me. You tried to take the things that meant the most to me. I couldn't walk away from that."

Astrid stepped in close as her next words were only for him. She could not keep the emotion from her voice.

"I win."

She raised Sven's knife and drove it into Magnus' throat.

FORTY-EIGHT

Cyneric's camp, Aedei lands, Forest of Salvaar

Twice they had caught sight of pursuers on their tail, and twice they had evaded them. No blood had been spilt, not even when Aeryn had one of the Catuvantuli in her sights and an arrow prepared to fly. The warrior had not seen them, and within moments the shaft was returned to its quiver. Kitara had asked her about it and the Aedei woman had merely shrugged.

"I kill to defend myself and others," Aeryn told her. "It is a heavy thing to take a life, and I would not do so absent cause. You ask this of me, yet I do not believe that you are one to kill for pleasure."

Kitara had met her stare and slowly nodded. "No, I am not," she replied. "I have only killed and will only kill to survive. Not for sport."

It took the better part of two days after the raid upon the slave camp for the three companions to reach Cyneric.

Aeryn whisked them through the Aedei encampment with few words. Kitara could feel eyes boring into them as they rode past the native warriors. One of their own, a moonseer, was held with the utmost respect. While a black-painted Káli warrior drew their curiosity, the girl with starlight hair, foreign clothing, who bore their own blue colours, drew their attention. For the first time that she could remember, Kitara felt no hostility from the people that surrounded her.

A great tent arose before them. It was covered in pelts and the skull and horns of a huge stag was attached over its entrance. Half a dozen heavily armed warriors stood at the base of the small incline leading to the tent. Their faces were awash with blue war paint. It was little wonder the Mierans called these people woads, for the swirling patterns of colour gave them an almost unearthly look.

"Welcome back, moonseer," called one of the guards.

"We need to see Cyneric," Aeryn told him, and she nodded over her shoulder to Kiernan. "This man must be heard."

"And her?" The guard flicked his gaze to Kitara.

Aeryn turned to face her companion before she replied, "She is with me."

"It will take us three days to reach the village of Oryn," Cyneric said as he glanced around at the men who filled his tent. "The Festival of Sylvaine begins in a matter of days. We will have to be quick, for there is no time to add to our numbers."

"We will make do with what we have, brother," Cailean told his brother. "Five hundred spears together with Bellec's men."

Cyneric slowly nodded. Lukas looked from man to man – the chief and his brother along with a third warrior, Bleddyn. A man who stood as the leader of Cyneric's guard was with them. Bellec, Sakkar and himself had been called upon, while the final member of the gathering was the black-painted Myrdren. The situation was growing desperate, yet there was nothing else to be done. The Káli man who had been with the chief upon his arrival, the one they called Myrdren, stood with them now. He had brought word from Vaylin that one of her villages had been taken by Henghis. The village was a vital borough created for the storage of grain. While her warriors were fighting along the eastern border of her lands, Henghis had sent men in from the south to claim it. Now Vaylin's army was stuck against her border, fending off the Icari and Malkor tribes. It meant they could only spare a few hundred warriors.

"Without us," Cyneric said after a moment, "the Káli will starve."

"Will we be enough though?" Lukas spoke up. "Even with the two hundred warriors that Vaylin has promised, we will have less than half their number. Not to mention we will be laying siege to a town."

Bellec snorted and glanced at the prince. "Numbers do not win a battle," he growled.

"No, they do not," Lukas replied with a glare. "I love a fight as much as the next fool, but if we are to do this, then the purpose and plan must be clear."

"You speak as if you have one." Cyneric frowned, gesturing towards the younger man. "What do you propose?"

The tent flaps opened, and words died in Lukas' mouth. One of Cyneric's guards peered in.

"Chief Cyneric, one of the moonseer has returned. She begs audience."

The great chief of the Aedei dipped his head in reply. The guard vanished and in walked an Aedei woman with silver eyes, a man of the Káli and Kitara. Lukas' jaw dropped. She was alive.

"Your return is a sight most welcome, moonseer," Cyneric said.

Kitara glanced at the massive warrior who, with his rich garb and proud pose, could only be the great chief himself. A few of the faces within the tent were unknown to her, yet she could barely restrain her surprise to see Sakkar, Bellec and Lukas once more.

"Kitara?" the Prince of Annora stammered. "You're alive."

"I would not be so easily from this world," Kitara told him.

Cyneric turned his gaze to Lukas. "You know this woman?" he asked.

He nodded in reply. "She rode with me, with us, from Miera. We would never have made it this far if not for her."

Kitara raised her eyebrows in surprise. Never had anyone been so quick to give her praise. The man who had taught her the sword, the one who hailed from Tarik, had once said that punishments should be handed out all at once so that it may give less offence. Praise should be handed out piece by piece so that it may be evermore relished. The beatings and bruises had been hard, yet every hurt was a lesson and had made her stronger for it. His praise kept her going.

"Chief Cyneric." Aeryn's voice brought her back to the present. The moonseer gestured to the Káli that they had freed days past. "This is Kiernan," Aeryn continued. "He rides with Morlag."

Cyneric's brow furrowed. "How did you get here? Vaylin believes you and her brother dead."

"We were taken, chief," the Káli warrior replied, "as slaves."

The air in the tent seemed to freeze.

"Impossible," Cailean growled. "Henghis would not go so far."

"He has not," Kiernan told them. "This is the work of his pet wanderer. He made a deal with those Medeans. Blood for slaves. Dozens have been captured, chief, bound for Aureia."

"Morlag lives?" the Káli who stood with Cyneric asked.

Kitara could not help but notice that, like Aeryn, his eyes were silver.

"He does, brother." Kiernan nodded to his kinsman. "We have to free him. All of them."

"Where?" Cyneric's voice boomed in anger.

"Two days ride south of here," Aeryn said. "There is a small camp. No less than fifty men. But they will be expecting an attack, chief."

"Fifty men, you say?"

The moonseer dipped her head as she spoke. "Their position is strong. Had Kiernan not been separated from the others, we could not have saved him."

The Aedei chief bared his teeth and snarled. "Then there is nothing we can do. Vaylin has called for aid, and I have sworn that we will be there. We are to ride tonight and meet her men at Oryn in four days' time."

"We cannot just abandon them to be sold as slaves!" Lukas cut in. The Annoran prince's eyes blazed as he turned to the chief in disbelief.

"I gave my word! Such a thing has meaning here." Cyneric ground his teeth. "I have barely five hundred men here. I cannot spare those it would take to do as you wish while still being able to aid the Káli. Henghis has a stranglehold on Vaylin's lands. If we do not ride at once, then the Káli may fall, and we would soon after suffer the same fate. There is only one path that we may take. We ride for Oryn. To the aid of our ally. When the Festival of Sylvaine is upon us, when the tribes gather, I shall tell Henghis of this barbarity. For I for one do not believe that this is of his knowledge or making."

"And what of the prisoners?" Cailean asked his brother. "What of Morlag?"

"They are in the hands of the spirits now."

Plans were made and the warriors in the tent went their separate ways to prepare.

"Kitara."

She turned back towards Lukas as she left the tent. He nodded to the side and gestured for her to follow him.

Kitara dipped her head before she looked to Aeryn. "I will see you soon?" she asked.

Aeryn lightly touched her arm. "Of course. Go."

With that, they parted. For the first time in near a week, they were separate. It felt almost strange to lose such a constant companion, even if for but a moment.

"How are you?" Lukas inquired once they were alone.

"Alive." Kitara smirked with a shrug. "A few cuts and bruises … Things that will heal with time. No more than that."

"I am sorry for what happened," he told her. "We wanted to find you but had no way of doing so."

"Have you ever known me to need saving?" Kitara allowed a chuckle. "But I am glad that you are alive. Truly."

Then she saw it. A shadow hidden behind his eyes. Paleness on his skin.

"There is something else?"

"Something has changed," Lukas said quietly. "It is not my place, but you deserve to know."

Kitara frowned. "Tell me."

The prince reached into one of his pouches and withdrew a thin chain. It was silver and held a ring. One most familiar to her. One that stood embellished with a sapphire. She took it from his grasp as emotion rolled within her. It was the twin of her mother's ring.

"How?" she stammered.

"The mercenary, Bellec," Lukas told her. "He is known by another name. Theron Malley. He was a captain in my father's guard over twenty ago when they rode to Salvaar. He is your father."

Anger. It was all Kitara felt as she stormed through the Aedei encampment. Her teeth were tightly clenched. She found the mercenaries easily enough, for they had set up camp alone.

Bellec – Theron – sat on a fallen tree beside the remnants of a fire. He was by himself. Kitara barely noticed Galadayne as he approached her. He could clearly see the dark intent in her eyes. He placed a warning hand out and grasped her shoulder. Kitara said not a world as she angrily shoved it off and pushed past.

"Bellec!" Galadayne yelled as Kitara took a hold of her sword and tore it free.

"GET ON YOUR FEET!" she roared as she charged towards

the man who claimed to be her blood.

Rage boiled within her as the mercenary slowly rose and turned to face her.

"Kitara–"

"Do not speak," she snarled as she crossed the distance between them and raised her blade.

She heard rustling feet and steel rasping from behind.

"Hold," Bellec commanded to the approaching threat.

No doubt Galadayne and the rest of his sellsword brothers were prepared to kill her if things went badly.

"Bellec–" Galadayne began.

"Galadayne, you will say nothing," Kitara commanded. She bared her teeth as emotion ran through her blood. She tossed Bellec the ring. "Is it true?" she snarled.

The mercenary met her eyes, revealing the truth before he at last spoke. His voice no more than a whisper.

"Yes. I did not believe it so. I thought your mother dead and you along with her."

There was pain in his voice, yet Kitara did not care. "You abandoned me," she snarled.

"I–"

"YOU ABANDONED ME!" Kitara bellowed as she raised her sword to his neck.

Bellec did not take his eyes from hers.

"I searched for you for fifteen years. Medea. Aureia. Larissa. Annora. Places beyond count."

"You actually expect me to believe you?"

Kitara felt emotion threaten to become tears. She held them back as she always had. She would not show this man such weakness.

"I swear it is the truth," he told her, sorrow etched in his voice. "I had given up hope. That is until word reached my ears that a golden-haired woman had been found in Miera. A woman with Salvaari blood who wielded a sword as well as any man. One who crossed from Annora. One of your age, my child's age."

He did not wince as Kitara pressed her blade closer. A single thrust would spill his blood and end his life.

"We were on our way to Carlian to learn the truth when we crossed paths. Had you not shown that boy your mother's ring, we would never have met."

Kitara gripped her sword tightly. She knew he spoke true. It was as clear as glass. The truth hurt.

"I grew up scared and alone because of you," Kitara cried. "I lost everything because of you!"

"Would that I could turn back the sun and save you from that fate," Bellec whispered.

"I should kill you. By the gods, you deserve it," she told him as she adjusted her grip.

The mercenary set his jaw. "You are my daughter and will always stand as such."

"Wanting something does not give you the right to have it," Kitara said through gritted teeth. She took a breath, and slowly lowered her sword. "Stay away from me," she ordered.

The camp grew quiet as the girl turned and began to march away, sheathing her sword.

Bellec started after her. "Kitara, I …"

She spun. Her hand snatched up her knife and launched it in a heartbeat.

Steel sliced through the air before the blade pierced the bark of a tree beside the mercenary. It sank in deep with a dull thud, level with Bellec's head.

"I said stay away!"

Kitara found Aeryn as the moonseer was making ready to leave. Two saddled horses stood with her.

"We ride together," the Aedei told Kitara before her expression changed and her eyes widened. She could see the pain in Kitara's gaze. "What happened?" Aeryn asked.

"Bellec ... he is my father. There is no lie."

Aeryn pursed her lips. "And how does that make you feel?"

Kitara met her eyes. One emotion had kept her going over the years. One thing had allowed her to survive the horrors that she had endured. It was that which tormented her each day and broke her sleep each night. One feeling directed at the man who had abandoned her. She felt it now rising deep inside. She could barely keep it in check.

"All I feel is hate."

They rode within the hour. A great line of horses and warriors headed west towards the lands of the Káli. They joined with Vaylin's force of two hundred a mere two days from Oryn. There, the commander who led the Káli, Eirian, met with the Aedei to forge a plan. Vaylin herself remained in the north besieged by the Icari. It was decided that the three moonseer in the army, Aeryn, another Aedei moonseer and Myrdren, would leave the column and deal with the enemy outriders and scouts. Meanwhile, an infantry attack led by Cyneric and Bleddyn would attack from the front. Two contingents of horsemen, led by Cailean and Eirian, would attack the village from the sides, for Oryn had no walls. Lukas would join the battle with Cyneric. The prince had some ideas. Ones that he had read about in books about the great Aureian generals of old.

The moonseer had been unleashed and so there was nothing to do but wait. Days passed by and the men grew restless. Then Myrdren returned. He was not alone. Lukas felt his jaw nearly fall from his face. With the Káli rode another man. One whom he knew well. Clad in brilliant silver armour, with a long red cloak and a longsword at his hip, was the most familiar of faces.

"Sir Garrik?" Lukas stammered as the master-at-arms dismounted with a grin. "What in the gods' name are you doing here?"

The knight fell to a knee before him and bowed his head. "Prince Lukas."

"Found him and his men a half a day west of Oryn. Barely three from the western border," Myrdren explained.

Lukas held out an arm and the Annorans embraced to the roar of the Salvaari, Aedei and Káli alike.

"We came looking for you," the knight told the prince as he clasped Lukas' shoulder.

"My father sent you into Salvaar alone?" Lukas frowned. That seemed most unlikely.

Garrik shook his head. "No, he did not. And alone, no. I ride with a complement of the guard."

"How many?"

"Three hundred strong. The king wanted us to wait in Sergova until we were reinforced," Garrik told him.

"Then you are well met indeed." Cyneric appeared at Lukas' side with a toothy grin.

The pair clasped arms.

"Thank the gods that your man found us when he did," the master-at-arms said with a nod to Myrdren. "I fear that we may well have attacked the Káli, thinking them to be our enemy, as we were once told."

Lukas frowned. "Why would the king send you to Sergova?"

"Much has changed, my prince," Garrik told him. "I will explain after the battle is won."

"Then go, return to your men." Eirian spoke up. "Once the battle is joined, ride in from the west. We will hammer them from every side, allowing no escape. Together we give the Catuvantuli battle. And together we shall drive them from these lands."

Lukas felt his heart quicken as they left the cover of the woods and began to close on the village. It lay not even one hundred paces away. Each step brought them closer to battle. Horns sounded within Oryn as they were spotted. Cyneric drew his sword and raised it above his head with a great roar. The war cry echoed down the line as one by one the warriors took up the shout. The village swarmed with activity as the Catuvantuli began to appear in droves. They banded together to face the army that had begun to descend upon them. The pace stayed the same. A steady walk to hold the line. Lukas had a plan. He could see the Catuvantuli clear as day as slowly one man became one hundred and then more. Kiernan had said that the red warriors numbered near to one thousand. Lukas adjusted his grip on his shield. Once plain, now it bore three great streaks of blue woad across its surface – an easy way to tell of his allegiance in the chaos of battle. Sakkar stood at his side with a small shield strapped to arm and his bow held firmly in his grasp. Lukas felt a tingle run down his spine as the Catuvantuli answered Cyneric's roar and began to charge towards them. They drew nearer and the prince's heart began to race.

Forty paces.

Thirty.

Twenty.

"SPEARS!" Lukas bellowed.

As one, the front two ranks of the Aedei let lose a volley of steal-tipped shafts. He could almost see the fear in the eyes of the Catuvantuli as the wave of spears ripped into their ranks. The steel killed many and sent dozens of men to the ground in a spray of blood. Lukas could barely keep at bay the savage grin that threatened to spread across his lips as the first row of red warriors was all but destroyed. The Aedei charged forth and crashed into the decimated front ranks of the Catuvantuli. The battle for Oryn had begun.

✦ ✦ ✦

Kitara's hair streamed behind her as they galloped through the trees. Aeryn rode at her side, while ahead was Cailean. They rode two hundred strong. All were covered in blue war paint. Under ash and oak, they rode as they swept around to the north of the village. They rode hard, for the cries of battle had already begun. Bellec and his men were with the Káli riders who at this moment would be circling around to the south. Cailean flicked his reins to change their course. Then they were hurtling to the south. Towards Oryn.

Houses flicked by as the riders charged into the town, their weapons held aloft and vicious cries upon their lips. The thunder of hooves drew the attention of the Catuvantuli who turned towards them. There was no sign of fear upon their faces. They formed a solid line. The streets made it hard for cavalry to manoeuvre and took away much of their advantage. Aeryn's bow sang. Her arrow ripped into a red-painted chest. With a roar, the cavalry swept into the Catuvantuli. They crashed into their foes with the force of a great wave.

"Keep moving!" Cailean bellowed after cutting down a man with a vicious thrust of his spear. "Use the streets. Surround them!"

Kitara kicked her heels in as the column divided. She raced down alleys and side streets in an attempt to contain the Catuvantuli. In moments, she rode with no more than twenty of the Aedei, their number growing fewer still by the moment. Half their number sped off down another alley. They vanished from sight and left no trace save the clash of steel. A large building of carved wood arose before them. A long hall. Its doors were barred shut from the outside. There was a bang, and the doors thudded. A scream followed.

"There are people in there," Kitara murmured.

"The villagers," one of the Aedei cursed.

Kitara bared her teeth and slid from her saddle. "We have to help them," Kitara cried.

One by one, the Aedei dismounted and followed her as she

made her way towards the hall. Aeryn ran to Kitara's side with an arrow nocked in her powerful bow. Their eyes were wary, and their heads moved on a swivel. This town was not yet safe.

"There," Aeryn said, nodding down one of the streets.

Catuvantuli warriors, perhaps a dozen, rounded a corner and saw them. Lips curled back into snarls. Weapons covered in blood. Bodies awash with red. Kitara adjusted the grip on her blade.

"My blood for Kerrigan!" the leader of the Aedei called as he thudded his axe into his round shield.

The rest of the warriors joined in. The chorus of their axes echoed around them.

"My heart for Yorath!"

The warriors cried out and Kitara felt her pulse quicken.

"My life for Sylvaine!"

The cry grew louder. Shields thudded and fists pounded.

"My sword for Tanris!"

The Aedei roared, and their foes charged to meet them. Aeryn felled the first man, an arrow deep into the depths of his throat. He fell. Kitara only felt calm as she stepped forwards. The street was open. There was no crowd. Here she could move. Here she was untouchable.

Lukas bellowed as he brought his warhammer down and caved in his enemy's chest. Blood washed over his face as the Catuvantuli vanished at his feet. The prince spun as he took a blow upon his shield. He shattered the man's skull in reply. His arm had begun to grow weary. Yet here, on the doorway between life and death, he felt the most alive. He had nearly laughed when Sir Garrik and the royal guard of Annora had crashed into the rear ranks of the red warriors. They had carved their path to Cyneric's men effortlessly. Cyneric's plan to encircle the Catuvantuli in a ring of steel had worked. They had begun to flee down the main road towards the safety of the forest. There they could have formed up and used their superior numbers. It had been then that the hidden Annoran cavalry had swooped in and hit the Catuvantuli as they fled. That strategy had been all Lukas. The Catuvantuli were falling in droves.

"ANNORA!"

The cry rang to the heavens. Garrik and a contingent of his men had forced a hole deep into the ranks of the Catuvantuli. The prince grinned as the Aedei surged forwards all around him. The battle was all but over. Garrik vanished in a blur as one of the red warriors leapt forwards and tackled him from his horse. He disappeared into the melee.

"WITH ME!" Lukas bellowed.

He raised his shield and barrelled forwards into the Catuvantuli line. He had to reach his friend and mentor. Sakkar tightened his grip on his blood-covered khopesh and charged after his prince. The Catuvantuli line buckled, and Lukas pushed his way through. He all but ignored the men he passed. The Aedei rushed to his side. Their number barely halted the wave of swords and spears that descended towards him. He saw a flicker of movement through the crowd. Garrik's back was to a wall as he fought three men. A fourth man rushed towards the prince. Lukas roared as he hurled himself forwards.

He slammed his shield into the man's oncoming sword. His fire-filled blood gave him strength and he barely felt the blow. His hammer cut a path through the air and knocked the man's blade aside. Lukas' shield hammered into the man's face and sent him from his feet. Lukas let loose a battle cry and he drove his weapon down. The prince abandoned the hammer and savagely pulled his sword free. He tossed his shield aside even as Sir Garrik cut down one of his foes. The Catuvantuli fell. He was dead before he hit the ground. Garrik turned to the last. Too late. The bladed point of a spear drove towards his flank. Garrik spun. He danced aside as the steel glanced off his armour. Surprise flashed across the Catuvantuli's eyes before Garrik's sword drove deep into his vitals. The knight did not see the red warrior come at him from behind. Too late did he hear the footsteps in the mud and the snarl rising above the din of battle. Garrik turned to see the hate-filled eyes and the axe held aloft. Garrik raised his blade. Lukas' sword skewered the Catuvantuli from behind. The tip of his blade pierced his back and erupted from the Catuvantuli's chest in a fountain of blood. The prince heaved his sword free and pushed the lifeless corpse to the ground with a roar. He gazed at the master-at-arms.

"This is no place to die," he told Sir Garrik.

The streets ran red with blood as the last of the Catuvantuli fell to the blades of the Aedei and Káli. Lukas found himself walking absent-mindedly through Oryn. He was alone save for the sword in his hand. The steel was, like him, slick with blood. He heard a thud come from a nearby house. Lukas frowned and made his way towards the building. It was as plain as any, just another pagan hovel. He tried the door, but it was barred from the inside. His frown deepened. Lukas slammed his boot into the wood. Whatever had kept the door locked snapped, and it flung open. The house smelt strange. He entered the darkness. It was musky. A thin tendril of light slipped through the cracks of a closed window. He heard a light footfall followed by the unmistakable whoosh of moving cloth. Something glimmered and Lukas instinctively angled his sword up.

Steel rang as Lukas barely blocked the axe aimed at his neck. Hot breath assaulted his face, and he saw bared teeth and wild eyes. Lukas drove forwards with all his strength and pushed the axe aside. He lashed out. His sword narrowly missed the stomach of the warrior before him. He had given himself enough space to see the room though. A large cell filled most of it, and behind those steel bars knelt a woman. Her eyes were closed and from her lips she mumbled some kind of chant. The Catuvantuli attacked without warning and heaved his axe forwards. Lukas deflected the blow. The Catuvantuli's fist crashed into the prince's jaw. The pain was fleeting as the punch rocked him backwards. The prince stumbled to the side and spat out a mouthful of blood. The taste of iron filled his senses. It engulfed him. It fuelled him. Lukas' eyes turned back to the warrior as anger rolled through his body. He raised his sword and levelled its tip at the man. Lukas thrust his sword as he leapt towards his attacker. The Catuvantuli's axe was deflected to the side and sent away from his centre line as Lukas had planned. The prince tackled the man and sent them both crashing to the ground. Steel rang as sword and axe bounced across the floor. The red warrior beneath him lashed out, but Lukas knocked the fist aside. The prince drove his freshly drawn dagger forwards and punched it deep into the man's chest. The warrior screamed. Lukas met the warrior's eyes and saw a flicker of fear. He drove the dagger down again. Again, and again, and again. Each blow sent forth a new wave of blood. Lukas stared into the eyes of the red warrior as he stabbed. Ten times. A dozen. He did not care. The light had long since left his gaze. The prince tossed aside his knife and slowly rose to his feet. His face was a mask of crimson. His breathing was laboured.

Lukas snatched up the keys that adorned the dead man's belt. He turned his attention to the cage and saw that the woman was watching him with curious eyes. Her lips were curled into something of a smirk. It was as if his actions had amused her. Those green eyes of hers seemed shrouded in darkness. Her ebony hair was wild and filled with braids covered in beads. A line of black paint was splashed across her face. Her dark dress was sleeveless, baring her rune-covered arms. Short bracers and an arm ring adorned her wrists. A curling snake-shaped bangle was wrapped around her bicep. There was something about her. She had some kind of an aura. She walked like a panther as she made her way over to the cage bars. Her emerald gaze peered deep into Lukas' soul.

"Who are you?" the prince asked.

He was unable to lower his gaze as he slid the key into the lock. Her eyes were like a bottomless pit that drew him in and ensnared him.

"A witch, some call me," the woman replied, and her tongue was as smooth as that of a snake. "Others, a priestess." The musical sound of her voice sent a shiver through Lukas' body. "I serve Tanris. Hear me. Know me for who I am. Venture into the dark so that you may awaken. I am Maevin."

Lukas turned the key.

FORTY-NINE

Sergova, Duchy of Aloys, Medea

"What do you mean gone?"

Prince Dayne of Annora kept his tone calm and his face expressionless. He had come all this way and expected the master-at-arms to be here with three hundred men. He had expected to ride into Salvaar, and war, together. Yet Sir Garrik was absent the city.

"Sir Garrik and his men rode out shortly after arriving, my prince," Alejandro Aloys replied.

Dayne clasped his hands together. He did not let even a flicker of his irritation show. He had mastered his emotions long ago.

"Where?" Prince Dayne asked.

"East," the duke told him.

The duke turned to face a great banner embellished with his family's crest. A mighty white lion atop a golden field.

"Now, I require a favour," the duke said.

Dayne met the man's eyes. He was searching for any hint, any sign, of falsehood.

"Then speak it," Dayne said.

"The time has come for my son to be blooded. When you ride for Salvaar, Emilian will travel at your side, along with five hundred of my own guard."

"As you will."

Dayne pushed all thoughts of annoyance from his mind as he left the duke's palace. Instead, he turned his thoughts to the task at hand.

Plans always changed. Whether you wanted them to or not. Once more he was forced to adapt. He arrived at his command tent as a new plan began to form. Edmund Hornwood, Elion Montbard and another of the Annoran nobles, Harold Robare, had joined him. They met him first in Alejandro's court, for they were his commanders, and then again in Dayne's own tent. Together their lordships controlled most of western Aethela. Vast plains that merged into the Steppe of Miera. As such, their people had adapted over the centuries and their armies formed much of the feared Annoran heavy cavalry. A force that was as vital to the crown as life itself.

"The tides have changed," Dayne told them, "and so must our path."

"What do you suggest, lord?" Edmund asked while stroking his chin.

The crown prince glanced at the man as he clasped his hands. Hornwood was ten years his senior and had served in Salvaar and countless other battles. Though not known for his skill at politics, his skill as a warrior was a thing well admired. He would be needed in the days to come.

"What I suggest, Lord Hornwood, is that we do not wait for Sir Tristayn to reinforce our position. For if we do, three hundred of our brothers may be lost. Together the three of us here have two thousand horses at our command. In the last war with Salvaar, our heavy cavalry changed everything. Aloys has also pledged half his guard. Sir Garrik marches straight into the lion's den – snake pit even. For he rides into Káli lands, and to those vile poison worshippers', cruelty knows no bounds. We must act. We must ride."

"Once more those pagans will know our steel." Hornwood

nodded as a hungry light flashed across his eyes.

"Indeed," Harold Robare added. "This time we are wise to their tricks."

Dayne looked from man to man. He felt a tingle run down his spine. Once more he would be tested. Once more he would prove his worth. He was ready. He had studied the works of each Salvaari tribe in great detail. In so doing, he knew them better than he knew himself.

"And so, in the wake of our kinsmen, we take the road east. We go with the gods," Dayne said.

Lukas closed his eyes as he splashed water over his battle-stained face to cleanse it of blood. Drop by drop, the iron-tasting red mask slid from his features to once more reveal the face of a prince. He looked into the barrel of water as he washed. He could see his reflection on its rippling surface. Lukas frowned for a moment. His lips pursed. He was satisfied with what he saw. He was more weathered than he had been a month ago. His face was slightly thinner and the beginnings of a beard had begun to grow.

"Well fought, prince." Chief Cyneric clapped the younger man on the shoulder. "My father once told me that a single raindrop can raise the sea. Perhaps one man can make a difference after all."

Lukas placed a hand on the Aedei chieftain's forearm. "I did not fight alone. This victory belongs to your people, and those of the Káli."

"Aye." Cyneric nodded thoughtfully as he removed his hand from Lukas' shoulder. "Surrounding them was my idea, containing the Catuvantuli to the streets where they could not use their numbers. But giving them a single path out and then catching them as they fled – that was your strategy."

"A cornered beast will fight back harder than one who thinks he can escape," Lukas told him.

"Where did you learn that?"

Lukas met his eyes and forced back the grin that threatened. He knew exactly what Cyneric's response would be.

"I read about it."

The chief frowned for a moment before a massive grin spread across his lips and a laugh erupted from them. "Keep your secrets then. It is clear that the spirits favour you."

Slowly, the leaders of the alliance began to sift into the town square. Bleddyn, ever the constant companion to Cyneric, Eirian and the black-painted Káli trudged into the square. Cailean appeared from the north and dismounted from his powerful steed. Lukas gave his friend a nod in greeting.

"The few survivors have fled, chief," the warrior called out as he approached. "Leaving with their tails between legs."

"A day they will not soon forget, I am sure," Cyneric replied.

The cry of a hawk came from the heavens. All eyes went to the bird as it soared above their heads. Lukas did not need to look to know who the bird called to. Sakkar held an arm aloft as he gave a single whistle. Sabra glided down towards his master before gracefully perching atop the Larissan's proffered arm. Sakkar stroked the bird's beak and nodded down the street.

"They come," he said.

The prince turned to see Aeryn appear. She rounded the corner, bow in hand, and began to make her way towards the square. At her side was Kitara. Her face was covered in the woad of her people. They were not alone. Eight Aedei warriors were with them, and in their wake were dozens of Káli. Men, women, old folk and children. Few among them stood as warriors.

"The people of Oryn," Bleddyn murmured.

Eirian grinned as he strode towards his kinsmen. It was hard for Lukas not to smile as the Káli general clasped arms and hands with his people. Many it appeared knew the man. Perhaps he had been from here long ago.

"Found them locked in a hall," Kitara explained when she reached Lukas.

"They're free now," Cailean said as elation spread across his face.

Sakkar thumped a fist on the Aedei's shoulder. "Aye, that they are, big man," Sakkar said.

Sir Garrik and the other Annorans began to emerge from the streets. Blood had turned their armour to the colour of their cloaks.

They rode tall and proud. Eirian strode up the four stairs that lead to the great pillar in the very centre of the town square.

"My friends," the Káli general called in his mother tongue, silencing the caw of the crowd. "In three nights, the festival of the Great Queen Sylvaine will be upon us. The skies will be painted and once more the streets will be filled with celebration. I beg you, do not let the events of days gone by cloud your mind. For this night, we drink. We laugh. We honour the dead. The village of Oryn has been reclaimed for the Káli!"

A great roar swept the square and fists were thrown skyward. Friend embraced friend, and brother embraced brother.

"He speaks true," Cyneric told Lukas. "With the festival fast approaching, we must ride for the grove come dawn. There is no time for delay."

"Understood," the prince replied.

"Your highness." A voice called above the crowd.

Lukas turned to see Sir Garrik making his way through the Salvaari. Three other guardsmen stood with him, while another, covered head to toe in a red cloak, walked in their midst. There was something clouding the master-at arms' face.

"What is it?" Lukas asked with a frown.

Garrik stepped aside and the shorter figure in the red cloak tipped back the hood.

"Kassie?"

His voice was incredulous. His face paled. The princess threw herself into her brother's arms. She wrapped her limbs tightly around him. Lukas returned the embrace as he fought to compose himself. He had missed her greatly. Questions assaulted his mind. Her hair was rugged and hung no further than her shoulders. Her face and clothing were stained by travel, and she looked half exhausted.

"I've missed you," her muffled voice said.

"I've missed you too," Lukas told her as he stepped back. "But you should not be here. Why are you not in Palen-Tor? Why are you not with our father?"

Kassandra looked him in the eye. She looked more confident than she ever had in the palace. "I had to find you."

"Lord, I–" Garrik began.

Lukas turned his murderous eyes upon the older man as he cut him off.

"You brought her here? You brought her onto a battlefield?" The prince dropped a hand to his sword. "If so much as a hair on her head had been harmed, you would have died screaming. As it is–"

"I am fine," Kassandra interrupted. She placed a calming hand on her brother's arm, and with her other hand took his cheek. "Do not blame Sir Garrik for my choices. I ordered him to bring me here."

"You should not have listened," Lukas told the knight as his anger burned. "Do you even know what you put at risk?"

"Lord, I made a vow to the Twins to protect your family. I would sooner take my own life than see harm befall your sister. I tried to send her home," the master-at-arms replied. "I tried."

"Only if he had," Kassandra added, "I would have been forced to tell Father that his most trusted advisor had taken his only daughter. How do you think he would have reacted to that?"

"That was cruel," Lukas told her. He ground his teeth together. His anger had given way to annoyance. Finally, something of a smile tugged at his lips. "You are becoming a fine schemer it would seem. Dayne would be proud," Lukas said.

Kassie snorted sarcastically and shot her brother a glare.

"Sir Garrik, you have my apologies. You risked more than your life to help me, and for that I am indebted," Lukas told the knight with a nod. "What you have done here and for keeping my sister safe, it shall not be forgotten."

"I only did my duty, lord. For you and for the Lady of Annora," Garrik replied.

Prince Lukas gestured towards a nearby house. "Now come. Tell me everything."

Come nightfall the bodies of the dead, on both sides, had been burnt and sent through the veil into the spirit realm. The city had not yet been repaired of damage, yet the drink flowed, and the music grew louder by the moment. The people of Oryn danced and celebrated in the streets beneath the stars. They embraced Aedei and Annoran alike as brother. The mercenary, Kompton, who rode with Bellec had pulled forth his lute and now his music filled the town. Kitara could not help but grin as she made her way through the crowd. They were a happy people, these Salvaari, a people that lived life with each breath. They cared not for race or religion, only for the next person that they could share drink with.

Sakkar sat by one of the brilliant fires. He had gathered up a pair of torches and set them ablaze. All watched on with wide eyes as the Larissan began to move. Slowly at first, yet full of grace. He moved in time to the music, and his dance grew faster. His torches spun through the sky and seemed to ignite the darkness. He launched one of his burning brands skyward. Sakkar's boots slid across the earth, and he caught the torch. He twirled it with a flick of his wrists. Kitara made her way over to Lukas as Sakkar became a whirlwind of flames.

"Your man always must be the very centre of attention," she told him with a grin.

"If there was another way to live, he would not know it," the prince replied as he held out his drink.

Kitara smacked her cup against his, and then together they drank.

"You're the one who bested my brother with a sword?" the girl next to Lukas asked.

The girl's gaze was on Kitara. Kitara nearly choked as she attempted to hold back the bursting laugh. She ran her eyes over the young girl with short brown hair. The stranger was wearing the cloak of an Annoran royal guard.

"And quite handedly too, I might add," Cailean said as he appeared through the crowd with a grin covering his lips.

Lukas glared at the girl. "She got lucky," Lukas said.

"Then you should not press your luck," Kitara countered, and she gave him a devilish smile before she turned to the young lady who sat at his side. "And you must be this Princess of Annora that I have heard so much about. The one who all but lead three hundred fierce knights to her brother's aid."

Kassandra grinned as her cheeks burned. "Her, I like," she told Lukas.

The drums grew faster. Sakkar whirled and dropped to his knees. He raised a torch, its flames near licking his lips. Then he breathed out and sent a jet of fire through the air as if it was his own breath. The crowd roared their approval.

As the night wore on, Kitara found herself sitting alone in the woods atop a fallen tree. She pulled a knee to her chest as she perched on its smooth bark. Her eyes peered out into the forest. Something tickled her ear. Her hand went to her knife as she spun around, only to see Aeryn standing behind her. The moonseer held an arrow in her hand and wore a mischievous grin upon her lips.

Kitara felt a laugh leave her mouth as she released her blade. The moonseer had tickled her ear with the feathers of her arrow.

"You're back." Kitara smiled as the silver-eyed woman joined her on the tree.

Aeryn nodded as she returned arrow to quiver. "The eastern road is silent and will hold no threats when we leave here tomorrow," Aeryn said.

"That is good," Kitara murmured. She gave her friend a sidelong glance. She had missed Aeryn's company in the wake of the celebration.

"You have not spoken of it," the moonseer said after a moment.

"Hmmm?"

"By the bank of the river … What you saw," Aeryn said as she met Kitara's gaze. "Your eyes."

Kitara shrugged as they drifted into silence for a moment. What she had seen and felt had only happened twice before in her life.

"In truth," she began, "I do not understand it. For a moment, it is like I can feel everything around me, the plants and animals, the trees and even the air itself. That much sight, that much knowledge, it hurts. I cannot control it. Before, I thought that it would only come at night and wake me from my sleep. Yet it is not a dream."

"A dream of a dream perhaps," Aeryn said quietly, and she pursed her lips. "You say it gives you sight?"

Kitara nodded. "The man who came upon us, the Catuvantuli, I knew of his presence long before he left the cover of those trees. Before even you knew of him."

"And in that moment, your mind was not your own," the moonseer murmured.

"I could hardly think let alone act upon what I had seen," Kitara told her.

She could remember the almost blinding pain. It had felt as though her mind was being ripped in two.

Aeryn reached out and gently placed her hand atop Kitara's.

"I believe that whatever this vision is, it is a gift that cannot be ignored. You could learn to control it. Direct it even. When we are first found as moonseer and are taken for training ... when the sight first comes, it terrifies you in deepest night. We are taught to not think about it ... It is the fear of what is happening. The fear of what you are that gives you pain. Too many thoughts, no? When you learn to empty your mind and think only of this gift, then it shall become as such."

"Those words you spoke by the river, the ones in your own tongue that pulled me from the dream ... Can you teach me?"

"Of course." The moonseer smiled.

Kitara ran her thumb over Aeryn's hand. She was comforted by the woman's touch.

"Aeryn?"

The moonseer met her eyes. Kitara bit her lip. She finally felt the pain, the rage, fade. The anger was a part of who she was. It was a thing that had always clouded her.

"You asked me once what I feared most of all. I told you nothing, but that was a lie. What I fear most strongly is that I am not worthy and will never be worthy of anything or anyone."

"Then let me tell you something." Aeryn leaned close. Kitara could feel her breath hot upon her cheek as their foreheads touched. "For all that you have lost, for all that you have suffered, you have remained true to who you are. You are worthy. And soon they will all see it."

Kitara felt emotion stir once more, but this time it was not anger or rage. It was in that silver gaze that she felt the new emotion come to life. Those mysterious yet compassionate eyes, more beautiful than anything she had seen before. The curl of lips when she laughed. Kitara gently ran a thumb across Aeryn's cheek. She pressed her lips to those of the moonseer. She felt Aeryn smile as the Aedei returned the kiss.

✦ ✦ ✦

Lukas found himself lost in thought. His empty cup was held loosely in his hand. Sir Garrik and his sister had informed him of his father's plan for Kassandra. As it had happened, Kassie had overheard the discussion between Dayne and Dorian by using one of the secret passages that ran through the palace, passages that Lukas himself had shown her in years past. The idea of a marriage between Annora and Aloys bothered him. More so the fact that his father had finally sent forth his army. This time, King Dorian would not be leading his men north. This time, it would not be a man so accepting of pagan ideal that led them. It would be Dayne. A brother who Lukas loved with all his heart, yet a man whose blood ran with that of the Twins. He would be leading the heavy cavalry in advance of the main army. Men who found leadership under the likes of Edmund Hornwood. A man with a sworn hatred of all things Salvaari and all things heathen.

Lukas caught a pair of emerald eyes staring at him through the crowd, a gaze so green and dark that it seemed to pierce his flesh. The gaze belonged to Maevin. The woman whom he had freed. She beckoned him with a nod. A shiver ran down his spine as Lukas rose to his feet. He was drawn in by the strange aura that surrounded her. Cailean grabbed his wrist as he began to make his way towards her.

"Be careful, prince. She is dangerous."

Lukas placed his cup down and dipped his head towards the Aedei. If one of the Salvaari, if a man such as Cailean, said that this woman was dangerous, then he would be on his guard. He buckled on his sword and set off after the woman.

He found Maevin alone at a fire where she stood awaiting his arrival.

"You have the blood of a king," she said smoothly.

Her voice was as dark and mysterious as its bearer. She began to circle the flames and Lukas began to do the same.

"And king's blood holds power," she purred. "You know who I am?"

Lukas' hand stayed atop his sword as he moved across the earth. It was as if he was in a kind of dance with the Káli woman. Maevin looked through the flames and met his eyes.

"The Dark One has shown me a great many things. Things that were and things that may be. You walk a treacherous path, Lukas of Annora."

The prince clamped his hand down on the sword at his hip to stop a tremble from rolling through his body. It was not fear. Of that he was certain. He could not place the feeling.

"Who are you?"

Maevin's face flickered as shadows met the light of the flames. She looked savage as her lips twitched into an almost malicious smile. Maevin pulled something out of one of her pouches and Lukas could see the grains of some kind of sand fall through her fingers. The witch chanted something in her own tongue before she hurled the sand into the flames. Orange and crimson turned to the brightest green.

"A priestess," she told him as she circled the fire.

It was as if she was stalking him. The light of the fire washed over her skin showing the dark symbols that covered her arms.

"A seer, a witch, a lover. I am whatever my lord Tanris needs me to be."

"What do you want?" Lukas asked as he stared through the emerald flames.

"I know who you are, Prince of Annora. Who you really are," she told him. "More than just the second son to the crown, the child of a mother long past. Eclipsed by a brother whose deeds become songs that are sang in every hall. Beholden to rules that seek to make you their servant. Forced to turn away from the impulses and instincts that drive you. Behind that mask that you wear so well, behind the lies that you tell, falsehoods that even you believe. I know you. You who remains in the shadows cast by other men. You who longs for the light, yet only darkness can reveal you."

"Tell me what you know," the prince said. He was unable to take his eyes from hers.

"You did not come to these lands for the sake of honour. You came because you cannot be held to the law of man. Because defying those who believe themselves your betters is intoxicating. You know in your heart what you are. And it longs to be set free," she replied.

Her feet glided across the soil as she circled the flames.

"You take a joy from killing. In taking life from another. I have seen it, for did you not take pleasure in striking down the man who had locked me behind bars? It was in your eyes, in your very heart. I have seen it. Tanris has seen it."

Lukas took a deep breath. He could still see the Catuvantuli's eyes. He could still see the fear in them. He had struck him again and again. He had revelled in the sight. It was all he could do to keep the vicious smile from his blood-covered lips. It was a side that he had long since hidden behind composure and pleasant manner. Yet here, far from the walls of Palen-Tor and the rule of better men, it had begun to stir.

"I like to look into the eyes of my enemy," he said, his voice cold, "to see their souls … to see how they are afraid of me."

"There is darkness in everyone, yet so few are willing to taste it. Remove your mask, and with it your shackles," the priestess told him. "Let Tanris guide you. Stand aside from those who would call themselves your betters. Away from the rule of man. For the Dark One is beholden to no rule but that of his own. Only then will you be free to do as you will. Only then can you accomplish greatness."

FIFTY

North Sword's Peak, Valley of Odrysia

With the end of the journey in sight, the knights rode hard. North Sword's Peak, one of the twin mountains that stood as a gateway to the valley of Odrysia, stood less than half a day's ride away when they made camp for the final time. The last of the orange rays of the sun had slipped beyond the horizon and Matias wanted them well rested for whatever task lay ahead.

"Durandail, lend me the strength to see this through," Kyler murmured.

He knelt alone on the cold earth not far from the camp. His eyes were closed and in his hands he clasped his amulet.

"Show me your light, show me the way. For that is why I am here, to do your bidding."

The boy knelt in silence for a moment longer. He could feel the cool northerly breeze against his skin. He arose feeling a warmth kindle in his heart and in his soul. His faith gave him strength and protected him from the demons that plagued this world in their varying forms. For with all his being, Kyler knew that he who knelt before the gods could stand before anyone.

"Kyler."

The initiate couldn't help but smile as a warm hand slipped into his own. He had not heard Elena approach. He turned to face the woman who he had grown up with. The woman to whom he had long ago given his heart.

"What tomorrow brings, we do not know."

"It is in the hands of the gods," she told him, and she rested her head against his own. "I am prepared. We all are. Whatever happens, whatever comes with the dawn, know that you are half my soul and all of my heart."

"Just as mine belongs to you."

He gently ran a thumb across the soft skin of her cheek before lifting her chin and gazing deep into her amber eyes.

"In this life and the next. Forever," he whispered to her.

Kyler leaned down and kissed her. He felt nothing but joy as it washed through his veins. Here, beneath the stars, it was just the two of them. There were no thoughts outside of each other.

The great mountain arose before them as the midday sun reached its peak. Its rays shone brilliantly down upon the glistening armour of the Knights of Kil'kara. They rode in tight formation around the two maija. Their sapphire cloaks flew at their backs in a blue wave, and their eyes gazed fiercely at North Sword's Peak. The open plain gave way into a thin forest as they drew nearer. The hooves of their horses thundered against the earth. They were forced to slow their pace as the forest grew thicker. Kyler felt his heart begin to race as they rode. There was something about this place. The woods around them seemed to be alive. The column slowed and came to a halt as the ground beneath began to rise into the base of the mountain.

"What is it?" Sir Corvo asked as he looked to Elena who had given the signal.

"I'm not sure," she replied as she bit her lip. "The path we now take is that of the clue. It takes us to the south side of North Sword's Peak. There in the shadows it lies still, what was lost shall be found, by Durandail's will. I think this message left by Duran speaks of more than just a cave. What if there is some kind of chasm, something to cut off the light of the sun? What if ..."

Elena let her sentence fade as she peered into the forest. Nearby, some kind of bird cried out and then flew from the canopy. Kyler heard it too, or rather he felt it. Everything had grown silent. Corvo turned his gaze to the ground and with a frown, he dismounted. His boots dug into the soft soil beneath. He moved away from the column and crouched.

"Matias," the Sword of Kil'kara called out.

His eyes went from the ground into the forest. His voice was tense. The warden slid from his saddle and made his way over to Corvo.

"Tracks," Sir Corvo told him.

A few of the other knights followed their companions to the ground and began to explore the clearing. Hands lingered atop swords.

"Here," Sir Neph cried. He dropped to knee as he caught sight of something. Kyler shared a glance with Elena before he dismounted and followed the Larissan. A chill ran down Kyler's spine as he saw what the man had discovered. The remnants of a campfire.

"The ash is still warm," Neph muttered as he ran a hand through the remains. "They are close."

Sir Corvo rose to his feet. His dark eyes gazed out into the forest. "SHIELDS ON ME!" he roared as something took his gaze.

Instinct took over as the knights sprang into action. They dashed to Corvo's side and brought their shields to bear. Kyler tightened the straps around his arm as his eyes followed Corvo's gaze. He saw a glimmer of silver, and then they trickled out of the trees. Men clad in the rough attire of mercenaries. They were armed with an assortment of sharp swords, axes and long spears. Five men became ten. Ten became twenty. More. They were outnumbered. That much was certain.

"SWORDS!" bellowed Sir Alarik from further down the line. His powerful voice echoed around the clearing. "SWORDS!"

As one, the knights drew their blades and locked their shields together in an impenetrable wall of steel and wood. The hungry eyes of the bandits lit up as they began to advance upon the knights.

"We hold them," Sir Alarik commanded as he angled the blade of his sword atop his shield. "We give no ground!"

The mercenaries began to advance without so much as a word. They were here for one purpose alone: to kill the Knights of Kil'kara.

"THE GODS ARE WITH US!" shouted Sir Matias.

Kyler's blood began to race as the mercenaries charged.

"KIL'KARA!" the warden bellowed.

"KIL'KARA!" the knights echoed.

The two sides came together in a bloody collision.

Kyler slammed his shield forwards and punched it into the face of his attacker. The dazed man stumbled back half a step and Kyler's sword found his throat. Hard training paid off as the Medean moved on instinct alone. He used his shield as a weapon as much as he did his sword. Another warrior took the fallen man's place. He drove his axe hard into Kyler's shield.

"PUSH!" Sir Alarik roared.

Kyler gritted his teeth and drove his shield forward. The line of knights rippled as they heaved and sent their enemies back a step. Shields slipped to the side and swords darted out. Many drove home into the flesh of the mercenaries. Blood washed over Kyler's hand as his blade sank deep into a man's stomach. He pulled his sword free, and his shield came back to bear. The wall reformed.

"FORWARD!" the battlemaster cried.

The knights roared and stepped forwards. Once more they met the mercenary line. Their enemy drove forwards once more and pushed against the shield wall with all their strength. Kyler grimaced. He could feel his muscles strain as he fought to hold ground.

"PUSH!"

He heaved and threw the man back. His sword moved fast. It darted forwards and sliced through the flesh of the mercenary's thigh. The man cried out in pain as Kyler retracted his blade.

"BREAK!"

The knights charged forwards. The wall disintegrated as they crashed into their foes. Space began to open up in the battlefield as the knights surged into their all but defeated enemy. Kyler deflected with sword and shield as he traded blows with a man. He did not notice the sweat that coated his body nor did he feel the blood hot upon his face. He threw his shield up to block an overhead strike. Kyler snarled as he took the full force of the blow. It left his foe exposed. Kyler plunged his sword deep into the mercenary's chest. He savagely wrenched steel through the man's vitals before he tore his blade free. Kyler stepped back as the man crashed to the ground. He gazed around the clearing as the last of their attackers were cut down by Corvo's blade. The Sword of Kil'kara pulled his crimson weapon free and viciously knocked the dead man down with his shield. Something flickered through the trees.

"MORE COME!" Sir Alarik bellowed as more brigands made themselves known.

Sir Corvo clamped his hand down on the battlemaster's shoulder. "Go, brother, that is an order," Corvo said. "Take eight men and the maija and see this task done. I will hold them here. Leave now!"

The brigands charged as the knights once more formed a wall of steel, this time between their brothers and the enemy.

Kyler snatched up his reins and leapt onto Asena's back. Sir Alarik set a brisk pace. He led them on a gallop through the dense forest as it rose to meet the mountain. Kyler rode with the battlemaster, along with Matias, Emir, Neph, Torin and three of the other knights. The mountain had begun to grow steep when they came across the thin entrance to some kind of chasm. It was all but hidden in the side of the rocky mountain and barely passable in single file. The knights had dismounted not far from the chasm and left their horses in the cover of the tree line. From there they had made their way to the crevice. A small crescent moon and sun had been carved into the stone.

"It's here. Has to be," Quinn murmured as he ran a hand over the carving.

"Neph, Emir." Alarik glanced at the two warriors. "Watch the doorway."

"Sir," they replied.

Matias gathered up three branches and wrapped a strip of cloth around each of them. One by one, the torches were lit with flint stones and handed out. Then, with a drawn sword, Alarik led the way into the mountain.

The chasm was dark. It cut off the rays of the sun within ten feet. Only the flames of the torches gave them any kind of light. The air began to grow still as they walked. The stones underfoot echoed with each step. Chills coursed through Kyler's body as the walls of the chasm seemed to close in around them. They were alone save for the gods. He made a silent prayer and tightened his grip on his torch. Slowly, the chasm grew wider.

"By the gods," Sir Alarik murmured from the head of the column.

Kyler felt his breath stop as he walked into the opening. There, barely five paces away, was some kind of stone door. Carvings covered its surface. A great crescent moon wrapped around a flaming sun with rays that drove out in every direction.

Elena pursed her lips and approached the stone. Her eyes peered at a small hole that plunged deep into the rock beside the moon. "It's a keyhole," she said.

"But what key?" Torin asked with a frown, and with wide eyes he suddenly turned to Quinn. "The cryptex."

All eyes went to the maija as he reached into his satchel and withdrew the wooden object. Slowly, he began to work. He slid the segments of the cryptex around and one by one they clicked into place. Kyler fought to contain his excitement as finally Quinn glanced up at the knights. He turned a final segment.

Click.

A small piece of wood popped up from the middle of the object. Quinn pulled it free with a tug. Kyler brought his torch closer at a gesture from the maija. Something within the cryptex glimmered. Quinn reached in and pulled it forth. There, in the palm of his hand, sat a key. He handed it to Elena who, without hesitation, inserted it into the hole and turned it. Something grated within the bowels of the stone and dust shot out from around the door. The stone door moved back slightly and then halted. Sir Alarik bit his lip before he planted his shoulder against the stone. He heaved with all his strength. Stone squealed. The door opened.

Sir Neph gazed around. His eyes flicked through the trees that surrounded them as they stood sentinel over the chasm. Whatever lay within the cave, he prayed it was something that could finally unite their faith under one banner. He gave Emir a nod as the pair locked eyes for a moment. His hand never strayed from his sword. Whatever happened, whoever found them first, whether it be more mercenaries or Sir Corvo, he was ready. He had been ready for this moment for all his life. Neph cast his gaze around. How he hated the woods. Who knew what threat lay beyond the next tree. His hand tightened on his sword. He barely heard the sound of fabric move. Then he felt pain. Steel slid into the side of his throat. It carved a path through his unprotected neck. He tried to cry out as he fell, but all he could manage was a splutter. The last thing his fading eyes saw was a dark flicker as a shadow stepped over his body and launched a blood-soaked knife. It ripped into Emir's neck with eagle-like precision. The Berenithian knight crashed to the ground.

✦ ✦ ✦

The orange light of the torches flickered against the walls of the cave illuminating the carvings that adorned the straight stone walls. There were images of Durandail and Azaria, images of the first Knights of Kil'kara, the original seven who banded together as warriors of their great faith. The cave was shaped as a circle and every inch of the stone walls was perfectly aligned. One by one, the torch-bearing knights all placed their blazing brands in brackets that adorned the walls. The entire chamber filled with light. The magnificent carvings that ran along the walls were forgotten as the knights and maija saw a sight that took their breath away.

"It cannot be," Kyler murmured as he laid eyes upon it.

He felt both his heart soul soar. At the end of the chamber, atop a small stone dais, stood a pair of statues. Both were forged with stone. Both were as alive as the people who gazed at them. One stood as a woman. She wore the robes of one far greater than even the arc'maija. A band of steel, encrusted with a large diamond moon, was wrapped around her brow. An open book was carved into one of her hands, while her other hand lingered over that of the statue to left. She stood as Azaria. To her side stood a warrior in his full glory. He was clad in brilliant armour with a sheathed sword at his side and a golden sun upon his breastplate. Like the woman, a crown sat atop his head. It was imbued with a similar gemstone in the shape of the sun. He gazed to his left where his hand stretched out towards the woman. Both their eyes locked on an object that their hands held tightly. A great spear of the purest silver.

Matias dropped to his knees before the figures and bent his head low in deference. All the company did the same.

"Durandail, Father of all Fathers," the great knight said as he closed his eyes, "you have shown us the way into the light, your light. Durandail, Father of all Fathers, for this gift, we will offer you no shame. Help us to right our path and to restore the honour of our creed."

Sir Matias rose to his feet and his brothers joined him. The warden gestured towards the silver lance.

"Sir Alarik, the honour is yours, brother. See it done. Bring us Durandail's Spear."

The battlemaster gave his friend a nod before he made his way towards the dais. Kyler could not take his eyes from his mentor, just as he could not stop his breath from stilling. This was a mighty gift that they had been granted.

Sir Alarik bowed low to the figures of Durandail and Azaria before he reached out to wrap his fingers around the shining spear. The knight gave it a tug before he pulled it from its stone embrace. The silver shaft flickered in the firelight. It shone gloriously before them.

"Behold, Durandail's Spear," the battlemaster said as he held the weapon aloft.

Kyler felt his heart fill at the sight. He did not see the small silver canister as it was hurled into the chamber. He only heard the thud of it striking the ground. An explosion assaulted his ears. The room filled with smoke.

Grey mist was belched forth. It swallowed everything from sight. It filled Kyler's eyes, his nose and lungs. He coughed and gasped for breath as he pulled his sword free. The light of the torches flickered through the smoke and painted the scene an eerie shade of orange. The screams began. Kyler could see neither knight nor maija. Not even his own feet. Chainmail rang as a body thudded to the ground. Kyler felt fear threaten to engulf him. One by one, their cries lit the chamber and were all too soon extinguished.

Footsteps.

Kyler whirled around and brought his sword to bear. Something heavy struck the ground at his feet. He glanced down and an icy chill of dread seeped into his bones. It was Torin. The man who had found him in that godforsaken tavern in Malcia. The knight who had been as friend, a brother even. He lay still. His eyes were unseeing. Blood pooled from his ruined throat.

Instinct made Kyler turn, and the sound of moving air made his blade slice up. Steel rang as sword met sword. Too fast was his foe. A blade hammered down and struck his own weapon from his grasp. It bit into his leg as he tried to step back. Kyler screamed. He stumbled back and fought to catch a glimpse of his attacker. The mist was too thick, and all he could see was a man-shaped shadow. The sword lashed at his face. It sliced across his helmet as he tried to evade the steel. Kyler fell back and crashed into a stone pillar. The pommel of a sword cracked into his face. It split his lips and slammed his head back into stone. Again and again he was struck. He lost track of thought and memory as the blows rained down on his helmet and unprotected lips. Blood covered his ruined face. It spilled down from his nose and mouth. Only his helmet stopped his brains from being spilled. Blood ran through his hair and trickled from the back of his scalp. The hilt smashed into the side of his head. His vision flickered.

Then he fell. Kyler struck the hard ground with a sickening thud. He couldn't move. He could barely breathe. He gasped for breath. Everything blurred as darkness descended, yet he could see. The smoke began to fade around the chamber and slowly filtered away into nothing.

Sir Matias stood alone between the dark-clad man and the Spear. Their attacker gazed at the knight, a longsword held tightly in his grasp. A dark, padded gambeson covered his chest and upper arms. Steel bracers adorned his wrists, while a long knife sat at his belt. His head was covered by a brown hood, while an equally as dark cloth covered his face. Only his eyes were left bare. A short cloak hung over his left shoulder. He stood as a demon belched from the depths of hell as he materialised from the smoke. Wa'rith. The shadow. Only Sir Matias stood against him. The rest lay scattered around the bloody chamber, lifeless to the last. Every blow that they had received had been true. Not just the knights had fallen. Quinn too lay bereft of breath. Sir Alarik lay against a pillar gasping for breath as he tried to force his wounded body to rise. Behind Matias was Elena, knife in hand as she stared at the man who had killed so many. He moved. Blood dripped from his sword as he levelled it at the warden.

"KIL'KARA!" Sir Matias cried as he wrapped both hands around his blade.

Kyler could only watch as the knight charged forth. His sword arced towards the dark man's neck. Wa'rith nimbly stepped aside and let the weapon slice harmlessly by. His body flowed as he countered. Steel rang as the blades were joined in deadly contest. Sickening dread took a hold of Kyler as one of the best warriors in his order was pushed back step by step, blow by blow. Wa'rith slipped through his opponent's defence and struck the warden hard upon his wrist. Only the steel armour stopped the sword from piercing flesh, but it was enough. Wa'rith lunged forwards and used his left hand to latch onto Matias' shoulder. He stopped the knight's counter while he drove his blade forward. The chamber had not finished echoing from the warden's snarl when steel drove deep into Matias' throat.

The chamber faded into silence. It was only broken by the ringing of the warden's sword as it hit the stones. Wa'rith ripped his blade free as the knight's lifeblood washed across steel and stone. Matias fell. Wa'rith, the monster who plagued the knights' dreams, stepped towards Elena. Kyler gritted his teeth and felt blood seep into his mouth. His feeling returned as he forced himself to move.

"YOU!" Sir Alarik's powerful voice boomed. "Fight me or die on your knees!"

The battlemaster had risen to his feet. Despite the blood, despite the wounds, despite the pain, he stood against his enemy. Wa'rith turned from Elena without a word and moved towards Sir Alarik. Steel met steel as one of Durandail's chosen met with this demon.

Kyler struggled. He had to help. Alarik's blade was knocked to the side. The knight was barely able to hold on as he was pushed back. Matias had fallen to this demon's sword uninjured, and now the veteran stood alone covered in his own blood. Unyielding. He was ready to give his life for his gods.

Someday, I'll be a knight.

Those words echoed in Kyler's mind. Words that he had spoken as a child. Words that had changed everything. His hands balled into fists as a new strength filled his veins.

Wa'rith struck his sword down into Alarik's raised guard and locked steel against steel. His free hand clamped down on the blade of the battlemaster's weapon as he stepped to the side. Wa'rith angled his sword and flicked his wrists. With a savage wrench, he pulled Sir Alarik's blade from his grasp.

Someday, I'll be a knight.

Kyler pushed himself to his feet. Wa'rith dropped his own sword and wrapped both hands around the blade of Sir Alarik's. The hilt of the battlemaster's sword, now in the grasp of his enemy, slammed into his head. Alarik fell to his knees. Blood ran from the knight's ruined lips as Wa'rith spun the weapon and took it by its hilt. He raised the sword to finish the battlemaster.

Kyler roared as he barrelled into the man. He took the demon from his feet and then they both crashed down. Steel flew from his enemy's hand. Kyler rolled and reached for Wa'rith, but the man had already gained his footing. Kyler took out his dagger and sliced at him. Steel kissed air as Wa'rith leapt back. He reached out. Searching, his hand found leather. Alarik's sword. Kyler snatched it up and lashed out. Wa'rith dived to the side and rolled as he hit the ground. Kyler gasped for breath and bared his teeth. His head pounded as a sliver of blood ran down from his wound. He planted Alarik's sword on the hard earth and heaved. He used the strength of the blade to help him rise unsteadily to his feet. The battlemaster lay at Kyler's back, weeping from a thousand wounds.

Kyler lifted the sword and tightly wrapped his hands around its hilt. His breathing was heavy, and his body ached. Yet still he stood. He would not back down. He would not turn from his mentor. He would not turn from his gods.

Kyler's bloody lips curled into a snarl as he roared, "KIL'KARA!"

Wa'rith turned to face him. His hands clasped the weapon of a lifeless knight. He held the fallen warrior's crossbow. Kyler's eyes barely had time to widen as the bolt hit him. Air was driven from his lungs as a great weight slammed into his chest. He tried to move. His sword fell from his grasp. He tried to speak. Blood burst from his lips. The pain washed through his body like fire as he stumbled and then crashed down. He heard Elena scream. Darkness took him.

FIFTY-ONE

The Sacred Grove, Forest of Salvaar

The days that followed the battle of Oryn were filled with wariness. The scouts were sent out by the day and the moonseer patrolled with them. Eyes watched the trees as the Aedei column rode east. After four days of doubt and hard riding, the night gathered around them. The moon was at its peak. It began. The moonseer returned as the sun slipped beyond the horizon, for the sacred peace had begun.

Cailean's mount snorted beneath him. The first sign that things were about to change. They had nearly reached one of the great lakes, barely three miles from the Sacred Grove, when Cyneric held up a hand and turned to face his companions. Bleddyn and Cailean rode at his side, while behind were the Larissan clansman, Kitara, Aeryn and the Prince of Annora. Bellec and his second rode further down the column with the rest of the sellswords.

"It begins," the chief said as he slowed his horse to a walk.

Lukas turned his gaze skyward and peered into the thick canopy above. His heart raced and anticipation flooded his body. A purple glow had begun in the night sky. The trees shielded it, yet it became clear as they continued on their path. The colour grew brighter by the moment.

Cyneric led them from the cover of the trees to the very banks of the great lake itself. Not one eye gave the waters a second glance.

Lukas' eyes widened and he heard the Aedei mumbling prayers in their own tongue. The sky had been painted the richest purple. Great rays of violet light danced through the night. It took his breath away, for such was its beauty.

"I have never seen such a sight," Lukas murmured.

"It is a glorious thing when Sylvaine paints the heavens," Cailean said with awe as he stared high above. "Now do you believe?"

The prince could not help his head from nodding ever so slightly. Perhaps the stories that he had been told, the fables he had heard, did in fact have a hint of truth behind them. These people, this place, this magic interested him a great deal.

"Perhaps the stories are more than just stories after all," he conceded.

Cailean snorted as he replied, "Perhaps."

The tribes gathered at the Grove one by one. The paint on their faces separated them. Despite the war that still raged, both sides met in harmony. Drinks were shared between Aedei and Icari, Sagailean and Catuvantuli. Such was their respect for the spirit mother Sylvaine. Large campfires roared to life, as the drink flowed, and lit the forest with orange and red. Song, dance and laughter echoed through the trees as the Salvaari gave themselves over to their sacred festival. Lukas glanced at Kitara and Sakkar who sat around one of the great fires. Like him, they knew nothing of this culture nor of the spirits.

"Tell us about Sylvaine," Lukas said, looking to Cailean.

"Sylvaine was born five thousand years ago. She was the first woman," the Aedei told him, gazing deep into the flames. "Everything we are, everything you see around us – the trees, the wind, the sky – she forged it all."

"She is a queen," Cyneric added. "A queen of spirits, of magic. Of the moon. Of life itself. Sylvaine is both mother and prophetess. But most of all, she is freedom, in every sense of the word."

Lukas frowned as they spoke. "And these spirits ... they rule everything?" he asked.

Cailean grinned at the prince. "No, my friend. They give us the freedom to choose. We are not made to bow or submit. They command us only to be wise. To live life with every breath, with all your heart," Cailean said.

Lukas slowly nodded as he fingered the sun and moon amulet beneath his shirt. The spirits were not as harsh and severe as Durandail and Azaria. They did not demand that you conform to their rules and wishes as the priests of the Twins so commanded.

"And this magic?" Lukas asked.

Across the fire, Kitara and Aeryn exchanged a glance before the moonseer looked at Lukas.

"Sylvaine painted the heavens. Tell me, is this gift not some form of magic in your eyes?" Aeryn asked.

"I suppose."

All eyes turned as the sound of footsteps drew near. There was half a dozen of them. Faces painted green, bodies covered in sleeveless tunics and woven vests. Thick woollen sashes were looped from shoulder to hip, while their frames were muscular and strong.

The red-haired woman who led them spoke first. "Greetings, Chief Cyneric."

"Etain of the Icari." Cyneric dipped his head in respect.

So, this was the one who Cailean had once spoken of, Lukas remembered. The one who stood as a fearsome warrior. The one beloved by the people.

"My men wish to share drink," Etain told them before she turned her gaze to Cailean. "And I would break words with you."

"So, you have returned." Etain glanced at Cailean as they walked beneath the trees. "And with the aid of Annora, no less."

He nodded. "Few enough have come. For better or worse, I do

not know."

"Have faith," the Icari chief said and gently wrapped her fingers around Cailean's wrist. "Have faith in the spirits, in your tribe."

"Everything I have done I have done for my people. To end this war or die in the attempt," Cailean murmured. "I know my path." He placed his hand on top of hers.

"The spirits came to me last night." Etain met his eyes. "The winds have changed. Can you feel it?"

"With all of my heart, I know it to be true. The spirits grow restless, and the trees whisper. Something has happened," Cailean replied. He had felt it upon his return to Salvaar, and he could still feel it in his blood. "Everything is about to change," he said.

"No matter what happens we are bound. You and I."

"Always."

Kitara spun as her sword sliced through the air. She marvelled at the blazing violet light of the sky dancing across her blade. She kept her movements slow and precise as she worked. Each form was as perfect as the last. It was often said that duels were won in the first few seconds of the conflict, whether it be by the sword or the mind.

Aeryn sat against a tree and gazed intently at her hands as she worked. The Aedei moonseer held a lump of wood in one hand and carved into it with purpose. Her hands knew exactly what they were doing.

"This place is beautiful," Kitara said as she slowly sheathed her sword. She gazed into the purple sky for a moment before she closed her eyes and breathed it all in. "Wild and dangerous perhaps," she continued with a smirk. "Yet peaceful like the eye of a storm."

The moonseer looked up at her and bit her lip.

"There is so much here that I do not understand and maybe I never will." Kitara frowned and waved her arms. "I don't know. I'm not a poet."

Aeryn gave her a sly smile. "I can see that."

Kitara returned the look. "What I do know is that this place is the first that I have known an untroubled sleep in many years."

"You belong to this place," the moonseer told her. "Same as me."

"Aye, I think I do."

Kitara saw Aeryn's ears prick long before she heard anything. She followed the moonseer's gaze to see a man gliding across the earth towards them. He almost rocked from side to side as he walked, while the deep hood of his gnarled robes was pulled over his head. A pair of black orbs gazed out from within, eyes that drew Kitara's stare. Aeryn slowly rose to her feet as he approached.

"Peace be with you this night, daughter of the moon," came the man's melody of a voice.

As he drew closer, Kitara could see the runes painted upon his flesh and the scarring carved through the skin of his face.

"What is it you desire, druid?" Aeryn asked, unable to tear her gaze from the man.

Aeryn's voice held a trace of fear. So, this was one of the druids that Kitara had heard so much about. Men who served the spirits and did their bidding. Men who crossed into the other plain to commune with their deities. Dark men.

"It is not of you that I require anything, moonseer, nor have the spirits called your name" he said, turning his soulless eyes towards Kitara. "The spirits' voice is in the wind, in the earth, in the rivers. The voice was clear, and I hear very clearly. The Great Queen Sylvaine has summoned you. You who is daughter to the forest, yet outcast to all. You who is no one of nothing, yet the spirits themselves have called your name."

Kitara felt a very real shiver run down her spine as the druid spoke. His words were powerful, as if another force spoke through him. He looked into her eyes, through them, into her very soul.

"I need you to come with me, and I need you to come with me now."

Kitara shared a glance with Aeryn before she alone followed the druid into the forest. For when the druids spoke, you obeyed.

The druid led the way through to the Sacred Grove without breaking a word. At the base of the hill, they met with the twelve leaders of the Salvaari tribes. Nearly twenty others also gathered there. Surprised looks mixed with glares turned towards Kitara as they approached. A few of the chieftains mumbled among themselves. Kitara ignored the looks and made her way over to Cyneric. The Aedei chief frowned as he saw her approach and turned from the three who stood with him.

"The druids summoned me," Kitara explained. "I do not know why."

"You will not speak of what happens next," Cyneric told her fiercely. "It is sacred to our people, and you must not utter a single word about which you bear witness too."

"I understand," Kitara replied.

Yet it was a lie. She did not understand at all.

"It is exceedingly rare, yet not unheard of," a dark-haired woman said, slowly circling Kitara, "that others are chosen."

Her face was coloured with black paint, while her tongue was smooth. Her full lips seemed to curl halfway between that of a suitor and that of scorn. This was Vaylin of the Káli, and no doubt the other two tribal leaders who stood with Cyneric were those of the Coventina and Sagailean.

Kitara flinched as Vaylin ran a finger through her blonde hair. She met the Káli chief's gaze with a dark glare. If the druids had not taken her weapons, she might have drawn steel. Vaylin's lips twitched, and her eyes flashed daringly.

"The druids are the eyes of the spirits," Balor of the Sagailean cut in and nodded towards those who did not stand as chief, "and like them, they must think you have some part to play."

Kitara turned her gaze from the Káli chief to the group of Salvaari. They came from all clans, and she recognised none among them. None save for Lukas Raynor.

"Yes, they chose him too," Cyneric told her. "Though why, I do not know."

"It is time," one of the druids called as he gestured to the path that ran up the slope of the hill.

The druids led the way in silence, and Kitara could see awe upon the faces of the twelve chiefs. Whatever this ritual was, it was of great importance. They reached the top of the hill upon which sat a huge tree ringed with a circle of stone.

"As one cycle ends, so another begins," the man who stood as shaman called out in his own language as his dark eyes stared towards the crowd. "You must now surrender yourselves to the spirits. For we stand under their gaze beneath the moon and burning skies."

He slammed his staff into the ground. The chanting began. The musical voices of the druids rose in their own tongue. The tongue of Salvaar.

Cyneric glanced to Kitara and Lukas who stood at his side, and quietly translated the words.

"Hail to she who was the first. Hail to she who is the prophetess."

The chanting grew louder by the word until it filled the night.

Kitara stared at the druids as the sound drew her in. Her blood ran as fire.

"Hail to the Great Queen. Hail to the Mother. Hail to Sylvaine!"

Silence.

Then she appeared, almost materialising out of the darkness. A woman. Her eyes blazed the same violet that danced in the sky. Her hair was raven black, and her face, ethereal and beautiful beyond measure. A long black skirt hung from her hips, while equally as dark wrappings covered her shoulders and breasts. Beaded necklaces hung from her throat and leather bindings adorned her arms. Her right hand clasped a large wooden staff. Its surface was covered in intricate carvings, while its end was twisted. The shaman and druids bowed first, and then the chieftains and the chosen followed. Her bare feet made not a sound as she glided over the earth and walked into the very centre of the stone circle before the great tree.

"My children," she said in the tongue of Salvaar, "the time has come again. The time of rebirth, and so the torch must be passed once more. Here and now at the turning of the tides. Here and now when everything is about to turn dark." Sylvaine turned to the druids who stood around another. "Bring forth the girl."

Kitara watched as the druids stood aside and revealed a woman no older than she. Her long red hair was pushed back, and a thin braid ran down behind an ear. From her clothing alone, Kitara knew her to be Icari. Her sleeveless tunic revealed strong, muscular arms, while a red and green sash ran across her body from shoulder to hip. A wide belt held it in place, while a silver brooch attached it to her shoulder. Unlike Sylvaine, the girl's eyes were nought but hazel. Like the spirit, she was a great beauty. Sylvaine planted her staff in the ground and beckoned the Icari woman. They stood mere inches apart. They were face to face and their eyes were locked as the younger woman spoke.

"I am prepared."

Balor of the Sagailean thumped his fist into his chest. One by one, the other leaders followed suit.

Thud. Thud. Thud.

The druids once more began to chant. The shaman himself joined in. Ravens cried out in the trees above. A wolf howled. The grove sounded as a great heartbeat rolled through the earth and echoed across the stars. Kitara found herself adding to the chorus with her fist. Everything slowed.

Thud. Thud. Thud.

Sylvaine leaned towards the Icari girl as the sound grew ever louder. Their lips near touched as the great Salvaari spirit breathed out. A grey mist spilled from her throat. It rolled like a wave against the other woman's face. The Icari opened her mouth and drew the mist in. The chanting grew deafening as the ravens and wolves sang.

Sylvaine collapsed. She crashed to the ground as if lifeless. The Icari girl fell to her knees. Her eyes slammed shut.

Thud. Thud. Thud.

Her eyes opened. They blazed with purple light. The chanting ceased. The thumping stopped. The cries of bird and beast ended. Silence.

The girl screamed.

She rose to her feet. Her hair fell like fire to her back. She took up the staff and gazed towards the assembled.

"HAIL SYLVAINE!" they roared.

The girl was merely a vessel, Kitara realised as she gazed towards the spirit mother.

The druids helped up the fallen woman who had moments ago stood as Sylvaine. The violet of her eyes had faded and was replaced with nought but green.

"Tomorrow there will be a bloodmoon," Sylvaine said, her voice strong and filled with power. "And many more in the days to come. My children, great things draw near, and you must be prepared to sacrifice everything. For if you do not, the sun will not rise again."

Sylvaine slowly, in almost a trance, walked down the line. The Salvaari dropped to a knee and bowed in deference as their spirit mother extended a hand and let it glide mere inches above their heads. She said not a word, yet something about her silence spoke only of unyielding strength. Then Sylvaine stopped for a moment. Her hand hovered over Kitara's head.

"I am sorry, my child," she murmured in the common tongue. It was all she said before she moved on.

Kitara felt her blood freeze as the words echoed through her mind. She had never been one to believe in any spiritual force or even magic for that matter, but there was something about Sylvaine. Something about what Kitara had just witnessed gave her great concern. It made her blood freeze.

The great spirit reached the end of the line and made her way back into the circle of stone. There she uttered something in Salvaari. Ravens once again cried out before flying down into the grove and circling the spirit queen. A wave of dark feathers engulfed her as she looked to the heavens. Then she vanished as suddenly as she had appeared.

"The new vessel stands as Icari," Dáire of the Coventina murmured as they rose to their feet. "The first since the great purge."

"What does that mean?" Lukas asked.

Cyneric could not tear his eyes from where Sylvaine had vanished into the night.

"The highlanders' blood runs with fire and their word is iron. They stand as the truest of warriors. This means war."

"Henghis," Cyneric called out as the assembly began to disperse. "A word."

The great chief of the Catuvantuli turned to face the Aedei. "And what word might that be?"

Many of the tribal leaders stopped to watch the confrontation between the two rivals, for the blood oath sworn a moon before still stood. Raigath still needed to be fulfilled.

"Slavery," Cyneric growled.

Cyneric angled his dark gaze towards the wanderer Kendrick who stood at Henghis' side. He raised a hand and pointed towards the man. "That snake is taking hostages and selling them to Medea."

"You dare impugn me, Cyneric?" Henghis snarled. "You know that you cannot weather this storm, so you spit upon everything we hold dear? Accuse me and mine of the most vile of barbarities? Have you no honour?"

Cyneric bared his teeth. "He is poison, Henghis, and will drag you to ruin. The Káli—"

"Broke their oath!" the Catuvantuli warlord bellowed.

"Because of that madman at your side," Cyneric spat. He stepped towards the wanderer, and his voice filled with loathing. "How do you answer, coward? Or have you given up your tongue as well as your spine?" Cyneric snarled.

Kendrick took a step closer to the Aedei. "I do not know of what you speak. To condemn others to slavery, to life behind bars," Kendrick murmured as he shook his head, "I am Salvaari."

Cyneric snorted as his lips curled. He met the worm's eyes. "Barely."

Many had stopped to watch the confrontation as it unfurled before them. The druids stood silent, and their dark eyes looked on.

"I tell you now," Cyneric said to all, "this man is not of the spirits. He is for himself alone and will do anything to sate his greed and dark appetites. And I ask you, where are those Medean knights that he brought to our land? For they are not here at their master's call. No, they deal in lives at this pretender's command."

Kendrick spat upon the earth. His hate-filled eyes bore into the Aedei chieftain. "You call me a pretender. You who became chief because of what I did. Your brother lies rotting in the mud, his body nothing but carrion for the crows. And oh, how they feast."

Cyneric felt rage boil up inside him. His face contorted with anger, and then he snatched out his dagger.

"NO!" roared one of the druids as Cyneric went for the wanderer, his eyes wild.

Rough hands took him and stopped the Aedei chief in his

tracks. He snarled and bared his teeth as he strained against those who held him.

Kendrick smiled darkly.

"You dare desecrate this place with steel this night?" the druid shouted as he strode towards them. "The spirits do not forget."

"Nor do I!" Cyneric bellowed as he tossed down his knife. He pushed off the hands that held him and glared towards the leader of the Catuvantuli. "Henghis, let us end this. I challenge you. Single combat. To the death. Beneath the gaze of the spirits. Come break of day, I will have your life."

Henghis met his eyes and set his powerful jaw. "So be it."

The square was formed as the first light of dawn crept over the horizon like a wave. The violet light of Sylvaine had long since slipped away. It was replaced once more with the sun's orange rays.

Cailean felt nought but nerves run through his body as he handed Cyneric his sword. The chief took it with a nod, and the two brothers touched their foreheads together.

"For Malakai," Cyneric murmured before he turned to face his foe.

Like the Aedei warlord, Henghis was stripped to the waist and covered in crimson red war paint that clashed against Cyneric's sapphire blue. Like his foe, he carried a round shield. He flexed his fingers around its grip as he took his sword from Kendrick.

Cailean backed away to the edge of the crowd. His hand tightly clasped the hilt of his own blade. He had seen many single combats before, but never had Cyneric fought in one.

Dozens had come once the word had spread. The chieftains of the twelve tribes as well as many of their people. Kitara, Aeryn, Lukas, Sakkar and even Bellec and his mercenaries watched on. The place they had chosen stood not far from the Sacred Grove.

The Stones of Tanris. It stood in a small clearing and its ground was paved with stones. Pillars carved with runes surrounded the square.

The air grew still as the two warriors faced off. Cyneric stood as a great bear. His body was covered in rippling muscle. Henghis stood as a panther. He was shorter and leaner, yet his gaze showed nothing but ice. Cyneric raised his sword, and the crowd cheered. Henghis lifted his own blade, and the cries grew deafening.

"Here upon the sacred Stones of Tanris will this grievance be made clear," the great shaman of Salvaar called. "Let the Dark One make his will known, and may we honour him with blood this day."

It began with a snarl as Cyneric charged forth. His sword arced through the air towards his hated foe's neck. Henghis took the blow on his shield and slid to the side as he retaliated in kind.

Sweat ran down Cyneric's powerful body as sword met with sword. The song of steel sounded through the clearing as they came together in a deadly dance. He punched out with his shield and threw his full power into the blow. It slammed into Henghis' buckler and sent him backwards. Henghis' feet scrambled for purchase on the stones. Cyneric continued forwards. He rained down blow after blow as he pushed his enemy back step by step. Inch by inch. Everything was blocked out by Cyneric. The roars of the crowd, even the rage inside him was far removed. Sword slid past shield and steel sliced across Henghis' arm.

The Aedei watching on cheered loud as their leader drew first blood. Their cries echoed deep into the realm of the spirits. Hope burned bright in Cailean's chest as his brother lunged forwards once more. If Henghis fell, this nightmare was at an end. They spun and twirled, their shields used as weapons as much as the steel that they clasped in their hands. Henghis ducked under Cyneric's sword as it sliced towards his head. His shield slammed into the Aedei's back as he moved past before he struck out with his own blade. Cyneric stumbled as the shield hit home. Pain flared to life. Steel sliced flesh. The Aedei felt a sliver of blood as it trickled down his back. He felt the small tingle of pain as it blossomed to life. Cyneric snarled. He had lost much, and this man would not beat him. He could not beat him. Blades came together. Cyneric remembered Malakai. He remembered their childhood. Remembered their days spent riding and hunting. Strength filled his veins as he pressed his assault. He had shared everything with his brother. Everything.

Henghis began to fall back. He took each blow upon his shield. He was composed and would not fall so easily. He was a chief. One of the greatest leaders the Catuvantuli had ever known. Blow after blow came down as Cyneric forced his foe back. They came together. Hot breath and the stench of sweat engulfed the Aedei. Henghis' bared teeth were mere inches from Cyneric's own. Cyneric carved his sword down. He threw the full power of his muscles behind the blow. The steel blade met with the lip of Henghis' shield and forced it aside. Blood flowed as the sword kissed the Catuvantuli's cheek. Henghis danced back as he countered. Cyneric caught the blade with his shield. Once. Twice. Henghis moved into a third stroke. Cyneric made to block. It was a feint. The Aedei leapt back as the razor-sharp tip of Henghis' sword drew a bloody line across his thigh. Henghis came at him before he could recover. Cyneric met steel with steel as Henghis aimed a cut towards his neck. The Aedei was ready, for he had anticipated the blow. He used his enemy's strength to parry the strike as he slipped inside Henghis' reach. His shield came up to fully cover his body as his sword arced over it. The Catuvantuli moved but he was too slow. Cyneric's blade lashed across Henghis' shoulder. It bit into muscle and flesh. The man staggered back. An opening came. Cyneric raised his sword. Weakness hit him like a hammer. The opening closed and Henghis charged. Cyneric gasped as he stumbled backwards. He was barely able to keep his footing. Something was wrong. His head began to swim as he took Henghis' sword upon his shield. It was knocked to the side. Cyneric felt his blade torn from his grasp. Steel drove home as Henghis lunged. The Catuvantuli pushed the tip of his sword through his enemy's chest. Cyneric's shield fell from his nerveless fingers as the blade carved through his vitals. Cyneric crashed to the ground as Henghis ripped steel free.

The crowd watched in stunned silence. They had all seen it. They had seen Cyneric suddenly grow weak. Henghis' face paled as he dropped into a crouch by the Aedei leader's body.

"Why?" Cyneric wheezed as he gazed up at his foe.

The Catuvantuli dropped his sword and bowed his head. Blood drained from his face as realisation hit him. The ringing of steel upon stone was the last Cyneric heard as life left his eyes.

"POISON!" Cailean roared as he pulled his sword free and made for Henghis.

The man who had now murdered both of his brothers. His blood kin.

"Seize the murderer!" Cailean bellowed.

Henghis leapt to his feet and stepped back. His face was pale with shock. Warriors rushed onto the stones and weapons leapt into hands.

"HALT!" Henghis bellowed to his own people.

The Catuvantuli leader held up a hand to stop them even as Cailean pressed the tip of his sword to Henghis' throat.

"Traitor," Cailean spat. He bared his teeth as he prepared to kill the Catuvantuli.

"I had no hand in this," Henghis growled.

"You lie!"

The chief met his dark glare and lifted his chin. "If you actually believe that, then you kill me now. Take my life upon these sacred stones, water them with my blood."

Cailean tensed his arm and adjusted his grip on the sword. He fought back the anger that threatened to engulf him. Red filled his gaze, and then he remembered.

"My father often told me that Henghis of the Catuvantuli is the most honourable of men." Cailean ground his teeth. "A man worth fighting beside. Why would such a man use tricks for which there is no honour?" Slowly, hesitantly, Cailean began to lower his blade. "Who gave you the sword?" Cailean asked.

Henghis turned his eyes to Kendrick and in that moment, he understood.

"You!"

"Lord, I ..." the wanderer splattered.

"TAKE HIM!" Henghis roared as his eyes filled with malice.

The druids seized him by the arms.

"On your knees, seed of evil," one of them snarled.

The leader of the Catuvantuli took up his sword once more. However, this time he turned it upon Kendrick.

"What other lies have you whispered in my ear, wanderer? What other falsehoods? You kiss my ring only to stab me in the back, and those knights, this supposed slavery? You have humiliated me."

"I am your servant," Kendrick growled back. "In all things. Poison is a coward's weapon. I would not–"

"He is lying," Kitara interrupted.

Kendrick spat to the side. "I will not be accused by a foreign barbarian. Chief Henghis, I know nothing of this."

"Another lie," was all Kitara said.

Henghis bit his lip and turned to Cailean. "Do you trust this woman?" Henghis asked.

"I do."

The Catuvantuli chief nodded slowly and gestured to Kitara. "Then speak," Henghis said.

Kitara crouched before the wanderer. She searched his eyes as he glared at her.

"I was born among liars. Raised by liars. Taught by liars. You think you can lie? No, even now your eyes reveal the truth. He poisoned the blade. That much is certain."

"Everything you said. Everything you told me. All of it was a lie." Henghis glared down at him. "Your only master is yourself."

"I serve you. No one but you."

Cailean saw something in Kendrick's eyes in that moment. A flicker of fear. Cailean ran his eyes down the wanderer's robes. His gaze locked upon something.

"Check his pouches," Cailean said.

Kendrick had no time to react before Henghis skewered his blade through the small bag and ripped it open. The stones rang as golden coins spilled upon its surface. Coins with the face of a man well known. A gasp ran through the crowd as Henghis took up one of the pieces.

"Aloys ..." With a snort, he flicked the coin down at the wanderer's feet. "You serve no one but Medea. Tell me true, did Malakai of the Aedei break the peace?" Henghis asked. "SPEAK!"

The answer was written all over Kendrick's face. It had all been a lie.

"Send his soul to Tanris," snarled Vaylin as she turned her serpent-like eyes down upon the wanderer.

The Salvaari roared, cheering for blood.

"No!" another of the chieftains snapped. Her hair was of starlight, while a crude breastplate of steel adorned her body. Upon her face were the colours of the Belcar. "If he dies, the truth dies with him."

Cailean growled as silence gripped his kin. If Kendrick fell now, then they may never know the truth behind his actions.

"Morrigana is right," Cailean said, and he set his jaw, glancing at the Belcar chief. "We need him."

"Wait," one of the druids called as he turned his dark eyes towards one among the crowd. "This creature's pets are still here."

The druid nodded towards the man, one of the few who had accompanied the wanderer to the grove. Rough hands seized the man as horror lit up his face.

"Free his tongue, yet as for the wanderer, the spirits are owed sacrifice," the druid said.

Henghis stared at the accused man and gave a curt nod. "Give him to the Káli," Henghis said.

Vaylin's lips curled into a savage grin as the words caressed her ears.

"No ..." Kendrick's man begged as fear set in.

His face was suddenly painted white. One of Vaylin's people took up a length of cloth and used it to roughly gag him. The Káli could make a man tell secrets that he did not know to begin with.

Vaylin walked towards her prisoner and stared deep into his eyes. "You will speak while you still have a tongue," Vaylin sneered. "You will know my face while you still have eyes to see. When at last the poison has done its work and freed the truth from your lips, you will beg for death before the end. Yet it will not be over so swiftly. That, I swear."

Henghis turned to his people. "I have been blind to this demon for too long," he said, "but now I see ever more clearly. Those demons of the west strike at our heart place and seek to divide us. No more. Cailean, his life belongs to you. We can get the knowledge that we seek from his men."

The chief nodded to Cailean and stepped back, allowing the Aedei to stand before Kendrick.

"For all that you have done. For all that you are. The worms shall feast," Cailean told him, and he pressed his sword against the wanderer's throat. "I curse you."

He drove the blade home and spilt Kendrick's blood upon the stones.

FIFTY-TWO

Aeryn sat down beside Kitara as she looked into the waters of the stream before them.

"What you did today saved many lives," the moonseer told her.

Kitara bit her lip and placed a hand on Aeryn's. "Enough had suffered because of Kendrick's lies," Kitara replied.

The moonseer squeezed her hand before she delved into the depths of her cloak.

"I have something for you." Aeryn said. "If you want it."

Curious, Kitara glanced at the one she cared so deeply about. Aeryn held up a band of silver that glinted in the sunlight. It was carved in such a way to look corded. It had a wolf's head at each end. It was a Salvaari arm ring. It was simple yet beautiful to the eye.

"Are you sure?" Kitara asked.

She was almost taken aback by the gesture. She knew how much symbols meant to the Salvaari, and their arm rings were their honour.

"You are one of us," Aeryn told her with a shrug. "You belong here."

Kitara smiled as she took the ring. She gazed down at it for a moment.

"This means everything to me," she said truthfully as she slid the arm ring onto her wrist. She finally had a place. A home, even.

"As it does to me," Aeryn murmured.

"That's why I …"

The words got stuck in Kitara's throat. Saying them made it real, yet saying them had been her undoing in the past.

"That's why I trust you," Kitara finished.

"I know how hard that must be for you," Aeryn murmured.

The moonseer met her eyes, and Kitara knew that she understood. Trust was foreign to Kitara. A thing that she had lived without for so long. A thing that had caused her so much misery. Aeryn ran a gentle finger across Kitara's cheek and pushed back a strand of golden hair. She caressed the cool yet smooth skin beneath the palm of her hand. Kitara leaned in and felt Aeryn's dark hair tickle her face as their lips touched. She embraced the kiss. She let it engulf her. For the first time since she could remember, Kitara felt whole.

They stayed together a while before Aeryn left in search of food.

Serenity encompassed Kitara as she drew her sword. Her eyes were closed, and the rays of the sun warmed her cheeks. She was alone, at peace, as she slowly carved her sword through the air. Kitara's body flowed like water as her muscles began to move as one. She easily took the weight of the heavy steel. It was a thing that had grown to be as a feather. Kitara twirled the blade. She pivoted her boots and slid atop the grassy earth below. Her footwork shifted as she changed the angle of the blade. She was its master. Her body and her sword obeyed her without question.

Kitara heard the light snapping of a branch as she shifted posture. The sound was accompanied by the gentle ring of chainmail and the beat of hooves. She did not react. Instead, she flowed from one move to the next. Her hands adjusted the grip on the hilt of her sword, and her breathing slowed.

"You." The voice rang through the small clearing and broke the silence like thunder.

Kitara froze. She completed her move and perfected her form. The voice seemed familiar and had the unmistakable ring of a Medean accent.

She turned. Her eyes flicked around the clearing. Eight mounted men stared back. Mercenary knights from Medea. Paid and bought by the worm, Kendrick. As one, they dismounted.

Kitara lowered her blade but kept the fingers of her right hand tightly about its hilt. Calmness washed through her body as she faced the leader of the knights. He stood covered head to toe in steel armour with his hand clamped tightly down upon the sword at his hip. Kitara could almost feel the anger that burned in his eyes.

"I know you." She frowned slightly as she remembered his armour clear as day. "You were at that slave camp."

"Aye." The knight nodded as his men began to close in around her like a wall of steel. "And you undid everything."

Kitara snorted. She did not shift her gaze from the man. She could hear the others as they moved closer. Their footsteps were so loud she could have found them in the largest of crowds. They were no more than ten paces from her.

"If liberating those condemned to slavery and death is a crime, then it is one that I shall gladly repeat," Kitara said.

The knight drew his sword and shook his head. "We had them. We had all of them suckling at our breast like children. In a few more moons these heathens–"

"I am one of these heathens," Kitara shot back.

"Then you will join them."

Steel echoed through the clearing as blades were drawn all around her. Still Kitara did not move. Everything seemed to slow as the lead knight extended his hand.

"Your sword," he commanded.

"With pleasure." Kitara flicked her wrist and edged her blade upwards ever so slightly.

All eyes went to her weapon. It took their gaze from her free hand. A feint. Her dagger sliced through the air before the knights could blink. Kitara lunged towards their leader. She angled her sword up and gripped it with both hands. The knife caught the man high on his arm and glanced off his armour as he swivelled to avoid it. Kitara lashed out and knocked his sword aside with her own. Her body changed as did her footwork. Muscles tightened. Steel came up. She struck hard into the knight's helm as he stumbled back. A whistle of steel sliced through the air and forced her to duck as the second man reached her. Kitara slid back two steps. She blocked equal the amount of strikes. She deflected a third, and her response was as lightning. The tip of her sword carved a bloody path across his arm, wetting her steel for the first time. Another blow came at her. It was stopped by the flick of a wrist. She countered, and her sword bit into the unprotected flesh of his left thigh. Her backswing followed and sliced open his right leg. His footwork failed. Kitara stuck his helm with her crossguard and then he stumbled. Her boot hooked his foot and took away what little balance he had left.

The knight began to fall, and her sword helped him on his way. She carved a bloody path down the side of his neck and shattered his collarbone. He crashed to the ground with a scream. The icy tip of a sword ripped through her thigh as Kitara danced back. She grimaced and bit back the pain. It was a shallow wound, but now once more the knights had closed in. She blocked a blow and slid back to counter that of another of her foes. He stepped back to avoid the razor-sharp steel of her blade. The crossguard of a sword slammed into the side of her head. The world grew blurry as she stumbled. She was barely able to hold her footing. She swung her weapon. She feebly deflected the next blow as it came towards her head. Kitara twirled. An armoured fist smashed into her face. Blood burst from her lips. Kitara fell to the ground as the world began to fade. The lead knight stood over her. His sword pressed to her throat.

"Take her," he said.

A boot came down, and darkness came with it.

Bellec and his men came upon the blood-soaked clearing as the sun reached its peak. The sight of a fallen knight had caught him off guard. The sword that lay not far from him near caused his heart to stop. It belonged to Kitara. The mercenary dismounted from his horse and crouched by the bloody blade as he gazed around the clearing.

"He's alive," Galadayne called as he held his dagger to the man's nose and lips.

The faint mist left by a man's breathing was barely visible upon the steel, but it was there.

"The steel does not lie, but he does not have long to live."

Bellec snatched up Kitara's sword and rose to his feet. He gazed into the woods.

What had happened here?

"What have you done?"

The mercenaries whirled around, and steel flew into their hands. Aeryn emerged from the trees atop her horse, bow in hand, the flights of an arrow pressed to her cheek. She did not use her hands to so much as direct the horse beneath, for they were as one. The bladed tip of her arrow was angled for Bellec. The mercenary leader held his hands out wide.

"I came to talk, no more than that. One of your people said she was here. We found him," Bellec said as he nodded to the fallen knight.

Aeryn glared at him for a moment before she lowered her bow and slipped from her saddle. The moonseer ran over to the fallen knight as her mind went to work. "This man cannot die." She gazed around the clearing, her silver eyes searching for something. Anything. Her gaze was drawn to the footprints left by armoured boots.

"Tracks. They lead north. They have horses." She met Bellec's eyes as she spoke. "We have to go now."

The mercenary, Kitara's father, nodded and glanced to Galadayne.

"Stay with the Medean. Above all else, he must be kept alive," Bellec commanded.

They rode hard and pushed their mounts to the limit. Aeryn led the way, for her sight was far above that of her companions. The sun began to slide down towards the horizon and its rays turned into orange light. It cast down through the thick canopy onto the party of riders below.

They had been riding for hours when they came to the burning remnants of a palisaded campsite. It was just like the one that the moonseer had discovered weeks ago.

"Another camp," Aeryn muttered as she gazed into the ruins.

"They have a wagon," Bellec growled and gestured down to the new set of tracks.

The moonseer circled her horse around the large divots in the road. The tracks were now unmistakable on the soft earth. She flicked her wrists and kicked her heels in.

"We're gaining."

The forest began to thin as the cool sea breeze seeped through the trees and whipped through Aeryn's dark hair. The light began to grow as stride by stride the trees grew sparse. Then they erupted from the tree line. The powerful muscles of their horses finally pushed them into a full gallop. They saw the ship within moments. It was anchored barely two hundred paces from the shore. Aeryn felt her heart begin to pound and she pushed her mare faster still. Grass-covered earth gave way to sand as they hurtled after the crystal-clear tracks that lined it. They saw the wagon first. Its caged doors were opened at the back as it was left abandoned on the beach.

"THERE!" Bellec roared as he thrust an arm out to the sea.

There, carving their way through the waves out towards the anchored ship, was a trio of oared boats. Each moment, the small wooden vessels drew further from the beach. The dusk sun glinted upon armour and revealed some of the passengers to be knights. The others stood as slaves.

Aeryn spurred her horse into the water even as she took up her bow and nocked an arrow. Horror hit her. There was no way to make the boats turn back. No way to return Kitara to her arms.

"KITARA!" Bellec bellowed across the waves.

Aeryn released the bladed arrow. The shaft buzzed through the air with deadly precision. It came down and drove into the shoulder of the knight who stood at the prow. Aeryn saw him tip forwards and stagger before he regained his footing. The first tear spilled from her eye as she could only watch on as one by one the figures were pulled up on board of the ship.

"What now?" Aeryn murmured as her eyes hardened like silver ice.

Bellec growled from her side. "I failed her once. Never again. Not while I still hold breath."

He turned to face the moonseer and met her gaze. Rage filled his own as he set his jaw.

"I will never stop hunting them," Bellec swore.

Prince Dayne Raynor of Annora pulled up on his reins and brought his mount to a halt. There he sat, gazing towards the great Forest of Salvaar with two thousand heavily armed riders at his back. Above them flew the red eagle banners of Annora, mingled with the golden standard and silver lion of Aloys.

"What are you thinking?" Sir Elion Montbard asked their leader as he glanced at Prince Dayne.

"We hit them first and we hit them hard," Emilian Aloys cut in. "Take as many villages as we can before they know we are here."

Dayne snorted. "No. That is what the Inquisition did not understand. What King Balinor and my father did not understand. You do not defeat these people by killing their warriors and taking their towns. You do it by destroying their faith. So here we will divide. Yet we must remain on guard. Remember, these lands belong to the Káli. Our enemy, as that man Cailean once told us," Prince Dayne said, and he turned to face his commanders. "Lord Hornwood, take five hundred men and ride north. There is place of worship to one of their spirits, Yorath, I believe. A temple of stone as my father once wrote. Burn it to the ground."

"As you will, my prince."

"Lord Robare, Sir Elion, you will ride with me. Emilian, I will need your men to see this done." Dayne glanced at the Medean lord.

Emilian Aloys gave him a brief nod. "You have them," the duke's son replied.

"There is a Káli town used as a food store not three days east from here, and so we will take it," the Annoran prince continued. "From there, we can plan our raids. Do not forget: these people will fight to the last if we allow it. We can afford no mercy to their warriors, for they will rise and rise again."

"Aye, lord." Sir Elion nodded. "Though how do you know of this town?"

"My father wrote much about the Salvaari." Dayne shrugged

and held out a rolled-up map. "The town is called Oryn. Lord Hornwood, you will meet with us there once your task is complete."

FIFTY-THREE

Durandail's Vault, North Sword's Peak, Valley of Odrysia

Elena saw Kyler fall. She saw the blood spew from his lips as the heavy-tipped bolt ripped through his armour and flesh.

She screamed.

Pain. It was all she felt. It began in her heart and consumed her. It rolled through her in a wave. Tears ran down her cheeks as she gazed at Kyler's body. She barely noticed Wa'rith as he tossed the crossbow aside and began to walk towards her. She was the last person standing between him and the silver spear. It lay in the ground behind her, abandoned and all but forgotten by the woman who stood before it upon the dais.

Wa'rith took up his sword as he strode through the carnage. Blood soaked the chamber's hallowed floor. It leaked from the lifeless corpses of Durandail's chosen warriors. Not even Sir Matias had survived this man's onslaught.

Elena took a step back as he approached. She tightened her grip upon the knife in her hand. She could still hear Kyler's voice, his laughter, his smile. It was all she could feel. Not the tears on her cheeks, or the fragile beating of her shattered heart.

Wa'rith reached the steps of the dais and said not a word as he levelled his sword towards her. Elena glanced back and saw the spear. The very blade of Durandail. Whether it held power or not, it was the reason this demon was here. It was the reason that Kyler and the other's lay bereft of life. She would gladly give her own to ensure that this monster could be delayed for even a moment. Elena set her jaw and turned her empty gaze to the man as he reached the very top of the dais.

She was prepared.

"Areut talc cuun'ect!"

The age-old cry of the Knights of Kil'kara echoed through the chamber as boots rang atop sacred stone.

Wa'rith turned and Elena's eyes flicked up. Corvo Alaine charged into the vault, his sword in hand and knights at his back. The demon in brown snarled as he saw the tide of steel rush towards him.

The first knight to reach the dais lashed out. His sword arced towards the legs of the man who stood on higher ground. Wa'rith flipped to the side and launched himself from the dais as the blade passed harmlessly beneath. He landed on level footing to the knight and slipped aside from another blow. He blocked a third blow with skill, as a fourth from Corvo's own sword caught him. It sliced across his chest and carved a line through his gambeson.

Elena felt the first tremble run through her as she watched the knights corner Wa'rith. The creature that they feared most of all. His hand went to his belt where he took up a small silver orb. Sir Corvo raised his shield as Wa'rith dashed the canister upon the ground. The vault rang as the shell exploded against the stone ground. Smoke once more billowed forth and cast everything from sight. All Elena could hear was her own breathing and the footsteps of all around her. No muffled shouts or cries of pain. Nothing. The mist faded, and Wa'rith was gone with it. He had vanished into the darkness like the demon he was.

"He lives!" Sir Corvo called out as he crouched by Alarik's side.

Corvo placed a hand on his friend's shoulder. The stones rang as Elena cast her knife aside and rushed to Kyler. She fell to her knees by his blood-covered body. She reached out a hand and placed her fingers on his cheek. It was still warm. His breathing was shallow and within moments he would be gone. There was nothing neither healer nor physician, nor even maija, could do to delay death.

"Is he?" one of the knights said from her side as he glanced down at the fallen initiate.

"Give me room!" Elena shouted.

She turned a tear-filled glare upon the warrior. It was all she could do to stop herself shoving him back. This moment was for her and Kyler alone.

"You heard her," Sir Corvo called as he rose to his feet and switched his sword to his left hand. "That monster may yet return. Watch the doors."

"Aye, sir."

Elena turned her attention back to Kyler as the knight walked away. She did not spare a glance for Corvo as he took up Durandail's Spear nor for any of the others as they knelt by their fallen comrades and brothers. She did not feel the tears that ran down her cheeks, or the sobs that racked her body. Elena had eyes for only one person. The man she loved who lay beneath her heartbroken gaze. She loved him. She had since the days in the tavern so long ago. Before the Order, before she had answered her call. She cared not for what any of the Order would think if they knew who she really was, what she really was.

Elena gave the briefest of glances around the room. None were looking. She was not Elena of the maija. Nor even that Medean-born tavern girl. She placed a hand on the bolt that stood embedded in Kyler's chest. If she removed it, he would die within moments. If she did not, he would die regardless. If she did this, they would kill her. The Order would see her as no more than a beast.

Elena did not care.

She wrapped her hand around the bolt and took a deep breath. Her tears rang as they hit Kyler's armour. It was the only way. Elena gritted her teeth and with a sudden tug she pulled the shaft free. Blood spewed forth. She snatched up her knife and gave into her emotion as she had been taught long ago. She closed her eyes and stilled her breath. She thought only of Kyler and the future so wrongly stolen from them. Elena let her gaze flicker open, and when it did, no longer was it amber. Her eyes glowed with crimson light. She held her knife over Kyler's chest and, without so much as a blink, she wrapped the fingers of her spare hand around the blade and squeezed. Elena sliced the steel up. She felt it part skin and flesh. She gave not a grimace as she pulled the blade away, revealing the wicked wound that ran down her palm, a wound that pooled with fresh blood. Black blood. She placed her hand over Kyler's chest and pressed it down atop the hole left by the bolt. Neither science nor the healing arts could save him, but her blood could. The blood of one descended from the old ways. The blood of the ruskalan. Drop by drop, Kyler's wound began to knit back together.

"DEMON!"

The roar shook the cavern as she was discovered. She heard steel rasp as blades were drawn.

It was not yet time. If she did not finish …

Elena snarled as she sprung to her feet and bared her teeth. The knights looked on in horror as they saw the fangs that lined her maw. They came at her.

Kyler awoke to the warm rays of the dawn sun upon his face. He pushed a rogue strand of hair from his face as he took in his surroundings. White sheeted beds filled the room, the same as the one on which he now lay. Most were empty and only a single maija was in the room. The infirmary. Then he remembered the Vault. The Spear.

Wa'rith.

Kyler pushed himself up onto his elbows and pulled the sheet down to reveal the naked skin of his torso. There were no bandages. Not even some kind of poultice, and then he saw why.

Upon his chest was no mark. No scar or broken flesh. Kyler slowly, almost tentatively, ran a hand over his skin. He felt nothing. No pain. Not even so much as a dull ache. The surprise grew as he remembered the bolt ripping through his chest. He could still feel the pain as he was dealt a mortal wound. Yet somehow, he still breathed.

"Welcome back." Lady Lysandra's soft voice reached his ears.

Kyler glanced up as the head of the maija glided over to his bed. "I should be dead."

"And yet you are not," she replied with a smile. "A miracle. The Twins themselves must have some purpose for you."

Horror hit him as he met Lysandra's eyes.

"Elena?"

"She lives."

"Thank the gods," Kyler replied.

He did not see a dark look edge itself into Lysandra's gaze. The Medean bit his lip, and then it all came back to him. Torin was dead. Matias was dead. Neph and Emir. Kyler pushed himself up and made to get out of the bed. He had to find out what had happened in that cavern.

"Wa'rith ... the Spear ..."

Lysandra placed a hand upon his shoulder. The soft skin of her palm stopped him in his tracks.

"The Spear is safe. Sir Corvo took it upon himself to carry the burden. As for the Shadow, he has once more slipped from grasp. Though now we know the nightmare which has plagued our sleep. Men such as Wa'rith are strongest when they are feared, and now that fear is being unmasked."

Kyler nodded. He could feel fire fill his bones as a new purpose filled him.

"Then I will find him, for Torin, and all the other brothers he has taken from us."

Lysandra gave him an almost sad smile. "One day, perhaps you will. For now, though, rest. You will soon be able to take up your sword once more."

"I long for it."

"Lady Lysandra." A gruff voice that Kyler recognised well filled his ears. "A moment with the pisspot."

Kyler nearly grinned as Sir Alarik walked over to his bedside. His arm was in a sling and his face covered in bruising and a few shallow wounds. He wore no armour but a plain tunic and breeches, his sword as ever present at his side. The healer looked to the battlemaster as he approached.

"A moment then, and no more than that," Lysandra told him sternly before she flitted away to another of the wounded.

Alarik watched her go as he sat down on the edge of the bed.

"Of all the evils in the world, Pisspot, there is nothing that frightens me so much as a healer separated from her patient."

Kyler chuckled as his mentor gave him a smirk. "It is good to see you, sir."

Alarik's smile slowly faded. "It would take more than some shadow of a man to kill me."

"How long have I been out?"

The battlemaster met his eyes. "Near a week," Alarik told him.

"And the others?"

In his heart, Kyler already knew the answer. Alarik merely shook his head.

"We would be too if not for Corvo. You saved my life, Pisspot. I will not forget."

Kyler dipped his head. He had known Torin dead from the moment he had fallen at his feet. Yet he could not believe all of them were gone.

"What happened in that cave?" Kyler asked.

"Whoever he is, Wa'rith knows his craft and he knows it well. Each blow was to the leg, neck and under the arm. To do so with such speed and skill – in all my years, I have only seen its likeness once before. And that lies with Sir Corvo."

Alarik's face paled and he placed a hand on Kyler's arm.

"There are some things in this world, forces at work, that are beyond us." The battlemaster's face darkened as he spoke. "Pisspot, the earth has shifted beneath our feet. Much has changed in your slumber. Amaris is dead."

"The grand master? How?"

"They found him two days after we left Kilgareth. The maija are saying that he passed peacefully in the night," Alarik told him. "We have lost our great leader at a most perilous time. The Spear of Durandail has been recovered and the birds have flown. It will only be a matter of time before the cardinal calls for another holy crusade. Once more, the armies of faith will assemble."

Kyler felt his blood chill. This could be a chance for him to finally prove his worth.

He held his amulet ever tighter as he murmured, "When the fires of the Citadel are lit, the Knights of Kil'kara shall ride again."

The battlemaster nodded before looking to the door. "It is time," Sir Alarik said.

Kyler followed his gaze as the maija quartermaster, Lorencio, walked into the chamber. A shiver ran down the boy's spine as he saw what the maija carried. A helmet. Steel of shining silver that glistened in the light was topped by a brilliant blue plume.

Alarik took the helm from Lorencio and rose to his feet.

"This journey has shown me the man you can become, Landrey. For good judgement, honour and courage in battle, you are to be knighted. In the name of Durandail, Father of all Fathers, and Azaria, the Lady of Silver, I welcome you into our Order, brother." He handed the helm to Kyler. "May you serve well," the battlemaster said.

"I won't let you down, sir," the Medean vowed as he took the gift.

"The ceremony shall take place when you are recovered," Alarik said as he dipped his head in respect. "I expect you to be back upon the field in two days, Landrey."

Landrey, he had said. Not Pisspot.

With that, Alarik turned and made for the door of the hospital. His voice interrupted Kyler's thoughts once more. This time his growl was quieter and held some kind of pity.

"When you're ready, we will talk about Elena."

Elara, the jewel of the Sacasian, great merchant city and mother of the League of Trecento, basked in the sun's rays. Its markets and harbours were filled to bursting with traders, vendors and merchants from all walks of life. Once little more than an Aurean colony, now it stood as a rival to the great city of Aureia itself.

Far below, in the maze of tunnels that ran beneath, one man walked alone. The stone corridors echoed with each footstep. His shoulder cloak and hood were as dark as his clothing, while his cloth mask was pulled up just shy of his eyes. A long, curved knife was sheathed at his back, while a second, straighter blade was buckled to his boot. He found the door locked when he came upon it, for he would allow no one access. He pulled a small key from a pouch and turned it in the keyhole. Metal clinked as the lock was forced open. He opened the door and walked into the room lit by torches upon the walls. The room was filled with tables and shelves covered in books and maps. A weapons rack stood to one side. A small table laden with potions, elixirs and powders. There were recipe books and the ingredients he required for his smoke bombs. At the back of the room, there was another door. One which led above ground. Wa'rith pulled off his mask of cloth and pushed his hood back. Messy, black hair fell to his shoulders. The dark eyes of an Annoran were revealed, as was his short, roughly trimmed beard. The back door creaked open, and had he not known the scent of rose petals, then the intruder would have been greeted by the sharp edge of a knife.

"Mellisanthi?"

He knew her scent as well as he knew her voice.

"Your information was correct?" the Larissan woman asked as she watched him enter.

The man flicked his gaze over her as he unbuckled his sword belt and placed it upon a bench. Her black hair was as beautiful and wild as a storm, and it fell in wavy tresses down her bare shoulders. A crimson corset was wrapped around her slender waist, while an equally as red dress fell to the floor. Her attire was trimmed in white and left her forearms as naked as her face. Her lips were full, and her dark eyes were of glistening copper. A single golden ring hung from her left ear. She was his closest friend and companion. She stood as a pillar of grace.

"It always is," he replied.

"And?"

He pushed back his hood and let his untamed hair cascade down the sides of his face. He clenched his fists and felt a slight sting come from the barely healed wound upon his chest.

"I failed. They have the artefact."

"How?"

Wa'rith near spat and his lips curled in anger. "They were reinforced before I could take it. Surrounded, outnumbered and without a sword. There was nothing to be done."

It hurt him to say it, yet it was so. Perhaps he could have sent two or three to see their gods, yet it would have cost him his life. Then the Spear would have been forever from his grasp.

"I followed them back to Kilgareth, but they left nothing to chance."

"I see." Mellisanthi pursed her lips. "What are you going to do about it?"

He met the eyes of the Larissan woman. "The most important thing that every man should know is what he would die for. I would gladly give my life to see an end to that evil which they hold most dear."

Mellisanthi slowly walked around the table and placed a hand on his arm.

"When does it end, Markus?" she asked, and her voice filled with sorrow. "If you continue down this path, you will find that you are the only one walking it."

He shrugged her hand away. "So be it."